"You trust too mu
stepped closer.

"I think you're right," she replied. "I trust people I don't even know. Like you. I trust you when I shouldn't. I don't even know you."

How could he make her understand he was here to help her? But that wasn't true, either. What was he thinking? Helping Gemma Rollins had never been part of his mission parameters. He was here to finish this, to find the man who was not only responsible for Bill's death but who was also the head of a large wildlife trafficking ring.

"Listen, Gemma, I was looking for you to tell you about an idea I came up with."

Her eyes brightened. "You came up with an idea for me? What—"

A rumble above cut off her question. Rocks shifted overhead, crashed against the cliffside, and echoed across the mountain and through the trees.

"Look out!" Grayson grabbed Gemma, cane and all, and pressed her beneath a protruding part of the rock wall, covering her with his body. Protecting her. Her breaths came hard and fast against his neck as her fear mingled with his own.

God, please protect her. Protect us!

Elizabeth Goddard is an award-winning author of more than twenty novels, including the romantic mystery *The Camera Never Lies*–winner of a prestigious Carol Award in 2011. After acquiring her computer science degree, she worked at a software firm before eventually retiring to raise her four children and become a professional writer. In addition to writing, she homeschools her children and serves with her husband in ministry.

Visit the Author Profile page at Harlequin.com.

UNDERCOVER PROTECTOR

ELIZABETH GODDARD

HARLEQUIN® LOVE INSPIRED® SUSPENSE

Recycling programs
for this product may
not exist in your area.

LOVE INSPIRED BOOKS

ISBN-13: 978-0-373-45681-9

Undercover Protector

Copyright © 2017 by Elizabeth Goddard

www.Harlequin.com

Printed in U.S.A.

A righteous man has regard for the life of his animal,
But even the compassion of the wicked is cruel.
—Proverbs 12:10

For Mom

Acknowledgments

Thanks to my many dear writing friends
who have encouraged me along this journey.
I'm so blessed that God brought us together. I'm grateful
that God planted a dream in my heart and then made my
dream of telling stories come true. Special thanks to Jeri at
Crown Ridge Tiger Sanctuary for answering my questions
about these wonderful big cats and what it's like to
care for them in a sanctuary. I'm more than blessed to
have an editor who believes in my stories—thank you,
Elizabeth Mazer—and an agent who saw something in me
years ago—thank you, Steve Laube.

ONE

Siskiyou Mountains, southwest Oregon

Gemma Rollins shifted gears as her beloved Jeep CJ bounced over the narrow gravel road carved from the mountain. With this torrential downpour, she was glad she'd opted for the hard cover and doors on this older model.

But she should have gotten the mud tires too.

This was just like when the Pineapple Express came through southern Oregon a decade ago. Except spring was the wrong time of year for the tropical moisture to be sweeping in from the Hawaiian Islands. The meteorological phenomenon occurred in the winter.

And the tigers in her sanctuary, fifteen beautiful creatures she knew by name, wouldn't be happy in this inclement weather either.

Gemma downshifted, slowing at the curve on the steep one-lane road, her pulse edging up as the rain pounded harder. This was a lot more like the kind of weather she'd see in Houston, Texas, rather than southwest Oregon. And too much rain might cause flooding in the sanctuary. With a USDA inspection coming up in three weeks, she so did *not* need more hurdles in her goal of getting Tiger Mountain accredited as a big cat sanctuary.

She pressed her foot against the brakes as she came up on the switchback. Suddenly, the steering refused to turn. What was happening? The sharp bend approached. She would never make it!

Throwing her entire body into turning the steering wheel, Gemma's effort paid off. The CJ slid around the bend, though still much too close to the edge of the ravine.

Trees and rocks would slow anything trying to take a fall, but that didn't reassure her. Nearing the next curve, she pumped the brakes. They weren't working so well either.

She was behind in vehicle maintenance, no doubt there, but her CJ had never let her down before. Another curve in the road approached, and she shifted to the lowest gear, gripped the wheel with both hands and groaned with the effort to make the turn.

She'd driven the road that bordered the fenced-in area of the sanctuary enough times to know what to expect—more switchbacks. The road was dangerous on a good day. She hit the brakes harder. Still the CJ picked up more speed. She turned the steering wheel left, barely making another switchback.

Her beloved CJ was out of control.

Heart hammering, the realization slammed her—this was a matter of survival.

She might actually die. The possibility sucked her breath away.

Mud oozed from the rocky wall to her left as it poured from the hillside above. *God, please help me! I don't want to die today. And please keep the sanctuary intact. Please don't let those fences give way.*

She couldn't imagine that would happen, but, then again, she hadn't dreamed her steering would give way on the same day as her brakes. What were the chances? A question rose from the shadows in her mind. Had this been intentional?

And on a treacherous, rainy day.

Images from that night long ago accosted her. Headlights glinting off a wall of water. The grinding crunch. The wreck that left her uncle dead, the Tiger Hills sanctuary her father had founded dismantled and Gemma with nerve damage and a limp.

Focus, Gemma! She gripped the steering wheel tighter, mentally skimming the road ahead. Another bend. She'd never make it with her steering out like this. But if she could make it around the next outcropping of the rocky wall—before the dangerous bend—and remain on the road, there was an incline to her right, a turn out that she could use to slow the CJ to a stop.

Would it be enough?

Come on, come on, come on...

"God, if You're listening, and You don't want me to die today, I need some help." Gemma wrestled the wheel even harder and yanked the emergency brake, getting no return for her efforts.

Up ahead, mud and rocks washed over the road.

A mudslide!

Though it could be dangerous, deadly even, she could use the mudslide to slow the CJ, except she would have another battle for survival. But it was moving slowly enough she might just be able to make it.

Was that the answer to her prayer?

The incline appeared ahead in the thick of the mud. She pumped the brakes again, but they were completely dead. Gemma shifted into a higher gear and sped over the mud before it carried her away.

The roar of the torrential rain and the sight of the mudslide filled her with dread and morbid memories, erasing all other rational thought. Gemma fought the rising terror.

She gripped the wheel and steered toward the incline, shifting down once she'd gained enough momentum because she'd need to stop this vehicle, once and for all, on the other side of the mud.

Regardless of her momentum, the CJ shifted as the mud gripped the tires, but Gemma persevered and evened out the pressure on the accelerator, adjusting her steering until the vehicle lifted up, the front tires gaining traction on the ground that rose above the mud, and sped forward.

But fast, much too fast.

The CJ slammed into a tree. Her body ricocheted against the seat belt. There were no airbags in an old Jeep CJ.

Stunned, Gemma blinked. Sucked in a breath. *I'm alive!*

Then she groaned.

"I'm alive." She breathed slowly to calm herself. "I'm…alive." It could have been much worse.

Gemma squeezed her eyes shut as memories overwhelmed her. Déjà vu. Her uncle had been driving the night he lost control of the vehicle and they hit a tree. He'd died and Gemma had lived. Why had she lived—then and now?

Drawing in a few more calming breaths until she could breathe normally, she shook away the daze. Felt the ache from her skin to her bones. But that was good news. She could feel everything, even the nerve damage pain in her left leg from the wreck that took Uncle Dave's life.

The CJ jerked to the right. What was going on?

Gemma turned her attention to the environment around her. The rain and the mud had risen even more and caught her rear tires. She had to hurry!

She tried to unbuckle her seat belt. Stuck. She searched for something sharp to cut herself out, but, strapped in the seat, she couldn't reach the tool kit in the back. Regardless, she tried to open the door, but it wouldn't budge. The front end had crumpled as the CJ twisted against the tree. Since she'd opted for a hard top, she couldn't cut her way out through the top, even if she could escape the seat belt trapping her inside.

She spied her cell phone—out of reach on the floorboard on the passenger side.

Gemma was going to die today, after all.

Grayson Wilde had picked the worst day for surveillance of the Tiger Mountain sanctuary. Now he paid the price as he searched for cover on the hillside to wait out the storm. He had an appointment in an hour to interview with Gemma Rollins, Tiger Mountain's founder, for a part-time volunteer position. A senior special agent for the United States Fish and Wildlife Service, Gray worked undercover to investigate and infiltrate a wildlife trafficking ring.

Shivering in the cold, he pushed deeper into a shallow cave to shield himself from the brunt of the wind and rain while he waited it out. He scraped a hand over his face and wiped away the water. As miserable as it was to be in this place right at this moment, he reminded himself of the importance of his assignment. For starters, his mission in life was to thwart wildlife traffickers and poachers abusing God's creations. It was crucial, dangerous work, considering illegal exotic pet trade and trafficking had become a multi-billion dollar industry, and came in right under drugs, firearms and human trafficking. And, as a source of funding for terrorist groups, it was a significant threat to both global and national security. But even aside from that, Gray had his own reasons for shadowing this sanctuary.

He'd gotten a tip from an informant that the person responsible for killing game warden Bill Garland—Gray's friend and mentor—was connected with the project. It was the kind of tip he'd been waiting on for what seemed like a lifetime. Bill had stumbled on a potential trafficking ring years ago, and turned the information over to the feds then ended up dead. With only two hundred fifty USFWS special agents to investigate the entire country, justice was never fully served.

And Gray needed a chance to make things right.

He had started as a game warden but worked his way to becoming a federal agent and he finally had a solid lead on his ongoing investigation. Someone to connect with an extensive trafficking ring, though he didn't yet have a name.

His new mission was to gain Gemma Rollin's confidence and work the business with her so he could discover the truth. Find the person responsible for Bill's death. Arrest him and everyone else involved.

He might have to show up for the interview soaking wet, but that could work in his favor.

Over the deluge he thought he heard a cry for help. Who would possibly venture out in weather like this? Well, other than himself. But unless they were conducting surveillance and working undercover, nobody should be out in the wilderness region that hedged the tiger sanctuary.

Gray quieted his thoughts and listened.

There it was again, only this time it was not a cry for help but an actual scream.

He darted from the cave back into the rain, wishing for goggles—a snorkel and a pair of flippers might even work. "Where are you?"

But he wasn't sure how he could have heard the scream over the torrent to begin with and doubted they'd heard his response.

Careful of the slick ground, Gray made his way in the direction from which he thought the screams were coming. Then he found the road circling the tiger sanctuary.

That made sense. Someone could have been driving this and he wouldn't have seen it from his perch. He jogged down the twisted, muddy road, water pouring from the rocky wall to his left. The screams came louder but were muffled.

Gray ran around a curve in the road and saw the mud rushing down the mountain, eating away this portion of the road.

And he saw an old Jeep CJ shoved up into a tree. He searched for thin places in the rush of water and mud and did a dance with the forces of nature as he hopped, skipped, jumped and charged like a bull intent on his target. He caught the bumper, gripped it, holding on against the force of the liquid earth sliding under his feet. He made his way to the driver's side door.

A frantic woman sat inside, her mouth wide and halfway through the word *help* when she caught sight of him. She stopped and closed her mouth.

Assessing the situation, Gray didn't need her to explain the urgency or that she couldn't get her door open. He doubted climbing out the other side was even an option, since the vehicle hung precariously near the edge on the passenger side. He tried the door, using brute strength, and then kicked at it, but it wouldn't budge. If he'd brought his weapon, he might have been able to shoot the door mechanism so it would release.

Instead, he grabbed a large rock.

Her troubled eyes grew wide again.

"Unbuckle your seat belt!" he yelled over the roar. "And move out of the way."

"I can't!"

"I'm going to smash the window."

She nodded. Covering her face, she leaned away.

Gray hit the window. Glass shattered, falling everywhere inside the vehicle, including on the woman. She carefully tossed aside the bigger chunks, and Gray helped remove the rest. He pulled out his Buck knife from his jeans pocket, cut her seat belt and then tugged off his jacket, laying it over the window jamb to protect her. Gray planned to pull her out, but she climbed out herself, her agility surprising him until she fell to the ground. Her left leg appeared stiff, her expression one of agony.

"You're hurt!" He crouched next to her. Of course, she would be hurt after her Jeep had slammed into the tree.

Rain beating down on her, she tried to stand on her own but failed and slipped back, mere inches from the spreading river of mud.

"We have to get out of here before the mud carries us away along with your Jeep." Gray scooped her into his arms.

She struggled against him and reached for the vehicle. "No, wait! I need—"

"Unless you've got a child in there—" and Gray hadn't seen anyone else in the vehicle "—someone else whose life is in danger, we're getting out of here."

"But—!"

Ignoring her, Gray headed away from the ensnared vehicle and the mudslide. He focused all his energy and strength into hiking over slippery boulders while holding a 115-pound woman with an injury. Behind him, he half expected to hear the telltale sound of the old Jeep CJ being carried away down the mountain, but that sound never came.

Carrying her solid but small form, he reached the road she'd been driving on when she'd hit the mud. He couldn't imagine how terrifying that must have been. She was in her twenties, he'd guess, a few years younger than his thirty-two years. Was she a volunteer who he would work with? He'd have to explain what he'd been doing out here. But first they had to get somewhere safe and dry.

He hadn't made it twenty yards when the rain slowed. "You can put me down now."

"You sure?"

She nodded. "I appreciate the help, but I can manage from here."

He set her on the still-slick road and put his hand out, ready to catch her if necessary. "Careful now."

Pushing her wet strands out of the way, she looked up at him, studying his face with her bright hazel eyes. Raindrops slid over her forehead and over her cheeks, revealing a pretty, natural face with a few freckles across the bridge of her nose and cheeks. Her dark hair hung long down her back and was so waterlogged that he couldn't tell for sure what color it was, but he was almost certain it was dark brown to match her perfectly shaped eyebrows.

He glanced up at the ashen sky and received droplets in his eyes. He wiped them out and then looked at the woman. "I suppose I should introduce myself. It's not every day I carry a woman down the mountain."

"I'm *walking* down the mountain," she corrected. "But I'm sure it's not every day you have to pull a woman trapped in a mud-strapped, tree-slammed Jeep."

"You got that right."

"Well, what's your name, stranger?"

"Grayson Wilson. But you can call me Gray." Though working undercover, he'd keep his first name. Easy enough to answer to that. Wilde would be off the books.

"I'm Gemma Rollins. I run Tiger Mountain, the sanctuary on the other side of this road. You might have noticed it since you were out wandering the area." Her tone sounded suspicious.

Gemma Rollins. Tiger Mountain's founder.

So much for his surveillance efforts. He should have known, though she looked nothing like the pictures, where she always had on sunglasses. Her eyes would have been a dead giveaway.

She shifted her focus to the road and then turned to him. "Well, are you coming? I want to get someplace dry."

"And then you'll call the sheriff, right?" The county maintained the mountain road, and she might want the report for her insurance.

Calling the sheriff was the right move for her, so Gray ignored the twinge he felt at the thought. Gray hadn't wanted to run into the man so soon on this operation, but Sheriff Kruse would likely send a deputy out instead and, in that case, Gray could keep his cover unless it was Deputy Callahan. In theory, it would be safe enough to read in the local cops on his investigation…but in practice, it was a whole different story. Sometimes, even law enforcement could be involved in trafficking.

"Yes. We need to let the county know about the mud and trees on the road."

She continued to favor her right leg over her left.

Gray asked, "Are you sure you're not hurt? You're limping."

Gemma stopped and turned to look at him, staring at him with her determined and enormous, crystal-clear hazel eyes. Why hadn't he known about the eyes beforehand?

Like that would have kept them from affecting him now. He didn't want to stop looking at them.

"I was injured years ago. Nerve damage. My limp is part of me now. If you had let me grab my cane out of the Jeep, I'd be using that to walk."

Gray was embarrassed. Why hadn't he noticed a cane in the few pictures he'd seen? "I'm so sorry. I didn't know." He almost offered to assist her in walking, but the set of her jaw told him that would be the wrong thing to do.

"It's okay. I understand. You were being a hero, and you couldn't have known you were rescuing a debilitated damsel. Honestly, I didn't expect anyone to hear my cries for help, much less a stranger to arrive to whisk me out of the Jeep. Thank you for that." Her soft smile wiped away the furrow in her brow but not the anguish—the deep-seated agony—behind her eyes.

Gray had come here to bring this woman down if she was involved in the trafficking ring—and especially if she was involved, even indirectly, in Bill's death. It seemed more than likely that she was part of the trafficking ring as founder of the sanctuary that was somehow connected.

How could she not be aware of the trafficking going on right under her nose? But looking at her now, Gray doubted his certainty. He could clearly see there was so much more going on in that head of hers. Finding answers would not be as easy as he'd hoped.

Especially when his natural drive to protect the innocent ignited for Gemma. Because if she wasn't involved in the ring, then she could be in danger.

All he knew was that he had a feeling Gemma Rollins had just reversed their roles and she was about to make trouble for Gray. Either that or he had just made a world of trouble for himself in coming here.

TWO

Gemma kept up the warm and friendly banter while she shared the mountain road with Gray. She appreciated his assistance out of the CJ. She could have died without Gray's help.

But she kept the conversation superficial. Gray was still a stranger and she didn't know what he could have been doing on the mountain or on the road during this storm. She had even more reason to be wary given the saboteurs who had caused her too many problems already in the form of vandalism to the property. They hoped to sabotage her efforts to provide a reputable sanctuary for tigers. Could Gray be connected to them? It was certainly possible.

Pain throbbed up her leg, pain that seemed to ignite in full force when she was stressed in any way. And with all the stress in her life lately, that meant a lot of over-the-counter painkillers. She'd managed so far without prescription painkillers and wouldn't start now, if she could help it.

She must have flinched because she saw him eyeing her with concern. "So what happened back there, anyway?" he asked. "You come around that curve too fast? Or was it the muddy deluge in the road that took you out?"

Gemma scoffed. "Let's just say it was the perfect storm. My steering went out and the brakes couldn't handle the slope." She didn't want to go on, fearing he might berate her for her lack of vehicle maintenance. She tried to ignore that gnawing in the back of her mind that it was something more threatening.

His demeanor changed—a subtle shift, but it was there.

Gemma shouldn't have revealed so much. "I know, I know. Vintage doesn't have to be unsafe."

He cracked a grin.

Gray might be a stranger on this mountain, but he elicited a smile from her in return. She glanced at him. Covered in mud, he was kind of scruffy-looking, his hair hanging to his shoulders and making him resemble a character in an epic fantasy movie. He'd been there, right when she'd needed him. But…she was itching to ask what he'd been doing on the road.

Gemma wished she wasn't a conspiracy theorist. Hoped that she was being entirely too suspicions, but she'd been through so much already. And where was this guy's vehicle? Either something didn't add up or Gemma didn't have all the information necessary to fill in the equation. She suspected the first but hoped for the latter.

A vicious cramp shot pain up her leg and Gemma slipped and fell, letting out a yelp.

Humiliation scoured her. If not for her limp, she wouldn't have gone down. Pebbles and rocks bit into her backside, adding to the mud already there.

Gray whisked her up and into his arms before she could protest. The concern in his face, the compassion in his warm brown eyes, told her she had nothing to fear from him. But she had never trusted her own judgment when it came to men like Gray—handsome men, whom Gemma could be attracted to if she let herself. Fortunately, her single-minded focus on her work meant she hadn't run into that many men like Gray. Warmth spread through her as she rested in his arms and against his broad chest, or was the warmth from the embarrassment of her fall?

He grinned, though the distant rumble of trouble boiled in his gaze. "It's okay, Gemma. I'm handy to have around at times like these."

The guy made her laugh, easing her humiliation. "I see that."

"And I know my timing is off, but—" he cleared his throat "—it's about time for my interview. You want to interview me here and now or wait until we get to headquarters?"

Huh?

He must have noticed her bewilderment because he laughed. "I'm interested in your volunteer position."

Gemma slapped her hand onto her head. "Oh! Oh, this is…well…put me down now."

Without argument, he set her on her feet. "I'm just trying to show that I can be useful as a volunteer."

Through the woods, Gemma spotted the main sprawl of buildings. "We're close. Let's get inside, dry off and warm up, and we'll talk about volunteer work over a hot cup of cocoa. Is that all right?"

"Sounds perfect." He flashed a nice set of teeth.

At least she had a reason to hope that he wasn't connected with the saboteurs now. It didn't make sense that someone would volunteer to help her if he really wanted to hurt someone. But the thought caused a shadow in her heart. She didn't want that to be the case for Gray Wilson. She could ask any hard questions—What he was doing on the road? Where was his vehicle?—once they were inside with the others. But she didn't want to think he was up to no good. His actions had proven otherwise so far.

Gemma led him through the side door of the main facility they hoped to open up for public education and training in the next few weeks. "This is the resource building. There's a big fire roaring in the fireplace for days like this. So have a seat. I'll get you a towel to dry off and a blanket to get warm."

The faux leather couches could be wiped clean of mud and debris.

She disappeared down a hall toward her office, where she found Cara, her friend and employee, busy working on the computer recording data for the tigers and ordering supplies.

She glanced up at Gemma and gasped. "What happened?"

"It's a long story. I have a guy out there, Gray Wilson, who says he was coming in for an interview today?"

Cara nodded. "Yeah. I left a message on your voice mail. He called this morning, and you said you needed help and, well, I thought you'd be back in time."

"I met him on the mountain."

"What?"

"Yeah. I crashed the CJ into a tree. Gray was there to help me out."

"Oh, Gemma, are you okay, honey? Do you need to see a doctor?"

"No, I'm good."

Cara didn't look convinced. "What about that old Jeep you love? You want me to call the sheriff for you? You'll need an official report so insurance will cover it."

"It's not like the insurance is going to pay." She only had liability. "But call the county to let them know about the road."

She dried her hair with one of the towels they kept on hand. Their work at the sanctuary was hands on, dirty work. Grabbing a couple of blankets from a closet, Gemma wrapped one around herself, wishing she had time to run over to her cabin to shower, change clothes and grab a sweatshirt. "Find my other cane for me, if you would, please? I don't want to keep him waiting."

Cara nodded. "I'll find it."

"Well, I'm off to see if we can use him."

But Gemma already knew the answer. He was definitely sturdy and able. But she was more curious about his background and what brought him to Tiger Mountain than anything.

She made her way to Gray, who stood by the fire, and offered him the blanket. "Wrap this around you. I can offer you coffee or hot chocolate."

He was indecisive behind his frown. "I don't want to trouble you."

"I'm getting some for myself, so it's no trouble."

"Then let me do it for you."

"Mr. Wilson, you're not a volunteer here yet. You're my guest. Now, would you like some or not?"

"Hot chocolate's fine. And…please call me Gray."

The mundane act of getting hot chocolate let Gemma compose her thoughts and settle her heart after wrecking the CJ and being carried by a stranger. Blanket still hanging on her shoulders, Gemma carried two cups of hot cocoa out to where Gray waited, hoping he would not look at her leg. There wasn't anything to see, really. Not like it was hideous or mangled. Instead it was stiff and aching.

She tried to smile to cover the pain. He'd settled on the big old orange couch next to the fire and appeared mesmerized by the flames, deep in thought. Good, he hadn't watched her limping walk.

"Here you go."

Slowly he turned his head to her, seeming to shake off his daze. "Thanks."

She handed the mug off. Of course their fingers brushed. But Gemma had already been up close and personal with Gray, so she didn't understand the current she suddenly felt. She wondered what he might look like when he was all cleaned up. Where had that come from? *Ignore, ignore, ignore.* "Well, we're off to an awkward start."

He quirked a brow and flashed a dimpled half grin. "At least it wasn't uneventful."

Gemma's heart hammered again at the reminder. At least she thought it was the reminder of her crash that elevated her heart rate and not his dimpled grin.

His smile suddenly dropped away. "I shouldn't have made a joke about it. You could have died. It could have been much worse."

Shaking her head slightly, she slurped in the warm cocoa. This was definitely what she needed. Get her core temperature back up and her brain working. It might be spring in southwest Oregon, but the rain dropped cold in the mountains.

"It worked out because you were there, at the right place at the right time. You've proven that you're physically strong enough to handle working for us, but tell me about your background—who are you, where do you come from, why do you want to volunteer and what experience do you have with animals, specifically big cats?"

"That's a lot of questions in one breath."

Gemma was botching the interview, but it all came rushing out and then she let the one question burning her mind spill.

"And why were you on the mountain today?" It wasn't like he'd simply shown up for an interview early. He'd been on the sanctuary property up in the mountains. The thought made her bristle.

Whoa with all the questions at once. But at least he'd anticipated them, even her last one. He had thought of an answer for that one while she'd gone to get the blankets. He hadn't expected for anyone to see him on the mountain or to rescue Gemma from a Jeep.

Without hesitation, he said, "I parked my truck where the county road meets Highway 101 and then hiked in. I was early for the interview and like to see the lay of the land where I'm going to work." It was as simple as that. And completely truthful. "Or, um…volunteer. But whether I'm salaried or not, I always take my work seriously."

"But you were on private property."

"Actually, I wasn't. I was still in the Wild Rogue Wilderness when I heard your cries for help. Only then did I cross over onto your property." Sure, he'd been checking the tigers and facilities from a distance with a set of binoculars—left behind when he'd run after her. Still, by the look on her face, he might have said too much.

She cocked a brow. "Getting the lay of the land, huh?"

Time to switch the topic. "I recently rented a house on the coast from a friend. I wanted a change of scenery from my place in Portland. I have a biology degree and worked in wildlife conservation before. I know that tigers are the most imperiled of the wild cats. Three subspecies are already extinct. There's only about three thousand left, living in the wild."

She arched a brow. Impressed? Or maybe he was trying too hard. He needed this volunteer position. But he couldn't let her see just how much.

"It's because I believe in what you're doing that I wanted to volunteer my time while I'm between contracts. It makes me angry when I read about the dwindling endangered species populations and abused animals. You're doing a good thing here. I believe in your cause." Okay, now he was repeating himself. His pulse was beginning to roar in his ears. He'd better shut this down or he'd go off again and she would think he was too crazy to keep around.

But he didn't have to worry as he saw the suspicion drain from her face. And all because he said he believed in her cause.

She limped closer to the fire and, without thinking, he offered a hand. "Are you sure you're okay?" Then remembered she'd said her limp was part of her now. She didn't want his help. "Since you were in an accident today, maybe you should see a doctor."

Her look silenced him on the matter. "I've already told you what happened. The reason for my limp." She bent over to stoke the fire, her long hair hanging down.

"You didn't, actually. Just that you had an injury. How did it happen?"

"I was in another car wreck." She straightened up. A distant look came into her eyes.

"I'm sorry to hear that."

Gray almost tossed out a joke about her skills as a driver but thought better of it. As she stood by the fire to warm up, her eyes grew bright, flames dancing in them. He'd never seen anyone more alive than

Gemma Rollins. And she truly seemed to be passionate about sheltering the abused wildlife and caring for them. Yet someone at this sanctuary was involved in crimes against the tigers. To use a sanctuary as a cover for trafficking was about as low as a person could go in Gray's opinion. Was there any chance someone else was behind the trafficking? Who would have the authority or access to do so without Gemma noticing? The simplest answer was the one he didn't want to believe—that she was involved in the trafficking after all. He could hardly believe the conflicting emotions she stirred in him. But it was time for him to push them aside and get to know the real Gemma Rollins and what she was really up to with the sanctuary.

"Thanks. It happened a long time ago." With a frown she refocused on him. "What do you do, Gray, when you're not volunteering? You mentioned you're between contracts."

"I'm a computer programming whiz."

She angled her head, confusion in her eyes.

He chuckled. "I know what you're thinking. I have a biology degree and I'm a computer whiz? As it turns out, learning to code is an important skill for biologists or any other science field, especially those who spend most of their time crunching data. I had a heads up on that skill. Growing up, I spent too much time playing video games and ended up learning to code early on as a side hobby. Though when I wasn't playing games, the rest of the time I was outdoors, exploring nature. I love animals, and I want to do something meaningful with my life." There. He hadn't even had to lie to keep his cover. He was currently working on installing new accounting software for Wilderness, Inc., a wilderness survival training company run by his brother, Cooper, though he'd had to put that aside temporarily to investigate Tiger Mountain.

Gray was only a silent partner at Wilderness, Inc. anyway. He invested in the business but didn't want to make decisions or be involved in running the place.

He'd been at the Wilderness, Inc. office in Gideon when he'd received the tip about Tiger Mountain. With this new tip, he believed he was close to solving this case, and he was geographically close as well.

Gemma sat on the sofa and he did the same, across from her. She studied him over the rim of her cup of hot chocolate.

Gray shrugged. "Any more questions?"

"Nope. You have any for me?"

Yep. I have plenty of questions. But he had to be careful and ask the simple questions a volunteer, a wildlife enthusiast, would ask.

"I'm a hands-on kind of guy. I like to learn the ropes as I work. So any questions I have for you can be answered while I'm working. Oh, well, I guess there is one question. You going to let me volunteer or not?"

She gave him her soft and simple smile, the same one he'd seen on the road. It kindled a feeling he hadn't experienced in a long time and he didn't want to feel that again. He'd have to be careful around Gemma.

"You're hired," she said.

A woman appeared from the hallway and came over to them. Gemma introduced Cara as a Tiger Mountain employee. She handed a cane to Gemma. "Found it."

Gemma's faced colored. She'd said that her limp was part of her, but she didn't appear that comfortable with it. "Maybe I can get my other one from the CJ, if it's even salvageable."

Gray glanced out the window, noting the rain had

finally and completely stopped. How long that would last, he didn't know. "Mind if I start work today? You can give me a tour of the place and show me what you need me for later, but right now maybe I can get your Jeep down the mountain."

Her eyes went even brighter. "Are you serious?"

"Sure, if you have a truck with a winch around here. Or, if not, we can call a wrecker, but I'll take care of it. You can get back to doing what's important." Gray found that, despite his true reason for being at Tiger Mountain, he honestly wanted to be useful to Gemma. But he reminded himself he wasn't here for her. He was working undercover to expose illegal activities at Tiger Mountain.

Gemma gave him the go-ahead and introduced him to Tom, a full-time staffer who had a four-wheel drive with a winch, which came in handy at a big cat sanctuary. Gray rode with Tom so he could show him where the vehicle had ended up.

Tom slowed the truck when they came to the mud slick in the road. A chunk of mountain seemed to have slid across the way. Tom sighed. "Gemma is not going to like this. Not one bit. She's already had a tough time here. I tell you, if it's not one thing, it's another."

Gray wanted to ask Tom more about what troubles Gemma had, but they were here. "This is where her CJ went into the tree. If you look to your left and up a bit, you'll see it just over the rise."

"I can see the bumper from here and hopefully the rest is still attached."

"Only one way to find out." When Gray stepped onto the road, his thoughts reverted to saving Gemma, holding her against him and hiking over the rocks and road.

He remembered her mentioning the perfect storm,

her brakes quitting during the drive while the power steering had gone out as well. She would have shifted to the lowest gear, no doubt, and possibly tried the parking brake, but going down a steep mountain road would have worked against her. Even if it hadn't been raining and even without a mudslide, that could have been deadly. The Jeep CJ rested right where he'd left it, only it was steeped in thick, clotting mud. The vehicle was decades old and the brake hose was likely just as ancient and could have given out. But the steering, too, on the same day?

In such situations, he often referred to Occam's Razor, a principle of philosophy—the simplest explanation was the right one—and in this case, the chance that both the brakes and the steering went out at the same time on their own was unlikely. In which case he wanted to get a closer look. Had the vehicle been sabotaged?

Tigers were worth more dead than alive, their parts bringing money in excess of a hundred grand, thanks to the demand for traditional Asian medicine. All it took was finding a buyer on the black market and someone needing money could easily make it in spades.

Gemma Rollins might be standing in the way of that. If Gray discovered her life was in danger, he would not only work undercover, but serve as her protector.

THREE

Gemma exited the shower, glad to finally be free of the grime and mud. But she wished she could shake the disquiet the crash had left her with. The sun had finally set and she'd hurried home—a cabin across from the main facilities—to clean up. Tom had texted that he and Gray had been able to get her CJ to Carl's body shop.

With the Jeep taken care of for now, she had the freedom to focus her energies elsewhere—such as on her wish list, which was more like a needs list for the sanctuary. Two-way radios for everyone went on the top of the list. If Gray hadn't showed up, radios would have come in handy. They didn't require a cell signal and would provide essential communication with the habitats so spread out. She wrote that down.

She had so many hopes and dreams for making Tiger Mountain great to build a legacy and fulfill the dreams her parents had for a big cat sanctuary. Dreams that had been dashed when they'd died in a plane crash, and ultimately, with her uncle's death after that.

And this time, Gemma would not allow rumors of abuse to spoil their reputation. Her parents had not exploited the animals and endangered their sanctuary status by putting the cats on display or allowing pictures to be taken with the animals. Or people to pet the cubs because they had no cubs. They were not breeding the animals! Nor had they abused the animals by under-feeding them.

Still those rumors had destroyed their donor base and her parents were returning from a trip to meet with an investor who could revive their private foundation that supported Tiger Hills when their plane had crashed.

She'd never understood why someone had started the rumors.

Or who.

But after their death, her uncle had worked tirelessly to hold things together under great pressure. After the car accident in which he died, and with Gemma in the hospital undergoing multiple surgeries, there had been no one left to manage Tiger Hills or answer the untrue rumors of abuse that continued. The rumors meant do-nors fell away and without funding to keep the animals fed, the rumors would become true.

There had been no funding left to even pay for staff, and she didn't want the possibility that a full-scale in-vestigation would further humiliate her family so she didn't stand in the way when the powers-that-be re-moved the animals and transferred them to other sanc-tuaries while she remained in the hospital.

Gemma spent several debilitated months going through two surgeries for her leg. She'd been devas-tated, broken both physically and emotionally over her losses. But once she was free to think about her future, she went to Oregon State University, got her conser-vation biology degree and masters in nonprofit man-agement with the help of a financial grant and student loans, and planned for the day when she could start all over. Building something new and untainted as a way of restoring all that was lost to her family.

Her father had started Tiger Hill one tiger at a time when she was only five. Ten years later, he'd died in a plane crash. At twenty-eight, building a new sanctuary was the only way Gemma could think to get back the only life she'd ever known.

The process of creating a nonprofit foundation to support the new sanctuary, all the paperwork and certifications, building new enclosures and creating protocols, hiring staff and finding volunteers had taken several years. Once they'd met the licensing requirements, they starting acquiring the animals. Now with all their animals in place, they were ready for the USDA inspection—she was that close to realizing her dream.

She had seven people to help, including Gray. With fifteen tigers to care for, she wanted three more people to even out the workload. With a high turnover rate lately, was that even possible?

Clyde, her father and uncle's longtime friend, seemed to think so. She'd understood him to be a silent partner in the old sanctuary, but he'd been out of the country involved with his conservation organization during the time of their deaths. She hadn't seen him since she was very young, but he'd come to her rescue and invested a lot of money into her project of opening a new sanctuary. He was all she had left now—well, that and Tiger Mountain.

From her cabin across from the Tiger Mountain facilities, Gemma could hear one of the tigers roar. Their roars could be heard up to two miles away. She didn't understand why Emil Atkins, the rancher whose property ran next to the sanctuary, found the tiger sounds disconcerting. Maybe it was more that his horses and cattle were disturbed, spurring him to lobby against the sanctuary, stirring up the other rural neighbors and ranchers.

Personally, Gemma found the sounds useful, since they let her know when something was upsetting one of the tigers. Maybe someone tampered with the cages, disturbing her tigers.

Or maybe it was more vandalism.

Irritation prickled the back of her neck.

Maybe it was Emil. Gemma needed to check. Grabbing a jacket, she paused to stare out the window into the pitch black of night. She couldn't see a thing. The sense that someone watched her crawled over her. Reaching for the drapes to pull them shut, she paused when lightning flashed in the distance and thunder followed, rumbling through Gemma's core.

Before she could close the drapes, someone knocked on the door, startling her.

She calmed her pounding heart and rushed to the door. A quick glance through the peephole into the darkness revealed nothing. Gemma flipped on the porch light.

Gray Wilson.

She frowned. What did he want?

Gemma opened the door. He'd cleaned himself up and wore jeans and a light black jacket over a blue polo shirt. His shaggy hair was neat and combed. She held back her smile. A gust of wind blew in and carried the scent of soap. He smelled nice too. "Gray, what brings you here?"

His expression grew somber. "Mind if I come in for a minute?"

"Actually, I was on my way out to check on the tigers. Heard one of them roaring."

"Another storm's approaching. Can't it wait?"

"What? Afraid of getting wet again?" She teased him, but the concern in his eyes increased her sense of uneasiness.

"We need to talk." He grabbed her arm and guided her inside. Oddly enough, his action didn't scare or offend her but confirmed the seriousness of the situation.

Suddenly, the room seemed too dark.

Gemma flicked on a lamp. "What is it, Gray?"

"While the Jeep was propped up on the wrecker, I took a look underneath. You mentioned the brakes and the steering went out at the same time. That's unusual enough that I wanted to tinker. Look a little harder."

Goosebumps rose on her arms. "And?"

"I think someone tampered with your brakes."

Gemma stiffened. She'd been on suspicion overload and hadn't wanted to think about that possibility. But she held on to the hope that he was wrong. "What makes you the expert? If the mechanic didn't see it?"

"I helped my dad restore an old hot rod and a few other vehicles. I know my way around cars."

"That still doesn't explain why you would find it and the mechanic wouldn't." She wanted to remain in denial. Find a reason he could be mistaken.

"Carl's a nice guy, but he gave it a passing glance. I didn't, that's all. Nor did I point it out to him."

Interesting. "Because…?"

"Because someone worked hard to make this look like an accident. And they might lash out or get desperate if word spreads that you know it wasn't. But I think you should call the sheriff about this—discreetly. Someone tampered with your brakes. Knew that they would be completely out by the time you were swerving around the dangerous bends in the mountain road. I would have called him myself, but I left that up to you. It's your business."

"And the steering? Anybody tamper with that? With no brakes and no real way to steer, I should have gone right over the edge." Then she allowed the truth she'd wanted to ignore to sink in. Gemma was sitting on the sofa before she even realized it. *Somebody tried to kill me?*

"No." Gray huffed a laugh. "The steering was just shot. That was just unfortunate." Gray frowned.

A chill crawled up her spine and around her throat. Gemma pressed her hand to her neck. When Gray took a step toward her, she instinctively stood from the couch and stepped around it, putting the furniture between her and Gray Wilson. It had been sheer chance that her steering had failed—and then sheer chance that she'd survived. That she'd been able to keep the Jeep from going over the road. That she'd screamed for help and someone had come. Chance...or was it? He had appeared out of nowhere today.

She studied him even as he watched her. Had he been the one to tamper with her brakes? He would have had to follow her up the mountain. Done his work while she'd left the Jeep alone. He'd definitely had the opportunity. But what about motive? Why do that only to save her?

"You were conveniently on the mountain today." What was she doing? She shouldn't accuse him right here and now, but she had to know. And in her heart of hearts, she didn't believe he would do such a thing. But if not Gray, then who?

"What? You think..." Gray threw up his hands. "You think I did that? I don't even know you. And if I wanted you to crash, why would I try to save you or tell you someone tampered with the vehicle and that you should call the sheriff to start an investigation?"

"Why indeed." To gain her confidence? Gemma scraped her hands through her hair. "I'm sorry. I know it sounds absurd, but I had to bring it up. You know the sheriff will."

Gray tensed. "Yeah, he'll ask if you bring it up."

"I won't have to. He'll want to know about anyone new who is working on the sanctuary." Gemma looked again out the window.

"Just anyone new? Why's that?"

"He's already looked into anyone who has been here longer than two months. Checking on the neighbors too."

"Why? What aren't you telling me?"

"I didn't want to scare you off so soon. There have been a few happenings."

"Happenings?"

"Up to now, it's just been vandalism and a little petty theft." She hadn't wanted to get into this with Gray before he even had a chance to meet the tigers and fall in love with them. "There are a few people around who don't want the sanctuary to succeed. So, once in a while, we have trouble. Vandalism that amounts to sabotage." *Please don't ask me more…*

"But do you think they would go so far as to try to kill you?"

"No. I can't believe that. Or, at least, I couldn't until just now. I don't…I don't know anymore. And I don't know why you would care so much."

Gray closed the drapes for her. "I'm just a volunteer who happened to show up on the day someone tried to kill you, Gemma. I want to help you—keep you from getting hurt. And that's why I'm telling you that you need to call the sheriff. And be on your guard. Keep your blinds and curtains drawn. And keep your head about you. Be careful around strangers."

Gray Wilson was a stranger to her, so it seemed odd he would say that, though it was good advice. He arched a brow.

"And be even more vigilant around people you know."

Gray watched Gemma's reaction to his warning.

Wariness lurked behind her gaze. Lightning flashed again and thunder sounded as though it was on top of them.

"I didn't mean to scare you by telling you about the brakes. But you needed to know."

"I'm not sure whether to thank you or not." She gave a nervous laugh and then released a long sigh.

Through a cracked window, he heard the tiger roar. Gemma glanced over, apparently still worried about the big cats—maybe even more than she worried about herself. That could be dangerous, but he admired her dedication.

"Why don't you wait to go out there until the worst of the storm passes? I'll go see the tigers with you. After all, that's what I volunteered for." He grinned, hoping to lighten the mood.

She smiled in return, appearing to relax. The only trouble was Gray didn't want her to relax too much. She needed to take the brake tampering seriously. Gray hoped the sheriff encouraged her in that. He'd met Sheriff Kruse but didn't know him as well as Cooper did. He hoped that the sheriff was a man who could be trusted. Gray didn't think anyone in local law enforcement was involved, but there was no way to know for sure—that was why it was so important that his cover remain intact, so he'd have to be conveniently absent when the sheriff showed up. And while working undercover, he could do a little investigating into the saboteurs she'd mentioned and anyone else who might want the sanctuary to fail. More importantly, he needed to learn why someone would want Gemma dead.

Were the vandalism and the attempt on her life connected? The two acts seemed different enough that they could be from two different people. Gray had a friend—a forensic investigator—who might be able to offer advice on the profiles of who might be behind these two very different crimes.

But first, he'd need to ask her what sort of things the saboteurs had done. Why the sheriff hadn't stopped them. But then he'd come across as an investigator. Besides, the way she shivered and hugged herself, he wanted to dial down the fear and tension. He needed to gain her confidence before he moved too fast.

He had taken a step out of his role as a nobody volunteer in coming to her cabin. In making the disclosure about her brakes. Maybe it would have suited his purposes better to keep the information to himself to see what developed, but he had a moral and ethical obligation to let her know what kind of danger she was potentially in.

"We can head over to the resource building while we wait. Get the keys for one of the utility vehicles. It's quicker to get in and out," she said.

"I guess now would be a good time for you to give me that tour I never got today."

"Maybe. Except it's dark out. You can't see everything. But, yeah, I can show you some things."

Gray followed Gemma, who was ably walking with

her cane, noting she hadn't locked her door. "Aren't you going to lock up?"

She paused, turned to face him. "What? No... I—"

"You don't usually lock up?"

She shook her head. "Never had a reason to."

"Until now. You are taking me seriously, aren't you?"

Frowning, she headed into the house and returned with keys and locked the door. "There. Satisfied?"

"Yes."

She headed toward the main building. Gray caught up to her in two long strides. "I know it's kind of awkward and all. First I pull you from the wreckage and carry you across a mudslide to safety only to learn that you're the woman I'm supposed to interview with. And now I show up at your cabin and tell you someone tampered with your brakes. Believe me, it's weird for me too."

"I'll admit it's a lot to happen in one day." Gemma paused beneath the security light on the porch of the main office and tried the door. It didn't open, and she jingled the keys. "Good thing I went back for them. Someone locked up."

"I hope that's the usual practice."

"It is—I'd just lost track of the time, or I would have remembered to grab the keys in the first place. Wouldn't do to have computers or paperwork stolen."

"Especially with the saboteurs running around."

"Exactly."

"But you're not worried about your cabin."

"No, I wasn't. Not until you showed up tonight. I didn't think they would go that far. I don't keep anything of real value in the cabin."

Once inside, Gemma grabbed a set of keys out of a key box and then led him out the side door to a commercial carport, where two utility vehicles—old Gators—were parked along with some other equipment. Gemma had a thing for old equipment, it seemed. Either that or limited funding.

"You could use a fence around this to make sure nobody steals this equipment."

"It's on my wish list. I'm making a list to give to the man who helped me establish the private foundation and funded most of it to get Tiger Mountain up and running—Clyde Morris. He's been out of town. Out of the country, rather, but he'll be here tomorrow and I need to be ready with the list. At some point, I won't have to depend on him so much. We're working on building our donor base but it takes time."

His pulse hiked up.

Clyde Morris.

Gray was definitely listening. Could this be the guy he was after? A single primary funder was unusual for an expensive operation like this one. The man had to have some reason for investing so heavily in the tiger sanctuary. Was it so he could use the animals for his smuggling? Gray knew better than to jump to conclusions—but it was still a lead worth following. "Why don't you tell me what's happened? You keep mentioning someone is trying to sabotage the sanctuary."

Ignoring him, Gemma grabbed a couple of flashlights and climbed into the utility vehicle. "You coming or what?"

"I thought we were going to wait for the storm."

"I think it's a lot of noise and threats. It might not even rain, and I don't have all night. I need to check on that tiger."

After Gray got in, he held on when she took off. She might struggle to walk and need a cane, but she had no trouble driving or shifting gears. That made him smile. "Well, tell me more about the issues. As a volunteer, I should know. You're not really afraid you're going to scare me off, are you?"

Waiting for her answer, he studied her profile. At least a few security lights had been installed at strategic points.

She glanced over at him. "You got me."

"Really? I was only joking."

"I've already lost an intern and two volunteers over this stuff."

Wow. "Look, Gemma. I'm a big boy. I can handle anything you have to say. Anything you think is going to happen. In fact, I'll go so far as to say maybe I'm supposed to be here to protect you. Keep you safe."

The Gator slammed to a stop, almost sending Gray flying. He jerked his head to Gemma. Had she done that on purpose? Gemma hopped from the vehicle, holding a flashlight. He followed her down the paved trail and she let them in through a gated fence—the first enclosure to surround the sanctuary, nesting two more fenced areas, he noticed. She unlocked and opened the gate to yet another fenced area.

"We have twenty main habitats the animals have access to. Each habitat has a lot of space with trees and grass, rocks and a pool. All the habitats connect to indoor buildings with stalls—four habitats to each of the indoor buildings. We call the indoor buildings Habitats A, B, C, D and E. Five buildings total. We have fifteen cats right now, but eventually, I hope to add more."

She led him down the path that wove through well-kept grounds with large secured areas. He saw now why her vehicles were old. She put all her money into the habitats and care of the animals. "During the day, the tigers are locked outside in their habitats while we clean the holding areas. I need your help with all of it. The cleaning, the feeding. We have an older cat, Caesar, who requires special care and takes extra time. I know it doesn't seem like much, but with so many cats and so few people it can be exhausting. And dealing with the daily maintenance has put me behind on administrative tasks. I have to work on proposals and grants and educating the public and most importantly getting ready for the upcoming USDA inspection. We have to always be prepared for surprise inspections, as well, but it's all I can do to take care of the big cats."

She looked at him, waiting for his reaction, he supposed. He shrugged. "I'm good with anything you throw at me. Lead on."

Gemma walked in front of him, and he couldn't help but notice that, with her cane, she had a gentle, rolling gait, almost like a tiger.

"At night, they have full access to their habitats, both inside and out."

Gray stopped to watch as a tiger he could barely see in the dark disappeared inside. "Do all the habitats have these multilevel platforms and pools?"

"Yep. We don't want the cats getting bored. We also rotate them so they are able to explore new habitats every few days. Wouldn't want them to get bored or start pacing like you see in zoos."

"You're encouraging them toward naturalistic behaviors."

She smiled. "You sound like a press kit. How are you at public speaking?"

He shrugged. "Okay, I guess. Why do you ask?"

"I could use help educating the public about what we're doing here. I want them to know why the cats need this place. I want to teach everyone about the endangerments the big cats face in the wild and in captivity. And about poaching and trafficking."

"Now *that* I can do." He wondered if he sounded a little too eager, too knowledgeable about the topic that was the basis of his career. But Gemma had no reason to suspect he was a special agent investigating Tiger Mountain, unless, of course, she was guilty.

Gemma led him deeper into the sanctuary, the moon finally filtering through the storm clouds and casting odd, dappled shadows through the refuge. Would it rain or not? Gemma still used her flashlight to chase away the shadows, and, by the way she continually shined the light into the dark corners, he knew she was taking his warnings seriously. Or her wariness could have to do with the vandalism, whatever trouble the saboteurs had been causing for her.

Finally they came upon a habitat with a pacing tiger and when the growl came, Gray knew this tiger was the one causing the ruckus. Pausing at the cage, Gemma sighed. "This is Kayla. She came from El Paso where she was chained in a too-small concrete cage for a roadside attraction at a truck stop. Someone bred tigers there too and sold the cubs to people who stopped in to get gas. She's usually very calm. Something's disturbed her."

He heard the frustration in her voice and more—she expected to find something wrong, such as more vandalism. Gemma walked the perimeter of the enclosure, shining her flashlight around.

Gray kept up with her, leaning in close to whisper. "I'm thinking now would be a good time to tell me what you're expecting to find. What has someone been doing to scare you like this?"

She gasped and jumped into him, dropping the flashlight. "That. That's what I'm looking for." Gemma pointed at something inside the habitat.

"Stay back." Gray grabbed the flashlight and pushed her behind him, not having a clue what she'd seen.

Then he found it. What was it, exactly? His mind was slow to wrap around it.

"It's a doll. Supposed to be me, slashed up and covered with blood."

Frowning, Gray shook his head, wishing he could have removed the doll before Gemma had seen it. But, considering her certainty after just one look, he realized she'd seen this kind of thing before. What he didn't know was if the person or persons responsible also had murder on their mind.

His first impression of her—that she was about to make trouble for him—had been all wrong. No. Gemma Rollins wasn't making trouble.

She was *in* trouble. In deep.

FOUR

"Is this the sort of thing that has your staff and volunteers leaving?"

"Yes and no. The attacks aren't always so...creative." This had her skin crawling, even though it wasn't the first of its kind. She used the clicker she kept in her pocket, signaling Kayla to go inside and remain there. Though the sanctuary's purpose was to offer a natural environment, some training was required for the tigers to live in captivity.

She took the flashlight from him and shined it around. "Looks like Kayla has gone inside. Now would be a good time to shut her in so we can get the doll out for evidence."

"Wait. Shouldn't we leave it like it is so the sheriff can see it?" Gray asked.

"You mean cordon it off as a crime scene and all that?" Gemma laughed. "That's exactly what they want so they can mess with my tigers. And by *they* I mean the neighboring ranchers. I'd have to shuffle the tigers around, disrupt the routine and I'd be short a habitat until Sheriff Kruse and his deputies could get to it. I'm almost of a mind not to call it in at all. Let them try to scare me. I'm not so easily scared."

A noise startled her. Gemma gasped. *Right. She's not so easily scared.* Sounded like a large object, maybe a garbage can, being knocked over. "Do you think whoever left this is still here?"

She started off toward the noise, but Gray grabbed her arm. "No. It's too dangerous. I would suggest waiting in the vehicle, but the Gator isn't going to provide any protection." He looked as if he wanted to run toward the sound himself but was visibly hesitating. "No way am I leaving you here alone."

While she was glad he didn't plan on leaving her, she hadn't exactly asked for his protection.

He hurried in the direction of the sound, leaving Gemma to keep up with him the best she could with a cane. Who was this guy anyway? Taking over like he owned the place. Gemma should be indignant, but Gray's actions kind of warmed her heart. Still, it didn't wash away her fury at the vandalism. Didn't these people realize the animals had already been abused in one way or another? They didn't need to be tormented anymore. Gemma followed Gray around a corner, watching as he flashed the beam of light with his own flashlight, searching the shadows while she hoped for a signal to call the sheriff's office on her cell. Finally, she got one and stood in place to keep it. She wondered what it meant that the number was saved on her phone.

She left a message with Laura, the dispatcher, about a new incident. Seeing an effigy of herself had only happened once before. Usually the trouble involved more mundane things like dismantling half the fence for a tiger's habitat or spray-painting vulgar words on the buildings. All of it was meant to wear her down. Didn't these people realize the extent of her commitment?

They found an overturned garbage can near a small

utility building. Gray put his hand up. "Don't take another step." He flashed the light around the ground. "Maybe someone was here and left some tracks. The sheriff can use that."

"Whatever you say." She waited a beat. "See any yet?"

"It's too dark out. With all the rain of late and mud, though, we're bound to find a few."

"Right, but you're going to see tracks belonging to volunteers and staff as well."

"Has anyone been out here since the rain stopped this afternoon?"

"Of course. Tigers still need to be cared for. Things don't stop because it rains." She thought back to this afternoon. Well, maybe things do stop a little when you have an accident. That had thrown off her afternoon—and Tom's too, when he went to haul the Jeep into town. "Look, Gray, I appreciate you trying to turn all detective and everything, but I think finding a distinctive shoe print in this mud is a lost cause. Besides, Sheriff Kruse is already investigating. He could have his own list of suspects, but I think it's the rancher neighbors. None of them are happy that we're here. The most vocal has been Emil Atkins. He hasn't been shy about letting me know what he thinks about the sanctuary. He doesn't like it so close to his ranch. He's threatened me a few times, but they were idle threats. So now he's escalated to foolhardy attempts to scare me off."

The way Gray looked at her told Gemma he was thinking about her brakes.

"Once Sheriff Kruse hears about this, he'll send one of his deputies out here to get the doll for evidence. Then one of them will visit the ranchers and ask questions and throw a few warnings out. It's a game we've been playing for a long time."

She waited and watched his reaction with only the dim light of the distant security lamp illuminating his face. But his frown was easy to see. He looked up at the sky as though expecting to watch the stars but instead found disappointing darkness in the clouds that hadn't yet dumped their burden. How strange. Even stranger, Gemma could totally relate to that.

Finally, Gray dropped his gaze to her. "I'm sorry you're going through this, Gemma. I know we've only just met, and you don't know me, but I'm here to help if I can."

And Gemma believed him. That was the problem—she usually believed people, whether she should or not. Gemma had been such a poor judge of character, and she shouldn't rely on that inner sense that told her Gray was trustworthy.

"Let's go and get the effigy out of the habitat and then head back to the Gator so we can leave here." This made her sick, absolutely sick.

Once they were in the Gator and Kayla's habitat was effigy-free so the big cat could roam at will, Gray glanced at Gemma. "I'd really like to hear about the other incidents."

"I know, Gray, but I really don't want to talk about them right now, if that's all right. Besides, I didn't hire you to investigate or even protect me. I hired you to shovel manure, clean out habitats while the cats are outside and maybe, if you're a good speaker, help me educate the public and convince the neighbors that we are no danger to them."

Her tone was hard, she knew that, but he seemed to take it in stride, understanding her mood. She was somewhat surprised at his determination to stay after everything he'd seen. And yet, Gray Wilson was still here, eager to help.

But Gemma had a big question burning in her mind. A question she wasn't willing to voice and barely willing to think about. After losing her parents and her uncle, was Gemma willing to stay—to build Tiger Mountain and keep it thriving—in the face of warnings and threats on her life? Her greatest fear was that she wasn't strong enough to see it through, to build a new sanctuary to match or even surpass what her father had built years ago. But if she was strong enough to stay, she hoped to restore her family's reputation destroyed by vicious rumors.

Who had started them?

Gemma steered the Gator into the covered garage and parked, hating how her mood had soured.

"I'll walk you to your cabin."

"No need, really," she protested weakly. Gemma was too tired to fight him, if he persisted.

"Well, my truck is parked that way anyway." He grinned.

Gemma could easily grow to like that grin. But she didn't like it yet. No. Not yet.

He strolled next to her. "Listen, the big cats are important to you. I get that. But who's going to take care of the tigers if you don't care of yourself?"

At her porch, she turned to him. "What are you trying to say?"

"When the sheriff or a deputy comes tomorrow to get the effigy and dismiss it as just another childish prank, tell them about your brakes. Promise me?"

"I don't have to promise you, Gray." Why was he

making this so personal? "But I'll tell him. I appreciate you thinking of the tigers."

And of me...

She nodded her goodbye and went inside her cabin. Shutting the door behind her, she leaned against it.

"Who's going to take care of the tigers if you don't take care of yourself, indeed?" She mumbled the question.

Why would someone try to kill her? It made no sense.

Her parents' tragic deaths had been followed by her uncle's just three short years later. Ten years later, Gemma was still haunted by the accident that killed Uncle Dave. Had his death been cold-blooded murder engineered to look like an accident?

At his temporary living quarters—the rental house on the beach—Gray tossed his keys on the table.

The accommodations were sparsely furnished but served his purpose. At least it wasn't too close to Gideon, Oregon, where his siblings, Cooper and Alice, worked at Wilderness, Inc., providing excursions and survival training. If he was any closer, he feared he would run into someone who could give his true identity away. He had to keep his distance from Sheriff Kruse, as it was.

Still, he hadn't worked in southwest Oregon when he'd been a game warden, so he shouldn't run into too many people he knew, other than the sheriff's department. When he'd been offered the job with the federal government as a special agent with the USFWS, then he'd worked out of the Portland, Oregon, regional office and traveled throughout Pacific Northwest.

Now, Gray was a senior special agent hoping for a management position as a Resident Agent in Charge.

That could mean a move to another regional office or even to headquarters in Falls Church, Virginia. The selection process was competitive and if Gray was promoted…well, maybe then Dad would be proud of him.

His stomach soured at the thought of his father. He thought he'd extricated that need for approval from his life. Gray had always believed he was the black sheep of the family until Jeremy committed suicide. Nothing compared to that. Still, Cooper was the son their dad was proud of. Not Gray.

He sighed and grabbed a soda from the fridge, noticing his cell buzzed.

Ten minutes later he finished a call with his superior, Mark Jenkins. Gray filled him in on the new developments. He hadn't come into this expecting to discover that someone was trying to kill Gemma.

Why had the mechanic been so quick to overlook the sabotaged brakes? Was he involved somehow? What about the sheriff's department? Why weren't they taking the earlier threats against Gemma seriously?

From what Gray knew of Sheriff Kruse, he believed the sheriff was a good man. But he had too much square acreage to cover with a few deputies and even less funding. So Gray could give him some grace, but he didn't like what sounded like a well-developed routine of letting Gemma's neighbors get away with harassment with nothing more than a slap on the wrist and the hope that it would stop on its own.

Fury boiled up in Gray's gut. He crushed the soda can in his hand. When the time was right, Gray would talk to the sheriff but not yet. Not until he had the information he needed. Gemma didn't know just how fortuitous Gray's arrival was.

Will you listen to yourself?

He hadn't come here to help her. He'd come to Tiger Mountain as a way to slip into the trafficking organization and work with them while garnering the information he'd required for arrests. He should be looking into the man Gemma had mentioned today—the investor, Clyde Morris, in addition to the other staff and volunteers.

After grabbing another can of soda, Gray sat at his laptop to work. It was going to be a long night. First, he sent off an email to Kit Howard, the forensic investigator, and detailed what he'd learned so far. He wanted to hear what Kit made of it. Could the vandalism Gemma equated to sabotage—that the sheriff's department didn't take seriously—be related to attempted murder via tampered brakes?

Then he started in on his research on Clyde Morris who headed up an organization called Conservation International. However, the sanctuary had been funded through another company, Investments Conglomerate. What a vague name. A shell company owned by Clyde Morris, perhaps? That's why Gray hadn't known about him. And that would make it easy to launder and traffic any kind of contraband. Wildlife trafficking and anonymous companies went hand in hand.

Mark was using his channels to pull additional information on Clyde and send it to Gray. He had his work cut out for him tonight. The man himself would show up tomorrow, and Gray needed to know everything he could. He wanted to either draw attention to himself in the right way or stay invisible and observe.

He started with the Tiger Mountain website. Immediately images of Gemma's tigers popped up. A few pictures of Gemma were in the photo gallery but always with the sunglasses, and that got Gray thinking about her eyes.

Those gorgeous eyes...

She was an amazing woman. But he wouldn't let that distract him. He had to keep his head clear to get justice for Bill. And if closing this case put him in a good position for the promotion that might finally earn his father's approval, then that would just be the proverbial buttercream icing on the red velvet cake.

The next day Gray found himself partnering with Wes—the intern working at the sanctuary for college credit this semester—to learn about the daily rigors of cleaning the habitats and feeding the tigers, just like Gemma had told him he would last night. She'd said it as though he might be surprised or unwilling to do the mundane and lowly work of shoveling muck, but he'd done enough volunteer work around animals to know the drill. He hadn't seen her today, but that was probably for the best. He had to stay focused.

He should get to know all the volunteers and staff. Cara and Tom were full-time. Jill, Mavis and Ernie were volunteers like Gray and worked varied shifts. Gemma detailed the daily schedules and chores on a whiteboard in the kitchen slash conference room of the resource building where everyone gathered for their morning meetings, supplies throughout the day, and for weekly and monthly meetings. Every single thing they did for the tigers was written in task-specific binders. Meticulous, grueling work, as far as Gray could tell. But everyone he'd met seemed committed to the cause and loved the tigers. He could almost doubt the tip he'd received.

Then there was Clyde, whom Gray had yet to meet but according to Gemma would arrive today. Someone from the sheriff's office was also coming this morning to investigate the effigy doll and the tampered brakes. At least, he hoped Gemma would tell them about the brakes. He'd call in the information himself, but he didn't want to risk being recognized by Sheriff Kruse. But with his head down as he walked the habitat, tidying and picking up old bones, he was sure no one would notice him. This was perfect. He could watch the others like one of the cats stalking its prey. Gray's prey was suspicious activity.

Wes snuck up behind him in the grass. "I finished with Caesar's habitat. Once you're done here, we can finish the other two and then let the cats back out and clean their stalls. Then feed them. After this, we move on to the next habitat building. Need help here or you want to finish this one on your own?"

"I'm good. You go ahead and start on the next one."

Wes gestured toward the fence. "There's Deputy Callahan now, coming to check out Kayla's habitat."

Gemma walked next to the deputy, showing him where they'd discovered the effigy last night.

Great. Gray knew the deputy. He would definitely be recognized if he got too close and then what?

Gray kept his head down and headed into the taller grass to the other side, where he still needed to clean. For some reason, Wes followed him.

"Gemma mentioned some incidents, but she didn't share too much," Gray said. "What do you know about who is behind this?"

Wes shrugged. "We all think it's probably Emil Atkins—or that he's the ringleader, if it's a group of people. He claims that the sounds and scents of the tigers disturb his horses and cattle. He seems to think if he messes with Gemma enough she might get tired of it and leave. Or if he causes her some problems, she might have to shut the sanctuary down. We have our first official USDA inspection coming up and then, we'll get surprise inspections, you know."

Gray seriously wanted a reason to meet Mr. Atkins. Wes paused before heading up the trail to the gate. "I heard you were with her last night when you found the doll."

"Yep. It scared her, but she's a strong person and got over it pretty quickly."

"Maybe the deputy needs to talk to you too."

Great. All he needed was Wes butting into it. "I'm sure they know where to find me if they want me."

The intern nodded and then left Gray to his work. But he didn't trust Wes not to fetch the deputy. Gray slipped out of the habitat and headed in the opposite direction. He'd have to make up an excuse to give Wes later.

He made his way to the resource building, avoiding others. He didn't want anyone questioning his exit. After grabbing some water, he made small talk with Cara, so she'd pass the word on to Gemma that Gray would return later. He hoped Deputy Callahan would make short work of his investigation and leave.

But as he stepped out of the office, Gemma and Deputy Callahan entered through the main door. Gray froze. He whirled around to head out the back.

A man he didn't recognize stood in his way. "Everything all right?"

"Sure, yes. I just realized I forgot something up at the habitat where I was working." Yeah, he hadn't finished his task. "Just heading there now."

The man cocked a brow. The look in his eyes told Gray he didn't believe him.

Why?

Gray started to walk around, hearing Gemma and the deputy's conversation growing louder. Gemma sounded frustrated, her voice louder than he would have expected, and the deputy's tone seemed to brush off her accusations.

He wanted to turn around and face off with that man behind the badge. Give him a piece of his mind. Meanwhile this guy…this man who stood in his path had to be Clyde Morris, himself. Gray was not making a good first impression.

It was now or never. Gray thrust out his hand. "I don't believe we've met. I'm Gray Wilson."

Clyde's hand came up to meet Gray's, though slowly, hesitantly. "Clyde Morris."

"Mr. Morris, I still have some work to do. Care to walk with me?"

Clyde looked over Gray's shoulder, weighing his options. Something like disdain flashed in the man's gaze and then he looked at Gray. "Let's go for that walk. And please, call me Clyde."

Interesting. Clyde Morris didn't want a run-in with Deputy Callahan any more than Gray did, but he'd wager, for far different reasons. He pushed through the back exit and held the door for Clyde.

"I'm volunteering. Just started yesterday. How about you, Clyde? You a volunteer or a staffer? What do you do at Tiger Mountain?"

Clyde kept the brisk pace with Gray. "I'm the bread and butter here. I'm the man who funded the initiative to get this place going. Hopefully, Gemma will be able to gain the attention of wildlife philanthropists and raise more funds on her own."

"What about the reason Deputy Callahan is here?

Got any ideas on what to do about this troublemaker, whoever he is?"

Clyde stopped walking so Gray stopped too. "Oh, I know who you are now. Gemma told me about you. You're the guy who was with her last night when she found that effigy."

"That's right. You don't think this Emil Atkins might actually try to harm her physically, do you?"

Clyde frowned. "Why so interested?"

Gray shrugged. "Why not? She seems like a nice lady. I don't want to see her get hurt."

Now, here was the rub. Should Gray ask Clyde about Gemma's brakes? He didn't want to give Clyde any reason to look at him too closely. Maybe he should wait on that conversation. Might as well play dumb as long as he could.

To his surprise, Clyde clapped him on the back. "I don't either, Gray. I don't either. Gemma is like a daughter to me. At least now, anyway, that her family is gone. I funded this project of hers because years ago I was friends with her father and uncle. We shared a few business ventures, interests and wildlife conservation efforts, including the original sanctuary right on this same property. Then, we called it Tiger Hills. When Gemma's parents died, her uncle stepped in to care for her and keep their sanctuary going. But then he died, too. I was involved in a project on another continent and wasn't here to offer much help, financially or otherwise, during either tragedy. When she came to me with her idea to build a new sanctuary—with a new name and a fresh start—how could I say no?"

Gray studied the man. "I see your point."

"Bottom line is that I won't idly stand by while people threaten Gemma, nor will I allow her to get hurt. By you or anyone else. That's why I'm here—to investigate who's behind this harassment and stop it."

Funny that he didn't want to talk to the deputy. That should have been his natural response. It would have been Gray's too, if he weren't working undercover.

Clyde squeezed Gray's shoulder blade. Gray almost winced. What was that about? But the man had certainly got his attention. He looked him straight in the eye.

"Gemma has enough on her plate. If you see anything suspicious, anything at all, will you come to me first?"

What was he going to say? No? Nodding, Gray said, "I will."

Gray had already decided he needed to stick close to Gemma as much as possible, to keep her safe. Clyde's words had surprised him. Hadn't he come here to investigate crimes that might involve someone like this man who'd funded Tiger Mountain? And now, it turned out that Clyde was here at Tiger Mountain to conduct his own investigation.

Another twist in Gray's investigation.

FIVE

Gemma watched Clyde walk alongside Gray as they made their way into the sanctuary and habitats. She didn't know why it mattered, but she was glad to see them walking along like they were friends. She'd wanted Clyde to meet Gray. For some reason she couldn't fathom, she wanted him to like Gray too. She couldn't help but wonder if adding Gray or Clyde to this conversation with Deputy Callahan would make a difference. Without anyone there to be on her side, talking with the deputy clawed over her nerves.

Turning her attention back to Deputy Callahan, as they stood at his vehicle, she listened to his last words. "I'll write all this up in my report, Gemma, but there's not much I can do about it until we know who's behind it. We can only speculate and that's not good enough."

Like she hadn't heard those words a million times. "I'll see about getting some security cameras going. But it's just another expense to add to my wish list."

"If you want some real evidence we can use, better make those cameras a priority."

"I don't get it. It seems like I'm the one being punished here. I have to pay for security cameras to catch these guys while harassing me doesn't cost them a thing.

You have an idea who is behind it. Why can't you just stop him?"

The way he snapped his small writing pad closed made it clear he hadn't liked her insinuation that he wasn't doing his job. He arched a brow. "Anything else you can think of, Gemma?"

She frowned. The sheriff's office heard from her often and now, with each new incident, she felt like her complaints were being relegated to a low priority. Discouraged, she sighed. The image of Gray walking with Clyde entered her mind. And then his words.

Tell them about the attempt on your life. Tell them about your brakes. Promise me?

She hadn't promised him because she hadn't wanted to, but now she found herself responding to his request. "Actually, there is something else."

If she expected the deputy to take her seriously, then there were things that Gemma needed to take seriously as well. Deputy Callahan's reaction would be interesting to see.

"Well?"

"I had a wreck yesterday on the county road that runs through the property."

"And you're just reporting it now? What happened?" Deputy Callahan flipped open his little notebook again, the sheriff's department funds too low to bring them into the millennium. Or perhaps Callahan preferred pen and paper. Gemma got that. She used a whiteboard.

"Someone tampered with my brakes."

His entire forehead creased as he raised his brows. "Say again?"

"My brakes. I think someone tampered with them so I wouldn't be able to stop and I'd go over the edge."

"Are you saying someone tried to kill you?"

"Yes."

"And you know this how?"

"One of my new volunteers helped Tom tow the CJ over to Carl's. He checked out the Jeep when they arrived."

"And what did Carl say?"

Oh, why had she brought it up? She should have talked to Carl first, but Gray said the mechanic only gave the brakes a passing glance.

"I'm going to have Carl look at it again. I don't think he looked it over very carefully."

The deputy wrote some more in his notepad. Then he flipped it closed, concern in his eyes. That surprised Gemma.

"I'll stop by and talk to the mechanic myself." The deputy put his hands on his hips and gave her a pointed look. "Why would someone want to kill you, Gemma?"

"I don't… I don't know. You don't think it's just whoever has been harassing the sanctuary hoping I would shut things down and leave, do you?"

He shook his head. "Everything else so far has just been pranks. I don't think this prankster is the murdering type. The harassing type, yes, but I don't think he would kill someone. That said, you've made some people pretty angry with what you've decided to do here. Maybe you should have considered the neighbors when you decided to start this thing up again. Sure, it's a new name and new management but it's the same old thing. You should have thought about the trouble your parents had here, your uncle too, before they died."

His words cut through her. She didn't know what to make of them.

"Still, let me talk to the sheriff about this. I think it's high time we crack down on the harassment against you, and I know you want it to stop. It's taking up too much of my time and I want it stopped, too." Something flashed in Callahan's eyes, too quickly for her to read, before he stared at the ground. Then when he looked back up to her, the emotion was gone. "In the meantime, you'd better keep an eye out. Beware of strangers."

"What about…what about people I know?"

"Say again?"

"I'm just thinking that maybe it wasn't a stranger who tampered with my brakes. Maybe it was someone I know."

"And I'll ask again, any reason someone you know would want to kill you? Make it look like an accident?"

She shook her head.

Thoughts of her parents' plane crash rattled through her along with images of the wreck that killed her uncle, crushing her chest so she couldn't breathe.

"Gemma, you okay?"

She drew in a breath, composed herself. "Yes, I'm fine. How's…how's Sandy? I'm sorry I didn't ask you right off." Through all of this she'd discovered that his wife was fighting cancer, but she hadn't learned more than that.

His expression turned grim. "Hanging in there. Thank you for asking." He hung his head. Then when he glanced back up to Gemma, more feelings that she couldn't decipher briefly appeared in his eyes. "I'm sorry you're going through this, Gemma."

"I wish I knew something more to tell you."

He nodded and started to get into his vehicle.

"Um… Deputy Callahan?"

"Yes?" He paused, halfway into the vehicle.

"The night my uncle was killed, he was about to tell me something. I have always had the feeling it was something big. I've wondered if maybe someone had wanted him dead and somehow caused the wreck. Do you think that's possible?"

"You were how old then? Seventeen?"

"I'd just turned eighteen."

"It was a traumatic event, and you were at that age when everything seems like it's life-or-death important. Maybe you imagined the importance of what he planned to tell you. Blew things out of proportion. I wouldn't make too much of it. The crash was ruled an accident. Remember, hon, it was a rainy night and a treacherous road."

He pursed his lips and studied her, like he was concerned about her mental state, which might plant doubts in his mind about everything Gemma had said. She wished now she hadn't brought it up.

"Get some rest, Gemma. Take a few days off." He climbed into his vehicle and drove off.

Right, like she could take time off when she had so much to do. She was almost certain not all of the habitats had been cleaned today, and they still had to butcher a slab of beef to feed the tigers this evening. And chickens for Caesar. He only liked chicken. Tomorrow the vet was coming to check on the old tiger. He might have liver cancer.

Gemma rubbed her arms and searched the woods that surrounded the sanctuary. The Wild Rogue Wilderness, where Gray said he'd been when he'd heard her shouting for help.

Movement drew her gaze to the carport shadows next to the main building.

Wes was talking to Emil Atkins! What was Emil even doing here? What was Wes doing *with* him?

He'd better be telling the man to get lost.

Gemma wished Deputy Callahan had stayed a few minutes longer.

She squeezed her cane until her knuckles were white. Her heartbeat thudding through her, she marched toward the building. When the two men disappeared behind the wall, she rushed forward, her leg aching with the effort, and called out. By the time she made the side of the building, both men had disappeared.

Fury coursed through her. Could Wes be involved with Emil? Was this the connection? Had he been the one to leave the effigy in Kayla's habitat?

Clyde had taken a phone call, leaving Gray free to finish cleaning the habitat while thinking about their strange conversation. He wished he could have lingered to listen in on the call. Clyde wasn't the man that Gray had expected. That's what he got for bringing his presumptions with him. He'd assumed the man was guilty based on limited information, but Clyde came across as innocent and genuinely concerned about Gemma. Still, Gray knew better than to trust Clyde. After all these years, if he were heading up the ring, the man had to be practiced in living his persona as an upstanding citizen. Someone fighting for the conservation of endangered tigers.

A true sanctuary stood in direct contrast to trafficking by rescuing abused or neglected animals, providing care. A true sanctuary didn't commercialize the tigers. Didn't buy, sell or trade the animals except where necessary for the tiger's quality of life.

Those thoughts brought him back to the task. He had a responsibility here in addition to his investigation.

The big cats were still in their stalls and off their schedule. He searched for Wes, but the guy was nowhere to be found. Gray didn't want to tackle the stalls without knowing the exact mechanism and procedure for releasing the tigers outside and locking them out of the stalls. He could probably figure it out on his own, but if he got it wrong that situation could turn dangerous. Even deadly.

Still, the work needed to be done. Where was Wes? He could ask one of the others to show him, but he had a feeling Wes wouldn't appreciate it. He didn't want to make enemies.

Frowning, Gray instead went in search of Gemma. He wanted to find out about her conversation with the deputy and keep an eye on her in general. She hadn't asked Gray to protect her, and he had no reason to be too worried for her safety in the middle of the day with the volunteers and staff about, except Gray couldn't find her anywhere.

Inside the resource building, Gray headed to the office and spotted Cara through the window walking to her parked car. It was only midafternoon—where was she going? Gray followed her outside.

"Cara!" He picked up his pace to catch her.

She paused next to her Honda Civic. "What's up?"

"Have you seen Gemma?"

"She was with the deputy, but I haven't seen her since." She frowned. "Why?"

He shrugged. "I wanted to talk to her, and I can't find her."

"I'm sure she's around somewhere. I know she wanted to check on Kayla after Deputy Callahan left. Maybe check the habitat."

"Sure thing." But he had just been there and no Gemma.

Cara got in her car and drove away. Gray stood there

and scanned the woods. From here he couldn't see much of the sanctuary behind the trees. Off in the distance, he spotted movement on a trail.

Gemma?

Per his mission, he needed to make inroads with Gemma and, now, Clyde. And he had a good excuse to talk to her. He could ask how it went with the deputy. Plus, he'd come up with an idea for educating the public. She didn't have to know the specifics about his years of experience in the wildlife arena. He trailed after her hoping to catch up with her. This particular path hedged the sanctuary expansion program—a vision to bring in more big cats and perhaps one day add other abused wildlife. It had beautiful views overlooking the Wild Rogue Wilderness region—rugged gorges and old-growth forests. The deeper into the forest on the trail, the thicker and taller the oaks, madrone, tan oak and chinquapin trees grew…the darker the forest.

Was she hiking the trail, which couldn't be easy with her cane, because she needed some time to herself?

Gray reconsidered interrupting her, but decided that he would follow behind, just to watch out for her. It didn't seem to him that Gemma was all that concerned about her life. Had she forgotten someone had tampered with her brakes? Didn't she understand what a bloodied effigy meant?

Did she realize that even Clyde appeared concerned for her? Though, come to think of it, could the man's concern for Gemma be an act?

Hands in his pockets, Gray hiked the trail, staying back to give Gemma the space she needed. And he thought about Clyde.

Could the man be behind the trafficking, using Tiger Mountain, and yet still care about Gemma as if she was a daughter? To Gray's way of thinking, those two undertakings were diametrically opposed. Gemma loved the sanctuary and the cats; any attempt to harm them would be painful to her. Things weren't adding up. As he walked, the trees closed in and the trail narrowed, littered with rocks and pebbles and gnarled tree roots. Hard for a woman with a cane, but Gemma had it figured out. And Gray thought he might have her figured out. She must doubt his assessment of the brakes or that someone had tampered with them. That someone was trying to kill her. She wasn't taking this seriously. Either that or it was simply too difficult for her to imagine someone harming her in broad daylight.

The woods around him suddenly turned quiet as the birdsong and chatter of squirrels and forest animals stilled. Leaves shuddered with a breeze. The sense that someone watched them set his teeth on edge.

His years in law enforcement, on top of his experience in the forests, sent warning signals resounding through him. The trail twisted around a cliffside, switching back above him. Pebbles trickled and Gray looked straight up the rocky wall. Was someone up there?

Gemma could be in danger.

He refocused on the trail and Gemma stood there, glaring at him.

"What are you doing here, Gray? Are you following me?"

"You got me. I followed you." He didn't mean to grin, exactly, because he wanted to remind her she shouldn't be hiking alone, but she somehow made him smile. Her long brown hair glistened in a ray of sun that broke through the trees. Beautiful. Gray found it hard to concentrate. He had the sudden urge to run his fingers through the tendrils. He shifted his gaze to her eyes and caught his mistake too late. Her eyes would always be a distraction for him.

To his surprise, Gemma's face softened. "You did?" Her question was soft. Warm even.

"Yes," Gray said, his voice softer too. *What are you doing, man? You can't be flirting with this woman!* But her eyes stared back at him, so full of goodness and purpose and worry all tangled up together. "You shouldn't go places alone. Remember, someone tried to kill you."

"I've walked this trail a hundred times."

"That was before someone tampered with your brakes."

Gemma sagged a little. "Oh, that. I wish you would quit reminding me. I needed to think about something else."

But he could see it in her eyes—even if she wasn't thinking about the brakes, she was brooding over something else that bothered her. How had he become so in tune with Gemma Rollins? "What happened, Gemma?"

She leaned harder on her cane, propped between two rocks. "Nothing. I wanted to clear my thoughts. I don't know who I can trust anymore."

"What did the deputy say? You did tell him about the brakes, didn't you?"

She nodded. "He said he would talk to Carl and see what he thinks. You said Carl gave it a cursory glance. Do you think he'll look again and find the same thing you saw? Or did I just make a fool of myself in front of a deputy who already doesn't take me seriously? Sometimes I even wonder if he wants the sanctuary gone, too."

Gemma leaned on the cane with both hands now and it was all Gray could do not to rush to her and hold her up. But she was much too independent to accept that from him. He didn't doubt she could hold her own, either. It was just that…maybe she had never had to face this kind of pressure from all sides.

He didn't want to give up his cover. Not yet. "I don't want to think Carl's involved, but if he doesn't tell the deputy the truth, then we'll know at least one person involved in this."

She shook her head. "I've known him much too long. I would never believe that."

And that was Gemma's problem. "You trust too much, Gemma." Gray stepped closer. He could catch her if she fell, but not for one minute did he believe she would.

"I think you're right," she replied. "I trust people I don't even know. Like you. I trust you when I shouldn't. I don't even know you."

How could he make her understand he was here to help her? But that wasn't true either. What was he thinking? Helping Gemma Rollins had never been part of his mission parameters. He was here to finish this, to find the person who was not only responsible for Bill's death but also the head of a large wildlife trafficking ring.

What would he do if that person turned out to be Clyde Morris, the man whom Gemma considered a father figure? From the information he'd read on Clyde, the man had long been a part of the Rollins family clan, though he hadn't been much support for Gemma when her parents and then her uncle were killed.

"Listen, Gemma, I'm sorry about the deputy. And about everything that's happening. But I do have some good news. I came up with an idea for educating the public. I wanted to tell you about that when I saw you on the trail. Then I realized that maybe you wanted some privacy so I tried to give you that while following you to make sure you were all right."

Her eyes brightened. "You came up with an idea for me? What—"

A rumble above cut off her question. Rocks shifted above, crashed against the cliffside and echoed across the mountain and through the trees.

"Look out!" Gray grabbed Gemma, cane and all, and pressed her beneath a protruding part of the rock wall, covering her with his body. Protecting her. Her breaths came hard and fast against his neck as her fear mingled with his own.

God, please protect her. Protect us!

SIX

The roar of boulders, rocks and dirt falling resounded through her ears and rumbled through her core. The rock wall behind her shook as if the whole earth quaked.

Gray's weight pressed against her as he pushed her harder against the granite. He was covering her, protecting her—making sure she didn't get hurt. This was a matter of life and death, after all. Gemma tried to shove the panic down, but a cry escaped anyway, betraying her. She squeezed her eyes shut as though that would help her keep the danger at bay, but whimpering groans fought their way out.

The rockslide seemed to take an eternity.

Gemma had never been more terrified, except in the crash with her uncle. What was happening to her already tumultuous life?

Finally, quiet replaced the roar in her ears. Well, quiet and her gulps for air along with Gray's.

Gray whispered into her ear, his warm breath accompanying his words. "I hope I didn't hurt you."

The fear and panic drained away, taking all her energy with it. Gemma was certain she would collapse if it weren't for the rock-hard pillar holding her up—and the powerfully built man. This wasn't the first time she'd felt the strength in Gray's shoulders and the sculpted muscles in his chest and abdomen. She'd been more than aware of his physique when he'd briefly carried her. She had to distract herself.

"Is it over?" she asked in a whisper.

"I think so." Gray slowly moved away from her. "Did I hurt you?" His tenderness was nearly her undoing. What did he think? That she would blame him for the pain she endured while being pressed against the rocks? He'd saved her life. Again. "No. I'm okay."

Did he suspect her lie? So what if the rock wall had likely left a few bruises on her back? At least she and Gray were still alive. Before stepping away from the wall, Gray twisted his neck to look behind him. They were partially pinned in by the rockslide. The way he tensed, she could practically feel the anger surging through him.

With all the rain they'd gotten, the rocks had no doubt shifted easily from their centuries-long resting place. A rockslide wasn't all that improbable, but what were the chances one would happen at the exact moment Gemma and Gray stood at that spot on the trail? Especially in light of her near death experience yesterday.

"Are you going to take this seriously now?"

Gemma couldn't help her quick intake of breath. The man didn't mince words. His question told her he had been thinking the same thing. This was no accident. "You don't think someone did this on purpose, do you?" The question sounded silly. But Gemma held on to a sliver of hope.

"We have to consider that a strong possibility." Gray turned to her, their faces impossibly close. "Gemma, why would someone want to kill you?"

"I don't know. All I can think is they don't want the sanctuary here. But is that worth ending my life?"

"The reasons people kill rarely make sense. Nothing is worth a person's life. Still, I want you to think hard about this. If you died, who would be left to run the sanctuary? Or would it die with you?"

At his words, a shudder ran over her. He didn't sound like a contract programmer who volunteered at a wildlife sanctuary in his free time. He sounded like someone who dealt with life-or-death issues every day.

Clearly sensing that she needed a minute to think through her response, he stepped away and assisted her around the large heap of rocks and dirt that must weigh a ton or more. They could have been crushed where they stood. Gray watched the area, alert and aware of his surroundings, to make sure they were no longer being threatened, she presumed. In a way, he reminded her of the tigers, always watching and patrolling their habitats, maintaining control of their territories. But that didn't boost her confidence in this predicament.

Would Gemma survive this?

Did she have the fortitude to stay and champion the sanctuary for the tigers' sake even when it could cost her life? "I'm the one with the vision. It's my dream. But Clyde was behind this too, and he wants the sanctuary. He could keep it going if something happened." *This time...* But she kept those words to herself.

She didn't know why he hadn't stepped in before. Maybe things were too far gone by the time he'd received the news. Or maybe he hadn't had the time or money and was too far away. She didn't know and she hadn't asked.

He'd only been a silent partner to begin with.

By the time she'd emerged from the hospital, her

body, heart and mind broken, it had been much too late. She hadn't looked back because it was too painful so moved forward with her life.

But her heart always went back to wanting to provide a home for endangered animals. Big cats. So after school, she'd gone to him with her idea to start a new sanctuary and had been more than relieved with his excitement at her idea. For the first time in a very long time, Gemma had been happy.

Still, she wished she hadn't answered Gray's question, said the words out loud, as though saying them would seal her fate, somehow. And now, her wounded leg ached more than ever, pain brought on by the strain of the hike and the stress of the rockslide. Gray handed over her cane as though sensing her suffering. He'd protected it? Kept it intact in the face of a rockslide? She looked up into his warm, brown eyes. "Thank you."

He nodded. "You're welcome."

Something unexpected—forbidden even—passed between them. Gemma couldn't say what. Oh, that wasn't true. She knew exactly what it was—an attraction, both physical and spiritual. A deep, emotional need for one another. She turned from him. She wouldn't let him see the answering response in her gaze. She couldn't trust him like that. Somehow, she had to recover her resolve. People hid who they really were. Gray had shown up yesterday and look how far he'd maneuvered himself into her life. The way he made her feel took her back to Ellis, the intern who had come to help at the sanctuary when her uncle was alive and running things. Gemma had been young and naive and let herself fall for him in a big way. He'd seemed to return her affections. She would have given him everything. Gone anywhere and done anything with him. Perhaps he would have taken advantage of that, if he'd had more time—but then his fiancée showed up at the sanctuary. He'd kept the news that he was engaged to himself until that moment. And then Ellis had the nerve to beg Gemma not to say anything about their relationship. It would ruin his life with the woman he really loved. If Gemma loved him, he'd said, then she would want him to be happy.

A rock shifted in the pile, jolting her back to the present. Gray studied her.

Using her cane and ignoring her trembling leg, she stepped away from him and just kept going. She needed to get down to the buildings, to her friends, both the staff and volunteers. People she knew. Gray might have saved her twice now, but who was he really? Strange that supposed attempts on her life all started happening when he showed up.

He, too, was hiding something, just like they all had been doing. Her parents, her uncle. Ellis, whom she'd fallen in love with when she was too young to know better. But she was much older, much wiser now.

"Hey, wait up."

Gemma kept walking. Though Gray had protected her and assisted her around the pile of boulders that now blocked her favorite trail, Gemma needed air and space. A small part of her knew she was hurting him by rejecting his help. But she didn't know him. Suspicion and paranoia whirled inside, easily invading her thoughts.

"Gemma, don't go alone. Please, don't ever be alone again until we find out who is behind this. Stick close to someone you trust, if not me."

Gray wasn't far behind her, fulfilling his self-proclaimed role as protector, but at least he was giving her the option to choose.

look in his father's eyes. He'd seen him give Coop the look. Gray had wanted that too. He'd given the bow and arrow to his father, only to have Cooper rush in and steal all the attention away with an announcement of some award he'd won. His father had put Gray's gift on the table without a second glance and given Cooper that look.

Gray had grabbed the present, run out the door and thrown it in the trash outside. That day, he stopped expecting anything from his father—his approval or attention—and resolved that he would forge his own way and never again need anyone.

But Gray hadn't realized just how messed up he'd been over the way his father treated him until he finally fell in love in his midtwenties. Yeah, it had taken him that long to find what he'd thought was the right woman. And then… Gray ruined it all by expecting something from her. Approval, validation? He wasn't sure. But when he showed up at her door with a ring—a diamond solitaire engagement ring—and saw her kissing another guy through the front window, he went right back to that day with his dad. It was the same thing all over again. Him counting on someone else to love him and make him feel valued.

Never again. He'd said the words before, and he wouldn't be fooled twice. Now? He made it his job to protect the innocent—the animals and endangered species—while always keeping his distance emotionally. Trying to get closer to another person would only lead to disaster.

One of the tigers growled and roared, yanking Gray back to the moment.

Gray shifted, moving his night vision binoculars to the habitats. Had he missed something? Or was the

sound just a—there it was again. No. That was definitely a growl. The big cat was in defensive mode.

Gray wanted to go and investigate, but he could see
more if he stayed where he was and watched. Otherwise, he might miss the culprit, if someone was there
causing trouble for Gemma by messing with her big
cats. Fury stirred in Gray's stomach. This was the moment he'd been out here waiting for, night after night.
Still…

The vandalism had to stop! He started to climb down
so he could catch them in the act.

In the distance to his left, he heard the distinctive
sound of a door shutting. He whirled and turned his
binoculars to the cabin, spotting Gemma as she exited.

Oh, no! *Gemma, what are you doing?*

That was it. Gray scrambled from his perch between
the boulders to head her off. With everything that had
happened, she didn't need to walk the grounds alone.

He hadn't felt the buzz of his cell phone. Why hadn't
she called him? At the very least, he'd thought she'd understood he would be there to protect her.

He pushed the disappointment aside. She didn't trust
him, that's why. Gray wanted to call out to her, but he
was too far away and he might alert whoever was at
the habitat stirring up trouble. Gray couldn't be certain
someone was there, but the cat's angry growls continued.

What's more, the way Gemma marched, even with her
cane—that determined set of her chin and shoulders—
said that she wasn't thinking past her anger and frustration to her own safety. He slid down a boulder and vaulted
around a huge, thick cedar with gnarly roots until, finally,
his boots hit flat ground. Gray took off after Gemma.

"Gemma," he called softly. "Wait for me."

He wasn't sure how he was going to explain his sudden appearance, but her safety was more important. Still she was too far ahead of him, and she quickly disappeared in the shadows. He heard the telltale sound of the gate opening and shutting. Saw the beam of her flashlight as she walked the paths within the main habitat settings. She would be looking for the troubled tiger and would find the problem and could expect—what? Another effigy?

Or could this lead to her death this time? Could the same person who had tampered with her brakes to kill her also be the person who was sabotaging the sanctuary? It seemed unlikely. Kit suggested otherwise, and even the sheriff's department considered the vandalism a simple matter of pranks.

Through the woods, in the distance, he spotted headlights from a vehicle driving up the road that led to the sanctuary. At the main gate, Gray slipped inside and shut the gate behind him before searching for the beam of light from Gemma's flashlight.

"Gemma!" he called out this time. He didn't care if he scared off the person behind the sabotage. In fact, he hoped they would be long gone by now. He didn't want to see Gemma hurt.

Taking the path, he rounded the corner of one of the large habitats. "Gemma!"

"Don't move." Her voice was low and measured.

He immediately stopped, heeding the warning in her tone. A question formed on his lips, but he never spoke the words. He didn't have to ask. He could see perfectly well the tiger standing in his path, tail swishing.

SEVEN

Gray remained frozen, his blood draining from his brain and heart into his feet. He couldn't move if he wanted to.

He'd experienced many things as a game warden and in his position as a USFWS special agent, but never had he faced off with a seven hundred pound cat. Never stared into a set of menacing tiger eyes without a protective barrier.

The animal he recognized as Raja studied him, moving his tail.

Swish, swish.

Swish, swish.

Gray thought he could see Raja trying to decide if Gray was prey—that is, dinner—or if he was a predator and a threat to Raja's territory. Either conclusion did not bode well for the outcome of this encounter. Gray considered his best course of action, the options playing through his mind all at once. He shoved aside any thoughts of his own safety—the natural fight-or-flight human response and survival instinct—and focused on Gemma. His Glock was shoved in a holster to his side, hidden away. It wouldn't do for Gemma to see that.

He'd have even more explaining to do. But he'd use it, if necessary, to protect her life.

Eyes wide, she had her hands out, palms down, as though the action would keep everyone calm, including the tiger. "Raja, let's go back to where you're safe. Where you have food and water," she spoke softly to the beast.

To Gray, she said, "I raised Raja from a cub. He was only six months old when the owners lost their home and had to move into an apartment. A tiger cub wasn't something they could care for. He was our first cat here at the sanctuary and is two years old now."

Raja started chuffing—the sound tigers made instead of purring. Gray understood this to be a happy sound. Maybe Raja had lost interest in Gray. The tension in his shoulders eased but not too much.

Slowly dropping her hands, Gemma appeared to relax. "Raja…" She dragged his name out in a singsong fashion.

Raja moved toward her and rubbed his head against her legs and waist and continued chuffing. Gemma patted his side like the big cat was a friendly Labrador retriever. She rubbed his head and played with his ears. "Are you a good boy, Raja?"

Yeah. Labrador retriever.

Sierra, the tiger in the habitat nearest them, paced along the fence. Next to her, Layla and Lilly, sister tigers who lived in the same habitat, paced as well. Gray hoped the beasts didn't growl or cause Raja to hurt Gemma. One could never forget that a tiger—no matter how it was raised—was a wild animal. A deadly wild animal. Raja clearly loved and responded to Gemma, but Gray knew things could turn dangerous in an instant. Raja could simply play with Gemma and then hurt her. Kill her. It happened all too often—trainers playing with tigers like they were small kitty cats and then the tiger attacked. Zookeepers and workers simply doing their jobs.

Be careful, Gemma...

Gray wanted to speak, to urge Gemma to be cautious and not careless. But she was the expert, and knew what she was doing, not him. He was more than nervous this close to a tiger. He also wanted to ask the best way to lure Raja into his habitat. What they needed was someone else to help. Someone who could either get at the tranquilizer gun or offer food to entice the tiger.

A sudden gush of water from a large hose blasted Raja in the face. A man held the hose, spraying the tiger. If Raja had been attacking Gemma, then this might have been enough to free Gemma from the tiger's attack. But, instead, the tiger, who had been calm and playful a moment before, roared and slashed his paws through the air. Gray looked on in shock as Gemma was thrown back, her body landing on the concrete, head slamming against it. She didn't move.

"Nooooo!" Gray rushed forward to Gemma as the rush of water forced the tiger to retreat to the fence.

He lifted Gemma in his arms, searching for injuries. He saw no claw marks or blood, and her pulse was strong, but she didn't stir.

"What are you doing?" he yelled at the man. He recognized Wes. He must have been in the approaching vehicle.

Wes might have thought he was helping the situation, but the tiger was angry and frightened. And with no one else there to help lure the big cat away, someone was going to die if Gray didn't do something and fast.

"Keep the water on him. I'll get the dart gun."

Lifting Gemma, he carried her limp form as he rushed to the emergency lockbox, which was much too far away for comfort. He laid her down next to the box. She groaned. Good, she was waking up. Gray wanted nothing more than to hold her and reassure her. Comfort her. But he had no time.

It hit him that the lockbox was called a lockbox for a reason. "The key—I don't have a key." Gemma stared at him, confusion in her eyes. "Please, do you have keys to the lockbox?" *Come on, Gemma, snap out of it. I need your help here.*

Gray didn't want to have to put the big cat down with his Glock. Gemma would never forgive him. That bothered him more than he would have liked—a fact he found both confusing and surprising.

He started searching her for keys before she could react. "I'm sorry. I have to find the keys."

He found them attached to her belt loop. Gemma finally shook off her stupor, helping him.

"This one," she said.

His momentary relief faded when he heard the spray of water turn to a drizzle and then nothing at all. Had Wes somehow forced Raja into his habitat and locked the gate?

In answer to his question, the roar of an angry tiger on the loose filled the quiet sanctuary.

Gemma pressed her hand against the knot at the back of her head, but her thoughts were on Raja. Gray inserted darts into the gun.

"Let me do it. I'm trained in this. I don't want you hurting Raja." She sat up.

"How's your vision? Seeing double?"

Gemma frowned. Gray helped her up as dizziness swept over her. "I don't know."

Gray frowned. "Under the circumstances, I think I'm the one to do it."

Still, Gemma reached for the gun.

He held it just out of her reach but caught her as she stumbled. "Trust me, Gemma. I won't hurt Raja. It pains me to see him going through this too."

Gazing into Gray's eyes, she saw the truth of it there. He really did care about the big cats. He cared about her too, though she couldn't fathom why. And even stranger, Gemma felt herself drawn to this man she barely knew.

"I'm sorry that I wasn't able to grab your cane too. I'm sure it's still there somewhere. But I had to get you to safety."

"Thanks for that," she said, though she was still considering her response to his request to trust him.

Gray grabbed her arm and pulled her behind him. "Let's get this situation contained before anyone, including Raja, gets hurt."

"I don't understand what happened. How did Raja get out of his habitat?"

Gray paused and they both listened for sounds of the tiger or of Wes. "I think we both know the answer to that," he said.

Gemma hadn't wanted to admit that this could be the work of the saboteurs again, but neither did she wish for the other possibilities—that a volunteer or staff worker had been negligent and left a habitat open. "If that's true, then this is going too far. Two tigers released in a week. The saboteur has never done anything like this before."

"You said saboteur this time. Singular. You mean Emil, don't you? You really think an old rancher is doing this, putting himself and his animals at risk?" Doubt suffused Gray's tone.

In the distance, Raja roared and growled his displeasure. He was confused, perhaps looking for a way to escape the sanctuary completely. *God, please no.* That would be disastrous. She could lose her license and funding completely. And Raja could lose his life outside of these walls. Bad enough he'd escaped into the sanctuary at large. "I hope Wes has found a safe place to hide."

"I'm not sure what happened. Did he purposefully turn the water off and if so, why?" Gray asked.

Gemma followed him, limping as she went. He headed toward Raja's bellows, cautiously watching the environment. She wasn't sure why she was letting him take the lead, but he projected so much confidence, while she still hadn't gained solid footing and wouldn't until she had her cane once again. No, that wasn't true. Even then, she would likely let him lead. Her brain still felt scrambled, and her limbs shook from the unexpected encounter with Raja. She was grateful that Raja had been the one to escape and not one of the more aggressive tigers like Zeus. He'd been terribly abused and didn't like or trust any of them. At least, not yet.

As her thoughts grew clear, something niggling at the recesses of her mind came into focus. "What was Wes doing here, Gray?"

"I saw a car approaching as I ran to the sanctuary. I think that might have been him, but I don't know. We'll ask when we find him. But he has a cabin in the back, doesn't he?"

"Yeah, we offered it to him, but he doesn't use it. His family lives nearby."

"That's what I thought."

"But, then, why were you here? What were you doing here?"

Gray turned to her then and she regretted her insinuation.

"I didn't let Raja out of his habitat, if that's what you mean."

"Then why? You weren't following me again, were you?"

His chest deflated with his breath. "Can we talk about this later? I had a good reason for being here."

Gemma knew she shouldn't trust a stranger, but something about Gray compelled her to follow him now in her sanctuary to dart her tiger and to trust that he had good reasons. Was she losing her mind? Wes suddenly appeared behind them.

Gray stopped. "Where'd you come from?"

He pointed. "Over there. I was hiding from Raja."

"What were you doing here?" Gemma and Gray asked simultaneously.

Wes stepped back and held his hands up as though protecting himself from invisible darts. "I lost my cell phone and came to search for it in case I dropped it here. I knocked on your door, Gemma. With everything going on, I wanted you to know why I was in the sanctuary at night. Then I saw the flashlight beam in the sanctuary and came to investigate. Since you weren't home I thought you might be here and could help me find my cell."

"You could have called first," Gray said.

"Um...not without the numbers on my cell."

Good point. Gemma wanted to believe him, but she'd seen the man with Emil. She'd questioned him about it earlier, but he claimed he'd simply confronted the neighbor and reported the incident to Cara. Gemma didn't want to work with people whom she couldn't trust, but letting an intern go based on suspicions wasn't right either. She'd suffered from the suspicions of others with the rumors about her parents' sanctuary. She wouldn't stoop to dismiss someone based on circumstantial evidence. Still, she'd tried to keep an eye on him. And here he was in the middle of suspicious activity.

Just like Gray.

And then Raja lumbered through the grass next to the path. *Poor Raja!* Gray lifted the dart gun. "Take cover. Raja could run when he's hit. I don't want you to be in his path."

"Hand it over, Gray." Gemma held out her hand. "I know what I'm doing. You're not officially trained. Technical training is crucial. If news got out that you were the one to use the dart gun, we'd have to answer a lot of questions."

"Are you sure you're okay?" he asked.

She nodded, hating they had to resort to chemical capture. "These darts have enough anesthesia to immobilize Raja. I'll be fine. You and Wes get back."

Gemma backed up with them until she was behind a tree next to the main habitat building where they could run and hide if necessary. But the tranquilizer should only take a few seconds to kick in. Anger coursed through her at what had happened. But she shoved that out of the way. Cleared her thoughts. Focused her aim on Raja's hind limb. Her hand slicked against the dart gun as she pulled the trigger.

The dart went into Raja, giving Gemma a small sense of satisfaction, but it didn't counteract her guilt and fury over Raja's situation, especially when she watched the big cat groan and drop.

* * *

The next morning, Gemma nursed a large mug of black coffee in the kitchen, waiting for the others to arrive. Her head ached and she popped two ibuprofens. She'd already detailed the chores and schedules for the day on the whiteboard. Logged the previous night's incident in the notebook. Called the sheriff's office to report what had happened again.

The USDA inspection was a few days away. If she didn't find a way to stop this dangerous vandalism, someone was going to get hurt or killed. And, of course, she understood now that was the whole point. Someone wanted her to get hurt. Her, specifically—she was the target.

She thought she could build the sanctuary, under the new name of Tiger Mountain, into something as grand and glorious as the sanctuary her parents had run that had housed and cared for thirty animals. But, instead, someone wanted to shut down Tiger Mountain and wanted Gemma gone too, preferably dead. She could feel her dreams slipping away from her. Tiger Mountain slipping away.

Turning on the small wide-screen television mounted on the wall, she set it on the local news station but lowered the sound. She wasn't sure she could stomach very much noise this morning. She'd barely gotten any sleep last night and when she'd finally drifted off, her rest had been fitful at best. Too many questions running through her overactive mind.

Like why had Gray been there? He'd said he would explain, but he never had. She thought she could guess what his answer might be—that he was watching her, following her to make sure she was okay.

Gemma didn't know how she felt about that. She

continued to have the eerie sense that someone watched her. Had it been Gray all this time? And who had left Raja's habitat open?

An image of a tiger on the television screen drew her attention. Gemma froze. In dismay, she stared.

She turned up the sound and watched in horror as photographs of Raja on the loose in the sanctuary filled the screen. "These pictures were taken just last night at the sanctuary known as Tiger Mountain, where a tiger apparently escaped and was on the loose for an undisclosed period of time," a reporter said, his face looming large in the TV screen. An investigative reporter had caught everything on camera? Who had he interviewed? How did he know?

The coffee mug slipped from her fingers and shattered on the floor.

EIGHT

Last night's incident still fresh in his mind, Gray parked his truck, a black Silverado and answered a call from Coop as he made his way to the Tiger Mountain facilities. He noted another vehicle parked in front of the main building.

"Saw the news this morning. You okay?"

Gray took a hesitant step and then stopped. "News? What news?"

"It's all over the news that a tiger got out last night at Tiger Mountain. There's some footage showing Gemma darting the tiger." Coop continued to explain, describing what the reporter had said about Gemma and Tiger Mountain and the supposed threat that the sanctuary presented to the local community.

Gray came close to swearing under his breath, but he bit back the words. That answered his biggest question—had it been an accident or planned? Of course, he'd suspected all along that it had been deliberate, but he hadn't had any definitive proof. Now it sounded like it had not only been planned but staged if a reporter was there to film the entire thing. Bile rose in his throat.

There's no way Gray had escaped being seen in the video. Had the reporter identified him? Was his cover blown? "Did you see me in the footage?"

"No. I know you're working undercover there, though."

Kicking a rock, Gray watched it roll across the still-moist ground. "I have to be in the footage. Most of the time, I was standing right next to Gemma. For part of it, when she got hurt, I was even carrying her. There's no way I could have escaped. The reporter saw me."

"But does he know who you really are? That's the big question."

"Maybe not. Why would he?" But if Sheriff Kruse looked at the entirety of the footage, then his cover would be blown, at least with the sheriff. Maybe that wouldn't be such a bad thing if he later required backup—which was possible since the situation kept getting more and more dangerous. But he needed more time to think about it. Needed to make sure no one within the department, like Deputy Callahan, for instance, was involved in any of the sabotage.

Gray wondered if the saboteur understood the risk of deliberately releasing Callie and Raja, or if they had intended to increase the danger. And with that thought, Gray had to question Kit's initial assessment and seriously consider that the vandalism and threats on Gemma's life could be connected. Committed by the same person or group. Regardless, someone wanted this sanctuary gone, even—or was it especially?—if that meant Gemma's life. It might be time for Gray to visit the neighboring rancher himself. Emil Atkins.

But he had to admit Wes was also suspect in the vandalism. He'd been there last night, though he claimed to have a reason. And while he might have been genuinely trying to help, his actions had definitely made the situation worse. Gemma wouldn't have needed to tranq Raja if it hadn't been for Wes.

But an even bigger question—what did any of this have to do with the trafficking ring he'd come here to investigate? Was there a connection? There were too many issues going on here. Did he refer once again to Occam's Razor, which would mean the simplest answer was the right one? That would suggest that only one entity was behind the vandalism, the attacks on Gemma's life and the trafficking ring. Could it be true?

All of these thoughts swirled in through his mind in a matter of seconds.

"Anything I can do to help?" Coop asked, pulling Gray from his thoughts.

Gray and Coop had their issues going all the way back to childhood, like all siblings did. Gray hated Cooper at times. Resented that their father favored him over Gray. But he'd made his peace with his brother, realizing that his issues with their father were between him and his father and were not the fault of anyone else. As adults, they'd left behind petty sibling rivalry and they had each other's back. Together, they watched over Alice, their only sister, and now Hadley, Coop's wife, was part of the family. After losing Jeremy, they only had each other. His suicide had brought them closer.

"Gray?" Coop's voice reminded Gray that he waited for an answer.

"No. Not yet. Your involvement at this juncture would raise too many questions."

"Okay then. Well, hurry and wrap this up so you can work your computer skills on this new system. Give me a Buck knife and throw me in the wilderness, and I'll survive just fine. Just don't put me in front of a computer accounting system."

Gray snorted.

"And Gray?"

"Yeah."

"Be careful."

"Always."

He ended the call, glad for the warning about the news, and headed to the resource building. It was still early but Gray couldn't sleep and he figured Gemma couldn't either. As he walked, he continued to chew over the questions about the previous evening's sabotage. Gray had already accepted that Raja's release had been deliberate rather than human error, especially with a news reporter ready and waiting, but had Gemma realized it? She had been fortunate Raja had been the tiger. Gray needed to think on that. Did that mean that whoever was threatening Gemma didn't work at Tiger Mountain, so the culprit wasn't familiar enough to expect Raja's positive reaction to Gemma? What had this person expected to happen? And what had the news crew come to see? Thrusting his cell into his pocket, he thought back to Cooper's call. Had Gemma even seen the news?

Finding it unlocked, he pressed through the front door and got the answer to his question.

Clyde hugged Gemma to him like a father would, comforting her. "We're going to overcome the bad press, Gemma. Don't you worry about it. This is why I'm here, and I'll stay as long as you need me to set things right. We'll find out who is behind this."

Gray felt awkward walking into the middle of this. If he wasn't undercover, he would have excused himself and found something else to do. But he needed to be in the middle to make sure he didn't miss any vital information, so he waited where he was.

The man noticed Gray standing there, suspicion and anger pouring from his gaze. Gray wasn't sure any of

it was meant for him, personally, but it was clear that
Clyde was frustrated with what had happened. No
matter that the man was suspected of running a huge
trafficking ring—he also had sunk money into this
sanctuary and, like any businessman, he wouldn't want
to have it fail. Gray averted his gaze. Thinking of Clyde
Morris involved in trafficking animal parts, and who
knew what else, and as the guy also serving as the main
venture capitalist behind a sanctuary twisted Gray's gut.

Clyde released Gemma, who wiped at her eyes. She
turned them on Gray, surprise in her gaze. He held
it. The sight of those big, clear hazel eyes—now red-
rimmed—clawed at his heart. Whoever was doing this
was going to answer to Gray. He would get Bill's killer,
and he would get the person behind these attacks on
Gemma and her tiger sanctuary.

But what he didn't know, what he couldn't be sure
of, was it the same person behind it all?

"Gray." The one word—his name—was breathy as
it escaped her lips. She stepped forward. "Have you
seen..." She trailed off as Gray nodded.

There was no need for her to complete the sentence.
"The bad press, the way that reporter twisted the story
to make it sound like Tiger Mountain is unsafe for any
visitors, which you don't allow anyway, and for people
living in the area? Yeah." He frowned. He hadn't seen
it but he heard all he needed to hear from Coop. "It's
scare tactics, trying to get people into a mob mind-set,
too driven by fear to realize they're being manipulated
to turn against you."

She shook her head, unshed tears in her eyes. "This
could kill my efforts. Everything I've done so far. Everything we've done."

Clyde shifted. "All we need is some good press.

Show some goodwill, public education. Anything to smooth things over."

"And we need to find who's behind this," Gray said. He eyed the kitchen down the hall behind them. He could use a strong cup of coffee to fuel his mind.

As if reading his thoughts, Gemma headed down the hallway. Clyde and Gray followed.

"I think we should let Wes go," Clyde said.

That news surprised Gray. In his undercover investigation, he'd tried to find out as much as he could about everyone working at Tiger Mountain. Clyde had been the one to bring Wes on. Now he wanted to let him go?

Gemma poured Gray a cup. "I don't know. He could be completely innocent. My family has lived under suspicion and scrutiny for too long, and I don't want to live my life doing that to others—blaming them because of circumstantial evidence against them. The whole point of building Tiger Mountain—a whole new name with a fresh start—was to erase the past filled with suspicions." Her voice broke.

And snagged a little piece of Gray's heart. Over in the corner, he spotted a broom and pieces of a broken cup swept into a pile on the floor.

"You saw him talking to the neighbor, Gemma," Clyde said as he sugared his coffee. "And now this. We can't trust him. Just tell him we don't need him anymore."

Gray gulped too quickly and almost choked. "Wait, you saw him talking to the neighbor? The same man you believe is behind things?"

"There's more than one neighbor and I think they might even all be in it together, with him as their leader," Gemma admitted. "Emil hasn't made it a secret that he wants the sanctuary gone."

"I'm going to have a talk with him myself." Clyde slammed his cup on the table. "And the intern has to go."

"I can't afford to lose more help, Clyde. You know that."

"I'm not sure you can afford to keep him." Gray wasn't sure if Wes had played a role in anything, and he'd prefer to gather evidence against him or catch him in the act, but he wouldn't let Gemma remain in danger, if Wes was responsible. "I think Clyde is right."

"Thanks for your input." Clyde nodded, amusement in his eyes. Like Clyde was so secure in his certainty of Gemma's trust that it was funny to think of himself needing Gray's vote of confidence. "Which brings me to another question. What were you doing in the sanctuary last night, Gray?"

Oh, boy. Gemma had asked him the same question and he had put her off because he had to focus on securing the tiger, but he had hoped to explain himself to Gemma alone. "I won't lie. I wanted to be the hero. I thought I could watch the sanctuary at night. Keep an eye out and wait for whoever is causing the problems— catch them in the act."

Was Gray holding his breath, waiting for Clyde's reaction? For Gemma's? He released it slowly, so they wouldn't notice. And now if Clyde was the man he'd been hunting, he'd just revealed his surveillance, and maybe even lost any chance he'd have of catching him in illicit activity.

Finally, Clyde nodded. "And your actions saved Gemma's life."

"It was Raja, Clyde. I would have been fine."

"Not with that idiot Wes spraying the cat with water. Gray was there to help you. Thanks for taking care of my Gemma." There was something more behind the man's eyes, but Gray wouldn't say it was gratitude.

Gray fought to read it, to understand the look there. Was he playing with Gray? Toying with him? Like a cat might play with a lizard he caught before killing it?

Other staff began to mosey in, grabbing coffee as needed. Cara entered the kitchen and hugged Gemma. Questions arose about the incident. Most were relieved all had ended well, but Gray didn't miss the wariness in their eyes.

He left Gemma with the volunteers and headed to the sanctuary grounds to search for clues. He'd leave the compound before anyone from the sheriff's office arrived to investigate that someone had purposefully left the tiger's habitat open. He hoped they'd question that reporter too. Eventually, Gray would have to make contact with Sheriff Kruse and share what he knew, but Gray would avoid that as long as he could. Gemma needed the support of the sheriff's department now and bringing his investigation into the mix—an investigation in which Gemma, on paper, still looked like a viable suspect—would just confuse matters.

That evening, Gray went to the nearest Laundromat to wash a load of clothes. Working at the wildlife sanctuary had him burning through two sets of clothes a day. Laundry had never been something he enjoyed doing, but he had to admit that he was glad for this downtime to sort through his thoughts. This investigation had turned into something much different than he'd expected. All he could think about was helping Gemma and Tiger Mountain. His thoughts had moved far from what they were when he'd first arrived.

He stuffed quarters into the drier, hoping he'd be out of here in the next thirty minutes. Was he losing sight of the real goal? His main purpose here? When his supervisor, Mark, called, Gray wasn't sure he was ready to talk to him and almost let the call go to voice mail.

But he answered and stepped outside into the starry night to talk in private. "Yeah."

"There's been an arrest made for the sale of tiger parts."

What? "When?"

"This morning. We believe it's connected to your trafficking ring. No way for you to be in more than one place at a time, Gray, so don't beat yourself up."

Gray hadn't made the arrest and it burned him. This was his investigation. Frustration grated him. "Why arrest the guy? If I'm about to close in on the head of the ring, I don't want him running scared off to some other country."

"The sale was made in Chicago, far removed from your suspect. It couldn't be ignored. The agent couldn't let it go. But I don't think you need to worry. Maybe your guy will make a few mistakes if he gets nervous."

He ended the call. Mark's words should put him back on track. With this arrest and the increased incidents, pressure building up at Tiger Mountain, Gray could sense his time was running out. The person he was after might back off or disappear completely before he could gather the evidence to catch them in the act.

Unfortunately, Clyde hadn't made any suspicious moves. Yet. But Gray now had two diametrically opposed goals—to keep Gemma safe as he helped her save Tiger Mountain and to bring down Clyde, the venture capitalist behind the sanctuary. How could he do both?

Gray returned to the Laundromat and found a guy

stuffing his clothes into a sack. "What...what are you doing, man? Those are my clothes!"

The guy shrugged. "I thought you left them and weren't coming back."

"I was right outside, dude." Frowning, Gray snatched the sack from the guy and made sure all the clothes had been scraped from the drier. "Of course you knew I was coming. I wouldn't leave my clothes behind."

The guy was an opportunist, that was all—looking to get as much as he could, without sparing a thought for the well-being of anyone else. If Clyde was truly the one responsible for the trafficking ring, then he was the same way. Benefiting from the tigers without a thought of how he was harming either the rare and precious creatures themselves or Gemma, who he claimed to love like a daughter and who would defend those tigers with her life.

Shaking his head, Gray headed out the door.

Climbing into his truck, something else wound through his thoughts.

Gemma would defend the tigers with her life...

He popped the steering wheel and sat back. Clyde was after what he could get—and that meant the tiger parts that he could sell to the highest bidder. If that was the goal, it seemed that whoever was behind the threats on Gemma and the harassment—the same person to call the investigative reporter—didn't want the sanctuary gone. They wanted Gemma gone one way or another in order to leave the tigers unprotected.

And then, he had the connection he needed between the sabotage, the attempts on her life and the trafficking ring.

Either she would leave on her own, fed up with the harassment and struggles.

Or she would stay and die.

* * *

Standing at the utility closet in one of the habitat's indoor facilities, Gemma absently selected a broom as she glanced at the text she'd sent a few minutes ago and Gray's ready response:

I'll be right there.

Had she been right to text him and ask him to meet her? Being alone wasn't safe, as he'd repeatedly warned her and now she finally agreed. She'd said goodbye to Cara as she'd left, and Gemma had headed to the habitat to make sure the tigers were safe. One last time.

God, please don't let anyone tamper with things.

Though she'd prayed the silent prayer in her heart, she didn't expect a response. The prayer had been a desperate cry for help as the overwhelming feeling she was about to lose everything she'd worked for weighed on her.

Nor could she leave the heaviness behind, especially when it wasn't safe to even walk the sanctuary grounds or a trail in the woods alone. So she needed protection.

An image of Gray—his wide shoulders and warm, brown eyes—had popped into her head so she'd texted him.

Part of her wanted him to be here with her to help protect the sanctuary from those who wanted it gone. But, if she was honest with herself, she also wanted to see Gray for reasons that had nothing to do with that. Even though she hadn't known him long, there was something about him that made her feel safe. Add to that—was she making a list?—that he had a sense of purpose about him that she liked and admired. Gray had also mentioned he had ideas about public education.

With everything that had happened, they had hardly had time to sit down and discuss his ideas. Or maybe Gemma was only now desperate enough to admit she needed his help. She was willing to listen to ideas from an outsider because, with the current bad press, Tiger Mountain was at a critical juncture. She'd had a PR brainstorming meeting this morning with Clyde, but even he seemed preoccupied and they'd come up with the usual, tired ideas that left them both unenthusiastic.

Needing to work, she flipped on the rest of the lights in the building that served four tigers, disturbing Raja, who had abandoned his chuffing from last night for angry groans today. Maybe she should have picked a different building to work in, but she desperately wanted the tiger to trust her again.

The whole incident had left Gemma feeling sick to her stomach.

But that's why she was here now. She couldn't sit around with so many frustrating thoughts converging on her. She needed to be proactive. Gemma had experienced trials and tribulations in her life and she'd never been one to give up.

But now…now she didn't know how much more she could take.

At least there was a bit of good news. Caesar was old and had issues, but the vet had confirmed he didn't have liver cancer, so they could expect him to stay around a few more years.

A noise startled her. Her heart jumped. Gray's sturdy form stepped into the hallway that ran next to the tiger stalls. He'd made pretty good time. Had only taken him fifteen minutes to get here. "Hey, I wish you would have waited for me before you came here alone."

She wouldn't tell him she'd already been here when

she'd texted. "I'll try to remember that next time." As if there would be more of these meetings with him.

He tugged off his black jacket, revealing a tan polo shirt that stretched tight over his broad chest.

Looking good, better than a man had a right to, he jammed his hands into his jeans and strode toward her, glancing at the broom in her hands. "Are we cleaning? Or are we going to talk about my ideas?"

"Can't we do both?"

He chuckled. "Sure. But it seems to me you've already had a long, exhausting day, not to mention last night."

Gemma sagged. It didn't take a brain surgeon to know that she was tired, but, still, she felt like Gray understood her. And that pushed her to be a bit more honest in her reply than she otherwise might have been. "I have to keep busy. It helps me to get my mind off things. I want to hear all your ideas about educating the public. We have a lot of work to do." She huffed and then glanced to him. "I say *we*, but you're only a volunteer. I don't mean to assume you'll want to put so much time and energy into saving Tiger Mountain." She'd said the words, but could he see her desperate pleas for help reflecting in her eyes?

He grabbed the broom, his hand pressing over hers. "Gemma."

The way his gaze searched hers, Gemma felt like he'd caressed her. Emotion welled up, taking her breath away. Stepping back, she released the broom to him. But Gray stepped forward, staying close.

"I'll do whatever you want or need done to help keep Tiger Mountain going. I hope by now you believe me."

Still grappling with the whirl of emotions that his nearness stirred, she said, "I don't know how much more of this I can take, but, maybe with your help, I can…"

"Gemma. If only—" He lifted his hand as though he might cup her cheek and then dropped it. "But there's more going on here than just the need to keep the sanctuary going. Something sinister and dangerous. I'm more worried about your safety. I don't know if you should stay here at all."

"I know what you're doing. You're backing out on me, aren't you?" She'd already lost volunteers and staffers over the last few weeks and months.

"What?" He frowned. "I didn't say that. There's something I need to tell—" Gray suddenly frowned, his gaze shifting to something beyond her.

"What's the matter?" she asked.

Gray gently urged Gemma to move behind him. "I'm not sure."

Someone else was there, or at least had been there, tampering again. She just knew it. Fear and anger surged through her. She wanted to rush around Gray and see what was going on. See who was behind all her troubles. "Well, what are you waiting on?"

"Just…listen."

Craning her neck, she tried to see as well as listen. What had Gray heard that had him tensing? Grabbing his side? Was he somehow injured last night?

"Oh no!" Gray rushed forward. "Stay close to me!"

"What…" But her words dropped away when she saw the orange and yellow flickers through the glass window of the door to the room where they stored supplies and processed meals for the tigers. The pungent scent of acrid smoke reached her nose.

NINE

Flames licked higher on the other side of the door. The sight momentarily stunned Gray. Low groans and frantic growls echoed through the shelter from the tigers who'd come indoors for the evening.

Gray's own panic rose. They had to put the fire out. He followed Gemma. On the wall hung an extinguisher. Or where a fire extinguisher should have been. Gemma glanced at him. "It's…gone."

Go figure.

He pursed his lips, fear and anger boiling inside. Gray peeked through the window into the room. How could the fire have grown so fast without some sort of accelerant? That, and the absent extinguisher, pointed to the conclusion that someone had planned this. "We have to get out of here."

"The animals!"

"We need to call 911 to get the fire department here."

Wild with fear, Gemma's eyes held him in place. As if that wasn't enough, she gripped the collar of his shirt. "They're too far away. What if they don't make it in time?"

"You can't panic, Gemma. These animals are depending on you."

Nodding her agreement, she stood tall and determined and then started checking that all the habitats were open to the outside, which they normally should have been. But this situation was far from normal. All things considered, if someone had started this fire, there was the possibility they had locked the tigers in. Gemma must have been thinking the same thing. Then she moved to each caged stall, making sure each tiger had fled, and closed the cage doors to lock them out. They had all fled except for Caesar, the geriatric tiger.

Gray would have assisted her to speed the process, but when he got a signal on his phone—always difficult in this area—he remained in place so he wouldn't lose it and dialed the number. Her face reflected her distress as she tried to urge the old tiger to get up and move outside, away from the very real danger.

Each ring of the phone—as Gray waited for someone on the other end of the emergency number to answer—seemed to take an eternity. Why was it taking so long? He watched Gemma as she tried to urge Caesar outside, using a clicker.

Finally, dispatch answered.

Gray started right in. "There's a fire at Tiger Mountain at Habitat B." The county fire department should have the detailed information regarding the layout of the tiger sanctuary. After answering a few more questions, Gray ended the call.

"I can't get Caesar to move."

"He'll move, Gemma. It's instinctive, pure and simple."

Appearing unconvinced, she pursed her lips. Other than being the oldest tiger in the sanctuary, was Caesar hurting or injured in a way that made him unable to exit the stall?

The stakes had just grown higher if they couldn't get Caesar out. "What is the fire escape plan?"

They hadn't been over that important detail yet, though he'd been told it was reviewed once a month at the weekly staff meeting. Gray hadn't been here that long.

"Prevention, detection and suppression, in that order." Gemma headed to the door that separated them from the fire. The fire had grown and would soon choke them out of this room before the flames even got to them.

"And if none of that works?" Gray asked.

Gemma coughed and covered her mouth and nose. "Their outdoor habitats should be enough space for the cats to stay safe unless things get out of hand."

None of that mattered for Caesar if he was unable to get far enough away. And as for the other big cats, if Gray and Gemma didn't get control and the fire began burning the habitats, then what? There was one reason to be thankful for all the rain they'd received this season. He hoped the wetter-than-normal conditions would be enough to slow the fire.

"And if it does get out of hand?"

She glowered at him. "It won't. But worst case, the fencing surrounding the entire sanctuary could keep the tigers in, if we're forced to release the animals from even their outside habitats. It would be better to have the others here to help transfer them to cages and transport them to the other side of the sanctuary or away from the danger. I'll text Cara and ask her to round up some help, but we don't have time to wait. We can use the hose and pump from the pond."

Agreed. "Then hurry. Let's get out of here." A sense of dread snaked up his spine. It wasn't going to be as simple as that, especially if this was arson. This fire had been planned, staged to burn hot, fast and out of control. It wouldn't be easily contained.

"But what about Caesar?"

"We have to trust he'll move, but in the meantime we have to put out the fire." He grabbed her hand to pull her through the door as he pushed against the exit.

Locked.

Gemma's pulse spiked even higher. But she couldn't let panic set in. Keeping her head would make the difference between life and death.

"Over there." She led him as they ran to the opposite end. "There are three exits in this building. Something has to be open."

Right. The door Gray had just walked through was now locked. She'd been an idiot to let this happen. They tried the other door. Also locked. And the third door was now engulfed in flames.

Gray eyed Gemma. "Can we unlock them?"

"There's no way to do that from the inside. Why would there be?" Gemma's eyes and throat burned. They'd definitely need to rethink the locks on these buildings in the future in case someone was trapped inside. Whoever did this had known they would be locked inside with no escape.

Smoke began filling the room, sneaking beneath the crack of the door from the room engulfed in flames. At this rate, the smoke would overcome them long before the flames reached them.

"The habitats." Gray paced next to the bars, reminding her of the tigers. "We go out through one of the habitats."

"That could put us in harm's way from the cats."

"Take your pick. Either way, we're in danger. For

certain, we'll die in here. We have to take our chances with the tigers."

"It's dangerous, but you're right. I don't see another way out."

"But which tiger?" He started opening an enclosure.

"No, wait," she said. "Let's go out with Caesar. We can coax him out and he's not likely to hurt us. He's relatively tame by comparison to some of the others. He's been with us almost as long as Raja and I think he'll understand we only want to help."

Gray's eyes widened. "I don't know, Gemma. The only time I've been that close to him he was sedated for the vet. He's huge."

"Like size would matter. Even the smallest one here could take you out with one swat. Besides, we need to get him out of here. He isn't moving. You said we should go out through the tiger stalls—now let's go. It's the only way."

Coughs racked Gemma as she made her way toward Caesar's stall. "You go out one of the other habitats and you'll be taking your chances with more dangerous animals. Caesar is older and weaker and he trusts me." Though she didn't make it a regular practice to pet the animals—Tiger Mountain was about being a true sanctuary and creating a natural environment—there had to be a measure of trust between the big cats and their caretakers.

"Caesar it is."

The flames had conquered the door and now climbed the walls. Heat flashed over her and smoke billowed. Gray nodded and followed Gemma. She gently spoke to Caesar, slowly entering his stall and letting the big cat know she was coming into his space. Despite the training she'd given him to receive care and feeding, she had never been with him in the stall. That was simply too dangerous.

Caesar released long, low moans but made no effort to move. That concerned her as much as the fire. Why hadn't he moved out on his own, instinctively distancing himself from the fire? Gray started into the stall, but she gestured for him to wait.

"Let me lead him out first. He doesn't know you like he knows me."

"You'd better hurry if we're going to get to the hose and save anything in this habitat, including ourselves and Caesar."

Gemma had her clicker in her pocket as always, and she stepped out of the stall into the outside of Caesar's habitat. If only she had some food with her. She clicked three times and waited just outside of the door. Beyond the cage, Gray coughed. She had to hurry.

"Come on, Caesar. We need to get you some place safe." Three more clicks and Caesar growled and grumbled but in a nonthreatening way, and then he got up and lumbered out the door. "Good boy, Caesar. Good boy."

This wasn't a circus, and Gemma didn't pet the old cat on his head or rub his ears as she'd done with Raja last night. That had been under completely different circumstances. She hadn't told Gray, but Raja might have attacked him had she not drawn the big cat's attention and relied on his familiarity with her. It had been a calculated ploy on her part. There was no need to take further risks with Caesar, especially given that the fire could have already set him on edge.

"Gemma," Gray called. "I'm coming through."

Gray had already entered and left the stall. He headed for the gate of the habitat, the exit into the sanctuary at large. Gemma wanted to lure Caesar farther away from the building in flames. She glanced at Gray. He waited by the gate, a question in his eyes.

Should he get the hose now and start putting out the flames? Was Gemma okay alone in the habitat with Caesar?

She nodded. *Go. I'll be okay.*

As soon as she knew Caesar was safe, she'd see to her own safety and exit the habitat so she could help Gray. Now that Caesar was up and moving, he didn't need much encouragement to continue to the far end of his enclosure. He slowly lumbered away, disappearing into the grass.

Relief swooshed through her for Caesar, but one glance back at the flames and her heart tumbled over itself.

Gemma was more grateful than ever that the enclosures were large and spacious, giving the animals plenty of room to roam and, in this case, to be far from the flames. She hoped and prayed the volunteer fire department would soon arrive with their truck filled with two thousand gallons of water and put out the flames before the animals were harmed. The building itself was another story.

The flames were quickly dashing her hope they could salvage most of the structure. Another glance at the area where she'd last seen Caesar reassured her he was safe for now. She headed to the gate so she could help Gray bring in the water hose. In the distance, beneath a security light, she spotted him already going toward the building. Determined to beat the flames, she picked up her pace, hating her cane now like never before.

Glancing toward the building, she watched the hot glow of the fire escaping the structure light up the night.

And across the way, she saw a figure slip out of the ring of light into the shadows.

TEN

Holding the hose, Gray doused the flames, grateful for the water pressure, but he doubted his efforts would be enough. In the distance, lights flashed as emergency vehicles headed up the road into the property. Other vehicle headlights followed, likely bringing the other staffers to help.

God, please let it be so.

Where was Gemma? Had she secured Caesar yet?

To his relief, he saw her silhouette rushing toward him with her cane, the inferno at her back.

Bending over her knees, she caught her breath. "I saw... I saw someone." She pointed to the other side of the building. "Just over there. He ran away. Do you hear me, Gray? Someone was there and then ran into the shadows."

"Did you see who it was?"

"No..." She gulped a few more breaths and then finally stood tall. "It was just a figure. A glimpse of someone. They stepped into the shadows as though they knew I had seen them. Maybe I'm getting paranoid. I started to search—"

"No!" Gray almost handed the hose over to Gemma so he could search, but he wouldn't leave her alone with the flames. He wouldn't leave her alone, period. "No, it's too dangerous. Whoever it was, they probably started the fire. It's too risky to try to corner someone who's willing to go to such insane lengths. That's why it's important that you try to think, try to remember if you recognized them."

The fire truck finally arrived. The firemen steered it all the way up into the sanctuary through double gates thrown wide open. One of the Tiger Mountain staffers must have opened it for them. Gray continued using the hose, spraying the flames as well as the rest of the building and the animal habitats to protect them, unconcerned about depleting the pond water, considering all the rain they'd received. But when he realized he was standing in the way of the more experienced firemen, he turned off his hose and moved to the side. He stood back and watched with Gemma and the others—Cara, Tom, Jill, Mavis and Ernie—who had arrived. Clyde had supposedly released Wes from his service at Tiger Mountain earlier in the day. They all stood, looking on in horror.

Everyone except Clyde. He wasn't here.

Gray leaned in to whisper. "Does Clyde know?"

She nodded. "I texted him. But if I remember correctly, he's in Portland. Cara called the others. They're all here, except…except for Wes, of course."

Gemma hadn't wanted to let him go.

She put one hand over her mouth and crossed her arm over her body. Her eyes glistened with unshed tears. "This is the absolute worst thing that could happen. The worst. I don't understand why this is happening. This will be a huge setback."

"Yeah, not to mention the cleanup. We could barely

keep on top of caring for the tigers in the first place."
Anger flashed in Tom's gaze.

Cara shot him a glare, but it went unnoticed by
Gemma. This wasn't the time to complain about the
extra work that would be needed to restore the habitat and to reassure the animals agitated by the chaos
and flames.

"It's not the worst thing, Gemma," Gray said. "The
flames will be put out before they can harm any of the
tigers. It could have been much worse." But he wasn't
sure his reassurances helped much.

Still, the animals might not be physically harmed, but
they had to be distressed by the smell of smoke, sensing the danger. Their growls and pacing confirmed it.
From here Gray could tell that at least two of the stalls
had been consumed by flames. A few more minutes of
burning unchecked and the fire would have hit the lush
foliage in the outdoor habitats. Some of it was still wet,
but the sun and wind had dried out the trees and grasses.

He thought of the figure Gemma claimed to have
seen stepping deeper into the shadows. Fury blew
through his veins. Gray grabbed a flashlight from Tom.
He'd bet that figure was the arsonist, and he stomped
off to search.

"Where are you going?" Gemma limped after him.

"Stay here. You need to stay with the staff and keep
safe."

"You're going to look for him, aren't you?"

"Him, Gemma? So you saw at least that much?"

"I—I think it was a guy, yes. That was my first impression. Is that where you're going? To look for him?"

"Yes. And I want you to stay here."

Had it been Emil Atkins or Wes, whom she had recently let go? What about Clyde? Sure, he was suppos-

edly out of town, but Gray wouldn't believe that alibi without proof. No matter who it was, Gray was determined to find him. But had he already wasted too much time? Maybe the guy had fled the scene. It was possible, but he doubted it. The arsonist would likely want to hang around to watch the show and view the damage he'd created.

Gray took off, heading in the direction where Gemma had pointed moments before. He heard her efforts to keep up with him and hated himself. All he had to do to lose her was start running, but that would be completely heartless. He slowed and turned to face her.

Eyes blazing, she caught up to him.

"What are you doing, Gemma? It's dark and dangerous, and…and…" He could make better time without her. But he wouldn't say the words.

"I want to find him. I want to know who did this. I want this to end." She nearly broke then, as her voice cracked, but she didn't lose her composure in front of him.

So strong and beautiful, even when her life was in upheaval. Gray could hardly stand to watch her go through it.

He couldn't help himself. He closed the distance between them and wrapped her in his arms. "You don't always have to be so strong, you know?"

A shudder ran through her. Was she crying? Releasing her pent-up anxiety and fury? Whatever it was, Gray sensed Gemma needed him to hold her. She needed human contact and, if he was honest with himself, he did too. He lifted his hand and felt the softness of her long and luscious hair.

She pressed her face against his shoulder. An image of Clyde holding her in a similar fashion flashed through him, but this was not a friendly, fatherly—or even brotherly—hug. No. With Gemma in his arms, his protective nature ignited more fiercely than he could have imagined even as he struggled to ignore the attraction he had for this woman. But it was more than that. Comforting her, keeping her safe, had warmth swimming around his heart and he knew he cared for her in a deeper way. He wanted something lasting with her.

But he couldn't let that longing go any further. He forced his attention onto the damaged building. Reminded of why he was here working undercover at Tiger Mountain.

He noted the flames were finally out at the building. Gemma seemed to sense a change in the atmosphere and she stepped back from him but not too far. He still held her. "If I'm not strong, who will be? Who will take care of these tigers? Who will build the legacy that should have belonged to my parents?"

He understood her then. Even with Clyde's support, she thought she was all alone in her efforts to build something lasting and good. In that moment Gray wanted to tell her everything. Who he was and why he was really here. She was so open in that moment that it made him feel low and petty for ever lying to her or keeping anything from her. Gray wanted to join Gemma in her cause. They were on the same side, after all—to protect endangered and abused animals from evil, wicked men. What could it hurt to tell her everything?

He was letting her get to him. With the moonlight shining brightly in her eyes, he had the strange desire to kiss her. Kiss away her worries like they were in some fairy tale.

Right. Like that would work in real life. Gray drew in a breath, catching the fetid scent of the water-soaked, charred building. Good. Reality was coming back to him. He remembered why he'd come to stand here. He wanted to find the arsonist. The man standing in the shadows.

The dark forest of the Wild Rogue Wilderness loomed behind them, and the back of his neck tingled.

Someone was watching them.

The next day Gemma wasn't sure how she would have pulled her heartbroken, aching body out of bed, if it wasn't for the animals who depended on her. She'd gotten up before dawn so she could be ready to give special attention to all the tigers today. Her nerves were on edge at the thought of the damage she would see once the morning sun illuminated last night's disaster.

She detailed the chores and schedules on the whiteboard and found she could use an additional one. There was simply too much to do. Still, she did her best so that no one would have any questions about what should be done or what she expected from them. She wished Clyde hadn't let Wes go. She could use his help.

She held on to a sliver of hope that some people in the community would assist with the cleanup, but first, the cause of the fire had to be investigated. She and Gray had shared what they knew with the firemen last night.

Gemma had always thought of herself as a positive person. Someone who chose to take the proverbial lemons and make lemonade, despite the many hurdles life had thrown in her path. But she couldn't deny that her positivity had been running on fumes. And now this—a fire set to trap her and Gray inside and either burn them alive or force them into the habitats with the tigers, where they faced death of a different kind. She struggled to keep from crumbling. Who wouldn't give up under such circumstances? She wanted to keep strong and stay the course, but her confidence had been shaken.

If she could just hold on until the sheriff learned who was behind these attacks, then Tiger Mountain could go forward. To that end, she thought about the tigers and their need for a home.

Somehow, they would be ready for the fast approaching USDA inspection that would give her the ability to continue forward. She could only hope they would overlook the decimated habitat.

And Clyde would encourage her when he got here. He always did. And there was someone else, someone unexpected, who encouraged her now as well.

Gray.

The thought of him filled her with warmth and left her confused.

The front door opened and shut. Gemma glanced over from the whiteboard and spotted Clyde ambling toward her, his shoulders slumped. Defeat in his expression.

Gemma absently put the marker aside, the look in Clyde's eyes scaring her. "Clyde?"

He placed his hands on her shoulders. "I'm so sorry I wasn't there to help you last night."

"It's okay. You said you were in Portland. You can't be two places at once."

"I was raising funds for Tiger Mountain." He hung his head.

"What is it? What's wrong?" Gemma sensed more had gone wrong than just the fire.

"I know this is going to be hard for you to hear, but, with this setback, we're going to have to downsize."

"What do you mean?" Gemma held her breath.

"Not for long. Just until we can get this behind us. I've already arranged for two tigers to be moved to another sanctuary."

Gemma stepped away from him, causing him to drop his hands.

"Now, Gemma, you know it's the only way. We've lost an entire habitat building. How are you going to manage the tigers otherwise?"

"We have the extra habitat that we use for rotation."

"And then our standard of care drops and they all suffer."

He was right. She had been holding on to false hope. She wasn't sure how she felt that he'd made this decision without even discussing it with her. But he was her benefactor and silent partner. Older, wiser and more experienced. Who was she to challenge him?

"Let me think about the tigers, then. Which two are better suited for travel and more able to adapt to a new environment. Kayla is young and healthy and hasn't been with us long enough to feel a sense of loss. And there's Sierra…"

Clyde grabbed her hand to stop her pacing. "Caesar, Gemma. Caesar costs us a lot of time and money. And Raja. It'll be better for our public image if he's gone— the community sees him as a threat after the news story of him running loose."

Heart crashing against her chest, she yanked her hand away. "You already decided? These are my decisions to make. Clyde, I know these animals better than you do. Moving Caesar to a new environment at this stage in his life will be too hard on him. No—" She shook her head "—I won't allow it."

His mouth flatlined, his face morphing from compassionate to stern. "The decision has already been made. And tell no one else. I don't want the drama."

Clyde turned and walked out.

What?

She gulped for air. What had just happened? As Clyde exited, Cara walked through the door, followed by Ernie and Mavis, their faces grim. It was up to Gemma to project a positive can-do attitude. Tiger Mountain depended on it. A dark cloud of depression and hopelessness loomed over her, but she kept it at bay. Standing tall, she welcomed everyone and went over the duties she'd outlined on the whiteboard.

"We can't do a lot in the way of cleanup until the fire investigator gives us the go-ahead, but we can tend to the tigers like it's any other day until then." She smiled, hoping the act would bring her heart around.

Gemma was disappointed that Gray hadn't joined the morning crew. Hadn't she just been thinking that he encouraged her? That's what she got for counting on someone. She knew better than to rely on anyone besides herself and Clyde. "Anyone know if Gray is coming in?" And now she'd asked about him.

"I saw him in the sanctuary," Cara said. "I think he's looking things over."

A measure of relief lifted her spirits. She'd misjudged him.

"Thanks for letting me know. I'll join you guys in a few minutes." She nodded her dismissal.

Cara led everyone outdoors to get busy with the usual chores. Gemma just needed a moment alone to gather her composure. But the truth was she was postponing the moment when she would see the damage in the light of day. Clyde's pronouncement that he was letting two tigers to go to another facility hadn't helped her frame of mind. Her leg throbbed like never before, forcing her to admit the stress came close to overwhelming her.

The man had been like family but while he was like a father to her in some ways, in others he was more like a distant relative. He had only planned to be here for a few weeks and then he would be gone again to work on foreign soil regarding his wildlife preservation efforts.

And then… Gemma would be alone again. Abandoned. The fact that someone wanted her dead drove the loneliness into her marrow.

Life shouldn't be so hard, should it? She was trying to do a good thing in this world.

She stared at the whiteboard, which was covered in so much ink you couldn't exactly call it white anymore.

It's not about me. If I just put my thoughts and energy into the sanctuary and into those working with me, then I won't be lonely.

There. She couldn't procrastinate any longer. To the sanctuary, then, to get her work done and view the damage done by last night's fire.

Someone came through the door just as Gemma put aside the marker. She turned to see Gray striding toward her. Her heart tripped, if only a little. Strange how he always seemed to show up when she was feeling down. He'd been there that day on the trail when she'd been frustrated and wanted time to think. It was like he sensed when she needed him. But that was ridiculous. Absurd! And she couldn't think about him like that. Of all the people she worked with, she knew Gray the least.

Then why did she find herself wanting to trust him?

Arms crossed, giving her a glimpse of his well-developed biceps, he stood near and studied her, his downturned mouth shifting into a half grin. "Don't look so sad, Gemma. It's going to be okay. You'll see. We're all going to pitch in."

Those were the words she'd expected to hear from Clyde. "What are you doing here?"

It was obvious he'd come in search of her, but she wanted to know why.

"I thought I'd walk with you to see the damage."

"But you've already seen it, haven't you?" Gemma remembered Cara telling her earlier.

"Yes." He offered a hand. "And, now, I'm going back with you to see it."

Gray was the one to reassure her and to build her confidence this time. Not Clyde. Gemma, normally the positive one, was now the one who needed coaxing to face the day.

Unsure why, she slipped her hands into his reassuring grip. Her breath caught. Ridiculous. "Is it…is it bad?"

"It could have been much worse. So while you're viewing the damage, remember the tigers survived and you will simply rebuild. The habitats can be replaced. You care about the tigers and it's why you saved them. It's what I like about you."

What he liked about her? Why should his confession send warm tingles through her? Tingles and warning signals. And yet, she left her hand in his as he led her out and into the sanctuary, up the hill toward the damaged habitat. Smoke still tainted the air, but the sun shone with the promise of a new start. If she tried, Gemma could imagine a bright future. This was just another hurdle. The sheriff would find the culprit and the sabotage would end. Tiger Mountain would pass the inspection. That day couldn't come soon enough. She allowed a ray of happiness to brighten her mood.

Gray slowed until he stopped. "The sheriff is here."

Good—the sooner he found a lead for his investigation, the faster this could all be resolved. But then she heard a deep, guttural scream that sliced through her hope.

"Come, quick. Over here!" someone yelled. It was Cara.

Gray hurried along with Gemma. She knew she slowed him down with her cane, but she was grateful he didn't let her go. Near the woods where she'd seen someone in the shadows lay Wes's body.

ELEVEN

Why had he lied to Gemma? Everything wasn't going to be okay no matter how many people pitched in. With Wes's murder, things had spiraled from bad to worse.

Gray marched through the door into Sheriff Kruse's office and shut it behind him.

The sheriff looked up in surprise. "Well, well, well, Special Agent Gray Wilde. What brings you here?"

"You need to interview all the volunteers and staff at Tiger Mountain, don't you?"

The sheriff's brows rose and then flattened. "Yes, why?"

"I'm one of the volunteers. Gray Wilson."

Slowly, the sheriff nodded his head. "Now I understand why Mr. Wilson was so sneaky and got away from the sanctuary before I could question him. I heard he went to search the woods where Gemma had seen someone last night. Now we've found a body. Sounds awfully suspicious to me."

"May I?" Gray gestured at one of two chairs in the sheriff's sparse office.

"Go ahead. Make yourself comfortable. How about some coffee to go along with your story, which I'm sure is going to be a good one."

The man's sarcasm rang through loud and clear. He hadn't appreciated that Gray's brother, Cooper Wilde, had taken it on himself to protect a woman being chased by an assassin and hadn't bothered to contact the sheriff on the matter earlier that year. The truth was that Cooper had tried, but the department was spread too thin, and there hadn't been time to wait on their response. Add to that, the sheriff suspected Gray had known about the woman's situation and kept it to himself—which was partially true. He had helped his brother when Coop had called him, even though he hadn't been told all the details. But, seriously, had the sheriff thought he and his department had the skills to face an actual international assassin entangled in CIA affairs?

"No thanks on the coffee." Gray eased into the chair. He had to choose his words carefully. The last thing he wanted to do was plant suspicions that sheriff would then direct at Gemma. "I'm working undercover at Tiger Mountain."

Sheriff Kruse poured himself coffee as he considered his reply. "Care to share more than that with me? I might know something that can help."

He sat and then leaned back in the chair as he drank.

Scratching his jaw, Gray thought about how much he should share. He didn't want the sheriff interfering, but neither did he want the man tracking him down because he hadn't been questioned. The timing on this couldn't have been worse.

"I got some intel that said someone at Tiger Mountain is involved in wildlife trafficking. Specifically tiger parts. I'm sure you're aware how much money that can bring in."

"A wildlife sanctuary involved in trafficking. Haven't heard that one before."

Gray recognized that the man was baiting him. He

chose not to take the bait. He wasn't going to share what he'd learned about Gemma's partner, Clyde Morris.

"Look, I can't really tell you more than that. Please just give me the space to work."

"And the threats on Gemma's life? What do they have to do with your investigation?"

He hesitated. "I—I can't be sure yet. She believes her neighbors would like the sanctuary gone, but I think someone wants her out of the picture completely because she is too close to the tigers and it's hard to move the animals when someone cares like she does." Now, why had he gone on about her like that?

"Sounds like she isn't the only one who cares." Sheriff Kruse lifted a brow.

When Gray said nothing, the sheriff leaned forward and put his elbows on his desk. "What about her safety, Gray? I need to investigate who murdered Wes Stimpson, and also learn who is trying to kill Gemma. How am I supposed to give you space?"

"Keep your investigation restricted to the murder and the attempt on her life." Frowning, Gray leaned forward too. "But any investigation is likely to interfere with mine or speed up timetables. I think things are about to go down soon."

"Let me know if there is anything I can do to help. But I do know something that might be important."

"Yeah?"

"Wes has a sister who's ill. She needs surgery that will cost far more money than the family can pay even with insurance. They've been trying to raise funds. It was on the local news."

Gray listened, wondering what else the sheriff had to add.

"I talked to the mother, gave her the news this morning of his death."

"I'm sorry."

"Part of the job, but it doesn't make it easier. She told me she'd heard him talking about the tigers and how much the parts could bring."

Stunned, Gray sat back. Wes? He couldn't be heading up a trafficking ring, could he? No, he was too young—this ring had been in place since before Bill's investigation started all those years ago. Wes would have been just a kid at the time. This didn't make sense.

"Of course, she scolded him for talking like that, she said. And then, apparently, he was released from working at the sanctuary. Hours later, someone tries to burn down one of the habitats. I'd say Wes did it. He had no legitimate reason to be there, and it wouldn't be surprising if he held a grudge after being released. But if he set the fire, then who killed him?"

Gray didn't like the insinuation in his tone. As if Gray had anything to do with it. "So he *was* murdered."

"The ME strongly suspects his death wasn't accidental but I haven't seen the report yet.

Gray nodded. "We can work together to find out."

The sheriff studied him.

Maybe Wes had learned something he wasn't supposed to know about the trafficking ring. If he was talking tiger parts, that would make sense. He'd gotten in too deep. Gray guessed the sheriff might be thinking the same thing.

"How does an intern get fired?" Sheriff Kruse asked.

"Gemma didn't want to let him go, but Clyde insisted on it. She'd seen Wes talking to Emil Atkins, the neighbor she suspects of harassing her and the tigers." Gray thought to ask the sheriff why he hadn't done more about that, but he needed the man on his side and didn't want to stir up trouble.

Sheriff Kruse stood, signaling their clandestine meeting was over. "I'll keep your cover, Gray. No need to worry about that. But in return I expect you to fill me in on anything that can help me solve this. I figure whoever is responsible for killing Wes is the same person behind the fire and also the attempts on Gemma's life. What I find interesting, though, is that each time she's been in trouble, you've been there to save her. The brakes, the rockslide and, last night, the fire."

Gray stood too. Interesting Sheriff Kruse knew about the rockslide. Had Gemma told him or someone else in the department? News traveled faster than one could imagine in rural areas.

"What do you make of that?" the sheriff finally asked.

Was the man accusing him of some crime? "I suppose it was just great timing on my part. Someone up there is looking out for her."

"Are you sure it's not more than that?"

Maybe the sheriff wasn't accusing him so much as getting him to see things from a different perspective. And then he understood.

Sheriff Kruse nodded. He must have seen in Gray's eyes that he finally got it.

When the brakes went out, Gray had been there to save Gemma by happenstance, but the other times? He and Gemma had been together when someone had tried to kill her.

Kill *them*.

Someone wanted him dead too. Did someone know his true identity?

Three brutal days later, Gemma exited the shower at the end of many long hours of work, finally free from the dirt and grime and soot that came from not only her normal labor at Tiger Mountain but from cleaning up the scorched habitat.

At least the tigers were calming after the chaos the fire had caused. She dried off and got dressed, trying not to think about Caesar. The big, old cat had been caged and carted off this evening, after most of the volunteers and staffers had left for the day, including Gray who had promised to return later in his self-appointed role as her protector. But Ernie had stayed behind to help. He was the only one who knew. Clyde had asked him to stay and assist.

She'd wanted to share her displeasure with Clyde and perhaps get the chance to convince him they should move another tiger. But Clyde had left again, returning to Portland shortly before Caesar—groaning and distressed—had disappeared into the truck.

Gemma stayed with the cat, comforting and reassuring him the best she could, right until the doors of the truck were closed. Seeing him go had left her discouraged. And while Gemma would have preferred to leave Ernie with the impression it was for the best, instead huge tears had taken her hostage. Before she embarrassed herself, she offered up a lame excuse and hurried back to her cabin. The place had served to keep her close and in the middle of life on the sanctuary, but never before had it served as an escape. A hiding place.

What did other people do when everything in their lives seemed to be falling apart?

She definitely needed to talk to someone. Before, she would have turned to Clyde. But he had been so remote that she wasn't sure she even knew the man anymore. His years of experience traveling the world had put distance between them, not only physically but emotionally.

She saw that now.

Besides, how could she talk to him when she was so angry with him for arranging to move the tigers out without even a discussion? What gave him the right—well, besides the fact he was the money behind Tiger Mountain? Still, he'd left Gemma to manage the sanctuary.

Right. Look how great that was going.

Venting the only way she could at the moment, she grabbed a throw pillow and tossed it hard across the bedroom. Releasing some of the frustration helped, but she had a long way to go. Gemma moved to the kitchen and heated a bowl of soup in the microwave, but she wasn't hungry.

In the living room she dropped to the sofa and tugged on jogging shoes—the kind of shoes she could no longer use for their intended purpose since the accident—wanting to go for a good long walk. Alone. But that was too dangerous.

She couldn't run. She couldn't hike.

She couldn't even drive her CJ!

But that had nothing to do with danger. The vehicle had been totaled. Everything she loved was slowly being destroyed. Images of the damaged habitat accosted her mind. The fire had to be arson. Add the death of Wes into the mix and Gemma could barely think straight.

Why did life have to be so hard?

Guilt suffused her for the thought. *She* was alive. Wes hadn't fared so well.

What had happened? Had he gotten in the way of the arsonists who wanted Gemma dead? Why had he even been at Tiger Mountain?

Nausea swirled inside. Hugging herself, she stared out the window. It was still a couple of hours until night set in and the woods around the cabin would be dark. Was she safe? The sheriff mentioned she might think of leaving town for her own safety. His department simply wasn't staffed to provide a protection detail. But Gemma couldn't leave the tigers she'd devoted her life to. Besides, Gray insisted on continuing to watch over the sanctuary, and her, at night. He'd been there to save her life every time.

She stared out the window, remembering he'd instructed her to keep the curtains drawn.

The forest grew darker and, while she loved the view, she once again had the sense of someone watching her. Gemma reached for the drapes to close them, but her eyes caught on a figure moving in the shadows between the trees. She paused, staring out, searching the woods.

Someone was out there. Had they been watching her? Was it the person who wanted her dead?

She gulped for breath.

It was all the encouragement Gemma needed to leave.

Grabbing her cane and bag, she headed for the door and left the cabin, remembering to lock the door behind her. Of course, Gray's face came to mind as she remembered the night he'd scolded her about locking her door. The night he'd shown up to tell her about the brakes. She shoved thoughts of him away and hurried to the truck Tom left for her to use, which was parked beneath the carport. She hadn't gotten around to replacing the CJ with all that was going on. In her bag, she searched for the keys.

Why did she have to use such a big bag? She could swear she'd stuck the giant key ring with her copy of all the important keys in the side pocket. She resisted the urge to dump the contents out on the ground. Gemma glanced behind her to make sure she was still alone. Maybe she was overreacting again and someone had been out taking a walk. Even though everyone had gone home for the day, at least there was still some daylight left. Gemma drew a measure of comfort from that. Still, she didn't like the shadows lurking in the carport. But she'd never find the keys with her hands shaking like this.

Sucking in calming breaths, she steeled her mind against the panic. *You have to stop freaking out!*

And then jangling, the familiar feel of metal.

The keys!

Finally.

She gripped them in her sweaty palm to unlock the truck door. Her hand trembled and she struggled to get it right, the keys clanking, announcing to the quiet evening that Gemma was afraid of what lurked in the woods. When the key engaged the lock, and she opened the door, she climbed in and sighed with relief. Starting the ignition, she drove down the road out of the sanctuary.

The county road ended at Highway 101, which ran along the Oregon coast. If she headed south, she would hit Gold Beach, where the Rogue River emptied into the Pacific, in about twenty miles. Gemma headed north.

Then it started to rain and hard.

Again?

Turning on the windshield wipers, she glanced in the rearview mirror. Had another vehicle just turned out off the infrequently traveled county road? She couldn't be sure with the downpour, but that gray sedan remained behind her. She turned her attention to watching the road that hugged the coast.

Rain pelted the windshield, and she adjusted the windshield wipers to accommodate.

Where was the rain when the habitat was burning? They could have used it. As she drove the slick, curvy road, all the wrong that had happened swirled in a vortex in her head.

Her uncle Dave's voice came back to her from that night.

On this road.

In the rain.

Gemma, there's something I have to tell you. I've put it off much too long. It's about—what's happening? The brakes! I can't—I can't control it. I can't control the car. This is all my fault! He'd glanced over at her, horror and certainty in his eyes. *Gemma! I'm sorry... Gemma—*

The car had crashed into a tree, silencing him forever. Leaving Gemma alive but with a severely broken leg and nerve damage.

She sucked in a breath. The sheriff had ruled the wreck an accident. But Uncle Dave had been scared that night. He hadn't said as much, but she could hear it in his tone. Sense it. What if the wreck hadn't been an accident—what if it had been orchestrated by the same person who was now targeting her? She hadn't gotten around to asking Clyde about this possibility, but maybe she would the next time she saw him.

She continued on for a few more miles and noticed the same vehicle still following her. Could be nothing. But Gemma needed no other nudging to steer down the short drive to the house Gray had given for his address, realizing this had been her intended destination all along. She couldn't even trust herself to keep her distance. Despite her common sense, her resolve. Despite knowing she couldn't get involved with the guy and should avoid him. None of that made any difference. Her resolve was no match against her desire to see him.

Gray had a way of encouraging her, and Gemma had never been more desperate for it. Her positive nature had been decimated with the events of the last few weeks. Of course, tonight when she'd turned to lock her door, an image of Gray's face had come to mind. But if she was honest, he was never too far from her thoughts. She found herself thinking about him often. Her heart danced a little each day when he first showed up. And when she saw him leave for the day, the light seemed to fade, if only a little. Why was she thinking about him like this? She knew better.

She *knew* better. It would only end in heartache. Everyone had secrets and Gray certainly had his. She stopped in front of the cozy, cute house painted in light shades of blue and trimmed in white. Then she felt ridiculous. Nobody followed her down the drive. Had she imagined it? A sense of awkwardness settled over her. Was it rude of her to show up uninvited?

Oh, what am I doing here?

Gemma shifted into reverse. Maybe she could just drive away before he even noticed. Too late. Hands on his hips, he stood on the porch. His jacket on, he looked as if he'd been about to leave the house. Her heart did that thing. See, even the rain had stopped for him.

Okay. Shift already.

But no. She couldn't exactly leave now that he'd seen her and, in fact, stood there staring. Was he grinning? And oh…yeah, she needed Gray. What would he say if he knew how much she needed to be here right now?

Gray bounded down the porch steps and over to the

truck door. He opened it. "Are you okay?" Deep concern filled his gaze.

"Yeah, I just…I just…" She couldn't bring herself to tell him about her complete paranoia. About seeing someone in the woods near her cabin and her fear she'd been followed. The gray sedan hadn't trailed her down this road.

"Well, don't just sit there. Get out and come in. We can sit on the porch and talk. It's a beautiful evening, especially since the rain stopped."

His kindness nearly undid her. Oh, good grief. She nodded and slipped out, forcing the sudden surge of tears back into the dungeon. She wanted to trust Gray, really wanted to trust him. The urge was frighteningly persistent. In fact, she had a feeling that she already trusted him but just didn't want to admit to what extent.

Once on his porch, he gestured at the wicker chairs with floral pads. He'd mentioned renting, so this obviously belonged to someone else. She couldn't see him picking this pattern out. But how would she know? She hadn't known him long enough to find out.

"I have lemonade, believe it or not. Or if you want something warm, how about hot chocolate or coffee?"

"No, thank you. Gray… I'm sorry for the intrusion. I—"

He sat next to her on the wicker sofa and took her hand. Her throat constricted.

"Something's bothering you. Tell me what happened."

Hanging her head, she shook it, feeling ridiculous for coming here. "Nothing's happened. It's not one thing. It's everything. And I needed someone to talk to."

He released her hand. "Why don't we take a stroll on the beach?"

He hadn't asked about her cane or if that would be a problem for her. He knew better by now. "I think I'd like that."

Taking her hand, he led her down the steps and the hundred yards to the beach. "What it must be like to have such a great view every day," she commented. "It's just beautiful here."

Gray shrugged. "It's okay. I prefer the views at Tiger Mountain though." He squeezed her hand.

Her heart flipped at his words. What had he meant by that? Or was she reading too much into it? She had to steer this walk and conversation to another place. But then the sun was setting, and Gray and Gemma stopped to watch. Sea stacks, rocky and beautiful, dotted the coast. Waves licked the shore at their feet, soothing her nerves.

"Nothing more amazing than the sunset on the Pacific." He released a breathy sigh.

Gemma wanted to be in his arms. But all she had was his hand. It was enough.

What am I doing? What am I thinking? I can't fall for this man, or any man.

She needed to talk to Gray about everything. That's why she was here.

"On the way here, I had a flashback. A memory of the night my uncle was killed."

Gray turned to look at her. "The accident that injured your leg?"

"Yes. I passed by the same exact spot today where his brakes went out and we slammed into a tree. It was raining that night too, so of course I would think of it."

He tugged her along with him and continued their walk. "Did you say the brakes went out?"

"I remembered tonight that he'd complained about

the brakes right before the crash. But the officials said the vehicle hydroplaned. He lost control of the car. It was an accident."

Gray stopped and faced her. "Do you believe that?"

"I did at the time. I was young. Had just turned eighteen. I don't know what to believe now, but I remember I had a bad feeling about what he was going to tell me. I don't know—something about that night was weird. I was scared even before the car went off the road. My uncle had been afraid there would be an investigation because of accusations about abuse. Rumors. Lies. It was all lies, Gray. And here I am, going through this all over again in a manner of speaking. All I've ever wanted was to have my family back. The people I've loved but lost. I thought if I built a sanctuary for my parents and my uncle, maybe I could have some of what I lost back. I could rebuild their legacy as well as do my part in this world."

She glanced at him—saw the raw emotion there, the understanding—and then dropped her gaze to the waves rushing forward, chasing her feet. If she didn't step away, she'd get wet. It was the same with Gray. She was getting much too close to him. Why had she told him any of it? Why had she been this transparent and vulnerable? Or thought she should come here?

"I don't know why I'm telling you this. I don't even know you. Not really."

"Gemma." The way he said her name… She had to look up to him. His eyes reflected emotion. Compassion and something much more—it touched the deepest place in her heart. She hadn't known she wanted that from him, or needed it.

But could she let herself accept it?

No. She had to pull away.

TWELVE

"Gemma." Gray grabbed her arm, careful he didn't knock her off balance, but she seemed determined to leave him there. "Where are you going? Why are you so afraid to open up? I promise, I'm not going to hurt you."

She stared at him. Did she see the truth there—that he was hiding things from her and that he wouldn't allow himself to get close to her? Is that what had her scared to share with him like she'd just done? Her gaze, those hazel eyes of hers, laid him bare, revealing the truth he didn't want to admit—he couldn't make that kind of promise. And in her eyes, maybe that was answer enough, reason enough for her not to trust him.

When he'd made his resolution to never need anyone, he hadn't known he would meet Gemma Rollins. Hadn't known how she would affect him. But looking at her now, Gray thought he might just need this woman. Need Gemma.

He released her arm. Who was he to keep her when she clearly wanted to go?

Images washed over him—the engagement ring, Julia, the woman he wanted to marry kissing another. He couldn't allow himself to fall for anyone like that again. He stepped back, putting space between them but not enough. Not nearly enough when he was still fighting his urge to be closer to Gemma. Gray wanted to pull her to him and reassure her, wipe her fears and doubts away. Run his fingers through her long dark hair again.

He shut his eyes.

Whispered her name. Thought of that moment when he'd had his hands in her hair. Warmth suffused him. A wave rushed up near his feet, cold seawater splashing him, jarring him out of the trance she'd put him in.

No. Gray had to stay focused. Someone was trying to kill her. Someone was trying to kill them both. He'd been heading out to take up the night shift to watch over Tiger Mountain when he'd gotten a call from Sheriff Kruse. He wanted to meet Gray tonight, but he wouldn't say more on the phone. Then Gemma had driven up. She needed him right now and he had to focus on what was best for her, not what he wanted for himself. Besides, getting involved with her during this investigation was all kinds of wrong. His emotional involvement could cloud his judgment and ruin this investigation down the road, if anyone was charged.

She marched on ahead of him.

"Gemma, wait!" Gray caught up easily. "You're shivering. Come inside and have some hot chocolate."

As the setting sun ushered in dusk, Gray realized he didn't want her to return to her dark, lonely cabin.

Head lowered, Gemma kept walking.

"Come on, what do you say?"

She shrugged. "Yeah, sure. Okay."

He hadn't known her long, but he'd never seen her this down and it disturbed him more than it should. But she had every reason to struggle right now. Gray wasn't doing anything to help her. In fact, he was keeping a secret from her, as an undercover agent. If only he could tell her the truth.

Inside the house, he settled her on the sofa and made hot chocolate for them both. Gemma took the mug from him, her expression somber, her features pale. He understood all too well. Everything she cared about had been targeted. He wanted to question her further about the night her uncle died. His death could very well have been murder. Could he have been about to give her information about the trafficking ring that had been in operation for far too long? Was that why he had been killed? If it was murder and Clyde Morris was responsible, how would Gemma react when she found out the truth? It would be devastating for her to learn that Clyde was behind it all. A man she held in high esteem.

He watched her sip on the drink a bit until the color came back into her cheeks. The silence wasn't deafening, like he might have expected, but comfortable. Two old friends sharing hot chocolate and listening to the waves crashing against the shore.

Gray broke the quiet with his words. "You're too hard on yourself, Gemma. You're always up, you stay positive and it's what draws people to you, but it's okay to be upset sometimes. It's okay to grieve." What was he? A therapist? But he was compelled to share what he could. "You're going through a lot right now, and if there's anything I can do to help, I will. I'm mostly concerned for your safety. Did the sheriff say anything to you? Did he suggest you get out of town for a while or at least stay with a friend instead of alone in your cabin?" This was Gray's way of making the suggestion, if the sheriff hadn't done that much. Gray watched over her cabin every night. Watched over the sanctuary. But standing watch hadn't been enough to stop the culprit so far and Gray still needed evidence to make an arrest.

"Yes, he made the suggestion. But I can't just up and leave Tiger Mountain. There's no one trained to take my place in the day-to-day management. And I guess I thought it was enough that you were watching the place at night." She sighed, then, "Thanks for that, by the way. I don't know how you do it all. And, thanks for listening, Gray. I guess I feel like I can talk to you. I've known Cara much longer, but I didn't want her to see me like this."

Despite her earlier reaction and doubts about revealing so much, talking to him when she really didn't know him, she apparently believed she could trust Gray enough to show him this side of herself. The real side.

He wasn't sure how he felt about that. "I understand. I'm here if you want to talk."

"Why is this happening?"

The question surprised him. He wasn't sure what she was asking, exactly. "What do you mean?"

She lifted her gaze. "Do you believe in God, Gray?"

Kind of sad she had to ask. That should be something easily seen in a person. "Of course I do."

"Well, I do too. For the longest time I've been hoping He would answer my prayers for the sanctuary. But He hasn't. Not as far as I can tell. So now instead of an answer to my prayers, I just want to know why all this is happening to me."

Wow. She was really unloading some deep stuff on him. He had to rub his jaw on that one. Boy, what did he say to that? Leaning back in the chair, he considered his words. *Lord, please help me to say the right thing.*

"I wish I had an answer for you. My brother committed suicide a few years ago, and I've always wondered the same thing. Why didn't God stop him? Why didn't He help *us* to stop Jeremy? To see how bad things had gotten. All I know is that we live in a fallen world and bad things happen. And maybe…maybe we can pray and God answers in ways we can't see and it doesn't all happen instantaneously. Maybe it's about the journey too."

She didn't respond, and he spent a minute worrying that he'd said the wrong thing. Maybe he should offer to pray with her? Or would that be insulting, implying that God was more likely to listen to him than to her?

"I wasn't expecting a real answer. Just expressing my thoughts. And why should I care so much about Tiger Mountain succeeding when someone is dead? Someone was murdered there. Someone tried to kill me too. And now Caesar is gone. Raja goes tomorrow."

"Wait. What?"

"Clyde wanted as few people to know as possible, but he's moving two tigers. He says we can't afford to keep all of them with the rebuilding expenses and the loss of space. He took Caesar this evening and I cried over that. I cried over a tiger when I should be more devastated over Wes. And I am. Maybe it's just the culmination of everything."

Pulse roaring in his ears at the news Clyde was moving Caesar, Gray struggled to listen to Gemma. Too much going on at once.

"Gray, are you listening?"

He rose, rubbing the back of his neck. He needed to make a call. "Yes, of course!"

He quickly sat right next to Gemma and grabbed her hands because he really did care about her, but moving the tigers could be the break in the case he'd been waiting on. "Where was Clyde taking the tigers? Why didn't I know about this?"

She tugged her hands free. "Why do you care so much? What's going on?"

He stood again and grabbed their cups. "Nothing. I'm just surprised I didn't know, that's all. I could have been there to help you. I'm sure it was hard. And I would've wanted to tell the old guy goodbye. Want some more hot chocolate?" Gray had overreacted at the news and had to play things down now.

Shaking her head, she said, "I've told you a lot about myself tonight, Gray. I don't know much about you. How about you reciprocate? Tell me something about you that I don't know, which is pretty much everything. I'd prefer to feel like this conversation isn't so one-sided."

"You know where I live." He grinned. And he did want to tell her everything. To be honest with her. She deserved it, but he was so close to ending this. Indecision tore through him.

When his cell rang, he glanced at the number. Mark, his superior. "Gemma, I have to take this call. And then… I'll tell you everything you want to know."

And maybe a few things she didn't.

Gray went out the front door and onto the porch to answer his call, leaving her alone.

This evening, Gray had been there for her once more. He's saved her again only this time it wasn't from physical harm as much as emotional angst. She'd been desperate or she never would have revealed so much of herself, but Gemma was glad she had shared. Gray had come through if only by listening. Was it so wrong to need someone who would listen and encourage you?

She'd been that person for most everyone, and now she needed that too.

Except, with Gray, Gemma had to admit it went much deeper. Her heart had somehow gotten tangled up with him. Just being with him—walking or sitting, drinking hot chocolate or cleaning out a tiger habitat—made Gemma's heart lighter. She could almost wish he had never volunteered because she had been doing just fine before he showed up. Now on top of everything going on at Tiger Mountain, she had a thing for the guy right when a distraction was the last thing she needed.

And he was a stranger, to boot. Rising from the sofa, she peeked out the front window. Still on the phone and in a serious conversation by the tone in his voice. *I wonder who that is?* See, she didn't know enough about him to even make a guess.

Was it…was it his girlfriend? Did he already have a special woman in his life, the way that Ellis had? How would she know? While she didn't like to snoop, she had to know whom she could trust. She'd just spilled everything to this guy, even about the night Uncle Dave was killed.

That was it. She had to know if a secret fiancée was going to show up, if he was the man he claimed to be. Pacing around the small living room, she looked at the sparse decor of a rental home. Gray hadn't left anything personal.

Who are you, Gray Wilson?

She meandered around the small beachfront home to find the restroom and, next to that, a bedroom. The door was shut. Why shut the bedroom door in a house where you lived alone unless you wanted to keep out guests? Indecision pressed in on her. Should she open it or not? Moisture slicked her palms, but determination drove her forward. Gemma had to know who Gray was. She grabbed the doorknob and twisted.

Inside the room, his things were scattered. A duffel bag crumpled on the floor in the corner. Shirts and jeans were spread out on the bed as if recently laundered but not yet put away. He hadn't expected company, that was for sure. Listening to him around the corner, she could tell he was still deep in the conversation, but that could end any minute.

She'd come to him, desperately needing his knack for reassurance, and now she would repay him by snooping. Another desperate need—to know the truth. Ellis had been hiding something, and she couldn't let herself go any deeper with Gray, a man she'd only just met, when there was still so much she didn't know about him. It wasn't like she had to go digging through his things. Everything was laid out for her to see on the small desk against the wall. A laptop was open but in sleep mode. A stack of papers and a thick file. His wallet.

And a gun.

Not so unusual out in the wilderness, but, still, seeing it made her nervous.

Next to the desk, a black leather briefcase. Slowly, she flipped his wallet open and there she found a badge and ID. US Fish and Wildlife Service Special Agent? What was that? The FBI of game wardens?

Special Agent Grayson Wilde.

Gemma dropped the badge, stunned at the discovery.

A federal agent working at Tiger Mountain under a false identity? She pressed her hands to her lips. What was going on?

And he'd lied to her. Kept this all to himself. He was obviously working undercover.

Pain scorched her heart. Right. She'd known not to

trust or care for anyone. She'd been through this before. Maybe she hadn't discovered a hidden fiancée, which he could still very well have, but she had learned he was lying about everything else. Lying about the reason he was at Tiger Mountain and about his true identity.

Gemma let fury boil up and compel her forward.

She had to get out of here.

But she didn't want to exit through the front door where he would see her and try to stop her. There had to be a back door in the place and she could sneak around the house to her truck before he saw her. She found it through the kitchen and carefully hurried down the steps hidden in the shadows. Darkness had settled in for the night, except for the light from a crescent moon now that the clouds had moved out again. Gemma made her way around the house, spotting the truck sitting only a few yards away. On this side of the house, moonlight guided her way.

Pain ached up her leg, the nerve endings firing off, slowing her efforts. Making her clumsy. So weird how the pain was connected to her emotions this way.

"Gemma!" Gray called from the porch. "Gemma, wait."

Footfalls approached behind her. If only she could reach the truck before he got to her. Climb in and drive off before she had to face him. She hadn't wanted to admit just how much she needed Gray, needed to trust him, but the depth of the pain in her heart proved it.

Her cane wobbled to the right, the pain in her leg causing her to crumple. Sparkling sand came at her as she fell, but strong arms swooped her up and in against Gray. *No, please no, not again.*

"Let me go!" She twisted away and he gently re-leased her.

"What's wrong, Gemma?"

Now that she had her balance back, she continued to her truck and opened the door. No thanks to Gray—it was because of him her balance had been off in the first place.

He held the door, so she couldn't shut it. "Are you going to tell me what's going on? Why you're so angry?"

He wouldn't let her go? Fine, they'd just have to get the confrontation out of the way right now. "I don't appreciate being lied to, that's what. I want to know the truth, Gray *Wilde*. Why are you at Tiger Mountain?"

THIRTEEN

Gray had done this to her.

He was the one to put those huge tears in her eyes, pouring over and sliding down her soft cheeks. He'd never thought he'd be so vulnerable to a woman's tears, but he could hardly stand to watch. They weren't tears of sadness or of grief. No. Gemma had now found herself again. She was the strong woman he'd met that first day. Anger blazed in her eyes instead.

She held up a fist and he knew she wanted to hit him. But she held back the fury carving lines through her beautiful face and then dropped her fist. "You lied to me!"

He said nothing because it was true. That's what one did when working undercover. But there was one thing he could say.

"Thank you."

"For what?" she snapped.

"For not hitting me."

"You don't think you deserve it?"

Maybe he did, and he hesitated before he answered. She couldn't understand what he'd gone through, growing close to her and keeping this to himself.

"I hope you realize that I have to tell Clyde. He's my

main investor and the support behind this whole endeavor. He needs to know we're under investigation."

If Clyde Morris found out about his investigation, it could ruin everything. Not only would it put the investigation at risk, but it might actually make Clyde lash out at Gemma. He had to tell her everything and convince her to stay quiet, at least for now.

His feelings, her feelings—it all had to take a backseat to the investigation.

"No. You can't tell anyone. It's for your own safety. Do you understand?"

"I won't understand until you tell me everything, and this time, I want the truth. Who are you, really? Why are you at Tiger Mountain?"

"I wanted to tell you. In fact, before the call, I was about to tell you who I am."

"Right."

She tried to tug the door shut, but Gray remained where he stood. In her way. He couldn't let her run off until they had an understanding.

"Now that you know, we need to talk. I need you to listen. Can you please step out of the truck and come inside?" He hadn't meant his tone to sound so forceful and cold, but he had to get a handle on this before all was lost.

Fear shone in her eyes, hitting him like a fist to the gut. When he spoke again, he was careful to soften his tone.

"Gemma, you know me. You know the real me. Whoever I am, you know me as a person. I'm the same Gray that you've come to know and work with at Tiger Mountain. It's just my job that you didn't know about. Please give me the chance to explain. I'm here to help you, and I have been ever since I found you stranded in the Jeep."

Would his earnest words spoken in a gentle tone be enough to convince her to come inside? She blew out a breath. Hung her head back and looked at the stars, in obvious indecision. The tears streaking her face almost had a fluorescent glow about them in the moonlight. When she dropped her gaze to him, he saw the deep pain there as her eyes searched his.

He couldn't help himself. He wiped away a tear with his thumb, brushing the soft skin of her cheek. She shuddered. Was that from his touch? He was getting in too deep, much too deep. He pulled away. "Well?"

"How can I believe anything you say?"

"How about I share my story and then you can decide?"

Frowning, she averted her gaze. "How can I argue with that?"

She couldn't. "Then come inside and I'll tell you everything. Answer all your questions."

She frowned, considering…and then nodded.

He slowly released a breath and relaxed his shoulders. At least he'd convinced her to give him more time to explain. But, in the meantime, a tiger was getting away. Gray needed to protect Gemma and also find Caesar. If it was too late to get him, then Gray would have to be on hand when Raja was taken away, tomorrow. He knew enough now that he could be on top of it when it happened. But for everything to work as planned, he needed Gemma's silence.

Once inside the house, Gemma settled in the same place he'd left her before her mad escape.

"How did you find out?"

Her eyes widened. "You left your ID and badge on the desk in your room."

"And you were in my room why?" Now it was his turn to be furious, and not just at Gemma but at himself. How could he be so stupid? But he couldn't think straight when he was with her.

Her gaze darted around the room as she looked at anything but Gray. "With everything that's happened, I needed to know who I could trust. I needed to know for sure. I wanted to trust you, to believe in you—can't you see that? But you were so secretive, even after I told you my story. I wanted to find out what you were hiding."

"And now you know."

"Not really. It's not making sense to me yet. You are stalling. Tell me everything, Gray."

"The reason I'm working undercover is because I received a tip that someone involved with Tiger Mountain is also involved in a wildlife trafficking ring. They planned to use your sanctuary to traffic tigers, specifically tiger body parts. And now, it sounds like that is actually happening."

She gasped. "You can't be serious. How is that possible? Who would do such a thing?"

"Gemma, please tell me you're not involved."

She stood then, stunned at his suggestion. He held his hands up in surrender. "I don't believe you are. I just had to ask."

"No, you didn't have to ask. Are you investigating me? Do you know what an investigation will do to us if the public finds out? Rumors of animal abuse killed our funding before. Without funding, yeah, it's hard to take care of animals. Clyde expects me to raise my own donor base, which I won't be able to do if we're under investigation. I can't believe this. I thought I could build something new. It's like I can never escape the past. This is like what happened before."

"Yes, it is, and who was involved then besides your now deceased family members?"

Those tears again, surging in her eyes, but she didn't allow them to overflow their boundaries. Gray hated doing this to her. Wanted to pull her into his arms as if that could make everything go away.

Her gaze held his. She didn't say the words, but he could see the moment she realized the truth.

Clyde Morris. He'd been the one all along.

"I…how could I not have seen? How could I not know?"

He'd asked the same questions when he first arrived, but then he saw how Clyde operated, leaving Gemma to the day-to-day running of the sanctuary. This sanctuary was only one small piece of Clyde's extensive trafficking operation. Looked like Clyde was happy to let Gemma have her sanctuary as long as he could use it for his own purposes. He'd been much more than a silent partner.

And Gemma had fallen in love with the tigers and gotten in the way.

"I can't believe Clyde would try to kill me, though. Gray, no, this can't be the truth. Please, there has to be someone else. Besides, *why* would he try to kill me? He needs me to run the sanctuary."

More questions without answers. He ached for her. Her expression shifted to one of terror. Horror even. "Caesar!"

Grimly, he nodded. "Yes, Caesar. While we sit here and talk, Caesar is likely being taken to slaughter." To be divided into parts and sold to the highest bidder in the traditional Asian medicine market. But he kept that to himself.

She jumped to her feet. "We have to stop it. We have to save Caesar."

He grabbed her shoulders. "Whoa. There's no 'we' about this. I'm the government operative with the training to deal with this. You need to stay out of it. You've faced too much danger already. Let me do my job, and maybe I can save Caesar."

"Wait a minute." She pressed a finger to her lips. "I might be able to help. The company that took him away—we've worked with that specific trucking company before. I can search the files on the computer. See if I can find something about their base of operations that you can use or maybe their delivery destination. Find out where they might take Caesar."

He shook his head. "That would be too dangerous, Gemma."

"I'm already in danger. Someone has already tried to kill me. But nobody will suspect me of doing something secretive on the office computer. You, however, someone would suspect."

"You said Clyde had gone to Portland. When is he due back?"

"Tomorrow. So there's time. We can do this."

"Are you sure?" He paced again. "And, then, what about tomorrow and the day after that? I'm not sure how long you can keep up this ruse without letting on that you know." He rubbed his eyes, wishing Gemma could come up with an excuse to leave town, but she was integral to Tiger Mountain, especially in their current predicament.

"Then we have to finish this. You have to find the evidence you need before it's too late."

He nodded. "Tonight then. See what you can find on the computer tonight. I'll catch up with you at the office. I need to make some calls and see if we can find out where Caesar is going from my end. Let my superior know what is going on. Get a hold of Sheriff Kruse. This is happening and soon." He couldn't help the hope that rose at the very real possibility he would find the evidence to bring Clyde Morris and his trafficking ring down.

But something troubled him, dousing his momentary rush. Gemma was selfless and might have been thinking about Caesar, but Gray was thinking about her. He had to finish this before she got hurt. Gemma's life was still in danger.

"Gemma, this is dangerous. You understand that, right?"

"I've been in danger since the day we met, Gray. Nothing has changed except that now I know the truth and I can protect myself." She hesitated.

"What?"

"I didn't tell you this before. I saw someone in the woods near my cabin tonight. I was afraid they were watching me so I got in the truck. And then I thought someone followed me. That's when I came to your house."

"Why didn't you tell me?"

"I don't know if I'm being paranoid or not."

"You have every reason to be cautious. That does it. I can't let you go back there tonight."

But Gray had let her return to the sanctuary. That's because Gemma had come up with the bright idea to hang out with Cara. Clyde was in Portland, as it was, so having Cara with her at all times seemed like overkill. Still, Gray had cautioned she couldn't be too careful. He was meeting with the sheriff and then would catch up with her here.

In the meantime, Gemma didn't know what she would do without Cara. Her friend had agreed to hang out with her this evening while Gemma worked. She'd given the true excuse that she was afraid to be alone with everything that had been going on. Cara had gone so far as to invite Gemma to stay with her and her husband until she was out of danger and things settled down.

She was feeling a lot better, and her positivity was beginning to return. But she wouldn't put Cara in any further danger and kept the details to herself.

"I haven't seen that in a while, you know?" Cara leaned against the doorjamb.

"What's that?" But Gemma had a feeling she knew.

"Your smile."

"It's not a real smile. I can't really smile until this is over."

"I hear you. I'm making a pot of coffee. You want some?"

She shook her head. "That would keep me up all night. On second thought, yes."

Gemma booted up the new desktop in the back office that Clyde had taken over while he was here. He mentioned leaving the machine behind for general use once he was done. A new computer, compliments of Clyde. She could replace the older one in her office with the latest model. She really was beholden to him, which made her snooping around in the files feel wrong. Surely there was some mistake. Clyde couldn't be the one behind the trafficking ring. And even if he was, why would he put anything on this machine that could be remotely incriminating? He knew she had access to it. He'd given her the password to log on, when Cara was busy in her office, inputting the data on each tiger. Another thing that had been bothering her: if Clyde was the man who wanted her dead, then who had she seen in the woods? Who had followed her? Maybe she really was being paranoid and it was nothing to be worried about.

Leaning her chin forward against her hand, she huffed.

What am I doing? Clyde can't be involved. He simply can't be. Regardless, she'd assured Gray she wouldn't reveal his identity to Clyde. She'd been here before. Someone else long ago had begged her not to tell the truth. To keep his secret hidden. She shoved the thoughts away. This was completely different.

Believing that Clyde was innocent gave her a new resolve. She would prove he wasn't part of a trafficking ring. To that end, she would search through the files, starting with information about the trucking company that had transported Caesar today, to see if she could find out where they might have taken him. She could even put in a call about the delivery.

The prospect of finally getting some answers was exciting. Now she understood Gray better. Solving a mystery and catching bad guys might even be addictive.

The truck that had taken Caesar was with Beacon Transport. She found the file, a trucking company specializing in wild animal transportation, no less. She was familiar with the company to a point, but they hadn't needed animals transported very often. Once tigers arrived, they rarely left until they died. That was the way a sanctuary was supposed to be—their home for life. That's why the idea of trafficking animals via a sanctuary didn't make sense to her, but, in that way, perhaps it was the perfect cover. And the fire had conveniently necessitated the moving of tigers.

The company was scheduled to transport Caesar to another sanctuary in Colorado, so the information said, but, oddly enough, the payment didn't match up with the cost of travel to Colorado. Looked like they were only getting paid to haul Caesar a short distance.

Her heart stumbled.

Gemma frowned. Finding a pad of paper, she searched for a pencil to write down the information. There weren't any on the desk and when she tried a drawer, it was locked. Why lock a desk drawer unless there was something to hide? If she broke into the drawer, she would actually be snooping on something Clyde believed important enough to lock. But he shouldn't hide anything from Gemma regarding Tiger Mountain. Using a paper clip, she picked the lock easily enough. So much for security.

Gray should be on his way by now. She wished he would hurry up.

Inside the drawer was a bill of lading regarding the transportation of two tigers to…a…warehouse? So Clyde *was* involved. The hurt she felt over his duplicity blurred her vision.

Voices resounded in the hall.

Not Gray.

Gemma froze.

Clyde.

How could that be?

He was supposed to be in Portland!

Gemma shoved the drawer closed and looked at the computer screen, pulling up a blank document. Pulse pounding, she started typing out a letter to whomever it may concern.

Clyde meandered into the office. "Gemma! What a surprise to see you here."

Cara appeared in the doorway behind him. "Hey Gem, I'm going to head on out now. Ted burned the lasagna. Now that Clyde is here, you don't have to worry about being on your own."

Gemma nodded. What could she say to keep her friend here with Clyde looking on? "Okay. Enjoy your dinner."

Glancing up at him, she couldn't even rouse a smile. "I thought you were still in Portland raising money?"

He slid onto the edge of the desk and studied her. With him looming over her like that, she'd never felt so uncomfortable under his scrutiny. But then, had she ever been under his scrutiny like this?

"Are you okay, Gemma?"

Could he smell fear?

No, I'm not okay! She'd thought of this man as a father, especially since losing her parents and then her uncle. Even from a distance, he'd filled that place for her as though he'd wanted to. Calling to check on her now and then. As though she truly mattered to him. But had he simply been using her? "I'm fine, Clyde. Still missing Caesar, that's all." She rubbed her face, revealing how tired she truly was, trying to act completely normal. "So what's up? Why'd you come back early?"

"I finished my business. With the fire and the recent problems, the funding isn't exactly flowing in like it should. I ended up talking to the sheriff tonight. You'll be glad to hear that he believes Wes might have been behind the attempts on your life and the other troubles."

She didn't see it. "Why would he do that?"

"While you were busy putting out the proverbial and literal fires, he could transport a tiger or two. But obviously things got out of hand. Didn't go as he planned."

"Why try to kill me?" And who had killed Wes? But she didn't say it out loud. She didn't want an actual conversation with Clyde and had already asked too many questions. The sooner he left, the better.

"Because you didn't make it easy for him to grab one of the cats, the way that he wanted. You were too close. At any hint of a disturbance, you left your cabin to check on the tigers. But with you out of the way, he might have had a chance. His sister is dying, and he needed the money."

She focused on the screen, typing her fake letter, wondering if Gray had known about Wes's sister.

"Why do you say that?"

"What?" She glanced at him.

"Why did you ask if Gray knew about Wes?"

Oh no. Had she said that out loud? Heart pounding, she scrambled for an answer. "Gray has taken it upon himself to protect me."

"He's done a lousy job, if you ask me."

Well, she hadn't asked him. And she was still alive thanks to Gray, so there. Gemma filed the document away and then shut down the computer. "Look, Clyde, I'll admit that I kind of like him. I don't mind him being around so much even if I no longer need protection." With that, Gemma was able to find a reason to smile, and it had the unexpected effect of putting Clyde off.

He didn't even crack a grin.

He was giving off strange vibes. Was she acting suspiciously? Did he realize she'd figured him out? He'd practically caught her snooping in his office. She'd never been more terrified. It was like she was seeing him for the first time. Who was this man?

Could Clyde see in her eyes what chilled her to the marrow?

Gemma was afraid for her life.

FOURTEEN

Clyde angled his head as if considering what to say. He obviously hadn't expected to find her in here like this after hours. And in his eyes, she saw what she dreaded.

He suspected she'd learned the truth about him.

She had to act as though nothing was out of the ordinary. Get out of here before it was too late. Stay calm. Just stay calm. "Well, I'm tired. It's been a long day and I need to head home." Gemma eased out of the chair and struggled to steady her breathing.

Could he hear her heart pounding in cadence with her rising panic? Where was Gray? He was supposed to be here by now.

The man she once thought was like family to her said nothing. He simply watched her as she walked out the door and headed down the hallway. She knew what he would do next. He would open his computer and try to see what she'd been up to—what files she had accessed. Then he would search his desk drawer and find it unlocked. She had a few seconds to escape. If only her leg didn't ache with her stress, adding to an already precarious situation. With the pain, her leg stiffened and it was like walking with a leg in a cast.

Heart pounding to get free of her chest, she pushed through the front door.

Run!

But she couldn't run; she could only hobble along. She had no intention of going back to her cabin. No. She would leave in the truck and meet Gray. But once she was at the vehicle, she realized she'd left the keys sitting on the desk in Clyde's office. Idiot! It had been all she could do to grab her cane and leave. She was doing the worst job of pretending everything was all right.

No way could she go inside and face Clyde.

Feeling her disability like never before, she carefully made her way through the woods in between the resource building and her cabin and tried to keep hidden as she headed for the road. Tugging her cell from her pocket, she tried to reach Gray to warn him and ask him to hurry.

She was in trouble!

But she couldn't get a signal here. Gemma pushed on, hugging the edge of the woods, heading away from the sanctuary. She had loved living here. Loved the hope that ignited in her heart that she could once again create something of what she knew growing up, create a legacy for the family that she'd lost. But she couldn't have been more wrong.

Exhausted, Gemma paused and looked at her phone. Finding a signal at last, she called Gray again.

He answered. She never thought his voice could sound so good.

"Where are you?" she practically screamed through the phone.

"What's wrong?"

"Come and get me now. I'll be hiking down the road to the main highway. Please hurry."

"I'm on my way already. Tell me what's happened."

"It's Clyde. He walked in on me on the computer. He didn't say anything, but by the look in his eyes, he suspects I know. And Cara thought I'd be fine with him there, so she left."

"What?"

"She didn't know I was afraid of Clyde. She thought when he got there she could leave." Clyde wouldn't have done anything in front of Cara unless he suspected she knew something too. Instead, she'd made it clear she was oblivious.

"Okay, stay hidden. I'll be right there. I've been on the phone with my superior. I was just with the sheriff. The medical examiner said the chemical etorphine had killed Wes."

His tone sounded almost accusing.

"What?" Oh, that made her sick. That tranquilizer was meant for big animals like elephants and rhinos. It wasn't legal for her to use it at the sanctuary. And it would have killed Wes instantly. "That's not what we use in our tranquilizer guns. We use ketamine."

"I know who used it, Gemma. It's a prominent tranquilizer among wildlife traffickers. And as soon as Sheriff Kruse said Clyde had stopped in to speak with him tonight, I tried to call your cell and warn you."

"I had trouble even getting this signal."

"The sheriff was headed over to see Emil Atkins to question him about Wes and the fire. Clyde has really done a number on him, but then he got called to an emergency. I'll call 911, but it will take a deputy time to get there. I'm on my way. And, Gemma?"

"Yes?"

"Stay alive."

"I promise I'll do my best. What are you going to

tell the emergency dispatcher? You don't have any evidence to arrest Clyde yet, Gray. This will ruin your investigation. And Clyde will run after tonight. I'm sure of it. My life will always be in danger."

"I'll tell them you're afraid for your life. You're more important to me than this investigation. I'm only a few minutes—"

"Gray?" She glanced at the phone.

She'd lost the signal.

Please, God, if you answer one prayer, please answer this one. Help me get to safety. Help Gray make it in time.

But doubt suffused her. She'd already been through so much and where had God been? Where was He now?

Her cane and stiff leg hampered her efforts to put distance between her and Clyde, and the terrain at night made her travel all the more difficult. All the hurdles life had thrown her had now been reduced to tangled and gnarled tree roots, boulders and rocks and slippery moss—the smallest of hindrances seemed insurmountable to her.

"Gemma!" Clyde's voice echoed through the dark woods—the forest she loved had now turned menacing.

No, no, no. He can't find me. Come on, Gray!

That Clyde would use the sanctuary for his own trafficking purposes—a man who claimed he made wildlife conservation his mission in life—seemed surreal to her. But she'd seen the evidence herself. If only she had thought to grab the documentation. But there had not been time. He'd shown up, appearing out of nowhere, as if he knew she'd discovered the truth. How could she have been so blind?

She had no more doubts that Clyde was involved in illegal trafficking, using Tiger Mountain—the words screamed through her head. He'd been more than exuberant when she'd come to him four years ago with her request for his help in building a new sanctuary.

Now she suspected that the night Uncle Dave died, he had been going to tell her the truth about Clyde. Gray had implied that the trafficking ring went back that far. An awful question suddenly occurred to her—if Uncle Dave really had been planning to tell her about Clyde, was it a truth he himself had discovered? Or had he been working with Clyde? She couldn't know.

Had Gray called 911? Where was he? What was taking so long?

Clyde called after her again. "Gemma, what are you doing? Where did you go? Are you hurt?"

He sounded so normal, just the way he always had. He was trying to make her think she was crazy, and that everything was all right. That he wasn't a killer. She wasn't about to listen. Twigs scraped her face as she hurried.

A protruding root caught her foot and she fell forward with a jar, stifling a cry. She'd never make it down the road at this rate. Gemma would have to hide in the sanctuary itself, until Gray or the sheriff arrived to help her. But what would happen once they came? Until Clyde physically harmed her, it would only look like she had lost her mind. Clyde would find an angle to spin everything against her, especially given he'd gone out of his way to speak with the sheriff tonight already. She realized now that he had manipulated everything and had the situation well under control.

God, please no. Please, help me to bring him down. He'd gotten away with too much for far too long. And Gemma had been stupid and naive.

A drop pelted her. And then another.

Of course. Of course it would rain now, making the slow-going even more slow and miserable. Still, that could help her, making it more difficult for Clyde to spot her. But it could also hurt her. She had to hide and stay hidden.

The only place she could think to hide was within the sanctuary itself. That could buy her some time, especially since she knew the space much better than Clyde did. Before the rain came down too hard, before her cell died completely, she texted Gray her plans to hide and wait Clyde out. When she got a signal, the text would go through.

"I know you're in the woods. You know with your leg that you can't get away from me." His call echoed through the gloomy forest. "Don't make me look for you. Come out and I promise I won't hurt you. Come on, Gemma. I'm practically family."

A deep, throbbing ache coursed through her at his words. He'd as much as admitted he was guilty. *Family?* she cried out on the inside. *You killed my family!* She had no evidence of this, but she knew in her heart that it was true. And if she got away, she would find the proof. The truth had to come out.

What about Wes? Did you kill him? Did you tell him those words? she wanted to cry out. *What about Caesar and Raja?* But calling out would only give away her location.

But it didn't matter. Clyde's voice revealed he was heading in her general direction.

He was close, entirely too close.

Gray slowly steered his Silverado down the county road that cut through the sanctuary, windshield wipers squeaking back and forth as he searched for Gemma, hoping she would step out into his headlights when she realized it was him. The beams of his lights would only go so far, and outside of that circle of light, darkness loomed in the woods, making it all but impossible for him to see anything. Tree branches stretched out across the road, shadows turning them into ghoulish arms reaching for frightened trespassers.

She had to be terrified out there alone in the dark with Clyde possibly onto her. Gray silently berated himself. He should have anticipated the man wouldn't have gone so far as Portland when a tiger was being moved. He probably lied to Gemma about his travel plans so he could conduct his trafficking transaction without drawing attention.

Where are you, Gemma?

She was expecting him and was supposed to wait in the woods. But he'd already made it to the resource building and hadn't seen Gemma.

Why hadn't she taken Tom's truck out? Clyde must have somehow prevented her. Where was the man? Gray checked the cell again and found a text from Gemma.

I'm hiding in the sanctuary.

Clyde was obviously stalking her. How long could she hope to elude him? Maybe the habitats would assist her in staying hidden. Gray texted her, hoping it wouldn't come through at an inappropriate moment.

I'm here. Where are you exactly?

He didn't wait for a response. Donned his jacket, made sure his Glock was in his shoulder holster and his extra pistol in his ankle holster. He never removed the small knife hidden in his belt. Confirming no one lurked in the shadows around his truck, he got out and headed toward the habitats. Clyde would have seen Gray's vehicle approach. Gray wouldn't go in through the front gates of the fenced-in portion, where Gemma was hiding. That would be too obvious and Clyde could be monitoring the gate and then take Gray out.

He'd have to walk the perimeter and climb over—not a little daunting. Regardless, it had to be done fast. Clyde could already have found Gemma and hurt her, or worse, killed her. Panic and fear for her urged him through the shadows, between the trees and over to the fence, though he remained in darkness.

Where was the sheriff's department when you needed them?

At least the rain had eased up into a fine mist. He hurried until he was a least five hundred yards from the resource building and against the outer fence. Then he'd have another fence to conquer—all part of the protective measures to keep the tigers in place. Now to breach the split-rail fencing and keep the chain-link from rattling so he wouldn't broadcast his location to Clyde. That meant Gray had to ascend both quietly and quickly.

Near the top he slipped, catching himself before he plummeted to the ground but not without making an entire section of fence clang. He stilled, holding his breath as if that could make him look like one of the rails between sections. On this dreary night, anything was possible.

Finally he made his way over the top, which included another section tilted at a forty-five degree angle to make things even more complicated. He climbed down until it was comfortable to simply drop to the ground. Immediately, he began to jog between the interior and exterior fencing, seeking another entry point. He'd made too much noise back there, even with the rain to cover the sound.

He scaled the next fence and just before he released his hold on the fence he hesitated. Movement in his peripheral vision caught his attention.

Gray froze and watched.

Something moved near a thicket of trees. Something large and…catlike.

Great. Had someone let a tiger out? Had it been Gemma or Clyde? Was she even in the sanctuary anymore? Gray dropped to the ground with a thud, again making more noise than he would have liked. He remained still, waiting and watching for any signs of Clyde, Gemma or tigers. Then he quietly rushed to the side of a building. Without knowing where she'd hidden, finding Gemma could take a while. At least most of the acreage was fenced in to contain each tiger. He wouldn't be looking there. Not yet.

Squeezing his eyes shut, he tried to picture her and imagine where she might hide from Clyde. A place that he also wouldn't guess.

Obviously, Clyde realized his game was up and the father figure had now turned dangerous and deadly. He wouldn't let anything interfere with his operation, which was worth millions and which provided him with a niche in which he'd thrived for decades.

Gray could almost be happy that the noose was tightening around Clyde's neck, except he didn't want anyone else to die because of the trafficking ring. And this time he might lose a woman he cared deeply about. Even if she'd never forgive him for lying about his reasons for coming to Tiger Mountain.

Trust, once lost, was hard to regain. He'd seen that

well enough with the tigers, especially with Raja who'd been blindsided and now no longer trusted Gemma.

Gray peered around the building and saw not one but two tigers prowling through the thicket. Tigers were normally solitary creatures. These could be the sisters, Layla and Lilly.

Great, just great.

Tigers were generally stealth hunters, but given that these animals had been abused before coming to Tiger Mountain, he wasn't exactly sure what he could expect with them. Would he become their prey? Or a toy to be played with?

A security light illuminated a habitat building about fifty yards from him, and next to a tree Gray spotted someone. Though it was too far and too dark to see clearly, he could at least see the person was taller and thicker than Gemma.

Clyde.

His gut churning, Gray searched his immediate area and then backtracked around the building. Maybe he could come up behind the man and stop him. Glancing through the fence and trees and toward the county road, he wished he would see headlights approaching or hear sirens. Something. Looked like the cavalry wasn't coming. One thing he was certain of: he couldn't *do* this alone. Too many dangers were converging at one place and time. Too much could go wrong.

God, I know You're always with me, but tonight I'm going to need Your help in a big way. Maybe tonight can be the night You answer some of Gemma's prayers. She believes. She hasn't lost faith or turned away from You. She's waiting on You.

And I'm waiting on You too.

He needed to get evidence and arrest Clyde, but all

he could think about was Gemma. Her hazel eyes that could pierce right through his soul and search him out. He had a feeling that she'd known all along he was hiding something. He wished he hadn't kept things from her. If he'd been honest sooner, maybe they could have avoided this predicament with Clyde. Gray couldn't let her get hurt physically or otherwise.

Please, God!

She'd already been through so much, and he couldn't help but admire her strength in the face of great obstacles. Her determination to make a home for abused tigers, something that was bigger than herself. Bigger than one person.

Her passion to make a difference in the world.

God had charged mankind, beginning with Adam, with caring for the garden and the animals. Gray didn't think anything about that task had changed. Sure, people needed to love one another, but they also needed to care for and be responsible for the earth and God's creatures. All Gemma wanted was to do good work—and yet all of this tragedy had fallen on her head.

Gray edged to the corner of the building and gulped a breath. He peered around the corner.

Clyde was gone. And no Gemma either.

And right now God, I have to save one of Your creatures. Help me to do it. Help me to find her.

FIFTEEN

Cold chilled her to the bone. The kind that crawled under her skin to stay when she'd been out in the elements too long. Her rain-soaked clothes didn't help. Pressing deeper into the shadows between the trees, Gemma hugged herself and shivered.

All she could think about was finding some place warm and dry.

Where was Gray?

He should be here by now. Had he arrived without her noticing? She hadn't been able to keep an eye on the road. At first, she'd thought to hide in one of the buildings, but she'd left the key ring behind—the same key ring with the truck key. She decided hiding in one of the cat buildings would disturb the tigers too much, anyway, and she couldn't risk drawing attention. Then she thought back to the night someone had locked her and Gray inside and started a fire. She wouldn't put herself in that position again.

And now, Clyde had released a few of the tigers. Lured them outside with meat and completely opened up their fenced-off spaces, leaving them to roam outside of their own habitats. He had effectively turned the sanctuary into the danger zone.

What was the man trying to do? Kill them all? He could just as easily be mauled by a tiger.

Then she spotted Clyde. He stood beneath a tree near the trunk. A security light illuminated his form, and she could just make out his weapon. From here, she couldn't tell if it was a dart gun or a real gun. He shifted in the light. Wait…it was bigger than their dart guns.

He carried a large pistol.

Her breath caught. Since when did he carry a gun? She felt like she didn't even know him. Had she ever? How could she trust another human being if even the man who had been a close family friend betrayed her like this? Had he also betrayed her parents? Her uncle? She tasted the bile in her throat.

What was it with people who pretended to be someone else?

Remaining in the shadows so he wouldn't see her, she could only hope—and yes, pray—one of the tigers didn't sniff her out and reveal her presence to the man with the gun.

Gray, where are you?

Where would he think I would go to hide? Her cell had long ago died, so she couldn't text her location. With Clyde effectively flushing her out by opening up habitats and luring tigers out, she couldn't stay hidden much longer.

A raucous noise drew her attention. Through the trees she could see Layla and Lilly fighting over the hunk of meat Clyde had thrown in their direction. Gemma glanced back at the tree. Clyde was no longer there. She searched the buildings and bushes, habitats and the shadows, but she couldn't see Clyde. Behind her, mud squished.

Her heart jumped up her throat. Panic engulfed her.

Had Clyde found her? Though adrenaline pumped through her veins, Gemma was afraid to respond to her body's need to fight or run. When she could no longer stand it, she prepared to launch from the tree and spring—or hobble with her cane. But just before she shoved off, another possibility hit her.

Maybe it wasn't Clyde but instead was a tiger. They stalked their prey, getting close as possible before they pounced. She didn't want to believe that they would pounce on *her*, though. These were her tigers—not pets, no, but she had a relationship with them. She loved them. Gave them the space they deserved as God's creatures, food and shelter. Took care of them until she was too tired to move at the end of the day. In turn, they seemed to know her. Like her. Appreciate her. But they were still inherently wild all the same, and hadn't she brought them to Tiger Mountain so they could revert to their natural instinctive behaviors? They were innocent animals caught up in this and once again used for selfish purposes—something from which she'd tried, and failed, to save them. If she ran now, maybe a tiger would chase her down. But she wouldn't let Clyde catch her.

She wouldn't give him the satisfaction.

Except all her resolve was for nothing. She was too terrified to move. Gemma opened her mouth to scream, unable to push down the terror invading her thoughts.

A hand covered her mouth, muffling the sound.

Not a tiger but Clyde! Gemma fought, but a familiar voice whispered in her ear.

"It's me, Gemma. It's Gray." Strong arms turned her to face him, as if seeing him was the only way she could believe.

Relief swooshed through her so violently that she almost collapsed, but between Gray and the tree, her body wasn't allowed to drop. "Gray," she gasped.

"Shh." He leaned in close and whispered so low that she could barely hear him. Right. They had to be completely quiet. Clyde might be close, or one of the tigers even closer.

Gray had found her. Oh, he'd found her!
Thank You, God.
Shivering, she appeared frail and distraught, but he knew her appearance belied her strength. He pulled her to him and held her in his arms until she stopped trembling. He wished he could chase the fear and grief right out of her, but any hope of that would have to wait until their escape. Still, for the moment, he would rejoice in the small things.

Despite an armed man hunting her and bent on killing her, and despite dangerous tigers free and stalking them in the sanctuary, Gemma had stayed hidden and alive like Gray had asked.

Like he had prayed for.

He wasn't sure how she had managed, and this was not the time to ask. Finding that out could wait. Right now, they needed to get out of here.

A voice called out—loud and angry. "Gemma, you're trapped. You have no escape."

Clenching his jaw, Gray held back the anger and let it burn in his gut. The man had some nerve, trapping her inside the sanctuary with the tigers like this. A woman he'd said was like a daughter to him. Clyde hadn't mentioned Gray's name. Did that mean he hadn't seen Gray's approach? Or just that he hoped they hadn't found each other yet? Either way, Clyde clearly expected Gemma to be alone and defenseless. Gray could use that. But not yet.

"Come on," Gray whispered. "We're getting out of here while he talks."

He urged Gemma onto his back so they could move faster, surprised she didn't protest.

"Be careful of the tigers, Gray."

Clyde continued, "In case you haven't noticed, the tigers are roaming around outside their habitats, so you can't wait it out. I've taken your dart guns. There's only one way out and I'm standing here at your only exit. So you'll have to go through me. But why are you afraid? You've always been family. I'm not going to hurt you. I'll let you go if you come on out without causing me any more trouble. I never wanted it to come to this, Gemma. You have to believe me. Now come out and let's talk it out."

That settled it for Gray. The man was crazy. Did he even hear himself?

But keep talking, dude, just keep talking. Nothing like a villain's monologue when one needed to escape.

Gemma clung to his back, holding her cane, and Gray kept his weapon out. The last thing he wanted to do was harm one of her tigers, but he would protect Gemma whatever it took. He crept between trees and around buildings, watching for Raja, the bigger, male tiger who recently lost any trust he'd had in his human caretakers.

Across the path, he spotted the sisters. They'd finished off the meat and settled into the grass, but he suspected their current pose wouldn't last long. They wouldn't be able to pass up the opportunity to explore new and forbidden territory. Gray headed away from the big cats and the sound of Clyde's voice. He wanted to put as much distance as he could between them and Clyde. When they started climbing the fence, they might give themselves away and Clyde would come looking—and possibly shooting.

A growl resounded through the sanctuary, much too close for comfort.

"It's Raja," Gemma whispered in his ear. "He's acted erratically since the night he got out. We need to climb the fence now. If he decides he wants to mess with us, then we're done."

Gray refrained from mentioning he had a weapon. She had to see it. But she was ignoring it, not even bringing up the option of him using it. He didn't want things to end that way either. None of this was Raja's fault. He sidled up to the fence and let Gemma down.

"Gemma!" Clyde called again. This time it sounded like it was coming from a megaphone. "Don't make me come in there to get you. I'll have to kill some of your precious tigers when I do."

Fury filled her eyes. The way she fisted her hands, dropping her cane, Gray sensed she was about to render an explosive retort. He grabbed her arms and held her steady, capturing her gaze.

"Don't give our position away," he said. "We have seconds before Clyde or a tiger finds us." He wasn't sure the tigers were exactly looking, but they were wandering about, exploring, maybe hungry and irritated. Even if they just wanted to play… Not a great scenario for any fragile human that was in their path.

Something stirred in the bushes a few yards away.

Ignoring the surprise in her eyes, Gray grabbed her waist and lifted her high onto the fence. "Grab hold the best you can and climb over."

She could have done that herself, but he wanted to give her a head start.

She glanced at him. Nodded. He read the meaning in her eyes. *I've got this.*

More agile than he would have thought, she moved up and across the height of the fence as if she were a child on the monkey bars. But though she moved quickly, she made too much noise. Grabbing her cane, Gray joined her. He couldn't wait for her to go over first. They were out of time.

Once they dropped to the other side, a tiger jumped onto the fence and then back down.

"Raja!" Gemma almost reached for him but held herself back. "What if Clyde goes in to look for me? What if he kills tigers to force me out of hiding? Gray, I can't let him do that."

"Nor can you give yourself up, Gemma." He gripped her shoulders, fearing that Clyde would soon discover their escape. "I care about these animals too. Remember, I chose a career in protecting wildlife. Don't worry. Clyde isn't going to shoot any tigers. It would damage the goods. He wants them healthy and happy until it's time to sell them."

As disturbing as that sounded, it was the truth and worked to appease her. Together they climbed the outer fence and then descended on the other side until it was safe to drop to the ground.

Gray grabbed her cane and held it. "Now get on. I'm going to hide you and then return for Clyde."

She stared into the woods, where there were no security lights.

"It's dark out there, Gray. So dark."

"I have a flashlight. But we won't use it until we have to."

With her on his back, traveling in darkness over the rough terrain, he had to be careful so he moved much slower than he would have liked. Since Clyde had the sanctuary exits blocked, that meant Gray couldn't access the vehicles near the gate without risking Gemma's life. Despite his need to take Clyde down, Gemma's safety was Gray's priority.

Once he found a place where she could hide and stay relatively warm and dry, then he would go back for Clyde. He was under no illusions that the man would surrender without a fight. Considering they both had weapons, Gray didn't want this to end in a shoot-out with Gemma caught in the middle. She was proactive and determined, and he could imagine her trying to insert herself in the middle to try to talk the two of them down. Gray would hide her away to protect her from herself.

Entering the Wild Rogue Wilderness area that bordered to the sanctuary, Gray thought about Coop. He wished he had called his brother for backup. Cooper would have arrived much faster than anyone from the sheriff's department. But then asking for help would be like admitting he wasn't good enough, after all. Wasn't as strong or as smart as Cooper. Those thoughts sent him right back to his childhood, messing with his confidence.

Bad timing.

And so was the sudden downpour as the mist shifted to something more tangible. Even with her jacket on, Gemma would be too wet and cold. She'd been outside in the wet for ages—she had to be freezing. He'd wanted to make it to the old berm cabin that he remembered being in the area, not terribly far from here, but then he remembered an assassin had blown it up while pursuing Hadley Mason, who later became Cooper's wife.

"How much farther?" she asked.

"Not much."

Coming up on a ridge, Gray shined the flashlight and searched for the other hiding place he'd spotted when hiking the area as he surveyed the sanctuary from a distance. A small fissure in the rocky wall—just large enough to slide into and stay dry and, eventually, get warm.

"This will have to do. You stay here and hide. I'm going back to get Clyde."

"No, wait." Gemma pulled him toward her, inside the fissure cave. "I don't want you to get hurt, Gray."

"I know what I'm doing. This is my job."

"Don't leave me here—I'm cold." She pressed into him, wrapped her arms around him.

He had a job to do, as he'd already said, and tried to ignore her attempts to keep him here. But for another moment, he held her. A cold rainy night like this, and what if Gray got hurt when he returned to the sanctuary and didn't make it back? What if Clyde got the best of him? Then Gemma would have to spend the night out here, maybe even get hypothermia. He had to get her at least a little warmer before he left.

"You didn't have to take me so far from the sanctuary. I know what you're trying to do now." Her cheek pressed against his chest, her voice sounding muffled.

"Protect you, that's what." Warming her up was important, but he knew he was staying there too long, much too long. Unfortunately, he could get used to holding her in his arms like this. "You hold on to the flashlight. Keep it off, as much as possible. I don't want anyone following the light."

Would Clyde still be at the sanctuary? Was he gone by now, on the run? Or was he searching for Gemma, figuring out that Gray was helping her?

At least Gray had saved the girl. And God willing, he would get the bad guy. A twig snapped behind him.

Pain ignited in his head. Darkness edged his vision and then everything went black.

SIXTEEN

Gray stiffened and then his body went limp against her and the flashlight fell away, igniting ghostly shadows.

"Gray?" What—

His weight pulled her down, down, down... His arms fell away.

Hands desperately gripping him, she tried to hold him up. Her pulse roared in her ears. What was happening?

Despite her efforts, he dropped to the ground. Gemma was helpless to stop him, her mind scrambling to comprehend.

A face came into view. The reason for Gray's collapse became clear when she saw the gun in his attacker's hand, held with the butt out. He must have struck Gray on the head. Gemma screamed and pressed deeper into the fissure, the rock wall cutting into her back. Light from Gray's dropped flashlight carved dark-shadowed lines across the face she recognized.

How had he followed them so closely? Found them in this dark, rainy night? Gray had been so careful. But carrying Gemma had slowed him down and distracted them both.

"Clyde?" her voice creaked out, constricted with fear.

He glared at her. "You couldn't just leave well enough alone, could you?"

Gemma wasn't sure what he was talking about, exactly. She didn't want to aggravate him or cause him to hurt Gray again, but she had never been one to idly stand by. And now, her life and Gray's might depend on her ability to protect them. Ignoring the sting of pain threading up her leg, Gemma launched at Clyde, screaming at him. Shrieking for all she was worth. Maybe someone else was out here and would hear her.

"Why are you doing this? Can't you just leave us alone?" *Leave the tigers and go!*

"Me? Why couldn't *you* just leave *me* alone? You've messed up my plans. I tried to steer you in the right direction. But you couldn't just stay the sweet and naive girl I'd always known." Clyde stepped over Gray and into the fissure, forcing her back against the wall. "And now, look what you've done. I'll have to sacrifice you in order to keep my network going. I'm on the verge of a very big deal."

He gripped her arm and squeezed. Pain radiated and Gemma winced as he tugged her out of the small cave and into the light rain. "Get your cane. I'm not going to carry you."

"And I'm not going anywhere with you."

"I'm going to drag you if you won't walk."

Gemma grabbed her cane, but she couldn't keep up with him. "What about Gray? We can't just leave him here." He could need medical attention.

Then she realized her mistake. *Idiot!* Gray would have been better off left behind.

"You're right, I have to make sure he's dead." He chambered a round.

"No!" Gemma threw herself on Gray, covering his body.

Clyde sighed. "You're determined to stand in my way at every turn, aren't you?"

He pulled her off Gray like she was a small sack of groceries. "I can't leave behind a dead federal agent. I made that mistake before with a game warden years ago. Better if he just goes missing along with you."

Gemma glared at him. Something in his face changed, morphed into…what—grief? "Gemma, I… This isn't how I wanted things to turn out."

"And I'm supposed to feel sorry for you?" She wished she had a cane that doubled as a weapon as some others did.

"I need you to help me carry him."

What? "How can I help carry him?"

"Do it, or I swear I'll shoot him now and be done with it."

Gemma slipped under Gray's arm on her right side and steadied herself with her cane on the left. Clyde took his other side. Traveling in the dark through the less than welcoming terrain forced them to move slowly, but Gemma did her best. She didn't want to give Clyde a reason to hurt Gray. Ignoring her own discomfort and her aching, trembling leg, she had no choice but to do as Clyde asked and pray her leg wouldn't give out. And she continued the prayer silently as they hiked.

God, please, help us. Save Gray. Help us out of this mess. And please…

Gemma nearly lost herself in a quiet sob, but she wouldn't give Clyde the satisfaction of seeing her cry.

Please, can you mend my heart? This man whom I loved like a father and thought I could trust has betrayed me in the worst way. Hadn't she known not to trust? And yet she'd thought Clyde was the exception to the rule. She'd known this man, her family had known and trusted him as well. If he would betray her, then whom could she trust?

Come on, Gray, wake up!

A lone figure hiked toward them, his form a mere shadow in the security lights from the sanctuary. Her heart jumped. Someone to help them? Except Clyde had a gun and would shoot before the person was the wiser.

"Help!" she called out. "Help us, please. But be careful. He's got a gun!"

But the figure continued toward them as though he hadn't heard her.

Clyde didn't scold her for calling out, nor did he lift his pistol to shoot the new arrival or act as though he should run and hide. Her mind finally admitted what her heart didn't want to see—this person was an accomplice, which meant that someone else at Tiger Mountain had betrayed her.

Even if Gray were to wake up now, he couldn't overpower two men. But who was it? Gemma wanted to face the other traitor. As he approached she could just make out a few things. He wore a cap tugged low and his jacket collar hid his face as he took over for Gemma, assisting Clyde in dragging Gray. And then she stood alone, watching the men drag him away toward the sanctuary. What had he told her? She was supposed to wait in the fissure for him to return and if he didn't come back, stay hidden until morning when others were at Tiger Mountain. She was sure Gray would instruct her to run now. To leave him and maybe even get help.

But where could she run in the dark forest? Without a working cell phone, she couldn't call for help. She would lose Gray forever when the men took him away. She had no idea where they would take him.

"Gemma, you can't hide from me so don't even try. Besides you don't want me to hurt Gray, do you?"

She'd been dreaming, that was all. She couldn't escape Clyde and he knew it. That's why he wasn't worried about her trailing behind them. And despite what he said, she knew he would hurt Gray, regardless. He would hurt them both. In the distance, she noticed a transport truck parked inside the habitat area.

"Oh no... Raja." They were transporting the tiger tonight. With that realization, she stopped.

Clyde seemed to sense she was no longer following. He released Gray to the other man, who dragged him forward and turned to her. "That's right. I've had to move up my timetable. And because you couldn't mind your own business, nobody will be here to oversee the care of the rest of the tigers tomorrow. Your volunteers rely heavily on you to direct them. How long do you think they'll hang around once you're gone?"

Letting her cane fall to the side, Gemma sank to her knees. "Oh, God, please, help us!"

She wasn't sure how long she remained there, but when she looked up Clyde was nowhere to be seen, nor was Gray. The man with the cap walked toward her and then held his hand out as if she would let him assist her to her feet.

"Come on, Gemma. Don't make this more difficult on yourself."

Gemma looked up into Deputy Callahan's eyes.

The flooring beneath him jarred and vibrated, stirring him.

Where am I?

Drums beat inside his skull, which ached so badly that he wasn't sure he cared where he was. He squinted, opening his eyes slowly and saw nothing but darkness. As he lay on a hard floor, the whole structure rattled and shook.

Moving. He was moving. Ignoring his throbbing head, he pushed himself upright, pausing until the nausea passed. What was the last thing that happened? The pain in his head made it challenging to concentrate, but Gray had to try. *Gemma.* He'd been with Gemma, trying to protect her from Clyde. He couldn't remember beyond carrying her through the woods.

Gray wanted to rub his face but realized his arms were secured behind his back. Great. And from what he could tell, he'd been relieved of both his weapons. "God, what happened to Gemma? Please keep her safe," he whispered into the darkness. He'd never felt so alone, so desolate. It was hard to believe God was going to help him.

"I'm right here." A soft voice whispered in response. "You prayed for me?"

Thank You, God. "Of course." He exhaled, feeling the weight of guilt fall away. But they weren't out of this yet, obviously. "What happened, Gemma? Where are we going?"

He heard the scuffle of knees and the creak of the floor and then felt Gemma's soft body draw close to him. He assumed her hands were tied behind her back too.

"Are you okay?" she asked. "I was so worried you would never wake up."

He wouldn't complain about his head. That was the least of his worries. "I'm fine, except I don't know what's going on. What happened tonight? All I remember is trying to get you to safety." Clearly he'd failed miserably.

"It was Clyde. He followed us to the fissure and, while your back was turned, he hit you over the head with his gun. You collapsed and then he almost killed you. Was going to shoot you, but he changed his mind. Instead, he made me drag you. Now we're in the truck with Raja. Clyde made sure to tranquilize him because he is beyond aggravated, but just be aware we're sharing this space with a caged tiger."

His spine stiffened. They had to escape. But how? "I'm so sorry you're here. That I messed up and now you're in the middle of this."

"Don't blame yourself. I was in the middle of this for years—I just didn't know it. I've been naive for far too long. It's my own fault. I just didn't want to think the worst of the closest thing to family I had left."

What kind of person does that to someone he loved? Family or friend. It was something Gray had never been able to understand, even though he knew it happened all the time. Family members were usually the first suspects when loved ones were abused, robbed, killed or went missing. A sad state of affairs.

But her earlier words wouldn't let him go. He had to know.

"There's something—"

"So why *didn't* he kill me, Gemma?" He'd cut her off. He needed an answer.

"Oh, Gray… I wouldn't let him shoot you. I threw myself over you to protect you and then…then he mentioned he couldn't leave another agent dead in the woods. He'd done it before. Better to have you go missing. I don't remember his exact words. I…"

"You shouldn't have done that, Gemma. I don't want you risking your life for me. Do you hear me?"

"But, Gray…"

Gray hung his head, letting the fury blast through him. "I'm sorry, Gemma. I shouldn't have taken my frustration out on you like that. You saved my life, and

I'm grateful. As for his reference to the other agent he'd killed, I was right then. I had a friend and mentor who worked with me when I was a game warden. He came across what he thought was a trafficking ring in this area. I wanted to go with him to try to snag the guy, but Bill got a lead while I was out of town. He was later found dead. And now…now I know that was Clyde. I've been searching for the man heading up this ring, the man responsible for Bill's death. Searching for a way to find him ever since Bill was murdered."

"I'm so sorry to hear that."

"It was years ago, Gemma. But his murder was never solved. Justice was never served. I worked my way up to the federal level so I could cover more ground and find Bill's killer and make up, in a small way, for not being there when he needed me."

"What are you talking about?"

"I should have been there to watch Bill's back. All I could think ever since then was that Bill might be alive today if I had."

Gray had never let go. Never forgotten.

"I think that's the most you've ever said to me about yourself." Her voice was soft in the darkness. "And you think that your friend is the one Clyde killed. The man he was talking about."

"Yes. It's one of the main reasons I hoped to infiltrate near the top of the trafficking ring. Then I received a tip from an informant that sent me to Tiger Mountain."

"Then we need to finish this."

We? "Gemma…" Her name came out breathy. "I wanted to protect you. I tried. And now you're here where you shouldn't be. Things could turn bad and fast, do you understand?"

"Look at us now, Gray. I think they already have. But what can we do with our hands tied?"

"Maybe we can fix that. I keep a small knife in my belt." At least he hoped they hadn't searched him that thoroughly. "I'm going to need your help to get it out."

"Okay."

"Position yourself with your back and your hands toward me and then I'll talk you through it."

Gray maneuvered himself so that Gemma could search for the small knife tucked on the inside of his belt. It was far from easy. Once she had it in her fingers, he turned so she could hand it over to him. He worked it open and cut away his ties and then hers.

She rubbed her wrist. "What are we going to do now?"

The truck downshifted and turned, slowly rolling over a few potholes. "Did you learn anything on the computer or did Clyde say anything about where he had the tigers delivered?"

"Yes. The trucking company was delivering to a warehouse. It didn't have an address so much as directions. Something about Smith's Flat Road, then five miles up County Road 493 and then Forest Road 22."

"Oh, that's just great." He'd definitely need to get ahold of Cooper, who knew this region better than anyone, even the sheriff's department.

"At least we've only been in the truck for a couple of hours, so it isn't that far."

"Maybe he'd been going there instead of Portland, like he told you."

"Could be," Gemma agreed. "But if that's where we're going now, then we should be almost there."

The sound and feel of the driver steering the truck

into a warehouse confirmed her words. Someone opened and closed the door of the cab.

"Okay," he whispered. "Time to keep our voices down."

Men talked and laughed. Not good. How many men were here?

The muffled sound of a tiger in distress had Gemma squirming. Gray gripped her arm. "We have to get out of here before they open the truck."

He detected the subtle shake of her head as her hair tickled his cheek. "How can we get out? It's locked from the outside."

Then someone jostled with the lock on the only exit. Gray's heart pounded. "Let's go."

Quietly they crawled around the tiger's cage to hide behind it, but hiding would only work for so long. Gray prepared himself to take the men down one at a time. He had the advantage of surprise. They weren't expecting him to be untied or armed, even if it was just with a small knife. He hoped he would only have to face one man.

The voices sounded as if most of the men were headed off in another direction. He released the breath he'd held. At least he wouldn't have to face them all at once.

The door of the truck rolled up and stopped a third of the way. It looked like there was only one man standing there.

Someone drew the lone man's attention. He stepped from the truck, leaving the door open, and moved to the side. Gray heard him speaking with another man about an urgent timeline for the delivery of the tiger parts. He cringed. Had Gemma heard too?

He leaned in and spoke quietly into her ear. "Now's our chance." Eyes wide, she shook her head.

He sent her a look. They had no other choice. She gave him a subtle nod.

The light from the warehouse illuminated a good portion of the back of the truck, eliminating Gray's advantage of surprise. One finger to his lips conveyed a silent message. *Keep as quiet as possible.* Then he tugged her hand and gently pulled her out from behind the cage. By the look of it, her permanently injured leg did not want to cooperate, but she made her steps as smooth and silent as she could manage. Hopefully the men would just think the tiger or their captives were stirring. They did not seem concerned and continued their increasingly heated discussion. Gray could use that to his advantage.

They had to be quiet and yet move quickly. At the edge of the trailer, Gray peered out of the small opening the partially raised door afforded them to make sure they could escape without notice. He stealthily hopped down and held his arms out for Gemma. He had to get her somewhere safe and contact his superiors and the authorities to let them know what was going on.

Otherwise, no one would find Gemma or Gray until it was far too late for them or the tigers.

The man who had opened the door suddenly appeared at Gray's side, surprise evident in his features as he lifted his weapon.

SEVENTEEN

Gemma froze, fear cutting off her scream.

Gray slammed his hand into the man's throat and disabled his weapon before the man even had a chance to call out to his friend. He caught the man before he slumped to the ground. This special agent who had infiltrated Tiger Mountain had skills that she should have expected but instead left her surprised. The speed at which he'd acted took her breath away.

She thought back to the many times at the sanctuary he'd acted quickly or handled a situation with confidence, like saving her from the rockslide. She should have suspected then that there was much more to him than a computer programmer who loved wildlife.

Gray's biceps distended and his face turned hard as he lifted the man, pulling her from her thoughts. Assisting him, she helped slide the man up inside the truck.

Then Gray helped her out of the truck. He tucked the man's weapon into his belt. Searched him quickly and found a radio, then looked at her, studying her. It seemed there was much more in his assessment than merely making sure she wasn't hurt. What was it? Admiration? Whatever it was, her heart warmed.

Stop it! She was too vulnerable when she was near him. But nothing she could do about that now.

He gestured that they were going to make a run for it, a question in his eyes.

Are you ready?

No. Never. She would never be ready for this, but what choice did they have? She nodded.

He gripped her hand and peered around the side of the truck. For the moment, they were alone in the warehouse, except for another tiger in a cage in the far corner. Caesar!

Before she could react, Gray lifted her in his arms. In all that had gone on, she'd lost her cane, but it didn't matter. He crept quickly, closing the distance between the truck and a stack of crates against the wall. In the shadows behind the crates, Gray gently put her on her feet.

"Why didn't you let me ride on your back?" she whispered.

"You'd be too exposed if someone shot at us."

He thought of everything, this guy.

But what did their meager attempt to hide do for them? "They're going to discover us gone when they come for the tiger."

He nodded his agreement, but he didn't seem to be in a rush. Maybe he thought they had a few minutes until anyone came to check on the guy Gray had fought. Had Gray killed the man with the strike to his throat? Gemma didn't know. She hadn't asked, and she wasn't sure she *wanted* to know.

He grasped her arms and leaned in close to whisper softly. "We need to get out of this warehouse, but I need to contact my superiors. You're sure there wasn't an actual address?"

She nodded. GPS couldn't find that address out here, hence the shoddy directions. Regardless, this was going down tonight. But it seemed to her that Gray was taking too long to decide what they should do next. She could imagine what he might be thinking. Get Gemma to safety or call for help? Even if he could hide her somewhere, they couldn't get far enough away before they were discovered missing. Clyde would find her in these mountains, just like he had earlier that night. "I have an idea," she said.

He held her gaze, waiting.

She pointed at the crates. "I can hide in there. I'll be safe and you don't have to worry about me when you go to call for help."

He frowned and opened his mouth, but she cut him off. He couldn't keep carrying her around. And she couldn't move fast enough to keep up with him on her own.

"It's the only way."

Finally, he nodded and, together, they found an almost empty crate of wood chips surrounded with other crates that could shield her from sight. Gemma climbed inside. At least it was large enough she could stretch her legs. But she wondered what else the crates held. Tiger body parts? Nausea swirled. She ignored it, willing it to pass.

"This is an old lumber mill, isn't it?" she asked.

"I think you're right. Now that we're out of the truck, I can smell the sawdust, chips and bark. They probably still have the saws..." Gray's voice trailed away.

She understood why he didn't want to finish the sentence. "Hurry, Gray. We have to get out of here."

He nodded his agreement.

Just before he shut her in, he leaned close. "Stay

hidden in the crate. No matter what you hear, don't come out."

He was so close that she trembled. Maybe that was her fear of what this night might hold for either of them. Or maybe it was something else. Something she still wasn't ready to admit. His face hovered right at her cheek, and she caught a whiff of his musky scent. Gray pressed his lips softly against hers. Then he backed away. Closed the crate and loosely secured it.

Tonight, they would stop the trafficking insanity, at least, Tiger Mountain's involvement, and possibly the larger trafficking ring would be exposed as well. She had to believe that. Cling to that hope.

To distract herself from the danger she knew she was in, she pressed her finger against her lips where he'd kissed her. Why had he done that? Was he afraid something would happen to him and he just wanted to say goodbye to her—a friend in the war against wildlife trafficking? Or had there been more behind the kiss, just like there was more behind the man? Gemma found herself hoping and praying for the latter but quickly hid it away inside a dark crate in her mind. Hadn't she learned already that she couldn't truly trust anyone? No matter how long or how well she thought she knew them. Not even law enforcement.

Like Deputy Callahan. Yet another person… Oh, no. She'd been about to tell Gray when he'd demanded to know why Clyde had changed his mind about killing him. His questions had led the conversation elsewhere, and Gemma had forgotten. Did Gray already know he couldn't trust Deputy Callahan? Gemma cupped her hand over her mouth to stifle her gasps. She should have tried harder to warn him!

Oh, Gray, be careful.

Though closed up inside the crate, she wasn't completely in the dark. Light spilled through the slats. Through a gap in the boards she noticed a thin space between the crates from which she could observe part of the warehouse. She heard voices. The men were returning. Soon they'd be searching for their missing partner-in-crime.

The rolling door on the truck slid open. Then shouts resounded.

Gray, please get out of here!

With the shouts, Gray knew he'd lost the element of surprise.

Skirting the wall of the lumber mill warehouse, he remained in the shadows. Five men ran into the warehouse, spilling through a side door. Where was Clyde? Had he remained at the warehouse to make sure the tigers, as well as his human captives, were dealt with appropriately? Gray suspected he would question them both to learn what they knew and who they had told before they were disposed of. And there was a good chance that Clyde would be shutting down this arm of his operation until things settled down again. Was that what had happened years ago when Gemma's uncle had died? And then when things were quiet and suspicions had died, he'd seized the opportunity to work with Gemma to build Tiger Mountain?

If Gray took the man into custody, cutting the proverbial head off the snake, then he could likely gain control of the warehouse tonight. But he absolutely could not let the head of the trafficking ring get away.

Where are you, Clyde?

Standing here wouldn't help him find the man. So,

for now, he needed to focus on his other priority—calling for backup.

Gray quickly slipped out the door through which the men had entered and searched for an office with a phone or computer or even a two-way radio. With the radio he'd retrieved from the man at the truck, he could possibly monitor the other men's movements but he couldn't call out for help with it. Fluorescent lights flickered and popped in the hallway, one of them going dark. He held his weapon out, ready to use it. With each door he passed, he waited and listened, and then he tried the door.

Finally he found one unlocked and empty. It was full of cleaning supplies. The scent of Pine-Sol accosted him.

At the sound of rushing footsteps, he slipped inside and closed the door, remaining there until the hall was empty again.

Why hadn't the sheriff or a deputy shown up to prevent Clyde from abducting Gemma and Gray in the first place? Irritation had him grinding his teeth. Even if he made contact and called for help, it might take too long for help to get here if they weren't already on their way. He could only hope that Sheriff Kruse would discover the directions to the warehouse as Gemma had and then maybe recognize the old lumber mill.

Regardless, if Gray had only one chance at a callout, then it had better be good.

He stepped out of the cleaning closet and tried a couple more doors, the last one revealing an office with a desk and filing cabinet.

Yes! At least their disappearance from the truck had summoned everyone to the main room of the warehouse, leaving this office unguarded and giving him the opportunity to find and use a phone. He hoped no one thought to look inside the crates.

God, please keep Gemma safe. Please help us to stop this.

Gray shoved away his worry. He couldn't help Gemma if he didn't stay on task, sharp and focused.

He locked the door behind him and then hurried to the desk, hoping to find a phone.

In this region of the forest, there were no telephone poles hence a landline phone couldn't be installed. And a cell phone would be difficult if it worked at all. But if he were running an operation like this, he would at least have Internet connected via satellite and use VoIP— voice over Internet protocol—for his phone. Though it wasn't optimal, it was better than trying to get a cell signal and a satellite phone needed line-to-sight. In these woods that would be troublesome as well.

And there, on the desk, sat the phone he'd suspected he would find. He called his brother Coop and left a voice message with all the details. He wished he would have gotten his brother in person, but he could count on Coop to find the county road address of the old lumber mill hidden away in the mountains and get Gray all the help he needed here as quickly as he could.

Then Gray called Mark, his superior, and got the man. He communicated what was happening and, as he stirred the desktop computer awake, he realized he had hit the mother lode. The information he saw before him could serve to cripple the trafficking ring if not completely shut it down.

Someone tried the doorknob and found it locked.

Gray set the phone on the desk without disconnecting, so that Mark could hear everything, and grabbed his weapon. Had they heard his conversation?

He stepped away from the computer and hid behind the filing cabinet. Cursing resounded outside the door. A familiar voice but not Clyde's. Who was it?

He didn't have to wonder too long. The man kicked in the door and stepped inside, holding his weapon out. Gray sagged in relief and stepped out from behind the cabinet, lowering his own weapon.

"I'm so glad you found us." Took them long enough.

Deputy Callahan's sturdy form filled the door.

EIGHTEEN

Dressed in his everyday clothes and wearing a baseball cap, Deputy Callahan kept his weapon pointed at Gray. "Put your gun on the ground and kick it over. Then keep your hands where I can see them and step away from the cabinet."

Gray would never give his brothers in law enforcement any trouble, but… "Wait, what are you doing? I'm a special agent working this case. Trying to stop this trafficking ring. Didn't Kruse tell you? I called for assistance at Tiger Mountain earlier tonight." Wasn't Callahan answering that call for help, following the clues to the warehouse?

"Drop the gun now, Wilde."

Gray did as the man asked, kicking his gun forward but not enough to send it straight into Callahan. The gun stopped about halfway between them. The man glared at him.

"Callahan. What are you doing?"

Whose side was Callahan on anyway? The sinking feeling in Gray's gut told him that he already knew the answer to that. He always went into things suspecting everyone, including law enforcement individuals. And Callahan, in particular, had always rubbed him the wrong way. Still, he'd give the guy the benefit of a doubt. "So we're good, right? Can I have my gun back now?"

Regret surged in the deputy's gaze. "I'm sorry, Wilde."

Clyde stepped into the room behind Callahan. "I went through your things at your rental house and found out who you are. I knew you were up to something."

Glowering at Deputy Callahan for his duplicity, Gray considered his weapon on the floor. Could he make a grab for it? "I guess this means the law isn't coming."

"That's right," Clyde gloated.

"I'm all you're going to get for now," Callahan said.

Gray saw that uncertainty hung in Callahan's gaze. Was he in on this for the profit? Or was he being coerced into helping Clyde with this operation? Gray could guess how things had gone down. He'd seen it all too often. Maybe Callahan had been paid a little to look the other way. Needed the extra money. Didn't think it would harm anyone. But then he was in too deep, and Clyde had him by the throat, able to ruin his reputation or even get him arrested by revealing the bribes he'd taken. And holding that threat over Callahan's head would just force him to fall deeper and deeper into the crimes.

"Where's Gemma?" Clyde asked.

"She's long gone." Gray had to get them apart, distract them somehow so he could go for the gun. "You'll never catch her."

Clyde laughed. Had the man ever cared about her? To Callahan, he said, "Tell the men to keep searching the woods. She couldn't have made it very far."

Callahan nodded and then disappeared through the door.

"You make me sick," Gray said to Clyde. "Don't you

care about her? When we first met you told me she was like a daughter to you. You tried to convince me you had her best interest at heart and you didn't want anyone to hurt her. Now look who's hurting her." Gray spat the words, hoping to distract Clyde with his animosity.

"Of course I care about her, but not more than I care about myself. I wouldn't have hurt her if you hadn't forced my hand. Without you sticking your nose in, she would still be safe at the cabin tonight, remaining clueless in her naïveté. Clueless and happy."

He let the anguish he felt at the truth of Clyde's words show. Except, the harassment started before he'd ever shown his face at Tiger Mountain. Before he said more, he waited until he heard the deputy exit through the door. "Don't kid yourself. She would have learned the truth sooner or later."

"You're the one who stole her life from her, Special Agent Grayson Wilde. And when I'm done with the two of you, you won't have time to even try to forgive yourself before you die."

Gray dove for the gun. A round had already been chambered and he fired at Clyde—who pulled his own weapon—before rolling behind the desk. Gunfire clanked against the metal desk. Gray ducked. He heard scuffling as Clyde tried to exit through the door, but Gray aimed and fired again, trying to stop his retreat. Clyde whirled and shot at Gray.

Gray remained in position and aimed for center mass, shooting a third time, and hitting Clyde in the chest. The man dropped.

He didn't move.

Now, to stop the others. Except Gray heard footfalls in the hallway. Callahan? No, no, no. He didn't want to shoot the man if he didn't have to. He remained hidden behind the desk and waited. Gemma stepped awkwardly into the room, her arm twisted at an angle, and then Callahan completed the image.

"What the—" Callahan started to say before taking the scene in at a glance. He pressed his weapon to Gemma's head. "Come out, or I'll kill her."

He didn't think Callahan wanted to kill Gemma and get himself in even deeper water. But desperation often caused men to do terrible things they wouldn't otherwise do.

Sweat slicked Gray's palms. Clyde's words echoed through his ears, reminding him that if Gemma died tonight, it would be his fault. Just like it was his fault for not being there for Bill.

No. He couldn't let himself think like that. Gemma was still alive right here and right now—and Gray was going to see to it that she stayed that way. This time, Gray knew what to do. He wasn't about to give up his advantage or risk her life. He aimed at Callahan's head, dead center, and fired his weapon. Callahan dropped next to Clyde.

Gemma screamed and fell to her knees. Cupping her hand over her mouth, she sobbed at the horror of what she saw, sorrow in her gaze taking in Clyde's still form.

Gray rushed to her side.

Clyde reached out and grabbed her wrist, eliciting a yelp from her. So he wasn't dead. Yet. He wouldn't survive that shot without serious medical attention. Gray pulled off his jacket and pressed it against the wound in his chest to staunch the flow. He pressed Gemma's hand in place. "Hold it there."

"Clyde," she said through tears. "How could you do this? I trusted you."

Checking Callahan, Gray confirmed what he already

knew. The deputy was dead. Gray blew out a breath and stood to his feet, positioning himself in the doorjamb. He watched the door at the end of the hallway in case any other hostiles decided to join the party.

"I feel sorry for you, Gemma," Clyde said. "Sorry you trusted a man like me. You were right that your uncle was murdered. He wanted a bigger percentage of the cut. When the rumors started that the animals were mistreated, the sanctuary came under a lot of scrutiny. Your uncle was afraid of an investigation. And then he got so scared that everything was going to fall apart that he decided he was going to tell you everything. That's why he took you for a drive that night. And that's why I had to sabotage the car. You should have died then too."

"No. You're not saying he was part of it. I don't believe you."

Clyde licked his lips and shook his head. "Doesn't matter what you believe."

"And my parents? You're not going to tell me they were in on the trafficking as well, are you?"

Gray could hardly stand to hear the deep ache that cut through her voice.

"No. And they died because of it. They wanted no part of an extremely lucrative operation even though they were struggling—your father believed the next big donor would show up soon. I knew I had to get them out of the way. With my black market connections, it wasn't so hard to find someone who knew how to sabotage a plane. With your parents out of the way, your uncle and I would be able to do business together. But then he started making demands. And I had to start the rumors and put the pressure on him. You see, there's nothing to tie me to anything on paper. I'm a silent partner via my shell companies."

Another sob escaped Gemma. "So many lives lost and for what?"

Clyde coughed. "I started out smuggling wildlife. It was too easy. One tiger or one rhino here or there brought crazy money. Over time, I realized that I had established a large pipeline in the black market. There was no limit to what I could smuggle through my shell companies. And then I had you, Gemma. I felt I owed you since I took your family from you. And Tiger Mountain could supply me with a tiger here and there, as I needed. And over time, the money would earn back my investment and more. The sanctuary would provide leverage for the movement of other wildlife. A tiger, perhaps, that never made it to Tiger Mountain. But I knew better than to think you'd agree to the operation, so I decided we'd all be happy as long as I kept you in the dark. But then you started questioning things, asking about the night your uncle died. Spending too much time with agent man there."

"You tried to kill me too. Why?"

"You were in the way. I couldn't let you ruin everything I had spent a lifetime building. I tried to scare you away, but you were determined to stay."

"Wait…wait a minute. That was you? The effigies. The vandalism. Releasing the tigers?"

"Some of it. I got the idea from the neighbor. Emil Atkins. His teenage grandson started the vandalism to help his grandfather, hoping you'd get a clue and leave. I just took it to the next level. It was only a matter of time before you would learn the truth if you stayed—" Clyde nodded at Gray then "—just like the agent said. Sooner or later. I'd hoped you would give up, but when I knew you wouldn't leave on your own, I tried to make it look like an accident. But your agent stood in the way. He…protected you."

"What about Wes, Clyde? Why did you kill him?" Gray asked. He wanted to know everything before the answers died with the man.

"I brought him in. He needed money. Sick relative or something. So I paid him on the side. He was the one to leave the effigies, to escalate the trouble. Then he decided he wanted more money or he was going to go to the sheriff."

"So just like when my uncle wanted more, you killed him."

Clyde didn't answer. He let out one last breath and then…nothing more.

Shouts resounded again in the warehouse and boots clomped toward the door. Even with two extra weapons— Clyde and Callahan's—Gray wasn't sure he had enough rounds to hold off half a dozen armed men until help arrived.

He glanced to Gemma. Her wide eyes told him she knew their time had run out.

Gemma gagged on the pungent scent of cleaning supplies that overwhelmed the closet.

"Hurry!" Gray urged her all the way inside. He followed her and shut the door behind them. Her eyes adjusted as light filtered in from under the door.

On the other side of it, men burst through and rushed into the hallway. She sucked in a breath.

They must have been searching the woods and heard the gunfire. They'd returned and would scour the mill until they found them.

This could not end well, especially when they found

Clyde and Deputy Callahan dead in the office down the hall.

Her breaths came too fast. Would her hyperventilating give them away? She held her breath. Gray must have sensed her tension and slid his arms around her, tugging her close. She melted into him, needing his reassurance, anything to stop the trembling. But his nearness did things to her insides, and she desperately wanted to protect herself from him. From everyone.

With Clyde's betrayal, Gemma knew she couldn't trust anyone. Not even this man whom she cared about deeply, in spite of herself.

Still, she couldn't bring herself to move away. There wasn't anywhere for her to go anyway. In mere seconds they could be discovered. Shot and killed.

If these were her last moments… Gemma let herself cling to him, her face pressed against his chest. Felt his heart beating there.

He held her and whispered near her ear. What was that? Was he…was he praying? Gemma's throat constricted.

How many times had she prayed, hoping that God heard her prayers, her cries for help? Did Gray believe that would work? Or was this an act of desperation, knowing they had no other chance to survive this? He couldn't face off with that many men and guns.

Still, Clyde's words came back to her. This man had protected her and been there each time she'd needed him. Had God been there watching over her, after all? Sending Gray to protect her when she hadn't known who the real enemy was?

Well, even if God had sent him, even Gray was praying for help now.

More than anything, she wanted to trust Gray. To

have someone to believe in. But look where that had gotten her in the past?

Gemma shoved the thoughts aside. The only thing that mattered right now was that the two of them survived this and escaped Clyde's men.

Voices resounded, and she felt Gray stiffen in surprise.

"Wait here," Gray whispered and then released her.

He opened the door.

And stepped out into the hallway.

NINETEEN

Gray shut the door behind him and hurried toward the door leading to the two dead men. Inside the room five men crowded around the bodies, but Gray only had eyes for one.

"Coop, I'm here."

Then all eyes turned to him.

And weapons.

Relief flooded his brother's features. "I thought I wasn't going to make it in time and then when I saw this I thought… I thought that I was too late. But then I remembered that you can take care of yourself."

Coop grabbed Gray in a bear hug. Patted him on the back, good and hard and brotherly. When Cooper released him, Gray's superior, Mark, stepped forward. "I heard most of this on the phone while en route, though it was spotty. Thanks to your brother, we found our way here."

GPS was especially erroneous in the wilderness and mountain back roads. Mark gave the other men instructions about the crime scene and gathering the evidence from the computers. Gray hoped it would be enough to identify and capture the rest of those involved. But that could still take years.

Coop tugged Gray aside and out of the way. "I won't stay long. This is your case and I don't want to be in the way. But I do want to congratulate you on a job well done. I know how long you've been working on getting this guy who took Bill down. I know how long you've blamed yourself for that, as well."

Gray was speechless. Sure, he could count on his brother, but he always felt like he walked in the man's shadow. He'd never thought he'd do anything to make Cooper actually admire *him*.

"And in case you didn't know, Dad is proud of you too. I know he doesn't say it often enough."

"Yeah, something about wanting to keep me tough." Gray had made his own way, or liked to think he had, and he didn't need his father's approval anymore. At least he would keep telling himself that. But in the meantime… "Wait here."

Gray left Mark, Cooper and the other agents and jogged to the closet. He opened the door and found it empty. "Gemma," he huffed out. He'd left her there in case he was wrong about who he would find, but he'd intended for her to stay put.

Then he looked down the hallway. "Gemma!" he called.

But Gray knew where she'd gone. He headed toward the main part of the mill. Once inside, he spotted her at Caesar's cage. The big cat chuffed, clearly pleased to see Gemma again. That's all that mattered to Gray, as well. Okay, that wasn't true. He strolled her way, giving her some time to process. Maybe she didn't want him to interfere.

For years, nothing else had mattered to him except getting justice for Bill, but he wasn't sure that he'd gotten that today. He'd seen the heartbreak and pain in

Gemma's eyes when Clyde had died. The man had used her and her family, killed them. The betrayal had devastated her. And seeing her go through that touched a forbidden place in his heart. He'd ached for her and with her. Gemma had broken through his resolve to never love again.

As he slowly approached, she finally turned from Caesar and Raja, both still alive and well, to look at Gray. A soft smile emerged. Along with it, her eyes held admiration—the approval he thought he didn't need from anyone. He'd lied to himself. He'd always longed to see it come from someone who mattered to him, and there it was in Gemma's eyes.

He stepped forward, closing the distance, and simply gazed into her face, her eyes—they had captivated him from the beginning. A tear leaked out the corner and streamed down her cheek.

"You saved us. You saved Caesar and Raja and…me. Thank you for that."

"You're welcome. I think the credit should go to God."

"I heard your praying in the closet, Gray. I think it's great that you reached out like that and, yeah, I think He answered you."

"He answered your prayers, too, Gemma. Caesar and Raja are safe. This whole thing is over."

She hung her head. He had a feeling he understood her struggle—as glad as she was that she and her tigers were safe, she'd lost Clyde, a family friend. Someone she'd counted on for almost her entire life. This wasn't the time to do this, but he might never get the chance to express himself, what he was feeling.

He cupped her chin and brought her face up. Gray leaned in and gently kissed her soft lips. He had to know if she felt the same way. She drew closer and responded eagerly. Still, was it just heightened emotions and her need for reassurance, or something more?

He had to give this a chance, them a chance. But first, Gemma needed a chance. She needed time and he would give that to her.

Approaching footfalls broke the moment, followed by a loud smack on the back. Mark smiled and shook Gemma's hand by way of introduction.

"This man is one of our best agents. I think you have that management position at headquarters in Virginia wrapped up now, Gray."

Hadn't Gray always wanted that? Some way to prove himself in his competition with Coop for their father's attention? Maybe that was what he'd wanted a few weeks ago, but he'd grown out of that. Didn't need it. Mark said the words, but Gray hadn't taken his eyes from Gemma. He saw in them her disappointment— she knew that with no reason to stay, he would be leaving Tiger Mountain.

And Gray knew he couldn't have both worlds.

One month later, Gemma sat on a rock at Rogue Point, overlooking the Tiger Mountain sanctuary. To her right the Wild Rogue Wilderness region ran up against the sanctuary and to the left were a few neighboring ranches and farms. In the distance, if it were night, she could just make out a few lights coming off Gold Beach.

The last month had been bittersweet. She'd finally learned to trust God. Saw now that He was there working in her life and had been all along. Even when the bad things came by the hands of evil men—free will and all that—God was working things out for her good. And that was the only reason that Gemma could now let go of Tiger Mountain. She had already turned the venture over to new management, new owners, new everything. That was the only way to keep her dream alive—by letting go. The public, donors and government entities would never accept Tiger Mountain as a responsible and authentic sanctuary with everything that had happened. Not with a Rollins in charge.

She let the tears she hated flow freely now, thinking back to the tigers to whom she'd already said her goodbyes. They would have a good home now. And it would be better for everyone that she not be there. It was even better for her, since walking around the sanctuary just upset her now. Sure, she'd built the place, but she didn't like to think of Clyde's investment and the advantage he'd taken of the sanctuary. She couldn't think about that side of things.

And those animals weren't the only thing she'd had to let go of—there was also Gray Wilde.

He'd kissed her, and she'd longed for that. She'd felt the promise of a future there, but it ended like things always ended for Gemma, with better opportunities elsewhere, like that job his boss had mentioned. Even if he weren't promoted, he was a special agent and traveled wherever his job took him.

And any glimmer of hope she'd held in her heart that he might be the one to stay with her instead of leaving her behind like everyone else had died away at that moment. She'd been a fool to harbor any hope at all, with her history. Gray wasn't too different from the others whom she could never trust—he had lied to her, though she understood why he'd done it. To find the truth and to fight for the innocent.

To bring justice.

It was why she could forgive him.

But why the kiss? It must have been to say goodbye. She'd conjured the hope of a future while he was kissing her goodbye.

That was it.

End of story.

And then… Gray stepped into view on the hilltop, as if she'd conjured him with her thoughts. He climbed all the way up to her. Gemma watched and waited, taking in this new addition to the view—her heart dancing. She'd thought she didn't want to see him again, that it would only lead to more pain. But, oh yes, she *did* want to see him again. She wanted to never stop looking at him.

She couldn't sit and wait anymore and stood, pacing the small flat space, worn by years of people climbing here to look at the incredible view. Gray finally rose to stand next to her.

"Gray."

"Gemma." His smile was tenuous.

"What are you doing here?"

"Don't you know?"

Shaking her head, she looked away—over at the wilderness region. She could just make out a bit of the Rogue River from here. "I don't know. I thought you were moving to the east coast or somewhere."

"Gemma," Gray turned her to face him. "I'm going to take a risk here. Go out on a limb. I don't know if you want me here or not. But I wanted you to know that I'm not taking that job in Virginia."

That news surprised her. She angled her head and studied this man, this beautiful man. Her heart pounded erratically. She feared speaking would give her away. She wanted to say something like *why would I care?* But it would be hurtful and a lie. So she said nothing at all.

"Don't you know by now…?" He began but trailed off.

She sucked in a breath. What was he trying to say? She wished he would just say it.

He pulled her close. Her senses were filled with the scent of him, a cool breeze swirled around them as if cocooning them together. "I love you."

Her heart jumped again. "You do?"

"Yes. And I'm hoping you feel the same way, because I already quit my job."

"You quit your job? For me?"

He nodded. "Do you love me, Gemma?"

Though it was difficult for her to say the words, Gemma couldn't deny the truth. "I love you, Gray Wilde. But why would you quit your job for me?"

"I know trusting has been hard for you. So I took the first step. A leap of faith, hoping you'd believe in me. Give us a chance, more than a chance. And anyway, the job would take me away from you. Too much travel. I'll work on a contract basis as a consultant, but I quit because I want to build something with you, Gemma. I want to make a difference, a lasting difference. We could start another animal refuge, and with my connections we could likely take care of the worst cases."

That all sounded good, but Gray was talking long term. Did he mean it?

"But I'm getting off track here." Gray leaned in and pressed his lips against hers. Gemma thrilled at the love pouring from him, as her senses heightened to every breath, every scent and every sound, and everything that was Gray.

He ended the kiss much too soon for her. "I love you, Gemma. I'm hoping you'll want me around for a long time."

"I've lost so much," she said. "I'm afraid of losing

again, but on the other hand I know life is too short to let go of a good thing when I've found it. Thank you for coming back for me, Gray. For giving it all up for me. I'd like for you to stick around for a long time."

He leaned in and brushed his lips against hers. "I don't want to rush you, Gemma, but do you think you could marry me?"

The question took her breath away, but she quickly found it again. Before she could reply, he interrupted.

"It's okay if you need more time. I'm not going anywhere unless you say otherwise."

"Oh, Gray, I've been through so much tragedy. I know that life can end in a moment. I love you and I can't think of anything I'd rather do than become your wife."

* * * * *

Don't miss the first exciting story in the
WILDERNESS, INC. *miniseries*
by Elizabeth Goddard:

TARGETED FOR MURDER

Find more great reads at www.LoveInspired.com

Dear Reader,

Thank you so much for joining me on this adventure. I hope you enjoyed the story. I set my story in the beautiful region surrounding the Rogue River in southwest Oregon—my old stomping grounds.

As always when researching a story, I learn so much more than I can ever put into the novel. What I learned about wildlife trafficking and how poachers are decimating entire species was disheartening. Whether you're an animal lover or not, God put Adam in the garden to care for the earth—the plants and animals—and God's directive for man hasn't changed.

On a more spiritual note, Gemma has had her share of tragedy and she keeps moving forward in life because she focuses on something bigger than herself. She has a cause and others (the tigers) are counting on her. Still, she struggles in that she doesn't have the sense that God hears her or answers her prayers. In the end she realizes that God was with her all along, working things out for her good.

We live in a fallen world and bad men do bad things, but we know that God is always there working things out for good on our behalf. Don't ever forget that. If you struggle with knowing this, ask Him to open the eyes of your heart.

It's always my hope and prayer that my stories will entertain you and provide a powerful emotional experience, but more importantly that they will bring you closer to the One who holds you.

Once again, thank you for reading *Undercover Protector*. For something extra, if you'd like to see pictures of the Wild Rogue Wilderness region, you can visit my Pinterest board at www.pinterest.com/bethrachg /wild-rogue-wilderness-series/ and look at tigers at www.pinterest.com/bethrachg/wilderness-inc-book-2/.

Be sure to visit my website at www.elizabeth goddard.com to find out about my books and sign up for my newsletter.

Many blessings!
Elizabeth Goddard

COMING NEXT MONTH FROM
Love Inspired® Suspense

Available February 7, 2017

THE ONLY WITNESS
Callahan Confidential • by Laura Scott
Paige Olson's five-year-old daughter may have witnessed her father's murder, but she won't talk about it—and now a gunman's hunting them down. Homicide detective Miles Callahan will do anything to protect Paige and her little girl...even if it means breaking police protocol.

SHADOW OF SUSPICION • by Christy Barritt
Framed for kidnapping her neighbor's daughter, computer specialist Laney Ryan needs help to prove her innocence. But as she and police detective Mark James dig into the case, they become the targets of an unknown threat.

DESERT SECRETS • by Lisa Harris
Kidnapped and tormented into revealing the location of her brother—and the money he stole—Lexi Shannon's convinced she'll be killed...until pilot Colton Landry comes to her rescue. But after their plane's shot down as they attempt to escape, they're thrust into a deadly desert pursuit.

RESCUE AT CEDAR LAKE
True North Bodyguards • by Maggie K. Black
When Theresa Vaughan is attacked at a remote snowbound cottage by a masked man seeking a secret from her past, her only hope of survival is Alex Dean, the daring bodyguard whose heart she broke when she ended their engagement.

PERILOUS HOMECOMING • by Sarah Varland
As the sole witness to a murder, Kelsey Jackson finds herself in a killer's crosshairs. But with the help of her high school rival, Sawyer Hamilton, she's determined to catch the murderer before she becomes the next victim.

PRESUMED DEAD • by Angela Ruth Strong
Preston Tyler's supposed to be dead...so Holly Fontaine can't believe the former soldier just rescued her from a bomb planted in her cabin. And with a killer after her, the childhood sweetheart she believed was gone forever is the only man who can save her.

SPECIAL EXCERPT FROM

Love Inspired®
SUSPENSE

Paige Olson's five-year-old daughter may have witnessed her father's murder, but she won't talk about it—and now a gunman's hunting them down. Homicide detective Miles Callahan will do anything to protect Paige and her little girl...even if it means breaking police protocol.

Read on for a sneak preview of
THE ONLY WITNESS
by **Laura Scott**, *available February 2017*
from Love Inspired Suspense!

"I looked up the license plate of the black sedan from the restaurant," Miles said, his expression grim. "The sedan is registered to Sci-Tech."

"They sent gunmen after us?" Paige asked in a strained whisper.

"Yeah, that's what it looks like."

"They're after me because of my ex-husband, aren't they?"

"I think so, yes." Miles reached over and cradled her icy hands in his. "I'm sorry."

Paige gripped his hands tightly. "You have to find Travis before it's too late."

He didn't want to point out that it might already be too late. Whatever Abby had seen on the tablet had frightened her to the point she wouldn't speak. Had Travis told her to keep quiet? Or had she seen something horrible? He found himself hoping for the first option, but feared the latter.

LISEXP0117

"I'm not sure where to look for Travis," he admitted. "There's no way to know where he'd go to hide if he thought he was in danger."

"Did you give the police the list of names I gave you?" Paige asked. "I know they're only a few names, but…"

"I've been searching on their names, but I haven't found anything yet. At least we have another link to Sci-Tech. No wonder they were stonewalling me."

"I might be able to get inside the building," Paige offered.

"No." His knee-jerk reaction surprised him, and he tried to backpedal. "I mean, if they're the ones behind this, then it's not safe for you to go there. Besides, how would you get in?"

She lifted her uncertain gaze to his. "I know a couple of the security guards pretty well. If I waited until after-hours, when there's only one security guard manning the desk, I might be able to convince them to let me in."

"I know you want to help, but it's not worth the risk." He couldn't stand the idea of Paige walking into the equivalent of the lion's den. "You don't know for sure which security guard would be on duty. And besides, if anything happened—Abby would be lost without you."

She blinked, and he thought he saw the glint of tears. "Logically, I know you're right, but it's hard to sit back and do nothing, not even trying."

"I'll find a way to do something while keeping you and Abby safe." He couldn't stand the thought of her worrying about things she couldn't change. He'd protect her, no matter what.

Don't miss
THE ONLY WITNESS
by Laura Scott, available February 2017 wherever
Love Inspired® Suspense books and ebooks are sold.

www.LoveInspired.com

Praise for Sara Douglass

"Sara Douglas is the best and most exciting writer of commercial fantasy fiction to emerge from Australia. . . . A skilled writer of short fiction, Sara also has the breadth of vision necessary to create sweeping epics and the storyteller's gift that makes readers love her." —*Locus*

"*The Wayfarer Redemption* has richness and color in a background balancing between Norse saga and the best of Robert E. Howard." —David Drake

"Douglass is at least as good as early Terry Goodkind or David Eddings, and she is currently Australia's most popular fantasist. With this skillfully handled tale, she may find success in the U.S. too." —*Booklist*

"Sara Douglass' *The Wayfarer Redemption* is a fast-paced tale packed with action and intrigue, mysticism and romance. Readers will be delighted to discover it is only the first in a six book series set in the intriguing realm of Tencendor. Douglass' fertile imagination gives life to several very different races that inhabit this ice-threatened land. Their interactions and conflicts, set against the background of an ancient prophecy, make *The Wayfarer Redemption* a compelling story. Sara Douglass blends traditional elements of mythology and folklore with her own highly original ideas to produce a tale with both depth and immediacy. I recommend this series to lovers of epic fantasy." —Juliet Marillier, author of *Daughter of the Forest*

"Powerful, hard-driving storytelling makes *The Wayfarer Redemption* a real page-turner of a novel. Sara Douglass gives us real people struggling in the face of dark rising doom, old prophecies, cliffhangers galore, and hard-won slivers of hope. Brother Ogden and Brother Veremund are particular delights among a large cast of splendidly-drawn characters, but there are many gems here. Bring on the sequels!" —Ed Greenwood, author of *The Kingless Land*

The
Wayfarer
Redemption

Sara Douglass

TOR®
fantasy

A TOM DOHERTY ASSOCIATES BOOK
NEW YORK

This is a work of fiction. All the characters and events portrayed in this book are either products of the author's imagination or are used fictitiously.

THE WAYFARER REDEMPTION

First published in Australia under the title *Battleaxe: Book One of the Axis Trilogy* in 1995 by Harper Collins Publishers (Australia) Pty Limited Group.

Maps by Miguel Roces

A Tor Book
Published by Tom Doherty Associates, LLC
175 Fifth Avenue
New York, NY 10010

www.tor-forge.com

Tor® is a registered trademark of Tom Doherty Associates, LLC.

ISBN-13: 978-0-7653-4130-3
ISBN-10: 0-7653-4130-1

First U.S. Edition: March 2001
First Mass Market Edition: September 2001

Printed in the United States of America

0 9 8 7 6

Dedication

The six books of *The Wayfarer Redemption* are for A. Lynn Martin, Tim Stretton and Frances Thiele, who have regarded with amiable tolerance their colleague's slow drift into the Star Dance.

Contents

viii ᐤ **Contents**

When will the hundred summers die,
And thought and time be born again,
And newer knowledge, drawing nigh,
Bring truth that sways the soul of men?
Here all things in their place remain,
As were all order'd, ages since.
Come, Care and Pleasure, Hope and Pain,
And bring the fated fairy Prince.

—Alfred Lord Tennyson,
"The Sleeping Palace"

N

KEEP

GORKEN FORT

RETREAT

SQUARE

GORKENTOWN

ISKR

ICEBEAR

Deadwood
Forest

RAVENSBUND

SKRAELINOS

GORKEN PASS

GLACIER

R. ANDAKILS

GORKENFORT
AND TOWN

TALON
SPUR

SEAL
BAY

ICHTAR

STRAUM
ISLAND

URQHART
HILLS

SI

SEA

WEST
ICHTAR

R. ICHTAR

R. AZLE

SEF
LAN

R. AZLE

ALDENI

MURKLE BAY

MURKLE
MOUNTAINS

R. FLURIAT

EL OCEAN

UNMAPPED TUNDRA

COAST

GLACIER

ICESCARP ALPS

ESCARP BARREN

SKRAELINGS

SHADOWSWARD (AVARINHEIM)

R. NORDRA

FORTRESS RANGES

WILD DOG PLAINS

WIDOWMAKER SEA

HOLT

OIS ING

HOLDHARD PASS

R. NORDRA

FORBIDDEN VALLEY

TAILEM BEND

SMYRTON

SEAGRASS PLAINS

The Prophecy of the Destroyer

A day will come when born will be
Two babes whose blood will tie them.
That born to Wing and Horn will hate
The one they call the StarMan.
Destroyer! rises in the north
And drives his Ghostmen south;
Defenseless lie both flesh and field
Before Gorgrael's ice.
To meet this threat you must release
The StarMan from his lies,
Revive Tencendor, fast and sure
Forget the ancient war,
For if Plough, Wing and Horn can't find
The bridge to understanding,
Then will Gorgrael earn his name
And bring Destruction hither.

StarMan, listen, heed me well,
Your power will destroy you
If you should wield it in the fray
'Ere these prophecies are met:
The Sentinels will walk abroad
'Til power corrupt their hearts;
A child will turn her head and cry
Revealing ancient arts;
A wife will hold in joy at night
The slayer of her husband;
Age-old souls, long in cribs,
Will sing o'er mortal land;
The remade dead, fat with child
Will birth abomination;
A darker power will prove to be
The father of salvation.
Then waters will release bright eyes
To form the Rainbow Scepter.

StarMan, listen, for I know
That you can wield the scepter
To bring Gorgrael to his knees
And break the ice asunder.
But even with the power in hand
Your pathway is not sure:
A Traitor from within your camp
Will seek and plot to harm you;
Let not your Lover's pain distract
For this will mean your death;
Destroyer's might lies in his hate
Yet you must never follow;
Forgiveness is the thing assured
To save Tencendor's soul.

Prologue

$\mathcal{T}$he woman struggled through the knee-deep snow, the bundle of dead wood she had tied to her back almost as great a burden as the weight of the child she carried in her belly. Her breath rasped in her throat before frosting heavily in the bitterly cold southerly wind. She was short and strong, her legs and shoulders finely muscled by twenty-eight years of hard-won survival in her harsh homeland. But she had always had the help and company of her people to aid her. Now she was alone, and this, her third child, she would have to bear without assistance.

This would be her last trip across the valley. The severe winter storms of the past few weeks had kept her iced into her shelter so that her supply of the precious hot-burning Timewood was almost exhausted; if she did not have enough wood and dry stores remaining for her confinement, then she would die and her child would die with her. Only in the past day had the weather broken sufficiently to allow her to struggle through the snow to reach the Timewood trees. Now the wind was growing harsher and the snow heavier and she knew she had only a short time to reach her shelter. The knowledge that once the baby was born she would not be able to travel far from her shelter drove her on.

Although her current solitude was a path she had chosen freely, worry ate at her bones.

And worry about her child also gnawed at her. Her previous two pregnancies had been uncomfortable, especially in the final weeks, but she had borne those children with little fuss. Her body had recuperated quickly and had healed cleanly each time. With this child she feared her labor more than the lonely winter ahead. It was too large, too . . . angry. Sometimes at night when she was trying to sleep it twisted and beat at the sides of her womb with such frantic fists and heels that she moaned in pain, rocking herself from side to side in a futile bid to escape its rage.

She paused briefly, adjusting the burden of wood on her back, wishing she could ease the load of the child as easily. Last night it had shifted down into the pit of her belly, seeking the birth canal. The birth was close. Perhaps tonight, perhaps tomorrow. She could feel the bones of her pelvis grating apart with the pressure of the child's head each time she took a step, making it hard to walk.

She squinted through the snow to the thick line of conifers about three hundred paces ahead. She had done her best with her camp. It was sheltered well behind the tree line in the lee of a rocky hill that, jutting above the peaks of the trees, was the first in a long range of hills leading into the distant Icescarp Alps. Well before her pregnancy had begun to show, she'd slipped away from her friends and family and travelled the Avarinheim to reach this lonely spot far to the north of her usual forest home. From the first of the autumn months, DeadLeaf-month, she had occupied her days with gathering and storing as many berries, nuts and seeds as she could. As hard as she searched, however, she had found only small amounts of malfari, the sweet fibrous tubers that provided her people with most of their winter sustenance. She had been forced to go without, and fears of what malnourishment might do to her and the child kept her awake at nights. The remains of a few scrawny rabbits, dried into leathery strips, were all she had for meat. She sighed and absently rubbed her belly, trying to ignore the fiery ache in her legs and pelvis, desperately wishing for a few chickens or a goat to supplement her diet.

She should never have tried to carry this child to term. Had she remained with her people she would not have been allowed to. It was a Beltide child, conceived during the drunken revelry of the spring rites, a time when her people, the forest dwellers, and the people of the Icescarp Alps assembled in the groves where mountain and forest met. There they celebrated the renewal of life in the thawing land with religious rites, followed, invariably, by an enthusiastic excess of whatever wine was left over from long winter nights huddled by home fires. Beltide was the one night of the year when both peoples relaxed sufficiently to carry interracial relations to extremes never practiced throughout the rest of the year.

Every Beltide night for the past three years she had watched him, wanted him. He came down to the groves with his people, his skin as pale and fine as the ice vaults of his home, his hair the fine summer gold of the life-giving sun that both their peoples worshipped. As the most powerful Enchanter of his kind he led the Beltide rites with the leading Banes of her own people; his power and magic awed and frightened her yet she craved his skill, beauty and grace. This last Beltide night past, eight months ago now, she had drunk enough wine to loosen her inhibitions and buttress her courage. She was a striking woman, at the peak of her beauty and fitness, her nut-brown hair waving thick down her back. When he'd seen her striding across the clearing of the grove toward him his eyes had crinkled and then widened, and he had smiled and held his hand out to her. Eyes trapped by his, she had taken his outstretched fingers, marveling at the feel of his silken skin against her own work-callused palm. He was kind for an Enchanter, and had murmured gentle words before leading her to a secluded spot beneath the spinning stars.

"StarDrifter," she whispered, running her tongue along the split skin of her lips.

The snow that had been drifting down for the past few hours was now falling heavily, and she roused from her reverie to find she could hardly see the tree line through the driving snow. She must hurry. His child dragging her down, she stumbled a little as she tried to move faster.

His hands had been strong and confident on her body, and she was not surprised that her womb had quickened with his child. A child of his would be so amazing, so exceptional. But although both peoples accepted the excesses and the drunken unions between the races on Beltide night, both also insisted that any child conceived of such a union was an abomination. For most of her life she had been aware of the women who, some four to six weeks after Beltide, went out of their way along the dim forest paths to collect the herbs necessary to rid their bodies of any child conceived that night.

Somehow she had not been able to force herself to swallow the steaming concoction she brewed herself time and time again. And finally she had decided that she would carry the child to term. Once the child was born, once her people could see that it was a babe like any other (except more beautiful, more powerful, as any child of an Enchanter would be), they would accept it. No child of his could be an abomination.

She'd had to spend the last long months of her pregnancy alone, lest her people force the child from her body. Now she wondered if the child would be as wondrous as she had first supposed, whether she'd made a mistake.

She clenched her jaws against the discomfort and forced her feet to take one step after another through the snow drifts. She would manage. She had to. She did not want to die.

Suddenly a strange whisper, barely discernible in the heightening storm, ran along the edge of the wind.

She stopped, every nerve in her body afire. Her gloved hands pushed fine strands of hair from her eyes, and she concentrated hard, peering through the gloom, listening for any unusual sounds.

There. Again. A soft whisper along the wind . . . a soft whisper and a hiccup. Skraelings!

"Ah," she moaned, involuntarily, terror clenching her stomach. After a moment frozen into the wind, she fumbled with the cumbersome straps holding the bundle of wood to her back, desperate to lose the burden. Her only hope of survival lay in outrunning the Skraelings. In reaching the trees before they reached her. They did not like the trees.

But she could not run at this point in her pregnancy. Not with this child.

The straps finally broke free, the wood tumbling about her feet, and she stumbled forward. Almost immediately she tripped and fell over, hitting the ground heavily, the impact forcing the breath from her body and sending a shaft of agony through her belly. The child kicked viciously.

The wind whispered again. Closer.

For a few moments she could do nothing but scrabble around in the snow, frantically trying to regain her breath and find some foot or handhold in the treacherous ground.

A small burble of laughter, low and barely audible above the wind, sounded a few paces to her left.

Sobbing with terror now, she lurched to her feet, everything but the need to get to the safety of the trees forgotten.

Two paces later another whisper, this time directly behind her, and she would have screamed except that her child kicked so suddenly and directly into her diaphragm that she was winded almost as badly as she had been when she fell.

Then, even more terrifying, a whisper directly in front of her.

"A pretty, pretty . . . a tasty, tasty." The wraith's insubstantial face appeared momentarily in the dusk light, its silver orbs glowing obscenely, its tooth-lined jaws hanging loose with desire.

Finally she found the breath to scream, the sound tearing through the dusk light, and she stumbled desperately to the right, fighting through the snow, arms waving in a futile effort to fend the wraiths off. She knew she was almost certainly doomed. The wraiths fed off fear as much as they fed off flesh, and they were growing as her terror grew. She could feel the strength draining out of her. They would chase her, taunt her, drain her, until even fear was gone. Then they would feed off her body.

The child churned in her belly as she lurched through the snow, as if intent on escaping the prison of her poor, doomed body. It flailed with its fists and heels and elbows, and every time one of the dreadful whispers of the wraiths reached it through the amniotic fluid of its mother's womb, it twisted and struck harder.

Even though she knew she was all but doomed, the primeval urge to keep making the effort to escape kept her moving through the snow, grunting with each step, jerking every time her child beat at the confines of her womb. But now the urge to escape consumed the child as much as its mother.

The five wraiths hung back a few paces in the snow, enjoying the woman's fear. The chase was going well. Then, strangely, the woman twisted and jerked mid-step and crashed to the ground, writhing and clutching at the heaving mound of her belly. The wraiths, surprised by this sudden development in the chase, had to sidestep quickly out of the way, and slowed to circle the woman at a safe distance just out of arm's reach.

She screamed. It was a sound of such terror, wrenched from the very depths of her body, that the wraiths moaned in ecstasy.

She turned to the nearest wraith, extending a hand for mercy. "Help me," she whispered. "Please, help me!"

The wraiths had never been asked for help before. They began to mill in confusion. Was she no longer afraid of them? Why was that? Wasn't every flesh and blood creature afraid of them? Their minds communed and they wondered if perhaps they should be afraid too.

The woman convulsed, and the snow stained bright red about her hips.

The smell and sight of warm blood reached the wraiths, reassuring them. This one was going to die more quickly than they had originally expected. Spontaneously. Without any help from their sharp pointed fangs. Sad, but she would still taste sweet. They drifted about in the freezing wind, watching, waiting, wanting.

After a few more minutes the woman moaned once, quietly, and then lay still, her face alabaster, her eyes opened and glazed, her hands slowly unclenching.

The wraiths bobbed as the wind gusted through them and considered. The chase had started so well. She had feared well. But she had died strangely.

The most courageous of the five drifted up to the woman and considered her silently for a moment longer. Finally, the coppery smell of warm blood decided it and it reached down an insubstantial claw to worry at the leather thongs of her tunic. After a moment's resistance the leather fell open—and the one adventuresome wraith was so surprised it leapt back to the safe circling distance of its comrades.

In the bloody mess that had once been the woman's belly lay a child, glaring defiantly at them, hate steeping from every one of its bloodied pores.

It had eaten its way out.

"Ooooh!" the wraiths cooed in delight, and the more courageous of them drifted forward again and picked up the bloody child.

"It hates," it whispered to the others. "Feel it?"

The other wraiths bobbed closer, emotion close to affection misting their orbs.

The child turned its tusked head and glared at the wraiths. It hiccupped, and a small bubble of blood frothed at the corner of its mouth.

"Aaah!" the wraiths cooed again, and huddled over the

baby. Without a word they made their momentous decision. They would take it home. They would feed it. In time they would learn to love it. And then, years into a future the wraiths could not yet discern, they would learn to worship it.

But now they were hungry and good food was cooling to one side. Appealing as it was, the baby was dumped unceremoniously in the snow, howling its rage, as the wraiths fed on its dead mother.

Six weeks later . . .

Separated by the length of the Alps and still more by race and circumstance, another woman struggled through the snowdrifts of the lower reaches of the western Icescarp Alps.

She fell badly over a rock hidden by the snow and tore the last fingernail from her once soft, white hands as she scrabbled for purchase. She huddled against a frozen rock and sucked her finger, moaning in frustration and almost crying through cold and sad-heartedness. For a day and a night she had battled to keep alive, ever since they had dumped her here in this barren landscape. These mountains could kill even the fittest man, and she was seriously weakened by the terrible birth of her son two days before.

And despite all her travail and prayers and tears and curses he had died during that birth, born so still and blue that the midwives had huddled him away, not letting her hold him or weep over him.

And as the midwives fled the birthing chamber, the two men had come in, their eyes cold and derisive, their mouths twisting with scorn. They had dragged her weeping and bleeding from the room, dragged her from her life of comfort and deference, dumped her into a splintered old cart and drove her throughout the day to this spot at the base of the Icescarp Alps. They had said not a word the entire way.

Finally they had unceremoniously tipped her out. No doubt they wished her dead, but neither had dared stain their hands with her blood. Better this way, where she could endure a slow death on the dreaded mountains, prey to the Forbidden Ones which crouched among the rocks, prey to the cold and the ice, and with time to contemplate the shame of her illegitimate child . . . her *dead* illegitimate child.

But she was determined not to die. There was one chance and one chance only. She would have to climb high into the Alps. Barely out of girlhood and clad only in tatters, she willed herself to succeed.

Her feet had gone to ice the first few hours and she now could no longer feel them. Her toes were black. Her fingernails, torn from her hands, had left gaping holes at the ends of her fingers that had iced over. Now they were turning black too. Her lips were so dry and frozen they had drawn back from her teeth and solidified into a ghastly rictus.

She huddled against the rock. Although she had started the climb in hope and determination, even she, her natural stubbornness notwithstanding, realized her situation was precarious. She had stopped shivering hours ago. A bad sign.

The creature had been watching the woman curiously for some hours now. It was far up the slopes of the mountain, peering down from its heights through eyes that could see a mouse burp at five leagues. Only the fact that she was below his favorite day roost made the creature stir, fluff out its feathers in the icy air, then spread its wings and launch itself abruptly into the swirling wind, angered by the intrusion. It would rather have spent the day preening itself in what weak sun there was. It was a vain creature.

* * *

She saw it circling far above her. She squinted into the sun, gray specks of exhaustion almost obscuring her sight.

"StarDrifter?" she whispered, hope strengthening her heart and her voice. Slowly, hesitatingly, she lifted a blackened hand toward the sky. "Is that you?"

1

The Tower of the Seneschal

Twenty-nine years later ...

The speckled blue eagle floated high in the sky above the hopes and works of mankind. With a wingspan as wide as a man was tall, it drifted lazily through the air thermals rising off the vast inland plains of the kingdom of Achar. Almost directly below lay the silver-blue expanse of Grail Lake, flowing into the great River Nordra as it coiled through Achar toward the Sea of Tyrre. The lake was enormous and rich in fish, and the eagle fed well there. But more than fish, the eagle fed on the refuse of the lake-side city of Carlon. Pristine as the ancient city might be with its pink and cream stone walls and gold and silver plated roofs; pretty as it might be with its tens of thousands of pennants and banners and flags fluttering in the wind, the Carlonites ate and shat like every other creature in creation, and the piles of refuse outside the city walls supported enough mice and rats to feed a thousand eagles and hawks.

The eagle had already feasted earlier that morning and was not interested in gorging again so soon. It let itself drift further east across Grail Lake until the white-walled seven-sided Tower of the Seneschal rose one hundred paces into the air to greet the sun. There the eagle tipped its wing and its balance, veering slowly to the north, looking for a shady afternoon roost. It was an old and wise eagle and knew that it would probably have to settle for the shady eaves of some farmer's barn in this most treeless of lands.

As it flew, it pondered the minds and ways of these men who feared trees so much that they'd cut down most of the ancient forests once covering this land. It was the way of the Axe and of the Plough.

Far below the eagle, Jayme, Brother-Leader of the Religious Brotherhood of the Seneschal, most senior mediator between the one god Artor the Ploughman and the hearts and souls of the Acharites, paced across his comfortable chamber in the upper reaches of the Tower of the Seneschal.

"The news grows more disturbing," he muttered, his kindly face crinkling into deep seams of worry. For years he'd refused to accept the office his fellow brothers had pressed on him, and now, five years after he'd finally bowed to their wishes and accepted that Artor himself must want him to hold supreme office within the Seneschal, Jayme feared that it would be he who might well have to see the Seneschal—nay, Achar itself—through its greatest crisis in a thousand years.

He sighed and turned to stare out the window. Even though it was only early DeadLeaf-month, the first week of the first month of autumn, the wind had turned icy several days before, and the windows were tightly shut against the cold. A fire blazed in the mottled green marble fireplace behind his desk, the light of the flames picking out the inlaid gold tracery in the stone and the silver, crystal and gold on the mantel.

The younger of his two assistants stepped forward. "Do you believe the reports to be true, Brother-Leader?"

Jayme turned to reassure Gilbert, whom he thought might yet prove to have a tendency toward alarm and panic. Who knew? Perhaps such tendencies would serve him well over the coming months. "My son, it has been so many generations since anyone has reliably spotted any of the Forbidden Ones that, for all we know, these reports might be occasioned only by superstitious peasants frightened by rabbits gambolling at dusk."

Gilbert rubbed his tonsured head anxiously and glanced across at Moryson, Jayme's senior assistant and first adviser, before speaking again. "But so many of these reports come from our own brothers, Brother-Leader."

Jayme resisted the impulse to retort that most of the brothers in the northern Retreat of Gorkentown, where many of these reports originated, were little more than superstitious peasants themselves. But Gilbert was young, and had never travelled far from the glamor and cultivation of Carlon, or the pious and intellectual atmosphere of the Tower of the Seneschal where he had been educated and admitted into holy orders to serve Artor.

And Jayme himself feared that it was more than rabbits that had frightened his Gorkentown brethren. There were reports coming out of the small village of Smyrton, far to the north-east, that needed to be considered as well.

Jayme sighed again and sat down in the comfortable chair at his desk. One of the benefits of the highest religious office in the land were the physical comforts of the Brother-Leader's quarters high in the Tower. Jayme was not hypocritical enough to pretend that, at his age, his aching joints did not appreciate the well-made and cushioned furniture, pleasing both to eye and to body, that decorated his quarters. Nor did he pretend not to appreciate the fine foods and the invitations to the best houses in Carlon.

When he did not have to attend to the administration of the Seneschal or to the social or religious duties of his position, there for the stimulation of his mind were thousands of leather-bound books lining the shelves of his quarters, with religious icons and portraits collected over past generations decorating every other spare space of wall and bringing some measure of peace and comfort to his soul. His bright blue eyes, still sharp after so many years spent seeking out the sins of the Acharites, travelled indulgently over one particularly fine representation of the Divine Artor on the occasion that he had presented mankind with the gift of The Plough, a gift that had enabled mankind to rise above the limits of barbarity and cultivate both land and mind.

Brother Moryson, a tall, lean man with a deeply furrowed brow, regarded his Brother-Leader with fondness and respect. They had known each other for many decades; having both been appointed as the Seneschal's representatives to the royal court in their youth. Later they had moved to the royal household itself. Too many years ago, thought Moryson, looking at Jayme's hair and beard which were now completely white. His own thin brown hair, he knew, had more than a few speckles of gray.

When Jayme had finally accepted the position of Brother-Leader, a post he would hold until his death, his first request had been that his old friend and companion Moryson join him as first assistant and adviser. His second request, one that upset many at court and in the royal household itself, was that his protégé, Axis, be appointed BattleAxe of the Axe-Wielders, the elite military and crusading wing of the Seneschal. Fume as King Priam might, the Axe-Wielders were under the control of the Seneschal, and within the Seneschal a Brother-Leader's requests were as law. Royal displeasure notwithstanding, Axis had become the youngest ever commander of the Axe-Wielders.

Moryson, who had kept out of the conversation to this point, stepped forward, knowing Jayme was waiting for his advice. "Brother-Leader," he said, bowing low from the

waist with unfeigned respect and tucking his hands inside
the voluminous sleeves of his habit, "perhaps it would help
if we reviewed the evidence for a moment. If we consider
all the reports that have come in over the past few months
perhaps we might see a pattern."

Jayme nodded and waved both his assistants into the intricately carved chairs that sat across from his desk.
Crafted generations ago from one of the ancient trees that
had dominated the landscape of Achar, the well-oiled
wood glowed comfortingly in the firelight. Better that
wood served man in this way than free-standing on land
that could be put to the Plough. Thick stands of trees were
always better cut down than left standing to offer shade
and shelter to the demons of the Forbidden.

"As always your logic comforts me, Brother Moryson.
Gilbert, perhaps you could indulge us with a summation of
events as you understand them thus far. You are the one, after all, to have read all the reports coming in from the
north."

Neither Jayme nor Moryson particularly liked Gilbert;
an unbrotherly sentiment, they knew, but Gilbert was a
rather pretentious youth from a high-born Carlonite family,
whose generally abrasive personality was not helped by a
sickly complexion, thin shanks and sweaty palms. Nevertheless, he had a razor-sharp mind that could absorb seemingly unrelated items of information from a thousand
different sources and correlate them into patterns well before anyone else could. He was also unbelievably ambitious, and both Jayme and Moryson felt he could be better
observed and controlled if he were under the eye of the
Brother-Leader himself.

Gilbert shuffled back into his seat until his spine was
ramrod straight against the back of the chair and prepared
to speak his mind. Both Moryson and Jayme repressed
small smiles, but they waited attentively.

"Brothers under Artor," Gilbert began, "since the unusually late thaw of this spring," both his listeners grimaced
uncomfortably, "the Seneschal has been receiving numer-

ous reports of . . . unusual . . . activities from the frontier regions of Achar. Firstly from our brethren in the religious Retreat in Gorkentown, who have reported that the commander of Gorkenfort has lost many men on patrol during this last winter." The small municipality of Gorkentown, two hundred leagues north, huddled for protection about the military garrison of Gorkenfort. Centuries previously, the monarchy of Achar had established the fort in Gorken Pass in northern Ichtar; it was then and remained the most vital link in Achar's northern defenses.

"One shouldn't expect every one of your men to come back from patrol when you send them out to wander the northern wastes during the depths of winter," Jayme muttered testily, but Gilbert only frowned slightly at this interruption and continued.

"An *unusual* number of men, Brother-Leader. The soldiers who are stationed at Gorkenfort are among the best in Achar. They come from the Duke of Ichtar's own home guard. Neither Duke Borneheld, nor Gorkenfort's commander, Lord Magariz, expect to get through the winter patrols unscathed, but neither do they expect to lose over eighty-six men. Normally it is the winter itself that is the garrison's enemy, but now both Duke Borneheld and Lord Magariz believe they may have another enemy out there amid the winter snows."

"Has the Duke Borneheld seen any evidence for this with his own eyes, Gilbert?" Moryson asked smoothly. "Over the past year Borneheld seems to have preferred fawning at the king's feet to inspecting his northern garrison."

Gilbert's eyes glinted briefly. These two old men might think he was a conceited fool, but he had good sources of information.

"Duke Borneheld returned to Ichtar during Flowermonth and Rose-month, Brother Moryson. Not only did he spend some weeks at Hsingard and Sigholt, but he also travelled to the far north to speak with Magariz and the soldiers of Gorkenfort to hear and see for himself what has been happening. Perhaps, Brother Moryson, you were too busy counting the tithes as they came in to be fully aware of events in the outside world."

"Gilbert!" The Brother-Leader's voice was rigid with rebuke, and Gilbert inclined his head in a show of apology to Moryson. Moryson caught Jayme's eye over Gilbert's bowed head and a sharp look passed between them. Gilbert would receive a far stronger censure from his Brother-Leader when Jayme had him alone.

"If I might continue, Brother-Leader," Gilbert said deferentially.

Jayme angrily jerked his head in assent, his age-spotted fingers almost white where they gripped the armrests of his chair.

"Lord Magariz was able to retrieve some of the bodies of those he had lost. It appears they had been . . . eaten. Chewed. Nibbled. Tasted." Gilbert's voice was dry, demonstrating an unexpected flair for the macabre. "There are no known animals in either northern Ichtar or Ravensbund that would attack, let alone eat, a grown man in armor and defended with sword and spear."

"The great icebears, perhaps?" Jayme asked, his anger fading as his perplexion grew. Occasionally stories filtered down about man-eating icebears in the extreme north of Ravensbund.

"Gorkenfort is too far inland for the icebears, Brother-Leader. They would either have to walk down the Gorken Pass for some sixty leagues or shortcut across the lesser arm of the Icescarp Alps to reach it." He paused, reflecting. "And icebears have no head for heights. No," Gilbert shook his head slowly, "I fear the icebears are not responsible."

"Then perhaps the Ravensbundmen themselves," suggested Moryson. Ravensbund was, theoretically, a province of Achar and under the administration of the Duke of Ichtar on behalf of the King of Achar. But Ravensbund was such an extraordinarily wild and barren place, inhabited by uncouth tribes who spent nearly all their time hunting seals and great icebears in the extreme north, that both the King of Achar, Priam, and his loyal liege, Duke Borneheld of Ichtar, generally left the place to its own devices. Consequently, the garrison at Gorkenfort was, to all intents and purposes, the northernmost point of effective Acharite administration and military power in the kingdom. Although the Ravensbundmen were not much trouble, most Acharites regarded them as little more than barbaric savages.

"I don't think so, Brother Moryson. Apparently the Ravensbundmen have suffered as badly, if not worse, than the garrison at Gorkenfort. Indeed, many of the Ravensbund tribes are moving south into Ichtar. The tales they tell are truly terrible."

"And they are?" Jayme prompted, his fingers gently tapping his bearded chin as he listened.

"Of the winter gone mad, and of the wind come alive. Of ice creatures all but invisible to the eye inhabiting the wind and hungering for human flesh. They say the only warning that comes before an attack is a whisper on the wind. Yet if these creatures are invisible before attack, then they are generally visible after. Once they have gorged, the creatures are slimed with the blood of their victims. The Ravensbundmen are afraid of them—afraid enough to move out of their homelands—and the Ravensbundmen, savages as they are, have never been afraid of anything before."

"Have they tried to attack them?"

"Yes. But the creatures are somehow . . . insubstantial. Steel passes through their bodies. And they do not fear. If any soldiers get close enough to attack them, it is generally the last thing they get to do in this life. Only a few have escaped encounters with these . . ."

"Forbidden Ones?" Moryson whispered, his amiable face reflecting the anxiety that such a term provoked in all of them. None of them had wanted to be the first to mention this possibility.

"Wait, Moryson," Jayme counselled. "Wait until we have heard all of what Gilbert has to say." All three men had forgotten the tension and anger that Gilbert's jibe had caused moments before.

"Magariz's soldiers have seen similar apparitions, although most who have been close enough to see them have died," Gilbert said slowly. "One man they found alive. Just. He died a few minutes after Magariz arrived. He said, and this report was Lord Magariz's own, that he had been attacked by creatures which had no form and which had suffered no wounds at the edge of his sword."

"And how did they wound this soldier? I thought the Gorkenfort garrison were among the best armored soldiers in the realm."

"Brother-Leader, Magariz understood from the soldier's last words that the creatures surrounded him—then simply oozed through the gaps in his armor until they lay between it and his skin. Then they began to eat."

Gilbert stopped for a moment, and all three men contemplated such a horrific death. Jayme closed his eyes; may Artor hold him and keep him in His care, he prayed silently.

"I wonder why they left him alive?" Moryson wondered softly.

Gilbert's voice was caustic when he replied. "They had already consumed the rest of his patrol. One assumes they were reasonably full."

Jayme abruptly pushed himself up from his chair and moved over to a wall cabinet. "I think Artor would forgive us if we imbibed a little wine this early in the afternoon, Brothers. Considering we still have the reports from Smyrton to review, I think we might need it."

He poured out three glass goblets of deep red wine and handed them out before reseating himself behind his desk.

"Furrow wide, furrow deep," he intoned.

"Furrow wide, furrow deep," Moryson and Gilbert answered together, repeating the ritual phrases that served all Artor-fearing Acharites as blessings and greetings for most occasions in life.

Both ritual and wine comforted the men, and soon they were ready to resume their considerations.

"And what else from the north, Gilbert?" Jayme asked, holding his glass between both palms to warm the remaining wine and hoping the wine he had already consumed would beat back the chill gnawing at his soul.

"Well, the winter was particularly severe. Even here we suffered from extreme cold during Raven-month and Hungry-month, while the thaw came in Flower-month, a month later than usual. In the north the cold was even more extreme, and I believe the winter snow and ice persisted in places above the Urqhart Hills throughout the summer." Even northern Ichtar usually thawed completely for the summer.

Jayme raised his eyebrows. Gilbert's intelligence was good indeed. Did he have sources that Jayme did not know about? No matter, what was important was that much of northern Ichtar had spent the summer encased in ice when usually the ice and snow disappeared by Thaw-month.

"If the ice persisted above the Urqhart Hills, then Gorkentown must also have remained in conditions close to winter," Jayme pondered. "Tell me, Gilbert, did the attacks continue through the warmer months?"

Gilbert shook his head and took another sip of wine. "No. The creatures appeared only during the most severe weather in the depths of winter. Perhaps they have gone again."

"And perhaps they have not. If the extreme north remained encased in ice during summer then I dread the winter ahead. And if they depend on extreme weather conditions, then does that mean they will be back?"

"We should also consider the reports of our brothers in the Retreat at Gorkentown, Brother-Leader." The Brotherhood of the Seneschal had a small retreat in Gorkentown for those brothers who preferred a more ascetic life, spent in contemplation of Artor, to the comfortable life of the Tower of the Seneschal.

"Yes, Gilbert. Perhaps we should."

"Our brothers believe that the Forbidden might be behind this."

"And their reasons for thinking so, Gilbert?"

"The reports and experiences of the garrison for one, Brother-Leader. But also several of the brothers have reported that demons inhabit their dreams on those nights when the wind is fiercest."

Jayme chuckled softly. "Not reliable. You give me bad dreams most nights, Gilbert, and I am not yet ready to class you as one of the Forbidden."

All three men smiled, Gilbert more stiffly than the other two. Moryson spoke gently, turning the younger brother's mind from Jayme's heavy-handed attempt at humor. "Have they reported *seeing* anything, Gilbert?"

"Neither Gorkenfort nor Gorkentown has been attacked; only small patrols or individuals outside the walls. No, the brothers have actually *seen* little. But they have observed the mood of the town and garrison, and they say that dark thoughts and moods lay heavily across the inhabitants. Extra prayers are offered to Artor every day, but the fear grows."

"If only there was someone alive who actually knew anything about the Forbidden!" Jayme was angry at his inability to understand the nature of the threat in northern Ichtar. He stood up from his chair again and paced restlessly across the chamber.

"Gilbert. Forget the mutterings of the brothers in Gorkentown for the moment. What news out of Smyrton?"

"Unusual happenings there, too, but not the same as in northern Ichtar."

Smyrton was a largish village at the extreme edge of the Seagrass Plains, the main grain-producing area of Achar. It was the closest settled area to the Forbidden Valley. If the Forbidden ever came swarming over Achar again, then the valley was the obvious place they would emerge, a natural conduit out of the Shadowsward, the darkest and most evil place bordering Achar. One day, thought Jayme, we'll take the axe to the Shadowsward as well.

"The local Plough-Keeper, Brother Hagen, has sent reports of strange creatures sighted near the Forbidden Valley and, more disturbing, near the village itself. There have been about five sightings over the past several months."

"Are they . . . ?" Moryson began, but Gilbert shook his head.

"Nothing like the strange creatures of ice and snow that the soldiers of Gorkenfort report, Brother Moryson. Yet in their own way, they are just as strange. Man-like—but somehow alien."

"In what way?" asked Jayme testily.

Gilbert had to swivel a little in his chair to follow the figure of his Brother-Leader as he paced the floor from window to fireplace and back again. "They are short and muscular, and very dark, making them extremely hard to see at night. They evade the villagers rather than seek them out. Each time one is spotted it has been carrying a child with it, and Brother Hagen reports that although no children from the village are missing, the villagers bolt their doors and windows fast at dusk. Perhaps they have stolen the children from somewhere else."

"You said, 'somehow alien'." Jayme stopped before Gilbert's chair and folded his arms in frustration. "What do you mean by that?"

Gilbert shrugged. "I only relate what Brother Hagen relates, Brother-Leader. He was not specific on that point."

Jayme sighed and patted Gilbert on the shoulder. "I cannot but think the Forbidden are moving again."

Spoken words about the Forbidden were enough to make all three men shiver with foreboding. Every Acharite living knew that a thousand years previously, during the Wars of the Axe, their forebears had driven the frightful races that had once dominated Achar with their evil sorcery back across the Fortress Ranges into the Shadowsward and the Icescarp Alps. Then, with the help of the Axe-Wielders, the Acharites had cut down the massive forests that had once harbored the Forbidden races, putting the cleared land under Plough and civilization. It was part of Acharite legend that one day the Forbidden would seethe back across the Fortress Ranges and slither down from the Icescarp Alps to try to reclaim the land that had once been theirs. Every parent scared their children with the threat.

Jayme walked slowly over to the fire, his shoulders stooped. He raised his cold hands to the flames until he noticed with horror that they were trembling, and quickly bunched them into fists and hid them in the folds of his gown. Though nothing as yet connected the two sets of reports from Gorkenfort and Smyrton, Jayme was scared they were connected. The responsibility of his position weighed heavily on him.

Moryson and Gilbert watched silently, both aware of the seriousness of these reports, both glad they were not the ones who had to make the decisions. Moryson scratched his chin reflectively. He knew dark events were upon them.

Slowly Jayme turned back to his assistants. "Tomorrow Carlon celebrates King Priam's nameday. The celebrations will end with a banquet in the royal palace to which Priam has extended me an invitation. He has also advised me that we will need to meet privately to discuss the problem at Gorkentown. Neither Priam nor the Seneschal can meet this threat alone. Achar will have to stand united as it never has before if we can hope to survive the threat of the Forbidden. Artor help us, now and forever."

"Now and forever," the other two echoed, draining the dregs of their wine.

2

At King Priam's Court

King Priam's nameday was an occasion of great celebra-
tion throughout Achar, but nowhere more than in the
city of Carlon where a general holiday was proclaimed. In
the morning Priam presided over a parade through the
winding streets of the ancient city, sitting under a heavily
embroidered canopy that usually kept sun from his regal
brow. Today it kept an unseasonable drizzle from his
closely curled head. Despite the unsettling rumors from the
north, the townsfolk lined the streets for the parade—an affair put on by the various guilds of Carlon to honor their
king. Priam waved cheerfully enough throughout the extended parade, although he was bored witless by the time
the fifty-seventh flower-draped cart passed him by. He
made a good-humored speech at its conclusion, thanking
the guilds for their efforts on his behalf, and saying some
graceful words about the large number of enthusiastic (but
largely talentless) children of guild members who had performed throughout the parade. The crowd cheered their
king warmly, Priam beamed and waved some more, and

then everyone hurried home, remarking on the cold weather and wondering whether it would affect the evening's festivities.

Priam's nameday was the one day of the year when he extended his royal largesse to all the citizens of Carlon, providing them with a free feast (although if they wanted to sit down they had to bring their own stools). With the tens of thousands of mouths that had to be fed, the public banquet involved many months of careful planning and preparation. As much as anything, the banquet was an opportunity for the lords of the various provinces of Achar to demonstrate their loyalty toward their liege. Earl Burdel of Arcness bred and transported five hundred substantial porkers, the gigantic Duke Roland the Walker (too fat to ride) of Aldeni supplied two hundred and thirty-five carts of vegetables and fruit, Baron Fulke of Romsdale supplied enough ale to keep the Carlonites off work for three days after the banquet, and two hundred and twenty barrels of his best red. Baron Ysgryff of Nor, understanding that the citizens of Carlon would need to have something to entertain them once they had drunk and eaten to sufficiency, donated the services of one hundred and eighty-five of the best whores and dancing boys from the streets of Ysbadd. All the lords contributed what they could, eager to impress the king, but the most generous of all was Borneheld, Duke of Ichtar, who donated an entire herd of his finest mutton and beef, and distributed amongst the guilds a fistful of diamonds and emeralds from his mines in the Urqhart Hills. Of course, muttered the assembled lords around goblets full of Baron Fulke's finest, Borneheld could afford to be the most generous since he controlled more territory than any four of them put together.

By nine in the evening the citizens of Carlon were happily gorging themselves at the various venues—the town hall, the market square, and seven of the massive guild halls. The whores and the dancing boys were starting to ply their business outside the eating halls. Well away from the street parties, a less rowdy and more decorous banquet was underway in Priam's cream and gold palace in the heart of Carlon.

The banquet hall of the palace, popularly known as the Chamber of the Moons, was a massive circular affair that doubled as an audience chamber on ordinary days of the week. Great alabaster columns supported a soaring domed roof, enamelled in a gorgeous deep blue with gold and silver representations of the moon in the various phases of its monthly cycle floating amid a myriad of begemmed stars (thus the popular sobriquet). The floor was equally spectacular—deep emerald-green marble shot through with veins of gold.

Tonight the floor was hardly visible beneath the dozens of tables crammed into the chamber, and (as yet) no one was drunk enough to be lying in such a position as to stare straight toward the magnificent domed roof. On the side of the chamber, directly opposite the entrance, was the slightly raised dais, where Priam normally sat to receive whoever had come calling, but which tonight supported the royal table. Priam was there with his immediate family (of whom not many were left) and the most important nobles of the realm with their wives. Jayme, Brother-Leader of the Seneschal, enjoyed a spot not far from the center of the table and was, despite the grim news from the north, determined to enjoy the banquet until he could discuss developments more privately with Priam.

Immediately below the royal party was a large table seating the sons and daughters of the highest nobles. From there the tables spread across the floor of the Chamber of the Moons with the least important guests cramped around rickety tables in the dim recesses behind the grand circle of columns.

Faraday, eighteen-year-old daughter of Earl Isend of Skarabost, sat soaking up the atmosphere with her intelligent green eyes. As she had only turned eighteen a half-year previously, this was the first time she had been invited to one of the grand royal banquets; indeed, this was the first time she had even been to Carlon. Although Faraday had not been raised in court, she was far from being out of her social and cultural depth. Her mother, Merlion, had spent years training her in the rituals and etiquette of court society, while the girl's own natural wit and composure gave her the skills to hold her own in most courtly company. Pleasant conversation notwithstanding, Faraday's green eyes, chestnut hair and fine bone structure held the promise of such great beauty that she had already caught the speculative eye of a number of young nobles seeking well-bred and wealthy wives.

Beside her sat her new friend, Devera, twenty-year-old daughter of Duke Roland the Walker. Devera had a blue-eyed, fair-haired prettiness that Faraday thought extraordinarily appealing.

Faraday leaned close to Devera, hoping that the intricate knot of her heavy hair, held together with only small pins of pearls and diamonds, would not tumble down. "Everyone looks so beautiful, Devera," she whispered, unable to completely hide her excitement. Her eyes slipped to the goblet of watered wine she held. Its golden cup was encrusted with small diamond chips. Noble she might have been, but Faraday was still young enough to be impressed by the extreme wealth and ostentation of Priam's court.

Devera smiled at Faraday. She remembered how she had felt when she first came to court two years ago, but she was not going to let Faraday know that. "You should try and look more bored, Faraday. If people suspect you are in awe of them they will seek to take advantage of you."

Faraday looked up from the goblet, her green eyes serious now. "Oh, Devera, surely you have read Artor's words in the Book of Field and Furrow? Taking advantage of people is not the Artor-fearing way." Besides teaching Faraday the courtly graces, Merlion had also made sure her daughter received strict religious instruction.

Devera suppressed a small grimace. Faraday sounded a little too devout for her liking. Everyone at court genuinely feared the wrath of Artor, and most respected the Brother-Leader, but they generally only paid lip service to the

Seneschal. Devotion to the Seneschal's Way of the Plough was a trifle too peasantish for most court nobility—indeed, most Carlonites. Besides, many nobles resented the interference of the Seneschal in the political affairs of Achar. Faraday would have to drop the expressions of devoutness if she was to hold the interest of one of the better-looking courtiers. Devera assumed Earl Isend had brought Faraday to court and decked her out in such an exquisite dark-gold silk dress and fine pearls in order to find her a husband. Devera herself was betrothed to one of the younger sons of Baron Fulke and would be wedded within the month. She looked forward to the event with lustful impatience.

Well, if Faraday was devout, then perhaps her father could arrange an audience with the Brother-Leader for her. Devera indicated the white-haired and stooped old man one place down from the king's left hand. "Have you met the Brother-Leader yet, Faraday?"

Faraday turned her gaze back toward the royal table and the leader of the Seneschal. He looked as noble as any other at the table with his well-groomed (and nontonsured) hair, his gently waved and perfumed beard and rich clothes. He wore a massive emerald ring on his left hand, and wielded his napkin with as much grace as the king himself. He had a kindly, intelligent face, though he seemed preoccupied with some grave concern.

"No." Faraday hesitated a moment. "Does he come from the royal family itself, Devera?"

Devera snorted behind her gravy-stained napkin. "Not he, Faraday. No, Brother-Leader Jayme comes from an undistinguished farming family somewhere in the depths of Arcness. Knowing that province, he probably has more than a passing knowledge of pigs, although he hides it well now. He was appointed chaplain to the royal household a few decades ago—that's where he learned his manners. Jayme was . . . is . . . an ambitious man, and he learnt well at court. Well enough, I suppose, to be appointed Brother-Leader."

Faraday was dismayed at the sacrilegious way Devera talked about the Brother-Leader. "Devera, you must not speak ill of the Brother-Leader. The Brotherhood of the Seneschal elects the Brother-Leader—the royal household has no influence at all."

Artor! but the girl had a lot to learn about the intrigues of both court and Seneschal, Devera though dryly, and decided to steer the conversation away from religious matters. "What do you think of King Priam, Faraday?"

Faraday smiled and her face looked truly beautiful. "He's handsome, Devera." Her eyes twinkled impishly. "But such curls!"

Devera laughed despite herself. Priam had inherited the regal good looks of his family as well as their magnificent dark auburn hair, but it really was a trifle ridiculous for a man in his late forties to continue to have his hair curled so tightly.

"That must be his wife, Queen Judith." Faraday indicated a woman of ethereal and fragile beauty sitting between Priam and the Brother-Leader. As they watched, Priam leaned over attentively and gave her the choicest meats from his own plate.

"Yes. It's so sad. They say that Priam loves her dearly, but that she cannot have children. Every year of their marriage but the past two she has fallen pregnant, only to lose the babe in the fourth or fifth month. Now, perhaps, she is too old."

Both girls fell silent for a few minutes as they contemplated this supreme tragedy. The primary purpose of any noblewoman was to bear her husband sons as quickly as possible. No matter the dowry, the connections or the beauty that a woman brought to her marriage bed, her life became meaningless if she could not produce heirs. Faraday picked up a piece of cloudberry cheese and nibbled delicately at its edges, a line of worry appearing between her eyes. "It would be a tragedy if King Priam does not have any sons to follow him."

"Ah," Devera took a healthy sip of wine, "that would leave the way open for his closest living relative. Now tell me, if you can, do you know who that is?"

Her tone irritated Faraday. "His nephew, Duke Borneheld of Ichtar," she retorted.

Faraday had arrived at court only the day before and had yet to be introduced to the King and his family. If she knew names, faces as yet meant little to her. To her humiliation, Faraday could not place Borneheld's face among the three or four noblemen at the royal table she still could not identify. *Which* one was he?

Devera savored Faraday's embarrassed confusion for a moment, then inclined her head toward the man sitting immediately at Priam's right hand.

"Ah," Faraday breathed, for now that Devera had pointed him out she could see some resemblance. Borneheld had Priam's gray eyes and his hair was precisely the same shade of auburn, although dressed in a soldier's close crop rather than Priam's court curls. He was a man in the prime of his life, about thirty, and as solid as he might be, it was clear that his bulk was all muscle. If Priam was a courtier, then it was obvious that Borneheld was a warrior, his body honed by years in the saddle and wielding the sword. He looked a formidable man. Her mother had been remarkably silent on Priam's immediate family.

"Borneheld is the child of Priam's only sister, Rivkah, who married Borneheld's father Searlas, the previous Duke," Devera explained.

Faraday paused in her contemplation of Borneheld to glance back at Devera. For a moment she thought that there was some hesitation, or some darker shadow, behind Devera's words, but she couldn't quite put her finger on it. "So, if Priam has no children, Borneheld will become king."

Devera shrugged and took another sip of wine. "Probably, unless the other Earls and Barons decided to fight him for the privilege."

"But that would mean civil war! Are you suggesting that

our fathers would be so disloyal?" Faraday valued loyalty above most other virtues.

"Well, the prize would be worth it, wouldn't it," Devera snapped, the wine she had drunk making her tongue dangerously loose.

Faraday turned her head away and concentrated on the food before her. Perhaps it were best if she let Devera chat to the youth on her right for a time.

Some twenty silent minutes later, Faraday became aware of a man moving quietly through the shadows behind the great columns, then weaving sinuously between the crowded tables and the darting, anxious serving men and women. Occasionally he bent to speak to a person or two seated at the tables.

She watched him, fascinated by his unusual grace and the suppleness of his movement. He was moving toward the dais where the royal table stood, and she wondered if he were one of the nobles. Faraday was enthralled.

Finally he stepped into the main body of the chamber and Faraday had her first clear look at him; she took a quick, sharp breath of surprise. Not even Priam commanded the same presence that this man did.

He was still a relatively young man, perhaps some ten or eleven years older than herself, striking rather than handsome. This was due partly to his lithe grace, but also to the unusual alien cast of his features. His shoulder-length hair, drawn back into a short tail in the nape of his neck, and his close-shaven beard were the color of sun-faded harvest wheat, his eyes an equally faded blue—but as penetrating as a bird of prey's. He was tall and lean, and wore a uniform unlike any that Faraday had seen before, either in her home of Skarabost or here in Carlon. Over slim-fitting black leather trousers and riding boots, he wore a black, close-fitting hip-length tunic coat of cleverly woven wool. Even the trimmings and the raised embroideries down the sleeves of his tunic were black. The only relief was a pair of crossed golden axes embroidered across his left breast. As he stepped into the brilliance of the central chamber the entire effect was as if a panther had suddenly strolled out of a dark jungle into the sunlight of a glade.

"Devera!" she whispered.

Devera turned and looked in the same direction. "Ah," she said, in understanding. Faraday's reaction was the same as every woman's the first time they laid eyes on the BattleAxe. It was a reaction the BattleAxe was fully aware he created and, if in the mood, capitalized on.

She sighed and tapped Faraday's hand to get her attention as the BattleAxe weaved through the last few tables toward the royal dais. "That is Axis, BattleAxe of the Axe-Wielders."

The Axe-Wielders! The legendary military wing of the Seneschal! And this was their commander! No wonder he had caught her attention. Faraday hadn't even hoped to lay eyes on one of the Axe-Wielders while she was in Carlon, since they generally stayed close to the Tower of the Seneschal across Grail Lake.

Devera's lips twitched. It was a shame to disillusion Faraday about this man, but if she didn't do it, then someone else soon would.

"Faraday. Look at Priam for a moment, and tell me if you see a resemblance."

Faraday did as Devera asked. "Oh! They're related— they must be. They have the same distinctive hairline and forehead."

"Yes. They are related. Axis is also Priam's nephew and Borneheld's half-brother, and Borneheld is just as unlikely to acknowledge that fact as Priam is to acknowledge Axis as his nephew. For the royal family, Axis is the ultimate embarrassment."

Faraday frowned, wondering why her mother had not told her of this man, but she did not take her eyes from the BattleAxe. He had stopped to laugh for a moment with a lady of minor nobility sitting at one of the tables close to theirs, and she did not want to take her eyes from him while he was so close. "I don't understand," she said.

Devera settled back in her chair and smiled. The story of Axis' birth was well known in Carlon—although it was not widespread elsewhere—and it was not often that she had the opportunity to tell the deliciously scandalous tale of Rivkah's shame to someone who knew nothing about the affair.

"Axis is the illegitimate son of Rivkah, Priam's sister," she said bluntly, and her words were finally enough for Faraday to tear her gaze from Axis and look at Devera.

"Really!" she breathed.

"Yes," Devera nodded sagely. "Rivkah was married at an early age, younger than you are now, to the aging Searlas, Duke of Ichtar. Within a year she had produced a son, Borneheld. Searlas was pleased. While Rivkah had the young babe to occupy her, he left her at the fort of Sigholt in the Urqhart Hills, safe enough one would think, while he went on an extensive tour of the northern fortifications at Gorkenfort and the River Andakilsa. He was gone a year. When he returned to Sigholt it was to find that Borneheld had grown into a strong, one-year-old boy, and the Princess Rivkah was holding court at Sigholt with a bulging eight-month belly. Can you imagine the scandal? Even the stableboys knew of the pregnancy before Searlas did."

Faraday's curiosity would not let the next question lie. "Who was the father?"

Devera's blue eyes twinkled and her mouth curved mischievously. She tossed her curls and her breasts jiggled in their too-tight bodice. "No one knows, Faraday. Rivkah flatly refused to tell. She had not wanted to marry Searlas in the first place, and most people assumed that this was her way of ending the marriage. Well, Searlas was furious—as he had a right to be. He had believed that Rivkah would be safe at Sigholt—there is no garrison bolted tighter in Achar—and his suspicions immediately fell upon the garrison guard and servants. It is said that he had half of them tortured before he came out of his black rage. He had

Rivkah sent to the Retreat in Gorkentown far to the north in a futile effort to keep the birth secret. Futile, because news of the pregnancy had already reached Carlon and the entire court knew that Scarlas was not the father. The old king Karel, Priam and Rivkah's father, was equally livid. He told Searlas that he could do with Rivkah what he wanted. But in the end Searlas didn't have to do anything. Rivkah died in childbirth."

Faraday's eyes misted and she twisted her napkin in her lap. "Oh, how tragic!"

"Tragic my foot," Devera snorted. "It was the best thing that could have happened. Well, the best thing that could have happened was that the bastard child had died at birth as well, but that was not to be. Searlas flatly refused to acknowledge him. King Karel, and then Priam after him, refused to even mention Rivkah's name, much less acknowledge that her bastard son is of their blood."

"But who took care of the baby? What became of him?"

"Brother-Leader Jayme, then attached to the royal household, was at the Retreat in Gorkentown when the boy was born. He took the child into the Seneschal as his protégé, hoping that the boy would eventually take orders and become a reclusive brother attached to some retreat in a dusty corner of Achar. It seemed the best solution and relieved both the King and the Duke of Ichtar of an embarrassing problem. But Axis had no penchant for the Brotherhood, and every penchant for the sword and the axe. After training in arms at a noble household for several years Axis joined the Seneschal's Axe-Wielders when he was seventeen and, five years ago when Jayme was elected to the position of Brother-Leader, Axis received the appointment of BattleAxe from his patron. Jayme pretended not to see the horrified looks at court, arguing that despite his relative youth Axis was the perfect man for the job—which he has certainly proved to be. So now the court has to live with a royal bastard, who everyone hoped would fade into obscurity, holding one of the most elite military posts within Achar. Rivkah's shame refuses to go away."

Faraday looked at the Brother-Leader. "Ah, I had heard that Brother Jayme was a good and kind man, but this story is proof of it. To take a young babe no one else wanted and give him home and family. Artor bless him for that."

Axis noticed the young woman staring at him when he passed by her table but thought little of it. He stepped lightly onto the dais, keenly aware of the sudden tension his arrival had caused in many members of the royal table. He clenched his right hand into a fist above the golden axes on his left breast in the traditional salute of the Axe-Wielders and bowed low before Priam.

"My King, may Artor hold you in his care."

"As He may you, BattleAxe," Priam replied tersely.

Axis straightened from his bow and looked Priam directly in the eye. Sheer courtesy on the king's part should have made him offer Axis food and wine and a place at the royal table at this point; the position of BattleAxe was one of great honor within the realm. But Axis noted with some grim humor that the king's sense of courtesy was noticeably absent when dealing with his sister's bastard. Queen Judith fidgeted nervously with a tassel on her velvet sleeve, staring at a distant point across the chamber. Her dead sister-in-law's fecundity, whether in or out of marriage, was a continual reproach to her own barrenness.

"Your presence is most unexpected," Priam said, carefully folding his napkin and dabbing delicately at the corner of his mouth.

Axis' mouth twitched. "Obviously sire, for I see you have begun dinner without me."

Priam stiffened, slowly lowering the napkin to the table. "And what has brought you home from Coroleas so precipitously, BattleAxe?"

Axis had taken six cohorts of Axe-Wielders south into the neighboring empire of Coroleas over two months earlier to help the Coroleas with their eternal problem of vicious summer raiders from across the eastern seas. It was a mission with dual purpose, to strengthen the diplomatic ties between Achar and Coroleas and, more importantly to Axis, to continue giving his own Axe-Wielders vital combat experience. Axis had now taken his command south on seven different occasions to help the Coroleans with both sea-raiders and internal rebellions. These successful forays had earned Axis his reputation as a brilliant commander in just five short years.

But eight days before Axis had received an urgent message from Jayme asking him to bring himself and his Axe-Wielders home. The message had not said what was wrong, and Axis had fretted about it for the five days it had taken the ships carrying the Axe-Wielders to sail from Coroleas to the port of Nordmuth in Achar. He had left his Axemen to travel at a more leisurely pace from Nordmuth and ridden virtually nonstop to the Tower of the Seneschal, exhausting himself in the effort. Arriving late this afternoon, only to find that Jayme was attending Priam's nameday banquet across the Grail Lake in Carlon, Axis had cursed the extra time it took to cross the lake. He sincerely hoped Jayme hadn't called him home just to add his own good wishes to Priam's nameday celebrations.

"I but follow the Brother-Leader's orders, sire." Bland as it was the remark was designed to irritate Priam. For many hundreds of years the Acharite monarchs had chafed that the Axe-Wielders, as a wing of the Brotherhood of the Seneschal, remained under the supreme control of the Brother-Leader rather than the monarch. Axis risked a glance toward Borneheld. His half-brother was furious to see him here, and was gripping the stem of his golden wine goblet so hard Axis thought it might bend or snap at any instant. There was nothing but bitter enmity between the two brothers.

Axis looked back at Priam, thinking that the man's curls made him look effeminate and ineffectual. "Sire. May I say that the passing years only add to your elegance and majesty? Permit me to offer my congratulations on your nameday celebrations. I'm sure you must find it a great comfort to be surrounded by your entire family on this joyous occasion." He paused, his level gaze once more on Priam, calmly ignoring the white faces at his slight stress on the word "entire." "If I might have your leave to speak with the Brother-Leader, sire."

Priam stared at Axis, his entire body rigid, then took a deep breath and dismissed him with a curt wave of his hand.

Axis bowed again. "Furrow wide, furrow deep, sire."

"Wide and deep," Priam muttered stiffly as Axis bowed again and moved around the table to speak with Jayme privately.

Borneheld let out a furious breath and turned to Priam. "Why in Artor's name did Jayme have to recall him!"

Priam laid a restraining hand on Borneheld's arm and spoke quietly, repressing his own temper at the BattleAxe's remarks. "No matter, nephew. It is as well, perhaps, that he is here. The latest news from the north is not good and we may well have to use both his expertise and that of his Axe-Wielders."

It was not the most diplomatic thing to say to Borneheld. Although control of Achar's regular army was theoretically in Priam's hands, Borneheld was their day-to-day commander. He had dedicated his life to the sword and was a clever military theorist if a somewhat untested combat commander. Priam had recently awarded Borneheld the title of WarLord of Achar; many said more in recognition of his position as heir to the throne than his demonstrated skill as a commander. To suggest that Borneheld might require Axis' assistance to cope with the threat from the frozen wastes to the north of Gorkenfort was to throw salt into a gaping wound. The Axe-Wielders followed Axis with a loyalty, a devotion and a single-mindedness that Borneheld both coveted and resented. Borneheld wanted nothing more than to see the Axe-Wielders disbanded and incorporated into his own command. But he could do nothing. And meantime he watched the reputation of the Axe-Wielders flower under the leadership of Axis. Because of their time spent fighting in the Corolean Empire, they had accumulated more real combat experience in five years than Borneheld had managed in fourteen years. It did not help that, while Borneheld was not an ill-featured man, it was Axis who had inherited most of his mother's (and perhaps father's) style and striking looks.

Yet of all the hatreds Borneheld bore Axis, it was the fact they shared the same mother that he resented the most. Even though Rivkah had betrayed both her husband and her elder son in conceiving and giving birth to a lover's child, Borneheld still revered her memory. And Axis had killed her. *Axis* had taken Rivkah away from Borneheld. Borneheld daily cursed Axis for causing his mother's death. One day, Borneheld thought viciously, he would meet this bastard brother of his in combat, and then the world would see once and for all who was the better man. Artor would judge who had better right to live. The stem of his goblet finally bent and it spun out of Borneheld's hand and onto the floor.

A servant scurried to replace it with another and mop up the mess, and for an instant Borneheld met Axis' eyes across the head of Priam and Judith. The hatred between them was naked enough for any to see.

Jayme gently touched Axis' arm and drew his attention away from Borneheld. He spoke quietly so that no one else would hear.

"My son, I am pleased and relieved that you managed to travel so quickly from Coroleas. I hardly dared expect you so soon."

Axis smiled at Jayme, his dislike of Borneheld fading before the gentle face of the Brother-Leader. "We were close to the Corolean Sound when your message reached me, Father." The title was one of deep respect tinged with some gratitude. Apart from his command, no one else accepted him the way the Brotherhood did. "It was relatively easy for us to extricate ourselves and put to sea for Achar."

The Coroleans had been angry to see them go when the threat from the sea-raiders had been at its worst but Axis' charm had smoothed diplomatic relations.

"Axis," Jayme said quietly, "nothing can be accomplished tonight. We cannot talk here and you are exhausted. Come to my rooms in the eastern wing of the palace at sunrise tomorrow morning. We can share prayers and then talk. I think we shall both be summoned to Priam's presence later."

Axis was silent for a moment. "It is the news from the north, then?"

Jayme smiled at his protégé. Even in Coroleas the BattleAxe had managed to keep his lines of information open. "Yes, my son. But let us not discuss it here in whispers. Better left till the morning."

"Besides," Axis whispered loudly in a stage whisper, glancing along the table with amused eyes, "if I stay here any longer I'll sour the cream in the trifle."

Jayme pinched Axis' arm sharply, but his eyes smiled. "Rest well, BattleAxe. Furrow wide, furrow deep."

"Furrow wide, furrow deep, Father," Axis replied, and kissed the Brother-Leader's emerald ring before he straightened and moved to the edge of the dais. He paused and bowed briefly to Priam before making his way out of the room. As he went he glanced again at the young woman who had stared at him earlier. She blushed and turned away. A moment later, at a table some three or four removed from the royal dais, his eye caught that of one of the noblewomen, the Lady of Tare, and she inclined her head slightly, a smile hovering around her lips.

3

The Lady of Tare

Embeth, Lady of Tare, made her way carefully along the darkened corridors of the palace. Most of the revellers were still enjoying themselves in the Chamber of the Moons, but she had finally managed to escape; courtly etiquette had kept everyone in their seats until the king and queen left.

She had not expected to see Axis at the banquet and had felt a jolt of surprise and pleasure when she saw him. He wasn't due back from Coroleas until Frost-month. She was pleased he was here at the palace instead of the forbidding Tower of the Seneschal. There were few places for them to meet privately at the Tower, and few excuses for her to be there in the first instance.

Embeth was some eight years older than Axis, a good-looking woman in her late thirties. They had been friends since Axis, as an eleven-year-old youth, had been sent by the Seneschal to train in arms at her husband's household in Tare. She had been young then too, and pleased to have

the opportunity to make friends with the silent young boy.
As her children had come, Axis had been a companion to
them as well, and now one of her own sons, Timozel,
served under Axis in the Axe-Wielders.

Five years before her husband had died and the friendship between her and Axis had deepened until now they
were also occasional lovers. Occasional not only because
they rarely had the opportunity to meet, but also because of
Axis' birth; Rivkah's shame clung close to her son as well.
The Lady of Tare had a reputation to protect for she was
still young enough to remarry and give another man sons.
Those rare nights they spent as lovers were accomplished
only with extreme secrecy—and were the sweeter, perhaps, because of it.

Embeth had not brought a candle with her, trusting that
the occasional lamp along the corridors would prove sufficient light. She lifted her skirts clear of the floor to prevent
them rustling, glad she had chosen her black silk for the
feast. She shivered a little in the cool night air, or perhaps it
was because she was drawing closer to Axis' room.

Thank Artor that as BattleAxe he warranted his own
room in the palace and was not sleeping in the barracks
with the common soldiers. Embeth smiled to herself a little
in the dim light—would she still have tried to sneak into
his bed in the barracks? She pictured herself being discovered in a room full of common soldiers in the dead of night
with her gown unlaced and her breasts bared, and just managed to repress her laughter.

Suddenly Embeth was caught from behind, a strong arm
pinning her around her waist, and a hand planted firmly
across her mouth to prevent her crying out. For a moment
she stiffened in shock, then she relaxed back against the
man who held her. She would know the feel of his hands
and the smell of him even in the darkest pit of the After-
Life. Axis.

"You walked right past my room," he whispered in her
ear, his breath warm against her cheek. "I wondered if

perhaps you had another assignation further along the corridor." He felt her lips smile against the palm of his hand.

He pulled her gently back a few steps until they reached a closed door. It opened silently with the pressure of his shoulder, and they stepped through into a plain chamber; Priam's palace steward had instructions not to allocate his king's bastard nephew a grander chamber in the main wing of the palace. After the door latched closed behind them, Embeth twisted in his arms and rested against his chest. They stood silently, holding each other, their deep friendship more important for the moment than desire.

Finally Embeth pushed herself back and looked carefully at Axis' face in the dim candlelight of the room. "You look exhausted, Axis. How far have you ridden?"

Axis grimaced and let her go, turning to pour them some wine. "From Nordmuth. Three days ago."

Embeth accepted the wine he gave her and took a small sip. From Nordmuth to Carlon was an exceptionally hard ride, and circumstances would have to be extreme to make Axis push himself and his horses like that. Axis' sudden reappearance when he should have stayed in Coroleas for another six weeks confirmed the rumors that something was gravely wrong. Embeth felt a pang of fear for Timozel. If Axis was involved then the trouble would also involve his command.

She turned away and walked a few steps into the small bedchamber. Axis had dumped his saddlebags and gear in one corner and Embeth resisted the urge to straighten things out. His small traveling harp, never far from his side, was set to one side of the bed. His axe, symbol of the Seneschal and of the Axe-Wielders themselves, was propped up against the far wall. But Axis, like most Axe-Wielders, also carried a sword and considered that his main weapon. It lay close to hand in its scabbard, which was slung over the bedhead. Embeth wondered how many men he had killed with it. How many men the Brother-Leader had ordered him to destroy in the name of Artor and the Plough. She loved and respected Axis, but she was more than a little in awe of his position as BattleAxe within the Seneschal, and more than a little scared of the power of the Seneschal and its Brother-Leader.

"Then the news is not good," she said softly, "if you had to ride back that far and that fast."

Axis walked up behind her and gently rubbed the back of her neck with his hand, marveling at how soft her skin was and how silky-slippery her glossy brown hair. "I know little, Embeth. I'm sure court rumor is about as accurate as me at this stage."

Embeth doubted that very much, but understood his reticence. Axis rarely talked about his position as BattleAxe and never talked about where and to what his duties led him. She let her head relax back against his gently massaging fingers. "Did Timozel do well in Coroleas, Axis?"

"Timozel continues to do well, my Lady of Tare, and you should be proud of him. If Ganelon," Embeth's dead husband, "were alive he would be proud of him also. Timozel grows tall," he kissed the back of Embeth's neck, "and strong," another kiss, "and wiser with each passing week." Axis slowly turned Embeth around and softly kissed her mouth. "He should be arriving back in Carlon with the other Axe-Wielders in two or three days time. But right now, my Lady of Tare, I fear I am far too exhausted to talk anymore."

Axis always found it hard talking of Timozel to Embeth. What would he tell her if Timozel ever found himself skewered on the wrong end of five handspans of sharpened steel? *How* would he tell her? He forced his mind away from the terrible image.

He was caught, unable to move, trapped by the thick hatred that seethed across the blackness and distance between them. He writhed desperately, trying to free his pinned arms and legs, frantic to run from the horror that drew closer with each breath he took.

"No," he whispered, "no . . . go away . . . no . . . I don't want you. You are not my father. Go away."

But the evil, disgusting presence only drew closer. In a few moments he knew that he would be able to smell its putrid breath. He gave up fighting to free himself and instead lay panting heavily, knowing he should garner his strength for the fight ahead.

"Go away!" he whispered again hoarsely.

It approached. He could feel it circling in the dark, could feel its loathsome presence.

"Axis, my son." Axis shuddered violently as the voice slithered through the dark spaces between them.

"No!" Axis whispered again. All he could feel from the other presence was hatred.

"My son," the voice repeated. "You should never have been allowed to reach birth. You are an abomination. You should have been aborted. You killed your mother . . . your beautiful mother."

The voice drooled over the word "beautiful," and Axis almost vomited with fear and loathing.

"Your *beautiful* mother. She died because of you, my son. You tore her apart. She cursed you in the end, you know, as you tore her apart. She swore she would drown you when she could finally get her hands on you. But you killed her first. She died with her life blood draining all over you. What a fiery baptism!" The voice rasped at its own joke in a ghastly parody of laughter, and its mad chuckles surrounded Axis like choking smoke.

He was crying now, crying because of the pain he had caused his mother, crying because she had cursed him, crying because he had never known her.

"I never wanted you, my son. If I had known she was pregnant I would have torn you from her body myself."

"You are not my father!" Axis cried, desperate not to believe it, but scared to the depths of his soul that this unspeakable voice was indeed his father. The muscles of his arms and legs bulged as they fought to escape the pressure of the invisible, magical bonds that bound him, but he re-

mained trapped . . . trapped in this dark unknowable space with his father. A father who hated him.

"You destroyed your mother, as you will destroy everyone about you. No one wants you, Axis, no one loves you. *You* should be dead instead of your beautiful mother."

Scores of dreadful red-hot teeth nibbled at his flesh, tearing strips of skin and muscle away from his body. Not enough to kill quickly, but enough to torture slowly to death. Axis battled with his sanity.

"See here," the voice soothed, suddenly solicitous, "my friends will help you. Tasty, tasty." The voice hardened with hate. "You are an abomination, Axis, you deserve to die. I have come to do what should have been done while you swam in your mother's womb. Tear you apart . . . piece by piece."

Axis lost control at that point, as he always did, and screamed. It was the only way he knew to escape.

The scream reverberated about the small chamber and brought Embeth out of her slumber with her heart in her mouth. She sat up and twisted around to Axis, who was rolling about on the bed, covered in sweat, his hands gripping the mattress.

"No," he whispered, his eyes wide open and staring at something that Embeth could not see, "you are not my father!"

Embeth's heart almost broke. She seized his shoulders, although his violent motions almost threw her off, and shook as hard as she could.

"Axis! *Axis!* Wake up. Wake up . . . it's all right, my love, it's all right . . . wake up!"

She remembered these dreams from the time he had first come to stay with her and Ganelon as an eleven-year-old. Once or twice a month they had punctuated his sleep, waking both her and Ganelon even though he was bedded down in the attic of their manor house.

But they had never been this bad . . . and she thought he

had grown out of them. "Axis," she cried desperately one more time, taking a hand from his shoulders and striking his face. *"Wake up!"*

Finally he was awake and out of whatever horror had gripped him. He grabbed Embeth's arms, startled, still desperately afraid, not knowing for a time who she was or where he was.

"Axis," she murmured, cradling his head against her breasts, "it's all right, it's all right, my love. I am here now, I am here."

Axis wrapped his arms about her as tightly as he dared, clinging to the love she represented. For a few moments they rocked back and forth on the bed, the one gently comforting, the other trying to reestablish some grip on sanity.

Tears streamed down Embeth's face as she gently stroked Axis' hair. "Shush," she crooned, feeling the fear wrack his shoulders, "shush." After a few minutes Axis pulled away and lay back against the disarranged bedclothes. Embeth said nothing, thinking it better that he speak first.

Eventually Axis took her hand. "Thank you for being here," he said softly, and Embeth wondered how many nights he had woken up to face this horror himself.

"It is the same dream you had as a child," she prodded.

He breathed deeply. "Yes. The same, but it has grown worse over the past few months. Infinitely worse."

He paused and Embeth stroked his face, feeling the sweat of fear starting to dry on his forehead and in his beard.

"Why does he hate me so much?" he asked no one in particular. "Why? I never asked to be born. How can it be my fault? Embeth?"

"Yes?" Fleetingly, Embeth thought Axis might tell her of his dream. Even as a child he had kept its details hidden from her, no matter how hard she probed.

Axis turned his head so he could look directly at her. He had been going to ask her if she had ever felt as if she were about to die during childbirth, and, if so, if she had ever blamed the child that was tormenting her body with pain. But just as he was about to speak the words he found he couldn't ask. To do that would be to reveal that every day of his life he lived with the guilt of killing his own mother. His beautiful mother.

Embeth watched the change come over his face, saw his face close over and knew that he needed to be on his own now. Axis had lived so much of his life unwanted by his own family that he found it hard to accept that others could love him for himself.

Embeth kissed his forehead a last time then slithered out of his bed, finding her clothes on the floor where she had discarded them. She dressed quickly in the chill early morning air, and wound her hair back on top of her head in a rough knot that would stand a cursory inspection by any curious eyes.

Axis lay still on the bed watching her, grateful that she had asked no more questions and that she recognized his need to be alone. Before she left Embeth paused by the bed, not touching him.

"Let me know if you need me again," she murmured, "and I will come."

He nodded, and Embeth smiled briefly, sadly. Without another word or look she turned and slipped quietly from the room.

Axis was left alone in the dark.

4

At the Foot of the Fortress Ranges

The two women sat closely together in the cold air, their plain woollen wraps tight about their shoulders, watching the sky begin to lighten over the Fortress Ranges. They had been sitting talking most of the night, and each knew they would have to move soon so that the younger could be back in her bed undiscovered by dawn.

The older woman turned her eyes from the sky. She had fine features, and such incredibly thick and wavy hair that it threatened to break free of the pins holding it protesting in its coil. From the widow's peak on her forehead a startling swathe of gold, two-fingers wide, ran back through her silvery hair. She smiled gently at the younger woman, who had risked a lot to meet her here tonight.

"You are very generous to offer to help us, my dear."

The younger woman looked at her companion. "You still do not trust me."

The older woman's eyes were as sooty-gray as the smoke from a damp wood fire. They held as many sparks, too. "You understand the reasons for that, surely."

The young woman sighed and rubbed her arms. "Yes. I do. But what can I do to make you trust me? What?"

"Trust cannot be bought, or hurried. It always takes time."

"But you do not have time."

The silver-haired woman paused. "We've never had enough time, Azhure. We have never had enough space. We have never had enough respect. And though we need the help of people like you, we must remain wary."

Disappointed at the rebuff, Azhure turned and waved her hand toward the distant village. "They hate anything they do not understand. It is the Way of the Plough."

The older woman rested a hand on Azhure's arm comfortingly and said, her voice filled with sadness, "I know, Azhure, I know."

"GoldFeather, you *must* trust me. Please! You desperately need help with the children."

GoldFeather shook her head slowly, resigned. "No, Azhure. It is too late. The only one that can save us from the Destroyer is lost and cannot be found. The Sentinels do not yet walk the land and Tree Friend has yet to be found. Soon winter comes. Ice will come to claim us. Tencendor cannot fight divided."

Her eyes glittered with tears. "You must return to your home before it is too late. Sing well and fly high, Azhure, and may you find some kind of peace in this most treeless of lands." She leaned forward and kissed Azhure's pale cheek.

5

In the Palace of the King

Axis lay awake for another hour after Embeth left, then, as the sky began to lighten toward dawn, cursed silently and stood up. He still felt exhausted. He'd only had an hour or two of sleep before the nightmare had claimed him and he'd needed a good eight or nine after the hard ride.

He splashed himself with cold water to rid himself of the stale sweat of his nightmare and dressed silently in the dark, not bothering to light a candle. He dreaded what Jayme might tell him this morning.

Jayme was already up and at prayer when Axis slipped into his quarters. The Brother-Leader was kneeling at the altar in his room, praying before an exquisite silver and gold icon of Artor the Ploughman. Axis knelt quietly behind him and bowed his head in prayer, trying to find some ease of mind in the rhythms of the ancient words and rituals. But prayers could not comfort him this morning, not after the nightmare he had endured, and after a few minutes his thoughts drifted to the daily problems of commanding a force of four thousand men.

A little later Axis realized Jayme was standing beside him, his hand resting comfortingly on his shoulder. He sighed inwardly—Jayme's interruption had distracted him from calculating the logistics needed to move six cohorts of Axe-Wielders from Nordmuth to Carlon.

"My son, you must not pray so devoutly, otherwise it might be said that the BattleAxe is more devout than the Brother-Leader . . . and we cannot have that."

Axis smiled and gripped Jayme's hand as it lay on his shoulder. "I find great comfort in prayer, Father, but there is no man who serves Artor more reverently and faithfully than you."

Jayme helped Axis to his feet and the two men embraced warmly, Jayme touching Axis' forehead briefly in blessing. "Well, at least I've managed to impress someone!" he said. "Come, I have fruit and bread, and some delicious fresh warm milk sent up for us to break fast with." Jayme had arranged their breakfast at a small table by a window overlooking the twisting streets of Carlon far below the palace.

The sun was just beginning to rise above the horizon and, although thick snow clouds blanketed much of the sky, a few rays managed to catch the glittering rooftops of the city's buildings. Jayme turned and looked out across the beautiful view for a moment, watching the myriad of colorful pennants and banners snap in the stiff breeze. What fruit trees there were in the city waved their bare branches at the sky. They had lost their leaves weeks earlier. Axis noticed that Jayme's face seemed older and more tired in the early morning light, and he wondered how haggard he looked himself.

Jayme's tone turned serious as soon as they seated themselves. "Axis, you probably know something of what is happening in the north."

"Something, but mostly rumor."

Jayme was silent a moment longer, then he sighed. "Unfortunately, Axis, much of what you've heard is probably more truth than not. Gilbert and Moryson will give you exact military details later, and I have yet to hear what Priam's intelligence is, but let me tell you what I know."

For the next twenty minutes or so, while Axis ate his breakfast, his chewing becoming slower with each passing minute, Jayme outlined what he knew.

"So, my BattleAxe," Jayme finished with a sad smile, "are your Axemen ready to face unbodied wraiths that can kill the most experienced soldier?"

Axis put down the piece of bread he had been turning over and over in his hand. What he had heard horrified him. Lord Magariz was an exceptional commander and his Gorkenfort units were among the best in Achar. If he was losing men in this manner then the situation was more than serious.

"Is there a possibility that the events of last winter were isolated, Father?"

Jayme frowned. "The Forbidden, or whatever they are, are starting to move south. Last winter . . ."

"Last winter they were simply probing," Axis finished for him, speaking slowly, thinking it out. "This winter there is every possibility that they will come in force."

"Yes," Jayme nodded. "I think so, and so, I believe, do Priam and Borneheld. These past few weeks they've been as jumpy as cats. Borneheld travelled to Gorkenfort over the summer months to assess the situation for himself. Now he is starting to move large units of infantrymen and cavalry north; for the past ten days all the merchant rowing transports on the River Nordra have been busy with men and armor rather than grain. And, as the good brothers of Gorkentown reported, the mood is not good. Nor is it here in Carlon. Even the traditional drunken revelry in the streets following the public nameday banquet for Priam was less than enthusiastic last night. Men preferred to return to their wives rather than take advantage of other, um, offers. And over the past week or so my brothers in the city and surrounding districts have been performing more marriages than usual. Those soldiers moving north are making sure their affairs are in order."

Axis' face was grim. "Will Priam and Borneheld ask for our help?"

"If it truly is the Forbidden that they face . . . then they'll have to." He paused a moment. "Axis, I am more than pleased you managed to return to Achar so quickly. I have a feeling that we will need you desperately over the coming months."

Axis met Jayme's eyes above the remains of breakfast. After a moment both men looked back out over the city view. At first Axis had been puzzled by Jayme's insistence on eating breakfast by the window when the warm fire beckoned, but as he gazed out he realized that Jayme had probably wanted him to have a good look at the weather. DeadLeaf-month was too early by eight weeks for heavy snowclouds.

6

In the King's Privy Chamber

Priam had requested that Jayme and Axis meet him in his Privy Chamber mid-morning, and Moryson accompanied them, to advise the Brother-Leader and swell the numbers of the Seneschal.

The Privy Chamber was one of the largest chambers in the royal palace, smaller only than the Chamber of the Moons. It was lit by narrow windows high in walls which sported as their only decoration the nine standards of the major provinces of Achar. At the center of the chamber sat a massive round table that, according to legend, was made from a single section of an immense oak tree which had stood on the site of the palace many hundreds of years before.

The moment they stepped into the stone chamber the three men sensed the tension among those present. There were five men sitting at the table, Priam, Borneheld, Earl Isend of Skarabost, Duke Roland of Aldeni and Earl Jorge of Avonsdale. Behind Borneheld stood his lieutenant, Gautier, while Duke Roland's lieutenant, Nevelon, stood behind his lord's chair. There were no servants in the Council chamber—unusual, because normally Priam had at least one clerk present to record the discussions and decisions of the King's Privy Council. Nor was this a full meeting of the Privy Council, which normally contained the nine lords of the provinces and their advisers. The significance of those who were present was not lost on either Jayme or Axis. Borneheld, Duke of Ichtar and WarLord of Achar; the darkly handsome but foppish Earl Isend and the bulky Duke Roland, the lords of the two provinces that lay directly below Ichtar; and the wiry and gray-headed Earl Jorge, a cunning and experienced campaigner with a lifetime of advice to give. This was nothing less than a war council consisting of the most senior commanders in Achar as well as those lords whose provinces would be most affected by any incursions into Ichtar.

Isend and Roland looked visibly relieved to see them enter, as though the previous few minutes had been spent in uncomfortable silence. Borneheld looked darkly resentful at Axis' presence, Jorge looked impatient, and Priam looked so haggard that Axis wondered if night-demons were invading his sleep as well.

Priam nodded at Jayme and Axis and waved them toward two chairs. Moryson stood a few feet behind his Brother-Leader's chair, waiting to be called upon if needed.

Jayme inclined his head toward Priam. "My apologies if we have kept you waiting, Priam." As spiritual leader of Achar, Jayme felt he was the King's equal and rarely accorded him his title, something that grated with Priam.

Borneheld broke in before Priam could speak. "Is it necessary for the Brother-Leader's lackies to attend this Council, sire?"

"Borneheld, the BattleAxe is here at my invitation, and I have no objection if Moryson stays," Priam said, passing a hand over his reddened eyes. Now that Axis was closer he could swear that Priam had hardly slept the previous night. His face had deep lines carved from nose to mouth, his auburn curls hung loose and unattended, and his clothes had the look of garments hastily thrown on simply to avoid nakedness. Not the fastidious Priam's normal appearance. Axis grew more apprehensive.

Priam took a deep breath and sat up in his high-backed chair, his hands splayed out on the table before him, his eyes studiously avoiding those of the other men about the table.

"Let us begin, and let us not waste words," he said quietly. "We all know of the troubles in the northern-most regions of Ichtar, and the reported sightings of the Forbidden by the villagers of Smyrton near the Forbidden Valley. Lord Magariz lost close to ninety good men while on patrol from Gorkenfort this past winter. Whatever attacked them has also devastated the Ravensbundmen. Over the past six months many thousands of them have been moving into northern Ichtar through Gorken Pass. Whatever we may think of the Ravensbundmen—"

"Carrion-eating barbarians," Earl Jorge muttered.

"—we know they are not cowards." Priam finished, as though he had not been interrupted. "Attacks on patrols have eased over the past months, have they not, Borneheld?"

Borneheld nodded. "I heard from Magariz last week. Over summer, such as it was, he lost only three men. But over the past two weeks the number of Ravensbundmen moving down from the north has increased dramatically. At the same time the weather is deteriorating badly in the north. Perhaps coincidence, perhaps not."

"And now winter stands before us again." Axis said quietly. He looked up from the table where his fingers had been idly tracing the ancient whorls in the wood.

Borneheld stared at him as Priam spoke again, his voice stronger. "Borneheld, you are the only one of us who has been to Gorkenfort. We would appreciate your understanding of what is going on there."

Borneheld shifted in his chair and deliberately addressed his answer to every man at the table but Axis. "No man has seen anything like this before. A foe who lives and breathes the winter, who has no form or substance, who advertises his presence only with a whisper on the wind. A foe who laughs at naked steel and who has no respect for the bravery of soldiers. A foe who apparently despises a clean kill and who prefers to inflict as much pain as possible; harrying his victim over hours, watching him bleed to death by degrees rather than killing with a clean stroke. The Ravensbundmen say that it feeds as much off its victims' fear as it does off their flesh. What is it we face? I do not know. All I know is that, no matter the skill, bravery and determination of those who have faced it, no one has ever killed one of them. If they ever come in force, Artor help us."

Earl Isend shifted in his seat. "You've been sending more soldiers to Gorkenfort over the past weeks, Borneheld."

"Yes. I have to anticipate that they'll come back with the winter snows."

Priam slowly rested his face in his hands on the table, and Axis glanced worriedly at him, but Priam looked up after a moment. His eyes looked even worse. "Do you think these creatures are the Forbidden?" he asked Jayme. "Is this what we face?"

Axis had never seen Jayme look lost for words, but he did so now. "I am embarrassed to say that I do not know, Priam. It has been so long, a thousand years, since they were penned behind the Fortress Ranges and in the Icescarp Alps. Most of the ancient lore regarding them has been lost or is hidden in riddles. But if you want an answer, then, yes, I am afraid to the very depths of my being that these are the Forbidden. What else *could* they be?"

"Achar, *Ichtar*, stands in dire peril and you sit there and weep and wail and say, very sorry, but it's been too long! You can't remember! Then tell me, Brother-Leader," Borneheld snarled, half rising out of his seat as he leaned menacingly across the table, "of what use are you when it is my men dying out there in the snow? Do you think mumbled platitudes will stop the Forbidden? Have *they* forgotten exactly what it is they hunt?"

Jayme flinched, but waved Axis back as he started to rise from his chair. "I feel as frustrated as you do, Borneheld, and I can only assure you that I and the entire Seneschal will do everything in our power to assist you."

Even Axis, much as he hated to admit it to himself, felt the inadequacy of Jayme's reply. Moryson shifted slightly behind his Brother-Leader as if he meant to step forward in Jayme's defense, but thought better of it as Borneheld glared at him.

Priam held a hand in the air. "There is more I have to tell you, and I have found it hard to find the courage to speak of it."

Every eye in the chamber fixed itself on the King.

Priam stared straight ahead, avoiding eye contact, his features looking even more ravaged. "In the early hours of this morning I received intelligence from Gorkenfort. A message, flown down by carrier bird." Priam glanced at Borneheld, who looked surprised. "Yes, I know Borneheld, normally you would have received such a message, but the contents were so," Priam paused and his face visibly paled, "terrible, that it was addressed to me personally."

Roland and Jorge exchanged glances. Terrible news received almost nine hours ago? Why had Priam waited this long to call them together?

"My friends," and now everyone in the room felt dread pierce their heart, for Priam had never addressed them so before, "four nights ago both Gorkenfort and the Retreat in Gorkentown suffered devastating attacks from creatures such as no one has ever seen before."

Both Borneheld and Jayme leaned forward as Priam continued. "Lord Magariz was attacked personally in his quarters. He escaped but was severely wounded and several of his guards were torn to shreds."

"But how?" Borneheld's face was a mask of confused anger. "Gorkenfort is impregnable. How could anyone have attacked Magariz in his quarters with no alarm sounding?"

"There is worse," Priam whispered, and Axis felt a finger of ice trace through his bowels.

"It appears that the attack on Magariz was only a blind for the real attack—a ruse to keep the garrison's attention focused inward. A much stronger force overran the Seneschal's Retreat in Gorkentown."

Jayme groaned and gripped the top of the table. If these creatures had penetrated into the heart of the highly defended Gorkenfort, then what they could have done in the brothers' Retreat horrified him.

Priam looked at Jayme. "Brother-Leader, I am most sorry, but most of the brothers were slaughtered as they sought to flee. Only two escaped with their lives. The carnage was . . . terrible." He fell silent for a moment.

"But that's not all." Priam's voice dropped to a whisper and his face blanched to a sickly yellow. "It appears that these creatures had two specific purposes in attacking the Retreat. They completely destroyed all the books and records of the Retreat, although that was not their first or main target." Jayme's head sank down to rest on the table and his shoulders shuddered once, heavily. "First . . . first," Priam's voice almost broke, and he had to clear his throat; Jayme pushed himself back upright and stared at Priam. "First, they broke into the crypt of the Retreat and . . . stole . . . my . . . sister's . . . body. They stole Rivkah's body. Then they desecrated her tomb with their excrement and the blood and entrails of those brothers they had slaughtered."

Apart from Priam and Borneheld, all eyes in the room swivelled toward Axis then, an instant later, swivelled away again. Rivkah had been buried in the crypt of the Retreat after she had died giving birth to Axis.

Jayme and Moryson exchanged shocked, silent glances as Priam spoke, but Jayme recovered himself enough to turn to Axis and lay a warm hand on his arm. "My son, I am so sorry," he said quietly.

So closely was Axis associated with his mother that for a

moment no one remembered that Rivkah was Borneheld's mother as well.

They were quickly reminded. As soon as the words were out of Priam's mouth Borneheld leapt to his feet, his chair clattering to the floor behind him. His hand automatically reached for his sword, until halfway there he remembered that he had left it in the antechamber.

"They stole my mother!" he screamed, his eyes wild, his hand still half-raised.

Axis felt as though Priam's news had driven a sword through his soul. He was stunned, and for an instant was propelled back into that black nothingness where the demon who claimed to be his father tormented him. He stared sightlessly ahead, oblivious to Borneheld's reaction, but after a moment he half turned his head toward Jayme and gropingly placed his own hand on top of the Brother-Leader's where it rested on his arm. "It's all right," he murmured.

Borneheld, still with one hand raised, took a step toward his half-brother. "It's all right?" he whispered incredulously, his face slowly turning dark red. "Is that how you react to the news that some demon-spawned fiends have stolen my mother's body? Is that all you can say?"

He kicked his chair away from his feet and took a step toward Axis. "Is that all you can say when it was you who killed her and put her in that stone tomb?" he screamed, and lunged around the table past Jayme, grabbing Axis by the throat and driving him to the floor of the chamber.

As the others leapt to their feet Jorge and Gautier dragged Borneheld away while Nevelon held Axis back. Both men had taken punishment, although Axis, at a disadvantage of weight and muscle, came out of it slightly worse. He managed to regain control of himself though and shrugged off Nevelon's restraining hands, dusting down his tunic coat and wiping some blood from his mouth with the back of one hand. He looked across at Borneheld who had blood streaming from a cut above his eye.

"At least Rivkah loved and respected my father enough

not to betray him," Axis said quietly, his eyes blazing fiercely as they locked with Borneheld's. "Would that your father had received such love and respect from our mother."

His quiet words sent Borneheld into a frenzy, and it was all that Jorge and Gautier could do to hold him back from attacking Axis a second time.

"By Artor!" snarled Roland, stepping between the two men, his massive flesh quivering with anger. "Is it not enough that we face this peril from the northern wastes? How can we face outside dangers when we tear ourselves to pieces within?" He turned to Borneheld and abruptly slapped him across the face, sending droplets of blood scattering across the floor. "Is this how a WarLord acts in the heat of battle? What will you do when your *foes* taunt you across the battlefield, if this is how you react in the King's Privy Council?"

Roland stared at Borneheld until Borneheld dropped his eyes and ceased to struggle against Jorge and Gautier. Then, belying his bulk, Roland whipped around to face Axis. "BattleAxe!" he snapped, and Axis straightened up from the wall, his gaze challenging. "Such a taunt belongs in the women's chamber, and if you have to resort to that level of remark among this company then perhaps that's where you belong!"

Axis' face hardened, but he held his tongue. Roland stepped back and glanced at both men. "Well. Enough. I would scarcely have expected this behavior from such high commanders. If you lead men, both of you, then you will have to learn a little more self-control. Am I right?"

There was silence for a moment, then Priam stepped forward. "I think the news was grim enough to make anyone lose their wits for a moment. But the Duke of Aldeni speaks wisely, and I am glad that at least one cool head remains in this room. I fear that over the next few months we will have news as bad or worse, and I think that we should all make the decision now to meet whatever the future holds for us united with all the courage and resourcefulness that we can muster. Now, perhaps we can retake our seats."

After a moment's awkward silence, Moryson stepped forward hesitantly. "Sire, if I might speak?" Priam nodded.

"Sire, has there been any report about what kind of creature attacked both Gorkenfort and the Retreat?"

"Yes. The two brothers who managed to escape the slaughter in the Retreat and several guards who rushed to Magariz's quarters related what they saw. Magariz was attacked by creatures no one has seen previously, or at least lived to report seeing, while three more of these same creatures led the attack on the Retreat."

Duke Roland wheezed and grunted as he shifted uncomfortably in his chair. "And these strange creatures are . . . ?"

"Large creatures, as large as the wraiths but far more substantial. Taller than a man, but man-shaped. They appeared to be made of old bones held together by yellowish ice; with very little actual flesh. Each had a skull of a strange tusked beast for a head, their eyes silvery orbs, beaks instead of mouths. Leathery wings tipped with talons. Frightening creatures. Huge raking claws for hands. And odd bits of white fur stuck over their bodies. Two led the attack on Magariz, three the attack on the Retreat."

"This is terrible," muttered Isend, "terrible." His dark eyes shifted nervously about the other men in the room.

"But what did they want, sire? Was it just—" Axis paused for a moment, choosing his words carefully, "the body, or was that just a random happenchance?"

Priam shook his head, his eyes haunted. "No. The two brothers who escaped the room where the creatures slaughtered most of the brothers said that they whispered Rivkah's name as they attacked. It was only after they had taken her body that they returned to the scriptorium and destroyed most of the books and records that were there."

Jayme and Moryson again exchanged glances. "And the brothers saw the creatures carry off her body?" Jayme asked.

"No," Priam replied. "They fled to a closet when the Retreat came under attack. They heard the creatures go down to the crypt, then up the stairs to the scriptorium. After destroying the scriptorium and its contents they feasted on the bodies of the brothers. Only after an hour's silence did the two left alive emerge to discover the complete carnage."

"Why?" whispered Borneheld. "Why?"

No one could answer him. Priam spread his hands helplessly. Jayme, his face as white as fine parchment, rested his head heavily in one hand. Jorge looked about him for a moment, then leaned forward, his voice low and intense, but growing louder and more angry with each word.

"I am dismayed by the reaction here in this room, and I am now old enough not to care if I insult each and every one of you in saying that. Is this a war council? Or is every last man of you like the young virgin who, when confronted by a rapist, knows not whether to run screaming or to smile politely and lift her skirts for the invasion?"

Jorge glared about the table, his gray eyebrows bristling with indignation. "Every one of you seems to have missed the point that the greater tragedy would have been if Magariz had been killed or taken. *Magariz* is the man who currently holds the fate of Achar in his hands. He is the one who, until he can be relieved, must hold these creatures back."

Jorge leaned still further across the table and stabbed his finger at each of the men sitting there. Now his voice was low and intense. "I am aware that Rivkah was either sister or mother to three of you and I am aware that the loss of the brothers upsets the Seneschal deeply. But Achar faces an unimaginable threat from an unknown foe. We cannot weep and wail over a body that is thirty-years' cold. Pull yourselves together! Act like men and the leaders of Achar that you are supposed to be!"

Jorge leaned back in his chair, his weather-lined face defiant. He was disgusted with the way Priam had acted. Priam was supposed to be the man to provide the leadership for the whole nation, but had instead sat in his chair and gone into a fugue over the loss of his sister's body. And as for Borneheld . . . he had always harbored doubts about Priam's wisdom in appointing the untested Borneheld as WarLord, and Borneheld's behavior today had only deepened them. Jorge shifted his gaze to Axis, who was relaxed back in his chair, his eyes half-lidded.

Jorge spoke again into the silence. "BattleAxe. What is the danger?" *Let me see just how good he is*, he thought to himself.

"You have said yourself," Axis replied calmly. "The danger is that Achar is about to be overrun by creatures whom we do not understand and who threaten to break through Gorkenfort's defenses. In a manner of speaking they have already done so."

"Yes," Jorge said, "and I think that—"

"And furthermore," Axis continued, over him, "*I* think that perhaps Gorkenfort is not the only flashpoint. One of the indications we had that these creatures would renew their attacks was the number of Ravensbundmen migrating down from the north during past weeks. Is it possible that the sightings of strangers about Smyrton, emerging from the Forbidden Valley, is another indication of the same thing? That the creatures who are pushing the Ravensbundmen from the north are also pushing the creatures of the forest south from the Shadowsward?"

Jorge nodded slowly. But Jayme looked anxious and concerned. "But Axis, are not the Forbidden in the Icescarp Alps and the Forbidden in the Shadowsward the same? Are they fighting among themselves?"

"Or is there something stranger still than the Forbidden, stronger than the Forbidden? More frightening than the Forbidden?" Roland asked.

"Damn it, we just don't know!" Jorge was angry with himself as much as anyone else. "We just have no idea what it is that we face. Now, what are we going to do about it?"

Borneheld slapped the table with his open hand, attracting everyone's attention. If he had lost his temper earlier, then he appeared cool and decisive now. "We move, and we move fast. Whether or not we face a threat from the Shadowsward or not I have yet to be convinced," he shot Axis a brief look of simmering ill-will, "but we do know that we face a threat from above Gorkenfort. If these creatures are wanting to move south through Ichtar then they will have to come through Gorken Pass, it is the only way past the River Andakilsa and the Icescarp Alps. There they will run straight into Gorkenfort. Earl Jorge speaks well. This young virgin is not going to run squealing, nor is she going to lift her skirts. We fight, and it is obvious that this winter the battle will be over Gorkenfort. I have moved many units, both of infantry and of cavalry, to Gorkenfort over the past few weeks. That will not be enough. I propose that as it can be organized, and I think it will only take a few days, I will move another seven thousand men to Gorkenfort. And I will move as many of them as I can the fast way. By ship through the Andeis Sea and then up the River Andakilsa."

"But those seas are unpredictable in autumn," said Priam.

"And would you have me move them the slow way, by rowboat up the Nordra and then by forced march across the plains of Ichtar? That journey will take close to six weeks and they will be exhausted when they get there. We need to move now, we need to move as fast as we can, and we need the men relatively fresh when we get there. If I commandeer as many ships as I can in Nordmuth then I could be there in under three weeks from the time we leave Carlon. It will take more than a week to organize the units and transport." Borneheld thought for a moment. "Myself and the greater part of the force can be at Gorkenfort ready to fight by mid to late Bone-month; the remainder of the force can go via the Nordra and be in Gorkenfort in early Frost-month, early Snow-month at the latest. *I* am ready."

Axis sat up straight and directed a level look at his halfbrother. "The Axe-Wielders also stand ready to defend Achar." He did not want anyone in this chamber to think that Borneheld commanded the only force capable of meeting the threat from the north.

Borneheld started to say something, but Jayme leaned forward and held up his hand. "No, BattleAxe. I think you are needed elsewhere. I am ashamed that I cannot provide Priam and Borneheld with the information that they need to fight these creatures. But there is one place where we might still find the information."

He glanced at Moryson, who nodded slowly. "The Silent Woman Keep."

There were nervous glances among several of the other men. Over the past forty generations few men, and certainly none in the room, had ever visited the Silent Woman Keep. The Keep stood solid and dark in the center of the only remaining forest in Achar, the Silent Woman Woods. Many whispered that although the Brotherhood of the Seneschal preached that all forests were evil, they allowed the Silent Woman Woods to remain simply to protect the secrets of the Silent Woman Keep. Few Acharites would ever willingly venture within leagues of the Silent Woman Woods. And no one professed any curiosity about the Silent Woman Keep or the small band of brothers who kept vigil there.

"Yes," Jayme agreed. "I suggest that you should reinforce the WarLord by all means, but do so by a circuitous route. Take the majority of the Axe-Wielders and travel to the Silent Woman Keep. Our brothers there have access to ancient records and chronicles from the time of the Wars of the Axe. Learn what you can about the Forbidden. From there, travel onto Smyrton via Arcness and Skarabost to assess the danger. Then," Jayme turned back to face Priam and Borneheld, "leave some of your Axe-Wielders at Smyrton and travel to Gorkenfort. Borneheld will need both your information and your men if the danger is as bad as it appears."

Borneheld's face darkened and he opened his mouth to say something, but he was interrupted by Priam. "A sensi-

ble plan, Jayme. We need to know more about these creatures."

Jorge nodded again. Sensible indeed. It kept Borneheld
and Axis apart for as long as possible before the likelihood
of real fighting in the north. Even going via the circuitous
route Axis could still be at Gorkenfort by the beginning of
winter. Winter would be the time these creatures struck in
force, if they kept to their previous pattern. And, if Artor
were with them, then Axis might also arrive with some information about exactly what it was that they faced. Hopefully, once Borneheld and Axis had a real foe to face they
would forget their private enmity.

Borneheld did not look so happy about the arrangement.
"Sire, my forces are perfectly capable of—"

Jayme broke in smoothly. "And, of course, when the
BattleAxe and the Axe-Wielders arrive in Gorkenfort, War-
Lord, they will be under your command."

An expression of deep contentment filled Borneheld's
broad face. "Yes," he said. "Yes. That would be satisfac-
tory. I'm sure that I'll be able to use your men somewhere,
BattleAxe. And yourself, of course."

Axis turned to Jayme, a look of angry incredulity over
his face. The cloth he had been using to wipe his lip was
clenched tightly in his fist. "Brother-Leader—"

Jayme took Axis' arm. "We have much to discuss in private, BattleAxe. Let it rest." His painful grip belied his genial face.

Axis took a deep breath and sat back in his chair, avoiding Borneheld's triumphant gaze, his mouth white and
pinched. He would rather burn in the everlasting fire pits of
the AfterLife before he handed control of the Axe-Wielders
over to Borneheld.

"So," Priam said, relieved that some decisions had been
made, "then we have at least made a start. Roland, Jorge, I
can count on you to support Borneheld with troops, supplies, and perhaps your own persons and advice? Good.
Gentlemen, if we can adjourn for the moment? I'm sure

that each of us has enough to keep us busy. Furrow wide, furrow deep, and may Artor guide our steps over the coming weeks and months."

As the group left the room, Earl Isend caught up with Borneheld and tweaked his elbow. "Duke Borneheld, if I may speak with you for a moment?"

Borneheld pulled his elbow away roughly, annoyed, and walked a little faster. He did not like the foppish Earl Isend very much.

Isend wet his lips nervously and struggled to keep step with Borneheld as he strode down the corridor. "Duke Borneheld? It is about my daughter . . . Faraday."

Borneheld stopped abruptly and turned to look at Isend, a speculative gleam in his eye. He'd taken particular note of Faraday when she had been presented to Priam the night before. Most men in the Chamber of the Moons had.

7

In the Brother-Leader's Palace Apartment

Axis retrieved his axe from the antechamber outside the Privy Chamber and fell into step behind Jayme and Moryson, his anger and resentment at Jayme's decision increasing with every stride. Why, after hundreds of years, was a Brother-Leader passing control of the Axe-Wielders into the hands of a secular commander? And Borneheld! Axis shoved his axe into his weapon belt with a furious thrust. He rarely disagreed with Jayme and had never raised his voice to him in anger before, but now he'd made a disastrous decision and Axis meant to tell him so, Brother-Leader or not.

He brushed past Isend and Borneheld talking in low tones in the corridor. Surely the dandified Isend wasn't offering to fight alongside him? As far as Axis knew the closest he'd ever come to a weapon was the fruit knife that he constantly carried with him, hanging from his begemmed belt on a small silver chain. He turned the corner behind Jayme and Moryson, who were discussing whether or not to send Gilbert along on the journey to the Silent Woman

Keep. Axis didn't give a damn about whether or not Gilbert accompanied him, all he wanted was future control of his Axe-Wielders back again.

A fat white cat that had rubbed about Axis' legs at breakfast now scrambled along the corridor behind him. As he shut the door of Jayme's apartment, he almost caught the cat's tail as she slipped in between his legs. Jayme and Moryson turned to look at him, their faces expressionless.

"Father, I will not relinquish control of my command to Borneheld at Gorkenfort!"

"Axis," Jayme began, stepping forward, but Axis was now so furious that he interrupted his Brother-Leader. "Have you gone mad? Do you know what you have done? You will inform Borneheld that you were mistaken and that control of the Axe-Wielders will remain with me."

Jayme halted a few paces from Axis, and bright spots of red blossomed in his cheeks; his eyes sparked as angrily as Axis.' "Remember who you speak to, BattleAxe! You do not question the orders of the Brother-Leader *nor* do you presume to offer him orders yourself!"

Axis took a quick deep breath and squared his shoulders, staring defiantly at Jayme, his fists clenched at his sides. Moryson stepped forward, worried, ready to intervene if he had to.

"I have not spent my life in the Axe-Wielders to see them led by someone other than me! I have not spent the past five years harrying them into the most effective fighting force they have been in generations to watch you squander their abilities so thoughtlessly!" Axis hissed, now so infuriated he was past caring if he insulted Jayme. "Do you know what you do, old man? Are your senses fading along with your strength?"

Jayme's nostrils flared, utterly shocked by Axis' disrespect. "Give me one good reason why I shouldn't hand over command of the Axe-Wielders to Borneheld *right now!*"

Axis was silent for a moment, his mouth twisting as he tried to reign in his temper. "Give me one good reason why

I should hand over control to Borneheld in Gorkenfort," he said in a quieter voice, though it still vibrated with anger.

For a moment longer Jayme stared at him, then he too took a deep breath and spoke in a calmer tone. "Because Achar needs to be united to face this threat, BattleAxe. When you get to Gorkenfort there must only be one force, one commander. That is the only way the Seneschal and the forces of Achar defeated the Forbidden a thousand years ago and it is the only way we can do it now." His voice rose a little. "Do you understand what I am saying, Axis? I do not want to sacrifice Achar to save your cursed pride!"

Axis stared at him, his fists slowly clenching and un-clenching at his sides. "I understand what you say, Brother-Leader, and I can try to accept the reasons behind it. But it doesn't mean I agree it's the right thing to do."

Moryson glanced between the two men. He hoped Jayme would accept Axis' words, for he did not think Axis would back down any further. As it was, only the years of deep affection between them and the respect Axis held for Jayme had made him back down this far. Moryson did not think that he would have done it for any other man. He must have got his damned pride from his father, Moryson thought dourly.

"All I want is your word that you will obey my instructions, BattleAxe," Jayme said quietly, his eyes holding Axis' in a vice-like grip.

After a moment Axis gave a curt nod. "You have it." He refused to lower his eyes before Jayme's stare.

The cat suddenly spat at Jayme, its fur standing on end. The distraction broke the tension in the room and Jayme forced a little laugh. "Well, at least the cat seems to agree with you, Axis."

Axis bent down and scooped the cat into his arms, pet-ting her back with long, slow strokes. The cat relaxed, her bright blue eyes blinking and then narrowing as she started to purr. She nuzzled his hand in affection.

After a moment's awkward silence Moryson cleared his throat. "Perhaps we need to talk about your journey, Axis."

The men walked over to the fire, Jayme waving the other two into chairs.

Moryson leaned forward to warm his hands. "The Brother in charge of the records in the Silent Woman Keep is named Ogden, Axis. He has been at the Keep many years and is the most knowledgeable of the brothers who study there. I know him well, he is a good man, dedicated to his duty. He will help you."

"Ogden is almost as damned independent and proud as you are, Axis," Jayme muttered. "I will send a rider off today to make sure he is aware of your coming."

"And we will send Gilbert with you, Axis," Moryson said. "When you continue on for Smyrton, Gilbert can return to us with what information Ogden and you've found." The plan was sensible enough, and an added benefit was that Jayme and Moryson had a few weeks free of Gilbert.

Axis closed his eyes and let the fire warm his face, idly stroking the cat as he thought.

Moryson and Jayme exchanged glances for a moment before Jayme asked, "When will you be able to leave, Axis? And how long do you think the trip to the Woods and then Smyrton will take you?"

Axis thought for a moment longer then opened his eyes. The firelight caught peculiar golden glints deep in his blue eyes. "How many of the Axe-Wielders do you want me to take?"

Jayme considered, his fingers steepled against his nose. "Most, I think. There is little point in leaving more than a token force at the Tower of the Seneschal. Take seven cohorts and leave one here. Depending on what you find at Smyrton you might need to leave several units there. Take the rest onto Gorkenfort."

"The six cohorts that I took down to Coroleas will arrive here within a day. They have been traveling for over a week, so I'll need to rest them and their horses a few days. I'll use that time to organize our support and supplies. We can leave within five days, six at the most. From here to the Silent Woman Woods—two weeks at a solid pace. From the Silent Woman Woods to Smyrton," Axis paused as he calculated the distance, "perhaps a month if we travel through Arcen and across the River Bracken."

"And from Smyrton to Gorkenfort?"

"That is a harder and longer journey. If the reports of ice above the Urqhart Hills are true then it will be even harder. Especially if the winter closes in early." Jayme and Moryson, who were in a position to see the window, nervously glanced at the heavy snowclouds. "Perhaps twenty days. If all goes smoothly and I am not detained too long at Smyrton, then I should be at Gorkenfort by early to mid-Snow-month."

Jayme looked concerned. "That's very late. Winter may well be there before you."

Axis' gaze was steady. "It's the best I can do given the number of cohorts and the route you suggest."

"Could he send a cohort or two directly to Gorkenfort via the River Nordra, Brother-Leader? They could be there several weeks ahead of the main force of Axe-Wielders that come via Smyrton," said Moryson.

"The force stays intact and it stays with me," said Axis fiercely.

Jayme hesitated, then nodded. "I will grant you that, BattleAxe. Borneheld will have enough troops there soon enough, and he will be ably supported by Jorge and Roland. No, all seven cohorts go with you, Axis."

Axis relaxed. "Good. Then, if you will excuse me, Brother-Leader, I have an expedition to organize."

Jayme nodded and waved a sketchy blessing with his right hand. "Furrow wide, furrow deep, BattleAxe."

"Furrow wide, furrow deep, Brother-Leader," Axis replied, standing. The cat jumped down and sat before the fire. Axis bowed slightly to Jayme and Moryson, his right fist clenched over the golden axes on his breast, then he strode from the room, his boot heels clicking sharply on the stone floor.

*　*　*

"Well," said Moryson quietly, after Axis had closed the door behind him.

"Well, indeed," Jayme replied equally as softly.

"Can we trust him?" Moryson asked.

Jayme took a deep breath. "Yes. Yes. He won't like passing over command of the Axe-Wielders, but he will do it in the end. It would look peculiar if we didn't send the Axe-Wielders to help in the defense of Achar, and even more peculiar if we didn't send their BattleAxe with them."

"What will he find out?" Moryson asked.

Jayme squirmed in his chair, and the cat paused in her washing to gaze at him. "Hopefully nothing. With luck his rivalry with Borneheld and the threat of the Forbidden will keep him occupied. Moryson—"

"I know, old friend, I know. Priam's news shocked me as much as it shocked you. What did those creatures want with Rivkah's body?"

Jayme looked up and caught Moryson's gaze. His eyes were cold and calculating and his face no longer wore its usual kindly mien. "And what will they do when they discover it wasn't hers?"

Moryson suddenly looked ten years older, his already hollow cheeks deepening further. "My friend, I think they already know that. I think that's why they destroyed the scriptorium in a rage."

Jayme smiled bleakly. "Then in that at least they did us a favor. For years I have wanted those records destroyed. We can only hope that the two brothers who survived were two of the younger brothers—with no memory that stretches back thirty years."

The cat paused briefly, her head still bent over her tail, but her bright eyes fixed on Jayme. Then she flipped over and began washing her protruding stomach.

"But it doesn't answer the question," Moryson said, his voice revealing the strain he was under, "why did they want Rivkah's body? Why?"

Jayme did not, could not, answer. The cat stretched and sat for a moment, regarding them both with level blue eyes. Then she rose to her feet and stepped languidly over to the door, scratching to be let out. Moryson obliged.

8

Faraday's Betrothal

Faraday sat at the lead-paned window in her father's apartment and gazed down at the activities in the palace courtyard below her. For the past five days the palace, and Carlon itself, had been bustling with activity as soldiers, archers, pikemen and cavalry arrived, formed into their units and then dispersed. Four days ago, six cohorts of Axe-Wielders had finally arrived from Coroleas. One more cohort had come from the Tower of the Seneschal to swell their numbers. Both Axe-Wielders and regular soldiers were billeted out across Carlon as war and transport plans were made, supplies obtained, horses shod and gear cleaned. In the palace itself there was almost no room to move. The cooks complained, the officers shouted, the dogs barked, the serving girls scurried from place to place with red spots in their cheeks, and numerous important-looking palace officials strode along the palace corridors carrying wads of thick documents under their arms. Those nobles resident in the palace for the festivities surrounding

Priam's nameday gathered in small groups and whispered the day away.

Faraday had done little but sit in her window and watch the activities below her. She caught frequent glimpses of the BattleAxe, and on those occasions she leaned a little closer to the frosty panes of glass, watching him as he conferred with his officers or chatted and smiled with his men. Sometimes a broken strap or a slow servant would make him lose his temper momentarily and shout, the sound of his voice just managing to drift to her ears. At his heels trotted a large white cat, as faithful as a dog. Faraday had actually forgotten her own troubles enough to laugh out loud when the cat tripped the BattleAxe up and he fell into a pile of straw the stable lads had just mucked out. Even the BattleAxe had enough of a sense of humor to smile wryly, and the cat had leapt into his lap as he sat in the hay, butting her head against his chin in a feline display of affection.

As the dusk set in she could just make out her father below in the courtyard talking to Axis. Axis was shaking his head firmly and her father was gesturing animatedly with both his hands. They had been standing there for some twenty minutes and Faraday could see that Axis was impatient to get away. But her father was persistent, and after a few more minutes, as Faraday pressed her forehead to the glass in order to see, Axis gave in and reluctantly nodded his head to whatever her father was planning. When Borneheld strode into the courtyard to join her father, Axis turned on his heel and left them to confer quietly in the shadows.

As she watched her father and Borneheld, Faraday's lovely face lost much of its animation. When she had first arrived in Carlon everything had seemed a grand adventure. She had wanted to visit court all her life, and had been quietly excited when her father and mother had told her she was to come to the king's nameday feast this year. The weeks of fittings for clothes grand enough to wear at court had entertained her, while the journey to Carlon had exposed her to landscapes and people she had not imagined existed. The clothes, the jewels, the sights and sounds of the court, the noisy crowds thronging the streets of Carlon—it all seemed a dream.

But three days ago the dream had ended and Faraday had come down to earth with a shock. Three days ago her father had come to her, his eyes bright and a great beam of pleasure lighting his face. He had arranged a marriage for her. Faraday had known that one day she would marry, and had realized that one of the reasons her parents had brought her to Carlon was to present her to the court as an eligible daughter, but she had vaguely assumed that marriage still lay a year or two into the future. But whatever had thrown the palace into a fever of activity had apparently also hastened her parents' plans. And hastened her prospective bridegroom's fervor.

Borneheld. She was to become the Duchess of Ichtar. It was, by anyone's reckoning, a splendid marriage for her. Borneheld was the most powerful noble in the realm and the current heir to the throne. Her parents were ecstatic. Devera was wide-eyed with amazement and had spent much of this morning with Faraday, chatting nonstop about clothes, servants and babies until Faraday's temper snapped and she asked Devera to leave. Devera had been offended, and left muttering about how Faraday would have to learn some manners when she was married to Borneheld.

Faraday shuddered. She'd had to pretend pleasure for her parents' sakes, but inside she felt hollow. She was very unsure of Borneheld; he was so large, so overbearing, and his manners were so gruff. They had met briefly the day before and had talked haltingly of this and that while her parents stood by, their faces mirroring their pride. Despite her best efforts, Faraday could not help comparing Borneheld to his half-brother. She was sure that conversation with Axis would not be peppered with the same embarrassing silences that her conversation with Borneheld was. Where Faraday could somehow imagine Axis being gentle and humorous, she could only foresee Borneheld being terse and impatient. She sighed. On the two occasions she had ventured a witty remark Borneheld had only stared at her uncomprehendingly.

Faraday shivered and gulped, trying desperately to hold back her tears. This afternoon was the formal betrothal ceremony and she could not afford to have swollen and reddened eyes. The usual niceties were being hurried because Borneheld would leave so soon for the north. The prenuptial contract, covering the legalities of dowry and jointure, had been signed yesterday. This afternoon her mother had dressed her in a gown of ivory silk that had left her shoulders bare and exposed so much of her breasts that Faraday thought it verged on the indecorous. Her thick chestnut hair had been left to flow down her back in virginal style.

Faraday suddenly realized that her father and Borneheld had disappeared from the courtyard. They must be on their way up here, she thought, her mouth suddenly dry, and she stood on wobbly legs just as the door to the apartment opened.

Her parents, Isend and Merlion, entered, and behind them came Borneheld, his lieutenant Gautier and Earl Burdel of Arcen. Faraday wet her lips and dipped into a curtsey as Borneheld crossed the room.

"My dear," he said awkwardly as she remained deep in her curtsey, her head bowed. He thrust his hand out clumsily, uncomfortable with courtly manners, and she took it lightly between her fingers, rising gracefully to her feet. She was a tall girl, and did not have to tip her head too far back to meet his eyes.

"My lord," she said softly but clearly, "I am honored by your offer of marriage." It was what her mother had told her to say this afternoon, and Faraday had no way of knowing that it was her father who had done all the offering and persuading. But Borneheld's greed and lust had made him listen and finally agree. Although Isend was not overly wealthy, Faraday was an heiress in her own right, due to inherit her maternal grandfather's estates. Faraday was not only pleasing to the eye but would bring rich lands to her marriage. Borneheld had not had to think overly hard about the offer.

"The honor is all mine," Borneheld replied after some considerable thought. Gautier grinned behind his master's back. That was the most courtly phrase he had heard pass Borneheld's lips in a number of years. Borneheld was always more comfortable cursing his soldiers than passing pleasant conversation with well-bred women.

"Ahem." Isend stepped forward. "I know how busy the Duke of Ichtar is, Faraday, so perhaps we can proceed with the ceremony. The Earl of Burdel and Lieutenant Gautier are here to act as witnesses."

Faraday's smile trembled a little, but she managed to keep her eyes level as Borneheld grasped her hand more firmly and began to speak the ancient ritual words of betrothal.

"I, Borneheld, son of Searlas, Duke of Ichtar, do plight thee, Faraday, daughter of Isend of Skarabost, my troth in marriage. Before Artor and these people here assembled I do promise to take thee as my wife and to give thee an honored place by my side. And to this I do freely consent."

Everyone waited expectantly. Faraday swallowed and wet her lips before repeating the vows. She hesitated a moment before finishing. "And to this I do freely consent."

Borneheld grinned a little lopsidedly, put his free hand into his pocket and withdrew a large ring of twisted dark gold mounted with a massive round ruby, fumbling slightly as he slid it onto the heart finger of Faraday's left hand. It fit perfectly. Faraday's eyes widened; the ruby was one of the largest stones she had ever seen.

"Oh, it's beautiful!" her mother whispered to one side.

Borneheld smiled happily and, placing his large strong hands on Faraday's shoulders, he leaned down and kissed her. Faraday tried not to tense under Borneheld's hands as his kiss lingered. He smelled of horses, leather and sweat and Faraday found his size and closeness intimidating. She trembled slightly as Borneheld finally leaned back, wishing she could respond to this man as spontaneously as she had been attracted to his brother.

Borneheld took her hesitancy as a compliment. "I can hardly wait until our marriage, my dear," he whispered. He dropped his hands from her shoulders, but did not seem to know what to say or do next.

Faraday forced a smile, likewise searching for some light remark. She supposed she would develop an easier rapport with Borneheld in the future, but for now she simply hoped that someone would do something that would bring this awkward occasion to an end.

Earl Burdel finally stepped up behind Borneheld and clapped him jovially on the shoulder. "I shall watch her like a hawk, Borneheld, and let no harm come to her. I'm sure that when you return from Gorkenfort you will want the marriage ceremony as soon as possible."

Faraday looked across at her father in confusion. Burdel? Surely she would remain with her parents until the marriage?

"My dear," Isend smiled at her confusion. "With the problems in the north both your affianced husband," he paused to bestow a wide grin on Borneheld, "and I believe that it might be too dangerous for you to return to Skarabost, and the court is no place for a young girl."

Oh no, Faraday thought in despair, please let me stay with you a while longer.

"So, I've decided to send you and your mother to stay with Burdel's family in Arcen. He will join you in a few short weeks once his business here is concluded. A sensible solution. But to get you there safely and in the quickest possible time, my dear, you will have to leave early in the morning."

Faraday looked even more confused.

"The Axe-Wielders ride for Smyrton through Arcness and I have managed to persuade the BattleAxe to let you and your mother ride with them. Three and a half thousand Axe-Wielders should provide a safe enough escort. The Lady of Tare will also be joining you for part of the way, so you will not be lacking for female company. Yes, yes, I know that they will be moving fast, but both you and your mother can ride well."

Borneheld stood to one side, pleased with the afternoon's events, but now impatient to get back to his men. In truth, he was not particularly happy that Axis should be the one to provide his future wife with an escort to Arcen, but as there were few men to spare as escort it would be foolish to ignore the service he could provide. Besides, Borneheld grinned to himself, Axis would have several weeks to envy the wife his elder brother had won. Axis would never be able to find a wife so well-bred or with such lands.

Isend stared at his daughter impatiently. "Well?"

Faraday looked between her father and Borneheld, feeling a confused mixture of emotions: relief, that she would not have to endure many more awkward moments with Borneheld in the near future; sadness, that she would not be returning home, and a welter of complex emotions about Axis. She managed to maintain a smile on her face, although she felt that everyone in the room must see how false it was.

"It sounds like the best solution," she finally said dutifully.

9

Leavetakings at Dawn

A xis strode about the courtyard in the predawn darkness, impatient to get moving and irritated beyond measure that he was to be saddled with a group of women. That one of them was the Lady of Tare did not diminish his displeasure one whit.

"Belial!" he shouted, frowning into the milling men and horses in the courtyard, trying to spot his lieutenant. "Belial!"

"Sir." Belial appeared at his side, a tall, well-built man with deeply set hazel eyes and a thick line of fine sandy hair over his tanned and beardless face. He wore a plain, gray woollen tunic coat over a white shirt and gray leather trousers, the normal uniform of the Axe-Wielders. Belial was some seven or eight years older than Axis, but despite his service, experience and undoubted expertise he had never harbored any ambition to lead the Axe-Wielders. He preferred that someone else have the ultimate responsibility and care, and he served happily under Axis.

"Why isn't everyone in formation!" Axis snapped. "It's late!"

Belial took no offense at his BattleAxe's short temper. He was always tense and irritable before they moved out. "This is the last cohort to form up. The other cohorts are waiting outside in the streets. In line. Packhorses loaded. Supplies accounted for. Geared up, fed, watered, weaponed, and ready to go."

Axis glared at Belial but there was so little light the effort was wasted. "Then where are these cursed women!" he growled.

"These cursed women are geared up, fed, watered, ah . . . packed, and ready to go," a feminine voice said from behind him.

Axis wheeled around. He could just make out Embeth in the dim light, but it was the huddle of female shapes behind her that caught his eye. Artor's arse! he thought, only avoiding swearing out loud through a supreme effort.

"I had not expected you to bring every single one of your seamstresses, laundresses and chambermaids with you, Lady Tare," he said curtly. "Do you think to teach my Axemen needlework about the fires at night?"

"The Lady of Skarabost, her daughter Faraday and I have brought our maids, BattleAxe. We do not travel without our attendants," Embeth replied firmly.

"Well I hope they can ride, because you'll have to travel without them if they fall off their cursed horses crossing the first overflowing gutter they come to!" Axis snarled, ignoring Embeth's gasp at his rough tone. Turning on his heel, Axis disappeared into the throng of men as they mounted and formed up.

Belial shrugged in sympathy at the women, then hurried off to fetch their horses. Embeth turned to the ladies Merlion and Faraday and smiled wryly. "I have heard that his temper improves as the sun rises, my friends. Let us hope that is truly the case!"

"No wonder Priam doesn't receive him!" Lady Merlion

muttered. She wished Isend had found them a more gracious escort—and one with a less unsavoury parentage.

Faraday wriggled in embarrassment at her mother's words, then abruptly giggled at the image of their maids floundering in a flooded gutter while Axis rode resolutely on.

Her mother was horrified. "Faraday!"

Embeth struggled for a moment, then she too started to laugh, wheezing with the effort of trying to keep it low. Finally she gave up and burst into a merry peal as Belial and several servants came back with their horses. "Onwards and forward, ladies," she chuckled, "onwards and forward!" and scrambled onto her horse.

Faraday was just settling her skirts after mounting her horse side-saddle when a rough hand touched her knee. "Borneheld," she gasped. The sun had just risen and a shaft of light shone directly into Borneheld's face as he squinted up at Faraday. "My dear. I had to see you safely off." Faraday was too high to lean down so that he could kiss her mouth, but Borneheld made up for it by patting her leg awkwardly through the skirts of her riding habit.

"I will count the days until I see you again, Borneheld," Faraday muttered, embarrassed by his attention in case Axis reappeared. She wriggled her leg slightly, hoping that Borneheld would drop his hand.

Although he ceased his patting, Borneheld kept his hand firmly in place as he peered about the courtyard. "Where is . . . ? Ah!"

The final cohort had formed up, and Axis appeared at one corner of the courtyard, mounted on his dappled-gray stallion, Belaguez. The horse was skittish in the early-morning cold, and his steel-clad hooves slipped and skidded over the slick cobbles of the courtyard as Axis rode across to Borneheld.

Faraday was now so mortified she wished that somehow Artor could find enough pity in his heart to reach down and snatch her from this life. She averted her eyes, her color rising, unable to look at the BattleAxe. Axis shot her a quick glance, recognising her from the banquet. He knew who she was now, since Earl Isend had spent the best part of an hour persuading him to accompany her and her mother to Arcness.

"Borneheld," he said flatly, his eyes flickering over his half-brother's hand resting on the young woman's knee. He felt a moment's sympathy for her.

Borneheld was unable to resist a sneer. "Don't lose too many of *my* Axe-Wielders before you arrive in Gorkenfort, BattleAxe."

Axis' mouth compressed and his hands tightened on Belaguez's reins, causing the stallion to half rear. "If you can't manage to drag your mind away from your forthcoming marriage, Borneheld, then I doubt that you'll survive long enough to lead even your horse to water."

Borneheld finally lifted his hand from Faraday's knee to pat her patronizingly on the arm. Seizing on the equine metaphor, he spoke without thinking, wanting only to irritate Axis. "Isend has handed me the reins of the finest mare in the stable, BattleAxe. You could never hope to own anything this well-bred." He laughed at his own wit and, dropping his hand, fondled Faraday's leg again.

Underneath her choking blanket of embarrassment, Faraday's temper flared into white-hot anger. She was no mare to be passed between men for the highest price! She dug her booted heel into her horse and viciously swiped it with the long whip that hung down the far side from Borneheld. The horse snorted and leaped sideways in surprise and indignation, and Borneheld lost his footing. He waved his arms and stumbled alarmingly, almost falling to his knees on the slippery cobbles.

"Borneheld!" Faraday cried, hoping her voice held a suitable degree of surprised anxiety. Her green eyes flickered momentarily to Axis before she hooded their triumphant gleam. Her mother gasped out in concern behind her, but Borneheld regained his balance and glanced at

Faraday, assuming she had momentarily lost control when the horse had shied at some imagined shadow.

Faraday splayed her hands in a display of helplessness and Borneheld smiled to reassure her. "My dear, it doesn't matter. When we are married I'll teach you to ride properly."

Axis had noticed Faraday's actions and glance and restrained a wry grin. The girl had spirit, it seemed. "And in return perhaps the Lady Faraday can teach you your dance steps, Borneheld. Your exhibition just now was hardly impressive."

Borneheld stiffened, wishing a biting retort would spring to his lips. "Do not tarry on your way to Gorkenfort, BattleAxe," he snapped finally, his color rising. He gave Faraday a final pat on the arm, then turned and strode back into the palace.

Although cheered by the BattleAxe's remark, Faraday nevertheless shook her head imperceptibly. Why had she acted so foolishly? She squared her shoulders, wondering at the antagonism between the two brothers.

"Axis." Jayme walked out from the shadows where he had been standing. Axis bowed from the saddle and gave his Brother-Leader the clenched fist salute of the Axe-Wielders. "Axis. Ride well and fast, my son. Find the answers that we so desperately need. And remember your promise."

Axis nodded, his eyes cold. The tension between the two had not dissipated completely over the past five days since their furious argument in the Brother-Leader's apartment. Axis edged his horse away from the Brother-Leader. "Furrow wide, furrow deep, Father."

"Wide and deep," Jayme replied. "May Artor hold you in His care now and for always, my son."

For a long moment their eyes caught above Belaguez's tossing head, then, as Jayme raised his hand in blessing, Axis wheeled his stallion around in a tight circle, sparks rising as the horse's hooves struck the cobbles.

"Axe-Wielders, are you ready?" he cried in a clear and penetrating voice.

From the courtyard and the streets beyond rose a single shout. "We follow your voice and are ready, BattleAxe!"

"Then let us ride!" Axis cried, and a shout rose from his men as the thunder of twenty thousand hooves filled Carlon, sending the eagles and hawks roosting on the city walls fluttering into the sky in feathered confusion.

10

Across the Plains of Tare

Embeth had heard stories all her life about the almost legendary ability of the Axe-Wielders to move fast and far, no matter the size of their column. She had never really believed them, thinking them soldiers' stories from the bottom of a jug of ale. But after riding five days from sun-up to sundown she realized the stories were all true.

The column of Axe-Wielders contained over three and a half thousand mounted men, at least three hundred pack-horses, several hundred riderless horses who were rotated among the riders each day, and, Embeth grimaced as they slowed down to make camp on the fifth night, seven very sore women (none of whom had fallen off at the first over-flowing gutter). There was also one equally sore Brother Gilbert and, unbelievably, a fat white cat which must have stowed away on one of the packhorses. Every evening it strolled out of the dark and wound around the BattleAxe's legs, purring loudly and contentedly despite his curses. Every morning it strolled off into the dawn and no one saw it again until the evening.

Embeth twisted around in her saddle. Gilbert was riding morosely along about twenty paces behind them. Still sulking at being sent to the Silent Woman Keep with the Axe-Wielders, Gilbert preferred not to spend his days in conversation if he could help it. Lady Merlion clutched grimly to the pommel of her saddle, no doubt cursing (well, perhaps not that) her husband for sending them along with the Axe-Wielders to Arcness. Faraday, younger and more flexible both in mind and body, was coping rather better. After the first day's ride she had abandoned the long trailing skirts of her riding habit and dressed herself in a more sensible divided skirt to ride astride. Her hair hung in a girlish fashion down her back in a thick plait. Lady Merlion had remonstrated with Faraday over both skirt and hair, but Faraday had managed to hold her ground. Embeth shifted in the saddle a little.

"We appear to be slowing down," she called, reining in her horse slightly so that Merlion and Faraday could draw level. "There's a hollow about five hundred paces ahead; perhaps the BattleAxe will be kind to us and decide to make camp there." She had seen several Axe-Wielders ride out ahead of the main body of the column, inspect the site, and report back to Axis, plainly visible on his gray stallion at the head of the leading unit.

"One can only hope so," Merlion grumbled, her wispy pale hair starting to drift loose from underneath her headdress. She looked tired and disheveled and fifteen years older than when she had set out. "The man obviously has no idea that women should not be made to travel so fast. My maids are so exhausted at night they can hardly attend to my needs."

Faraday exchanged a brief smile with Embeth. "This is no pleasure jaunt, mother. The BattleAxe rides at a soldier's pace."

Axis had studiously ignored the lot of them thus far. Although the soldiers pitched the women's tents close to Axis' personal campsite at night, he spent most of the time moving from campfire to campfire in the evening, talking to his men and conferring with his officers. He only returned to his bedroll late at night, and then only to collapse into an exhausted sleep. The women sat at their own campfire talking amongst themselves, a small pocket of femininity among the thousands of men surrounding them. While Merlion trusted her daughter to retain her virtue, she kept a careful eye on the maids who travelled with them. They had shown a disconcerting willingness to disappear from their bedrolls at night.

A horseman rode back from the head of the column and drew level with the women. "Timozel!" Embeth cried delightedly, for she had hardly seen her son on this march.

Timozel grinned at his mother and sketched a bow to the other two women. "My ladies, I trust you have enjoyed your excursion thus far."

Faraday smiled at Timozel, taking an instant liking to him. He was a year or two older than her, and still with the slightly thin and big-boned frame of a youth yet to fill out into maturity. He had the look of his mother with a shock of rich brown curls and dark blue eyes, but must have inherited the wide mobile mouth and hooked nose from his father. Despite his youth he handled his rangy bay gelding with the skill of an experienced horseman, and the axe and sword that hung to each side of his body gave him the look of a man rather than a boy.

Timozel looked at Faraday and his grin widened for a moment. Faraday reddened slightly, although her own smile widened to match his own and her eyes sparkled with pleasure. Embeth watched the exchange with some amusement. What a shame that Faraday had been betrothed before she could experience the simple enjoyments of flirting at court. Now she would never have the chance. Not with Borneheld to watch over her.

"Ladies, mother, I'm sure you'll be pleased to hear that we'll be stopping a little earlier today. There's a good campsite just ahead, with excellent shelter and water. The

BattleAxe is pleased with the progress we've made thus far and wants to take advantage of this campsite to rest both ourselves and our horses a little longer this evening."

"The man has mercy!" Merlion muttered, trying in vain to tuck her hair back into order beneath her headdress.

"The BattleAxe has requested that I extend an invitation on his behalf for the Ladies Merlion, Embeth and Faraday to join him at his campfire this evening to share the evening meal."

Timozel kept his tone light and charming, although he had his own reservations about the message he delivered. Though his mother did not realize it, Timozel had been aware for some time of her relationship with Axis. The knowledge had soured Timozel's previous admiration for his BattleAxe. But Timozel hid his doubts well, and neither Axis nor Embeth had any idea of the simmering resentment beneath his good-natured and courteous exterior.

Embeth's mouth twitched in amusement at Timozel's message. She doubted Axis had managed to put the invitation so politely. She turned to Merlion, who, as the senior lady present, would have to accept or refuse on their behalf.

Faraday's eyes pleaded with her mother. "Please, mother! The evenings have been so dull. Perhaps Timozel can join us."

"It would be my pleasure, my lady," Timozel smiled, inclining his head toward Faraday and then turning to bow politely at her mother.

Timozel's display of courtly manners impressed Merlion. If this youth would join them, well, perhaps they would have some polite conversation after all. Even Merlion had missed masculine company in the evenings. Brother Gilbert, if and where he joined them, hardly counted.

"We will accept the BattleAxe's gracious offer. Kindly tell him that we will be pleased to share the evening meal with him."

*　*　*

For a while after they finished eating the group watched the campfire spit and hiss in the chill evening air. Gilbert, Timozel and Belial had joined Axis and the three noblewomen so that, in the best courtly tradition, the number of men exceeded the number of women. There had been enough time, after making camp, for the women to wash with water brought from the nearby stream and to brush their hair out. While Merlion and Embeth had both dressed their hair on top of their heads, Faraday had left hers in the long braid, wispy tendrils brushing her cheeks.

The meal had been simple but good. Axis was in a fine mood, feeling more relaxed than he had since Jayme's urgent message reached him in Coroleas. This was the first time he had taken virtually the entire Axe-Wielders on such a hard and fast march, and he had fretted about their speed and a myriad of other small details. But things were going well and they were moving even faster than he had hoped. Years of planning and training were paying off. His men were doing him proud.

The large hollow, several hundred paces across, sheltered them from the cold wind. Axis stretched his legs out before the fire so that his booted feet could take maximum advantage of the flames, leaned back against a waist-high rock, and contemplated Faraday.

"My Lady Faraday," he said smoothly, "it has been bothering me that I should find your face so familiar when, to my knowledge, we have never met before this march." He wondered if she would admit to her ill-mannered stare the night of the banquet.

Faraday smiled uncertainly, her hands clutching her knees where they were drawn up to her chest. "Really? . . . ah . . ." Her voice trailed off. She wasn't sure how to address him. "BattleAxe" was so inappropriate in the relaxed mood about the fire, yet "Axis" seemed too familiar. She could hardly call him "my Lord", because to all intents and purposes his illegitimate birth placed him beyond that respectable and noble title.

"You undoubtedly saw me at Priam's nameday banquet

in the Chamber of the Moons. I'm afraid that I was staring. The Axe-Wielders have such a legendary reputation in Skarabost, indeed, around all Achar itself, that I have long desired to see one. I was fortunate that my first sight of an Axe-Wielder was of their BattleAxe himself. I apologize from my heart for my bad manners that night, Axis Rivkahson."

Embeth's mouth dropped open in shock—and hers was not the only one. Never had she known anyone to address Axis so. He was extraordinarily sensitive about the circumstances surrounding his birth, so that no one, *no one*, ever referred to his mother or to his illegitimate status to his face. Yet . . . yet . . . Embeth had to admit that she was stunned, not only by Faraday's explicit mention of Rivkah, but by the girl's exquisite handling of what was undoubtedly an embarrassing moment for her. In the end, Faraday had done the impossible; she had referred to Axis' illegitimate status in such a graceful manner as to make Axis' connection to his mother a virtue rather than an embarrassment.

Axis looked as stunned as Embeth felt, but Embeth could see that emotions battled inside him. His instant re-action had been a surge of anger and humiliation that Faraday had referred so openly to his illegitimacy, but now he was confused by the fact that neither her eyes nor her tone held any trace of mockery. He groped for something to say, but such a complex mix of emotions surged through him that he could find no words.

Faraday clearly understood what she had started and she understood as well that having started it she would have to lay it to rest. She spoke again into the absolute silence about the campfire, her voice gentle, her eyes fixed on Axis. "I have heard that the Princess Rivkah was a woman of remarkable qualities, Axis, and you must surely be proud to have had such a woman as your mother. Yet I am equally sure that she too would be proud to have you as her son, and to have you bear her name through these years that she is unable to live herself."

Embeth closed her eyes against the tears that pricked up in them. In the eighteen years she had known Axis she had never presumed upon their friendship enough to mention his mother to him so openly. And yet this young woman had spoken clearly and simply of Rivkah's pride and love for Axis as if it were undoubted fact. Embeth did not often feel so deeply moved, and especially by one so young. She opened her eyes again and looked between Axis and Faraday. Perhaps her reticence in past years had been a mistake.

Axis took a slow, deep breath, profoundly affected by Faraday's words. "Thank you, Faraday. It is rare that I hear anyone speak so well of my mother."

Faraday's beautiful smile lit up her face and Axis' eyes darkened perceptibly as they looked back at Faraday.

Embeth, watching the two of them, felt a sudden chill of premonition. "Dear Artor," she whispered to herself. "Not this . . . not this." Not with Faraday bound to Borneheld. Not with the contracts signed and the betrothal oaths taken before witnesses. Not with the bitterness that already existed between the two brothers. If it could be stopped before it went too much further then the tragedy might be averted. She would have to speak to Faraday, the sooner the better.

Embeth smiled and spoke lightly, deliberately breaking the look between them. "Axis, it is so rare that I have a chance to hear you play your harp. Will you play for us now? And Timozel, do you have your lute with you?"

There was a collective sigh of relief around the fire as the mood changed.

"Only if the ladies agree to accompany us with their voices," Timozel said, unsure what to think about the scene he had just witnessed.

For a man so given to the military arts, Axis had an unexpected flair for music and song. Embeth was never aware of who had taught Axis his skill on the harp—he was proficient even when he joined her and Ganelon at eleven. Although far less skilled, Timozel could accompany well enough and the three women were all practiced with their voices. The rest of the evening passed pleasantly with ballads and songs of love and adventure.

Gilbert, protesting his inability to keep a tune, sat silently throughout the evening, applauding the musicians and singers whenever they finished a song and smiling at their laughter. His sharp eyes, however, kept returning to Axis and Faraday. Jayme had told him to report everything he witnessed, *everything*, and Gilbert meant to do just that.

11

Unlocked Doors

Two days later they rode into Tare, the small town which sat on the border of the Plains of Tare and the small Province of Tarantaise. It was poor country, and even assiduous use of the Plough only yielded small returns in grain and vegetables, so Tare relied on the east-west trade across Achar for its primary income. When Embeth had first come to live in Tare as a young bride she had been overcome by the vast spaces of the sparsely grassed plains surrounding Tare. Now, after twenty years, she had come to love the town and appreciate the slow rhythms of Tarian life.

The townsfolk lined the town walls to watch them arrive, waving and cheering as the men rode around the town walls. The Tarians were round-eyed but not displeased to see so many Axe-Wielders. Soldiers, whether Axemen or regular soldiers, always meant money.

The majority of the Axemen would have to camp outside the town precinct, for there was no way they could be billeted in a town the size of Tare, but Embeth invited the women, Gilbert, Axis and Belial to stay at her castle. After some confusion, Axis told Timozel he too could stay with his mother while they were in Tare. It was a concession that pleased Timozel though he was resentful that he needed Axis' permission to sleep in his own house. Especially when Axis would no doubt make free use of the privacy of Embeth's home to take further advantage of her.

Axis planned to stop two days in Tare to replenish supplies and rest his men and their horses. After the first few days on a hard march there was always a mass of equipment needing repair, horses to be reshod, and men needed the chance to spend some solid hours at weapon practice. And if the reports drifting down from the north were true, then within a few short weeks they might not have the time to relax, and many might never have the chance to woo a serving girl over a jar of ale again. He told the unit commanders to let as many men as possible enjoy their evenings in town.

The Lady of Tare lived in a high, thick-walled castle sheltered against the fortified walls of the town and separated from the streets of Tare by a tall private wall. It sat on a small hill so that its walks and gardens looked down over the town. It was a large building and accommodated the women, their servants, the Brother and the three Axe-Wielders easily. Although Embeth had another son and a daughter—twins and a year younger than Timozel—both were still attending the court at Carlon.

Embeth desperately wanted to talk to Faraday before she departed, but Merlion had other ideas. For the two days they stayed with the Lady of Tare she kept Faraday closeted in her room, going over designs for dresses, and describing the duties and responsibilities she would have to assume once she became the Duchess of Ichtar.

Faraday would have liked to spend some time on her own or talking with Embeth. There was also the town to explore and the thrill of watching the Axe-Wielders at weapon practice. But Merlion kept her firmly under control, admonishing her that she would have no time for such frivolities once she was married to Borneheld. Merlion had brought with her lists of the major nobles in the realm, the names of their families out to the third cousin, and the type of property and income that each controlled. All this she would have Faraday learn. By heart, if possible. There were also the towns and villages of Ichtar to memorize, together with the names of Borneheld's retainers and senior household staff.

By the night of their second day in Tare, Faraday was despairing. They would be leaving at dawn the next morning and Merlion's demands on her time had left her feeling exhausted rather than refreshed. She sat up in her bed, relishing her privacy, and, gazing through the window at the clouds rushing across the moonlit night, let her thoughts drift toward her forthcoming marriage to Borneheld. Now that there was some physical distance between them Faraday felt she could think about it a little more dispassionately.

Faraday knew she had been bedazzled by her first sight of Axis, but she understood she could not let her fascination with the man ruin her marriage with Borneheld. Axis was surely a better looking man than Borneheld, and his reputation as BattleAxe lent him an aura of glamor that her affianced husband could not match, but Borneheld was no poor choice for husband by any means. As Duke of Ichtar, he was the richest man in the realm apart from Priam himself, *and* he was also WarLord and current heir to the throne of Achar. It was no wonder her parents were so excited with the match. She could do no better.

Faraday began to feel a little guilty about her behavior in the palace courtyard. Borneheld had not meant to insult her and had tried, in his own way, to be kind. She thought over what she knew of Borneheld's life. Perhaps his blunt nature owed much to his lack of a mother in childhood. Searlas had not only not remarried after Rivkah's death, but had died himself when Borneheld was fourteen, leaving the boy to assume the heavy responsibilities of the Dukedom of Ichtar at an extraordinarily early age. Perhaps all he needed was the gentle hand of a wife. Faraday tried to picture Borneheld as he might be after two years of marriage to her—still predominantly a fighting man perhaps, but with polished manners and easy conversation. Yes, Faraday smiled, perhaps all he needed was a bit of refinement in his life, and she would be the one to provide it.

She wondered what it had been like for Embeth when she first married Ganelon of Tare. Faraday knew Embeth was of a Carlonite family and that she'd married at an even younger age than Faraday was now. Perhaps she'd faced similar problems.

Faraday frowned and played with a tendril of her hair where it had escaped the braid wrapped about her head. She needed to speak to Embeth. Although it was late, perhaps she was not asleep yet. Would Embeth mind being disturbed? Faraday abruptly made up her mind and swung her legs out of the bed, wrapping a warm shawl about her shoulders against the cold night air.

The house was dark and quiet, for everyone had gone to bed early in preparation for the dawn start. Faraday walked slowly down the wide corridor, running her fingers along the wall for guidance, her feet cold where they touched the bare stone between the scattered floor rugs. She held her breath outside her mother's room, but all was quiet. Mentally Faraday cursed her mother's lists; if nothing else she would be able to recite the list of Borneheld's retainers to him on their wedding night. She wished her mother would tell her more about what a husband expected of a wife.

She paused outside Embeth's room. There was the vaguest suggestion of light coming from between the cracks in the door. Good, Embeth was still awake. Faraday tapped softly, listened carefully for a moment, then tapped again. Embeth's voice sounded softly, although what she said was indistinct. Faraday took it as an invitation to enter.

She twisted the door handle and stepped quickly into the room. Embeth was sitting on the edge of her bed swathed in a green woollen wrap, with a look of utter shock and disbelief on her face.

"Embeth," said Faraday, halfway across the room. "I'm sorry to disturb you so late but I want to ask you if . . ."

Too late she saw Axis standing naked by the fire. She stopped, stunned, unable to tear her eyes from him.

"Faraday," Embeth said desperately, rising from her bed and stretching a hand out toward the girl.

Faraday dragged her eyes back to Embeth. Her hands started to tremble where they held her shawl about her shoulders. How could she have been such a fool! Her eyes filled with mortified tears and she started to stumble back toward the door. "I'm so sorry," she whispered. "Please, excuse me!" Then she turned and fled before her tears could spill down her cheeks.

Axis took a step forward but Embeth stopped him with a look. "Wait here, I'll talk to her."

Embeth hurried as fast as she dared down the dark corridor. She dared not call out for fear she would wake Merlion and prayed that Faraday was not so angry that she would slam her bedroom door or, worse, bolt it after her. Fortunately Faraday did neither, and Embeth was able to hurry into the bedroom after her, closing the door securely behind them.

Faraday was huddled into her bed, her hands covering her face, her shoulders convulsing with sobs. Embeth sat down and wrapped her arms about her. "Faraday?"

Faraday dropped her hands from her tear-stained face. "Oh Embeth! I'm so sorry, I didn't realize . . . that . . ."

"Shush. It's all right. You did nothing wrong, Faraday. Axis and I were just foolish to take such a risk with so many guests here. Shush."

Faraday took a deep breath and made a determined effort to stop her tears. Artor, what a simpleton she was! "How long . . . how long . . . ?"

"Oh, on and off for about three years. Faraday, listen to me. Axis and I have been good friends for many years; now and again we are lovers. But we are not in love. Do you know what I am saying?"

Faraday nodded, drying her tears with the back of her hand. "I think so. But I still feel so stupid."

"Well," said Embeth dryly, "at least you have learnt one of the more important rules of court etiquette—not to go bursting into bedrooms late at night, even if the person inside is supposed to be alone."

Faraday smiled a little. "Mother didn't teach me that one."

Embeth squeezed Faraday's shoulders and then let her go, sitting back a little. "What did you want to see me about?"

"Well . . . can I ask you another question first? About what just happened?" Embeth nodded. "Do women at court sometimes take lovers, even though they are married to another?"

Ah, thought Embeth, and right here is where I have to be careful. It was not unusual for married noblewomen to take lovers, as did their husbands, but Embeth could foresee disaster should she tell Faraday that. "Faraday, sometimes it is not unknown for women to take lovers, but usually only after they are widowed." And may Artor forgive my dissembling tongue, she thought to herself.

"So you and Axis were not lovers while Ganelon was alive?"

"No. We only became lovers some time after Ganelon died. And, should I remarry, then I would be true to my husband." At least that is the truth, Embeth thought.

Faraday was silent for a moment. "I wanted to ask you about marriage, Embeth. How you felt, what it was like."

"Are you having doubts, Faraday?"

Faraday nodded a little, her bright hair slipping free of its braid and over her eyes.

"It is not uncommon for a girl to have doubts before her marriage. So much is unknown and uncertain. But Faraday, your parents have already signed the contracts between your family and Borneheld. Although you have not yet actually spoken the marriage vows, or consummated the union, there is no turning back. Legally you are now bound to Borneheld, as Borneheld is to you. Only death can break the bonds between you. You both freely consented to the marriage before witnesses and before Artor."

Faraday sighed and twisted her hair up out of her eyes. "I know, Embeth. But . . . but what if we are not happy together?"

"Faraday, your duty is to your husband, to look after his needs and his estate and to bear his children. If love also comes, then that is good. But whatever happens you must always respect and honor him. You will be Duchess of Ichtar one day, and possibly Queen. You will have responsibilities to many other people as well as to yourself and your immediate family. Happiness?" Embeth shrugged. "Happiness is not everything, but duty and respect surely is. Your duty lies clear before you, Faraday. Do not let any foolish, girlish, romantic notions come between you and your duty."

Faraday looked a little shaken at this plain speech, but she also looked determined. "I understand, Embeth. Tell me, did you have happiness with Ganelon?"

Embeth smiled a little, remembering. "He was a good man, and he cared for me. He also respected me. At first I did not love him, and I found it hard to be happy here. But as the years passed and our marriage grew stronger, love and happiness also came along. One day—after bearing him three children!—I woke up and realized that I was in love with Ganelon. Two years later I lost him to the ill-willed tusks of a wild boar." Embeth did not add that she had almost died with grief when her steward brought her news of Ganelon's death. For a moment her heart clenched, remembering the blood down the steward's tunic, the tears in his eyes.

Faraday smiled, comforted. This is what would happen between Borneheld and her. Love might not come at once, not even for a year or two. But come it would, and she would be as good a wife to Borneheld as Embeth had been to Ganelon. All it took was patience, respect, and a firm sense of duty.

"Thank you, Embeth. I'm glad that I had this talk with you."

"Artor rewards those who remain true to their duty. Now," Embeth tucked Faraday into her bed as she would have done her own daughter, "to sleep with you, for it is an early start in the morning."

When Embeth opened the door to her room a few moments later Axis was gone. She suddenly felt very sad, not wanting to spend this night alone after remembering her happiness with Ganelon. If Faraday had been betrothed to a Ganelon then Embeth would have no doubts about the outcome, but Borneheld was no Ganelon.

12

At the Edge of the Silent Woman
Woods

The journey from Tare to the Silent Woman Woods took five days. The first days of Bone-month were upon them and the weather was now bitterly cold. During the day dark clouds broiled across the sky, and the riders were hit with frequent bouts of heavy rain and sometimes hail. Snow could not be far away. The soldiers huddled inside their oiled sealskin cloaks, the collars turned up to their ears, trying to ignore the water that trickled down their necks. The plains of northern Tarantaise were bare of anything but league after league of scrubby grassland containing no life at all. There was no shelter to be found against the rain. Merlion huddled cold and miserable inside a voluminous cloak and again damned her husband's insistence that they ride with the Axe-Wielders. Even Faraday's spirits were dampened by the weather. Occasionally Timozel rode beside them, trying to cheer them up with amusing stories, but Merlion and Faraday would only smile politely, and eventually he'd gallop back to his unit.

Once or twice Axis tried to speak with Faraday. He

thought he ought to say something, even though Embeth had told him she'd explained everything. On the one occasion he'd managed to find Faraday without her mother attached to her side like a limpet, she had smiled, apologized graciously for interrupting Embeth and himself, and turned on her heel and walked away without another word. Axis shrugged. Well, she had to grow up sooner or later. Better sooner, before Borneheld got his hands on her.

On the evening of the fifth day, for once blessedly clear of rain although the clouds still hung low, the dark line of the Silent Woman Woods appeared on the horizon, spreading as far as the eye could see.

Belial rode up to Axis where he sat motionless on Belaguez, surveying the line of trees ahead. "It is enough to make an Artor-fearing man reach for his axe, is it not, BattleAxe?"

Axis nodded his head absently. He had only seen the Silent Woman Woods once before in his life, and had been glad to pass leagues to the south of them. Now, however, he would have to enter.

"We'll make camp another two hours' ride closer, Belial. Any closer and we'll all suffer nightmares. In the morning . . . in the morning we'll ride in."

Belial understood his commander's hesitation. The Woods were a frightening sight, and he dreaded to think what they would look like at a lesser distance. Let alone what they would look like while they were riding through them.

"All of us, BattleAxe?"

Axis laughed sympathetically at his lieutenant's question. "No, Belial. Only a few of us. Myself, Gilbert, and one or two others. Timozel, perhaps, and Arne," he said naming one of the cohort commanders. "You had better stay and assume command of the Axe-Wielders until I return, Belial."

Belial tried, unsuccessfully, to hide his relief. "As you wish, BattleAxe."

* * *

The Silent Woman Woods were even more unnerving from the vantage point of the campsite. The trees, dark, thick and gnarled, grew tight and close together. Their tops reared upwards for what seemed a hundred paces and stretched outward so far that their boughs intermingled one with the other ensuring that little sunlight ever reached the forest floor. Eyes seemed to gaze out at those who watched. A constant undertone of strange whispers and crackles issued forth for anyone who cared to listen. The men were silent as they made camp, and most kept their backs to the Woods as much as possible. More men than usual made a prominent display of weapon practice with their axes as the cooks hurried to prepare the evening meal.

Faraday, her cloak held tightly about her, strolled up to Axis and Gilbert as they stood surveying the Woods. "It's frightening," she said quietly as she reached them, her eyes wide and apprehensive. "It's so wild, so untamed, so un-civilised. What could live in there but demons?"

Gilbert tried to reassure her. "The Seneschal have the Silent Woman Woods well under control, Lady Faraday. Do not fear, Artor is with us."

"Now and forever," whispered Faraday in automatic response. She turned toward Axis. "And you have to ride in there tomorrow?"

Axis did not move his eyes from the dark Woods. "There is no other choice. Although how the brothers could live in there, Artor only knows."

Faraday turned back to Gilbert. "Why are they called the Silent Woman Woods?"

"Because they do not ask as many questions as most women!" Axis snapped at her before Gilbert could reply.

"I'm sorry if I disturbed you, BattleAxe," she said quietly, and turned and walked back to camp. The white cat wound about her heels. Axis glared at it.

It was a bad night for many in the camp that evening. Those that did drift off to sleep often woke sweating a few

minutes later, frightened by unidentifiable fears. After tossing and turning for what seemed like hours, the nightmare
claimed Axis.

He was in the dark place, naked and bound by invisible
bonds to the floor. He strained every muscle, every liga-
ment, trying to break free, knowing as he did so that he
should be saving his energy for the fight that lay ahead.
Sweat broke out from every pore on his body. His breathing grew heavy and labored as his fear deepened.

Suddenly he could feel the presence, surrounding him,
so powerful it might crush him.

"No," he whispered, "you are not my father!"

The presence grew strange. It did not speak. There was
not the hatred that he could usually feel. It felt . . . puzzled.

"Who are you?" Axis whispered. "Who are you?"

"Who are you?" an echo whispered back at him,
strangely hoarse and distorted by the darkness. "Who are
you?"

It felt strange—just as frightening and threatening, but
different. The bonds holding his arms and legs disappeared
and Axis leapt to his feet, trying desperately to discern
shape or movement in the darkness that surrounded him.
The ground felt cool and damp beneath his feet.

"We do not know who he is," a voice whispered behind
him, and Axis whirled in the dark, almost losing his balance. "Where has he come from? What is he doing here?
How did his feet find the paths? Who guided his feet to the
paths?"

"Who are you?" Axis whispered fiercely, looking
around for his sword or his axe.

There was a moment's silence. Axis could still feel the
puzzlement surrounding him. "We are who we are and we
have always been here. Who are you?"

"I am Axis Rivkahson," he said. "BattleAxe of the Axe-
Wielders."

Instantly he could feel the change about him. Puzzlement vanished in an instant as fury and hate surrounded

him in palpable waves. Whoever, *whatever*, was out there began to hiss and moan in equal amounts. Axis could feel himself being buffeted by the malevolence surrounding him. He clenched his fists and crouched, as ready as he could be for attack.

To one side a bright light bloomed and Axis twisted in that direction, squinting as the light hurt his eyes. There seemed to be a vague shape behind it.

"Go away Axis Rivkahson, BattleAxe of the Axe-Wielders!" a thousand voices suddenly boomed, surrounding him from every direction. Axis whimpered as the full force of their fury hit him. "Get you gone from this place! You are not welcome!"

The shape that held the light stepped forward and became more distinct. The light itself spread and grew stronger and Axis started to distinguish his surroundings. He was in a large grove in the middle of a forest, black trees pressed close about the edges of the circle of light. There were shapes, however, many shapes, moving restlessly among the trees. Axis was glad the light was not strong enough for him to see them properly. The creature holding the light was standing slightly to one side of the center of the grove, and as Axis focused on it he almost cried out in horror. Although it had the trunk and limbs of a muscular man, clad only in a brief loin cloth, the creature had the head of a full-grown stag. Massive antlers branched out from its forehead and its eyes were red with hate. It wove its head threateningly from side to side as it strode toward him, baring its broad yellow-stained teeth. "Leave!" it screamed, and Axis screamed with it. He sat bolt upright in his bedroll, still terrified. At first he thought that he had screamed aloud, but the other men about the campfire paid him no heed, trapped as they were in their own ill dreams. Axis leaned forward and put his face in his hands. Would it never end? He felt a warm shape bump into his side. His heart leapt in fear, before he realized it was only the cat. Axis pulled it up to his chest as he lay down and tried to get a few more hours' sleep before dawn. He slept soundly and dreamlessly until Belial awakened him just as the sun was staining the eastern horizon.

13

The Cauldron Lake

An hour after dawn the small group breakfasted and took their horses not fifty paces from the Silent Woman Woods. A biting wind blew over the land and they all shivered inside their cloaks. The horses shifted uneasily, the nervousness of their riders transmitting itself to them. Belial stared at the path leading into the Woods.

"It won't be wide enough for two of you to ride abreast, sir."

Axis sat still and silent, then said, "How far in is the Keep, Gilbert?"

Gilbert looked discomforted. "I'm not completely sure, BattleAxe."

"I thought you knew most things, Gilbert," Axis said dryly. "You do know exactly where the Keep is, don't you?"

Gilbert's face splotched a patchy red in embarrassment. "At the end of the path, BattleAxe."

Belial swore under his breath. "Is that all you've got to say, you useless lump of . . ."

"Belial," Axis said mildly, "it is not a good thing to curse the Brotherhood of the Seneschal. If Gilbert says the Keep is at the end of the path, then the Keep is at the end of the path. Of course, it might help if Gilbert knew how long this Artor-forsaken path is, wouldn't it, Gilbert?"

Gilbert swallowed. He wished he were back in the Tower of the Seneschal. "We have not had any communication with the Keep for some time, BattleAxe."

Axis frowned. "Jayme said he was going to send a rider in to tell them we were coming."

"The Brother-Leader sent a rider, it is true. . . . It's just that he hasn't come back out again."

All the men shifted nervously now. Timozel and Arne, the youngest men present, traded frightened looks and fingered their axes.

Axis remembered how unsure Jayme had seemed about the records the Keep contained. "And just how long is it since the Brother-Leader has heard anything from the Keep, Gilbert?"

Gilbert rolled his eyes skyward, as if he found something terribly interesting among the clouds. His skin was pasty-white in the dawn light. "Thirty-nine years."

"Thirty-nine years?" said Axis incredulous. "Gilbert, how does anyone know there *is* a Keep in there? Jayme told me that Brother Ogden was chief Brother in the Keep. How does he know that if there's been no communication for thirty-nine years?"

Arne, a dour-faced and dark-haired man, chuckled suddenly in grim humor. "Because that's who the Seneschal sent to take charge thirty-nine years ago, BattleAxe!"

Axis stared at Gilbert. "Is that right?"

Gilbert nodded unhappily. "The Brothers are an uncommunicative lot," he muttered.

Axis swore under his breath. Why hadn't Jayme told him this? "Belial. If we're not out in three days, send in a party after us. If that party doesn't come out within three days, then send no one else in. Break camp and go back to Carlon. You can tell Jayme that if anyone else has to go back into the Woods then it will have to be him. And if he doesn't want to go into the Woods, then he can go and stop the Forbidden at Gorkenfort."

Belial nodded and backed his horse off a little. "May Artor keep and hold you in His hand, BattleAxe."

"Now and forever," the others muttered.

Axis turned to the other three. "Arne, Timozel, are you ready?" They nodded. Axis turned to Gilbert. "Brother Gilbert, you may take the lead. Your prayers might help to keep the demons at bay. Timozel, you follow me; Arne, bring up the rear. Are you ready, AxeWielders?"

"We follow your voice and we are ready, BattleAxe!" Timozel and Arne shouted.

"Then let us ride," Axis cried and spurred Belaguez into a gallop.

Belial stood and watched them until they disappeared into the gloom of the Woods, then he slowly turned his horse. He would set guards by the trail night and day until his BattleAxe came back. Halfway back to camp he came across Faraday standing alone in the waving grass, watching the spot where the riders had disappeared.

The men slowed their horses to a walk once they entered the Woods. Within thirty paces of the tree line they were completely lost in gloom. Every man sat straight and tall in the saddle, eyes shifting constantly from side to side, expecting attack at any moment. They could hardly conceive of a world where there were no wide-open spaces, where the sky was not instantly visible. The three Axemen had pulled their swords from their weapon belts and held them at the ready. Gilbert occasionally whimpered in fear and would have stopped had not Axis kept Belaguez pressed against his horse's rump.

The gloom and the silence enveloped them. Not even birds called from the trees. About one hundred paces in, Timozel abruptly cried out from behind. "BattleAxe!"

Axis pulled Belaguez to a halt and whipped around in the saddle. "What is it?"

Timozel was bent double, half out of the saddle as he leaned further and further down his horse's off side. "It's my axe!" he gasped, "it's . . ."

Now Axis could feel it too, a massive weight hanging down by his right hip as if a gigantic hand had seized his axe by the haft and was pulling it toward the ground. He grunted and tried to pull the other way, but whatever had hold of his axe was too strong. The next moment he was pulled out of his saddle, and though he desperately grabbed the pommel he felt himself being dragged inexorably to the ground. Axis heard Gilbert cry out in horror, but he had no time to see what was wrong with him. The pressure on his axe increased—whatever invisible hand had hold of the haft was unbelievably strong—and, an instant after he heard Timozel hit the ground, Axis was pulled completely out of the saddle himself and hit the ground so hard that his breath was knocked out of his body.

Axis unbuckled his weapon belt to free himself of his axe almost as soon as he hit the ground, and the instant it was free he felt the immense pressure disappear. He jumped to his feet. Timozel and Arne lay struggling on the ground nearby, their horses a little further down the track, milling in confusion. Axis almost lost his footing as the ground swayed underneath his feet.

"Tim . . . Arne . . . unbuckle your weapon belts!" Axis shouted, stumbling in his efforts to reach his men still writhing helplessly on the ground. Timozel had been pulled halfway into the ground and Axis bent over him, the ground heaving beneath his feet, desperately trying to help Timozel free himself from his axe. Finally the weapon belt dropped free and Timozel grunted in relief. Axis hauled him to his feet then bent to help Arne, who had also unbuckled his weapon belt. All three turned to look for their axes, but the ground was heaving and buckling even more violently and their axes had completely disappeared underneath the loose covering of leaves and pines needles that littered the surface.

They all stepped back several paces to where the ground

was firm, legs shaking. "Artor save us!" Arne gasped, "they would have taken us with them!" For a few heartbeats longer they stood, swords in hand, chests heaving as they fought to recover their breath, watching the ground where their axes had disappeared, hardly able to comprehend what had happened. After a moment the ground settled down until even the leaf litter had ceased to shift. They exchanged frightened glances. What sort of place was this where the forest could eat axes? How could they fight the very earth itself?

"I wonder whether the rider that Jayme sent was wearing an axe," Timozel said quietly, his youthful face ashen. "And if he was, I wonder if he got his weapon belt off in time."

"And how many others are buried under the earth in this spot," Arne whispered.

That thought didn't bear thinking about, and Axis battled to regain his equilibrium. "Get back on your horses. I for one am going to feel a lot better with Belaguez underneath me again."

Gilbert rode back as the others remounted. "What happened?" he asked.

Axis swung into Belaguez's saddle. "We have been deprived of our axes, Brother Gilbert," he said, a lot more calmly than he felt. "We must hope that the forest does not eat us as well. Ride on."

Nothing else troubled them for the rest of the long ride, although the forest loomed still and dark around them and they were all tense and jumpy, snarling at each other whenever a twig snapped under hoof or a low-slung bough scraped at a head or a shoulder. Hands lay slippery with sweat on the hilts of swords, but the three Axemen were unwilling to wipe their hands along their cloaks in case the demons, or whatever other dark fiends inhabited these Woods, chose that moment to attack.

After they had been in the saddle almost eight hours, the

ground started to drop away underneath them, and they had to rein their horses back on the increasingly steep path in case they slipped and fell. An hour later Gilbert pulled his horse up and turned back to Axis, his face now so weary that deep lines of fatigue scored his pimply cheeks and forehead.

"BattleAxe," he waved ahead sketchily. "Water."

Axis peered through the gloom. Although it was difficult to see very far ahead, he could see a glint of water. "Keep going," he said. "The sooner we find somewhere to rest and eat the better."

"*If* we find somewhere to rest and eat," he heard Timozel mutter. Axis hefted his sword in his right hand, almost dropping it as his fingers cramped, and leaned further back in the saddle as Belaguez slipped a few paces down the slope. Artor, he thought, if we don't get some rest soon we'll have to lie down here in the very path.

And if we do that, will the ground swallow us as easily as it swallowed our axes?

Almost as soon as that thought crossed his mind, Gilbert's horse jumped a small obstacle and landed on level ground, Gilbert only managing to keep to his saddle by the most strenuous effort. Forewarned, Axis gripped the saddle with his knees just as Belaguez leaped across a small stream; he called a warning back to Timozel and Arne. The path broadened and flattened ahead and all four men allowed themselves a deep breath of relief at the increased space, Gilbert taking the first opportunity he'd had to rein his horse back from the lead position. Axis kneed Belaguez forward.

"The trees thin ahead," he said. "There's a lake."

A few moments later they had reined in at the shore of one of the most incredible sights they had ever seen. The entire forest sloped down into a deep circular basin, the mass of gray-green trees ending abruptly at the edge of an almost perfectly around lake. But it was the water itself that caught the party's attention. It shone a soft, gentle gold in the late afternoon light.

Axis turned to Gilbert. "Did you know this was here?"

Gilbert shook his head slowly from side to side, not taking his eyes from the water.

"It must be enchanted," Axis said flatly. "Water isn't gold."

"Perhaps it isn't water," said Timozel softly, making the sign of the Plough to ward off evil.

"Look," said Arne, pointing with his sword. "It's the cursed Keep."

The Keep sat virtually at the lake's edge, about a quarter of the way around, built of pale yellow stone that reflected the glow from the water. Its smooth cylindrical stone walls rose some thirty paces into the air, the walls only occasionally broken by narrow dark windows. It looked to be completely deserted.

"Well," Axis spurred Belaguez forward, "let us go find this lost tribe of brothers, shall we?"

The horses slipped and slid their way around the lake's edge, finally reaching the Keep just as the last rays of sun disappeared behind the tops of the forest trees. The Keep looked even more deserted closer up, and the men began to feel uneasy. No one wanted to spend the night outside in this damned forest.

Axis kicked his stallion up to the barred door and brought the hilt of his sword crashing down on it three times. "Open up in the name of Artor!" he shouted. "We have need of food and rest."

Nothing happened. Timozel and Arne exchanged looks, and Gilbert groaned quietly. Axis thundered at the door again, then edged Belaguez backwards a few steps so he could gaze up at the impassive stone walls.

"Damn you, open up," he whispered.

A small trapdoor at eye level in the barred door suddenly swung open. "Well?" a scratchy voice demanded.

Axis felt relief wash through him. He half fell from his saddle and staggered stiffly up to the door.

"I am Axis, BattleAxe of the Axe-Wielders. These are my two companions, Arne and Timozel, and Brother

Gilbert, assistant and adviser to the Brother-Leader, Jayme." There, he thought, let him think about that.

A pair of suspicious gray eyes darted back and forth across the group. "No, you're not, and no, he's not," he said abruptly, and slammed the trapdoor shut in Axis' face.

"What!" Axis hammered at the door again in angry frustration. "In the name of the Seneschal, open up!"

The trapdoor popped open again. "You're not the BattleAxe," the scratchy voice said belligerently, "Fingus is." The gray eyes shifted to Gilbert. "And he's not adviser or whatever to the Brother-Leader. I am."

The trapdoor slammed shut again.

Axis leaned wearily against the door, rubbing his hand over his eyes in exasperation. Fingus had been BattleAxe decades ago. These men had received no news from beyond the borders of the Silent Woman Woods for the past thirty-nine years.

He somehow raised the strength to hammer at the door again.

"Go away!" the voice called from behind the door.

"We are hungry, we are tired, and we need somewhere to stay the night," Axis said in what he hoped was a reasonable tone. "Please, will you give us aid?"

Finally there was the sound of bolts being pulled back and Axis stood up straight, just in time to avoid falling over as the door swung inward. A short, plump Brother of about seventy stood there, suspicion darkening the gray eyes in his round, cherubic face. Wispy white hair surrounded his head like a halo. "Well, why didn't you say so in the first place," he said irritably. "Come in, come in."

Timozel took the horses and tied them up loosely to a row of iron rings in the wall of the Keep, then he followed the others inside. The irritable Brother slammed the door shut behind him.

14

Inside the Silent Woman Keep

"Well? What are you doing here? What are you doing wandering the Silent Woman Woods?" he demanded.

Axis looked around. They were in a large, dimly lit circular room which seemed to take up the entire ground floor of the Keep. To one side a twisting iron staircase led to the upper levels. Various packing cases lay strewn across almost half of the floor space, while the other half was set up as a rude kitchen and eating area. A large wooden larder, propped up by bricks, leaned precariously against the stone wall, while a crude wooden table sat before a small fire in an iron grate. The fire provided the only light in the room. A small and utterly insufficient iron hood led some of the smoke away through a pipe in the wooden ceiling. The rest of the smoke simply drifted about the room.

Axis gave the Brother the Axe-Wielder's salute; he saw no point in insulting the man. "Brother Ogden?"

The Brother grunted and looked the group over. "That is my name."

"Brother Ogden, my name is Axis, BattleAxe of the Axe-Wielders. Wait!" He raised his hand slightly and took a step forward as Ogden started to shake his head. "Brother, it has been thirty-nine years since you had contact with the outside world and many things have changed since you were last at the Tower of the Seneschal. Fingus died many years ago. Now I am BattleAxe. King Karel likewise died many years ago and now Priam sits on the throne of Achar."

"He was a snotty-nosed toddler when I last saw him," Ogden grumbled. Timozel restrained a smile at the image of a snotty-nosed Priam, complete with auburn curls. The Brother looked at Axis sharply. "Who's the Brother-Leader did you say? Jayme?"

Axis nodded. Ogden frowned then smiled as if recalling something. "Well, well. Done well for a boy from the farm, hasn't he? I wonder what friends *he* made to reach such a high position?" He muttered to himself for another moment, his smile fading, then wandered over to the table. "Well, sit, sit. No use standing about like gawking peasants caught at court." He kicked out a couple of bare benches from underneath the table. "Courtesy dictates that we offer you some food while you tell us why you are here. Veremund!"

Ogden's sudden bellow caught the four men off-guard and Gilbert, who was closest to Ogden and in the act of sitting down on the dusty bench, tripped and would have fallen had not Timozel caught his arm.

"Veremund!" Ogden bellowed again, staring at the staircase where it disappeared into the darkness. There was a shuffling from above, then a figure hastened into view, lit by a small lamp that he was carrying. He hurried down the staircase, whispering to himself.

Veremund was as tall and spare as Ogden was short and fat, and unlike Ogden's pale gray eyes, his eyes were almost black in his pale face. His hair, however, was as white and as wispy as his fellow brother's. Ink stains ran down his dirty gray habit.

"Guests!" he exclaimed, as he caught sight of Axis and

his companions. "Ogden! We have guests!" He hurried over to the table and enthusiastically shook all four men's hands. "Charmed," he beamed. "Absolutely delighted, old chap." He patted Timozel on the head and clapped Gilbert on the shoulder, then he spied the insignia on the breast of Axis' coat.

"BattleAxe! We are indeed honored . . . aren't we, Ogden?" He looked expectantly at Ogden, who grumbled to himself again and shuffled over to the fire and pushed a large kettle closer to the flames. "Well," Veremund continued, a little deflated. "We *are* honored. It's been a long time. Please excuse Brother Ogden's poor manners, gentlemen. He does dislike to be disturbed from his contemplations, you see. But I am glad to have company." He waved at the men to sit down. "Please, sit . . . sit."

Ogden banged some dirty plates on the table, stared at them for a moment, then wiped them perfunctorily with the skirt of his habit, leaving even more smears. "They've not yet informed me why they're here, Veremund." He passed the plates about the table.

Veremund smiled broadly at the men. "Well, that doesn't matter, does it. We have plenty of time to hear their story." He paused, and a shadow crossed his face. "Gentlemen, forgive me if I ask this. But I can't help wondering if you had any trouble coming through the Woods?"

Ogden, who was rummaging in the larder behind their backs, paused and turned back to the table. His eyes briefly met Veremund's.

Axis glanced at Timozel and Arne. "We were not inside the trees a hundred paces when . . ." He paused. "When . . ."

"Ah," said Veremund softly, wringing his hands, a sad expression crossing his face. "The Woods, you see, they would not allow your axes in, would they?"

"Demons," said Arne darkly. "No woods or forests should be allowed to stand. It's an affront to Artor."

Ogden banged a cold honeyed ham on the table. He chortled. "Young man, the Seneschal have been trying to cut these woods down for a thousand years. Why—so it is said—one day Axemen five thousand strong surrounded the Woods with their axes and tried to cut their way through." He laughed again. "None survived the experience. . . . Axemen, I mean."

Axis looked at the others, startled. "But I thought these Woods were left standing because the Seneschal wanted the Keep left undisturbed."

Veremund sighed and sat down. "Unfortunately, the Seneschal is not yet strong enough to conquer these Woods, BattleAxe. The old magic is still too strong." Gilbert frowned at the casual mention of magic. Veremund looked back to Ogden, returning from the larder with a tray laden with food. The unspoken thought passed between them—why had the Woods taken the axes yet let the men live to reach the Keep? The Woods had let none live for . . . well, for many years.

The kettle whistled and Veremund busied himself setting some tea to steep while Ogden unloaded the tray. Their four guests exchanged surprised looks; the food that Ogden laid out was as fine as that of Priam's table itself. There were four different kinds of bread, an array of cold meats, pickles, mustards, fresh vegetables, various berry tarts and jellies, cream, butter, spiced fruits and a variety of cheeses.

Gilbert cleared his throat. "Excuse me, Brothers, but, ah, I was wondering how you manage to set such a fine table?"

Ogden and Veremund, sitting themselves down at the table, looked baffled. "Why, the food comes from the larder, of course," Ogden said.

"Yes," Gilbert pushed, wriggling a little on his bench, "but how does it get in there? I mean, do you butcher and bake all this yourself? There were no livestock outside, and we saw no gardens."

Ogden's eyes snapped. "Young whip-snake, the food comes from the larder. I presume Veremund puts it in there."

Veremund's eyes widened in denial. "Oh, no, no, no, Ogden! *You* put it in there. *I* don't."

Ogden turned on Veremund, absolutely furious at being contradicted. "No, I don't! You do!" His plump cheeks had gone pink with anger.

"Brothers," Axis said hastily to avoid further argument. "It really doesn't matter. I'm sorry if Brother Gilbert's question offended you. Please, the food is more than we could have expected."

"Well," Veremund huffed. "If you will excuse me, I will attend to your horses. There is a stable out the back. If you could perhaps leave your tale until I return I won't have to impose on you to repeat your words." He pushed himself back from the table and sniffed at Ogden. "Brother Ogden, perhaps you would be so kind as to pour the tea while I am gone." Then he stalked from the room, slamming the Keep door behind him.

An hour later the men were warm, fed and far more relaxed than previously. Veremund had stomped back inside and joined them at the table. He refused to eat, sipping only at a mug of steaming tea. Ogden leaned forward. "Now, young men, what brings the BattleAxe, two Axe-Wielders, and what you claim to be the Brother-Leader's adviser deep into the Silent Woman Woods to disturb two old men who would prefer to be left alone?"

Axis stared at his empty mug for a moment, then looked at Ogden and Veremund. "Brothers, we've come because the Seneschal, Achar itself, needs your help."

For almost an hour Axis talked, telling them everything he knew about the problems in the north. Occasionally he'd clarify a detail with Gilbert, and sometimes one or other of the two Brothers would ask a question. Finally he sat back. "Well, can you help us? Can you tell us how to defeat these unbodied wraiths?"

Ogden looked at Axis, then glanced about the rest of the table. His eyes were troubled. "My sons. The news you bring is grievous. I am afraid to tell you that I, we, believe the news is worse than you yet realize." He paused.

Axis face tightened. "Then tell me, man, tell me! Don't sit there and keep me guessing!"

"BattleAxe. At one point you mentioned the possibility that this danger from the north might not actually be the Forbidden themselves," said Veremund stumbling over the word "Forbidden", "but something else. You were correct. Brother Ogden and I are afraid that the danger you speak of might be the Destroyer, Gorgrael himself, driving his Ghostmen and his ice and cloud down from the north."

Axis glanced at Gilbert, but Gilbert looked as perplexed as he. "Veremund, what do you mean? Who is this Destroyer? This Gorgrael?"

Ogden answered instead. "Axis, first let me explain about this Keep a little." Axis nodded. "Jayme told you that the Keep contained records, ancient records, from the time when the Acharites penned the Forbidden behind the Fortress Ranges, is that right?"

Axis nodded again. "Jayme hoped that these records would contain valuable information about how to defeat the Forbidden."

Ogden blinked, amused. "Hardly, young man. The records that this Keep contains are the actual records of the Forbidden themselves. They extend back almost eight thousand years."

"What!" Gilbert was appalled. "They should have been burned hundreds of years ago!" Ever since the Forbidden had been penned behind the Fortress Ranges and the Icescarp Alps the Seneschal had done everything in their power to rid Achar of any sign or memory of the Forbidden, even discouraging people from repeating the old legends that included the Forbidden. No wonder the Seneschal did not encourage any interest in the Silent Woman Woods and Keep.

"Exactly why the Seneschal has not let it be widely known that they exist, you young simpleton!" Ogden snapped at Gilbert. "They might be the records of the Forbidden, but they are valuable for precisely that reason."

"But the Forbidden are brutes, hardly better than beasts, Ogden. How could they keep records?" Axis asked quietly, leaning forward so that the firelight glinted in his eyes and in the short hairs of his blond beard.

Veremund answered. "BattleAxe. The Forbidden, as you have so simplistically called them, had a written and oral culture that was far more complex than our own. Even after hundreds of years of brothers studying the records that remain, we can only dimly comprehend the complexity and beauty of their lives."

Arne studied both Brothers carefully. "You sound as if you admire them."

"Young man, it has been hard for Brother Ogden and myself to do anything but admire them. They were beautiful peoples."

"Sacrilege!" Gilbert hissed. "You are unworthy to wear the robes of the Seneschal!"

"Hush, Gilbert," Axis said tersely, though he sympathized with Gilbert's reactions. How could these Brothers *admire* the Forbidden when, as every Artor-fearing Acharite knew, the Forbidden had done their best to slaughter every man, woman and child in Achar? "You said 'peoples,' Veremund."

"The Forbidden are composed of two peoples. The Icarii, sometimes known as the people of the Wing, and the Avar, or the people of the Horn. The records here are mainly of the Icarii, although we do have some relating to the Avar as well."

"How can you read the language of the Forbidden, Brothers?" Gilbert asked suspiciously, ignoring Axis' admonition to keep quiet.

"All the races of this ancient land once lived together, Gilbert, and spoke the same language. It has scarcely altered over the centuries."

We speak the same language as the Forbidden? Axis raised his eyebrows, but he did not dwell on it. "And these records will tell us of what we face?"

Veremund nodded. "I believe so. But it might be better if

I show you rather than simply tell you. Ogden, do you think that would be best?"

"Yes, Veremund. I think that *would* be best."

Veremund inclined his head and stood up, taking the small lamp providing the only illumination in the room besides the fire, and climbed the circular iron steps until he disappeared from view.

Axis felt a premonition crawl down his spine and he reached instinctively for his axe. But it was gone, buried underneath the Woods, and his sword stood propped out of his reach against the wall of the Keep. He glanced at Arne and Timozel; both looked as nervous as he. How had they let their swords be placed out of their immediate reach?

Ogden noticed their tension. "Gentlemen, I assure you that there is no danger. Veremund has simply gone to fetch one of the Icarii books."

Soon the four men heard Veremund shuffling back down the steps. He had left his lamp behind, and grasped a large leather volume to his chest with both arms. He almost dropped the volume as he reached the table: clearly it was very heavy. Ogden turned the book around so that he could open it, squinting in the flickering light and muttering as he leafed through the pages. The others could see that each page was made of vellum, and contained an unfamiliar hand-written script and illuminations of incredible beauty. Whoever had written in this book had used inks of vivid hues, and gold and silver paints glittered among the rainbow enamels of the script.

"Ah," Ogden finally breathed, his fingers tracing lightly along the lines of a page. "Here we are. Both the Icarii and the Avar, often so dissimilar in nature, had a shared prophecy, a prophecy that dates back many thousands of years. All Icarii and Avar used to pray that they would not be alive when the prophecy came to fruition. Let me read it to you."

He took a deep breath and began to read, his voice taking on a peculiar musical aspect. "A day will come when born will be . . . Two babes whose blood . . . whose blood . . ." He stopped, rubbing his eyes. "Cursed firelight!" he growled. "You should have brought the lamp back with you, Veremund. Here, can you read this?"

Veremund shook his head from side to side. "Brother Ogden, you know that my eyes are weaker than yours—perhaps the BattleAxe?"

Axis looked startled, but Ogden waved him over. "The words won't bite you, BattleAxe, and you have a young man's eyes. I used to know these lines by heart, but 'tis so long since I had cause to remember them. . . . Here," his finger tapped the page impatiently as Axis sat down on the bench beside him. "The words start here."

Axis stared at the page for a moment, but the writing was so strange and alien that he could not make out the words. He looked up at Ogden. "Brother, I can't read this. The writing is foreign, and I—"

"Nonsense!" Ogden interrupted. "Look! Concentrate, and you'll be able to read it—you'll see."

Sighing, Axis turned back to the page. He let one finger lightly touch the page; it felt slightly warm. He stared at the writing. The letters were strange, curved and exotic, and the words all seemed to flow into one another. The vivid colors were distracting. It was impossible. He frowned and leaned a little closer, his temples throbbing in the poor light. A wave of dizziness passed over him, and, when he blinked and cleared his vision, the writing had somehow come into focus.

"Yes," he said quietly. "I can read it. It is very strange, but . . . but I can read it." A strange melody ran softly through his mind, but Axis ignored it.

"Then read it, BattleAxe, read it to us," said Ogden quietly, his eyes riveted on Axis' face.

Axis took a deep breath, and when he started to read, his voice took on a low-timbred musical quality, almost as if he were singing to himself.

A day will come when born will be
Two babes whose blood will tie them.
That born to Wing and Horn will hate

The one they call the StarMan.
Destroyer! rises in the north
And drives his Ghostmen south;
Defenseless lie both flesh and field
Before Gorgrael's ice.
To meet this threat you must release
The StarMan from his lies,
Revive Tencendor, fast and sure
Forget the ancient war,
For if Plough, Wing and Horn can't find
The bridge to understanding,·
Then will Gorgrael earn his name
And bring Destruction hither.

Axis paused a moment, although he didn't take his eyes from the page. "Tencendor?"

"I will explain in a moment," Ogden said quietly, placing a gentle hand on Axis' shoulder. "Finish. Please." Axis resumed reading.

StarMan, listen, heed me well,
Your power will destroy you
If you should wield it in the fray
'Ere these prophecies are met:
The Sentinels will walk abroad
'Til power corrupt their hearts;
A child will turn her head and cry
Revealing ancient arts;
A wife will hold in joy at night
The slayer of her husband;
Age-old souls, long in cribs,
Will sing o'er mortal land;
The remade dead, fat with child
Will birth abomination;
A darker power will prove to be
The father of salvation.
Then waters will release bright eyes
To form the Rainbow Scepter.

"There is a break," Axis said quietly, "then begins another verse." He felt very strange, almost as if he were in the grip of a dream. The melody running through his mind had become louder, more insistent. He was thankful for the pressure of Ogden's hand on his shoulder, and did not notice it tighten in shock the moment he continued to read.

StarMan, listen, for I know
That you can wield the scepter
To bring Gorgrael to his knees
And break the ice asunder.
But even with the power in hand
Your pathway is not sure:
A Traitor from within your camp
Will seek and plot to harm you;
Let not your Lover's pain distract
For this will mean your death;
Destroyer's might lies in his hate
Yet you must never follow;
Forgiveness is the thing assured
To save Tencendor's soul.

For a long moment there was silence. Then Axis reluctantly tore his eyes away from the beautiful page. His vision blurred, then cleared again as he blinked at Ogden. The melody had disappeared as strangely as it had come.

"I don't understand," Timozel said, his face confused. He looked apologetically at Ogden and Veremund. "I was never good at my book learning, Brothers. I preferred to spend time with my weapon instructor."

"Axis seems to have been very good at *his* book learning," Gilbert muttered very quietly to himself. Gilbert was sitting next to Axis as he read and yet as carefully as he had studied the page he could not decipher the writing—and he had far more training than Axis had ever had. How had Axis managed to read what he could not?

"Tencendor," said Veremund, "was the ancient name of

Achar when all three races lived together in harmony. The followers of the Plough, the Wing and the Horn. The Prophecy of the Destroyer, as these verses were known, refers to a time when Gorgrael, the Destroyer, will drive his forces of ice and cloud down from the north in an attempt to conquer Tencendor, ah, Achar."

"Destroyer rises in the north and drives his Ghostmen south," Axis mused. "Brothers, are these Ghostmen the wraith-like creatures that have been attacking the patrols? And the creatures made of ice that attacked Gorkenfort and Gorkentown . . . ice creatures of this Gorgrael?"

Ogden nodded.

"It's completely ridiculous!" Gilbert exclaimed, amazed that Axis could be taking these lines seriously. "This is a heretical book, BattleAxe! You *cannot* listen to these words!"

Axis turned his pale blue eyes on Gilbert. "I don't care if we listen to the words of a pox-ridden whore whose brain is riddled with the diseases of her trade, Gilbert, just as long as they make some kind of sense." He turned back to Ogden and Veremund. "Brothers, I can understand the reference to the Destroyer, and the troubles in the north, but the rest of it? It's a riddle."

"I'm afraid that prophecies tend to be a little like riddles, Axis. Easy enough to interpret when you know the answer, almost impossible when you don't." And dangerous, he thought, dangerous when you misinterpret them.

"But," Timozel frowned and leaned forward. "Doesn't the Prophecy refer to a man who can stop this Destroyer? The 'StarMan'?"

Veremund frowned. "And tied by blood to the Destroyer. A brother, perhaps."

Gilbert laughed incredulously, his pimply face scornful as he looked at the two elderly Brothers. "Oh? So you now tell us that we not only face some mythical Destroyer, a legend of the Forbidden, but that we have to put our trust in his *brother*? If the Destroyer is born of Wing and Horn then he is one of the Forbidden himself. His brother can only be of the Forbidden too. My friends, I think you have been too long closeted with your books. The Seneschal will not allow the Forbidden back into Achar. Never."

Veremund stood and started to clear away the dishes. He shuffled around the table, and placed his hands briefly on Arne and Timozel's shoulders. They had heard enough for one night. "My friends. You are tired after your long ride. It is late, and we need to sleep on this. All will seem clearer in the light of the morning."

Timozel yawned hugely and Arne followed suit an instant later. Both stretched. "Come," Veremund touched Axis lightly on the arm and brushed Gilbert's back with his fingers as he walked past. "I will prepare you a sleeping chamber on one of the upper levels. All will be well in the morning."

Axis finally felt his weariness come crashing about him. He realized he could no longer think clearly. Veremund spoke sense.

"I really think we should . . ." Gilbert began, but then his body was wracked with a gigantic yawn. "Perhaps you are right, Brother Veremund," he finished lamely. "I do feel somewhat tired."

"Then come," Veremund smiled. "Let me lead you to your beds."

Fifteen minutes later all four men were sound asleep in the small chamber Veremund had prepared for them. They had paused only long enough to remove their outer clothes and boots and had then crawled into their blankets. Veremund waited at the door until he could hear the men taking the deep, slow breaths of sleep, then walked thoughtfully back down the stairs.

Ogden was still sitting at the table by the slowly dying fire, his hand resting lovingly on the text of the Prophecy of the Destroyer. "Well, Brother," he said as Veremund sat slowly down at the table, careful of his arthritic limbs, "have we waited our time out?"

Veremund took a deep breath, his eyes on the embers in the grate. "No Acharite has been able to read those words for almost a thousand years." He raised his eyes to Ogden. "No one *can* read them, lest he or she be of Icarii blood." Veremund had told Gilbert only half the truth earlier when the Brother had asked him about the language of the Forbidden. Although all three races, Acharite, Icarii and Avar, spoke a common language, the Icarii also spoke a sacred language reserved only for the most holy or important occasions. The Prophecy had been composed in that sacred tongue.

"And, what is more, of the Icarii line of Enchanters. The final verse of the Prophecy was heavily warded. Not even we have heard it before now."

Both were silent for a moment, staring into each other's eyes.

"It is our task to be heedful," Ogden finally whispered.

"Watchful," Veremund whispered back.

Neither spoke out loud the thought that had gripped them the moment Axis had started to recite the words of the last verse—that final verse had been meant for the eyes of one person only. It had stood unread since the ink and the spells of warding were still wet on the page. Now the Prophecy of the Destroyer was awake and walking the ancient land of Tencendor. And, by the look of the BattleAxe, it had been doing so for some thirty years.

15

Silent Woman Night

Faraday lay sleepless in her bedroll, listening to her mother's gentle snores. The night lay heavily upon her, and Faraday felt oppressed, trapped in this tiny tent. She twisted over to her other side and closed her eyes, trying to find sleep, but ten minutes later she was twisting back the other way, eyes wide open again.

She sighed and sat up. What she needed was some fresh air. Quietly, so as not to wake her mother, she turned the blanket of the bedroll back and fumbled in the dark for her shoes. The air was cold, and once she stood up Faraday reached for her heavy cloak to wrap around her nightgown as she slipped through the flap in the tent. Outside she pulled the hood of the cloak over her face. No use attracting attention to herself.

Her tent was right in the middle of the encampment. About her lay the huddled forms of several thousand warriors. Faraday smiled to herself. Under what other circumstances would her mother consent to her bedding down amid so many men? She picked her way carefully through the camp. Clouds scudded across the night sky but enough moonlight broke through for Faraday to see her way.

At the edge of the camp Faraday paused. She had expected one of the sentries to stop her before now. But all was quiet. Not sure whether to go back to her tent, or to go on further, suddenly a glimpse of white in the grass a few paces in front of her caught Faraday's attention.

"Puss?" she whispered. "Puss?"

She hadn't seen the cat for a day or so. Perhaps if she took the warm cuddly animal back to bed it would help her to sleep. She stepped past the boundaries of the camp and reached down for the cat. But just as her fingers brushed its back the cat sprang forward a few more steps.

"Puss!" Faraday muttered irritably and walked after it, but the cat jumped away from her again. Faraday was now engrossed in catching the cat. Some time later she looked up and the fear gripped her heart for an instant, until she spun around and spotted the low campfires in the distance. She wasn't so far away, after all. The cat purred about her legs and she bent down and picked it up.

But as Faraday turned back to the camp several dark figures loomed out of the night. She squealed in terror and convulsively gripped the cat to her breast. It squawked with indignation and squirmed out of her arms. She turned to run, but tripped over her long cloak and tumbled down into the grass, skinning the heels of her hands as she fell.

A tall, dark figure bent down over her.

"Get away from me!" Faraday hissed, trying to scrabble out of his reach on her hands and buttocks.

The figure leaned back. " 'Tis only me, lady," a soft burred country voice said. "Jack the pig boy. Won't do no one no harm. Jack Simple's the name."

Faraday held her breath ready to scream. The clouds thinned over the moon and she caught a look at his face. He was in early middle-age, sparse blond hair tumbling down over his forehead, his skin weather-lined and tanned, friendly eyes over a wide grin. Faraday stared at him, try- ing to work out what was wrong with his face, then she realized. Jack the pig boy had the face of a friendly and completely harmless simpleton. In one hand he held a heavy wooden staff that topped him by a full handspan; it had a heavy carved knob of some kind of dark metal on its top. The other dark shapes behind him resolved themselves into large but equally harmless pigs, staring at her curiously.

The white cat, purring loudly enough to attract the attention of every sentry about the camp, was weaving itself ecstatically around Jack's legs. He bent down and picked the cat up.

"Pretty puss," he murmured, "pretty, pretty." Jack held her in the crook of his arm and stroked her back in long sensual strokes. He had nice hands, long fingers, square fingernails.

Faraday recovered her composure and scrambled to her feet. She pulled her cloak about her again and carefully tried to brush the dirt out of her grazed hands.

"What are you doing here?" she asked harshly, still not completely recovered from the shock he had given her.

Jack looked downcast and shuffled his feet a little. "Didn't mean you no harm, lady. Taking my friends for a walk, I was. Nice night, yes, for a walk."

Faraday looked at the pigs. There was a small herd of about fifteen standing patiently behind Jack. They all looked fat and well-fed. Faraday supposed he came from a distant farmstead, and perhaps spent most of his time minding the pigs as they roamed the plains, fattening themselves for market.

"You scared me," she said shortly, and wished as soon as she'd said it that she had not sounded so petty.

Jack looked contrite, lines of distress creasing his forehead. "M'lady. Please, I meant you no harm."

"It's all right, Jack. I know you meant no harm. Why," she said, to turn Jack's mind away from his guilt at startling her, "the cat adores you." To be honest, Faraday was feeling just a little jealous of the cat's attentions to Jack. Up to now the cat had showed a preference only for her or Axis. It had been a tie to bind them.

Jack smiled broadly, wiping away all the worry lines from his face. "Yr, her name is, Lady. It's been a long time since I saw Yr. Many, many years. More years than pigs I have here. Twice as many, surely."

Faraday smiled tolerantly at him. The cat had undoubtedly never been out of Carlon before this time, and was certainly not more than fifteen years old, let alone thirty. Poor Jack, he must live in a wonderful fantasy world.

"What are you doing here?" Faraday repeated, although she kept her voice light this time.

"We're come from the Woods, lovely lady."

Faraday gaped at Jack. "You've come from the Silent Woman Woods? Jack! Those Woods are bad! Don't you know that?"

"Woods are good, lady. People tell me the Woods are bad, but the Woods and I get along just fine. Pigs can find lots of nice nuts and cones to eat in the Woods. No, no," he shook his head emphatically, "people don't know what the Woods are really like."

Faraday glanced over his shoulder, finally realising just how close they were to the Woods. Worry lines etched her face.

"No, no, pretty lady," Jack said anxiously as he watched her frown. "No need to be afraid. Let Jack show you." He took her hand and started to pull her toward the Woods.

"No! I can't go in there!" Faraday cried. "Let my hand go!"

Jack instantly dropped her hand. "Lady, I mean you no harm! The Woods don't mean you no harm, neither. Not unless you mean them harm. No," Jack dropped his voice to a conspiratorial whisper, "trees'll tell you secrets, lady. They are magic trees. If you ask them nicely, sometimes they will tell you your future."

"Really?" asked Faraday doubtfully, her interest piqued nevertheless. What if she could find out her future? Would she see herself surrounded with her and Borneheld's children? Her husband loving and attentive at her side? Perhaps if she could see that it would still her fears about her marriage. "Really?" she asked Jack again, her tone less doubtful than curious. "How close do we have to get?"

The two creatures that had assumed the forms of Ogden and Veremund paused briefly at the door to the sleeping chamber. Their eyes glowed the soft gold of the lake outside.

"They are asleep," the one who called himself Ogden said quietly.

"Yes," said his companion. "They will sleep well."

They stepped lightly into the room and stood either side of Timozel, curled tightly in his blankets, only his tousled dark head showing. Veremund leaned down and placed his splayed hand and fingers over the man's face, covering it from chin to forehead.

"Ah," Veremund said softly. "This one has a good heart though it is shadowed with some unhappiness." He shook his head slightly. "He will endure yet more unhappiness and uncertainty. He will have troubled choices."

They moved on to Gilbert. Both hesitated above him, but finally Ogden leaned down and placed his hand over the man's sleeping face.

"Ah," he hissed almost instantly. "I knew I did not like this one. His heart is full of holes and snakes reside there. His mind is a maze, and waits to trap the innocent. He will *not* be true; Artor has too strong a hold on this one." Ogden let go of Gilbert's face with a grimace and wiped his hand down his habit. He looked at Veremund. "What can we do?"

Veremund shook his head sadly. "Our task is simply to watch and be heedful. We cannot act, though perhaps we can warn. Come," he stepped over to Arne, who lay arms akimbo atop his blankets. "I wonder if he will do?"

He bent down and rested his hand over Arne's face. "Another good-hearted man. Stolid, and it will take much to change his mind. He will not like what lies around the corner and the secrets that will be revealed. But in the end his loyalty will keep him true. He would follow his BattleAxe to the grave if that is where Axis asked him to go. Yes, he will do well." His voice changed slightly, and now he spoke directly to Arne. The tips of his fingers glowed slightly golden where they touched Arne's face. "Good man, listen to these words. One day your BattleAxe will face great danger. Watch carefully those around him, especially those who pretend friendship and profess loyalty. Treachery will dog his footsteps. Watch your lord's back, good man, and protect him from those who would do him harm."

Arne moaned slightly in his sleep, and his hands clenched convulsively. Veremund paused a moment longer, then he released Arne and stood up. "It is all we can do. And now . . ." both turned to look at Axis, "now . . ."

Axis lay fast in a deeper and more peaceful sleep than he'd had for many months. He looked years younger then he did when awake.

Ogden whispered and looked at Veremund pleadingly. "May I be the one to . . . ?"

Veremund bowed slightly to his companion. "Dear one, we can both do this. If you place your hand thus, and I place mine so, then we can both share this moment."

He took Ogden's hand and placed it over Axis' face then placed his own hand over Ogden's, but so that his own fingertips touched Axis' flesh between Ogden's spread fingers.

For a long moment both were completely still, their eyes perhaps glowing slightly more golden, as they listened to Axis' heart.

"Oh, yes, yes!" Veremund whispered, almost ecstatic. "Yes! I believe it is so! Oh! But wait, can you feel it?"

Ogden, his own face close to Veremund's, nodded slightly. "Yes. The Destroyer already seeks him out. He invades his dreams and seeks to create doubts. He seeks to create hate in his heart. And," Ogden paused briefly, "oh my goodness! This one had already touched the Sacred Grove!"

"All by himself," Veremund said incredulously. "It is a wonder they let him live! We must watch over him. Ah, my sweet friend, fate has him firmly in hand. No wonder the Silent Woman Woods let him through unscathed. They had to."

Both let go of Axis' face and sat back on their heels at his side.

"And yet there is so much we do not know. My friend, if we can find his father, then we might be able to learn more about the Destroyer."

Faraday paused nervously in front of the tree. Jack had assured her she would not actually have to enter the Woods, that it would only be necessary to touch the nearest tree. Still, now that she was this close she wondered if it had been unwise to allow Jack to talk her into this.

But Jack was grinning happily. Yr had followed them and now sat watching curiously from a few paces away. She blinked, her eyes bright blue even in moonlight, and Jack's smile, if possible, became even broader than previously. He turned back to Faraday.

"Lady? Lovely lady, let me take your pretty hand." Jacks hands were rough and work callused, but somehow comforting. Faraday relaxed slightly. Jack winked at her. His eyes were the most unusual shade of green. Faraday smiled. How could she not trust this simple-hearted man?

"Look, the trees are nervous too."

Faraday looked startled. "Nervous? Why?"

Jack's smile dimmed. "Axes, people bear axes. Trees do not like axes. Trees are afraid of people. They do not trust them. Lady, tell me, do you bear these trees ill-will in your heart?"

Faraday looked bemused. "No, no, Jack. I bear them no ill-will. But I feel a little silly about all this."

"Come, lady. Place your hand against the tree trunk. Here." He placed her hand on the rough bark, covering her small hand with his own roughened one.

"What am I supposed to do, Jack? How can I talk to the tree and ask it my question?"

"You must talk to it with your heart, lovely lady, not with words. Close your mouth and talk with your heart, with your feelings. Feel the tree, feel what it says to you."

The man was crazy, not just a simpleton, Faraday thought. Just to please him, she closed both her mouth and her eyes for good measure, and tried to let a stream of goodwill flow toward the tree. Then, just as she was about to step back, her eyes flew open.

"Jack!" she gasped. Something unbelievable had just happened. Just when she had started to relax suddenly she felt another presence, it was the only way she could explain it. She could feel the tree, feel its emotions, in her own heart. The palm of her hand tingled.

Jack smiled, and dropped his hand. Now Faraday pressed almost her entire body along the tree trunk.

"Jack," she said, her voice breathless with wonder, "it's singing to me!"

Jack's eyes filled with tears.

In the Keep, Ogden and Veremund were still crouched beside Axis. As the tree started to sing to Faraday their eyes widened and glowed so bright that the entire chamber was bathed in golden light.

"Dear one!" Ogden gasped, and Veremund groped for his hand. Both were filled with wonder.

"It's singing to me," Faraday whispered again. "I can feel it. Oh! It sings such a sad song. Oh Jack, it is so sad!"

Jack stepped close and embraced both tree and Faraday. Faraday began to weep and laugh at the same time, the tree's song was so sad yet so incredibly beautiful. "They are all singing to me," she whispered. "The entire forest is singing to me!"

Tears squeezed out of the corners of Yr's eyes as she watched them. Tree Friend had been found at last. At last.

Jack stepped back a little. "Ask of it what you will, Faraday my lovely lady, and if it can the tree will show you what it can see."

Faraday wondered fleetingly how Jack knew her name. She had never mentioned it. What did she want to ask the tree? Oh yes. Borneheld.

Tell me of my husband, she asked the tree, asking with her heart, not words.

For an instant the song faltered, then it started up again and an image so vivid filled Faraday's mind that the night and the forest disappeared entirely from her sight.

But the vision was not beautiful, and Faraday's face crumpled in despair. She was in the Chamber of the Moons in the palace in Carlon, but now the tables that had been there the night of Priam's nameday banquet had disappeared. The Chamber was bare, save for several hundred people who stood in a circle around its edges. Their faces were blurry, indistinct, their presence unimportant except as witnesses to the tragedy about to unfold. She felt herself held by the strong arms of Jorge, Earl of Avonsdale; although she strained against his arms to be free, reaching with her arms and hands into the center of the Chamber, Jorge was too strong for her. She was crying, terrified by what she saw.

The Tree Song altered, became harsher, and images began to flicker rapidly before her eyes.

She saw Borneheld, stepping down from the throne. Two men circling, swords drawn, faces twisted into snarling masks of rage fed by long-held hatreds. Borneheld and Axis. Both bleeding, both stumbling with weariness. Red. Everything was red. Even the silent watchers were clothed in a red veil. A bloodied sun hanging over a golden field. The heat. The heat! Faraday flinched as a gigantic fireball consumed her. Two men circling, trading blows, bleeding. A feather. Many of them, floating about her. The two men fighting. A mother weeping. A scream, as if of an angered bird of prey. Swords, notched with use. A heart, beating uselessly. A golden ring, flying through the air. A scream—hers. *"No!"* Borneheld lunging at Axis, forcing him to a knee. Music, strange music, as if stone were being dragged over stone. Blood. Blood, everywhere. Dark Man watching, crying with laughter. Axis, on his knees, his sword flying out of his hand and sliding uselessly across the floor. A feather, she felt as if she were choking on a feather. A woman, beating at prison bars, pleading for release. A darker woman at a table, keeping tally, watching. Blood—why was there so much blood? Axis? *Where was Axis?* Faraday twisted away, gagging in horror. He was *covered* in blood—it dripped from his body, it hung in congealing strings through his hair and beard. He reached out a hand, then a great gout of blood erupted that covered her as well. She could feel it trickling down between her breasts, and when she looked for Axis all she could see was a body lying before her, hacked apart, and a golden and white form, as if a spirit, slowly rising behind it.

The chamber rang with shouted accusations of murder and treachery.

And all the time, the blood.

She could feel it, smell it, *taste* it.

Driven to madness by the feel of the warm blood running down her body, Faraday began to scream.

She ripped her hands from the tree and screamed and screamed her horror, almost falling in her distress. Jack grabbed her before she could run away and held her as tightly as he could, muffling her screams against his chest.

"Naughty tree!" he said angrily, glaring at the tree. "Naughty, *naughty* tree! You made the lovely lady cry."

Now Faraday was sobbing uncontrollably, twisting feebly to free herself from Jack's arms. Jack tried ineffectually to pat her back. "Please, pretty lady, sometimes the trees play tricks, yes they do. They show us only snatches of the truth, not all of it. Sometimes they warp what is truth, yes they do. Yes they *do*!" he said, giving the tree another angry glare.

Faraday finally managed to tear herself free. "It was horrible, Jack. Horrible! I don't want that to happen ever. *Ever*!" She started to back away from the trees, tears staining her cheeks, then stumbled. "I wish you had never brought me here, Jack. Go away!"

Then she was gone, flying through the night, her cloak whipping back from her slim form, her white nightgown flapping about her legs. Yr gave Jack a reproachful look and then bounded after her.

Jack watched them disappear into the night, then turned back to the trees. "Well, my friends, I don't know what you showed her, but you scared her almost to death. Perhaps it was for the best. She needs to be awoken. She needs to have reason to fight. But I hope you haven't frightened her too much . . . she is your only hope."

16

Two White Donkeys

Axis woke feeling more refreshed than he could remember. For a long while he lay in his sleeping roll, too warm and relaxed to move. Then finally he sat up, slipped quietly out of his blankets and dressed; Gilbert and the two Axemen were still sound asleep. Stepping out of the chamber, Axis peered at the rusted iron staircase twisting far above his head into the upper reaches of the Keep. Eventually he lowered his eyes and walked down the staircase to the ground floor.

Ogden and Veremund were at the table, arguing quietly but heatedly over a pile of books. Stuffed saddlebags lay on either side of the table. "Good morning, Brothers," Axis called.

The two Brothers looked startled, for they had not heard him come down the stairwell. For one instant Axis thought they were going to bow, but the moment passed and both merely inclined their heads his way.

"Good morning, BattleAxe," they said simultaneously.

"What are you doing?" Axis asked, puzzled by their preparations for a journey.

"We've decided that we must come with you," Ogden said calmly.

"Oh, for Artor's sake!" Axis swore, annoyed. Not only women but doddery aged brothers as well? This was too much. "There's really nothing you can do and we're moving too fast and hard for you to keep up. All I need is the information you have about the Forbidden and this so-called Destroyer."

Veremund drew himself up to his full height, a good hand-span taller than Axis himself, looking both deeply offended and utterly smug at the same time. "If we were to tell you all we know, BattleAxe, we would keep you here a lifetime. And a lifetime you do not have. No, far better that we bring ourselves, our knowledge, and a few," he turned to glare at Ogden, "of our most important books so that we can respond to your queries as we go. What you need to know now may not be what you need to know once you reach Gorkenfort."

Ogden beamed at Axis, folding his hands across his ample belly. His habit looked filthy in the morning light; mold grew in some of the deeper creases. "The time has come for us to leave the Keep, BattleAxe. I'm sure that Jayme would agree with our decision if he were advised of it."

"I don't have spare horses for you to ride out of these Woods."

"Oh, we have our own mounts stabled here, BattleAxe. Now, the more speed the better." Ogden rubbed his hands together briskly and turned to his companion. "Veremund, we simply must take this volume. It contains vital information about the origins of the Avar people and their religious beliefs. . . ."

Axis hesitated, annoyed by the two Brothers' casual assumption that they would ride with him. Then he shook his head. Perhaps Veremund was right. Who knew what new questions he might have in six weeks' time? And if they

could not keep up, he could leave them in Arcen with Faraday and her mother.

Leaving them to argue over what books to take, Axis
strolled outside. It was still cloudy, but it looked as though
the rain would hold off for a while. He lowered his gaze to
the golden lake. Not even a ripple marred its surface.
Frowning, he squatted down at the water's edge and dipped
his hand in. He felt no sensation of wetness, and when he
pulled his hand out again it was still completely dry. He
quickly stepped back from the lake, making the sign of the
Plough in the air to ward off enchantments. He would be
glad to be gone from this place.

Inside the Keep, Timozel, Arne and Gilbert had joined
the two elderly Brothers. Gilbert was standing defiantly in
front of the fire with Ogden and Veremund facing him,
both obviously furious. Arne stood slightly to the side and
between the three men. Timozel stood well back from
them, not wanting to have anything to do with whatever the
argument was about.

Veremund turned as he heard Axis close the door. His
face was white with fury. "This . . . this *snake* was trying to
burn down the Keep, BattleAxe!"

Gilbert lifted his chin and stared at Axis defiantly.

Arne stepped forward. "I'm afraid it is true, BattleAxe. I
found Gilbert in one of the upper-level rooms, one choked
with musty old books. He had a tinderbox with him and
was trying to lay a fire with some old pages."

"He had torn up one of the most exquisite volumes we
have in the Keep for that very nefarious purpose!" Ogden
cried, almost apoplectic with rage. He stepped forward as
if to seize Gilbert, but Axis quickly laid a restraining hand
on his shoulder.

"Is that true, Gilbert?" he asked, his voice dangerously
quiet.

"BattleAxe. We both serve the Seneschal. How can you
let this cursed Keep and its contents stand?" Gilbert cried.
"These volumes are wicked—look how they have cor-

rupted our two poor Brothers," Veremund snorted, "to the point where they actually admire the Forbidden! Their minds are soft with age, they mumble about prophecies. Jayme would be horrified if he knew what was going on here. If he knew what this Keep really contained."

"Gilbert," Axis' voice trembled with rage, "it is not up to you to single-handedly determine to destroy what the Seneschal has maintained for a thousand years."

Veremund and Ogden glanced at each other. Best that Axis continue to believe that for the time being.

"If you go back to Jayme and give him your opinion that the lot should go up in flames, and if he should agree with you, then fine. I will light the pyre myself." Ogden winced, but kept still under Axis' hand as the BattleAxe continued. "But you have no right to destroy this building and its contents by your own judgment, Brother Gilbert. Do you understand me?"

Gilbert stared at him defiantly. "You are wrong, BattleAxe, but I must comply with your orders. My weak body is no match against your sword, and that of your two henchmen." His eyes swept over Arne and Timozel, then returned to Axis. "But I will inform the Brother-Leader of your unreasonable and, might I say, somewhat disturbing championship of these two old Brothers and their books. Perhaps their behavior can be excused by their weak minds, but you appear too ready to listen to words of the Forbidden, Axis, before those of the Seneschal."

"I keep an open mind," Axis snarled, "and I am willing to listen to all who are willing to talk to me. And if you want to run squealing to Jayme I cannot stop you. But, by Artor, the moment you are out of these woods you are on a fresh horse and heading back to the Tower of the Seneschal. And," Axis let go of Ogden's shoulder and stepped forward to seize the front of Gilbert's habit, "you'll take a copy of that Prophecy back to Jayme as well, if I have to brand it on your forehead. Do you understand me?"

Gilbert sneered into Axis' eyes. "You may be sure that I

will report *everything* that I have heard and observed when I get back to the Brother-Leader, BattleAxe. Everything."

Axis stared at him a moment longer, then let go of his habit, pushing the Brother back half a step as he did so. He turned to Arne. "And what were you doing in the upper levels, Arne?" he asked, his tone still low and dangerous.

Arne cleared his throat. "I heard a noise, commander, and I thought I'd investigate. I knew Brother Ogden and Brother Veremund were down here."

The two elderly Brothers regarded him benignly. He would do well.

Axis wasn't satisfied with Arne's explanation, but he wasn't prepared to push him in front of Gilbert. He shifted his hard stare to Timozel to search for any guilty expression, then turned back to Ogden and Veremund. "How long before you're ready?"

"We're all but ready now, BattleAxe. Give us a moment to pack some food and saddle our mounts and we will be ready."

"Make sure you are," Axis barked and turned to Arne and Timozel. "As you can see, Ogden and Veremund will be coming with us to render assistance as they may." Neither Arne and Timozel dared say anything in Axis' present mood. "I'm sure you're as eager as I am to get out of these Woods, so breakfast as quickly as you can and then saddle the horses."

Both Arne and Timozel understood the order as "forget breakfast and saddle the horses now!" and were quickly out the door. Axis then pulled out a bench with his foot and sat down. "Now, Gilbert. Shall we sit down and wait together?" He broke a piece of fresh bread and covered it with some bacon from a dish. "You'd better eat something, Gilbert," he said around a mouthful of bread and bacon. "You'll have a hard ride back to the Tower of the Seneschal if you want to get there as quickly as I think you do."

Gilbert merely stared at him and remained standing. Ogden and Veremund packed one remaining book into their already bulging saddlebags, stuffed a holdall with some of the food that remained on the table, and hurried outside as well.

They were ready in under half an hour. Axis took pity on Arne and Timozel and gave each of them some food after they'd finished saddling the horses. Leaving a sulking Gilbert with the two Axemen he then helped Ogden to close the Keep down; Veremund was behind the Keep saddling their horses.

"You must be sad to leave this Keep after so long," Axis remarked softly as Ogden poured water over the fire and spread the damp ashes out.

Ogden straightened up and looked at Axis. "Yes," he said. "Both Veremund and I have spent most of our lives here. We will be sad to leave," he waved his hand vaguely around him and looked toward the upper levels of the Keep, "all our books and records, for they have become friends to us."

Axis moved closer. "You can understand that I share some of Gilbert's sentiments, old man, can you not?" he said softly. Ogden nodded, for once speechless. "I am the BattleAxe of the Axe-Wielders," Axis continued so quietly that Ogden could barely hear him. "My duty is to protect the Seneschal and Achar itself from whatever threatens it. I find it . . . uncomfortable, to say the least, to hear you and Veremund talking of the Forbidden as though they are old friends. You would not let your rather dubious loyalties compromise any advice that you might give me in the future—would you, old man?"

It was not a question and Ogden fully realized it. How strange that this man should appear in the guise of the BattleAxe of the Axe-Wielders, he thought to himself.

"My lord," he said, and this time he did bow. Axis' eyes narrowed at both title and action. "I understand your loyalties to your land and to your people and I swear on all that I hold dear that I will never compromise those loyalties."

It was an ambiguous answer, but Axis believed that Ogden meant well.

"Don't call me 'my lord,' " he said shortly, and stalked out the door. Ogden paused briefly in the room. Both he and Veremund, as others, had waited eons for this moment and this man. They had sacrificed their lives for it. It was up to them to guide the future. Ogden made a quick gesture with his hands, his eyes glowing golden for an instant, then he turned and walked through the door without a backward glance.

He almost ran straight into Axis who had stopped dead in amazement at the scene before him. Gilbert, Arne and Timozel all sat on their horses. Timozel holding Belaguez's reins ready for him. Gilbert looked openly disdainful, while Arne and Timozel were looking everywhere but at Axis' face.

Veremund stood by the group of horsemen, holding the reins of two fat, long-eared, thoroughly amiable white donkeys. Both wore oversized saddles and had large crammed saddlebags, tied onto the backs of their saddles.

"You can't seriously expect to keep up riding those two donkeys," Axis said incredulously.

Ogden stalked past him and took the reins of his donkey from Veremund. "They will keep up, BattleAxe. They have impeccable breeding." He looked at his companion. "If you would be so kind, Veremund."

As Ogden put his foot into the stirrup and grasped the saddle with both hands, Veremund, his face completely expressionless, placed his hands underneath Ogden's ample posterior, and gave a single heave that almost sent his friend tumbling over the other side of the donkey.

After an anxious moment Ogden settled safely onto the donkey's back. His hair stuck out wildly and his habit had rucked up beneath his legs, but he seemed unperturbed. "See," he said triumphantly, gazing about the group. "As agile as any youth. No trouble at all."

Axis groaned and covered his face with his hands, and Timozel gave up trying not to smile and roared with laughter. Even Arne, normally not given to humor, twisted his mouth in wry amusement. Only Gilbert's face remained totally unamused.

"No trouble at all?" Axis repeated wearily. "No doubt that's why you were assigned this isolated post in the first place, Brother Ogden. For thirty-nine years you *have* been no trouble at all." He swung into Belaguez's saddle, checked that Veremund was safely mounted, then waved the small group out.

17

The Ancient Barrows

They rode out of the Woods at mid-afternoon to be met at the tree line by a profoundly relieved Belial and a small group of Axemen. Belial raised his eyebrows at the two brothers jogging along serenely on their white donkeys, but Axis, feeling exhilarated by the wide open spaces of the Tarantaise plains, kicked Belaguez into a gallop without a word. Arne slapped the rump of Gilbert's horse and with loud whoops, he and Timozel herded Gilbert back to camp at a similar speed. Belial and his Axemen sped after the party, while the two Brothers trotted their donkeys along behind, preferring to keep to a more sedate pace.

On their way to the Axe-Wielders' camp Ogden and Veremund paused briefly to share greetings and words with a genial pig boy, driving his pigs in an easterly direction around the rim of the Silent Woman Woods.

Faraday was so overwhelmed by the sight of Axis returning that she almost burst into tears, turning away quickly as he rode by her and not acknowledging his nod and smile. She had managed to return to her bedroll undetected the previous night, and had lain awake until dawn, Yr curled in her arms, reliving again and again the nightmarish vision the trees had shown her, feeling the heat consume her, hearing the ring of steel against steel, watching Axis, covered in blood, stretch out his hand toward her, experiencing over and over again the warm ticklish sensation of blood trickling down between her breasts.

When she arose she spent a full forty minutes scrubbing her body red with icy cold water, evading her mother's stares and questions. She was very quiet all day, and the cat stayed close to her.

After Axis' return, preparations began for breaking camp and moving out. Gilbert had been given no time to rest; Axis wanted him gone as soon as possible. He detailed five men to escort him back to the Tower of the Seneschal, giving their leader firm instructions to make sure that he got there. The packet of documents that Ogden and Veremund had made up for him was handed over with instructions that it be given straight to the Brother-Leader.

The next day the entire company moved out well before dawn. Ogden and Veremund had placed themselves at the head of the column, their donkeys surprisingly spritely and well able to keep up with the horses. But Axis was so frustrated with the two old men's continual arguing over trivialities that he sent Veremund back to ride with the women and kept Ogden with him to discuss the meaning of the prophecy.

Veremund joined the ladies happily enough, and both Merlion and Faraday thought him delightful company. Over the next two days Timozel often joined them, and, between Timozel and Veremund, Faraday sometimes found the heart to smile. But the ghastly vision that the Silent Woman Woods had sung for her refused to fade, and Faraday became deeply upset whenever Axis rode by or stopped to chat with them. She knew Axis was puzzled by her behavior, but every time she looked at him she could watch his sword spin uselessly across the stone floor of the Chamber of the Moons, could only see him as he stood before her, blood clotting through his hair and down his body, his hand extended in appeal toward her.

On the morning of the third day Timozel, in an effort to distract Faraday from whatever was depressing her, began to tell her about the prophecy, which had imprinted itself so vividly on his mind that he could recite it word for word. Well, all except for the final verse, which was a little hazy. Faraday was so fascinated that the hateful vision receded to the back of her mind for the first time in days. She asked many questions of Timozel and Veremund, wanting to know all Veremund could tell her about the Forbidden and the ancient land of Tencendor.

She pulled the collar of her cloak a little tighter in the cold wind and edged her horse closer to the elderly Brother jogging along on his white donkey. "Do you mean that the Forbidden and our people lived in harmony in Achar?"

"Tencendor, it was called then," Veremund corrected her. "Yes, dear one, for many thousands of years."

Faraday frowned. "But how could we live in peace with them when they are so terrible, so frightening?"

"The Seneschal teaches that the Icarii and the Avar are frightening. 'Twas only after the Seneschal gained influence in Tencendor, teaching the way of the Plough, that the rift between the races started."

Faraday did not like the implications of what Veremund was saying. "Do you mean that . . ." she paused, "that the . . . Icarii and the Avar were not at fault in the war between the followers of the Plough and themselves? That the Seneschal started it?"

"The Forbidden were evil creatures and *that* is why the Seneschal helped the armies of Achar drive them from this land and clear their filthy nests and forests," Merlion snapped.

Her words silenced the others for a moment, but Faraday turned back to Veremund. "Brother, what sort of creatures were the Icarii and the Avar?"

Veremund thought for a moment. "We have their songs and their records, but in actuality they tell us relatively little about what they looked like or how they lived. The Icarii preferred high places and studied the movements of the stars and of the sun and the moon. Perhaps that is why they were called the people of the Wing. They tended to live in the hills and mountains of Tencendor. The Avar, why, they were people of the forest and had a special relationship with the land. Some of the passages that Brother Ogden and I have read suggest that they could talk to the trees."

Faraday gasped and reined her horse back a pace or two from Veremund's donkey. "Mother was right," she said tightly, "they were evil creatures and it is right that the Seneschal drove them from this land."

That afternoon the long column of Axe-Wielders approached a series of massive mounds, each about one hundred paces high and two hundred long. Their sides were steep and covered with low bushes and turf; each with a flattened top that was covered in bright yellow and red flowers. There were almost thirty of them stretching in a crescent for over half a league. Axis called the column to a halt and turned to Belial who was riding beside him.

"Do you know what these are, Belial?"

Belial started to say something, but it was Ogden who answered from his position behind Axis. "It is said that these are the burial mounds of some of the ancient kings of Tencendor, BattleAxe."

Ogden kicked his donkey up beside the BattleAxe, and Axis stared flatly at him for a moment, dislike for the man simmering just below the surface. Over the past three days Ogden had talked about the ancient land of Tencendor, and each additional piece of information he gave made Axis feel increasingly uncomfortable. He had always vaguely assumed that the land he had lived in, the Seneschal and the way of the Plough had always been, but now he was discovering that Achar as he knew it had once not existed, the Seneschal had once never existed, and that his own race and those of the Forbidden had lived side by side in an ancient land called Tencendor. It was unsettling.

"So," he said smoothly after a moment, "men once ruled over the Forbidden, did they?"

Ogden smiled. "By no means, BattleAxe. The royal family of Tencendor came from the Icarii line. The House of SunSoar supplied the Talon, the King, for well over five thousand years. They were a prolific house."

Both Belial and Axis stared unbelievingly at Ogden. The Forbidden had ruled over mankind? It was unthinkable!

"Yes," Ogden said quietly, lost in thought as he gazed at the Barrows. "It was mankind, under the influence of the emerging Seneschal, who usurped the Icarii rule and drove both them and the Avar beyond the Fortress Ranges during the Wars of the Axe."

Axis turned back to stare at the Barrows, his face set like stone. "Well," he said grimly, "tonight the Icarii graves will provide shelter for mankind. They should be high enough to keep us from this Artor-cursed wind."

They camped in the sheltered crescent of the Barrows, grateful for the relief they gave them from the bitterly cruel northern wind. By now word of the prophecy had spread among most of the Axemen, and there were low discussions around most campfires that night about the meaning of the ancient riddle. More than one set of eyes was turned northwards toward the origins of the cruel wind and upwards toward the thick black clouds blanketing the sky. The rain and hail that had troubled them across the plains of Tare had mercifully abated, but the clouds had thickened, as if they bore within them a surfeit of ice and hatred, waiting for the moment when it could be unleashed upon the column of Axemen.

That evening Faraday picked at her meal at the campfire she and Merlion shared with Axis, Belial, and the two Brothers, then she excused herself and wandered off to sit alone in the night. Axis watched her. She had been acting

very strangely since he had returned from the Silent
Woman Woods.

Axis hoped it had been nothing of his doing. Faraday
had earned his grudging respect over the past three weeks
or so. Both she and her mother had kept up with the pace
with no complaints or petty requests for consideration because of their womanhood. They had caused his Axe-
Wielders virtually no trouble at all; indeed, Axis smiled to
himself, the Lady Merlion had kept a firm eye over their remaining two maids as well, to the disappointment of not a
few of the Axe-Wielders who'd hoped to have some extra
warmth in their bedrolls at night.

Axis had been surprised when he heard of Borneheld's
betrothal to the youngest daughter of Earl Isend of Skarabost. Borneheld had evaded the ties of matrimony for the
past ten years or so, preferring to keep a succession of
blowzy mistresses either at Sigholt or Gorkenfort when he
was in the north, or in the palace in Carlon when he was at
court. Axis had thought that Borneheld would finally accept the offer of one of the richer lords—even with her
grandfather's estates Faraday was not the richest heiress in
Achar. Surprised, that is, until the night Faraday had
smiled across the campfire at him. Pretty now, she would
be an extraordinary beauty one day, and was both graceful
and perceptive.

Well, Axis thought as he put his empty mug down at his
side, it was no concern of his. A shame, however, that
Isend had picked Borneheld. Borneheld did not deserve a
woman like Faraday—and certainly would not know how
to treat her. Faraday was a lively and intelligent woman,
and she would be miserable in the wilds of Ichtar; from
what Axis had gleaned from palace whispers his mother
had hated her life in the province. He hoped that life with
Borneheld would not rob Faraday of her honesty and di-
rectness. Glancing about the fire he saw that while he'd
been lost in thought the others had engaged themselves in
an energetic debate about whether or not Baron Ysgryff of
Nor had actually spent some of his youth as a pirate on Pi-

rate's Nest. Smiling to himself Axis stood up and left the campfire, walking in the same direction that Faraday had taken.

He found her sitting on a low boulder just beyond the perimeter of the camp, her back to him as he approached, staring at the silhouette of the Barrows against the dark night sky.

"Faraday," he said quietly, and she jumped to her feet at the sound of his voice, turning to face him. She had been crying.

"Excuse me," Faraday muttered, and tried to walk past him back into camp, but Axis caught her arm as she drew level with him.

"Faraday, what is it? What have I done to upset you?"

Faraday tilted her face up at him, her eyes gleaming with tears. "It's nothing you've done, Axis," she whispered. "Please, let me go." A tear escaped her eyes and trickled slowly down her cheek.

"Faraday," he said again. "Why do you cry?" With his free hand he gently reached up and wiped the tear from her cheek with the back of his fingers. Without thinking he let his fingertips trail down her cheek and underneath her chin.

Faraday tried to smile. "Because life plays such cruel tricks, and . . ." and oh, she should not say this, but Axis was so close and his fingers were so gentle on her skin that she could not help herself, "because I am betrothed to Borneheld when it is his brother that I want more than life itself."

"Faraday!" What was this girl saying? She was too young, too dangerous, and the timing was all wrong. He slipped his hand from her arm and into the small of her back, pressing her against his body. "Faraday," he whispered again, and then he leaned down and kissed her.

His touch was so light, so gentle, that Faraday found herself straining on her toes to maintain the contact. Slowly the kiss deepened, and for long moments they held each other, then Faraday finally broke the embrace, pushing her hands against his chest and drawing back with a small shaky laugh. "Forgive me, BattleAxe," she said a little unsteadily. "I'm not sure what came over me."

Axis let her go reluctantly. He gazed down at her left hand, where Borneheld's ring glinted in what little light there was. "Why?" he asked, softly.

Faraday followed his eyes and twisted the ruby out of sight, closing her fingers about it. "Because it is what my father wanted, and because the alliance will be good for my family. I freely gave my consent, Axis."

"But it is not what you want." Axis' eyes caught her own, forcing her to tell the truth.

"No," she said very softly, "it is not what I want, but in the needs of a nation one girl's wants are a very small thing. I will go ahead with the marriage, Axis. I have to. My honor binds me."

Axis' temper broke. "It is not the needs of a nation that want this, but the greed of your father and the lust of Borneheld. And you are young and innocent if you think that honor has anything to do with this marriage. Faraday, there are long months ahead before the marriage has to take place. Think about whether you want to marry Borneheld, or whether you might be prepared to risk spending your life with someone you could learn to love instead."

Then he turned on his heel and stalked back into camp, his shoulders stiff with anger and frustration.

Faraday held her breath for a moment. Then a step distracted her and she turned toward the sound. Veremund, the white cat curled in his arms, stepped out of the darkness. "Dear one, we have to talk," he said quietly. "We cannot allow this to go any further." His eyes were golden in the night.

18

The Sentinels Speak

Faraday took a step backwards, almost tripping over the low boulder she had been sitting on when Axis had disturbed her. *What was wrong with his eyes?* All the tales about the evil aspects of the Forbidden she had heard as a child came rushing back to her.

Veremund held out his hand to her. "Do not be afraid, dear one. We do not mean to hurt you. Come, take my hand."

Faraday, her heart beating wildly, stood looking at him.

"Please, dear one, take my hand."

His tone was soft and gentle, and Faraday found herself reaching her own trembling hand forth. The moment his fingers touched Faraday a feeling of tranquility flooded over her.

"Will you walk with us a while, dear one? The others are waiting to talk to you as well." He began to lead her toward the nearest Barrow.

"The others? Which others? What do you want to talk about?" Faraday suddenly realized that Veremund had witnessed her talk with Axis. "Oh, Veremund, please! What happened between Axis and myself just then was simply foolishness. It meant nothing! You won't tell Mother, will you?"

Veremund paused a moment to let Yr down, then turned back to Faraday. "No, child, I won't tell your mother. But what happened between you and the BattleAxe hardly meant nothing."

"Then it has nothing to do with you, Veremund! What happened between Axis and myself is our own business."

Veremund shook his head. "I think not, dear one. Neither you nor Axis will have very private lives in the future. Now, we have to climb a little. Save your breath for the slope."

Veremund still held onto her hand, and as they climbed the steep side of the Ancient Barrow Faraday found she needed more and more to reach down and steady herself with her free hand. "Where are we going?" she panted after some fifteen minutes. Yr bounded ahead of them with an apparently endless supply of feline grace and energy.

"Shhh," said Veremund, hardly breathing deeply at all, "we're almost there now."

A moment later they climbed onto the top of the Barrow. Even though they were in an exposed spot, the air was still and calm and not a breath of the cold north wind touched their faces. From Faraday's vantage point a hundred paces in the air the hundreds of campfires of the Axe-Wielders seemed like a necklace of diamonds and rubies nestling around the Barrows.

"Look," Veremund pointed. "They wait."

Faraday followed his finger. "Oh!" she exclaimed, surprised. About twenty paces away, in the very center of the small plateau on top of the Barrow, Ogden and Jack the pig boy sat inside a circle of white stones. Jack's heavy staff lay to one side outside the ring of white stones. "How did Jack get here?" she said, half to herself. "We rode so fast."

"Jack knows the land somewhat better than the Axemen with whom we ride," Veremund said mildly. "Come."

Faraday let herself be led toward the other two. Yr's small white form reappeared a few paces in front of them, and she sat down between Jack and Ogden just as Faraday and Veremund stepped up. Faraday stepped into the circle of white stones.

"Lovely lady," Jack smiled at her, although he did not rise, "it gladdens my heart to see you again." Faraday looked at him carefully. He did not look so simple tonight, although his good-hearted nature still shone forth at her. "Please, sit down within this our circle, and know that you are safe among us."

Faraday sat down cross-legged, tugging the skirt she had donned after the day's ride down over her knees and ankles. She turned to Veremund to say something, but the old man laid a soft finger across her lips as he sat down beside her. "Shush, dear one. For the moment you must simply watch and listen. We will answer all your questions in good time. Remember that you are in no danger."

Faraday looked about the group. All of their eyes glowed in a most unusual manner, almost as if there were colored lamps behind them. Ogden and Veremund's eyes shone golden, Jack's a brilliant emerald green, while Yr's glimmered a deep midnight blue.

"Let us begin," Yr said in a soft, burred voice, the end of her tail twitching slightly.

Faraday just managed to stifle a shocked gasp. The cat blinked slowly at her, then turned back to her companions.

"We are . . ." she began.

"Diligent," Ogden whispered in a tone reminiscent of brothers when they chanted the Service of the Plough.

"Careful," Jack whispered in the same tone.

"Heedful," Veremund chanted softly beside her.

Faraday's eyes were wide as the chant went on about her, each taking turns to carry the chant on.

"Attentive."

"Mindful."

"Regardful."

"Thoughtful."

"We are the . . ." Veremund chanted softly.

"Harborers."

"Keepers."

"Shelterers."

"Servants."

"We wait," they all chanted together, "for . . ."

"The One."

"The Appointed."

"The Savior."

"The StarMan," they all breathed as one. Then they all turned their startling eyes on Faraday.

"We are the Sentinels!" they suddenly finished with a shout. Overhead the clouds milled in sudden anger and lightening forked through them. Thunder cracked and roared so that the very Barrow they sat on trembled.

The mood was broken now, and Yr followed Faraday's eyes to the sky. "Ah," she said, "the Destroyer knows we have emerged to walk the land of Tencendor again. See his temper. He will seek us out, soon enough."

"What is this?" Faraday whispered, lowering her eyes. "Who are you? *What* are you?" She looked at Jack, for she could not talk directly to the cat. "How can Yr speak?"

Jack smiled gently at her confusion. "We all choose different forms, dear one. Yr," he turned and smiled affectionately at the cat, "prefers a form that will let her be stroked as much as possible. She has always been a sensual creature. Not all of us are so social, however. My other companions," nodding at Ogden and Veremund, "and myself generally prefer solitude to company, prefer the pursuits of the mind rather than the pleasures of the flesh." Looking at Ogden and Veremund's stained and tatty habits Faraday thought that they had totally ignored the basics of cleanliness as well as the pleasures of the flesh. Her nose wrinkled a little in distaste.

"As for what we are, sweet child," Ogden continued, the first time he had spoken directly to Faraday since she had sat down among them, "well, you do not need to know it all. But this we can tell you. We are creatures of the

Prophecy, recruited and recreated and bound to serve the Prophecy. We are watchers and waiters, it is true, but we are also in a manner servants."

Faraday forgot her distaste of a moment earlier and blinked in confusion, unable to take in all she had witnessed over the past few minutes. "But are you not the Brothers Ogden and Veremund? Or are you some kind of magical creatures?"

"No, we are not Ogden and Veremund as such. Ogden and Veremund were once Brothers of the Seneschal, it is true. But they died a long time ago when they tried to enter the Silent Woman Woods. Because any visitors to the Silent Woman Keep would have expected to find Brothers of the Seneschal in residence, we simply assumed the forms of Ogden and Veremund. And are we magical creatures?" Ogden shrugged a little. "Perhaps, but we wield very little magic ourselves, and each of us has slightly different talents."

Faraday shuddered and bit her lip. She did not want to hear anymore.

"You must hear it, lovely lady," Jack said, his tone firm. "We are creatures of the Prophecy and we serve the Prophecy. You are now also bound up in it, and you have no choice but to let the Prophecy bind you to its will."

"No, no," Faraday whispered. "This is madness!" She wanted desperately to get up and run, but her limbs felt heavy and refused to move for her.

"Listen to us, Faraday." Ogden spoke up again. "Remember the Prophecy as Timozel told you this morning. The Destroyer Gorgrael has arisen in the north. Driven by all-consuming hatred, aided by his powerful magic, he will overrun all of Achar, of Tencendor. The races of Icarii, Avar and mankind must unite. That is the only way that Gorgrael can be stopped. But only one man can do it."

"Axis," Faraday whispered. "Oh merciful Artor!"

"Merciful Artor can do nothing," Yr snapped. "It was His minions who drove the Icarii and the Avar from their homeland in the first place." Her tail swept in angry arcs behind her.

"Yr," Veremund remonstrated gently. "She cannot help her upbringing. Yet she will be true. She will do her duty."

"She must!" Yr said, only slightly mollified, still trapped in her hatred of the Seneschal. Of them all. Yr knew most about the internal machinations of the Seneschal, and the more she knew the more she loathed the Brotherhood.

Faraday frowned. "But if the Prophecy is correct, that makes Borneheld the Destroyer, doesn't it? Isn't the Star-Man the Destroyer's brother?"

"Borneheld and Axis share the same mother, dear one. The Destroyer and Axis share the same father."

Faraday looked at the Sentinels, calmly watching her. "Then who is his father?"

Yr's lips curled. "Not even we know that, child. Would that we did. It would make things so much clearer. We are creatures, servants only, of the Prophecy. Not even we understand all of its riddles."

"Faraday," Jack said gently, "before we go any further, we must know what the trees told you. What did you ask them, sweet child, and what did they sing for you?"

Tears rolled down Faraday's face as she remembered the dreadful vision the trees had shown her. "I asked them to show me my husband. I was unsure about my marriage to Borneheld."

"And what did they show you, Faraday?" Veremund rested a comforting hand on her shoulder. It gave Faraday strength. Haltingly, she described to them the dreadful images, leaving nothing out. Her voice grew ragged and distressed as she described the blood dripping through Axis' hair, his hand stretched out—in appeal, she supposed—and the great gout of blood that soaked her.

"Dear child," Ogden asked carefully, as she finally ground to a halt. "You asked the trees to show you your husband. Which man did you see first?"

Faraday frowned in thought. "Borneheld," she said finally. "It was Borneheld. Why? What does it matter?"

"Ah," said Veremund and Ogden together, unhelpfully. Yr blinked again and her tail gave a single twitch.

Jack shifted a little. Even such enchanted creatures as Sentinels apparently got sore buttocks if they sat too long in one place. "Remember what I said to you that night, Faraday, before you ran away? The trees show what will be, but they do not always show it all, or they show it in such incoherent images that it is impossible to sort them out. Beware you do not misinterpret what the trees showed you. Dear one, perhaps the images do not describe Axis' death. But if Borneheld does indeed kill Axis, then Tencendor is doomed. My sweet child, Axis is the *only* one who can meet Gorgrael. He must not be murdered before he can accomplish what he was born for."

"No," whispered Faraday, folding her arms tightly across her breasts, her body rocking backwards and forward slightly. Not murdered.

Veremund looked about at the others and they nodded to him. He turned back to Faraday. "Child, we believe that you also have a part to play in the Prophecy; in fact, we believe you have two very important tasks to perform, without which Axis will not succeed. Your first task is to stop Borneheld from killing Axis before he reaches his full potential. We know what you and Axis feel for each other, but if you follow your hearts now it will only result in Axis' death."

"Why?" Faraday whispered, although in her heart she knew the answer.

"Because if you break your betrothal vows to Borneheld and turn to Axis instead, it will enrage Borneheld so much that he might tear Achar to pieces in search of Axis. Do not become the spark that ignites Axis' funeral pyre."

"But Jack said the trees showed me truth. What *will* be. What does it matter if—"

"Faraday," Veremund's voice was sharp. "Axis and Borneheld will battle it out one day. The vision clearly showed that. But it must be at Axis' instigation and on Axis' terms. We, *you*, cannot afford to push Borneheld into challenging Axis now. If you marry Borneheld you will be in a position to moderate his hatred of Axis. To stay his hand. To allow Axis to grow into the man he must become."

"Faraday, listen to me," Yr said softly. "You will save Axis and you will save Tencendor as Borneheld's wife, not as Axis'. The *vision* showed you as Borneheld's wife, not Axis'. "

"You told Axis this evening that in the needs of a nation one girl's wants are a very small thing," Veremund said. "Then you meant Achar. But in Tencendor's needs, in the hopes of three races, your wants are but a tiny thing. Tencendor's hopes rest on whose bed you choose." Veremund thought for a moment, then came up with the crucial argument. "Axis' life depends on your becoming Borneheld's wife."

The weight of their arguments and the emotional strain was all too much. Faraday covered her face with her hands and started to sob. All she could think of was how it had felt when Axis had held her and kissed her.

Veremund cradled her gently, giving her what comfort he could. Faraday was so young, so innocent, and Veremund felt a twinge of guilt at how they were pushing the girl. Still, it had to be done. The Prophecy demanded it. The Sentinels were silent for a few minutes as Faraday wept, then, as the girl's sobs began to ease, Yr leaned forward. "Dear one, you must marry him as soon as you can."

"Oh no!" Faraday cried, her tear-streaked face horrified. "Please, give me time!"

Veremund's arms tightened about her for a moment. "Dear one, we cannot know it all, but we can see some things. Axis rides for Smyrton, where he will not be detained for long, then he rides for Gorkenfort. Sweet one, it is vital that you get there before him, and that when he arrives you will be Borneheld's wife. Gorkenfort will be the making or breaking of Axis. You must be there to restrain

Borneheld. He will be triumphant that you have come to him, and it will make him feel very powerful. If he feels powerful, if he feels as though he has triumphed over Axis, he will not feel the need to challenge him. Gorkenfort is a crucial test for Axis, Faraday."

In a strange way what the Sentinels told Faraday buttressed what Embeth had told her about duty. She took a deep breath and nodded reluctantly at the Sentinels. "I think I understand. But how can I get to Gorkenfort before Axis?"

The Sentinels relaxed. They had been uncertain whether or not Faraday would agree, and they could not force her into any action she was unwilling to undertake. Yr stood up and stretched, then walked across and butted her head against Faraday's knees. Faraday smiled a little and stroked Yr's back, grateful for the affection.

"You will travel with myself and Yr," Jack said. "Stay with Axis until you reach Arcen. That is as far as you would have gone with him anyway. Once Axis and the Axe-Wielders leave for Smyrton, then we will leave for Gorkenfort—secretly! Do not tell your mother about this!" he added.

Faraday laughed a little. "Tell my mother about this?" She waved her hand about the top of the Barrow. "About you? She would give me an enema to clear my wits!"

"Faraday, we would have you leave as soon as you can," Jack said. "Ideally, we would set out tonight—but when Axis realized you were missing in the morning he would have three and a half thousand men to search among these Barrows for you, and not even a Sentinel can hide from so many."

"I understand," Faraday said, then hesitated a little. "Tell me, does Axis know any of this?"

The Sentinels shook their heads. "No," Ogden replied for them all. "He must grow a little before more can be made clear to him. His path will be very different to yours. He must discover his own identity. Trust us on this."

"One more thing," Faraday said. "You said that there

were two important tasks for me to perform. One," she paused, "is to marry Borneheld. I understand that and I will try to accept it. But what is the other one?"

Veremund patted her shoulder. "Be assured, dear girl, that it will not be quite so distasteful as the first. But you have heard enough tonight. Jack and Yr can tell you more on your journey to Gorkenfort. Now," his eyes glowed bright gold, "will you be true to us and to Axis, dear one?"

"Yes," Faraday whispered. "Yes, I will be true, though I think you do not understand the sacrifice you ask of me."

"The Prophecy demands much from many people, Faraday. And no one will have to sacrifice more than the Sentinels. *No one*." His voice hardened. "Do not speak to *us* of sacrifice!"

"I'm sorry," Faraday whispered.

Veremund's eyes dimmed a little in contrition. "Yes, sweet child. I know you are sorry, and I know you will be true. And I, all of us, recognize that what we ask of you is indeed a sacrifice. Now, I'm sure you must be feeling very tired. Yr? Perhaps you will escort Faraday to her bed?"

Ogden, Veremund and Jack sat silently as Yr led Faraday down the side of the Barrow. After a few moments Jack spoke.

"So, it has begun, my friends. We have alerted the Destroyer to our presence, yet we still lack one of our number."

"Where is she?" asked Veremund. "Where is she? Why isn't she here?"

19

A Cloudy Day

Axis deliberately avoided Faraday the next morning, for which she was profoundly grateful. Although she could still remember the warmth of Axis' mouth, the strength of his arms, the events that had followed seemed a dream. When she'd awoken, her mother was already dressed and gone, and Yr was sitting on her vacant bedroll, smiling at Faraday.

Faraday managed a small smile back, uncertain what to do. "Good morning, Yr," she finally managed. The cat jumped across to Faraday's side of the tent, walking up Faraday's body until she stood on her chest. There she sat and began to knead uncomfortably. "Good morning, sweet one," she whispered in a burr that was all but inaudible. "May I suggest that now you bear me more respect you might be a little less tardy about enquiring after my breakfast?"

Faraday closed her eyes for a moment. It had been no dream. She remembered what she had agreed to do on top of the Barrow and shuddered. "Food!" hissed Yr.

An hour after daybreak the column of Axe-Wielders wended its way through the Barrows and out onto the exposed plains of Arcness. Overnight the weather had deteriorated and daybreak had seen the landscape lighten scarcely beyond a dim twilight. The wind had doubled in strength and the clouds to the north, which hung so low that in places they dragged along the ground, bubbled and broiled. Streaks of lightning shot through them at intervals and occasional rumbles of thunder reached the riders as they moved out. The mood within the column was grim, and even Veremund was sunk in uncharacteristic gloom. Occasionally he exchanged glances with Yr, huddled behind Faraday's saddle.

"Excuse me," Veremund said finally, booting his heels into his donkey's flanks, "I must talk to the BattleAxe."

Timozel turned to Faraday and raised his eyebrows, but she only turned to watch Veremund's back disappear toward the front of the column, a worried expression growing on her face.

Veremund cantered up to Ogden who was riding a few paces behind Axis and Belial.

"My friend, I do not like what is happening," he said softly.

Ogden gave him an anxious look. "No. It is not good. These clouds are not natural. We make a tempting target for Gorgrael—four Sentinels within the vicinity, Axis and Faraday."

"What can we do?"

Ogden shook his head. "We can but warn, Veremund, we can but warn. Yet I know not how to warn Axis against what looks like approaching."

They both booted their donkeys forward until they were riding next to Axis.

"BattleAxe." Ogden leaned forward. "I like not the look of this approaching storm. We are so exposed here—there is nowhere to shelter."

Axis glanced at him briefly. He had been thinking the same thing himself; over the past few minutes the wind had almost doubled in strength so that it now blew around them in malevolent gusts. He reined Belaguez to a sudden halt. "Belial, how far out are we from the Barrows?"

Belial considered a moment. "We have hardly seen the sun this morning, BattleAxe, so it is hard to estimate. But I would think that we have not been riding for much more than an hour."

Axis chewed his lip, berating himself for pulling out this morning at all. He had been so preoccupied with thoughts of Faraday, of the feel of her pressed against his body, that he had failed to consider the dangers of a march in this weather. What an Artor-cursed fool he was!

"And the storm, Belial, how far away do you think that is?"

The column of mounted Axemen had started to ride past them now, and the four men edged their mounts out of the way. Some of the men gave them anxious glances.

Belial squinted into the distance. "Less than an hour, BattleAxe. The horizon is already lost."

Axis quickly made his decision. "Belial, get this damned column turned around. Spread the men out as much as possible so that they don't ride each other down. And tell them to ride, damn it, ride as fast as they can. Those Barrows will give us the only shelter we're going to get!"

Belial turned his horse and started shouting at the men. Axis cursed again. It was well-nigh impossible to get such a large column turned around and moving fast without some degree of chaos. Belaguez fidgeted nervously, tossing his head and prancing as the column slowly, achingly slowly, started to wheel about and spread out over the plains.

"Go, damn you," Axis whispered. "Ride before this wind!"

The Axe-Wielders started in ones and twos to push their horses faster. Ogden leaned as close as he could to the prancing stallion and shouted to attract Axis' attention

above the increasing thunder of hooves. "Axis! BattleAxe!"

Axis only just heard him and looked down at the two
Brothers, still keeping him company on their placid white
donkeys. "Damn you! Ride!" he yelled at them. Belaguez
reared in excitement and fear. He wanted nothing more
than to stretch his powerful body out after the rest of the
horses fleeing before the wind.

Ogden wheeled his donkey out from under the stallion's
hooves. "Axis," he shouted again. "Listen to me! This is no
ordinary storm. This is the work of Gorgrael!"

"Then tell me how to fight it, man!" Axis almost
screamed at him, keeping his seat on Belaguez's plunging
back only through his remarkable gift of balance. "Tell me
how to save my Axemen from this demon-spawned nightmare!" The wind was now so strong that it tore Axis' blond
hair from its braid, whipping it wildly about his face.

"I don't know," Ogden whispered, terrified, "I don't
know."

Axis stared at him for a long moment, anger and fear
battling across his face, then he kicked the donkey's rump.
"Then ride, damn you, ride! It's our only chance!"

He finally let Belaguez have his head and the stallion
raced away after the rest of the Axe-Wielders. Ogden and
Veremund followed as fast as their donkeys' short legs
would allow. This was not how it was supposed to be.

Timozel turned Faraday and Merlion's horses about as
soon as it became apparent what was happening, and
screamed at their maids to do the same thing. He whipped
his sword out of his weapon belt and beat their horses'
rumps with the flat of the blade, his too-long hair falling
over his eyes. Every time he looked around the storm
clouds were closer, heavier, angrier. Never had he seen
clouds move in such a fashion, or boil in defiance of the
wind. Red, blue and silver flashes lit them from within.

Faraday gripped her horse's mane in her hands, terrified

by the sudden turn of events. She remembered the shot of
lightning and the anger of the thunder last night when the
Sentinels had shouted their presence at the sky, and she
knew that somehow these two events were connected. "Oh
Axis, please be safe," she cried to herself as she struggled
to keep her hands tangled in the horse's heaving mane,
"please be safe!" Behind her, Yr clung with her claws to the
saddle blanket, fighting to keep her balance on the horse's
wildly heaving back, her eyes glowing deep blue, her lips
pulled back in a snarl. "Jack!" she hissed, and her eyes
flashed as she spat the word. "Help us! Be there for us!"

It was every rider for him or herself in this made race.
Adding to the danger of a flat-out gallop of over three
thousand horsemen were the packhorses and relief horses,
most of which were running out of control. Faraday prayed
that her horse would not stumble and fall. A terrified shriek
sounded behind her. She turned and saw her mother's maid
disappear under the flashing hooves of the horses that
came behind her. She gave a cry and might have tried to
turn back, if Timozel had not grabbed her horse's head and
kept it moving forward.

"She's gone, Faraday!" he screamed at her. "There's
nothing you can do. Save your own life!"

Faraday glanced across at her mother who, white-faced,
was clinging grimly to the pommel of her saddle. Her fingers tightened in her horse's mane until the coarse black
hair started to cut deep into her flesh. She began to cry
soundlessly.

At the back of the mass of fleeing riders Axis finally managed to bring Belaguez under some control. He swung the
horse's head around to look for the two Brothers, but what
he saw drove all thoughts from his mind. The line of broil-
ing black clouds was now much, much closer. Frighteningly close. In their center a gigantic head had formed out
of the cloud mass. Vaguely manlike, although its bulging
forehead and massive beaked nose looked almost like

those of a bird of prey, it had a set of vicious tusks emerging from its cheeks that glinted wickedly as it twisted its head from side to side. Its mouth hung open, a too-large tongue protruding over its lower lip, canine fangs hanging from its upper gums. Huge silver orbs were sunk into deep eye sockets. Its skin was leathery and scaled, like a lizard's skin. The cloud head was the most terrifying thing Axis could imagine encountering.

And then it spoke. It saw the solitary man sitting on the gray stallion behind the fleeing riders and in front of the two small figures on the donkeys, and it spoke.

"Axis," it boomed across the distance. "My son."

"No," Axis whispered, lost again in his nightmare—except that this time the darkness had lifted, and he could see his tormentor. "You are not my father," he croaked from a mouth gone dry and papery with fear. He was no longer capable of rational thought. The writhing, twisting tusked head held him entrapped.

Ogden and Veremund reached him. "Axis!" Veremund screamed, standing tall in the stirrups of his saddle to reach up to Axis' face and slap him as hard as he could. "That is not your father, simply a likeness of Gorgrael created from cloud and ice! Axis! Listen to *me*! Do not listen to him—he speaks only lies!"

"I came to your mother like this," the voice said, long ropes of saliva twisted down from its tongue. "I came to your mother like this and she loved me as I am! Yes! She loved me! She *writhed* for me!"

Axis felt the evil presence of his dreams. Despair threatened to overwhelm him. There was nowhere to run. There was never anywhere to run.

"He won't listen to me!" Veremund turned to shout at Ogden. "What can we do? If he stays here he will die when that cloud rolls over him!"

Ogden thought frantically, then edged his donkey as close to Belaguez as he possibly could, stood as high in his stirrups as he dared and, eyes glowing, launched himself onto Belaguez's back, hauling himself up behind Axis. Belaguez plunged and danced at the unexpected weight, but Axis had him on such a tight rein that the stallion could do very little to dislodge the weight from his back.

"My boy," Ogden breathed into Axis' ear, "do you remember this tune?" He started to hum, a strange lilting tune that gained strength and thrived despite the howling wind. Axis blinked and turned his head slightly. Ogden continued humming, his voice becoming stronger with each phrase. Axis' eyes started to refocus and Ogden felt some of the tension draining out of his rigid muscles.

"Oh," Axis gasped, turning his eyes from the apparition of Gorgrael and hummed a few bars along with Ogden.

"Yes! Yes, that's it, m'boy. Sing! Sing with me!" Axis' voice grew stronger and Veremund finally recognized the tune. It was an ancient ward for protection that Icarii fathers sang to their babies while still in the womb. If Axis' father was of the line of Icarii Enchanters, then the ward of protection would be strong indeed. Very strong. It was the first gift Icarii fathers gave their sons, and, some said, the most valuable.

"Sing, Axis," Veremund whispered, tears in his eyes, "sing!"

And Axis did indeed sing, his voice now stronger than Ogden's, his eyes blazing in his face, the melody lilting above the wind. He took the melody beyond what Ogden had sung to him, adding new variations and creating strange new depths to the song. He sang words, alien words, rather than simply humming a melody. Now he was smiling, some distant memory resurfacing in his mind, and an expression of joy crossed his face. His voice was very beautiful and very moving.

Veremund gave a shout of triumph, and wheeled his donkey around so he could shake his fist at the head as it advanced toward them. "Did your father sing that to *you*, unloved one?" he screamed. "Did your father bother to sing that to you while you grew in your poor mother's womb? Did your father *love you enough to sing to you*?"

The head of Gorgrael gave a terrifying scream of rage,

viciously swinging its tusks from side to side, and for a moment Veremund thought that he had only provoked it into a more dreadful display of power. But as the scream died the head started to dissolve, reforming into simple cloud again. But the storm still came on. And it was as angry and as deadly as previously.

Veremund swung back to Axis and Ogden, still clinging precariously to Belaguez's back. "Ogden! Axis! Ride now!"

Turning Belaguez's head for the Barrows, Axis gave the long-suffering stallion his head. "That was *not* my father!" he whispered to himself.

Veremund kicked his white donkey after Belaguez, but Ogden's riderless donkey outraced them all.

20

The Storm

Few of the Axe-Wielders were aware of what was happening behind their backs, and Faraday, her mother and Timozel had completely missed it.

The first riders were now approaching the Barrows, but the storm was rapidly gaining on them. Already Axis, Ogden and Veremund were encased in heavy rain, their horses finding it harder and harder to keep their footing in the slippery mud churned up by the Axe-Wielders' mounts. The wind increased to gale force, screaming across the plains behind them, and Axis bent low over Belaguez's neck to give the horse as much assistance as possible. Ogden clung on grimly behind him. Because of the double weight that Belaguez carried, Veremund's donkey was able to keep pace. Ogden's white donkey had disappeared in the pelting rain.

As Timozel and Faraday approached the Barrows, Merlion and her maid close behind, Timozel grabbed the bridle of Faraday's horse and pulled it toward the shelter of one of the steep-walled Barrows. The rain was upon the Barrows now, streaming down from the sky in unnatural floods, driven by the brutal wind. Every rider was drenched to the skin whether they wore a heavy sealskin cloak or not. Men and horses scurried toward the most sheltered spots among the Barrows, and the air filled with the sounds of men shouting, horses neighing and the increasing fury of the storm as it swept over them.

Faraday pulled her horse to a halt and frantically looked about her. "Timozel!" she cried. "My mother?"

"Faraday, get off your horse. We've got to find some shelter. Now!" Timozel shouted as he slid off his bay gelding and stumbled across to Faraday.

But Faraday tugged at the reins of her exhausted horse, trying to kick it into the turmoil about her. "Mother?" she shouted, desperately searching. "Mother!"

Timozel reached up blindly, his eyes closed against the beating rain, fumbled for a moment with Faraday's soaked cloak, then seized her waist and hauled her unceremoniously off the horse.

"Timozel!" Faraday wailed, trying to twist out of his hands but overbalancing and falling to her knees in the mud. Her horse swerved back into the confusion of men and horses about them, causing Yr to leap from its back, feet and claws extended, wet fur standing in spikes all over her body. She landed squarely on the back of Timozel's head and neck.

"Ug!" grunted Timozel, collapsing on top of Faraday and pushing them both down into the ground.

Yr's leap undoubtedly saved all three of their lives. Just as Timozel collapsed on top of Faraday a great sheet of what appeared to be lightning speared through the sky, striking Faraday's horse as it turned to bolt into the storm.

Timozel rolled off Faraday and squinted through the rain. The horse lay completely still not four paces from them, its head shattered by a massive spear of thick ice. As Timozel gaped, unable to believe what he was seeing, more ice spears rained with vicious purpose from the sky; those men and horses still in the flat open space between the Barrows took the full impact of the dreadful deluge.

Timozel grabbed Faraday by the shoulders, pulling her half out of the mud. "Faraday! We've got to get out of here! Move!" He hauled her to her feet, Faraday having just enough time to grab Yr out of the mud as Timozel pulled her, hunched over as far as they could go, toward the lee of a Barrow about thirty paces distant. Dreadful screams of those transfixed by the ice spears rang out about them.

They had taken about fifteen faltering paces, buffeted by men, horses and the wind and pelting rain, when the dying body of a headless horse struck Timozel squarely on the shoulder.

"No!" Timozel screamed, as he and Faraday were pushed to their knees in the mud again. Timozel tried to drag Faraday up, but she shrieked in complete horror and wrenched herself out of his hands before he could haul her to her feet.

Timozel saw Faraday's shocked face, and followed her eyes down. Lying on the ground, so close that Faraday's knees were touching the body, was the lifeless form of Merlion. A few paces away was the body of her maid, crushed under her horse. An ice spear had caught Lady Merlion in the back as she ran toward the Barrow, and now protruded in jagged red-tipped spikes from her belly and breast. The rain had washed most of the blood from her face and her lifeless eyes stared into the murderous heavens, the heavy rain drops making small indentations on the surface of her eyeballs before running like tears of sorrow down her pale cheeks.

Tearing his eyes away from the dreadful sight, Timozel groped for Faraday's shoulders. Artor save them! he thought numbly, for surely nothing else would. His lips moved but no sound came. Faraday's initial scream had weakened into a series of heart-rending wails, and now she dropped Yr, her hands patting ineffectually at Merlion's body as if it was somehow possible to put her back together again.

"Faraday, Faraday," Timozel mumbled feebly, "come, we've got to go."

Faraday did not hear a word he said, and Timozel began to cry himself, overcome by the dead and dying about him, his tears mingling with the rain streaming down his face. This was not how he envisioned death, warriors should die nobly on the battlefield, fighting a flesh and blood foe—not this terror that rained down from a demonic sky. He closed his eyes and rested his face on Faraday's shoulder, resigned to their imminent death.

"Now, now," a soft burred voice said. "Time to move, young man. No use staying here in this weather. Come, lovely lady, take my hand."

Timozel slowly lifted his head, twisting to look behind him. A roughly dressed peasant, long heavy staff in his hand, was leaning down and smiling into his eyes. He appeared totally unmoved by the carnage about him. He must be simple, thought Timozel vaguely. What was a peasant doing here in this nightmare?

I have died, Timozel decided. None of this can be happening. I have died and gone for my sins into the crazed pits of the AfterLife.

"No, no," the man said, his smile widening for a moment. " 'Tis all happening, as true as the sun do rise every morning. Dreadful, dreadful, it is, that the Destroyer has reached this far. Too many of us here, there were, too enticing a target. Come, come, we must move. Don't know what his next trick might be."

Faraday's wails abated a little at the sight of him. "Jack," she whispered.

"Come, come," Jack repeated, gripping her hand, and now Timozel could sense some strain in his voice. As he pulled Faraday to her feet, Jack seized Timozel's arm and hauled him up as well. "Yr, you shall have to walk by yourself for a moment or two. If you stay close you should manage—the worst of the storm has passed."

The cat slunk close to Faraday's heels as Jack led them safely across the remaining ground to the side of the Barrow, stepping smoothly past the bodies of horses and men that littered their path. He kept up a soothing monologue about nothing in particular while they walked, calming both Faraday and Timozel. The ice spears had all but ceased and, while the wind and rain still beat at them, it now had the feel of a normal autumn gale rather than the supernatural force of a few minutes before. Jack stopped where several dozen men and one or two horses sheltered against the steepest part of the Barrow, and turned to Timozel.

"Young lord," he said deferentially, " 'Tis better you wait here with your fellow Axe-Wielders. Wait for your Battle-Axe. Wait for his orders. He will tell you what to do. I will take the lovely lady a little further along the Barrow, where she can grieve for her mother in private. You can rest now . . . you have been true."

He had such a soothing voice and for a moment his words made complete sense to Timozel. He nodded his head in agreement and Jack led Faraday away along the Barrow wall.

Timozel shut his eyes, rubbing his eyebrows with his hand, head bowed. "Faraday," he muttered to himself. Surely he should stay with her, she was all alone now. He opened his eyes and lifted his head. Faraday and Jack, the white cat still with them, were almost to the very end of the Barrow. Where was he taking her? Fear and suspicion flared bright in Timozel's mind and he turned to walk toward them, his feet strangely heavy and sluggish. Faraday—he had to save her. Something had to be saved from this dreadful day.

Jack stopped Faraday at the very end of the Barrow. "Dear one," he said quietly to Faraday, one arm about her shoulders, his face close to hers. "Do you remember that you promised us to be true?"

Faraday nodded her head. She really didn't care at the moment what she had promised to anyone.

"Dear one," Jack repeated, knowing how deeply she had been wounded by the sight of her mother's torn body. "In the slaughter and chaos of Gorgrael's storm it might be possible for us to begin our journey to Borneheld here, at this moment. If you disappear among the Barrows, Axis will suppose you dead and not search for you. That would be best, dear one, that he supposes you dead for the while."

Tears ran down Faraday's cheeks. Jack stroked her cheek comfortingly, his fingers wiping away both tears and soft rain. "Do not worry, lovely lady. All will be well. But for the moment, Yr and I think it best that you leave. He is too distracted by you, and you will serve him better at Borneheld's side."

"I understand," Faraday whispered.

"My dear," Jack said softly. "Lay your hand upon my staff, it will keep you safe. Yr, my shoulders, if you please."

The cat scrambled up his thick woollen cloak and crouched on his shoulder. "Hurry," she hissed softly.

Jack took his heavy staff in his free hand, waited until Faraday had grasped it in both her hands, then raised it slightly and knocked it three times on a piece of flat gray rock by their feet. The sound rang through the ornate knob at the top of the staff.

"Sing well, fly high, StarFarers. By your leave, let us pass the chamber of death and grant us entry to your Halls. In the name of the One who will walk with you one day we seek your aid this day." His eyes glowed emerald and his fingers whitened about the heavy staff.

Then everything seemed to happen at once.

Timozel clapped his hand on Jack's free shoulder. "What are you doing?" he began, his voice brusque and demanding. Jack whipped his head around, his emerald eyes blazing, his entire face a mask of white-hot anger. Yr hissed and struck out at Timozel with her claws, her own eyes brilliant with fury.

There was a sound of rumbling thunder from their feet, then the earth beneath them opened up into a yawning chasm and the entire end of the Barrow began to collapse about them. Faraday saw the black hole suddenly yawn under her feet and screamed, frantically trying to leap backwards. She was too late and the next instant felt herself falling head over heels into a chasm. Then something struck her head and blackness claimed her.

Axis and the two Brothers entered the Barrows just as the storm was beginning to fade. They had not fared badly, the Icarii ward protecting all three of them from the full force of the storm.

Axis was appalled at the carnage that met his eyes as he rode between the Barrows. Although most had escaped to shelter beside the steep walls of the ancient earth-covered tombs, hundreds of bodies lay scattered about in the wide exposed spaces between the Barrows. Both horses and men had died gruesomely. Others lay writhing in pain in the mud, their bodies pinned to the ground by the piercing ice, their life blood draining away. Puddles of blood and water mingled on the sodden ground as the ice spears melted, the continuing light rain adding to the spreading pink puddles.

Ogden looked up at Axis. "It is the work of Gorgrael, BattleAxe. The ice is his mark."

"What have I done?" whispered Axis, scarcely hearing Ogden. "What have I done to my men?" How could a storm wreak this much mayhem and death?

Veremund rode up, leading Ogden's donkey. "You could have done nothing more than what you did, BattleAxe. How could men fight the storm with swords and axes? If they had not retreated to the Barrows, then more—hundreds more—would have died on the plain. Here, at least, most found shelter."

His words did not comfort Axis. He should never have led his men out of the Barrows in the first place, but so wrapped was he in his thoughts of Faraday that . . .

Axis looked up, his eyes frantically searching among the

bodies scattered across the ground. His heels dug into the stallion's sides and Belaguez leaped forward.

Ogden and Veremund hurried after him, Ogden lifting his habit well clear of the bloodied mud as he leaped in ungainly bounds across the ground.

Axis had got to within fifty paces of the nearest Barrow when he saw Faraday, Timozel and a strange man standing huddled together in a group at its far end. He opened his mouth to call but just then the ground rumbled beneath Belaguez's hooves, and the stallion stumbled and almost fell. His hands clutching at Belaguez's mane, Axis' eyes did not waver from the sight before him. He saw Faraday cry out and clutch at the air, her whole body weaving backwards and forward. All three then toppled into the hole which opened at their feet. The entire side of the Barrow slid downwards and an immense shifting mass of mud, turf and boulders engulfed the spot where the three had disappeared. For as long as it took Axis to gallop Belaguez across the site, the landslide continued, then it rumbled grudgingly to an end as Axis slid off the stallion.

"No!" Axis screamed, tearing at the earth with his bare hands. "No!"

Ogden and Veremund reached him moments later. "It's too late," said Ogden, pulling Axis gently back from the mudslide. "They're gone."

Axis' hands were torn and bloody. "No," he whispered, his face ghostly pale.

Belial joined them, blood oozing from a deep wound in his shoulder. He waved Ogden and Veremund back with an abrupt movement of his hand, then squatted beside Axis and talked to him in a low voice, his eyes intense. After a moment Axis nodded curtly and stood up.

"I am going to ride north until I can face this Destroyer in battle," he said, his voice harsh, his eyes hard and cold, "and then I will tear him to pieces for what he has done here today."

21

Inside the Enchanter-Talon's Tomb

Faraday awoke, her head throbbing, every muscle and joint in her body aching. Someone held a hand close over her face.

"Mphh," she muttered, trying to brush away the irritating hand.

"I'm only wiping the dirt from your face. There. Can you open your eyes?"

With a great effort Faraday slowly opened her eyes. She blinked, trying to focus. Jack's concerned face swam above hers and she blinked again. Gradually his face came into focus.

"I hurt, everywhere," she muttered, trying to sit up.

"We came down more heavily than I had foreseen," Jack said, his worried face easing a little as Faraday began to move. "I didn't realize the Barrow would collapse so badly. Yr and I escaped the worst of it, but you and," his face hardened, "that Axe-Wielder were hit by some loose stones."

"Timozel!" Faraday sat up straight, too quickly for her

aching head to adjust, and groaned, catching at her head with her hands.

"Quietly," a woman's soft voice said behind her, and Faraday felt cool and soothing hands run gently across her brow. "You must not move so fast yet. Here, let me massage your head for a moment."

The woman's hands felt wonderful and for a few minutes Faraday sat, her eyes closed, letting the marvelous hands take away the worst of the throbbing.

"Thank you," she whispered eventually, opening her eyes and turning to thank the woman who had relieved her head of so much of the pain. "That feels . . ." Faraday's eyes widened in astonishment. Squatting behind her was a completely naked woman with long straight white-blond hair hanging to her waist.

"Why, Lady Faraday, do you not know me? I am Yr, and this is my human form."

Faraday's eyes widened even further. "You can change?"

Yr laughed, a low and throaty sound, "It is hard for me, for any of us, to change, and we need a little assistance to do so. This place," she waved her hand about, "still contains so much residual enchantment that the transformation was made easier for me." She laughed again merrily and winked at Jack. "Jack did not always approve of the cat. He thought it . . . inappropriate." She shrugged a little. "But a cat can go where no woman can, and can listen to conversations that any other man or woman would be killed for overhearing. I have stalked the corridors of Carlon for many years, sweet girl, and I have heard much."

"Enough," Jack said shortly. "Faraday, can you stand?"

Yr and Jack helped Faraday to her feet. Her head swam a little, then she looked about. They were standing at one end of a dimly lit rectangular stone chamber, perhaps forty paces by fifteen. In the center of the chamber stood a table-shaped solid block of stone, as high as a man's waist and pure white, almost gleaming in the poor light. Two copper lamps, one at either end of the chamber, glowed softly.

188 ᴥ Sara Douglass

Turning around Faraday saw that the wall behind them was half obscured by tumbled masonry and dirt.

"The landslide has blocked the passage down here completely, Faraday. No-one can follow," Jack said softly. "As far as those above are concerned we are dead, entombed in the mud and the rocks."

Faraday shivered. Axis thought she was dead. Well, it was for the best. She gasped suddenly as she saw Timozel's motionless form stretched along the floor immediately behind her. She stepped over and bent down by him. "Timozel!"

Yr and Jack looked at each other. It would have been better if Timozel had died in the landslide, but he had been largely protected by the magical aura of the staff as they fell down the chasm. His presence was a complication that they did not need. Still, as Ogden and Veremund were bound, so were they. They could suggest and advise, and sometimes they could manipulate events if they served the Prophecy, but they could not go so far as to interfere with life itself.

Jack sighed and bent down by Timozel. "Faraday, move your hand. I can help him as I did you."

Faraday watched as Jack moved his hand over Timozel's face, a faint green light emanating from the tips of his fingers. Gradually the color seeped back into Timozel's cheeks and after a few minutes he shifted slightly and began to moan.

"Faraday," Jack looked at her as she crouched the other side of Timozel. "You must persuade him that Yr and I pose no threat. As you can see, the boy is fully armed with sword and axe, and Yr and I are as vulnerable to steel as you or Axis. As Axis must not die, neither must we—for then all is lost."

Faraday nodded, her green eyes grave, and leaned one restraining hand on Timozel's chest.

Unlike Faraday, Timozel leapt from unconsciousness to full alertness. His eyes opened, both angry and indignant, and he lurched into a sitting position, brushing aside Faraday's restraining hand, his knees bending to rise. His hand gripped his sword, half unsheathing it from its scabbard. Both Yr and Jack flinched involuntarily at the sound of the steel sliding free from its prison.

"No!" Faraday cried, trying to wrap her arms around him. "Timozel, it's all right. We're safe!"

Timozel sat rigid for a moment, his hand still clenched about the hilt of his sword.

"Faraday?" he said, puzzled, "What happened?" He turned to look at her, his eyes losing some of their aggression.

"Shush, it's all right, Timozel." Faraday ran her fingers soothingly through his brown curls.

"Where are we?" he asked, turning to look around him. "What happened?" His face tightened as he saw Jack and remembered him trying to abduct Faraday; then his cheeks stained red as he fully realized that the strange woman standing next to Jack was completely naked. Yr's lips parted a little in a smile. She shook her hair back from her face and squared her shoulders slightly, leaning back against the stone block, her skin almost as white as the stone itself.

Timozel slid the sword back into its scabbard, his eyes still on Yr, and rose slowly to his feet.

"Yr," Jack rebuked gently. "This is not the time nor the place."

"But what can I do, Jack? I have no clothes," said Yr.

Timozel continued to stare at Yr, his eyes wary. "Here," he said finally, his face returning to its normal color. "You can have my cloak."

He slipped it from his shoulders and took a step toward Yr. Yr paused, teasing, then she languidly stretched forth a hand. "Ugh," she said disapprovingly, "it's wet."

"Take it!" Jack snapped, irritated by Yr's behavior. He wished she had retained her cat form; she could be infinite trouble in her womanly guise.

Yr sighed and slipped the cloak about her shoulders. "It will no doubt dry quickly enough," she said. "Thank you, Timozel."

Timozel was more relaxed now that Yr's nakedness was covered, and he sketched a courtly bow for her. "My lady," he smiled.

Faraday placed a gentle hand on Timozel's arm. "Tim, this is Jack and Yr. They are . . ." Faraday stopped, confused. What should she tell him? She looked at Jack for guidance.

Jack interrupted. "Timozel. Do you remember the Prophecy that you heard at the Silent Woman Keep?" Timozel nodded. "Well, Yr and I are two of the Sentinels mentioned within the Prophecy. We are part of the Prophecy, we are bound to it and serve it."

Timozel's eyes narrowed. The line of the Prophecy mentioning the Sentinels ran through his head, "The Sentinels will walk abroad," then he remembered its darker companion. When the Prophecy had been simply an abstract riddle Timozel had found it amusing if puzzling; now that it was taking flesh and blood form before him he did not think he liked it as much. Like all Acharites, he had been taught from a child in arms that all magic or enchantments were evil and used only by the Forbidden in order to harm Artor-fearing Acharites and undermine their faith in the Way of the Plough. His unease grew. The Prophecy also mentioned the remade dead and dark powers. Were these magical creatures now a threat to Faraday and himself? Timozel's hand crept a little closer to the hilt of his sword again.

"Timozel," Yr said, her voice soft and reasonable. Her eyes had lost their challenging look and were now reassuring. "Jack and I, as are our comrades, devote our lives to preserving this land, and to finding and supporting the StarMan, the one who will be able to stop Gorgrael the Destroyer. We mean you and Faraday no harm."

"Then why have you seized her?" Timozel demanded.

"They are taking me to Borneheld," Faraday said, "be-

cause they believe that he will be better able to hold the ice
creatures at Gorkenfort if I am at his side."

"Is he the one who will save Achar?" asked Timozel.

"He will be vitally important in Achar's defense," said
Jack. "He will need Faraday there to support him."

Timozel stared at Faraday, trying to think. Her hair hung
down about her shoulders in disarray and her eyes were
anxious as they looked into his. No doubt she couldn't wait
to reach her betrothed husband. The more he thought about
it, the more he believed it would be a good thing if Faraday
joined Borneheld. But it would be so dangerous at Gorkenfort.

Timozel made up his mind. "Yes," he nodded, "I can understand that Borneheld would need you by his side." Faraday visibly relaxed. "But," a frown crossed Timozel's face,
"I do not entirely trust your companions, either. What on
earth made them cast us down here?"

"Timozel, you know Axis. He had orders to take me to
Arcen and leave me there. Yet I wish for nothing else than
to join Borneheld." Artor forgive her for that lie, she
thought. "And see how the Destroyer attacked the Axe-
Wielders. It might have been dangerous for me to stay with
them. Jack and Yr thought it best that we leave now."

"Yes," Timozel nodded his head slowly, then abruptly
made up his mind. Artor must have pushed him to Faraday's side like this for a reason—to protect her. Artor was
giving Timozel the chance to prove what a great and honorable warrior he could be. He dropped down on one knee
before her and seized both her hands between his own.

"Lady," he said earnestly, "I pledge my life to your service." Faraday gasped, and her eyes flew to the impassive
Jack and Yr before returning to Timozel's face. "Know that
I will stand between you and harm, that I will guard both
your body and your honor before any regard of my own
safety, that I will champion your cause and seek only that
you walk in light for the rest of your life. Artor witness this
my holy vow; only my death or your wish will break it.
Lady Faraday, will you accept my service?"

Faraday did not know what to do. Warriors had been known to bind themselves as Champions to a noble lady, but, as far as she knew, it had not occurred for many years. She looked across to Jack for guidance.

Jack nodded slightly. Perhaps Timozel could protect her against some of the trauma ahead. She would need a friend.

Yr wondered if Timozel might get in the way more than he could help, but she too inclined her head. As Faraday's Champion, Timozel would prove a far more irresistible challenge for her.

Faraday took a deep breath and turned her eyes back to Timozel. She was touched by his offer and his genuine concern for her. She knew that the relationship between a lady and her Champion was never sexual; perhaps that was one of the reasons the nobles at court had discarded the ancient tradition as hopelessly idealistic and practically untenable. But Faraday also knew that a Champion was more than simply a protector. He was a friend, a confidant, a pillar to lean on, a man who would always believe her, strive to understand her, and do his utmost to support her in any decision that she made. She nodded slowly. Perhaps life at Borneheld's side would not prove so awful with Timozel there to turn to.

"I accept your offer of service, Timozel, and thank you from the depths of my heart. Let Artor witness that this bond shall hold until your death or my wish does break it. May Artor also guide both our steps in the future, and may He keep and hold us in the palm of His hand."

Timozel smiled and kissed her hands softly, then he let them go and stood up. Now this strange pair would know that Faraday had a protector, he thought. If they tried to harm her then he would cut them down where they stood.

Timozel squared his shoulders. He felt taller, as if his new role as Faraday's Champion had given him added stature along with the new meaning and direction of his life. He dismissed the thought of what his BattleAxe might say. It was more than time he started to shoulder some responsibility.

"Now," he said in as authoritative a tone as he could manage. "Perhaps you could explain where we are, Jack."

22

Evening by the Barrows

By nightfall Axis had resumed control and moved his men further into the Barrows. The Axe-Wielders had gathered their horses together quickly and reformed into their units. The two physicians who travelled with them tended the wounded while the dead were gathered and placed in graves hastily dug in an open area between two Barrows. "The Barrows can hold our dead as well as those of the Forbidden," Axis remarked bitterly when Veremund dared to raise an eyebrow in his direction. Later, the two Brothers, pressed by Axis' cold stare, mumbled the words of the Service for the Dead and managed, with a number of embarrassing stumbles, to commend the dead to Artor's care. The injured lay on stretchers, ready to be taken back to Tare by a small escort the next morning.

Later, soldiers sat about their campfires, either forcing down warm food, or cleaning gear muddied during the confusion of the storm. Axis spent much of the evening walking among his men, smiling and reassuring, asking and answering questions, putting a comforting hand to a shoulder when it was needed, laughing and joking when that was needed more. Despite the apparent attention Axis gave to the individual men of his command, his mind worried over the events of the day, trying to make some sense out of what had happened. He was grateful that no one had seen the raging head in the clouds; he did not think he could explain that to his men. What was it that had bubbled out of his subconscious to drive back the frightful apparition that seemed so intent on destroying him?

The more Axis thought about the implications of what had happened, the more unsure he became. Having lived so long with the uncertainty and shame of his parentage, Axis was not a man who enjoyed encountering uncertainty in other areas of his life.

Finally, Axis wound his way to Ogden and Veremund's campfire. The two old men were huddled inside their precious books in their lap. Both were so absorbed in their reading they did not hear Axis approach.

"And have you found the answers yet, old men? Can you tell me how to drive back another of those demon-spawned storms? Can you tell me how to protect my men from spears of ice that rain from the clouds?"

Ogden and Veremund looked up, startled. Axis stood the other side of the low fire, his stance aggressive. Both of his hands hovered close to the sword and axe in his weapon belt.

"Axis," said Veremund gently. "Sit down with us awhile. We should talk."

Axis stood a moment longer, then sat down cross-legged in one fluid motion. He has the Icarii grace, thought Ogden, and the temper to match.

"Yes." Axis said harshly, "we should talk. And will you tell me the truth, old men?"

"How much truth do you want to hear, BattleAxe?" Ogden snapped, before Veremund laid a hand on his arm and replied smoothly. "We have never told you anything but the truth, Axis."

Perhaps, thought Axis, but mostly couched in as many

riddles as your beloved Prophecy. He took a calming breath. "What was that in the clouds this morning? Was it the Destroyer your Prophecy speaks of?"

"It was his image," Ogden replied. "Not the Destroyer himself. He is not strong enough yet to make such a journey in the flesh."

"Why journey in the flesh when you can kill and maim as effectively with your cursed sorcery?" Axis said angrily.

"Axis, be calm. Learn from it, but do not waste your energies blaming yourself."

For a moment Axis battled with his temper; that Veremund had only spoken sense did not endear him to Axis. "Then tell me what to learn from it, man, tell me what to learn from it." Axis paused, his jaw clenched tightly. "Why did he attack us?"

"Because we are a danger to him," Veremund replied.

"Do you mean the Axe-Wielders are a danger to him?" Axis asked carefully.

"And you, BattleAxe," Veremund replied just as carefully. He did not want to give Axis too much information while he was in this state of angry self-denial. "You lead them, and you lead them toward Gorkenfort. Perhaps Gorgrael thought it worthwhile to risk an attack while you were still far from the icy north."

Axis accepted the answer. He would think about any further implications of Veremund's words later, when his heart did not burn with such fierce sorrow that he thought he could not bear it.

Both Ogden and Veremund knew what was going through his mind. They had also seen what had happened to Faraday, yet they, unlike Axis, knew that she was probably still alive. Neither were unkind creatures, but they knew it would be disastrous for Tencendor if Axis were diverted from the path of the Prophecy.

"And what happens when this Gorgrael, or his image, returns, old men? What then?" said Axis.

Ogden glanced at Veremund. They had discussed this earlier, and concurred in thinking that Gorgrael had risked this attack only because so many of the Sentinels, as well as Axis and Faraday, had been in one spot. Now that they were split, Gorgrael might well hang back. They suspected—hoped—that Gorgrael had seriously weakened himself in trying to attack this far south. Ogden turned back to Axis. "We hope he will not adventure so far south again. Axis, think a moment. The storm was vicious and deadly, but it lasted a few scant minutes once it reached the Axe-Wielders. If you were Gorgrael, would you have stopped with only a few hundred men?" Axis winced, but conceded the point. "Gorgrael could not press the attack home. Perhaps he has overreached himself with this effort. Hopefully we will be safe for the moment, and, who knows, perhaps we have even bought Gorkenfort time."

"Brothers, why has he appeared in my dreams?" Axis asked quietly, looking into the low flames of the fire.

"Gorgrael is a creature who thrives on hate, hate is his very existence, it drives his heart," said Veremund.

"Yes," Axis looked up from the flames. "I have felt that."

"And he hates most of all those who will stand before him, stand to deny him what he craves—the complete destruction of all lands below the line of year-long ice and snow."

"Why?" Axis interrupted. "Why would he want to do that?"

Ogden shrugged. "He simply hates, Axis. That is enough."

Axis nodded. He understood.

"Gorgrael will try everything in his power to drive uncertainty and fear into the hearts of those who oppose him, Axis. If it means invading your dreams to do so, then Gorgrael is perfectly capable of doing that."

There was a long pause. Ogden and Veremund both knew what Axis would ask next.

"What did I sing, Brothers? What did I sing out there?" His voice was barely above a whisper.

"Axis, you sang an ancient ward—"

"Sorcery!" Axis broke in, his voice horrified. Axis had

absorbed the Seneschal's fear and hatred of things magical at an early age.

"No, no," Veremund hastened. "Although some might consider it an enchantment, it is simply a ward against evil. No one can sing it, ward themselves against evil, unless it has been taught to them in the womb. Axis, your father sang that to you. He loved you so much that he gave you the gift of that song."

Axis passed a trembling hand across his eyes, turning his head slightly away from the two Brothers. Veremund caught a glint of tears. "Never doubt that you were loved and wanted, Axis. If your father has never claimed you then it is because circumstances greater than his love for you have kept him away."

Axis nodded his head curtly, acknowledging Veremund's words. Finally he looked back at Ogden and Veremund. Tears trailed down his cheeks despite his best efforts to hold them back. "Who was my father? *What* was my father?" he whispered.

Both of the older men rose and moved quietly around the fire, sitting either side of Axis. Veremund laid his hand on Axis' shoulder, but it was Ogden who spoke. "Axis, neither of us know exactly who he was." Neither felt the time was right to tell Axis that his father was almost certainly an Icarii Enchanter. "But if you find him then a great many questions will be answered."

"Ogden, when I read that Prophecy from the book in the Keep, I felt as though a dark, deep dungeon that had been locked all my life had been thrown open and flooded with light. Ogden," he looked Ogden deep in the eye, "I am not sure that I like what I can now see in that unlocked chamber. I am starting to wonder if it might have been better had it remained locked the rest of my life."

Axis held Ogden's eyes for a moment longer, then he shrugged off Veremund's hand and stood up with the same fluid grace with which he had sat down. "Brothers, sleep well tonight, for tomorrow we ride for Arcen, where we will reprovision, then ride for Smyrton with full haste. I will not let Gorgrael deflect me from riding north." He paused. "I will send riders with the injured back to Tare and then to Carlon with news of what has happened here this day." His voice hardened. "And to that purpose I must now write to the Lady of Tare telling her that her beloved eldest son is dead under a mountain of mud and rock. Would that I could tell her myself rather than entrust such news to a messenger."

23

The Star Gate

"We are in the tomb of the ninth of twenty-six Icarii Talons to be buried here, Timozel," said Jack.

Faraday and Timozel looked about them. Although obviously built by skilled masons, for the tomb of a King it seemed remarkably bare. Apart from the central stone block there was nothing else in the chamber. The four stone walls, relieved from outright starkness by false pillars, showed no sign of any opening.

"How do we get out?" asked Faraday.

Yr turned to Jack. "Jack, you know this place better than any of us. Do you know the way below?"

Jack turned to the stone block and laid a reverential hand upon it. "These Barrows were built for only twenty six of the Icarii Talons, Kings over all Tencendor. The Talons ruled Tencendor for over five thousand years, yet only twenty-six were laid to rest here. Thirty-one lie in more mundane surroundings."

Timozel stirred restlessly, but Jack raised his hand. "Be still, lad. You must know this. Only twenty-six. Under half the total number of Talons. The twenty-six who were not only Talons, but also of the line of Enchanters. These Barrows are very enchanted places."

"Enchanters?" Timozel's voice was stiff. "What do you mean?"

Jack looked at the boy. "Those of the Icarii who could cast enchantments, Timozel."

Timozel's eyes widened and he invoked the sign of the Plough against evil, shifting back a little toward the wall of the tomb. He did not like this talk of Enchanters and enchanted places.

Faraday moved to stand beside Jack at the stone block. "Is the Talon entombed beneath this block?" she asked, about to rest her hand on the stone, but thinking better of it.

"No." Jack paused, reflecting. "The Enchanter-Talon was laid out on this block when he died. But he has long since gone. And where he has gone, so must we."

"The Star Gate." Yr took a deep breath. "I have never seen it—but I yearn to. I have heard so much . . . so much."

Jack nodded. "Only I among the Sentinels has laid eyes on the Star Gate. And no one for the past thousand years has walked the paths of the StarFarers down to the Star Gate."

"Why do you call them StarFarers, Jack?" said Faraday.

"It is what the most powerful of the Icarii Enchanter-Talons were known as, although all Enchanters bear the word 'star' somewhere in the name. They honor the stars and the movements of the heavens. Much of their magic comes from the stars, or so it is said."

All this talk of magic was making Timozel uneasy. "Enough of that. Where are you taking us? What is this Star Gate?"

Jack hid his annoyance behind a bland smile. "What it is concerns you not, Timozel. If I thought I could get us out of here without passing by the Star Gate then I surely would. But all paths lead down to the Star Gate, and to find another path to the surface we will have to walk past the Star Gate."

"Is it dangerous?" Faraday asked.

Yr laughed. "Not unless you walk through, sweet child." She paused and regarded Jack a moment. "Jack has not explained well enough, I think. These Barrows are not actually tombs, for they hold not the bodies of the Enchanter-Talons. Each Barrow is instead an entranceway. A gate before the real gate, if you like. Whenever one of the twenty-six died their people would build for them a Barrow, with this chamber below it. Below the chamber they built a long stairwell that leads to the Star Gate. When the Barrow, chamber and stairwell were completely built, the body of the Enchanter-Talon was laid upon the stone block and the Barrows sealed. Once sealed in his tomb the Enchanter-Talon would eventually make his way down the stairwell into the Chamber of the Star Gate and walk through. Each had his own entrance to the Star Gate—thus twenty-six Barrows for twenty-six Enchanter-Talons. Twenty-six gates to the Star Gate. Once through the Star Gate, it is said the Enchanter-Talons wait."

"Wait for what?" Faraday's eyes were wide. She had not believed that anything the Forbidden did could be so hauntingly beautiful. Despite her devout upbringing, Faraday was rapidly losing her uneasiness with talk of things magical. This talk of the StarFarers and the Star Gate fascinated her.

Yr shrugged. "Who knows, darling girl? They wait for whatever concerns them."

Timozel didn't like the sound of this. How could these Enchanter-Talons make their way down a flight of stairs when they were dead? No wonder the Seneschal taught that magic was evil. Yr stepped over to him, resting a hand lightly on his shoulder and leaning close. "Who knows how these dead Enchanter-Talons made their way down, Timozel. I confess that it is the living who concern me." She rubbed her other hand gently against his chest and leaned against his body.

Timozel's face hardened and he seized her hand, lifting

it off his chest. Did she seek to enchant him with her charms? Yr shrugged and stepped back, clutching the cloak closed where it had gaped open. There would be time enough later.

"Enough," Jack said mildly. "It is time to descend. We have no food or water. The quicker we move through the quicker we can find something to eat."

Jack picked up his heavy staff and hefted it in his left hand, running his right hand gently over the metal knob at its apex. Faraday looked closely at the metal knob for the first time. It had deep lines etched into it, whirling in complicated patterns across the knob that was about the size of a man's clenched fist. The metal looked strange, blackened, tarnished almost. Then her attention was diverted from the knob to Jack. He was talking to the staff, very quietly so that his actual words could not be heard, but with a beautiful cadence underpinning his words. He almost seemed to be singing to it. Faint emerald light pulsed from his fingertips in rhythm with his voice. Yr stepped up softly behind Faraday. "Step back this way, Faraday," she whispered. "You must not get in the way."

Yr and Faraday joined Timozel by the far wall. He was staring at Jack, his eyes dark with suspicion, his hand resting lightly on the hilt of his sword.

Suddenly Jack seized the staff in both hands, whirled it at shoulder height three times around his body, then thrust the metal tip against a spot in the floor.

"Ecrez dontai StarFarer!" he cried, and instantly a large section of the stonework underfoot dropped several handspans and slid underneath the rest of the floor. Stone steps spiraled out of sight into the blackness below.

"I am impressed, Jack," Yr said very quietly. "You seemed to have learned well during your long wait for the StarMan." Jack raised his head from his contemplation of the steps. His jewel-like eyes were faintly satisfied. He nodded in acknowledgment of her compliment.

"Let us go. Timozel, you will bring up the rear with one

of the lamps. I will lead with the other. Yr and Faraday can come between us. The climb is long, I fear. Please be careful, the steps can sometimes be uneven."

They had to climb slowly. The stairs were steep and, as Jack had cautioned, uneven in places as the stairwell would down deep into the earth in tight spirals. Jack, Yr and Faraday had to carefully hold their cloaks out of the way lest they trip over their trailing hems, and Jack gave the lamp to Yr so that he could manage both his cloak and the heavy staff.

Faraday concentrated hard to avoid falling. The steps seemed to spiral down into infinity, and she lost all track of time. Her calves and knees ached after only a few minutes and, as they descended further, the ache intensified into a burning sensation. She was so lost in contemplation of her pain that she bumped heavily into Yr when she stopped in front of her.

"Pay attention!" Yr snapped. "Jack has called a rest."

Faraday mumbled an apology and sat down to massage her aching calves. "How much further, Jack?"

"We're about halfway down," Jack said. Faraday was glad to see that both he and Yr were also massaging their legs. Magical creatures they might be, but it didn't stop their muscles from complaining. Timozel was stoically pretending that his own legs didn't ache.

Yr began to comb out Faraday's wet and tangled hair with her fingers. Faraday smiled and closed her eyes. She would give two years of her life for a warm bath, she thought vaguely, lulled into tranquility by the touch of Yr's hands.

As Faraday's eyes closed Timozel surreptitiously stretched his legs across the width of the stairwell, his face grimacing with relief as the ache began to abate. He sighed and settled his shoulder comfortably against the stone wall.

For a while he watched Yr comb Faraday's hair, then his eyes, like Faraday's, slowly closed.

He was on a great beast—not a horse, something differ-

ent—that dipped and soared. It screamed with the voice of . . .

Timozel's eyes flew open and he sat forward, startled. For an instant he could have sworn that he was . . .

"What's wrong?" Jack's quiet voice asked, concerned. Yr and Faraday were too absorbed in each other to notice Timozel.

"Nothing," said Timozel tersely. "Nothing."

Jack stared a moment longer, then sat back, turning his face to the blackness below them. No wonder the Axe-Wielder is unsettled, he thought. This is a stairwell haunted by the memory of strange steps. He tried to rest, wishing that fate had not brought them to *this* Barrow. Prophecy.

Slowly Timozel leaned back against the wall. He closed his eyes.

He fought for a great Lord, and in the name of that Lord he commanded a mighty army that undulated for leagues in every direction.

Again Timozel's eyes flew open, but this time he kept still. Commanded a great army? He almost chuckled. Commanded a great army? Humph! Not if Axis had his way, he thought sourly. So determined is he not to favor me because he beds my mother I'll be lucky to achieve chief of the horse lines before I'm fifty. Timozel felt a stab of resentment, deeper than he'd ever felt before. He had a poor future in the Axe-Wielders.

He closed his eyes again.

The cold wind blew at his back as hundreds of thousands screamed his name and hurried to fulfill his every wish. Before him another army, his pitiful enemy, lay quavering in terror. They could not counter his brilliance. Their commander lay abed, unable to summon the courage to meet Timozel in just combat.

This must be a vision from Artor—a reward for taking the holy vows of Championship.

Remarkable victories were his for the taking.

"Yes," Timozel whispered.

In the name of his Lord he would clear Achar of the filth that invaded.

"Yes," he said, louder this time. He revelled in the power he would wield. His fist clenched by his side.

His name would live in legend forever.

"Timozel?" Faraday touched his hand. "Are you all right?"

Timozel hesitated, not wanting to let the vision go, then he opened his eyes and smiled at Faraday. "Yes. Yes, I will be all right."

All will be well.

I will be a *powerful* Champion, he thought, for people to scream my name thus. He muttered a quick prayer to Artor, thanking him for the vision.

"All will be well," he whispered.

"Let's move," Jack said finally, and they all rose stiftly to their feet. Yr had done her best with Faraday's hair, and now it lay coiled into a neat roll in the nape of her neck, the worst of the tangles and mud removed. Faraday turned to look at Timozel as they started to climb down again, his confident smile reassuring her. She thought she was going to like having her own personal Champion.

Timozel followed the others with new assurance. Artor's vision made him feel older, more purposeful. Harder. Ready to stand and defend Faraday—and Artor himself, if need be—at a moment's notice. A true Champion.

They continued to climb down the stairs, the only relief from complete blackness the dim glow provided by the lamps Yr and Timozel carried. Faraday shivered as she thought what it must have been like for a person to climb down this stairwell in total darkness. But then, perhaps these Enchanter-Talons made their own light.

Eventually they became aware of a faint sound of wind echoing up the stairs around them.

"What's that?" Faraday whispered, and felt Timozel touch her shoulder reassuringly.

"It is the sound of the Star Gate," Yr replied. Her voice

was stiff with barely suppressed excitement, and Faraday looked at Timozel, intrigued.

The sound grew louder as they got closer and a faint blue light began to augment that of their lamps. Finally the light was strong enough for Jack to ask Yr to douse her lamp, and after a moment's hesitation Timozel did the same. Yr was almost pushing Jack's back in her eagerness to get to the bottom of the stairwell.

"Peace, Yr, we're almost there," grumbled Jack though he was also keenly excited. He had seen the Star Gate on three previous occasions, yet three hundred viewings would never be enough for him.

As they rounded one more bend, the stairs abruptly ended in a long corridor that angled toward an open archway in the distance. Blue light and sound pulsed at them from the far side of the archway. Jack stopped them for a moment, although Yr looked so excited that for a moment Faraday thought she might break and run down the corridor toward the strange blue light. Her heart began to pound, and Timozel pulled her a little closer to his body, thinking she needed reassurance.

"There is no danger as long as you do not step through the Star Gate," Jack said, his eyes keen as they searched those of Faraday and Timozel. "But there are one or two things that I must warn you of. Yr? Do you listen as well?" Yr nodded her head impatiently, her eyes on the distant archway. Jack turned back to Faraday and Timozel. "No human has been down here for almost a thousand years, and in the time of the Icarii rule it was rare indeed that a human was allowed to see the Star Gate. This is one of the most sacred Icarii sites in this land, so treat it with due reverence. The Star Gate is very beautiful, and it will tempt you to step through. You can hear it sing now. But if you do that you will never come back. Do you understand?" Both Faraday and Timozel nodded.

"Well then, let us enter the Chamber of the Star Gate."

Timozel gripped Faraday's hand tightly as they followed

Jack and Yr. He was a Champion and he would lead great armies; there was no need to fear this blue light.

As soon as they stepped through the archway into the Chamber of the Star Gate, their ears were buffeted by the sound of a gale, although not a breath of wind touched their faces.

Faraday's first impression, after she had adjusted to the sound, was that the chamber was a smaller, if more exquisite, version of the Chamber of the Moons in the palace of Carlon. It was perfectly circular and surrounded by pillars and archways. Each of the pillars was carved from translucent white stone in the shape of a naked, winged man. Most of the men stood with their heads bowed and arms folded across their chests, wings lifted and outstretched so as to touch those of the men next to them, their touching wingtips forming the apex of the archways. Faraday noticed that an entire section of pillars across the far side of the chamber was different. These winged men had their heads up and their eyes wide open, golden orbs staring toward the center of the chamber, their arms uplifted in joy with their wings. She did not have to count to know that there were twenty-six.

"Faraday," Timozel whispered, and when she turned to look at him he pointed toward the vaulted ceiling of the chamber. Blue shadows leaped and chased each other across the white stone vault. Like demons, Timozel thought.

"Oh!" Faraday gasped, "it's beautiful!"

"It is not there you should be looking, lovely lady, but beneath the shadows," said Jack, standing halfway between the archway they had come through, his extended arm indicating what looked like the low rim of a large circular pool which occupied the center space of the floor.

Faraday walked toward the pool, dragging a reluctant Timozel with her. She was almost breathless with excitement. A few paces from the pool Timozel balked; he would go no further. Faraday let Timozel's hand go and walked to the rim, it was about knee height and wide enough to sit on comfortably. Without hesitation or a backward glance,

Faraday sat down. Deep blue light pulsed across her face and reflected far above on the stone vault.

Faraday's lips parted and her eyes widened. For a few moments she forgot to breathe. Yr and Jack joined her at the rim, and for long minutes all three stared transfixed into the Star Gate.

The circular pool contained no water; instead, to all intents and purposes, it contained the universe. The real one, not the faint shadow that lights the night sky. Stars reeled and danced, suns chased each other across galaxies, moons dipped and swayed through planetary systems, luminous comets threaded their mysterious paths through the cosmos. The sound of vast interstellar winds roared out into the chamber and a luminous deep blue light pulsed through the Star Gate. Its depths stretched into infinity.

Faraday opened her mouth to say something to Jack, sitting next to her, but there were no words to describe what she saw. She started to cry through sheer wonder at the incredible beauty and majesty of the Star Gate. No wonder the Icarii worshipped here and, when they could not be here, worshipped the Star Gate's reflection in the night sky. Artor paled into utter insignificance for Faraday as she battled to come to terms with what she saw. Nothing she had been taught about Artor and the Way of the Plough could compare with this. She envied with every fiber of her being the Enchanter-Talons who had stepped through this Gate. What incredible joy they must have felt as they slid over the rim of the pool and into infinity! Perhaps even now they joined the stars themselves as they danced through the universe. "Ah," she moaned, longing to join them, wondering if she would be good enough for the Gate to accept her. Her hands stretched toward the Star Gate.

Jack's arm slid about her shoulders. "No, sweet one. No, do not be tempted. It is not for you or I to step through this Gate. Only an Icarii Enchanter powerful beyond telling could ever hope to survive."

Faraday dragged her eyes away from the Star Gate and looked at Jack. His cheeks showed the trail of tears as well.

"So, it is not only the dead Enchanter-Talons who go through?"

Jack thought carefully before he replied. "No. It is said that one day the Icarii will breed an Enchanter powerful enough to journey through the Gate and manage to come back out again. I do not know what he would find there."

Or what he *did* find there, he thought. His eyes slipped momentarily to the line of twenty-six statues whose arms were uplifted in joy.

Faraday's eyes had drifted back to the Star Gate and she did not notice Jack's glance. "I do not know why he would ever want to come back out again," she whispered.

"It is good that you have seen this," Jack said quietly. "It will help you through the next years of your life. Remember it always."

"Always," Faraday echoed fiercely, and then Jack was pulling her back from the brink and handing her to Timozel who still refused to look into the Gate. "Keep her back, now, lad," Jack said, and Timozel nodded, annoyed at being called lad, but pleased that Jack had entrusted Faraday to his care.

Jack returned to the stone rim surrounding the Star Gate and spoke quietly to Yr, who still sat enraptured by the Gate. After a moment she reluctantly inclined her head and stood up, following Jack back to where Timozel and Faraday waited.

"Do each of these archways lead to a Barrow?" Timozel asked as Jack drew level with him. "There are more archways than Barrows."

"Only some of them lead to the Barrows. Others lead . . . elsewhere. The Icarii needed access to the Star Gate through doorways other than those of the Barrows of the Enchanter-Talons. And then there are others who ply their way to and from the Star Gate and use corridors still stranger than those the Icarii used. Come, make sure Faraday follows, and I will lead us out through another passage."

Jack took Yr's hand and led them toward one of the arches surrounded by sleeping winged men. As they passed under, Faraday roused, turning for one last look at the Chamber of the Star Gate.

"Why did they put wings on these men, Jack? Is it meant to symbolise their status as StarFarers?"

Jack turned around, his disbelief making him laugh a little. Did she not understand? "Symbolize? No, sweet heart, these pillars are accurate representations of the Icarii. Sweet lady, the Icarii are winged people."

24

Across the Plains of Arcness

If the climb down to the Star Gate was hard, the ascent
was a nightmare.

The stairwell that had led down from the tomb to the
Star Gate had been made of well-crafted stone, but the
stone corridor Jack took them through to escape the Star
Gate quickly degenerated into nothing more than a tunnel
carved out of the living earth, only the occasional wooden
strut looming out of the dark to relieve the uncertain lines
of the earthen walls. As they gradually came closer to the
surface, deep tree roots pierced the walls of the tunnel and
water dripped down from the roof. Caught in the fold of a
cloak or a skirt and then sucked free, the moisture provided
only bare relief from thirst. Along with the moisture, great
chunks of earth also fell periodically from the roof. To pre-
serve light Jack allowed only one lamp to glow at any
given time and Faraday clung close to Timozel as they
stumbled over the uneven floor, terrified that the tunnel
would collapse on her at any moment.

According to Jack, and how he knew neither Faraday

nor Timozel could fathom, it took them the best part of a day and a night to reach the surface. Jack explained that their ascent was taking a great deal longer because this particular tunnel led them to a spot far distant from the Barrows. It was the tunnel he had used on his previous three journeys to the Star Gate, he said, and had once been in much better repair—it had, in fact, been one of the main entrance ways to the Star Gate for the Icarii. But with the passing centuries the tunnel was slowly collapsing in on itself.

Faraday found herself spending long stretches of time thinking of her mother. Silent tears welled and flowed down her cheeks, and she brushed them aside, trying to be strong.

Timozel hardly spoke during their ascent. He stayed close by Faraday's side, lying down beside her to keep her warm whenever Jack called a rest and supporting her as they floundered through the dark tunnel, but unusually reticent whenever Faraday tried to talk to him.

Finally, when it seemed as though they could not go on, that they'd never see daylight again, they came to a solid earth wall blocking their path.

Timozel pushed past Yr to stand next to Jack, who was running his hands over the wall. "Can your magic get us past this, then?" he rasped, barely managing to get the words out through his parched throat. Timozel's dislike and distrust of Jack had grown with each step through the dark and dank tunnel.

Jack stared at him flatly. "No magic, boy, but your back and mine. This is the wall, perhaps some two paces thick, that conceals the entrance. We should be able to dig through it with just the two of us. Yr, Faraday, stand back, but be prepared to move quickly when I call."

Yr and Faraday took several paces back, as Jack began scraping at the wall with his hands but Timozel put a hand to his shoulder.

"Wait," he said. He pulled his axe from his weapon belt and started to hew into the earthen wall, standing well back and swinging his entire shoulders into the effort. Jack leaped out of the way as clods of earth flew in every direction.

"Be careful, you fool boy!" he croaked, choking on the loose dirt drifting through the air, "or you'll bring the whole tunnel down around our ears." He hefted his staff in his hand, as if he was debating with himself whether to strike Timozel or the earthen wall.

Timozel took no notice of Jack's warning and Faraday found herself praying, to whom she did not know or care, that Timozel would break through quickly. She felt as if she would die if she did not stretch her face to the sky soon.

Finally there was a rush of earth and the remaining lamp was smothered in dirt. Timozel stepped back, choking as the earth tumbled about his shoulders.

"Now!" cried Jack. The women hesitated, terrified by the sudden dark and the sounds of the earthfall before them, but both Jack and Timozel reached for their arms and hauled them through the shifting, collapsing mass of earth. For several terrifying heartbeats the four battled through the earthfall, trying as best they could to protect their heads and to prevent too much of the dirt from entering their noses and mouths.

Then, suddenly, miraculously, they were free into cold, gray daylight, stumbling through dry knee-high grass, coughing and choking as they tried to free their throats of dirt.

Faraday collapsed into the grass, retching and choking until she thought that she would vomit her entire stomach up through her mouth. Through her distress she could dimly hear the other three choking and retching as well. Eventually her heaving abated, and she rolled onto her back, wiping her streaming eyes with the backs of her hands. For long minutes Faraday lay still, staring at the clouds scudding across the late afternoon sky, drawing in as much of the clean air as she could manage.

Eventually she sat up, beginning to shiver in the frigid air. The other three were also stirring, wiping the dirt from their faces then running, shaking trembling fingers through their hair to rid it of as much earth as possible. Faraday looked back toward where they had come. There was a low hill in front of her, largely covered with small rosenberry bushes. Part of one side of it looked to have collapsed in on itself and, as she sat looking toward the hill, Faraday thought she could feel faint vibrations through the ground. Jack saw her looking at her hand as it rested on the ground. "The whole tunnel is collapsing," he rasped between dry coughs. "We got out just in time." It was the first time that Faraday had seen him even slightly rattled by events.

Timozel heaved himself to his feet and held out a hand for Faraday. "That we escaped with our lives from such a hole is enough. I care not if the entire Star Gate collapses in on itself. Faraday, are you all right?"

Faraday shook out her cloak and brushed her skirt and blouse as free from dirt as she could. Timozel was strangely calm considering the events of the last few minutes. He seemed older, more certain of himself. There was some undefinable quality about him she had not seen previously. Faraday shrugged, perhaps it was simply the dirt. No doubt they all looked vastly different to what they had several days ago before they had been exposed to storm and mud and a variety of earthfalls.

"Ah, my treasures!" Jack suddenly called happily, his voice stronger. "You have found me!"

Faraday looked up. Trotting across the plain were Jack's pigs, each and every one of them wearing a large grin of pleasure, their tiny eyes gleaming between rolls of fat. They heaved and grunted and rolled and ambled and almost bowled Jack over with exuberant affection when they reached him. The sight made everyone smile.

Yr turned to Faraday and Timozel. "Well, at least Jack's happy. But I, dear ones, could use a drink and a wash."

Jack stood up from petting his pigs. His face wore a huge amiable grin. "There's a stream not far from here, and we can drink and wash there."

"Food?" Timozel inquired, slipping his axe back into his weapon belt from where he had dropped it in the grass.

"Ah, well, food is a little further off. I have friends, good folk, some distance from here, who can provide us with food and shelter and, um," Jack's eyes slid across to Yr, "clothes. But they are some leagues distant, and we will have to walk most of the night and tomorrow morning to reach them."

"Isn't there anywhere closer?" Faraday asked despairingly. She did not think she could walk through the night. Not after the interminable hours spent tramping though the earth tunnel.

"You are going to have to get used to walking, my Lady Faraday," Yr said dryly, "unless you want to ride one of the pigs."

Jack led them to a stream some hundred paces away, and they all splashed as much of the dirt from their faces and arms as they could before lying prone along the stream's banks and slurping up great gulps of water. Jack allowed them a couple of hours to recover, but he wanted them to start moving before night fell. The wind was cold and the sky overcast. If they couldn't find adequate shelter then the best way to keep warm was to keep moving. None of them were dressed warmly enough to spend a night on the ground.

After they finished drinking, Timozel surprised Faraday by producing a short knife from his boot and asking her to cut his hair for him. It was too long, he complained, and the curls were flopping in his eyes. She did the best she could, hacking away at his thick brown hair with the knife, cutting it so that it lay flat against his scalp. After she finished Timozel took the knife from her hands and scraped away at his two-day-old growth of beard, but without hot water to assist him he left a dark shadow spreading across his cheeks. Sitting back watching him scrub at his cheeks with the knife, Faraday pondered that the Timozel sitting in the deepening dusk seemed vastly older and more self-possessed than the youth she had shared the long ride from Carlon to the ancient Barrows with.

Yr also sat, chin in hand, a thoughtful expression on her face as she regarded Timozel. The experience below had changed him in some undefinable way, she mused, but, unlike Faraday, she wondered if the change was more than just the simple maturing of a youth into a man. The Halls of the StarFarers had done stranger things before than merely make a youth grow up.

During the walk north through the night the small group were buffeted by freezing head winds which made them shiver and stumble. Jack kept them moving, striding at their head with the staff held high, his pigs trotting along at his heels. Timozel had resumed his appointed place by Faraday's side, supporting her whenever she lost her footing, and sometimes lending a hand to Yr as well. No one felt like talking; it took all their energy simply to keep placing one foot in front of the other.

The plains of western Arcness were as barren of life as the plains of Tarantaise had been. Most of these southern plains were used as grazing lands for cattle and sheep during the summer months, but as winter approached the shepherds and cattlemen drove their herds closer to the scattered villages for protection. According to Jack, only a few hardy pig herds still roamed the plains, and even they would be heading for their winter shelters soon enough.

Timozel, when he'd still had breath for conversation, had asked Jack where they were going, and how he planned on getting Faraday to Gorkenfort.

"North," Jack had replied tersely. "We head north in as direct a line as possible. If we can reach Tailem Bend on the River Nordra we may be able to hire horses at Jervois Landing for the last part of the journey through Ichtar. The route to Gorkenfort is well-marked and Duke Borneheld has, over the past few years, established plentiful supply stations along the way. With luck there should be few problems."

Timozel asked why Jack and Yr didn't simply take Faraday to one of the major towns or forts, perhaps Kastaleon, or even back to Carlon, where they could hire the type of transport her rank entitled her to. Jack looked at him as though he were a muddle-headed youth. "Because no one would understand her desperate desire to reach Borneheld," he snapped. "They'd do their utmost to prevent her going any further north than the safety of Carlon."

Timozel nodded quietly to himself. It was the answer he'd expected. He was not at all comfortable with this lonely journey north, and not at all comfortable with the companions that he and Faraday had landed. But if nothing else, Timozel understood Faraday's wish to be with Borneheld. Every Lady needed her Lord beside her and fretted the days while they were apart.

They had worked out a cover story should anyone meet them by chance in this lonely spot. The Lady Faraday, her maid Yr, and her escort had been heading across the plains of Arcness toward Arcen when they had been hit by the dreadful storm of several days previously. Timozel was the only one of her escort to escape the ice spears. All their horses had been killed. Lost in the featureless rolling plains, they had been spotted by Jack, driving his pigs north to shelter for the winter in the hills of the Bracken Range. Genial good-hearted fellow that he was, Jack was leading them toward closest civilization, the towns of Rhaetia to the northwest. It was a slender story, but it would have to do.

Jack let them rest again just as dawn was breaking to the east. Faraday had spent the last half a league leaning heavily on Timozel for support, while Yr had started to stumble badly every forty or fifty paces, grazing the skin from her hands and knees as she tumbled to the ground time after time. They huddled together in a tight group in the lee of a small rise, pigs gathered about, trying to keep as warm as they could in the freezing wind. Faraday clenched her chattering teeth. She would have to make the journey worthwhile; Axis' life depended on her keeping Borneheld's jealous temper under control. She wondered where Axis might be now, but was too exhausted to pursue the thought. Her head dropped on Timozel's shoulder and she lapsed into unconsciousness.

No sooner had she closed her eyes than Jack was calling for them to wake up and start walking again. Her aching body protesting, Faraday struggled to her feet. Timozel wrapped his arm about her waist, she was not sure whether to support her or to keep himself upright. Yr, head and shoulders slumped, could barely keep step behind them as they started to walk again. Once or twice Faraday heard a muffled thump behind her, but when she turned her head Yr was struggling to her feet again, a determined look on her smooth face. Jack was the freshest of them all, used to tramping these plains in all kinds of weather, though even he stumbled occasionally.

It was close to mid-morning when Jack finally waved them to a halt. Timozel and Faraday were in such a catatonic state, their bodies and minds attuned only to putting one foot before the other, that they almost crashed into Jack. Yr likewise stumbled into their backs, and Timozel reached around and put his arm about her to keep her from falling.

"There," Jack said, his voice showing signs of terrible strain, his hand too tired to do more than wave vaguely before them. "There. Goodman and Goodwife Renkin's farm."

Faraday peered ahead. About five hundred paces away lay a small farmlet nestled in a small dip in the plains. Tidy fields and gardens surrounded a long, low stone house, its thatched roof in good repair. A small amount of smoke came from the chimney, only to be whipped away in the gusting wind. She gritted her teeth and started walking. She hoped they had both fire and beds.

Goodman and Goodwife Renkin had both and more to offer. Startled from their comfortable spot by the fire, they hastened to the door to find their friend Jack Simple standing there with an exhausted noblewoman, her maid and, by Artor, an Axe-Wielder as escort! Apart from Jack's muddled explanation about finding the trio wandering the plains after the dreadful storm days before, all were clearly too exhausted to talk, so Goodwife Renkin hastened the two women to the big bed built against the far wall, while the Axe-Wielder and Jack slumped down on the wide wooden benches that ran along the wall by the fire, asleep almost before the Goodwife could throw blankets over them. For a moment the Goodman and his Goodwife simply looked at each other in amazement, then the Goodwife shrugged prosaically and walked over to the larder. She would have to bake some more bread if they were to have so many guests at once.

Faraday had never dreamed so wonderfully before. She was so happy, so free from pain and care. She sat in an exquisite grove, surrounded by trees that stretched into infinity above her and yet, when she raised her head to look, beyond them spun a myriad of stars almost as breathtaking as those of the Star Gate. She looked down. She was sitting cross-legged on sweet, cool grass in the center of the grove, wearing nothing but a soft linen shift, and at her breast suckled a newborn baby. Faraday's lips curved in a smile and she gently stroked the soft down covering the babe's round head. Tiny fingers, perfectly formed, kneaded at her breast. Faraday felt infinitely fortunate to be here in this place and with this babe, and she cuddled the baby as close as she dared, crooning to it as it continued to suck. A shadow fell across her lap and Faraday looked up, startled. She frowned a little at the intrusion, then smiled, for this strange beast with the body of a man and the head of a white stag was her friend. "You must leave here," he said. Faraday's frown returned. "No," she said. "I do not wish to. I am free of pain and betrayal here. I can trust you— only you." "You will come back one day," the man-beast said gently, his liquid-brown eyes loving, "and then, if you wish, you can stay." "No!" Faraday cried as she saw the grove start to fade around her. "No! I do not want to go!"

Timozel also dreamed, but his dream was far more unsettling. He was walking down a long ice tunnel, naked save for the gray trousers of his Axe-Wielder's uniform. Where he was Timozel did not know, but he knew that he was walking toward certain doom. Death lay at the end of the ice tunnel. There were strange-shaped creatures leaping and cavorting on the other side of the ice walls, their forms distorted by the ice, but Timozel could not see them very clearly, nor did he want to. He wanted to turn and run, but his feet would not obey him. A force greater than his own will had enslaved him and was drawing him down the tunnel. Closer and closer Timozel walked to the death that waited for him until finally he could see a massive wooden door set into the ice wall at the end of the tunnel. His teeth began to chatter in fear and he felt his bowels loosen. He halted before the door, and his hand, unaided, unasked for, rose of its own volition and rapped sharply upon the wood. "Come!" a dreadful voice boomed from the other side, and Timozel's treacherous hand slid down toward the door latch. He fought it with every muscle in his body, until he could feel himself sweating and trembling with the effort. Although he managed to slow his hand he could not stop it completely, and slowly his fingers closed about the metal latch. "Come!" the dreadful voice, impatient now, called again, and Timozel heard heavy steps approach from the other side of the door. He gibbered in fear as the handle began to twist open in his hand. "No!" he screamed, then everything started to fade about him as he slipped into blessed unconsciousness.

25

The Goodpeople Renkin

$\mathcal{F}$araday woke slowly, revelling in the warmth of the bed and the remaining comforting vestiges of her dream. She dozed a while, unwilling to open her eyes, feeling Yr still deep in sleep beside her, listening to the Goodpeople Renkin and their children move softly around the house. Finally the delicious smell of fresh baked bread roused her completely and she stirred and opened her eyes. Yr murmured sleepily in protest as Faraday sat up, hugging the warm comforter to her breasts as she looked about the room.

The Goodman and his Goodwife lived in a typical one-roomed farmhouse. At one end blazed a huge fire fed by the dried peat that country people dug from the marshes during the summer. A large cauldron hung suspended over the flames, and kettles and pots simmered on a grate before it. Two toddlers, twin boys, played cheerfully a safe distance from the flames and hot pots, while the Goodman dozed against the warm stones of the fireplace. The plump

Goodwife bustled between the pots and a solid table, scarred by the knives of countless generations.

The rest of the home was virtually bare of furniture, save for the bed itself, a number of benches, a large storage cupboard and two large iron chests. Shelves along the walls held the family's possessions. Wood, being rare and difficult to procure in Achar, was a precious item and these folk had undoubtedly had to save for many years to buy an item of furniture made from the small number of plantation trees grown in Achar. Cheeses, hams and ropes of dried onions hung from the exposed rafters of the thatch roof, well out of the way of dogs and children. On the wall a few paces from the fire a tightly swaddled baby hung suspended from a nail, lulled to sleep by the constricting linen wraps around its chest.

The Goodwife noticed Faraday awake and, smiling and nodding, ladled out a mug of broth from one of the pots.

"My Lady," she beamed as she brought it over, "you and your companions have slept away most of the day." She spoke with the soft country burr of southern Achar, more musical and easier on the ear than the harsher accents of Skarabost.

Faraday accepted the mug gratefully, wrapping her hands around it and taking a small sip. Jack and Timozel still lay asleep on the benches by the fire, Timozel tossing a little as if his sleep were disturbed.

"My Lady, you were very lucky to find our Jack," the Goodwife said as she noticed Faraday's eyes turn to the two men. "In this bad weather you would have perished had you found no shelter."

Faraday turned her gaze back to the Goodwife. She was in her early thirties, plump but clearly careworn by her hard life in this isolated farmstead. Stringy brown hair was pulled back into a functional knot at the nape of her neck. She wore the brown worsted dress preferred by most country folk, its sleeves rolled above her rough elbows, and covered with a rough, black-weave apron. Her reddened and chapped hands twisted together above her protruding stomach.

Faraday realized she had been staring and quickly smiled, trying to cover her bad manners. "We are all very grateful for your help, Goodwife Renkin," she said, reaching out and touching the woman's hand briefly. "For the past few days we have had very little to drink and no food at all. As you can see, our clothes were quite inadequate for the bitter winds and frosty nights. My, er, maid and myself were close to death until Jack led us to your door. Timozel, my escort, could barely support us himself because of his own exhaustion. Goodwife, I do not know how we can adequately repay you for the kindness you have shown us."

"Oh," the Goodwife beamed, " 'tis nothing more than any Artor-fearing soul would do." She paused, then found the courage to say what she wanted. "Oh, my Lady, you are so beautiful!" Faraday's brief touch had emboldened the country woman and she reached out an admiring hand and smoothed back Faraday's chestnut hair from her forehead. The Goodwife had never seen a noblewoman this close and she marveled at the softness and whiteness of Faraday's skin. Among those of her rank women had weather-lined faces by the time they were twenty, courtesy of the long months spent either in the field or helping their menfolk herd the livestock to pasture.

Faraday finished the broth and grimaced a little. "Goodwife, we are all so dirty. May I stretch my good fortune further and ask if perhaps we might have a wash? And if you have some clean clothes while we brush out our dirty ones . . . my maid has no clothes at all. She," Faraday improvised quickly, "was caught by the storm as she was washing in a stream and her own clothes were blown away. If you could spare her one of your work dresses I will repay you well for your trouble." Faraday wore a thin gold chain strung with five pearls about her neck that would more than adequately repay the Goodpeople Renkin for any food or clothes they might give them.

The Goodwife was so thrilled to have such a noble and

gracious guest that if Faraday had asked for all their possessions the Goodwife would have been hard put to refuse her. Faraday shook Yr out of her slumber and the Goodwife led them, Yr complaining under her breath about having been woken so abruptly, to a small shed behind the house where there were barrels of rainwater. The Goodwife gave them towels and blankets, a bar of rough yellow soap, two of her work dresses and short woollen capes as well as boots for Yr, and left them to scrub themselves as clean as they could with buckets of cold water. Faraday and Yr washed quickly but thoroughly, shivering in the cold, then scrambled into the rough woollen dresses, their skin red from the scrubbing they had given themselves and tinged blue in places from the cold. The dresses hung loosely on both women, and Faraday's ankles stuck out below the hem of the dress of the much shorter woman. Both smiled wryly at the sight of themselves, bunching the worsted material and cinching it tight to their waists with woollen ties, but the dresses were warm and Yr and Faraday decided to stay and wash their hair, taking it in turns to scrub and massage the scalp of the other.

When they reentered the farmhouse the Goodwife had woken Jack and Timozel who sat bleary-eyed before the fire, sipping mugs of warm broth. Faraday noticed that Jack had resumed his vacant, simple expression, and she marveled at how easily he did it. Who could not trust a man with such a transparent face, whose nature appeared so slow and witless as to be incapable of any deviousness, of plotting any harm? Poor Jack, good-natured Jack, doomed by his mental fog to spend the rest of his life herding pigs across the plains of Arcness. Hah!

Timozel had pulled his bench before the fire and was staring into the flames as he sipped his broth, his blue eyes dark. He had propped his axe and sword by the door as a gesture of goodwill toward the Renkin family, but Faraday noticed his short knife was still thrust into his boot within easy reach. Timozel's white woollen shirt and gray leather jerkin and trousers were dusty and stained with dirt, and his face was streaked where he had tried to wash at the stream the previous night. He acknowledged Faraday's presence with a small nod, but his eyes remained grave and his face unsmiling.

"Timozel," Faraday said quietly, "the Goodwife has left soap and towels by the water barrels in the shed behind the house. Draw yourself some water and wash. You will feel so much better."

Timozel drained his mug with a long draft and nodded again. He stood and handed the mug to the Goodwife who was hovering around her guests. Not only was her home being graced with the noble presence of such a fine Lady, but a handsome and awesome Axe-Wielder as well. What a tale she would have for her good friends when she went visiting! She beamed at Timozel and thrust one of her husband's clean and mended shirts at him.

Timozel treated the woman to a courtly bow. "Madam Goodwife, your hospitality overreaches any I have experienced before. I am humbled."

The Goodwife blushed with pleasure to the roots of her hair and sketched a small curtsey, although with her big boots and belly it was hardly the most elegant of gestures. She turned back to Faraday as Timozel left the house. "M'Lady," she said a trifle breathlessly, "you are so lucky to have such a courtly warrior to protect you!"

Faraday inclined her head gracefully, agreeing completely, then shook her long wet hair out before the fire to dry it.

Yr slipped noiselessly into the shed and stood quietly for several moments, arms folded, watching as Timozel, his back to her, sluiced water over his head and neck, and scrubbed away at the accumulated dirt and sweat. He was still perhaps too thin, but time and maturity would flesh out his rangy frame, and even now his body was handsomely muscled. Yr's eyes glowed brightly with desire as they

traced a slow path down Timozel's naked body, noting the
way his pale skin contrasted so wonderfully with the
patches of his darker body hair. She had been attracted to
him from the moment she saw him; that he had pledged
himself to Faraday as her Champion had made him completely irresistible. It was time for this youthful Axe-
Wielder to learn some new skills.

Yr scraped her foot across the earthen floor and Timozel
looked over his shoulder at the noise, expecting to see Jack
or the Goodman, or perhaps even the Goodwife herself. He
raised an eyebrow at Yr and turned around slowly, a washer
and the sudsy soap in his hands.

Yr narrowed her eyes at him, momentarily caught off
balance. This was not the reaction she had expected from
the man. He was yet young, and should have been discomforted by her frank observation of his nakedness. The trip
through the Chamber of the Star Gate *had* changed him, Yr
decided. She stepped forward and took the washer and
soap gently from his hands, tossing them back into the
bucket of water behind him, then bent her mouth to his
chest, running her tongue slowly over his skin, savoring the
mingled tastes of sweat and soap. Her hands trickled
lightly, teasingly, down his wet body, feeling his desire begin to grow against the touch of her body.

Yr laughed softly, pleased.

Suddenly Timozel seized her and roughly thrust her
back against the crude stone wall of the shed. His body
pressed hers tightly against the stone while his hands
groped with her skirts, bunching them about her hips.

"Is this what you were after, Yr? Have I understood you
correctly?" he said hoarsely, and proceeded to give her precisely what she had wanted from him ever since she had
paraded her nakedness before his eyes in the tomb of the
Icarii Enchanter-Talon. After a few long grasping, gasping,
frantic minutes it was done, and Timozel let Yr go as suddenly as he had seized her, turning back to complete his
wash. Yr, for once lost for words, still burning with his

touch, sank slowly to the floor and wondered if she had finally met her equal in matters of the flesh. The youth had
the vigor of a man.

Faraday looked up as they reentered the house, and
frowned. Something was different about them. Timozel
looked more relaxed, walking into the dimly lit house with
a slight swagger. He sat down, the Goodman's long heavy
shirt hanging loosely over his leather trousers, now with
most of the dirt brushed from them. Yr, her normal exuber-
ance a little more repressed than usual, sat down behind
her and, playing the part of lady's maid to perfection, began to comb out and then plait Faraday's thick hair into a
crown around her head. Jack had only needed one look at
the pair to know precisely what had happened. The only
uncertainty in his mind was which one of them looked the
more satisfied.

Because Jack was trapped in his role as idiot pig herder,
Faraday and Timozel took the lead in asking the Goodpeople if they could purchase some clothes, food and blankets
for their journey north to one of the towns of Rhaetia. Faraday unfastened the gold and pearl necklet and handed it to
the dumbstruck Goodman, anxiously inquiring if it would
be enough to repay them for the food and clothes.

The Goodman and his wife, the woman so stunned by
the offer of the necklet that she put the baby she was feeding down to sleep but forgot to tuck her breast decently out
of sight, gaped at the generous Lady. For the necklet, they
stammered, she could have a dozen blankets, food for a
week, and their trusty mule and his packs to carry it all for
them. They were abjectly apologetic that they had no gentle palfrey for the Lady, nor a high-stepping charger for the
courageous warrior, but the mule was sound, had a sweet
disposition and would carry their packs patiently, and perhaps the Lady herself. The Goodman and Goodwife
paused to gaze in wonder at each other. Not only would the
necklet pay for all the goods and the mule they would give

the Lady and her companions, but there would be enough left over to buy a team of oxen and some new furniture. The bargain was made, and everyone shook hands with great goodwill and genuine relief on the part of Faraday and Timozel. If they had to journey north through the deepening autumn, then at least they would have the means to survive.

Having eaten again (the Goodwife insisted they eat to seal the bargain, and no one truly objected), Timozel took charge and insisted they bed down early. They still needed to recoup some of the strength they had lost over the past several days, and he wanted them to get an early start in the morning. Faraday and Yr once again snuggled down into the Goodpeople's marital bed, Jack and Timozel wrapped themselves in blankets before the fire, and the Goodpeople Renkin themselves sat up for hours, quietly resolving exactly how they were going to spend the money the necklet would earn them.

26

"Belle My Wife!"

From the Ancient Barrows Axis led his Axe-Wielders hard and fast toward Arcen. There the Axe-Wielders reprovisioned and Axis explained to Earl Burdel's family, waiting for the Ladies Merlion and Faraday, what had happened to them. It was not an easy task, and Axis had left the Burdel townhouse feeling embarrassed and inadequate. He kept the Axe-Wielders in Arcen a day and two nights, during which he composed detailed reports of the incident at the Ancient Barrows to Jayme, Earl Isend and Borneheld to supplement the hurried messages he had sent from the Barrows. Axis, still grieving, dreaded explaining to Borneheld in person.

It was a relief to finally leave the city and ride north toward the narrow passes in the Bracken Ranges. From there it would be a straight run northeast to Smyrton. The first night out of Arcen, Axis halted his command a league south of the first of the passes. They had covered good ground that day and he did not want to negotiate the passes during the night hours.

Since leaving the Ancient Barrows Axis had taken no risks. He insisted that the Axe-Wielders ride lightly armored with mailshirts under their cloaks to give them the best chance against further ice-spears. At night, in camp, men slept fully clothed, weapons to hand, double sentries posted in case Gorgrael struck again. Ogden and Veremund might hope that Gorgrael had exhausted himself with his effort at the Ancient Barrows, but Axis wasn't prepared to risk it.

Axis felt in a reasonable mood as he sat before the campfire that night, his cohort commanders and Belial laughing and joking about some tavern brawl they had witnessed in Arcen, Ogden and Veremund sitting quietly to one side. Axis had virtually ignored the two old men since they had left the Barrows; everything had gone wrong since he had read the Prophecy. And though they had argued they would be useful to answer questions Axis might have, both gave such indistinct answers or such disturbing ones that Axis sometimes found himself wondering whether or not he should leave them behind.

However, over the past week the Brothers had proved surprisingly pleasant company about the campfire at night. They had respected Axis' wish to be left alone, and had proved to have such a repertoire of bawdy ballads that even Axis sometimes forgot his cares and dissolved into embarrassed laughter at their contributions to the campfire ballads.

But they were far more than they appeared. Axis leaned back into the shadows and narrowed his eyes as he stared at them. Perhaps what they said to him about not knowing the identity of his father was the truth, but Axis also had the distinct feeling that they did not tell him all they knew—and how had Ogden known the basic melody of that ward? Axis remembered how they had faltered over the Service for the Dead at the mass burial site at the Barrows. Was thirty-nine years long enough to completely forget the words (and yet still remember ancient enchantments)? It had been embarrassing and disrespectful toward the dead and Axis had fought hard to restrain his anger at them.

As the Axe-Wielders moved through Arcness and into Arcen itself, Ogden and Veremund avoided contact with any of the local Plough-Keepers, as the brothers who lived among and ministered to the people were known. Many among the Axe-Wielders had noted and commented on their peculiar behavior. Some of this could simply be the result of spending so long isolated in the Silent Woman Keep, perhaps combined with the onset of old-age senility, but Axis wasn't sure and he knew that Arne watched them closely as well.

But tonight everyone seemed in a relaxed mood. Belial had produced a harp and was laughingly trying to play the tune of a ballad he had heard in Arcen. Axis smiled. He liked Belial very much and respected him as a fighting man, but his attempts at the harp were appalling.

"My friend," Axis leaned back into the light and held out his hand. "That harp needs tuning. Let me see."

Belial grinned and handed the harp over. Axis' diplomatic remark had not fooled Belial who had deliberately mishandled the strings to prompt Axis into asking for the instrument. Axis had been too quiet since losing so many men at the Barrows, and Belial tried whenever he could to lift the man out of his dark moods.

Axis sat back with the harp, making a pretense of tightening the strings, then he looked around the campfire. "And what shall we sing tonight, my friends?" he asked softly.

"Belle my Wife!" one of his commanders called and the others laughed and clapped. It was a favorite ballad among the Acharites, yet one only a skilled musician could do justice.

Axis smiled with his men and strummed the opening chords.

This winter's weather, it waxeth cold
and frost it freezeth on every hill,
And Artor blows his blasts so bold
that all our cattle are like to spill.

Belle my Wife, she loves no strife
she said unto me quietly,

Rise up and save Cow Crumbocke's life!
man! put thy cloak about thee!

His voice was clear and strong, and the others let him sing the first four verses before they joined in. Soon the night rang with good-humored voices and when the ballad was finally sung to a close, after the fifth repetition of the final chorus, Axis joined his men in laughter and loud applause.

He played several more ballads, then, as the mood shifted, strummed soft tunes on the harp as his commanders talked about the ride north and about the danger they would shortly face. What *were* these creatures that had attacked Gorkenfort? Where did they come from? Who drove them?

"BattleAxe?" asked Baldwin, one of Axis' commanders. "What do you think about this Prophecy? Are the creatures that attack Gorkenfort the Ghostmen the Prophecy speaks of? Before we left Carlon we thought it was the Forbidden who were responsible. But now . . ." His voice drifted off.

There was silence as everyone waited for their BattleAxe to answer. Ogden and Veremund watched him carefully.

"Do *you* think that Gorgrael's Ghostmen attack Gorkenfort, Baldwin?" said Axis, turning the question back.

Baldwin hesitated. The Prophecy Timozel and Arne had brought out of the Silent Woman Woods had spread like wildfire through the ranks of the Axe-Wielders. Once heard, it was impossible to forget.

"I cannot get the Prophecy out of my mind," Baldwin admitted, and to one side Ogden nodded. It was enchanted. Once heard, few would be able to forget it—except the third verse, of course. Only one man could remember that. He restrained a smile as he thought of the enchantments that the Prophet had woven into his Prophecy. No doubt the Seneschal would find over the next few months that many Acharites were not so deeply committed to Artor as they thought.

"It seems to make sense," Baldwin continued softly, "that if Gorgrael is responsible for the attacks in the north, then perhaps he was also responsible for the storm that hit the Ancient Barrows."

Axis frowned and opened his mouth to speak, but another commander, Methuen, broke in.

"If it is Gorgrael in the north, then we need to find this StarMan to save us."

Axis, angry now, opened his mouth again, but was again forestalled.

"Axis," Belial asked gently. "What is that you play?"

Stunned by the question and by the circle of eyes gazing at him, Axis closed his mouth. What *was* it he played? Axis hadn't been paying any attention to what he actually strummed on the harp. Now he realized that he was playing a haunting melody he had never heard before. But it was more than that, for the style of music, its phrasing and beat, were completely alien to his ears.

"A silly tune, Belial, nothing more." He dropped the harp at his feet and hurriedly rose. "I have to check the sentries," he said, tersely, "to make sure they have the perimeter adequately covered."

Then he was gone.

Arne rose to follow him but Belial grabbed his arm. "No. Wait. Give him some time alone."

Axis inspected the sentries, then wandered a little distance from the camp, needing time to sort out his thoughts. What was happening to him?

The only good thing which could be said for his experiences since the Ancient Barrows was that his nightmares had finally completely disappeared. But if the lies of his nightmares no longer troubled Axis, thinking on the continuing enigma of his father made him deeply uncomfortable. What sort of man was this that could teach a growing fetus how to sing an enchanted ward to protect himself against evil later in life? Enchantments of any sort were evil, the Seneschal had taught him that. Even the herbal remedies that many country women used were frowned upon by the Brotherhood of the Seneschal, especially if the women used words or songs to aid the herbs in their healing powers, and Axis himself had been involved in several cases where he had to bring these women to the Tower of the Seneschal for trial and justice. Axis shuddered at the memory of what happened to those women who had been found guilty; death by the purification of fire had always been the sentence imposed by the Seneschal. Never would he forget the screams of the simple country women as the flames engulfed them; at least it had not been his role to light the fire.

And now he, the BattleAxe, was experiencing disturbing, long-buried memories out of that deep, dark place that the reading of the Prophecy had unlocked. Not only memories, but talents. The ward against evil that he had sung to the apparition of Gorgrael had been the most powerful thus far, but the strange alien melody he had played for his men this evening had been another example.

Where had his talent for the harp and the music come from in the first place? Axis could never remember actually learning the harp. He had simply always played. Even as a small child he had been more skillful than the court bards. If the Seneschal learned of these strange tunes and words that bubbled out of long-hidden memories, Axis himself might face the purifying flames, or, at the very least, be subjected to rigorous inquisition. For the first time in his life he was glad for the distance separating him and the Tower of the Seneschal.

He wandered slowly through the pitch-black night, listening to the soft sounds of the camp settling down for the night. Despite his best efforts, Axis' thoughts turned to Faraday and Timozel. Two such young and innocent people, both with such promise and zest for life. One the son of his closest female friend, the other a beautiful woman who had earned his respect and admiration. Axis had never been in love before, although he had never been slow to charm women into his bed, and had sometimes wondered if he was too cynical and bitter to ever open himself to the risks of love. But that night in the shadows of the Barrows, with the bones of the Icarii kings moldering beneath his feet and Faraday weeping in his arms, Axis had realized that perhaps, just perhaps, her freshness, innocence and above all, honesty, might be enough to break through the barriers he had spent years building around his heart.

Axis bent down and pulled a strand of grass from the ground, absently chewing it as he thought. What had he meant when he'd told Faraday to think about risking spending her life with someone she could learn to love? Had he meant himself? Yes, Axis admitted. Yes he had! He laughed bitterly. Had he really been so brazen as to suggest to the daughter of an Earl that she would forget a life of ease at court, possibly a life as Queen, for his bed? Borneheld's taunt in the palace courtyard had stung deep. Axis could never hope to win the hand of a noble heiress like Faraday. Was that why he had kissed her? Was he attracted to her only because it would be a triumph to win her away from Borneheld?

Axis wasn't sure. But he did know that he had never met another woman like her. Perhaps he had kissed her simply because she was Faraday and because she was close and warm and because he thought he might be falling in love with her.

Axis mouth twisted. Now she lay moldering with the Icarii kings along with her mother and over three hundred of his Axe-Wielders. In any event, what was love if it made him so careless that he condemned so many to death while he was lost in dreams of his would-be lover? Despite the reassurances of Ogden and Veremund, Axis still burned with guilt at leading the Axe-Wielders out of the Barrows that day.

"You must not blame yourself, Axis."

Axis spun around. Strolling out of the dark, Belial smiled and saluted casually, although the use of Axis' name implied he came as a friend, not as Axis' lieutenant. In front of their men Axis and Belial were always BattleAxe and Lieutenant; in private they were friends and companions.

Axis tried to be annoyed and angry at the interruption, but failed on both counts. "I *was* responsible," Axis said, turning away to look at the clouds. "There is no one else to blame."

Belial stood by him, watching the clouds as well, offering the simple comfort of his presence. There was nothing else to say about what had happened at the Barrows. It was the worst—in fact, the first—serious military defeat Axis had ever suffered and Belial knew that it would take time for Axis to come to terms with himself. Especially since the loss involved the Lady Faraday. Belial had not failed to notice his commander's attraction to the woman.

He turned his mind back to the storm. How could one call an altercation with a roiling storm a "military" defeat? Because Belial, like so many of the Axe-Wielders, had made the connection between the unnatural ice spears of the storm and the Gorgrael of the Prophecy. What else from the Prophecy would rise up and bark at their heels before this adventure was ended?

"Belial?"

Belial snapped out of his reverie and realized that Axis had called his name two or three times.

"Your introspection is catching, Axis," he laughed. "What is it?"

"Belial, what did I play there tonight?"

Belial gazed steadily at his friend, then clapped Axis on the shoulder and grinned. "Who knows, Axis? To play something that beautiful you must have the soul of a bard, and all know that only bards and pregnant women need never explain their actions."

To his relief Axis laughed and relaxed under his hand. "And you have the soul of a diplomat, Belial. What are you doing wandering about with the Axe-Wielders?"

"I'd look ridiculous in satins and ribbons, Axis, and I can't make a courtly bow to save my life. Now, to more mundane matters. I came out here with a purpose. The fifth cohort has a problem with its . . ."

"Belial!" Axis whispered, appalled, and Belial stopped short at the horror in Axis' voice.

Rolling down from the north, perhaps half a league away, were great churning clouds hanging to the ground, shot through with silver and blue lightning.

Gorgrael! Axis thought, furious with the Destroyer and with Ogden and Veremund for claiming Gorgrael would be too weak to strike soon. With his anger came fear. How could he save his men in these open spaces?

As one both men raced for the camp.

As they reached the first of the lines Axis grabbed Belial's arm. "Get word to the commanders," he shouted. "Tell the men to dig themselves as far into the ground as they can before the storm hits. It's our only hope!"

As Belial ran off, Axis looked back to the clouds, expecting to see the ghastly head of Gorgrael. But although they boiled with unnatural malevolence, they took no other form, and Axis turned back into camp.

Everywhere men were digging frantically with whatever came to hand—spades, swords, even pots and pans. Axis made himself walk slowly through the lines of men, stopping every now and then. Fear showed on every face.

The storm clouds were closer now, perhaps only a few minutes away. They were massive, dragging along the ground even as they boiled and tumbled among themselves, glowing and crackling in the night air with flashes of silver and blue lightning. It was one of the most frightening—and weird—sights Axis had ever seen.

"There's no wind, BattleAxe," Ogden shouted, grabbing at his arm. "Listen to me, Axis, Gorgrael can't—"

Axis threw his arm off, furious at the sight of the old man. "You told me that Gorgrael was too weak to strike again this far south. You were wrong then. Why should I listen to you now?"

"He *is* weak, Axis!" Veremund said, rushing up behind Ogden. "*Look* at those clouds. Do you sense the same power in those that infused the last storm?

"There is no wind, no fury, Axis. Gorgrael has weakened himself," Veremund continued more quietly.

"Then what is that I see approaching, gentlemen?" Axis snarled.

"It is a storm of fear," Ogden said very, very quietly. "The Destroyer knows he can cause as much damage with fear as he can with ice spears."

Axis knew he was right. Panic was as deadly to an army as were spears . . . of any description. Without another word he turned on his heel and strode further into the camp.

Veremund laid his hand on Ogden's shoulder. "We can make ourselves useful amongst the horses. If they panic when that cloud hits they will kill more effectively than any ice spears that Gorgrael can send our way."

Most men managed to dig themselves a small pit in the ground, dragging armor and cloaks over themselves, wriggling as close as they could into the earth.

When Belial indicated a small depression he had prepared for them Axis shook his head. "Hand me my cloak, Belial. I want nothing else. I will meet Gorgrael's fear on my feet."

He pushed Belial down, dragging a canvas ground sheet over him, then wrapped himself in his cloak and turned to face the clouds.

Already they had enveloped the outer edges of the Axe-Wielder lines and Axis could see the hunched forms of his men disappear as the clouds rolled forward.

Behind him Axis heard a horse neigh in terror, then a gentle whisper sounded and the horse snorted once and was quiet.

But he had eyes only for the clouds.

He wondered if death was like this. The clouds consumed everything before them. One moment a line of hunched shapes was clearly visible, the next it was simply gone as if it had never existed.

Suddenly Axis' face was lit with an eerie blue and silver light, the reflection of the glow of the clouds, and in the next instant they had consumed him as well.

A cloud of fear, Ogden had said, and the moment they rolled over his head Axis knew why.

It was as though he stood alone in all existence. The enveloping cloud, clinging to every curve of his body and seeping up his nostrils, cut him off from every other living creature. Even the stars and the earth were gone. Although Axis knew Belial lay in a depression at his very feet, *knew* he was there, yet he was not. Belial was gone and Axis was alone. There was nothing but this cloud, running its hungry, icy fingers over the exposed skin of his face, sending slivers of fear sliding into the darkest niches of his body.

The interior of the cloud was brighter than the hottest day. The silver and blue bolts of lightning somewhere deep in the cloud's interior reflected off every particle of water in its misty substance so that Axis had to squint to keep the light from hurting his eyes.

He began to tremble. There was *nothing* here in this cloud but himself. He was alone, isolated in existence.

Wrong. The whispers began again.

"Axis, Axis . . . pretty, pretty . . . tasty, tasty . . ."

Axis bit his tongue to stop himself from screaming. They were like yet unlike the whispery voices from his nightmares. The whispers of his nightmare had hot teeth which stripped his skin and flesh achingly slowly so that he died the most painful death possible. These whispers were simply hungry . . . and Axis could hear them seeking through the mist.

"Pretty, pretty."

"Tasty, tasty."

"Axis, Axis."

And then, horribly, from somewhere off to his right, Axis heard the click of claws. Click, click. Click, click. Click, click. As if some ghostly creature was scraping through the mist toward him.

He tried to tell himself that there was nothing there. Just voices. Just fear.

Click, click.

And, far away, the sweep of great wings through the air. And again.

"Axis, Axis."

Click, click. Click, click.

And the sweep of wings.

He felt a movement at his feet and thought it was a creature come to devour him. He jumped back, feeling his heart seize so violently he thought it would kill him.

"No," a soft voice moaned.

Belial! Axis took a deep breath. He was *not* alone! Not only Belial, but over three thousand of his men were out there.

How could he have forgotten that?

Again Axis breathed deep, clinging to the thought that he was not alone. Gradually he regained some measure of composure. Fear. That was all that Gorgrael could throw at him. Fear. Whispers in the cloud. Fear.

But Ogden was right. Fear could kill. If you allowed it to run away with your reason it would eventually persuade you to relinquish your hold on life.

And no doubt every one of the Axe-Wielders out there in their own private nightmares were as consumed with fear as he had just been.

Axis laughed, hard as it was, and reached down with his hand. He fumbled about then hauled the canvas off Belial. The rough feel of the material in his hand gave him added heart and even when a set of teeth snapped so close to his ear that he could feel their passing, Axis did not let it distract him.

"Belial? Belial, my friend!" Axis forced a hearty tone into his voice. "Why do you cower on your belly when you still have myriad adventures to face on your feet? Arise, my friend, and give me some company in this cursed mist."

"Axis?"

Axis flinched at the fear evident in Belial's voice. If Belial had succumbed this badly, then how were the rest of his men faring isolated in the mist?

Axis grasped Belial's hand. "Come, Belial, we still have a night of revelry ahead of us." He hauled Belial to his feet, appalled at the sickly blue hue over the man's face.

"Revelry," he repeated slowly, then suddenly he knew what he had to do. "Belial? Come, wake from your fugue." He snapped his fingers.

"Axis? What do you plan? A dance?" His voice was as forced as Axis' had been moments earlier, but at least he was making an effort.

"A dance, Belial? If I plan a dance then we need partners. Come," he gave Belial a shove that propelled him into the mist. "Wake those about us and we will have a night of revelry such as Gorgrael has never seen."

Pray keep your heart, my friend, Axis thought as Belial stumbled into the mist. Pray keep your heart.

Axis sat down, reached into the pack he could feel at his side, "Ah, here you are. Well, Gorgrael, do you know this little ditty, perhaps?"

He struck a chord on the harp, then began to sing merrily, his voice clear and sweet, cutting through both mist and whispers.

Belle my Wife, she loves no strife
she said unto me quietly,
Rise up and save Cow Crumbocke's life!
man! put thy cloak about thee!

Standing among horses, Veremund and Ogden stared at each other wide-eyed. They had been affected by the mist, but not as badly as the Axemen.

"I thought he would have sung—" Ogden began, but Veremund cut him off.

"No. No, this is perfect. Anything else would have been alien to his men's ears. This they know. This they can cling to."

"This," Ogden laughed, understanding, "they can sing along with."

> Cow Crumbocke is a very good cow
> she has always been good to the pail,
> She has helped us to butter and cheese, I trow
> and in other things she will not fail.

One by one men turned over in their pits. Many, like Axis, had been at the edge of madness. Some had teetered over.

Each of them had been alone with their fears and the dreadful whispers and scrapings of claws and beatings of wings. The mist, ghastly silver and blue and as dank and cold as a five-day corpse, had crept beneath armor and cloaks and had edged between tightly closed eyelids.

> For I would be loath to see her pine, so therefore, good
>   husband, hear me now
> Forsake the court and follow the Plough, man! take
>   thine old cloak about thee!

Men grabbed onto Axis' voice as they would a hand reached out to save them from a raging sea. "Belle my wife . . . she loves no strife . . ." then they heard another voice, and another, and yet another. Then *they* realized that they were not alone. There were *others* out there.

It was the ballad that linked them and that allowed courage to flow between them.

The cloud roiled and hissed and lightning shot from earth to sky, but the song went on, and a greater chorus of voices began to sing it.

> My cloak it is a very good cloak,
> it has always been good to the wear,

It has cost me many a groat,
and I've had it this forty-four year.

The ballad, three thousand voices strong, soared into the night.

The cloud began to disperse. The lightning slowed then disappeared. Whispers faded. Claws and wings withdrew into the night. Soon there was silence and single shreds of mist clinging stubbornly to a few shards of grass. Then there was simply nothing but the night and low pregnant clouds beginning to shed their load of snow.

Yet, despite the three thousand voices, Axis' voice still rang clear and sweet through the night, leading the choir.

Belle my Wife, she loves no strife
she said unto me quietly,
Rise up and save Cow Crumbocke's life!
man! put thy cloak about thee!

Some had been at the edge of madness. Some had teetered over.

But all came back.

27

Towards Fernbrake Lake

They left the next morning armed against the cold with clean clothes, new clothes and boots for Yr (and even an old but serviceable cloak that had once belonged to the Goodman's father), a plentiful supply of provisions, blankets, and, as promised, the trusty and sound mule to carry their newly acquired belongings. Jack set off in the lead, his vacant expression lasting only until they were out of sight of the Renkins' farmstead, his pigs trotting happily before him. Timozel followed, leading the placid mule, and the two women brought up the rear, walking with healthy strides now that their energies had been a little replenished. Although the snow continued to drift down about them, the wind had abated. Nevertheless, all were aware that mid-Bone-month was six weeks too early for snowfalls this far south. No one spoke his name, but the lingering menace of Gorgrael's threat shadowed their footsteps.

Although Faraday and Timozel had told the Goodpeople Renkin they were headed north for one of the towns of Rhaetia, Jack slowly led them north-east toward the Bracken

Ranges, the low and narrow mountain range that divided Skarabost from Arcen. As they approached the ranges their legs ached with the constant scrabbling up and then down low rolling hills. They met no one and encountered no insurmountable obstacles, although it rankled with Timozel that Jack was leading this expedition north when Artor's vision in the stairwell had clearly shown him to be a mighty warrior who would one day lead a great army. But Timozel said nothing. Artor would show him when the time was right. Meanwhile, as Faraday's Champion he devoted his days completely to her, making sure she had the most advantageous spot before their evening campfire and the choicest portions of food. His nights were devoted to other pursuits.

Faraday had become abruptly and uncomfortably aware of the new relationship between Yr and Timozel the first night they made camp. The covert movements and soft sounds drifting across the campfire from their blankets had first made her wriggle in embarrassment, and then struggle to suppress her own curious thoughts about what it would be like to bed with a man. Images of Axis and Borneheld mixed in her mind, confusing her, and she tossed uneasily, sleep eluding her for several hours.

Jack watched Faraday toss restlessly within her blankets from where he sat huddled watching the flames, his face unreadable. He was more concerned than ever at Timozel's presence with them, and wondered if the young man would disrupt their purpose. Ogden and Veremund had told him that Timozel had a good if troubled heart, but Jack wondered if that goodness had survived unscathed through the Chamber of the Star Gate. Like Yr, he had noticed the subtle changes in Timozel over the past few days, the increasing confidence and maturity, and wondered exactly what the changes would lead to. Jack could only hope that his devotion to Faraday would serve her well. That Timozel shared Yr's blankets and body at night meant nothing; Yr would eventually leave Timozel alone to pursue her purpose. Jack sighed and tossed a few more of the dead rosenberry branches into the fire. Even in this wet and cold weather, if one reached deep enough into the thick rosenberry bushes there was always dry and dead wood at hand for a small campfire. He hunkered down inside his blankets, grateful for the added warmth they gave him, closed his eyes and tried to snatch a few hours of sleep. They were only three or four days away from Fernbrake Lake, and he and Yr would have to talk to Faraday before they reached it. The Sentinels had told Faraday she had two very important tasks to perform without which Axis would not succeed in his battle against Gorgrael. The first was to keep Borneheld from murdering Axis in a fit of jealous rage. That she already understood. But at Fernbrake Lake Faraday would have to begin her journey toward fulfilling her second important task, that of Tree Friend.

After ten days of travel they reached the Bracken Ranges. Jack led them toward a narrow gully which would take them into the low mountains. It was the easiest passage, he explained patiently to a protesting Timozel, but Timozel walked off in a huff. Faraday sighed and made as if to walk after him, but Jack had held her back.

"Dear one, Yr and I need to speak with you for a moment. Let Timozel go."

Faraday gazed at Timozel striding ahead with the mule, upset at his constant arguing with Jack, but she nodded her head.

"Sweet child," Jack began soothingly, "you are the one that the Sentinels have trusted so much to. Aside from ourselves you are the only one who understands who the StarMan is. Faraday, please keep that trust. Do not tell Timozel too much; the lad might well betray Axis with an unwary word. Do you understand?"

It ached Faraday's heart to keep secrets from Timozel; he was, after all, her Champion.

Yr smiled and took Faraday's hand. "I will stay by your side for the time being, sweet girl. Share your doubts and secrets with me if you must speak them. It will be far safer that way."

Yr's touch reassured Faraday and she smiled a little and nodded. "I will do anything I can to protect Axis," she said softly. "You know that. I have told Timozel nothing and I will continue to keep Axis' true identity from him."

Jack looked ahead to check that Timozel was still out of earshot. "Sweet child, tomorrow we will reach a lovely lake in the center of the Bracken Ranges. While we are there we will show you some of what your second task will be."

Faraday frowned. The pass that Jack had indicated was only a few minutes' walk away. "You would not tell me what that was, Jack, when I asked before. Will you tell me now?"

Jack nodded. "Dear one, do you remember that night by the Silent Woman Woods when the trees sang to you?"

Faraday's face paled and Jack hastened on. "Remember that what the trees sing is often confusing. Their truth is sometimes not as we understand it. Remember that."

Faraday nodded curtly but Jack's words did not comfort her. None of the images the trees had shown her were positive. No matter how she rearranged them time and time again in her mind, Faraday could not see how the vision could depict anything except pain.

Jack and Yr watched Faraday's face close over. They hoped that her horror at the vision had not turned into a complete rejection of the singers.

Yr squeezed Faraday's hand gently as it lay in hers. "Dear one, no human has ever before heard Tree Song, and even very few of the Avar, the forest people, have. Faraday, it is important that the forest has a friend who can lead them to Axis. You must be Tree Friend."

"I *hate* the forest!" Faraday said tersely. "It is dark and evil and I will have nothing to do with it!" Her voice rose and Yr and Jack exchanged worried glances.

Jack placed a gentle hand on her shoulder and opened his mouth, but Faraday rounded on him. "Don't you *dare* enchant me into submissiveness," she said in a low fierce voice, her festering anxiety over the vision finding release in anger at Jack. Although Faraday genuinely liked Jack and Yr and was prepared to trust the Sentinels if it helped Axis, she wondered about the secrets they kept and occasionally resented their obvious manipulation of people about them.

Jack hastily removed his hand. "None of us will force you into anything," he said firmly, but Faraday turned on him again.

"You did not hesitate to trick me into placing my hand on that tree with your deceptively simple face, Jack." Faraday wrenched her hand from Yr's. "And if you worry about Timozel learning some of your dark secrets, then perhaps you should worry more about what Yr whispers into his ears during the long night than what I might innocently say to him during the day!" She glared at Yr for a moment, then turned back to Jack. "If your precious Prophecy needs a Tree Friend then it will have to find one elsewhere," she snapped and turned her back on the pair of them, lengthening her stride to catch up with Timozel.

Jack held Yr back from following her. "Leave her awhile," he muttered softly. "We will have only one chance at Fernbrake Lake. If we cannot present her to the Mother some time over the next few days then we are all doomed to endure the long dismal slide into complete destruction."

That evening they made camp well into the pass Jack called Pig Gully. They had followed the gully for about a league, deep into the mountains, before Jack had called a halt as it narrowed to an end. With the mountains on either side of them they were sheltered from the worst of the winds, and there were plenty of scattered bushes to provide a leaping fire.

While Timozel unpacked and rubbed down the mule, Yr prepared the evening meal, cutting thick slices from a smoke-cured ham and one of the remaining loaves Goodwife Renkin had packed for them. As she laid out the portions on plates Faraday joined her.

"I'm sorry for what I said earlier," Faraday said stiffly. "I was upset."

Yr looked up at her carefully, and motioned Jack closer. Faraday glanced at Jack as he approached and her stiffness increased. "I understand that you are bound to the Prophecy. I understand that. And I accept that I have my role to play." She paused, but neither Yr nor Jack said anything to help her. "Why do the trees need a friend? Why do they need *me?*"

"The trees and their people need someone to speak for them. They have picked you. Faraday, someone has to bring the trees behind Axis. He must unite Tencendor. If the trees do not join him then he cannot do that."

"Veremund assured me that my second task would be less distasteful than my first. Did he speak the truth?"

"Faraday. You will come to love the trees almost more than life itself." Yr paused, thinking. Tree Friend's role was far more than bringing the trees behind Axis. But it was not the Sentinels' place to tell Faraday that. "The trees have chosen you for a reason, Faraday, and that reason contains only joy. No sadness. Believe me."

A shadow crossed Faraday's face. "They were so sad," she whispered, remembering the Tree Song. "Yet so beautiful."

"They were slaughtered across Achar, dear one. Few remain. Lovely lady," Jack moved to change the subject, "tomorrow we will take you to Fernbrake Lake. But you must understand that Timozel cannot, *must* not, come with us. He is an Axe-Wielder and he would be in danger there."

Faraday looked alarmed, but Yr reassured her. "We will have to enchant him a little. He will know nothing. He will simply sleep, unaware, while we visit Fernbrake Lake. Trust us."

Faraday sighed and nodded. "I wish I had never left Skarabost," she said quietly and turned away.

28

Fernbrake Lake

Hours before dawn the next morning Yr raised herself from Timozel's side and looked about. Jack stood waiting silently a few paces away, staff in hand. Their glowing eyes met, but neither said a word. Yr looked down at Timozel, deep in sleep, his youthful face boyish in repose. She carefully spread her hand across his face, fingertips at his temples, thumb on the point of his chin. Blue light pulsed lightly from her fingertips. She glanced at Jack and he stepped forward and gently laid the knob of his staff on the back of Yr's hand where it rested on Timozel's face. The blue light around her fingertips intensified twenty-fold, and both squinted a little in the sudden brightness. Jack's lips moved silently, while Yr's face was a mask of concentration.

Faraday watched from a safe distance. Poor Timozel, caught up in an adventure that he had not wanted. Unwillingly subjected to an enchantment about which he knew nothing and that he would loathe and fear if he did know.

She fidgeted, feeling nervous about the day ahead. Why had the Prophecy sprung to life in hers and Axis' lifetimes?

Precisely because it is your lifetimes, a small voice echoed in her head, and she noticed Jack looking at her. Had he invaded her head as well?

Timozel's breathing slowed gradually until he breathed only once every minute. Yr scrambled to her feet and slipped her rough worsted dress over her head, cinching it tight about her waist at the same time as she wriggled her feet into her boots. She twisted her hair into a knot behind her neck.

"What have you done to him?" Faraday asked quietly as she stepped up beside the Sentinel.

Yr glanced at her. Faraday seemed drawn and pale in the faint light emitted by the coals left from last night's fire. "What I have done, with the help of Jack's staff, is to move him slightly outside the normal flow of time. What would normally be another three hours of sleep will now extend into three days, if not more. He will wake with no sense of having slept that long."

"Will he be all right? What if it rains . . . snows? How will he keep warm?"

Yr stroked Faraday's cheek soothingly. "Hush now, sweet child. We are well within the protection of Fernbrake Lake at this point. The Lake knows we are coming, and the Lake knows that Timozel, the pigs and even the mule require the same protection as ourselves. She will keep him in Her care until we return. He will stay warm and safe, and the mule and the pigs will remain close by. The worst of the weather will pass well overhead."

"She?" What did Yr mean, talking of the lake as if it were alive?

Jack stepped up behind them, handing them their cloaks. Protected or not, the air was still close to freezing. "Come. The Mother awaits."

Faraday shifted her eyes nervously between them. "The Mother?"

Jack smiled gently, and his eyes were soft. "Faraday, do

you remember how scared you felt before you walked into the unknown Chamber of the Star Gate?" Faraday nodded. "And do you remember how you felt when you gazed into the Star Gate itself?" Faraday nodded again, more strongly this time. She would never let that sight fade from her mind. "Faraday. The Star Gate is one of the most magical and powerful places in this land of Tencendor. Fernbrake Lake, or the Mother, as it is anciently known, is another. You are caught up in an adventure that you did not ask for and did not want. But, think on this sweet lady, you are witnessing wonders that none of your race have seen for close on a thousand years."

Faraday pondered Jack's words, and the stress lines on her face slowly began to ease. She had seen the Star Gate, and even if she never saw it again it was enough simply to know that it was there, that it existed.

"Yr, I know so little. Will you tell me of Tencendor as we walk?"

Yr took Faraday's hand between both of her own. "Gladly, sweet child. Gladly. Today we will see a part of Tencendor that still survives, that still lives much as it did before . . . before the Seneschal started to murder this beautiful land."

"Come," Jack's voice was brisk. "We will have to climb most of the day."

The two women shouldered the smallish packs that Jack had prepared for them. Faraday paused a moment by Timozel's side, then touched his check gently. "Rest well," she said softly. "I will return safely."

Jack finished checking the camp, hefted his own larger pack onto his back, and gestured impatiently. Yr led Faraday toward the end of Pig Gully where a trail wound up into the mountains. When they turned their backs Jack leaned swiftly down to Timozel's side and placed his hand over the man's face. Faint green light glowed at his fingertips. After a moment Jack lifted his hand off, puzzlement written over his face. He wiped his hand through his blond hair, considering. Veremund had told him clearly what he had felt when he had tested Timozel in the Silent Woman Keep. A good heart, but shadowed with unhappiness. The promise of troubled choices in his future. Yes, all that was there, but there was also a taint of something strange that Jack could not identify and that made him very uncomfortable, very uncomfortable indeed. He stood up and hurried after Yr and Faraday. Again he wished he had led Faraday and Timozel into some other Barrow than the one he had. Any Barrow but that of the ninth Enchanter-Talon. But Jack could not deny the Prophecy, and none of the marked could ever evade the Prophet's hand.

They climbed solidly until the sun crested the mountain ridges that rose far above them. No one had any breath left for talking once they started to bend their backs into the steep mountain path out of Pig Gully. For a long time the only sound was the crunch of their booted feet on the gravel of the path. Once the sun was well clear of the mountain ridges Jack called a halt. Yr and Faraday sank gratefully against the rocky mountain wall of the path, legs outstretched. Faraday wondered vaguely if all of Tencendor's wonders existed at the very top of the world or at the very bottom.

"All others have been destroyed," Yr gasped by her side. "Only those at the top and the bottom of the world have survived."

Faraday closed her eyes in weariness. She would never get used to the Sentinel's unnerving habit of reading thoughts. Yr leaned over and patted her hand. "We do not do it all the time, dear child," she muttered. "We try to be polite."

"Oh, Yr! What thoughts did you catch as you wandered the corridors of Priam's palace?"

Yr's grin faded a little. "Not always pretty ones, dear one, not always pretty ones." She thought about some of the more irksome and surprising knowledge she had picked up at the palace, not to mention the troubling se-

crets she had gathered on her regular forays to the Tower of
the Seneschal. Thank the Mother that Axis was away from
the Tower for the time being. Perhaps, just perhaps, his
journey north would open his eyes to some of the lies that
enveloped him. The sooner he was freed from their false-
hoods the sooner he would find his own truths.

Jack sat a little further up the track watching them. He
was immensely relieved that they had been able to leave
Timozel behind. When he and the other Sentinels had discussed spiriting Faraday away to Borneheld, they had
wanted the opportunity to train her as much as possible before events overtook them. But he and Yr had been severely restrained by Timozel's presence, and Faraday still
had to step firmly onto the path that the Prophecy had chosen for her.

He passed out thick slices of ham, crunchy currant bis-
cuits, and tawny, dried summer apples. If Timozel had
been an unplanned nuisance, then Goodwife Renkin had
served her purpose far better than he could have hoped.
"Yr," he muttered around a mouthful of ham, "perhaps
you can tell Faraday of the Sacred Lakes while we breakfast."

"Sacred Lakes?" Faraday's eyes were round. "Is the
Fernbrake, the Mother, one of them?"

"Yes, sweet child." Yr nibbled delicately at the core of
an apple. "There are four of them. The Fernbrake, or
Mother, whom we will visit today. Can you think of any
others?"

Faraday licked her fingers; the ham was exceedingly delicious. She wondered if it was smoked over peat or wood
fire. Perhaps the Goodpeople Renkin smoked it over dried
pig manure. She thought about that very hard for a moment, concentrating on forming a clear image in her mind.

Jack gagged and spat out the last mouthful of ham that
he had been chewing on. Faraday let the image go and
laughed delightedly, clapping her hands like a small child.
The two Sentinels looked wryly at each other. Caught.
"Not polite," Faraday laughed.

Yr repressed a smile. "The Lakes, dear child. Can you think of any others?"

Faraday concentrated. "Why, the Cauldron Lake. In the Silent Woman Woods. That must be one of them. Timozel told me how strange it was."

Yr inclined her head in agreement. "But there is one you know even better."

Faraday blinked her eyes in confusion. "What other strange lakes are there, Yr? There are no other large lakes in Achar except . . . oh! Surely not!"

"Ah," Jack winked at Yr. "I think she has it."

"Not Grail Lake," Faraday breathed.

"Precisely, my sweet. But Grail Lake has buried its enchantment deep over the past several hundred years. Of all the Sacred Lakes, it has been the most exposed to the works of man. And of the Seneschal."

"And the fourth?" Faraday asked.

"It lies far to the north." Jack smiled to himself. "But I think it is the most beautiful of all."

Faraday turned back to Yr. "Why are they sacred, Yr?"

Yr started to crunch her way through a currant biscuit, holding a hand beneath her chin to catch the crumbs. "Each has its own purpose, Faraday," she muttered ambigusly, "and its own secrets. Today, or perhaps tomorrow, you may see why it is that the Avar people particularly revere the Mother."

Faraday remembered what Veremund had told her about the Avar people. The people of the forest. He had also called the Icarii the people of the Wing, and now Jack had told her that, incredibly, the Icarii were actually winged people. "Yr, if the Icarii are referred to as the people of the Wing, and if they do indeed have wings, then what do the Avar look like if they are the people of the forest? Do they have leaves instead of hair?"

Now it was Jack and Yr's turn to laugh. "No, dear one," Jack said obscurely as he rose to his feet. "Hardly that. Come, it is time we were moving."

Just as they were beginning to climb again Faraday remembered what else Veremund had mentioned about the Avar, that perhaps they could speak to the trees. She looked about the slopes of the Bracken Ranges. The mountains were so named because of the dense growth of ferns and waist-high bracken that covered most of their lower slopes. But now Faraday wondered if the interior of the Ranges surrounding Fernbrake Lake supported plant life a little larger than bracken. Some of Faraday's nervousness returned. Her entire life up to this point had revolved about fear of the forest and the forbidden creatures it contained; despite her wonder at the Star Gate, it was not easy to let go of such ingrained fear.

Timozel, caught in his enchantment, dreamed. Again he walked down a long ice tunnel, enslaved, terrified, and again he approached the massive wooden door. Again a dreadful voice boomed from the other side of the door to enter and Timozel's treacherous hand closed firmly upon the latch, which twisted open. "No!" he screamed, but the latch continued to move and Timozel heard a click as the door lock gave way. Just as the door began to inch open his mind let go and Timozel slipped back into sleep.

After many hours of climbing, Jack, Yr and Faraday topped a ridge and Fernbrake Lake lay before them, a vast circular body of emerald water almost completely filling the collapsed peak of a mountain. Great ferns and bracken, as tall as a man, surrounded much of the lake, but around one end there stood a stand of massive trees towering into the dark and cloudy sky. Jack led them down the side of the ridge toward a smooth, well-grassed area between the trees and the water's edge.

Faraday was subdued as they scrambled down the side of the ridge onto a steep path hemmed in by the tall tree ferns. Fernbrake Lake, although beautiful, was not as wonderful as Jack and Yr had promised. It was certainly nothing like the Star Gate. And Faraday was depressed at the sight of the trees. For her they recalled the dreadful images of her vision, and she did not think she could bear it if they wanted to sing her another like it. Yr turned and smiled reassuringly at her. Yr had said that she would learn to love the trees almost more than life itself, but Faraday thought it would take all her efforts simply to learn to accept them. Even the myriad of birds that called from the bracken did not calm her.

It took them close to an hour to climb down the steep path and work their way around the lake toward the clear area in front of the trees. The clearing stretched some fifty paces between the tree line and the water's edge, extending in an almost perfect crescent around the eastern rim of the lake.

"This is a very sacred spot for the Avar people, dear one," Yr whispered to Faraday. "You see, the Avar revere the—"

"I do not think your explanations will be necessary, gentle one," Jack said, his voice very still, gazing toward the tree line. "I think that for once our luck has turned for the better. See, the Mother has an Avar Bane in attendance."

Both Yr and Faraday turned to look at the spot in the tree line where Jack's eyes were riveted. "A Bane," Yr whispered, awed. Faraday stared at the trees, but for a long moment she could see nothing. Then, just as her eyes adjusted to the shadows between the trees, a man, carrying a small child, walked into the cold daylight of the clearing.

Timozel was trapped again in his dream, trapped before the slowly opening door. He finally managed to force his hand from the door latch lest the opening door pull him precipitously into the room beyond. The person—the creature—who was opening the door was standing behind it, and all Timozel could see was his shadow stretching across the ice floor of the room beyond. Even the ill-defined shape of the shadow was ghastly enough for Timozel to finally wrench his mind from the power that held him and escape once more.

29

The Bane and the Child

Faraday shifted a little closer to Yr. "Who are they?" she
whispered.

"Shhh!" Yr hushed, and stepped up to stand beside Jack
as he stood, staff in hand.

Faraday looked back to the man and child. The man was
of an indeterminate age, a little shorter than Jack, about her
own height, and very muscular with smooth olive skin and
dark brown hair waving down about his neck. He wore a
short woven tunic with a subtle pattern around its hem that
Faraday could not quite make out and brown leggings underneath that. His face was broad, open and peculiarly
formed with a wide, almost lumpy, forehead above a long
aquiline nose, high cheekbones and a thin mobile mouth.
Of all his features, however, it was his eyes that demanded
most attention; they were so dark as to be almost black,
deep liquid pools that appeared to have witnessed both
great tragedy and indescribable joy. He was one of the
most compelling people Faraday had ever seen, with a
wild, alien air about him that almost vibrated. The child

was very young, no more than a toddler. She was of the
same race as the man who carried her, curly brown hair
above a similarly structured face and black eyes. She
smiled happily at the group before her as the man stopped
some five or six paces from them. At this distance Faraday
could see that the subtle pattern around the hem of his tunic was of leaping deer.

The man's eyes were disturbed as they shifted among
the three. He opened his mouth to speak, but both Jack and
Yr stopped him as they bowed deeply. Yr placed the heels
of both her hands on her forehead as she bowed, but Jack,
encumbered with his staff, placed only the heel of his left
hand on his brow. "Bane," they said simultaneously in
strong, clear voices, "we honor you and yours. May you always find shade to rest in, and may the paths to the Sacred
Grove remain always open to your feet."

The man was surprised by the formal greeting, but he
visibly rocked with astonishment when Jack and Yr both
stood straight again; their eyes glowed softly emerald and
sapphire. He placed the child gently on the ground and
bowed low before them, his hands over his eyes and forehead. "Sentinels. I greet you with honor." He straightened
and dropped his hands, his eyes unreadable. He sighed.
"And with mixed relief and fear. Your presence before the
Mother confirms to me and to mine that the Prophecy has
indeed awakened." His eyes shifted to Faraday questioningly.

She stared at the Bane. She could easily understand him,
although his accents were strange.

Jack's voice sounded instantly in her head. *All three
races once lived together in Tencendor, Faraday, and all
three still speak the same language*.

As Faraday hesitated Yr shot her a sharp glance from the
corner of her eyes and Faraday started a little. She was being rude. She bowed low and in the same manner as Jack
and Yr had, trying to repeat their greeting exactly. Then she
straightened and let her hands fall to her sides. "My name
is Faraday, daughter of Earl Isend of Skarabost."

The man frowned. She was a Plains Dweller and her presence before the Mother troubled him. But she accompanied the Sentinels. "Faraday, I greet you and welcome you before the Mother."

The girl-child was clinging to the man's legs and he picked her up again. "The child's name is Shra," he said, "and I am Raum, of the GhostTree Clan." Jack and Yr introduced themselves and then Jack motioned at the ground.

"Bane Raum, may we sit? We have been climbing into this valley for most of the day and our legs ache. We would have words with you."

Raum nodded and they sat down in a circle, Jack, Yr and Faraday slipping the packs off their backs. Faraday stretched her back and arms a little, glad to be relieved of the weight. The child Shra stood beside Raum as he sat cross-legged, her small hands holding onto his bended knee for support. She looked immeasurably curious at the presence of these strange visitors.

Jack smiled gently at her, and then looked back at Raum. "Have you presented her to the Mother yet?"

Raum glanced at Faraday again, but then looked back at Jack. "No, Sentinel. We only just arrived. The time will not be right until very early tomorrow morning."

"Good. Raum," Jack hesitated, "Yr and myself have brought Faraday to the Mother for the same purpose. But we are honored that you are here and would ask that when you present Shra you also present Faraday."

Raum's eyes widened and his nostrils flared in anger.

"She is a woman of the Plains! She does not understand the trees! *Only the Avar can tread this path!* Sentinel, you cannot mean what you ask!"

"Bane, one of your learning must understand the words of the Prophecy, yes?" Raum nodded stiffly. "And the Prophecy has chosen this young woman to serve too. She will serve the Prophecy by serving the trees—we are sure of that. Raum, will you test her? If you do not think she is worthy of this task then we will leave."

Faraday tensed as Raum eyed her angrily. The alien air

about him was magnified ten-fold and she clenched her hands to stop them from trembling. Abruptly Raum rose and stepped across the circle to squat before her. He reached out with both his hands and seized her head between them. Faraday went rigid as his powerful hands gripped her. Raum leaned forward until his black, hostile eyes were only inches from her terrified ones. Then she fell into blackness.

She was running, terrified, through an immense forest of trees that towered above her. Something appalling, undefinable, yet so dangerous that Faraday knew it would tear her to pieces if it caught her, chased her through the trees. The thick and crooked black trunks of the forest trees reared angrily from the lichen and leaf-covered soil of the forest floor, crowding in on Faraday as she ran, reaching out to trip her feet with their cunning twisted roots and snag her shoulders and arms with their sinister boughs until Faraday's white skin was scratched and bleeding. Faraday cried as she ran, desperately trying to find a way through the trees, but as hard and as fast as she ran the forest crowded thicker about her, striving to impede her progress. She could hear the beast that hated her, that wanted to kill her, gaining ground behind her, crashing unobstructed through the trees while she had to fight for every step. "Help me," she sobbed as she ran, but the malicious trees only intensified their efforts to hinder her progress, trying to hold her tight for whatever chased her through their midst. Faraday began to lose her temper, frustration slowly overcoming her fear as she pushed her way between the thick, black forest. Why should the trees hinder her and not the one who chased her? "Naughty trees," she muttered angrily, not realizing that she had copied Jack's tone when he berated the trees for frightening her during the long Silent Woman Night. "You should help me!" Perhaps they would tell her where she could hide if she asked them. Faraday lurched to a halt beside a massive Whalebone Oak, slapped it as hard as she could in her all-consuming rage, then leaned against it, palms tight against its rough bark. For a moment there was nothing but her rage, but then Faraday recalled how Jack had taught her to listen to the trees of Silent Woman Wood. "Damn you," she muttered. "listen to me now." She deliberately erased all feelings of anger from her heart, and tried to feel the tree's presence through her hands into her heart. For a long moment she concentrated hard, trying to ignore the sounds of her pursuer. Then, finally, just as she was beginning to despair, a tremendous sense of peace engulfed her and she started to hear the tree sing a Song of love and reassurance. Tears slipped out of her eyes, and she humbly apologized to the Whalebone Oak for hitting it in her anger. The sense of danger, of being hunted by some dreadful beast, completely disappeared; there was now no sound but that of the Tree Song. The forest no longer oppressed her; instead it held her and comforted her. A slow smile curved her lips as she felt its love, then she laughed delightedly and opened her eyes.

Raum, his eyes still wide, slowly let her head go and sat back on his heels. Faraday smiled at him in understanding. "It was you who chased me through the forest, wasn't it?"

Raum nodded, bewildered at what he had witnessed. He resumed his seat within the circle and looked at Jack and Yr. "She underwent the same test as do all those of our children who show the promise," he said hesitantly. "And yet we, the Avar, who live so close to the trees, lose so many in the test. All that they are required to do to pass the test is simply to think about asking the trees for help from the danger that threatens them. That is all. And yet we lose so many." Sorrow deepened his voice. "Most die of terror. Most never think about asking the trees for help. Of all that undergo the test in the Avarinheim, only a small number survive to make the trip to the Mother."

"What did Faraday do?" Jack asked, immensely relieved that Faraday had passed the test.

Raum smiled introspectively. "She stood, even as the danger was closing in on her, and let them sing to her, let them sing the danger away. None of our children have ever done that. Even after a lifetime of training few of our number are ever privileged to hear even a small part of the Tree Song." He paused. "They sang for her. They sang for her," he repeated, still amazed at what had happened. He looked across to Faraday, and his eyes now reflected awe. "What will they do for her once she has been presented to the Mother?"

Trapped again, all Timozel could see was the ghastly shadow stretching across the ice floor of the room beyond. The ill-defined shadow wavered as the creature behind the door stepped out into the light. "Who is it?" a dreadful voice asked. "Who comes to disturb my rest?" Timozel could feel hate oozing out of the creature's mouth along with its words, but he was so mesmerized by the slowly moving shadow that he had no heart to resist the question. "My name is Timozel," he whispered, "and I do not want to be here." Unfortunately, unconsciousness did not save him from the nightmare this time.

Raum fetched a bundle from the trees and unwrapped it to share some of his food with the others. Although Faraday recognized some of the berries and fruits that he offered her, the piece of flat bread that she ate tasted unusual, although not unpleasant. "What is it made from?" she asked.

"It is malfari bread, made not from the grains that you grow on the plains, but from a fibrous tuber we gather in the Avarinheim called malfari. We crush it and dry it and then bake it with herbs and cheese into flat bread. During winter it is the mainstay of our diet."

"The Avarinheim?" Faraday asked puzzled. Shra, her black eyes trusting, tottered over to her and curled up in her lap. Faraday stroked the child's head, but repeated her question. "What is the Avarinheim?"

Jack smiled at the Bane in apology. "Bane, we have had no time nor the opportunity to tell her anything. We have only just found her ourselves. Could you perhaps explain a little about your people, and particularly about yourself and the child and why you are here?"

"Shra and I are of the Avar people." Raum's mouth twisted in a bitter smile. "One of the two races you call the Forbidden. We live in the Avarinheim, the great forest that stretches from the Icescarp Alps to the Fortress Ranges—where your ancestors penned us a thousand years ago in the Wars of the Axe." Faraday's face brightened with embarrassment for her people, but she held Raum's eyes in a steady gaze. "You know the Avarinheim as the Shadowsward, and your Brotherhood of the Seneschal have taught your people to hate and fear it and all those who live within it."

Raum looked about the valley of the Fernbrake Lake, beginning to darken in the dusk light. "Here there stand a few remaining remnants of the Avarinheim, and I am told that there still stands a wood around Cauldron Lake." Jack nodded in confirmation. "Those are the last remaining stands of trees that once belonged to the Greater Avarinheim stretched from the Icescarp Alps to Widewall Bay and from the Widowmaker Sea to River Nordra. You and yours have killed much of our home, Faraday of Skarabost."

"Over these last few weeks I have learned that the past has many different interpretations, Raum," she said a little dryly.

Raum continued. "The Avar are a peaceful people, Faraday. We live in as great a harmony with the land as we can—unlike your race, which desecrates and scars and rapes the land for what it can give you, and yet give nothing back. Your Way of the Plough is an abomination, Faraday."

"Enough, Raum," Yr said softly. "Poor Faraday has not the shoulders to carry the guilt for her entire race."

Raum inclined his head at the Sentinel, but his eyes glinted with anger. "Sometimes, Sentinel Yr, it is hard for us to watch the land we loved and cared for carved up into barrenness under the dreadful plowshare." He turned back to Faraday and moderated his tone somewhat. "We live in harmony with the land," he repeated, "and with the seasons. We do not try to change or to warp, but to assist both land and seasons as best we can. Of all living things we revere the trees most of all. For us the forest, the Avarinheim, is a living being and we treasure it as we do our own families. Our most sacred rituals are those designed to assist the turn of the seasons and the regeneration of the land and forest. Some among us have the ability to become Banes, or images, and it is our duty to care for the forest with an even greater dedication than most Avar, and to conduct the rites of land and season."

"And those children you think might have the ability to serve as Banes you put to the test when very young?" Faraday's tone was hard enough to leave no one in doubt about what she thought about putting children through such a frightful experience.

"Faraday, life is sometimes cruel. We grieve for those children who are lost, for every one of them is precious to us. But without Banes to conduct the rites, the rites would lapse, and then the seasons would falter and the land would die."

"But why so young?" Faraday asked. "Shra cannot be above three."

"It is vital that we bring those children who have passed the test to the Mother to be presented while they are very young, otherwise their talents will not grow as they should."

"Why do you call this lake the Mother, Raum?"

Raum smiled and looked out over the lake. "Because it is said that life originated within this lake. For us, it is very magical. It is the beginning of a Bane's true life."

For a long time no one said anything. But then Faraday frowned. "Raum? How do you get here? Do you come across the Seagrass Plains of Skarabost?"

Raum nodded. "Every year or so we try to bring several children out to bathe them in the waters of the Mother. But we must travel at night and move as stealthily as we can. We avoid contact with humans. Skarabost is a sparsely populated region and most people remain inside after dark. We are helped in this by a woman of your race who lives with the Icarii. Some years she comes down to help us bring the children through. Because she is of your race she can travel openly with a well-cloaked child or two and attract little comment." He shrugged. "But it is hard. And we have not been able to bring as many children to the Mother as we would have liked. In the best of times we have hardly enough Banes to conduct the rites, but, now, as the seasons begin to fail around us and the land dies underneath its unnatural cover of snow and ice, we do not have the number of Banes to even attempt to halt the rot. Over the past few years, as the danger from the north has grown, we have tried to bring as many children through as we can . . . but it is hard, it is very hard."

Faraday opened her mouth to ask about the woman who lived with the Icarii, but Jack's voice leaped in before she had a chance to speak. "Bane, what do you mean? What has been happening in the Avarinheim?"

"Over the past two years, particularly this past year, the Skraeling wraiths from the northern wastes have been wandering in ever-increasing numbers along the border of the Avarinheim. They do not trouble us much because they still remain afraid of the trees, but it is worrying nevertheless. And, as you can see, the weather dies around us. There has been talk among us and the Icarii that the Prophecy of the Destroyer has awoken; none of us want to believe it . . . but," despair shone from his eyes, "your presence and words tell me that Gorgrael has indeed been born and that even now he prepares to spread his hatred southward. Tell me, if you can, have you found the StarMan? Will he save us?"

Again Faraday opened her mouth, but Jack silenced her with a hard look. "He still lies trapped within the lies that bind, Bane Raum, and it will be many long seasons before he can ride to Tencendor's defense. All we can do is trust in the wisdom of the Prophecy."

"I fear that the Skraelings, driven by Gorgrael, will launch their major attack through the north of Ichtar this winter, Raum," Yr said quietly. "I doubt if the Acharites alone will stop them. Do you think the Icarii will help?"

Raum massaged his forehead. For a moment Faraday thought she could see two tiny knobs of bone glistening within his hair, but then thought she must have been deceived by the low light.

"Would the Acharites accept their help, Sentinel? Or would they slaughter the Winged Ones before they had a chance to assist?" Raum said finally.

His words made Faraday wonder if perhaps she might have more than one role to play in Gorkenfort.

Timozel stood, riveted with fear. "My name is Timozel," he whispered, "and I do not want to be here." He closed his eyes as tight as he could, relieved that at least his eyelids still obeyed his conscious thought. He did not want to see what it was that stepped out from behind the door. "Timozel," the disgusting voice said slowly, as if its tongue had trouble with such a multisyllabled word. "You are a pretty boy. What magical path did you walk to find me, Timozel?" Timozel did not know what the voice was talking about; all he did know was that he dared not open his eyes. He wondered if he was going to be killed as he stood there. "Timozel. Will you be my friend, Timozel? I would like an

Axe-Wielder for my friend." The request was so strange and so unexpected that Timozel's eyes flew open. In front of him stood the most horrific and disgusting creature he'd ever seen. He screamed with such intensity that the kind blackness came to claim him again.

30

The Mother

As night fell Raum advised Faraday to take Shra and try
to get a few hours' sleep before the ceremony at the
Mother. Faraday looked for guidance to Jack and Yr, but
they told her to trust Raum in whatever he asked her to do,
so Faraday cradled the sleepy child in her arms and curled
up in one of the blankets. The last thing she saw before finally drifting off into sleep was Jack, Yr and Raum sitting
around a small campfire, deep in conversation.

Raum shook her awake some hours later. "It is time," he
said softly. Faraday sat up and rubbed her eyes. It was very
cold and she shivered when the blanket fell from her shoulders. For once the cloud cover had blown away and the
stars wheeled above them in their countless thousands,
while the full moon floated fat and complacent just above
the peaks of the mountains. Faraday woke the child who,
uncomplaining, wrapped her arms about Faraday's neck as
the young woman hefted her into her arms. "Where are
Jack and Yr?" she whispered.

Raum nodded to the tree line and Faraday could just

make out the huddled forms of the two Sentinels as they sat and watched under the nearest of the trees. "They will not disturb us," Raum said softly. "Now, do not say another word unless I ask it of you. Are you ready?"

Faraday nodded silently.

"Then come," Raum turned his back and started to walk down to the lake. Some twenty paces before the water's edge he stopped and turned to Faraday and Shra. "We must take our clothes off here," he said. "The Mother demands that we meet her as naked as the day we were born."

Faraday opened her mouth to protest, but Raum's eyes bored into her own so fiercely that eventually she nodded stiffly and slipped Shra out of her tunic and leggings. Putting the still placid child down on the ground, she slipped out of her rough woollen dress. The shock of the night air on Faraday's naked skin instantly raised goose-flesh and she shivered as she folded her dress. Unbidden by Raum, but feeling it was the right thing to do, Faraday unpinned her hair and shook it down her back. Turning around and picking Shra up again, Faraday averted her eyes from Raum's nakedness and was grateful that the dark of the night hid her own hot face. She suddenly thought about what her mother would have said about this, and for an instant her eyes stung with painful tears, but she blinked them away. Hugging the child to her, Faraday followed Raum down toward the water.

Raum turned as they reached the water's edge. "Remember, no sound unless I ask you. Put Shra down. She will have to stand on her own for this."

As Faraday slid the child down onto her feet, Raum quickly stooped and picked up something from a large flat rock at his feet. Faraday's eyes widened as she realized that he held a large hare in one hand and a sharp bone knife in the other. Again Raum's eyes met her own and Faraday bit her lip to stop herself from saying anything. Although its flickering ears indicated that it was still alive, the hare lay virtually motionless in Raum's arm.

"Thank you," he whispered almost inaudibly to the hare, "for this sacrifice that you are willing to make for us. Tonight, you will join with the Mother." Then, hefting the bone knife in his other hand, he made a long slit down into the hare's chest cavity. Blood welled out of the deep gash and shone darkly in the moonlight. Placing the knife back on the stone again, Raum dipped the fingers of one hand into the blood and bent down to Shra.

"With this blood, freely given by friend hare, I bind you with the Mother. Will you promise to serve her, to aid her, and never betray her?"

"I do so swear," Shra lisped, and Faraday realized that they were the first words she had heard the child speak.

"Then may the paths to the Sacred Grove always remain open to your feet, Shra," Raum said gently. He ran the fingers of his bloodied hand lightly along her face and chest, leaving three parallel lines running down her body. "With this blood you are bound."

Raum rose and faced Faraday. "With this blood, freely given by friend hare, I bind you with the Mother. Will you promise to serve her, to aid her, and never betray her?" Raum asked.

Faraday thought of her eighteen years of utter devotion to Artor and her complete trust in the Seneschal. She wondered what she was doing, how she could possibly have found herself in this situation? She opened her mouth to say the words, but for a moment nothing would come out. Gaping helplessly, she wondered if she should run, run as fast and as far as she could. Then, just as she was about to break from Raum's stare, Faraday remembered how she had felt at the Star Gate, how she had thought then that Artor was totally insignificant compared to the deeper mysteries of the Forbidden. There was more to life, and more beautiful, than the Seneschal's Way of the Plough.

"I do so swear," she said softly. Raum dipped his fingers into the blood again and raised them to her face, tracing three long trails of warm clotted blood down her forehead and the length of her face so that one trail ran down her nose and mouth to the point of her chin and the other two ran down either cheek.

"Then may the paths to the Sacred Groves always remain open to your feet, Faraday." Raum ran his fingers down Faraday's chest, leaving one trail of blood down her sternum, and the other two trails tracing down her breasts to her nipples. "With this blood you are bound."

Faraday closed her eyes, repulsed by the feel of the warm slick blood on her breasts, unable to stop herself remembering the feel of the hot blood as it had splattered and run down her breasts in her vision. When she opened them again Raum was still staring at her, but his eyes were sympathetic and Faraday realized he understood the feelings the blood had stirred in her. Feeling empowered as somewhere deep within her the Mother enriched her new daughter with strength and courage and understanding. Her doubts and fears faded.

Raum spoke gently. "Faraday, will you honor me with the Mother's marks?" He held the hare out slightly away from his body.

Faraday, no longer afraid or even cold, dipped her fingers into the hare's chest cavity, realising with a start that the animal's heart was still beating. She raised her dripping fingers and marked Raum as he had her, and then she smiled at him. "May this blood renew your bonds with the Mother," she said, "and may your feet hold firm to the paths of the Sacred Grove."

Raum smiled at her, pleased that she had bonded so well, and then reached down to the hare and tore its living heart out with an abrupt twist of his hand.

"Mother, with this heart's blood may you wake for us this night," he cried into the still night, hurling the still quivering heart into the lake. As soon as the heart and its blood drops spattered across the surface of the water the entire lake burst into a luminous deep emerald glow—the lake became a vast bowl of light. The sight was so beautiful that Faraday was unable to stop a gasp of wonder.

Raum turned from the lake, tossing aside the carcass of the hare, and touched Faraday's shoulder gently, his eyes reflecting the emerald light. "Behold the Mother," he smiled at her.

Faraday could not tear her eyes from the spectacular scene before her. The emerald lake lit up the entire mountain, and even the stars in the night sky reflected some of the luminous color of the water. Power seemed to vibrate from the lake, calling to Faraday, and at last she turned her eyes toward Raum in mute appeal.

"Yes," he whispered. "It is time to present you to the Mother." He leaned down to pick up Shra and then held out his hand for Faraday. "Take my hand, Faraday, and walk with me and Shra through the Mother and into the Sacred Grove. Be welcomed."

Faraday grasped his warm hand, and then they slowly began to walk down into the water.

Timozel again felt himself being pulled into the nightmare and he struggled against it, fought with his entire being until he thought that his heart would burst from his body, but it made not a whit of difference. He forced his eyes open. The hideous part-man, part-bird, part-beast stood before him, a full head taller than Timozel, and five times his weight in muscle. Power radiated from the creature's silver eyes and again it reached out a hand (or was it a claw?) in entreaty. "Timozel, will you be my friend?" it simpered. With what he thought would be his dying breath Timozel summoned what was left of his courage and screamed, "No! I would rather spend eternity in the fire pits of the AfterLife than be your friend!" The creature bellowed with rage, and clawed hands reached for Timozel.

As they stepped into the lake Faraday felt no sensation of wetness, only of power. It throbbed all about her, and she wondered what it would feel like when she was completely submerged. Raum's fingers tightened about her hand, but she smiled at him reassuringly, and stepped confidently by his side. Shra reached her plump arms out into the emerald lake, laughing with joy. As they walked further the emerald glow rose further up their bodies until it had reached the level of their chests. Raum held Shra so that her head still floated above the line of power. "Come," he said, and dipped beneath the surface of the lake, pulling Shra and Faraday down with him.

Faraday did not feel a moment's tension or worry as the surface of the lake closed over her head. She could still breathe without any effort and, as the lake bed fell away beneath her feet, she found that she could walk completely suspended in the deep emerald light without any support. She looked about her in amazement. Raum, Shra and herself were completely enclosed in the light and all traces of the shoreline and night sky had totally disappeared.

Raum looked at her, the blood on his face and chest burning blackly in the eerie glow; she turned away again and they walked further and further into the light.

Gradually Faraday became aware of a change in the light; it was growing darker and shadowed in some places, lighter in others. She again had the sensation that she was actually walking on solid ground and when she looked down she realized that her feet were walking through soft, ankle-high grass. The blurred green shapes about her resolved themselves into tall trees and after a lingering glow of emerald, all traces of the lake disappeared and Raum, Faraday and Shra found themselves walking down a narrow path through a deep forest. Overhead the stars spun through the night sky in a dazzling display of power beyond that which any man or woman could hope to hold.

Faraday felt very happy, very contented. She took a deep breath of complete exultation; she had seen the Star Gate, and now she had not only seen the Mother, the Fernbrake Lake, but this time she had been permitted to walk through. She had been blessed. At her side Raum felt her rapture, he lifted their joined hands and pressed the back of her hand against his chest for a moment. Shra reached down and grasped their hands and then all three of them laughed together for sheer joy.

The path led them, as Faraday somehow suspected it might, into the grove of her dream; except this was no dream. Raum stopped them at the edge of the large circular grove and motioned them to wait, then he walked into the center of the clearing, raised his arms above his shoulders, hands extended palm-up to the night sky, and spoke in a strong, clear voice. "Sacred Horned Ones, I bring you greetings from Avarinheim, and I present to you Shra and Faraday, who have passed through the terror of the forest and have been cleansed and blessed by the Light of the Mother." He turned and held his hands out for Shra and Faraday to join him. "One will grow tall and strong and will walk the shaded paths of Avarinheim, serving the Mother and your Sacred Selves, and the other will walk in the shadow of the Prophecy of the Destroyer and will, if her strength prevails, bring us through the other side. Please, Sacred Ones, step forth and grant both Shra and Faraday the courage of your strength and your blessing."

Faraday, standing at Raum's side, started to tremble with the sheer drift of power through the Grove. She could see forms slipping through the shadows of the surrounding trees and feel eyes slide over her naked body. It was strange that no fear, only exhilaration, filled her. She sensed that the same exhilaration filled Raum. She reached out a trembling hand and touched his hairline where she had earlier thought she had glimpsed little knobs of bone . . . there . . . they were the infant nubs of antlers. Raum turned his head slightly and looked at her. "Eventually I hope and pray to take my place with the Horned Ones," he whispered. Faraday smiled at him. "You will," she said softly, "you will."

When she dropped her hand and turned her head back to the Grove she saw that nine of the Sacred Horned Ones had joined them, standing in a rough semicircle some paces away. All had the muscular bodies, virtually naked save for brief loin cloths, that supported the magnificent stag heads and antlers. Most had thick brown or black pelts that grew down over their shoulders and mid-way down their backs. One of the Horned Ones had a striking silver pelt instead of the brown or black. Liquid-black eyes, like Raum and Shra's, gazed at her. All exuded tremendous power.

The silver-haired Horned One stepped forward, holding his hands out in greeting. "Welcome Shra, welcome Faraday. And welcome again to Raum, who serves us so well in the Avarinheim and with the Mother." He leaned forward and rubbed cheeks with Raum, picked up Shra to do the same with her, then stepped over to Faraday.

"Tree Friend," he said. "We are pleased beyond telling that you are finally here." He grasped her hands and leaned close. His furred cheek brushed briefly against Faraday's cheek, and her skin thrilled at the touch.

"May I stay?" she asked, a little afraid at asking so much. She knew what he would answer.

"You will come back one day," he said gently, "when your work and life are done, and then, if you wish, you may stay." His voice and words held the certainty of a benediction.

Faraday's eyes filled with tears of joy. He would not lie to her.

"But before that day arrives you may visit whenever you wish."

"Thank you," she whispered, and the Horned One let go of her hands. He turned to one of his younger companions and took something from his hands.

"Tree Friend. We would give you a talisman that will help you to grow into the person you need to become, and will also help you find us again if you are nowhere near the Mother. Grow in strength and understanding, Daughter, and never forget your service to the Mother."

He handed Faraday a wide shallow bowl that looked as if it had grown into its present shape rather than having been carved into it. The wood had a deep reddish color, almost glowing under the night sky, and it felt warm in her hands.

"Thank you," Faraday said, awed by the honor of the gift, and just then a falling star blazed across the firmament above them.

The Horned One looked at Raum. "Time grows short, young brother. Go in peace. Take care of yourself and the little one. There are too few of you in these times of need." He bent back down to Shra. "Peace, little sister. Serve the Mother well, and learn how to sing to the seasons and the land. If you learn well, then perhaps it will be your voice that will make the difference."

The little girl nodded seriously. "Will," she whispered, and both Raum and the Horned One smiled affectionately at her.

"She will do well," the Horned One said, then turned a final time to Faraday. "Be true," he said, and touched her forehead, sending a jolt of power through her. "You will have to be."

Then he turned and, all at once, the clearing was bare save for Faraday, Raum and Shra.

"Come," said Raum quietly, "it is time to go."

This time the blackness could not save Timozel. He felt the mad hatred of the creature reaching through the blackness for him just before fierce, clawed hands seized his throat and started to pull him back into the iced cavern that the creature called home. "No escape," it whispered, "no escape. If you will not be my friend then you will have to serve me as others do." The power of the creature forced Timozel to his knees and for a minute he cowered there. A hand grasped his head and forced him to look up. The creature bent over him, yellow gobs of phlegm oozing down its protruding tongue and spattering on the ice floor. "Timozel," it whispered, drooling over the word, "what a pretty boy! Yes! You will serve me well." Timozel felt a force unlike anything he had ever experienced before compelling

*him to pledge his service to the foul being before him. He
was completely and utterly powerless to resist. Except . . .
"Can't!" he choked. "What?" the creature spat, its eyes
glowing red for a moment. "What does it mean—can't?"
"Can't," Timozel whispered with the last of the strength in
his body. "Already pledged my life . . . my service . . ."
The creature howled in fury, raising itself to its full height
and shaking its entire body in a frenzy of rage. Timozel,
still held tightly in its grasp, was flung about like a wet rag.
His muscles and tendons screamed with the abuse they
were receiving. The creature shrieked again, infuriated.
"Who? Who have you pledged your life and service to?"
Timozel shook his head weakly; this the creature's power
could not compel him to answer—to do so would break his
oath of protection to Faraday. The creature hissed in mad-
dened frustration. "Listen to me, you crawling piece of excrement, listen to this. You will promise to serve me if you
are released from your other vow! Well?" It started to twist
Timozel's head about at such an unnatural angle that Timozel could feel his spinal column crack with the strain. Red
spots floated before his eyes. He could feel the unnatural
compulsion building again within his body. His resistance
to the power of the creature faded. "Yes, I do so swear," he
whispered, hating himself more foully than he hated this
creature before him. "I do so swear. If I am released from
my current pledge of service then I will serve you before
any other." Gorgrael smiled. He knew he would have Timozel in the end. He indicated a shadow behind him. "The
Dark Man bears witness, Timozel. Your vow binds you to
Gorgrael. On the day that you are freed from your current
vows you will come to me." He held Timozel a heartbeat
longer then let him go.*

Gorgrael turned to the cloaked figure behind him. "Did you
set his feet on the dream paths to find me?"

He felt rather than saw the smile from the hooded man.
"Then thank you, *thank you!*"

The Dark Man inclined his head, accepting Gorgrael's gratitude. "It is going well," he said. "Very well."

"Will you stay awhile?" asked Gorgrael.

"No. No, you know that I have duties elsewhere. All will be well."

The cloaked figure before Gorgrael vanished.

As they rose through the emerald light it began to thicken about them, until in the last few paces, when they could just see the brilliance of the stars in the night sky, it thickened into water, and they burst coughing and choking through the surface of the Fernbrake Lake about fifteen paces from the shore. Raum and Faraday were just tall enough to feel the bottom with their toes, and they carried Shra above them to the shore. Jack and Yr were waiting anxiously with blankets and wrapped them up as tightly as they could against the predawn ice.

Faraday hugged the blanket to her, feeling the wooden bowl press against the skin of her stomach.

All three of them slept for the rest of the morning, exhausted by the events of the predawn hours. When they finally rose, Raum and Shra immediately made preparations to leave for the Avarinheim.

Faraday hugged them both. "Take care. Do not let those Plains Dwellers snatch you."

Raum laughed at her. "We travel only at night, and few humans can catch sight of us at night.

"Listen to her, Raum," Yr said, seriously. "The Axe-Wielders will be in Smyrton sometime within the next few weeks on their way to Sigholt and Gorkenfort. Take care as you pass by on your way to the Avarinheim."

Jack, Yr and Faraday left for their camp in Pig Gully later that afternoon, arriving some time during the night. All seemed as they had left it; the mule and the pigs were close by and safe, Timozel lay asleep in his blankets. Yr slipped out of her clothes and snuggled down beside him, removing the enchantment. "He will wake as normal in the morning," she whispered. Jack and Faraday nodded and retired to their own blankets. Their sleep was sound that night. All seemed well.

31

Smyrton

On the first day of Frost-month, almost three weeks after traversing the passes in the Bracken Ranges, the BattleAxe rode at the head of his column into the large Skarabost village of Smyrton.

He was still on schedule to reach Gorkenfort at the beginning of Snow-month, but only just. He had been forced to slow the Axe-Wielders' advance through Skarabost; in places the horses had foundered in the deepening snow drifts. But there had been other frustrations and delays. The direct route from the Bracken Ranges to Smyrton would have taken Axis uncomfortably close to Earl Isend's estates in the southern part of the province. Although he knew the Earl was still in Carlon, Axis had taken the Axe-Wielders almost a day out of their way to avoid the estates. Although the grief he felt over Faraday's death was less keen than it had been, his guilt was no less painful. Axis could not bring himself to explain to Faraday's two elder sisters how he had managed to lose their mother and sister. So he led the Axe-Wielders a day to the east.

In itself that day's detour should not have caused any problems, but it brought them into a village that had, over the previous several months, been terrorised by a vicious gang of bandits some sixty strong. It had taken the Axe-Wielders two days to deal with the bandits, but, when added to the delays caused by the weather, it meant that Axis reached Smyrton close to six days later than he had wanted.

At least Gorgrael had not struck again since the night he had rolled his cloud of fear over the Axe-Wielders. The weather over Skarabost, while worsening toward an unnaturally early winter, had not had the feel of evil enchantment of the storm at the Ancient Barrows or the roiling cloud outside Arcen. His reaction to Gorgrael's cloud had reassured Axis. He had dealt with it without recourse to the strange music or songs that still haunted him from time to time.

As Axis rode into Smyrton, music and song were the last things on his mind. Smyrton was a village like any other village in the Seagrass Plains of Skarabost except that it was, perhaps, slightly larger than most. The lower taxes of the outpost regions attracted many settlers to this village, despite its proximity to the Forbidden Valley. Even in this distant outpost of civilization, the open fields that surrounded the village were well-tended and the road into the village were well-repaired and cleared of snow. The few villagers out in the snow-covered fields in the late afternoon waved excitedly as the long column of Axe-Wielders rode by.

There were sixty or seventy houses in the village; each with an ample garden containing vegetables and fruit trees as well as chickens and the occasional pig. Whitewashed picket fences kept stray children and animals from straying onto the roadway. Most of the village homes lay clustered about the well-built Worship Hall where the good people of Smyrton met every Seventh Day for the Service of the Plough. As the largest and most solidly built building in the village, the Worship Hall also served as courthouse, village hall and place of refuge should Smyrton come under attack. Close behind it stood the home of the local Plough-Keeper, and to one side a well-tended graveyard. A large market square was the only other notable feature of the village, and Axis wondered as he rode into the square what life must be like for country folk in these isolated regions.

There was a small knot of visibly excited people standing in the market square to greet them. The Plough-Keeper, clad in a flowing habit that wrapped about his legs in the stiff wind, was instantly recognisable at the head of the group. His fat cheeks were red; whether from the wind or from excitement, Axis knew not. Axis reined Belaguez to a halt in front of him, unable to resist the impulse to touch his heels to the stallion's flanks and make him slide to a halt in a half-rear so Axis could leap down to the ground in a fluid movement. Most of the village folk took two or three rapid steps back to avoid the stallion, but Axis noted that one woman, unusually striking for a country wife, had stood her ground and was now gazing at Axis with something approaching disdain.

Axis saluted the Plough-Keeper. "Brother Hagen, Brother-Leader Jayme sends personal regards and thanks for the reports you have been sending the Brotherhood of the Seneschal. They have been most valuable."

Brother Hagen beamed with pleasure and returned Axis' bow. "I am overcome that the Brother-Leader should send the BattleAxe and so many Axe-Wielders to investigate." Brother Hagen's smile faltered a little as he gazed anxiously at the number of men still arriving. "But I am unsure that our village can provide adequate hospitality for so many of your men, BattleAxe."

Axis smiled reassuringly at the man. No doubt he thought the Axe-Wielders would eat the entire village to the ground before they were through. "We will make camp well away from the village, good Brother. Be assured that all we will need from you is water from your well. We travel with our own provisions."

Brother Hagen looked visibly relieved. "Then might I

invite your good person to share my humble abode, BattleAxe? We cannot provide your entire command with
comfortable beds, but at least you and your officers will
sleep well."

"Myself and my officers will share the hard ground with
our Axe-Wielders, Brother Hagen." Axis caught a glimmer
of surprise across the face of the woman standing to one
side of Hagen. "But I would be glad for the opportunity to
share your table this evening. There are matters we should
discuss, I think." He did not want to offend the man by entirely refusing his hospitality.

"Excellent! Ah, BattleAxe, might I present some of
these Goodpeople?"

Axis smiled politely. Might as well get the introductions
over with as soon as possible.

Brother Hagen motioned two middle-aged men forth.
"BattleAxe, this is Goodman Hordley," a sandy-haired
stout fellow nodded, "and Goodman Garland," his companion, a bald-headed man with a pockmarked complexion
nodded at Axis, "the two senior men of the village. Their
Goodwives," Axis nodded politely at the two beaming,
plump women. A tall, thin man was introduced as Miller
Powle and the equally tall and thin young man by his side
as his son, Wainwald. Hagen paused and Axis glanced
across at the woman who had regarded him so disdainfully.
Most of the country folk of Skarabost were of fair coloring
with sandy or light brown hair, but this woman had the exotic features of a Nors woman with thick, raven hair waving back from a pale face, framing smoky blue eyes. She
wore the usual plain woollen dress of most country
women, although hers was of a soft blue shade that
matched her eyes, covered by a rough black-weave, full-
length apron.

"Ah," Hagen looked a little embarrassed. "This is my
daughter, Azhure."

Axis could not keep the surprise from his face. The
Seneschal generally encouraged their brothers to avoid
women and the responsibilities of a family so that they

could concentrate entirely on their duties in the Seneschal. Those that did marry, mostly country Plough-Keepers like Hagen, generally married one of the local folk. But from the look of Azhure, Hagen had gone out of his way to find an extraordinarily exotic wife. The Nors people were known for their somewhat relaxed attitude to morals and community standards, and few of the conservative northern Acharites would welcome a Nors woman into their homes, despite their considerable beauty. And Nors people rarely came this far north.

Axis realized he was staring at the woman. He turned back to Hagen and the other villagers. "I am pleased to meet you, Goodpeople," he said. "My name is Axis Rivkahson and this," indicating Belial, "is my lieutenant, Belial."

On the long ride north Axis had decided to accept the one gift Faraday had given him—the first glimmerings of pride in his birthright. From now on he would bear the metronymic of Rivkahson as a badge of honor.

Now he had surprised both Hagen and Azhure, although none of the other Goodpeople blinked at the use of the name. As a member of the Brotherhood of the Seneschal Hagen would know of the scandal attached to the BattleAxe, and presumably he had told Azhure as well. Axis held Hagen's eyes until the man blushed and came to his senses. "Ah, um, BattleAxe," said Hagen, obviously discomforted, "perhaps your good self and Belial would care to join me in my home to share some ale while we discuss, ah, recent developments?"

Axis narrowed his eyes at the man. Was his nervousness simply due to the presence of the Axe-Wielders, or was there something else?

Axis nodded his acceptance and turned and shouted for Arne. "Take the Axe-Wielders a good distance out of the village, Arne, and set up camp. Make sure you cause no damage to fences or outlying buildings. I'll join you later." Axis handed Belaguez's reins to a young Axe-Wielder, giving the horse a well-earned pat, and turned back to Hagen, pulling his leather gloves off. "Your offer of a draft of ale is deeply appreciated, Brother Hagen. Shall we go?"

Goodmen Hordley and Garland joined them inside the Brother's comfortable home. Although it followed the usual one-roomed design of most country homes, Brother Hagen and his family obviously enjoyed a slightly better standard of living than most country folk. Well-made furniture, and a goodly quantity of it, stood about the house, and the internal walls had even been plastered. The curtains and wall hangings reminded Axis of the designs he had seen for sale in the market places of Ysbadd in Nor, and he glanced again at Azhure as she poured foaming ale from a ceramic jug for the men sitting down at the well-crafted table in the center of the room. His eyes narrowed idly. She was of an age to be married yet she wore no ring.

"Is your mother not home at present, Azhure?"

Her eyes flashed a little at his casual use of her name; although she loathed the title, the use of 'Goodmistress' would have been considered polite. She hid her dislike carefully and smiled at this arrogant Carlonite. "My mother ran off with a traveling pedlar when I was five, BattleAxe. She obviously found the pace of life in Smyrton a little slow for her blood," she finished sweetly as she handed him a mug of ale.

Hagen looked both mortified and furious at the same time and Axis bit the inside of his cheek to keep from laughing. Artor! but Azhure must be a handful for the Plough-Keeper, he thought, amused. One could only hope that the bed sport with her mother had been worth the daughter. He noticed that Belial had almost choked on a mouthful of ale in his efforts to avoid laughing out loud. He took a draft and looked back at Hagen.

"My sympathies, Brother Hagen. The price these pedlars demand for their tin pots can sometimes be over-high," he said blandly, unable to refrain from commenting on the issue. Belial made a sound suspiciously like a chuckle into his mug. Hagen's color deepened and he angrily waved Azhure back into a corner by the fireplace. Axis quickly changed the subject. "Have you seen any other of the strange creatures you reported were coming out of the For-bidden Valley?"

Again the mood changed abruptly. Azhure's face tight-ened completely and she turned away to jab angrily at the fire with an iron poker. Goodmen Hordley and Garland both leaned forward, their eyes bright with excitement, barely restraining themselves from speech. Hagen forgot his embarrassment of a moment previously, and smiled in-dulgently at the BattleAxe.

"Why, yes, BattleAxe. Indeed we have. In fact, just four nights ago we managed to capture two of the frightful crea-tures as they tried to reenter the Forbidden Valley. We have them now, caged and guarded in the cellars of the Worship Hall. How fortuitous that you should arrive in time for their execution tomorrow morning."

32

The Prisoners

Axis stared at the man, his mug of ale raised, forgotten, halfway to his mouth. "You've what?" he barked in his astonishment. Belial put his own mug down carefully on the table, all traces of amusement wiped from his eyes.

Hagen looked well pleased with the reaction his news had caused. "Eight of the village men were out late checking the rabbit traps when they ran straight into the pair, trying to cower behind Goodman Harland's haystack."

Harland nodded vigorously. "It was a battle worthy of a bard in King Priam's court," he said proudly, omitting to mention that he and his family had hid underneath their bedstead until it was all over.

Hagen glared at him, then turned back to Axis. "The men trusted in Artor to save them from the Forbidden's dark magic, BattleAxe. We have brave men in this village."

In truth, the men had run in terror when they first discovered the Forbidden behind the haystack, fearing their dark magic, and one of the older men had tripped and dropped his lantern. The burning oil set the haystack ablaze and, in the ensuing panic, the Forbidden tried to escape but fell themselves. The village men would have skewered them then and there with their pitchforks had not Hagen, alerted by the fuss, arrived and ordered that the senseless man and the screaming child be imprisoned in the Worship Hall cellar. "He might tell us if there are other Forbidden about," Hagen had said. "Don't worry, Artor will protect us from his evil sorcery."

Hagen's words proved correct and, in the days since the capture, the villagers not only became increasingly bold about their prisoners but also reworked the story of their capture until it was their bravery that had captured the creatures, not a combination of panic and ill-luck.

Axis nodded impatiently. "Yes, yes. I'm sure your men are extraordinary." Two against eight did not seem a great battle to him. "Now, let me see these creatures." He almost pushed his chair over in his haste to rise. Belial was already hovering by the door.

Hagen rose more slowly. "We have interrogated them extensively, BattleAxe, but have learned nothing. The beasts refused to answer any of our questions. We will all be relieved when we can put them to the torch tomorrow."

Even in his haste to get to the door, Axis noted that Azhure had blanched at the mention of the burning.

Hagen led the group outside and across the courtyard to the Worship Hall. The back door was unlocked and Axis glanced questioningly at the Plough-Keeper.

"Be assured we have them under close guard, BattleAxe. They will not escape."

The Hall was empty of people and their steps echoed across the stone slab floor as Hagen took them across to a stairwell and then down to the cellar. Axis, his heart racing, almost pushed the brother in his impatience to reach the bottom of the steps.

But well before he reached the cellar a sickening stench caused him to choke momentarily. "What?" he began to ask, but Hagen was leading him off the stairs and across a large windowless cellar. The rear quarter of the cellar, partitioned off with sturdy metal bars and normally used as a lock-up for drunken husbands, was now being put to a more vile purpose. The stench that came from the barred cell was overwhelming, and Axis had to cover his nose and mouth until he acclimatized himself to the smell of old blood, stale urine and feces. Every time Axis encountered unnecessary cruelty it sickened him—and he could smell it now in this cell.

When he finally managed to look at the cell, he was not surprised to see that Ogden and Veremund had managed to find their way down there before himself. Hagen was obviously overjoyed to see two of his fellow brothers and exclaimed with delight as he hurried over to them, pointing into the cell as if showing off prized pets. Axis could see that both Ogden and Veremund were white with anger.

Axis finally gathered himself and looked more closely— and within the space of a heartbeat he completely and utterly lost his temper. Huddled in a corner, as far as they could get from the iron bars, were a dark man and a small female child of alien although attractive features. They were naked, filthy and covered with bruises and abrasions. Looking briefly at the long iron bars that the two village lads, acting as guards, held, Axis realized that Hagen's "interrogation" probably consisted simply of poking and prodding the two until pain made them confess to whatever crime Hagen had in mind. Obviously no one had been inside to clean the cell, or to offer the two the simple decency of a bucket for their bodily needs. Sores running across their lips and down their faces suggested they had not received any water in the four days since the good people of Smyrton had imprisoned them in this iron-barred chamber of horrors.

For an instant the strange man's eyes, full of velvet darkness, met Axis' through the iron bars of his cage.

"You curdled clot of whore's piss," Axis snarled, reaching over to Hagen with one hand and slamming him back against the bars of the cell. "In whose name do you dare to treat *anyone* like this?"

Hagen went as white as the underbelly of a fish. The BattleAxe's hands had him pinned so viciously by the throat that he could hardly breathe, and the BattleAxe was leaning over him with a look on his face that suggested Hagen was not long for this world. Blood trickled down his neck where his head had been pushed roughly against the iron bars. He could feel the hilt of Axis' sword pressing painfully into his ample belly.

"What?" he gulped, unable to comprehend why the BattleAxe had reacted like this. The two village lads on guard stood helplessly to one side, stopped from trying to pry the BattleAxe off their Plough-Keeper by his lieutenant, who looked almost as furious as the BattleAxe himself.

"In Artor's name," the Plough-Keeper finally managed to whisper. "They are filth, beasts, there is no point in treating them as if they understood what was going on. This is all they deserve."

Axis' face was white with fury. Did Artor call for such treatment of prisoners? "*You* are filth, Brother Hagen," he spat at the terrified man and, seizing him by his hair and the cloth of his habit, hurled him against the far wall of the cellar where he crashed senseless to the floor. The Goodmen Hordley and Garland cowered back against the steps of the stairwell, terrified that Axis would attack them next, but the woman Azhure stood her ground, retaining her composure before Axis' fierce stare. "I have brought water and food every day for the past four days," she said calmly, indicating a bucket and tray of food standing unused by the foot of the stairwell. "But Hagen would not let me minister to them."

"Then get the water now," Axis said gruffly, and turned on his heel to the two guards. Both of them backed up to the wall, patently horrified. What had they done wrong?

"Belial, will you get the keys to the lock off these craven deformities that think to call themselves men?" Axis said tightly. "I do not trust myself to get too close to them."

The guard holding the keys voided in sheer terror when

Belial snatched the keys from his hand. Belial turned and spun them through the air to Axis, their eyes meeting in complete understanding as Axis caught the keys. Whatever either might have thought about the people in this cell, no one ever treated prisoners like this, nor did anyone *ever* imprison a child that could barely walk.

Axis turned and slipped the key inside the lock; he felt Azhure at his shoulder with the bucket of water. Goodman Garland gasped in horror as the lock swung free. "They are dangerous, BattleAxe! Do not go in there!"

Axis turned and caught Garland's eyes. "You do not know what danger really means, Garland," he said quietly but menacingly. Garland paled and shut up.

Ogden grabbed Axis' arm. "Axis, I beg of you, let them go!" he whispered, his face completely distraught. Forgetting that Azhure was right behind him and within easy listening distance, Axis grabbed Ogden's hand and threw it off his arm. "That's hardly a sentiment the Seneschal would approve of is it, *Brother* Ogden?"

The woman frowned at the exchange, but the next moment Axis had thrown open the door of the cell, leaving his sword and axe by the door, and was walking slowly across the filthy space toward the pair huddled in the corner. Azhure slipped in behind him, and Belial stepped up to guard the door.

Axis turned and caught Azhure's arm as they were halfway across the cell. "Wait here," he said quietly, and took the bucket of water from her.

Axis hesitated before he moved over to the prisoners. He had always wondered how he would react to the Forbidden. Now, instead of the anger or fear that the Seneschal had taught him, Axis found himself regarding these two with sympathy and, even more confusingly, empathy. Looking into the great dark eyes of the man, Axis discovered that he was incapable of hating or even fearing this man.

Raum watched as Axis approached. He had recognized the black uniform emblazoned with the twin axes as soon as the man had stepped into the cellar. That uniform had not changed in over a thousand years, and every Avar was raised to fear and loathe it. Yet, just when Raum was about to commend himself and Shra to the Sacred Grove for eternity, everything had exploded in a direction that he could never have foreseen. The BattleAxe had seized the Plough-Keeper and had half-murdered him in a rage that would have done a Horned One proud. And now, after Raum and Shra had endured four days of unimaginable terror, pain and thirst, the BattleAxe had disarmed himself and was approaching with a bucket of water in his hands and sympathy in his eyes. Raum hugged Shra to his chest protectively. She had been unconscious for the past twelve hours and was now scarcely breathing.

Axis put the bucket on the floor and squatted down in front of the man.

"Do you understand me?" he said quietly. For a moment Raum did nothing, then he nodded tiredly.

Axis regarded the man. He was strong, very strong, and of strange features, but Axis could see nothing about him to warrant the tales of cruelty and evil that the Seneschal told about these men. What creature of evil could hold a child so lovingly? He remembered some of what Ogden had said about these people. "You are Avar?" he asked.

Raum's eyes widened a little. Then he nodded again, a little more strongly this time. Axis' eyes shifted to the girl. She had been brutally treated by the Smyrton villagers, and Axis could see that she was near death. Her breathing was shallow and irregular, gurgling through fluid-filled lungs, and her fingernails and lips had a bluish tinge. His throat constricted, and compassion for the little girl consumed him. Tears filled his eyes.

"Please," he said very quietly so that none but Raum or Azhure could hear him, "let me hold her."

After an instant's hesitation, Raum held out the little girl's limp body. She would need the BattleAxe's help if she were to survive the day. Axis gathered her gently into his arms. After a moment he dipped his hand into the bucket of water by his side and washed some of the dirt from her face.

Then softly, very, very softly, he began to sing for her. It was a strange song, almost with no melody, filled with breathy catches and lilts, but extraordinarily compelling and beautiful. It shocked Raum to the core of his being; he had heard this Song sung only once before in his life, and then it had been no human that had sung it. Only the most powerful of Icarii Enchanters could sing this enchantment; yet even they were normally too weak to make it work. He sank back against the wall of the cell, his eyes wide and unbelieving. Not even the Horned Ones could do this, and certainly no human could!

Azhure stood puzzled. What was the BattleAxe doing to the child?

Ogden and Veremund, however, could feel if not hear the Song. Tears welled in their eyes. "Oh dear one!" Veremund whispered almost inaudibly, "Save her!"

Raum had no eyes for anyone save Shra and Axis. Axis' voice began to grow in intensity, though not in volume, and then . . . then . . . Shra began to stir. Tiny, jerky actions at first, then stronger movements as the child visibly squirmed in the BattleAxe's arms. He stopped singing, stared quietly at the child for a moment, then looked up and smiled into Raum's eyes. "She lives," he said, genuine surprise in his voice. Raum had the strangest feeling that the BattleAxe did not quite know what he had done.

Raum held out his arms for Shra, but the BattleAxe continued to hold her tight. She was awake now and staring at Axis curiously, then she reached out and touched his beard. "I can get her out of the cell for the night," Axis said very softly to Raum, "but I am not sure that I can save your lives. I am bound by my oaths as BattleAxe to the Seneschal to destroy the Forbidden. And . . ." He frowned. Why was he even thinking about trying to save them? They were *Forbidden!*

Raum nodded. He understood that the BattleAxe of the

Seneschal was the last person in the land who would try to save them. Yet . . . what had he done for Shra? No BattleAxe could have sung that Song. He leaned out a hand and briefly ran his fingertips along Axis' cheek, ignoring Belial's sudden movement of concern. "I understand," he whispered, "but I do not know why one with the soul of an Icarii Enchanter wears the black and this badge of destruction. Surely the Icarii hate as much as we do? But I thank you for the Song that you sang for Shra." As he dropped his hand from Axis' face he briefly touched the twin axes on Axis' breast.

Axis' face hardened at the man's words and he abruptly stood up, fighting desperately not to think about what they meant. "Azhure," he said, turning and handing the child to her. "Look after her for the night." He glanced back down at the man lying amid the filth of the cell and then turned and walked from the cell. "Belial, get two of our men and get this place cleaned up!" He glared at the Plough-Keeper, who had regained consciousness, ignored Ogden and Veremund, and then strode out of the cellar without saying another word.

33

The Forbidden Valley

Azhure took the child back to the house she shared with the man she called her father. She was still bewildered, though she felt little sympathy for Hagen; the man was a coward and a fool, and cruel besides. She had hated and feared him ever since she could remember. His cruelty had driven her mother away and he had since made her own life unbearable. The violence the BattleAxe had dealt to Hagen had been only a fraction of the violence Hagen had meted out to her over the past twenty years. Up until this afternoon Azhure had included the Axe-Wielders in the hatred she bore for the entire Seneschal, a sentiment rivalled only by her hatred for Hagen. Now, a little uncomfortably, Azhure had to admit to a small amount of respect for the BattleAxe and his lieutenant. They had treated the man and child with both respect and sympathy.

As she cleaned and dressed the child Azhure continued to think, growing more and more excited. One of her secret dreams, held ever since her mother ran away, was that one day she, too, would find the opportunity to escape. Tonight seemed the perfect time. The village was distracted by the arrival of the Axe-Wielders and the altercation between Hagen and the BattleAxe. Azhure would not only escape but save both man and child in doing so. For the past few years she had been trying to persuade GoldFeather that she could be trusted to help with the Avar children. She wanted to help in whatever way she was able. Now she could.

Azhure had stumbled upon the secret of GoldFeather some twelve years before when she was fifteen. Driven by the need to escape Hagen, she would often slip out of the house in the middle of the night and sit watching the Fortress Ranges and the dark shadows of the forest beyond. One night she had caught the furtive shadows of people moving out of the Forbidden Valley and had followed the Acharite woman she had since come to know as Gold-Feather as she and one of the young Avar men took two children stealthily past Smyrton and into the Seagrass Plains. Over the next year or so she tracked and followed the woman again, until finally she made one noise too many and the woman had heard her.

Azhure had been lucky to escape with her life. The Avar man with GoldFeather became frighteningly angry, but GoldFeather had persuaded him against any action and had then reassured a frightened Azhure. They had later formed an intense friendship and, over the following years, they met maybe three times a year, and talked through the night. GoldFeather would tell her a little of the life of the Avar people, but, surprisingly, she never wanted to hear any tales of life in Achar. "My old life is dead and gone, Azhure," she would smile sadly, "and I have started a new life now." Azhure never told anyone in Smyrton of her new friend and, sometimes, when she was feeling very lonely, Azhure would pretend to herself that GoldFeather was her long lost mother.

Now Azhure smiled at the little girl she held in her arms. She was bruised and cut in several places, but she looked much better than she had. She gave the child something to eat, and was relieved when the little girl placidly took the food and water she was given. Azhure cuddled her close as the girl ate. One day she hoped to have a child of her own, but not if it meant one of the village oafs giving it to her! No, Azhure was going to escape this village and lead a life of adventure and purpose. She would find a hero to father her children. She smiled. She had absolutely no doubts that a hero would turn up precisely when needed.

She heard raised voices outside. It was Hagen, now recovered from the crack across his pate, and the BattleAxe (so *he* was the bastard son of the Princess Rivkah!). They were arguing about the Avar man. Finally the arguing ended and Azhure heard Axis stalk off. Hagen entered the house and glared at Azhure but simply went and lay down. Perhaps his head pained him. Azhure breathed a sigh of relief and relaxed her arms about the child. She knew she was lucky not to have received a beating for her earlier remark about her mother. She had only just recovered from the three broken ribs he had given her two months ago.

As Hagen began to snore Azhure sat by the fire, rocking the child to sleep, and planned.

She moved during the dark hours of the night. In the hours before dawn, when the human body and spirit were at their lowest ebb.

First she wrapped the sleeping child in a warm blanket, whispering to her to be quiet, then grabbed a cloak herself. She would have liked to take some food with her, but she dared not take the risk that it would weigh her down.

As Azhure bent down to lace her boots her nervous excitement grew.

Courage, Azhure, she berated herself. Another hour at the latest and you and the Avar man can be racing for the Forbidden Valley. And then you can spend the rest of your years wandering with GoldFeather. Free from Hagen.

Azhure swore silently as one of the boot laces stubbornly refused to tie. She had the child tucked under one arm and, combined with her nervousness, it made her fumble-fingered. Quickly laying the sleeping child on the floor, she began to relace the offending boot.

"Bitch!" Hagen grunted behind her and grabbed the child.

"No!" Azhure cried hoarsely, too frightened to scream. She tried to turn around, but overbalanced and fell to the floor.

Hagen threw the now crying child on the bed. Stepping over to the table he dealt Azhure a vicious kick in the ribs on the way.

"No!" Azhure wheezed, doubling up on her side, trying to draw breath. Hagen had kicked her in the very ribs he broke two months previously; now it felt like fire flickered up and down her ribcage. Her face contorted in agony, Azhure squinted toward Hagen.

He stood at the table, ignoring the wails of the child, riffling through the plates and cutlery that Azhure had washed earlier and had yet to put away.

"No," she whimpered. "No!" She had to move, she had to do something, but the pain in her ribs crippled her and she could hardly draw breath, let alone get to her feet.

Hagen grunted again, his hand clutching at a bone-handled knife.

"The Forbidden child dies now," he said conversationally, lifting the knife to inspect its edge.

He spent hours each week honing that knife.

Azhure knew how sharp it was.

He lifted the knife . . .

Azhure groaned and closed her eyes.

The flames cracked and popped.

She rolled over so that she was lying on her belly and pressed her face into the stone floor, desperate to escape both the scene before her and the memories fighting to break free.

The smell was terrible.

Hagen stepped over Azhure's still body and took another step toward the child on the bed.

The little girl. Frightened. Watching. Unable to escape.

He was not worried about Azhure. He had beaten her

into submission enough over the years to know that she would not act now. He had trained her well.

"Why not kill me?" she screamed.

Hagen reached the bed and began to pull the little girl's outer clothes apart.

"Because I like to see you suffer," he replied.

Azhure finally managed to rise to her knees, but she was still bent double with pain and fear. Not now. Not again!

"Shall I check the bandages this morning? See what's there?"

Hagen raised the knife.

Hagen raised the knife . . .

Azhure raised her hands to her head, rocking backwards and forward, keening under her breath. Not again! Not again!

This time she could stop it. This time *she* could save the child, and in doing so, save herself.

. . . and dug.

Azhure launched herself forward, grabbing frantically for the hem of Hagen's robe.

He heard her movement and half turned, the knife still raised, his face masked in rage.

Her grasping fingers caught at the hem of his robe, but the material slipped through.

Howling in anger now, Hagen raised his foot to stamp on Azhure's fingers, the knife glinting wickedly in his hand.

With the last of her strength Azhure grabbed his foot and twisted, took a desperate breath, and twisted again.

Hagen teetered backwards and forward, his face surprised rather than angry. Then, with a small "Oh!" of utter astonishment that Azhure would actually do this to him, he toppled to the floor.

Azhure rolled out of the way and scrambled to her feet, one hand clutching her ribs. But her breath was coming more easily now and she stood ready, sure that Hagen would leap to his feet with a savage roar, intent on her final murder.

But Hagen lay still, his right arm twisted under his body. The Avar girl's wails began to subside and Azhure quickly checked her. She was unharmed, but Hagen had come so close . . . so close . . .

Azhure took a quick, deep breath, fighting to forget the brief images that had flashed through her mind.

That never happened!

"No," she whispered, her mind slipping dangerously close to the edge of madness. "That never happened. Forget it, Azhure. Forget it. It was your imagination." In her battle to disremember the horror, Azhure unconsciously murmured the words that had been shouted at her for so many years. "Wicked child. That's what you are. Wicked."

She finally slammed the door on the memories, composing herself with great effort, and stared at Hagen. Had he knocked himself unconscious in the fall? Azhure hoped so. If he was unconscious then she and the child would still be able to scramble free.

Slowly, lest the man only be pretending, Azhure bent down and touched him quickly on the shoulder. He didn't react. She shoved him and leapt back. But still Hagen didn't move.

"Oh, no," Azhure whispered as she watched his still body, her stomach starting to churn. "Oh, no!"

On the bed Shra rolled over and sat up, her tear-streaked face curious.

Biting her tongue to stop herself from gagging, Azhure seized Hagen by the shoulder and rolled him over, grunting at the flare of pain in her ribs as she did so.

He was dead.

Everything told Azhure that: the spreading pool of blood beneath him; his staring eyes, comically surprised; his hand still grasped about the hilt of the knife, its blade stuck its entire length in his lower abdomen. As she watched, his dead hand slowly unclenched and slid to his side, hitting the floor with a sickening thud.

Azhure turned away and retched. Shra stared, then slid down from the bed, toddling over to the body. Almost overbalancing on her plump legs, she squatted down and rested both hands in the pool of blood.

"Azhure," she lisped and Azhure looked back, stunned to see the child with both her hands swimming in blood.

"No!" she cried and snatched the child from beside Hagen's body. What did she think she was doing?

Then the child did something even more strange. She lifted one hand to Azhure's forehead and ran her fat little fingers down the woman's face, leaving three trails of blood.

"Accepted," she said clearly. "Accepted."

Azhure sat trembling at the table for a very long time, the child in her lap, staring at Hagen's body.

She had killed him. She had *killed* him. The words ran through her mind over and over. Murder. There was no other way to dress it up.

And every time *that* thought ran through her head a wave of sickness enveloped her. Murder.

She had not wanted to kill him. She had simply wanted to protect the child and escape from him.

Eventually Azhure roused herself. She could not stay here now. The village people would undoubtedly lynch her the moment someone discovered the body. Then they would burn the Avar man and the little girl.

And Azhure would not have escaped Hagen at all.

Hurriedly she wiped her face and the child's hands, leaving the blood-streaked towel lying on the table. "Come," she whispered to the child. She rewrapped the girl, adjusted her own cloak and left the house she had called home for almost twenty-eight years behind her without a backward glance.

Outside Azhure recovered the cloak she had secreted for the Avar man and walked to the rear door of the Worship Hall.

Could she go through with the rest of the plan, when the initial stages had gone so disastrously wrong?

"I must," she murmured determinedly, "if I am to save this girl and the man. We are all dead if we stay."

She forced herself to think of what she needed to do. How many guards had been left to watch over the Avar man? She stepped down the stairs to the cell, making no effort to move silently. She did not want to appear to be sneaking.

When she walked into the cellar, the Avar girl-child held tightly in her arms, Azhure fixed a bright smile on her face. She breathed a quick sigh of relief. Only one man sat in here on guard, but as that one man turned to look at her Azhure's relief turned into dismay. It was Belial, the BattleAxe's lieutenant. Azhure hid her dismay by widening her smile. She rather liked Belial, he had a good-humored face yet acted decisively when needed. He might not be a hero, but he had kind hazel eyes that now crinkled at her in some puzzlement. She did not want to hurt Belial, but she would do what she had to do to save the Avar man.

"What are you doing here at this time of night?" he asked, rising to his feet, puzzled but not anxious. Good.

Azhure made a face and smiled at the child. "She wanted to see her father, and fretted at me for so long that I had to bring her." Azhure made her face fall, and she leaned a little closer to whisper to Belial. "And tomorrow morning . . . well, I couldn't refuse her one last hour spent with him, could I?"

Belial relaxed a little. Of all the Smyrton villagers in the cellar this afternoon Azhure had shown the most courage and independence; besides, she was very attractive. Belial was normally a little shy around beautiful women, but Azhure did not flaunt her beauty nor seek to use it to intimidate. He patted the child a little awkwardly on her head. "Poor little girl."

"Yes, I know." Azhure simply wanted to get this over and done with. She could see the Avar man begin to stir behind the bars. He had been given water to wash and was

warmly dressed against the night cold. Good. Azhure gritted her teeth a little, this was going to be hard. Courage,
girl, she repeated to herself. You have already killed once
tonight, and that a man you called father. Surely disabling
this stranger should not be a problem.

But Hagen had beaten her and abused her. Belial had
done nothing but treat her with kindness and respect and
now displayed touching tenderness toward the child in her
arms. Azhure stretched her smile until she thought she
must look like a grinning idiot. "Do you think perhaps . . . ?"
she said, tilting her head toward the door of the cell.

"Oh, of course," Belial smiled at her. "Let me get the
keys."

Azhure slipped the child down onto the floor and followed Belial across the cellar. As he bent down to pick the
keys up from the stool where he had left them, Azhure
pulled a fist-sized rock from the deep pocket in her black
apron. She raised it high above her head, her hand trembling, and, just as Belial was starting to rise, she brought it
down, dealing Belial a heavy blow to the back of his skull.
He twisted as he fell, his eyes registering a moment's surprise before they rolled up into his head and he collapsed
unmoving on the stone floor. Azhure stared at him for a
moment, unable to believe she had actually hit him. She
dropped the stone beside Belial's body and started to
shake, raising her hands to her face. What had she done?

"Quick!" a voice hissed behind her. "The keys!"

She turned and saw the Avar man standing by the cell
door, his eyes intense. "The keys!" he repeated. Azhure
reached across the floor to where they had fallen and slid
them over to the Avar man. He had the door open in an instant. He picked the child up and grabbed Azhure's arm.
"Come," he said, his voice quieter now, "you must come
with me. You know that your friends will kill you too,
now."

Azhure nodded and stood, her legs still weak with
shock. She glanced one more time at Belial, hoping he

wasn't dead. "Sorry," she whispered, then the Avar man was pulling her toward the stairs.

Axis could not sleep. He had tossed and turned in his bedroll, listening to the sounds of the night, until finally he decided that there was no use pretending he was going to sleep and rolled out of his blankets, slipped into his clothes, strapped on his weapon belt and headed into the night.

He nodded to the perimeter guards as he passed them. He still felt troubled by the events of the afternoon. The condition of the Avar man and child had appalled him. He had seen death and agony many times on the battlefield, but never before had he seen such wanton cruelty. And all in the name of the Seneschal, all in the name of Artor and the Way of the Plough. Axis had been repelled by the blood lust in the villagers' eyes, and now, as he was walking through the crisp cold air, he was repelled by the thought of the sight he would witness this morning.

He cursed himself as he wandered down the pathway approaching the Worship Hall. He needed to talk with Belial to calm his nerves.

The moment he descended into the cellar he knew what had happened. The cell door yawned wide and Belial lay sprawled in an unmoving heap over by the far wall. Axis crossed the cellar in five strides and gently rolled Belial over. He was still breathing, but he had a huge lump on the back of his head. Whoever had hit him had done a good job.

And Axis thought he knew who might have done it.

Axis took the stairs out of the cellar three at a time and ran the distance between the Worship Hall and Hagen's house in the space of six heartbeats. He burst through the door without bothering to knock. Hagen lay in a pool of blood beside the bed, a knife sticking out of his belly. A bloodied towel lay on the table; and Azhure and the Avar girl were nowhere to be seen. Axis cursed and checked the man's body—it was cool—and Axis cursed again.

He ran outside again and quickly orientated himself under the early morning sky. Azhure and the Avar man would have run for the Forbidden Valley . . . and Arne had set up the Axe-Wielders' camp on the opposite side of the village. There was no time to rouse their support, and Axis refused to consider rousing the Smyrton villagers. The Forbidden Valley was unpassable to horses, and the Avar and Azhure must be close to it by now. Axis cursed yet again, low and vicious, as he turned and sprinted out of the village, heading northeast. Although he had tried to save their lives, Axis thrust aside his previous sympathy for their plight and any thought of simply letting them escape. Hagen was dead and, even more damning in Axis' eyes, Belial lay assaulted and helpless after both he and Axis had trusted Azhure. His bonds and loyalties to the Seneschal demanded that the BattleAxe take revenge for the death of the Plough-Keeper, the assault of one of the most senior Axe-Wielders, and the escape of the Forbidden.

Axis was a strong and fit man, and once beyond the village he quickly settled into an easy stride. The entrance to the Forbidden Valley lay less than half a league from Smyrton along flat and easy terrain; Axis was determined to give the Avar man and Azhure a run for their pains.

Yet as he ran a small troubling voice nagged inside his head.

Why not let them escape? Why not simply say that you tried your best, and stop here, and let them escape into the night?

Damn it! Axis thought as the disturbing question would not go away. I cannot betray my trust to the Seneschal—it has protected me and supported me all my life.

And yet how strange that you wanted to save them from Hagen. How does that serve the Seneschal?

Axis panted for breath as he drew closer to the Forbidden Valley. Could he admit to himself that his guilt at earlier trying to save the Avar man and child now drove him desperately to catch the runaways? Before they had not killed, he told himself angrily, now they have.

Was it the Avar who killed or was it the Nors woman?

She killed for them. She killed to help them. And in accepting her offer of help they became accomplices in the murder of a Brother of the Seneschal. His blood stains their hands equally. I *am* doing the right thing, Axis told himself fiercely.

And how can you blame the man for taking the child and running, Axis Rivkahson, when the Seneschal was preparing to burn him today? What threat does he pose to the Seneschal, to Achar, that he should be burned?

He is one of the Forbidden! They are both of the Forbidden! I cannot betray the Seneschal's trust in me. Now Axis' lungs were beginning to burn with the effort of pulling in as much air as he could manage, and still it wasn't enough.

Remember how you found them, Axis, torn and filthy and denuded of all their self-respect. Did you see threat in the man's eyes when he looked into yours? He trusted you with the child. Let them go.

No! Axis kept forcing the sight of Belial's assaulted form lying senseless on the floor into his mind.

Raum could move far and fast, but not with the child and Azhure to slow him down. They had moved well to begin with, but the child started to fret soon after they had left the village and Azhure's ribs pained her so badly she could hardly run. Raum tried to remain calm, but he had visions of the Smyrton villagers hunting them down when they were within shouting distance of the Avarinheim. He carried the child and tried to hurry Azhure along as fast as she could go. Dawn was not far off, and he did not want to be caught out in the open after the sun had risen.

They entered the Forbidden Valley just as the sky was beginning to lighten toward dawn. Azhure gripped her side, her chest heaving as she fought for breath, forcing each leg forward despite the sharp spike of agony which shot up her side. She began to wonder if somehow Hagen's spirit was revenging itself on her for his murder. Ahead of her the Avar man still moved smoothly, gripping the girl to his hip. Even with the injuries that the sharp iron spikes of the villagers had inflicted on him, he had hidden reserves of strength. Azhure knew that he could have been deep within the Avarinheim by now if it hadn't been for her.

They were close to the Nordra now as it escaped the Shadowsward through the narrow valley. The River Nordra roared and leaped dangerously as it flowed through the narrow confines of the chasm of the Forbidden Valley, and Raum and Azhure had to slow down on the slippery and dangerous path that ran beside the river and the rocky chasm walls. There was barely enough room for their feet on the narrow and treacherous path, and Azhure's heart rose into her mouth every time she saw the Avar man's foot slip, or felt her own feet threaten to give way on the slippery, rocky surface. Only a pace below the path the waters of the Nordra roared, ready to consume them should they topple in.

After what seemed like an eternity of treading carefully, her clothes soaked through to the skin by the spray and mist that rose from the turbulent water, Azhure saw the Avar man pause.

"Look!" he shouted, trying to make himself heard above the roar of the river, "ahead lies the Avarinheim. We are almost home!"

Azhure peered ahead. The valley started to broaden some fifty or so paces ahead, and she thought she could see the darkness of close trees. They were almost safe! She turned her eyes back to the Avar man, relieved, but his eyes were now focused on something behind her and his expression was one of horror. Azhure turned around, almost losing her balance. The BattleAxe was close behind them, a bare twenty paces, his face set in determined anger.

Raum grabbed Azhure's shoulder and pushed Shra into her arms. "Get ahead of me," he said urgently. "Walk as fast as you dare. The path is wider and less wet just ahead. When you can run, *run*. Get the child into the Avarinheim. I can hold him back here."

Azhure started to protest, but Raum pushed her roughly past him. "*Go!*" he said fiercely, and Azhure tore her eyes away from the BattleAxe and moved as quickly as she could along the slippery path. She could feel the Avar man following her. Her breath came in terrified gasps. The BattleAxe, no matter what he might have thought of Hagen personally, would never let his murderer walk free. And Belial . . . ? He would be even less likely to forgive the murder of Belial than that of Hagen.

Azhure berated herself as she strode out. The footing was firmer now, the river bending away to her left, and the Avarinheim was no more than twenty paces ahead. They were going to make it after all! The Avar would protect them as soon as they were behind the tree line. The figure of a woman stepped a pace or two out of the trees, holding out her arms for the child. Azhure's heart leaped inside her chest—it was GoldFeather! The woman's silver hair burned brightly in the first rays of the sun as it rose above the walls of the chasm. They were safe!

And then everything went wrong. Azhure suddenly heard a shocked intake of breath and a sickening thud and crack some ten paces behind her. She whipped around, almost falling herself. The Avar man had hung back, trying to give her and the child time to reach the Avarinheim before the BattleAxe reached them. But, just as the BattleAxe had closed in on him, the Avar man had twisted his foot and slipped on what had to be the last remaining wet patch of path. He had fallen awkwardly, and Azhure saw by the white and pinched line of his mouth that he had hurt himself badly.

Without thinking Azhure started to scramble back toward him, forgetting even the child in her arms. Perhaps all it would take was to get the man on his feet again and they could still outrun the BattleAxe.

But it was too late, far too late. His sword drawn, the BattleAxe had reached the downed Avar man in two strides, and Azhure was now close enough to see that his left ankle lay bent and broken, the wicked gleam of white bone breaking the surface of his dark skin. "Ah, no," Azhure moaned, and she would have run to him had Gold-Feather not stepped up behind her and grabbed her shoulders.

"Azhure! No!" she cried sharply, her own eyes riveted by the scene before them.

Raum lay on the ground, Axis' booted foot on his chest, his sword pressed so hard against the Avar man's windpipe that the tip had broken the skin and a little trickle of blood had trailed down his neck. Both men heaved to catch their breath.

"Well," Axis panted between breaths, his eyes derisive as he stared at Azhure, "you've managed to surpass your mother's efforts quite nicely, haven't you, Azhure? Murdering your father and running off with one of the Forbidden far outclasses a simple midnight flit with a pedlar. And Belial . . ."

"Let him go," Azhure said urgently, her voice strained, her eyes intent on Raum as he lay fixed by the point of Axis' sword. "I truly didn't mean to kill Belial."

"You killed your *father*," Axis said shortly, "Belial still breathes."

"Ah," Azhure's voice regained some of its strength. She straightened her shoulders, lifting her eyes to meet Axis' hostile stare. "I'm glad that Belial lives, BattleAxe. Will you apologize to him for me?"

"Azhure," Raum whispered, twisting his head as far as he dared with Axis' sword to his throat. "Take the child and run. You can get her to safety. Leave me." His chest heaved for a few more breaths as he fought to conquer the agony that flared up his leg, and then he spoke to Axis. "You will let them go, BattleAxe. You did not recreate Shra's life to kill her now."

"He's right," the tall woman standing behind Azhure said, her voice calm and level. "Go now. Go on," as Azhure hesitated, her eyes still fixed on Raum as he lay under Axis' sword. "Go now. Take little Shra and go. Quickly! Her father waits. *Run*, Azhure!"

Azhure jumped at the command in GoldFeather's voice. Without another word or glance she turned and walked quickly into the forest, disappearing from sight within a stride or two of reaching the densely packed trees.

GoldFeather walked closer slowly, very, very slowly. She did not want to startle the BattleAxe into sliding the point of that sword through Raum's throat the moment he felt threatened. She stopped a few paces away. The man stared at her and his black uniform, the twin crossed axes, brought memories flooding back into GoldFeather's mind. It had been so long since she had seen one of the Axe-Wielders, and now here stood the BattleAxe himself, his foot and sword dishonoring one of the most powerful Banes the Avar people had trained for many generations. The man was young; what was the Brother-Leader thinking of appointing one so young to such an important position? Her eyes flickered over his face for a moment. But she was too concerned about Raum to look too closely.

GoldFeather bowed as graciously as her mother had taught her as a child. "BattleAxe, may Artor hold you in the palm of his hand and guide your steps always."

Axis frowned at the woman. She was a handsome woman of middle-age, and had a striking golden streak through her silver hair. Her manner was courtly and her voice gracious, her gray eyes calm and her demeanor composed even as she faced a man who could kill her with a single twist of his sword. What was such a woman doing running with the Forbidden?

"I would return the blessing," he said flatly, "except that Artor would surely have deserted any woman who runs with the Forbidden many years ago."

The woman's eyes hardened at his tone. The Axe-Wielders always thought they knew everything, and this BattleAxe seemed more arrogant than the one she had known in her youth. Why hadn't he killed Raum? Why was he hesitating?

"Does Artor demand Raum's life?" she asked softly, deliberately giving the BattleAxe the Avar man's name. It was always harder to kill a man whose name you knew than a complete stranger. "What has Raum done to deserve to die at the point of your sword?" Axis' face tightened, and GoldFeather could see that doubts did indeed beset him. "I do not know all of what has passed this night, but Azhure's words make me think that any violence was done at her hands. Do not murder this man to atone for her wrongs."

"I am the BattleAxe of the Brotherhood of the Seneschal. I have a duty to serve the Seneschal," Axis said, but his tone suggested that he needed to convince himself more than he needed to convince either GoldFeather or Raum.

"No," GoldFeather said very softly. "You need do only what your heart tells you is right. Not what the Seneschal has taught you must be done. Your duty should always be to do what *you* feel is right." She paused. "Does it feel right to hold that blade to Raum's neck, an honored and honorable man among his own people, when he has done you and yours no wrong?"

Her words provoked a strange reaction in the BattleAxe. He winced at her last phrase.

"But who are mine? Who *are* my people?" Axis whispered, his eyes swivelling back to Raum.

GoldFeather frowned. What was he whispering? The BattleAxe raised his head and looked back at her. His eyes were tormented. "Lady, do you know of the Icarii?"

She nodded slowly, surprised by the question, troubled by the expression on the BattleAxe's face. "I know them well."

"Then answer me this. Do they sing?"

GoldFeather's eyes deepened with memory and she smiled. "Yes," she said. "They sing magically. It is their gift to this land and to the stars. All Icarii sing, music courses through their blood, but their Enchanters sing with the power and the grace of the stars themselves."

The BattleAxe's face twisted with emotion. GoldFeather stepped forward to place a hand on his arm. But he flinched and tightened his grip on the hilt of the sword and she paused instantly, her hand left hanging in the air.

"Who am I?" he whispered in a tormented voice. "*What am I?*"

GoldFeather opened her mouth, but did not know what to say to comfort him. Axis stared at her a moment longer, then abruptly he stepped back from Raum and, lifting the sword from Raum's neck, jabbed the point of the blade into the dirt, leaning on it heavily.

"Go, Raum," he said, his voice now tired and colorless. "I have no right to hold you. Go now."

Raum rose slowly from the ground, his neck bloody and his face ashen from the pain of his shattered ankle. Gold-Feather bent down and helped him rise to his feet, taking most of his weight on her shoulder. They turned and started to hobble for the Avarinheim, but at the tree line Raum paused and turned back to the BattleAxe.

Axis was still standing, sword resting on the ground as he watched him, his face tired and drained of emotion, his eyes unreadable. Jack and Yr had told Raum of Faraday's love for this BattleAxe, and at the time Raum had been deeply troubled by it. He had questioned Jack and Yr closely about the BattleAxe, but they were reluctant to say anything about the man beyond that Faraday loved him. Since he had seen this man sing, seen him recreate Shra's life, Raum could understand why Faraday felt as she did. Raum was also deeply aware that he was twice indebted to this man for his and Shra's lives.

"For the gift of two lives I give you one life back," Raum called, his voice clear above the roar of the river, "and I will hold one to give you later." He paused. "Faraday lives." Then he turned and he and the woman disappeared into the trees of the Avarinheim.

34

GhostTree Clan

Within ten paces of stepping into the Avarinheim Azhure felt as though she had entered another world. All her life she had been taught that forests were places of fear, dark and impenetrable shadows that harbored wraiths who would suck you dry of your blood. Yet Azhure's first impression of the Avarinheim as she walked more slowly down the path before her, was of space, light and music. On either side of her, ancient evergreen trees reared toward the sky, the trunks straight and smooth for the first fifteen or twenty paces of their height before their limbs branched out. The entire effect was to draw the eye upward toward the canopy above, toward the light filtering down through the interlacing green leaves and vines. The shrubs and bushes that spread across the forest floor were low and colorful. With the lack of low branches or high undergrowth the Avarinheim was filled with space and fragrance, cool light and soothing music rather than the unnatural and evil atmosphere that the Seneschal preached pervaded the Shadowsward. Azhure's arms relaxed about Shra as she walked a few more steps into the forest, drawn by its beauty. It took her some minutes before she realized what the music was. In the background she could hear the crystal sounds of the Nordra as it tumbled over rocks nearby, with a dozen different birdsongs overlaying its sounds. Azhure smiled, her eyes filled with wonder. Acharites barely knew the beauty of birdsong as most species of birds had retreated before the axe. The songs of the sparrows and ravens of everyday life in Achar could not compare with the sounds that now filled Azhure's ears.

Azhure shook herself. The Avar man still fought for his life beyond the trees, and she had to get Shra to her father. Perhaps then she could return to help the man and Gold-Feather.

She walked briskly down the path, and within a few steps a man, as muscular and swarthy as Shra's companion but with gray streaked through his dark brown hair, suddenly leaped out of some purple flowering winterberry bushes to Azhure's right where he had been crouching and tore Shra from Azhure's arms.

Azhure gasped in shock and stepped back. The man had stopped some four or five paces from her, clutching Shra protectively to his chest, his dark eyes fierce, his entire body tense and ready to fight if need be. He was dressed in a tunic woven from wool and dyed a dark red with patterns of interlaced tree branches at its hem. Underneath he wore serviceable brown leggings, bound with leather thongs, and ankle-high leather boots. Shra cried out with delight when she saw the man, and then snuggled as close to his chest as she could.

Azhure spread her hands to try and look as nonthreatening as possible. The man had no idea what was going on, and as far as he was concerned she was one of the hated Acharites who had strayed into the Avarinheim, carrying his daughter. No wonder he looked tense.

"I mean no harm," Azhure said as reassuringly as she could, although she was scared by the man. What if he decided that she posed a threat?

The man's eyes narrowed still further and he took a step backwards. Azhure's head swivelled to her right as her eyes caught a new movement. A slim, dark-haired woman stepped out from behind a tree. She was much shorter than Azhure, and dressed in a long, pale-yellow robe, again subtly patterned at the hem, but this time with leaping deer like Raum's robe. While she was obviously wary of Azhure's presence, she still exuded power and confidence and stepped up to the man's shoulder.

"Grindle," she said softly, laying a small and delicate hand on his shoulder, "I think it is all right. Shra seems well and unafraid of this woman." She turned her eyes to Azhure. "I am Barsarbe, Bane of the Avar people." She inclined her head gracefully, but her eyes demanded an explanation from Azhure regarding her presence in the Avarinheim with the child Shra in her arms.

If anything, Azhure was more afraid of this small woman than she was of the man, Grindle, but she tilted her chin and tried to sound as confident and relaxed as this woman before her. "Greetings, Bane Barsarbe. My name is Azhure, and I have come from the village of Smyrton."

The woman nodded slightly. "GoldFeather has mentioned you."

Azhure breathed a little easier. "Yes. I have talked many times with GoldFeather over the years. Bane Barsarbe, please listen to me." Her voice became urgent—what were they doing standing here, passing pleasantries? "Shra and the Avar man she was with were caught by the villagers of Smyrton some days past. I could not free them until a few hours ago, but the BattleAxe of the Axe-Wielders, who arrived in Smyrton yesterday with his force, caught us just short of the treeline. The Avar man—"

"Raum," Barsarbe said quietly, her eyes worried as she listened to what Azhure had to say.

"Raum told me to take Shra and escape into the trees. He turned to fight the BattleAxe."

"Raum must be dead by now," said Grindle, preparing to run and help.

"Wait," Barsarbe counselled, "let her finish."

Azhure looked worriedly at the two of them. Would they be able to help Raum? "Raum fell and broke his ankle. He could not escape the BattleAxe. But GoldFeather was there, and is talking to the BattleAxe."

"Raum and GoldFeather are both dead," Grindle growled.

"He treated Raum and Shra well," Azhure pleaded, not sure why she was defending Axis. "And I think he would have liked to save them. He had Shra freed from the prison where she had been thrown. Perhaps he can be persuaded by argument."

"Maybe she is right," Barsarbe said. "And GoldFeather will know how to treat the BattleAxe. We can do nothing for the moment."

"We can do our best to save Raum!" the man cried. "How can we lose another Bane? He is my *brother!*"

Barsarbe's hand tightened on Grindle's shoulder. "I will *not* condone violence, Grindle, not even to save Raum. It is not the Avar way. And if you run out there and add your anger to the scene then Raum *will* probably die. Your presence will *not* serve to save him, Grindle. We must trust in GoldFeather."

Suddenly Barsarbe turned and stared down the path leading to the Forbidden Valley. Azhure strained her ears, but could hear nothing.

"It's GoldFeather and Raum," Grindle said shortly, thrusting Shra into Barsarbe's arms and running down the path. Barsarbe passed Shra to Azhure and ran after Grindle, her hands lifting her robe to her knees to enable her to run more freely.

Azhure found the four of them around the first bend. Grindle had lifted Raum into his arms and was striding toward her. Raum's face was a mask of agony, his neck dark with blood, his hands slipping from Grindle's shoulders where he tried to hang on. His foot swung limply at the end of his leg, bone glistening through the bloodied skin of his ankle. Azhure stepped to one side as Grindle hurried past and her throat constricted as she realized the extent of the break to Raum's ankle. She knew the injury was close to being fatal because of the undoubted infection that would set in.

Barsarbe, supporting GoldFeather who looked exhausted, brushed past Azhure. "Follow us," she grunted, and Azhure hurried forward and put her free arm about GoldFeather's waist, relieving Barsarbe of some of the taller woman's weight.

They walked through the forest for about an hour, moving deeper and deeper into the Avarinheim. Grindle disappeared out of sight within a few minutes; Azhure was amazed that he could move so fast while carrying Raum's weight. After a while GoldFeather recovered sufficiently to wave Barsarbe and Azhure back, and although she still walked a little unsteadily she refused any further support. As the older woman's color improved, Azhure ventured to ask her how she had managed to persuade the BattleAxe to let both go.

GoldFeather shrugged. "I do not know completely, Azhure." She shivered in memory. "His hand tightened on the hilt of the sword and I was sure that Raum was dead. But . . . then he asked me if the Icarii sang." She frowned. "When I told him that they did, he seemed, well, he seemed almost frightened and then he let me take Raum. He was a very strange BattleAxe. I must speak with Raum more when he is able. Perhaps he can tell me more."

"For a BattleAxe he has compassion," Azhure said quietly. "When he arrived in Smyrton yesterday he was so furious at the treatment Hagen had dealt to Raum and Shra that he attacked Hagen, gave Shra to me to tend, and had his lieutenant Belial personally supervise two Axe-Wielders who cleaned Raum's cell and made him comfortable."

"Belial . . . the man you attacked?"

Azhure looked uncomfortable. "Yes, GoldFeather."

Both GoldFeather and Barsarbe stared at Azhure for a moment as they walked, both frowning.

Azhure looked even more uncomfortable as her guilt

rose, and GoldFeather turned a little to Barsarbe. "There is much to speak of here, Barsarbe. Perhaps we can wait until we are in your camp and have tended to Raum. But whatever she did, remember that Azhure saved Raum's and Shra's lives."

Barsarbe's frown did not leave her face, but she turned her eyes from Azhure. Azhure remembered Barsarbe's remark to Grindle; obviously the Avar abhorred physical violence. What will they think when they find out I caused Hagen's death last night, Azhure thought frantically. Will they insist I leave the Avarinheim? They walked silently for some minutes, GoldFeather well aware of Azhure's increasing distress. Finally she touched Azhure's arm gently. "The Avar are a peaceable people, Azhure, but they will also be grateful for what you did for Raum and Shra. If you had to commit violence to save them, then they will take that into account."

Azhure relaxed a little. "I hope so, GoldFeather. I only wanted to help. I did not think that I would . . . that I would . . ."

GoldFeather smiled to reassure the girl. "Shush now, Azhure, I know how badly you have wanted to help."

Azhure was quiet for a moment. "GoldFeather, I cannot go home now. May I stay with the Avar?"

GoldFeather turned and raised her eyebrows in query at Barsarbe. "We will have to ask the Clan," Barsarbe said eventually, her voice terse.

Shortly afterwards they arrived in a modest camp in a small glade close by the banks of the Nordra. The camp consisted of two circular leather tents stretched over lightweight curved wooden supports. A small fire smouldered on a stone hearth before them, a pot simmering to one side of the coals. Grindle had laid Raum down beside the fire and two women and a number of children hovered anxiously about them, looking immeasurably relieved when Barsarbe and GoldFeather appeared. The children hung back shyly, uncertain about Azhure's presence, but the two Avar women continued to kneel by Raum's side, Grindle standing behind them looking as angry as he had when Azhure had first told him that he was injured.

Barsarbe pushed the younger of the Avar women to one side and crouched down, inspecting Raum's neck and ankle. She looked anxiously at the other woman. "I'll have to work quickly on this, Fleat. Can you find me some splints?" The woman nodded and rose and Barsarbe turned to one of the children, a boy about fourteen summers. "Helm, I'll need some pots of fresh water if you can heat me some, and Skali," to a girl a year or so younger than the boy, "will you fetch me my basket of herbs?" The boy and girl nodded and rushed off, and Barsarbe started to wipe some of the blood away from Raum's neck to inspect the gash made by Axis' sword. Raum was only barely conscious now. She looked up at Grindle. "Grindle, you will need to keep Raum still while I clean and set the ankle. Will you hold him?"

Grindle knelt down by Raum's shoulders. "Can you save him, Barsarbe?"

She smiled reassuringly at the man. "Grindle, I will do my best. At least the wound is fresh, it has not been left to fester. I have saved worse than this."

GoldFeather waved over the young Avar woman. Dressed in a tunic and leggings like Grindle, the woman was carrying a small infant strapped to her breast. She stepped up to GoldFeather and Azhure, and smiled as she saw that Azhure held Shra.

"Shra!" she exclaimed, relief flooding her face, and the little girl held out her arms to the woman. "She is well," Azhure reassured the woman.

GoldFeather smiled. "Pease is Shra's mother, Azhure, and Grindle is her father. Pease?" The woman looked up from her daughter. She looked too small and frail to hold both infant and daughter, yet she seemed to cope with ease, and Azhure thought that although the Avar women were much shorter and more fine-boned than their men folk their frail appearance hid considerable strength. "Pease," Gold-Feather continued. "This is Azhure, and she has helped re-

35

StarMan

Axis staggered out of the Forbidden Valley, his face expressionless, his sword still dangling naked in his hand, words and images jumbling chaotically through his mind. The Avar man had said he had the soul of an Enchanter . . . an *Icarii* Enchanter. The woman had said that all Icarii sang, that music coursed through their blood. He had sung and played music that no one had ever taught him. Now more music, strange songs, were surging to the surface of his mind from long-hidden traps within his soul. He had sung an ancient ward against evil to protect himself against the apparition of Gorgrael. He had sung again yesterday to the Avar child, and had done something to her that had shocked Raum. His instant reaction to the sight of the trapped Avar had been sympathy, not hatred.

Who was his father?

Axis did not want to make the connection, *could* not make the obvious connection, lest he drive himself mad. All he wanted to do was put one foot in front of the other and somehow get himself back to the Axe-Wielders, back to a world that he understood and that understood him.

How could he be the son of one of the Forbidden when he had dedicated his life to serving the Seneschal—whose foremost enemies were the Forbidden? How could he have Forbidden blood coursing through his veins when all his life he had hated and feared the Forbidden?

Had his sympathy for the Forbidden been prompted by the fact that he was Forbidden too?

"*No!*" he whispered, "it cannot be!"

And Raum had said that Faraday lived. How could that be? How could Raum have known that? If he let himself hope it were true, and it were not, then he would truly be damned.

"No," he whispered, "it cannot be."

"BattleAxe!"

Axis raised his head with a conscious effort. Arne was spurring his big roan gelding toward him, relief written across his face. Several Axe-Wielders followed close behind. Axis slowly straightened.

"BattleAxe! We found Belial hurt and Hagen murdered and the Avar missing. Are you all right?"

Axis grimaced. "The Avar escaped. With the help of Azhure." He sheathed his sword.

Arne's face twisted into a snarl. "That Artor-cursed bitch! She murdered her father and dealt Belial a grievous blow."

Axis wiped a tired hand across his eyes, almost staggering with the effort. "How is Belial?"

Arne looked down at his BattleAxe with concern. "Belial will live. Ogden and Veremund are with him now. They say they can help him."

"Ogden and Veremund." Axis' eyes gleamed. "Yes. I must speak to them," he said to himself, very quietly.

"And the Avar and Azhure?"

Axis sighed and looked over his shoulder into the Forbidden Valley. "They had too great a start on me. They disappeared into the Shadowsward."

"Cursed misbegotten animals!" Arne growled, and Axis flinched, losing even more color. He wavered slightly, and Arne lent down his hand. "Swing up behind me, commander."

The good people of Smyrton were standing about in the main street and square. Word had spread quickly about the murder of their Plough-Keeper and the escape of the Avar man and the child. None of them were unwilling to believe that it had been Azhure who had murdered her father, attacked the Axe-Wielder (and the lieutenant to the BattleAxe at that!), and then fled with the Avar man and child. No one doubted Azhure's part in the crime. No one had liked her, they all agreed, shaking their heads in a great public show of sorrow, she had never really fitted in, and wasn't this just like her mother? Except worse? Far, far worse. Never trust a Nors woman, they all clucked to each other. Hagen's infatuation with that woman had been his only fault, and, in the end, the death of him.

Hagen's corpse had been removed to Goodman Hordley's house, where several of the village Goodwives were weeping and wailing as they washed it (and stitched the evil wound in his belly) and dressed the Plough-Keeper in his best habit. Later the entire village would file past to view the body. In Hagen's home the floor had been mopped and scrubbed and the bed prepared for the grievously struck Axe-Wielder.

Still, if denied a burning, the villagers at least had a burial to entertain themselves with. How fortunate that the two other brothers were in the village to conduct the Service for the Dead.

Axis slipped off Arne's horse at the house of the Plough-Keeper. "Arne," he said, steadying himself against the horse's flank. "Who is inside?"

"Only Ogden, Veremund and Belial were in there when I left them, sir."

Axis nodded to himself. "Very well. Arne, stand guard

here for me. Let no one else in. I do not want to be disturbed for a while."

Arne nodded. One word from Axis was worth an entire
edict from King Priam as far as he was concerned.

Axis headed for the door. Would Arne still believe in
him if he knew who, *what*, he really was? He took a deep
breath. Now was the time for some direct questions for Ogden and Veremund. Axis was tired of vague answers. Now
was the time for these two . . . brothers . . . to tell him all
they knew.

For a moment he leaned against the door, trying to find
the courage to enter, then he slipped the door catch, shutting it very quietly behind him.

Ogden and Veremund did not notice his entrance. They
stood across the far side of the room, leaning over Belial
who was stretched out straight and still on the bed. Ogden
had his hand splayed over Belial's face and faint golden
light emanated from his fingertips. Veremund stood close
beside him, his hand on Ogden's shoulder, muttering very
quietly to himself.

Axis leaned against the closed door and looked at them.
Belial wasn't in any danger, otherwise he would have
rushed to his aid. Suddenly he felt a surge of anger. Ogden
and Veremund were very much *not* what they pretended to
be. Well, the time for playing games was over.

It was Veremund who noticed him first. He leaned over
to a side table to reach for a damp cloth to wipe Belial's
face when he spied Axis from the corner of one of his
faintly glowing golden eyes. Instantly the golden light
died. "Axis!" he breathed, and Ogden lifted his hand from
Belial's face. They both turned from Belial to stare at Axis,
both uncertain what to say and do. They had wanted to wait
longer yet before they revealed themselves.

Axis pushed himself off the door and strolled lazily
across the room, his stare holding both Ogden and Veremund's gaze until he pushed past them to Belial's side. He
dropped his eyes. Belial lay quiet on the bed, breathing
easily, a cool compress over his forehead and across the

back of his neck. As Axis watched, Belial opened his eyes and grimaced in self-reproach.

"BattleAxe. My apologies. I should never have turned my back on her."

A corner of Axis' mouth lifted at Belial's apology. "You were lucky she did not knife you. She has a steady hand, it seems, when it comes to murder."

"I did not expect it of her," Belial said quietly, gently touching the back of his head with a trembling hand.

"Well, if it's any comfort, she was distraught at the thought that she might have killed you—she sent her apologies. Your smile must have charmed her just enough to stop the killer blow."

"Always had a way with the women," Belial whispered, then closed his eyes again, a spasm of pain crossing his face.

"You spoke to them?" Ogden whispered anxiously at Axis' side.

Axis turned and moved so swiftly that Ogden was unprepared for his action. All he knew was that suddenly Axis had one hand buried in his hair, holding his head tilted back in a tight grip, while the other hand was at his throat with a short but lethal blade.

"And was she in your pay, old man?" Axis whispered fiercely, his own face not a handspan from Ogden's. "This has your smell all over it."

"Axis!" Belial whispered weakly from the bed. "Do not harm them! They have done my head good."

"As well they should, Belial," Axis said tightly, his eyes still staring into Ogden's. "I am not so sure they did not plan the whole escape."

"Axis!" Veremund fluttered helplessly at Ogden's side, unsure what to do, frightened that whatever he did might cause Axis to slide the blade a little too far into Ogden's neck.

"Will you answer my questions, old men?"

"Yes! Yes!" Veremund said, his hands flapping impotently. "Just let Brother Ogden go."

Axis let Ogden go so abruptly that the man slid to the floor, then sat down at the foot of the bed and sheathed the knife back into his boot. Belial, who had struggled into a half-sitting position, sank back upon the pillows again.

Ogden glanced at Belial anxiously. "Perhaps this would not be the best place, BattleAxe."

Axis took a deep breath and looked at his lieutenant momentarily. "No, old man, this is very much the right place. I would rather that Belial heard this. I will value his advice."

"Very well . . . Veremund, would you mind assisting me to a chair?"

The tall old man helped his plumper companion to sit in a chair facing the bed, then pulled up a chair beside him. Veremund turned to Axis. "What do you want to know, dear one?"

All the anger had drained from Axis' face. Now he simply looked tired. "Do you remember when we spoke the night of the attack at the Barrows?"

Ogden and Veremund nodded.

"I said then that reading the Prophecy had opened a dark dungeon that had previously been locked tight all my life. I said that I did not like what I saw in that dungeon. Well, old men, too many things have crawled out of that once dark hole for me to ignore, and unless I get some explanations from you I am going . . . to . . . go . . . insane."

His stress was so clear that Belial reached out a hand to him. Axis grasped it tight. His eyes, however, did not waver from Ogden and Veremund. "Old men, whatever you might be, I no longer believe this fiction that you are simple Brothers of the Seneschal, devoted to learning and driven halfway to dementia by your isolation of the last thirty-nine years. What are you?"

Again Ogden and Veremund exchanged glances, and they grasped hands too, unsure what to do. "Dear one," whispered Ogden, "is the time upon us?"

"You have no cursed choice!" Axis almost shouted from the bed. "Because if you do not tell me I will break free this knife again!"

Both Ogden and Veremund lifted their chins, their decision made. Their eyes, one set light gray and the other as dark as the night, suddenly glowed as golden as the setting sun. "We are the Sentinels," they said in unison, then Ogden spoke alone. "We are creatures of . . ."

"And serve . . ." Veremund broke in.

"The Prophecy of the Destroyer," both finished, again in perfect unison.

For a moment there was utter silence. The golden light in the Sentinels' eyes died as abruptly as it had flared, and again two old men sat across from Axis and Belial, looking unsure as to how their news had been received.

"Ah," Axis finally said. He had known that they were not whom they pretended to be . . . but he had expected nothing like this.

Belial laughed suddenly, the sound a little shocking in the absolute quiet of the room. "No wonder you couldn't remember a damn word from the Service for the Dead," he said. Sentinels? He gazed at the two men with vastly increased respect.

"So," Axis said very quietly, "we know that Gorgrael has arisen in the north. And now the Sentinels walk abroad." He dropped his eyes to the floor and was silent for a while, then he came to some decision and raised his eyes again. "Well, Sentinels, shall I tell you what I am?"

Both Ogden and Veremund held their breath.

Axis watched their expressions, then laughed bitterly. "I am the son of Rivkah," he said slowly, finding it hard to say the words. "The son of Rivkah, Princess of Achar, and . . . and an Icarii Enchanter." Axis felt a great relief at finally saying it aloud, and his shoulders slumped as if freed of a great weight. Belial stared at him in amazement.

Finally Veremund nodded slowly. "Yes. That is what we think, too. But that is all we know about your parentage, Axis. We do not know who your father is beyond that he is probably an Icarii Enchanter."

"How did you realize, BattleAxe?" Ogden asked quietly.

Axis took another deep breath, his shoulders trembling.

He turned to Belial for a moment, ignoring Ogden. "Well, Belial. What do you think of that? Here we are, Axemen committed to hunt down every Forbidden that we see, yet now you hear that your BattleAxe is of their blood. What do you say to that?"

Belial gripped Axis' hand, using its support to pull himself upright. The last few minutes had been confounding, confusing, and his mind swirled with what he had just seen and heard. Yet while Belial had been raised to fear the Forbidden, he had found the Avar man more worthy of his respect than of his hatred. And he did not see a hated Forbidden sitting beside him, but a friend who needed his support now as he had never needed it before.

"I say that you are my BattleAxe," Belial said, his eyes burning fiercely, daring Axis not to believe him. "I say that you are the best commander that I have ever served under, and I say that you are my friend, and that in choosing my friends I have never asked who their fathers were."

Axis' eyes gleamed with tears and he leaned forward and embraced Belial. Veremund almost fainted with relief; Belial had just accomplished what it might have taken Ogden and himself months to do.

"How did you realize?" Ogden asked again, very quietly.

Axis turned back to him, his mouth twisting. "The music that I remembered. The song I sang before Gorgrael, the song . . . the song I sang to the Avar girl." Axis paused and stared at the rafters for a moment, recalling. "The Avar man, Raum, said I had the soul of an Icarii Enchanter." He laughed shortly. "He asked me what I was doing wearing the black and these axes," Axis absently tapped the crossed axes on the breast of his tunic with his fingers, "when all the Icarii hated them as much as the Avar did. And when we were before the Shadowsward, when I had Raum at the point of my sword, a woman stepped forth from the trees."

Ogden and Veremund leaned forward. They still did not know what had happened earlier this morning. "What happened? What woman?" Veremund asked.

Axis briefly told them of his chase of Azhure and the Avar man across the fields and through the Forbidden Valley. "As for the woman, I do not know. Of our . . . well, of Acharite extraction. She was not Avar. I asked her if she knew the Icarii, and she said yes. I asked her if they sang. And she told me that they sang magically, that the Icarii had music coursing through their blood. And then I remembered my own skill at music . . . which has improved immeasurably since you have kept me company, gentlemen."

Ogden sat back in his chair. "We knew that you must be of Icarii blood when you read the Prophecy. The Prophet wrote it in the sacred tongue of the Icarii, rather than the common tongue of Tencendor. No one else but an Icarii could have read his words."

Axis rose and stood before the fire, staring into the flames for a long time. "Why else did you have me read the Prophecy, gentlemen?" he asked softly, not lifting his eyes from the flames. "Why not test Timozel, or Arne, or Gilbert? And why follow me all the way around Arcen and Skarabost? Why?"

Veremund hesitated. "Because we think that you are the One, Axis Rivkahson."

"The One?"

"The StarMan." It was Belial who answered. "The one who will unite the three races of Tencendor. The only one who can stop the Destroyer Gorgrael."

Ogden and Veremund nodded. Again Belial had surprised them. He would prove a valuable ally for Axis in the coming months. Briefly Veremund considered some of the deeper riddles of the Prophecy and wondered if any of them concerned Belial.

"I do not want this!" Axis suddenly hissed from the fireplace. His eyes flickered between Belial and the two Sentinels. *"I do not want this!"*

"Axis," Ogden began, but Axis broke in, turning and striking the stone wall of the fireplace with his tightly clenched fist in anger and confusion. "How can I be the one to unite this supposed realm of Tencendor? I am the *BattleAxe!* I serve the Seneschal, and the Seneschal is . . . is . . ."

"Is opposed to everything that you are, Axis!" Ogden leapt to his feet, his cheeks red and his gray eyes bright. "The Seneschal, driven by their devotion to Artor, spread lies among the Acharites to incite hatred of the Icarii and Avar. They drove them from this land and left it vulnerable to Gorgrael. Damn it, Axis! You *know* the Prophecy. The three races must unite again to defeat him and," he took an angry breath, "*you* are the One. You are a war leader, and you can lead Tencendor against whatever forces Gorgrael might throw against us. You carry the blood of Achar's royal line in you—and Priam should recognize that he has two heirs, not just one. You have compassion, as you have shown me time and time again, and you will need compassion before all else if you are to unite the races and destroy Gorgrael. And last, but not least, you have within you the makings of one of the most powerful Icarii Enchanters that ever lived—if you would only embrace it instead of fighting it!"

Axis' face worked with emotion. "You lie, old man. I cannot combat the sorcery of Gorgrael! I could not stop the storm that killed so many of my men!"

"No!" Ogden all but shouted, waving his plump fists about in the air. "At the moment you cannot! You need to find your father—because without the teaching of your father, and he is the *only* one that can teach you, you will never be strong enough to face Gorgrael. And *we* need your father, Axis, because he must also be the father of Gorgrael, and without the father we cannot find or know Gorgrael!"

There was silence. Ogden's passion slowly faded and he sank into his chair. Belial, with great effort, swung his legs over the side of the bed and sat there, fighting the dizziness that swept over him. Axis turned back to the fire. Veremund looked a little helplessly between them all, opening and shutting his mouth.

"What did I do to that Avar girl?" Axis eventually asked, turning his head so that he could see the Sentinels.

"You sang what is known as the Song of Re-creation, Axis," Veremund answered. "The child was almost dead. But when you held her in your arms, from somewhere, I know not where, you recalled the Song of Re-creation. How you could sing that without being taught it by your father, I do not know—it is hardly something he would sing to you while still in the womb. The Song of Re-creation is a very beautiful song, very haunting, because it recreates life itself. It takes as its music the intertwined breath of the person who is dying and the breath of the person who is singing and it uses the power of the Stars themselves to infuse the dying with life. No Icarii Enchanter has been able to sing that song so well for over three thousand years. None alive today could have saved that child as you did. Ogden and I," Veremund turned to smile at his companion, "well, we wept. We could not help ourselves. Raum was shocked. He is a Bane, one of the Avar who well understands the practice of enchantments, and he recognized the Song for what it was. He also knew how much power it took to sing it. No wonder he asked what you were doing inside that black uniform, dear one."

"But if," Belial's voice was weak and he had to clear his throat and start again. "But if Axis could recreate life in the Avar girl, and none can do that now, then why is he not powerful enough to meet Gorgrael and defeat him?"

Axis answered himself, his voice weary with resignation. "Because I do not know how I do it, Belial. I cannot help myself. I cannot stand here now and call on . . . on this 'talent' within me to perform some enchantment whenever I need it. I don't know where this power comes from. I cannot stand before Gorgrael, or even a three-legged mouse for that matter, and hope that some snatch of the appropriate song occurs to me before Gorgrael strikes." Axis hesitated. "Belle my Wife might rally my men from a mist-induced fugue, but I doubt it will drive Gorgrael screaming from my sight. Unless," he managed a wan grin,

"Belial is there to accompany me on the harp. Your skill is so dismal, my friend, even the Destroyer would flee your dark music."

Belial grinned, but Ogden was not to be distracted. "You need your father to teach you," he repeated. "The Icarii Enchanters usually pass on knowledge from parent to son or daughter, as the case may be. *No one* can teach a new Enchanter except another Enchanter from their family, and usually it is the closest blood relative—the Enchanter parent."

Axis' amusement was replaced by irritation. "And where, old man, am I going to be able to find my father to teach me those things I need to know?"

Ogden spread his hands, his face assuming a cherubic expression. "Who knows how the Prophecy will work itself out, dear one?"

"So what, oh-creature-of-the-Prophecy, do I do now?" Axis ground out, irritation in turn being replaced by anger.

Veremund shrugged. "You do as you were doing, Axis. On to Sigholt, and then to Gorkenfort. Both places, I might add, where you might find clues to your father's identity. At one you were conceived, and at one you were born. Who knows what marks of your father's existence remain there?"

Axis turned to Belial. "My friend, what should I do? How can I continue as BattleAxe of the Axe-Wielders, knowing what I know?"

Belial did not hesitate. "You have command of over three thousand men committed to defending Gorkenfort against the raids of Gorgrael. How does that compromise the purpose of either BattleAxe or Enchanter's son? You simply go on as you would have done. As I see it, now you go equipped with more knowledge, perhaps more weapons, than previously."

"He speaks well," said Veremund.

"Yes," Axis agreed, sighing again. He paused. "Veremund, Ogden, there is one more thing I have to tell you. When I let Raum go he told me that, as he owed me two lives, he was giving one back. He told me that Faraday lived. How would he know that?"

Ogden and Veremund were genuinely shocked. While they had been sure that Jack and Yr had managed to keep Faraday and Timozel alive in the landslide at the Barrows, they could not understand how Raum would have found out. But Axis must not know that Faraday was headed for Gorkenfort and Borneheld. There was still time for him to arrive before her and ruin all their plans. Yet they had promised not to lie to Axis. What should they do?

Veremund took Axis' hand. "It is possible that Faraday survived the fall into the Barrow. The ground is riddled with tunnels and tombs."

Axis looked distraught. "Then she could be wandering lost, trapped in those dark chambers!"

"No, no!" Veremund hastened, patting Axis' hand. "If Raum saw her, then it must have been above ground. Perhaps she is working her way north from the Barrows to her home in Skarabost. She must have mentioned you to him. Otherwise, why would Raum mention her to you? Axis, she may well be home by now, and if she has Timozel to protect her, then what could go wrong?"

Axis relaxed a little. "Yes, you are probably right. Well, Brothers of the Seneschal you may not be, but you are all that the poor villagers of Smyrton have right now. Gentlemen, you have a Service of the Dead to perform. At least you've had some recent practice."

Belial laughed, and then flinched and held his head, groaning.

Axis smiled at him, his thoughts on Faraday. He let himself hope a little.

36

The GhostTree Camp

It was two days before Barsarbe was satisfied enough with Raum's progress to let him out of the tent. And although Grindle and his family were eager to hear of his adventure through the Seagrass Plains and Shra's presentation to the Mother, Barsarbe was adamant that Raum needed sufficient rest before he could explain what had happened.

GoldFeather felt unsettled; she kept going over their conversation with the BattleAxe in her mind, analysing each expression that had crossed his face. There was something about his face that tugged at her memory . . . something . . . something. It finally came to GoldFeather with a sickening jolt. The man's face resembled Priam's in some characteristics. A thought so terrible occurred to GoldFeather that her stomach turned over and she almost gagged. Borneheld? *Had Borneheld become the BattleAxe?* He was about the right age, and Stars alone knew he could have inherited both his devotion to Artor and his military prowess from Searlas. But no. No. GoldFeather started to relax as she thought it through. It was very unlikely that a noble as high as the Duke of Ichtar would take the position of BattleAxe. And hadn't Azhure mentioned the man's name at some point? Axis, yes, that was it. Axis. She breathed a great sigh of relief. Not Borneheld. *That* would have been too frightful to contemplate. To meet Borneheld again after so many years? No. There was too much guilt associated with Borneheld for her to want to meet him again.

And he hadn't resembled Searlas at all. No. But the encounter still nagged at GoldFeather, shadowing her mind. There was *something* about the man's face. Those eyes . . . no! Stop it, GoldFeather told herself firmly. Stop it! You've made a clean break from the past, so why worry over it like a sore tooth now? The man was probably a distant cousin to the royal family of Achar. That would explain the slight resemblance to Priam. She managed a small smile, convincing herself. Stars knew some of the past kings had scattered their bastards far and wide.

While Barsarbe kept Raum inside the tent, refusing to allow discussion with him about anything but the most trivial queries about food or comfort, GoldFeather spent more and more time walking the trails of the Avarinheim, trying to turn her mind from the BattleAxe by thinking of her husband and daughter waiting for her return in the Icescarp Alps. Although GoldFeather freely gave of her time to help the Avar in whatever way she could, each year she spent months away from her own family, and each year she wondered if she was drifting too far from them. Yet, with the Skraeling wraiths intensifying their raids on the Avar, GoldFeather knew there was still work she had to do. Now more than any time in the previous twenty years, the Avar needed her help, and that of the Icarii.

Azhure spent most of the two days wandering about feeling totally useless. The question of her remaining within the Clan was still undecided, and she spent most of her time with Fleat and Pease. Fleat took pity on the Plains Dweller, and explained to Azhure what Raum and Shra, and all the other children Azhure had seen going past Smyrton over the past few years, had been doing.

"We revere the Mother as the giver of life," Fleat explained one evening as she and Pease were grinding dried malfari tubers for flour between flat quern stones before the fire. "Those children picked to be trained as Banes are presented to the Mother and form a special bond with her, enabling them to touch not only the Sacred Grove itself, but use the rhythms of life that surround us to heal and help grow. Both we and the Avarinheim," she paused in her grinding to look about her at the forest, "rely on them to keep the land and the seasons healthy, else we would all die."

Pease added dried berries, seasoning herbs and lard to the malfari flour the two women were grinding, rolling and slapping into small round loaves which she wrapped in the large waxy leaves of the odinfor bush and put in the hot coals of the fire to bake. "Our Clan is honored that Shra was chosen by the Banes to be presented to the Mother," she said, smiling affectionately at the little girl who had hardly left her mother's side since she'd come home. "Already the GhostTree Clan has Raum, Grindle's younger brother, as Bane, and now we will have Shra as well."

"Is Barsarbe of your Clan as well?" Azhure was still a little confused by the relationships within the Clan.

"No," Fleat replied. "She comes from the FlatRock Clan, but came with us to the edge of the Avarinheim to wait for Raum's return with Shra." She took a deep breath of relief. "Thank the Mother she did. Without her healing skills Raum would likely have died."

Azhure helped the women gut some fat-bellied trout caught from the Nordra. The older children spent much of their time helping their mothers in the time-consuming task of food gathering; they generally found time for play only in the early evening. As far as Azhure could see, the Avar did not bother to plant or crop at all, preferring to live off only what the Avarinheim provided for them. "Do all of your people live in Clans like the GhostTree Clan?" she asked, sucking a finger where the sharp blade of the bone-filleting knife had cut it open.

"Yes." Fleat passed a spare odinfor leaf across for Azhure to wrap her finger in. "We all live in small family groups. The Avar must live from what the Avarinheim chooses to give us, and we cannot survive in large villages like your people do. We spend most of the year traveling from spot to spot throughout the Avarinheim. This is really too close to the edge of the Avarinheim for our liking. We are here only because we were waiting for Raum and Shra to return."

"And soon we travel to the Yuletide Meet!" Pease said, her dark brown eyes gleaming with excitement.

Azhure frowned. "The Yuletide Meet?"

GoldFeather joined them, sitting down by the fire beside Azhure. "Each year the Avar and the Icarii meet for two important festivals. Although the Avar are close to the earth and the Icarii closer to the heavens, they share the Yuletide and Beltide festivals in common, and each year meet in the groves of the northern Avarinheim where the forest meets the mountains in order to celebrate these festivals. Yuletide is the most important of the rites. It is held at the winter solstice, only a few weeks away now, and both Avar Banes and Icarii Enchanters are needed to ensure the sun rises from its death and is reborn. The Beltide festival is a more joyous affair, and is held in early spring to celebrate the reawakening of the earth after the death of winter."

Pease's grin widened. "Many marriages are contracted at Beltide, Azhure. It was then that I joined the GhostTree Clan as Grindle's wife. Other unions and ambitions are consummated as well. Beltide is the one night of the year when Icarii and Avar indulge in temptations denied them the rest of the year. Beltide is a night when dreams and desires become reality. Tell me, Azhure, of what do *you* dream? Of *whom* do you dream?"

Azhure blushed and the other women laughed.

"Azhure will have no opportunity for Beltide excesses if she does not remain with us, Pease," Barsarbe broke in suddenly, standing at the entrance to the tent and looking coolly at Azhure. The two Avar women stopped laughing and looked away from Azhure although GoldFeather smiled reassuringly at the young woman. Barsarbe turned her attention to Grindle's senior wife. "Fleat, will you assist me? Raum refuses to lie abed any longer, and he insists on joining us for the evening meal. Well, I suppose it is time we heard what he has to say."

The two women supported a still-ashen Raum out of the tent. His leg was tightly bound and splinted, and he found it awkward to swing as he hobbled to the fire. Raum sank gratefully down by the fire. Obviously still in some pain, he managed to smile at the women and children gathering in some excitement about him. Grindle himself stalked back into camp and peered anxiously at Raum.

"Brother, are you well?"

"Thanks to the skill of Barsarbe and the good care of Fleat and Pease, yes, I will be well, Grindle." The deep lines around his mouth and the unnatural pallor of his skin partially belied his words, but the spark of life burned bright in his eyes, and his mouth retained a quirk of humor.

Grindle looked relieved and joined the others around the fire. "I would never have let an Axe-Wielder catch *me*, brother," he said mildly.

"He stayed behind so that me and Shra could escape," Azhure said, stung that Grindle should even jest about Raum's inability to flee the BattleAxe.

Both Grindle and Barsarbe looked at her sharply, annoyed that she had spoken, and Azhure subsided, regretting her interruption. Even the three older children aped their father and stared at her with a total lack of tolerance. GoldFeather patted Azhure's arm in sympathy; of all the others about this campfire, GoldFeather knew what it felt like to be an outsider among a people who had no understanding of the culture that had shaped her. GoldFeather had found her first years among the Icarii hard.

Fleat gave Raum a mug of the herbed tea the Avar brewed and drank at every opportunity, and the Bane drank it down gratefully. For a long moment he looked into the fire, then he sighed and spoke to the group.

"There is much I have to tell you," he said, "and much of it is bad. What is not bad is, to say the least, puzzling." He took Barsarbe's hand as she sat beside him. "Barsarbe, it is as we feared. The Prophecy is awake and walking. Gorgrael has indeed been born, and is even now preparing to push his forces south and destroy all before him."

Everyone about the fire gasped, save Azhure, who looked mystified. All the Avar knew of the Prophecy of the Destroyer, and the talk at the last Beltide Meet had been primarily concerned with the fear that the time of the Prophecy of the Destroyer was finally upon them.

"How can you be sure?" Barsarbe asked, after a worried glance at Grindle.

Raum took a deep breath. "The Sentinels walk abroad. Shra and I met two of them at the Mother." If Raum's previous statement had stunned the group, now they were wide-eyed with shock. Raum described his meeting with Jack and Yr at Fernbrake Lake and explained how they had told him that the Prophecy was awakened, and that the StarMan was even now beginning to stir to meet Gorgrael.

"Where is he?" Barsarbe asked urgently.

Raum shrugged. "I do not know. The Sentinels were reticent when it came to the actual identity of the StarMan. He walks, as does Gorgrael, but I had the sense from them that the time is not yet arrived that he can meet Gorgrael. Perhaps he has still to break through the walls that the lies have built about him."

"And what else did the Sentinels have to say, brother?"

Raum thought for a moment. "They talked of their two companions left traveling with the BattleAxe of the Axe-Wielders and of many other things, Grindle. But it is not so much what they had to say, Grindle, but who they had with them." He paused and looked at the ring of faces staring at him. "They were at the Mother for a specific purpose. They had brought with them a young Plains Dweller, a woman called Faraday, to present to the Mother."

"Sacrilege!" hissed Barsarbe.

Raum put his hand up. "That was how I reacted, Barsarbe. But the Sentinels invited me to test her and I did."

"You put her to the test?" Pease gasped.

Raum nodded. "She was exceptionally strong. My friends, the Sentinels believe, as I do now, that she is Tree Friend. The forest sang for her. That has never happened before."

For a while there was total silence as the other Avar digested this piece of news. Ever since the Wars of the Axe, when the Avar were pushed behind the Fortress Ranges and the southern Avarinheim slaughtered before the axe, it had been legend among the Avar that one day Tree Friend would appear; a man or woman who would lead them back across the Fortress Ranges and enable them to reestablish themselves and the Avarinheim on the barren plains that ran down to Widewall Bay. But that Tree Friend should be a Plains Dweller, of the race that had slaughtered both the Avar and the Avarinheim, was unthinkable!

Raum could see the thoughts and emotions running across the faces of his fellow Avar about the fire.

"After the test," he continued softly, knowing as he spoke that his companions did not really want to hear the words, "I bonded and presented her to the Mother as I did Shra. We walked the pathways to the Sacred Grove, and the Horned Ones were there and greeted her and called her Tree Friend."

He stopped and let them absorb the news. GoldFeather found the news easier to accept than the Avar did. She knew they placed all the hopes of their race in the long-hoped-for Tree Friend. To find that Tree Friend was of the hated Plains Dwellers was a hard blow for them to absorb. GoldFeather frowned a little as she remembered the name, Faraday—what was it that Raum had said to the BattleAxe about Faraday? Azhure still looked totally mystified, and GoldFeather looked at her and indicated that she would explain later. She looked back to Raum. Strange days were upon them.

"Where is Tree Friend now?" Barsarbe finally, reluctantly, asked.

"She is traveling north to Gorkenfort—"

GoldFeather's head rose sharply and she stared at Raum, her eyes hard.

"—Where she is to marry her betrothed, Duke Borneheld of Ichtar."

GoldFeather gave a strangled moan, her hands flying to her mouth, her eyes distressed, and everyone looked at her, startled. "What is it, GoldFeather?" Azhure asked, concerned. She had never seen GoldFeather anything less than totally composed.

GoldFeather took Azhure's hand and grasped it so strongly that she crunched the bones of Azhure's fingers. Azhure's mouth tightened a little with the pressure, but she said nothing.

Grindle leaned forward. "GoldFeather? What is it?"

GoldFeather fought to compose herself: While some of the Avar, mostly Banes, knew that she had come of a highborn Acharite family, none knew her true origins or name. GoldFeather had buried her past completely behind her when she'd gone to live with the Icarii. But now Borneheld . . . Borneheld. Before this morning she had hardly thought of him in almost thirty years, then first she had feared Borneheld was the BattleAxe, and now Raum mentioned his name again. Hardly coincidence. Was the Prophecy going to pull her into its frightening entanglements as well?

"I knew his father once," GoldFeather finally managed to say, trying to reassure the group with a small but unsuccessful smile. "He was a hard and humorless man, more comfortable in his armor with his enemy at the point of his sword than wasting time in needless pleasantries. I cannot imagine that Borneheld will be anything less than his father. The Prophecy moves in mysterious ways." Again the

Duchess of Ichtar will become friend to the Forbidden, she thought to herself.

Raum looked at GoldFeather, concerned by her sudden pallor, yet knowing that there was still more he had to tell the group. News that would confuse, perhaps frighten them, even more.

"My friends, Tree Friend is not the strangest news I have to tell you. You know that Shra and I were captured by the villagers of Smyrton. They imprisoned us for four days in foul conditions. Shra was near death." Pease looked stunned, and her arms tightened about the little girl, who was now awake and listening to Raum avidly. "On the afternoon of the fourth day the villagers brought the Seneschal's BattleAxe to see us. Shra was no more than an hour from death."

Barsarbe looked as if she wanted to say something, ask Raum some questions, but he stalled her with a raised hand. "No, Barsarbe, let me finish what I have to say to you. I held her in my arms and watched the BattleAxe walk across the cell toward us, and I thought we were dead. But then . . . but then he asked to hold Shra."

"And you let him?" Pease asked, her voice angry and hostile.

"Pease, you were not there. What I saw in the man's eyes was compassion, not hatred. I gave her to him. He held her for a moment, and then . . . then the BattleAxe of the Seneschal, the one man we have all been taught to hate and fear without thinking, sang for her the Song of Re-creation. He recreated Shra before my eyes."

The Avar group were stunned into total silence now. Eyes drifted to Shra, then back to Raum.

"My friends, I have never heard such power from an Icarii Enchanter previously. Not even from the most powerful alive today—StarDrifter. Within the body of the BattleAxe of the Seneschal, an Axe-Wielder, lies the soul of an Icarii Enchanter."

Her eyes wide and alarmed, GoldFeather battled to control the emotions within her. She realized why it had not just been the BattleAxe's resemblance to Priam that had made him so familiar. He had the facial bone structure and the eyes of an Icarii, and what GoldFeather had first thought was the arrogance born of ignorance which festered within the Seneschal she now recognized as the natural demeanor of an Icarii Enchanter. A crazy thought, so crazy, so disturbing that it threatened to drive her over the edge of sanity, started to drift out of her subconscious, but GoldFeather thrust it back into the darkness where it belonged. No! she thought. No! I will *not* consider it! He died . . . *died!*

"What does this mean?" Barsarbe said, her small hands twisting in her lap, her eyes distressed. "How could this be?"

Raum folded her hands in his own. "This must be presented to the Yuletide Meet, Barsarbe. The sooner both Avar and Icarii can discuss it the better."

Grindle nodded, but looked concerned. "Raum, we will have to start moving for the northern Avarinheim within a few days at the latest. Will you be able to travel?"

Raum's face tightened in determination. "I will have to manage. If you can fashion me some crutches then I should be able to keep up with you."

"We could make you a sled, Raum." Helm, quiet until now, spoke up. "It would be no trouble to pull you. The paths are clear most of the way to the north."

Grindle looked at his firstborn with affection and pride. "Well done, Helm. One day you will make a fine leader of the GhostTree Clan."

The lad's chest swelled with pride, and his sisters gazed at him admiringly. His mother nodded, clearly proud of her son.

"Um," Azhure broke in, unwilling to speak but her uncertainty about her own situation driving her to it. "What about me? Can I travel with you? I cannot go back to Smyrton now." Grindle had allowed Azhure to stay with his Clan until Raum told his story, but her place in the Avarinheim was still unresolved.

Barsarbe looked at her consideringly. "Perhaps it would be best if you tell us exactly why your villagers would not welcome you home, Azhure."

Azhure licked her lips, worried that the group would not understand the circumstances surrounding her father's death—Barsarbe had reacted badly before when Gold-Feather had suggested that Azhure had committed violence to free Raum. Her eyes flickered about the group, feeling their eyes upon her, feeling very alone. She turned to Gold-Feather, but the woman was so preoccupied that she offered her no comfort. "Well, I helped Raum and Shra escape. For that alone they would not welcome me. But," Azhure looked down at her hands, unconsciously cleaning imaginary blood from beneath her fingernails, unable for the moment to meet anyone's eyes. "But they would also not welcome me because during the escape I mistakenly caused the death of my father, Hagen, and knocked the Axe-Wielder who was guarding Raum unconscious." Her eyes flew up again, hoping they would understand. "I was desperate to help Raum and Shra escape! Please, understand."

But her own guilt about Hagen's death and Belial's injury shone from her face and hardened Barsarbe's heart.

"Wanton violence always results in heartbreak, Azhure." Barsarbe's voice was cold. "Your actions caused his death. Even though the act was not premeditated, it is still murder." The Avar, as wild as they were, abhorred physical violence, let alone murder; any brutal behavior was extraordinarily rare among them.

Azhure hung her head, too ashamed to meet Barsarbe's eyes. "Hagen was a violent man," she tried to explain. "He abused and maltreated me from the time my mother ran away. I did not mean to kill him . . . but . . . I was afraid of what he would do to Shra. He . . ." She paused, unwilling to show these people what she had never shown or spoken of to anyone else, but Azhure was desperate to make them understand why she had taken the foolhardy actions she had. "Look." If she had to, then she would. Her fingers started to fumble with the fastenings at the back of her dress, and GoldFeather roused enough to push Azhure's fingers aside and unfasten the gown herself. She undid the dress to Azhure's waist, startled at what she saw, then she folded the material over Azhure's shoulders to expose her back.

"Look," GoldFeather said, echoing Azhure, twisting the woman's upper body around with her hands so that the others could see.

The Avar gasped in horror. Running down Azhure's back were the raised and red scars that looked to be the result of years of repeated vicious beatings; running down either side of her spine their tracks ruined her pale skin. She was marked for life. Slowly GoldFeather slid the woollen material over Azhure's back again and hugged the tense woman to her for a moment. In all the years she had known Azhure, she had never, never mentioned this to her. GoldFeather raised her eyes to Barsarbe challengingly. "Well?"

Barsarbe was shocked. As a healer she had never seen anything like this. Abuse of children was rated close to murder within Avar society, but did it justify murder?

Shra scrambled out of her mother's lap and toddled across to Azhure. She touched the woman's forehead and then glanced back to Raum. "Accepted," she said, clearly.

Raum frowned. "Shra? What do you mean?"

"Accepted!" the child repeated, almost angrily now.

Azhure looked up, eyes still bright with the shame that the Avar had seen her back. "After Hagen . . . died . . . Shra did the strangest thing."

"What?" Raum and Barsarbe both said together, leaning forward.

"She wiped her fingers in Hagen's blood and then ran them down my forehead, and then she said, 'Accepted.'"

GoldFeather looked at the two Banes. "What does that mean?"

"I'm not entirely sure," Raum frowned, "but it perhaps indicates that she accepted Azhure's father's death as a sacrifice to the Mother. It is strange. I don't know exactly what Shra meant."

Shra walked over to stand by Azhure's side, regarding the rest of the group with great dark eyes. Raum paused, and then continued. "I do know that if it wasn't for Azhure then Shra and myself would not be here now. She showed great courage in first trying to make our imprisonment more comfortable, and then in freeing me from that hateful cell. I say, let her stay with us for the time. She cannot go back. If the Clan wishes it, then she will have to answer to the Yuletide Meet for the violence she has committed."

Barsarbe took a deep breath, considering, then she abruptly nodded. "I will accept that Shra has apparently approved of Azhure's actions, and I will accept that Azhure saved the life of Raum. I cannot easily accept the violence she has demonstrated, however. I will support what Raum says. Let Azhure stay with us, and she will answer to the Yuletide Meet for the death of her father and the assault on the Axe-Wielder."

Grindle nodded as well. "I accept that. You may stay with us, Azhure. Be well and welcomed to our Clan." For the first time he smiled at her, his face completely losing its normal austerity. For whatever reason Shra had accepted Azhure, so he would too.

Azhure smiled in relief. At least she could stay with the GhostTree Clan for the time being. "Thank you," she said. "Thank you."

37

Jervois Landing

After almost two weeks of travel Jack, Yr, Faraday and Timozel, plus assorted pigs, drew within sight of Jervois Landing on the River Nordra. All were footsore and weary and more than once tempers snapped and flared over trivial incidents.

They had travelled as inconspicuously as possible, skirting small villages and larger towns in the dark of night, sleeping during the day in whatever shelter they could find. Occasionally Yr had crept into a small hamlet, coming back with food to replenish their own dwindling supplies. Faraday did not ask how she had obtained the food, but gulped it down before whatever fire Jack would allow them.

The weather had become colder and more bitter. It snowed most days now, and for five days they had struggled through snow drifts, their legs aching with the effort. Sometimes Timozel would lift Faraday on top of the mule, but the poor beast labored so hard through the snow that Faraday soon leapt down again. All four wore blankets under their cloaks, and on those occasions when Jack thought it too dangerous to have a fire, they huddled together in the lee of a hill, or behind an outcrop of boulders, shivering in misery. Faraday kept her wooden bowl close by her, but she had little opportunity to study it and none whatsoever to use it. When Timozel asked where she had got it from, Faraday shrugged and inferred that Goodwife Renkin had given it to her. Over the past fortnight the sense of empowerment she'd felt when Raum bonded her to the Mother had gradually faded, although if she concentrated she thought she could still feel it somewhere deep within her. She hoped that when she tried she would be able to find her way back to the Sacred Grove through the Mother. The memory of that enchanted and powerful place remained with her, and she held it as a talisman against the cold and fatigue of the journey north. When she lay down to sleep she recalled the warmth and joy she had felt there, and it always comforted her enough to lull her into immediate sleep.

Timozel was becoming more dark and moody as the days went by. He shaved only rarely, and a light brown beard covered his cheeks. His eyes had sunk deep into their sockets, and sometimes looked so sorely troubled that Faraday would ask what was wrong, if she could help. Timozel would smile at her, and her presence would lighten his eyes for a while, but the moment she moved away the dark mood crept over him again. In the week after leaving Fernbrake Lake Yr had shared his blankets two or three times, but Timozel seemed too wrapped in his own thoughts to spare energy for Yr, and after a while she spent most of their rest time huddled against Faraday's back sharing her warmth with the girl.

Jervois Landing was a small trading town on the great elbow of the River Nordra known as Tailem Bend. From Jervois Landing the Nordra arched southwards. It was the spot where those of Borneheld's troops who had not travelled the quicker route to Gorkenfort by sea disembarked from the river boat transports and massed to begin the long overland march northwards. Previously a sleepy town, with the preparations for war Jervois Landing had expanded into a bustling little metropolis, the pitched tents of soldiers expanding the stone town six-fold. The wharves were constantly crowded with river boats disembarking men, horses and supplies, and the streets of the town were packed with soldiers spending the last of their leisure time in whatever amusing manner presented itself. The locals were making a fortune.

Faraday and her three companions stood late one afternoon on the far bank of the Nordra, surveying the scene.

"I can smell a clean bed, linen sheets and a bath from here," Faraday muttered.

Timozel turned and smiled at her. "And you shall have them, my Lady. Tonight we shall sleep in comfort, and in the morning I shall arrange transport for us with some of the troops traveling northwards to Gorkenfort. You will soon be reunited with Duke Borneheld."

Guilt and self-loathing seared through Timozel every time he remembered how he had pledged his service to Gorgrael. His only hold on reason was to remind himself that so long as he was bound to Faraday then Gorgrael could not touch him. His devotion to the girl deepened and Timozel spent every waking moment ensuring that she was well cared for and her wishes were attended to as soon as possible. He knew that sometimes Jack and Yr regarded him strangely, but he ignored the Sentinels as much as he could. Faraday was his only protection against Gorgrael. If he was to survive to become the heroic commander of Artor's vision, then it would be Faraday's doing.

"How will we manage?" Faraday asked, worried. "We have no money, and nothing left to sell." Timozel's eyes drifted toward Jack's pigs, but Jack glared at him. "What if we can't arrange for horses and an escort?" Faraday continued. "I don't think I can continue to walk north!"

Timozel took her hand. "Faraday," he said gently. "You are betrothed to Borneheld, Duke of Ichtar. This may be the southernmost point of his territory, but every innkeeper and unit commander within five leagues of this place is going to trip over himself in his eagerness to please you. You will shortly be their Duchess—do you think they are going to ignore you? They'll believe a single smile from you will ensure the success of their personal careers or businesses for the next ten years."

Faraday laughed. "Yes, I suppose so. But, Timozel, how will they know that I am betrothed to Borneheld?"

Timozel held her left hand. "Faraday, look at this ring. Every soldier, every inhabitant of Ichtar, will recognize it. It will buy you instant respect. And," his voice tightened, "if it doesn't then I will personally make sure that you receive it the very next moment."

"The youth is quite the man," Yr quipped. "Less talk and more action would please me right this minute."

"Yr," Faraday murmured. "Timozel will do his best for all of us. Be quiet now."

"There is a ferry a little further up the river on Tailem Bend itself," Timozel pointed out, ignoring Yr. "If we hurry we can cross before dark."

Jack frowned. "Wait. There is something I must say. Yr, you know that we are missing one of our number." Yr nodded. There should be five Sentinels, but only four walked abroad. Where was the fifth? Jack turned to Faraday and Timozel, standing huddled together against the wind. "Faraday, Timozel. I am going to leave you here." Jack smiled a little at Faraday's cry of protest. "Faraday, Timozel and Yr can look after you well enough from this point, and there is no place for a pig herder in Gorkenfort. Timozel will be your Champion, Yr your maid. She can show you everything you will need to know as well as I can." Faraday knew he was referring obliquely to what had happened at Fernbrake Lake. Jack turned to Yr. "Yr, I must look for the fifth. The Prophecy will be lost if I cannot find her. *I* will be lost if I cannot find her. We have come far enough together—and you know we will meet again."

Yr blinked back tears, but nodded. She stepped forward and they hugged fiercely. "Travel well and safely, beloved one," she whispered. "I will watch Faraday and guide her steps."

"Remember," Jack whispered for Yr's ears alone. "What happens at Gorkenfort is critical. Make sure that Axis, Faraday *and* yourself survive. I care not whether Timozel walks out of there alive or lies buried forever beneath the mud of the battlefield."

Yr nodded, then let Jack go, standing back, wiping her tears away with the back of her hand. Jack stepped over to Faraday and she hugged him almost as fiercely as Yr had. "Goodbye, sweet one," Jack said, his voice choking a little. "Remember to be true, and remember that we will be true for you, as well. Go with our blessing to comfort you." He paused, as if considering whether to say anymore or not, but decided against it, pulling back and kissing Faraday gently on her cheek. He smiled into her eyes, his own friendly and affectionate. "Find peace, Faraday."

Faraday sniffed, trying to hold back tears. "Will I see you again, Jack?"

"Yes, lovely lady, we will all meet again." Jack kissed her gently once more, then let her go and stepped over to Timozel. He held out his hand, and after a moment's hesitation Timozel gripped it. Snowflakes whirled in the air between them. "You only have Faraday's best interests at heart, Timozel. I know that, and I know you will do your best for her. Be true, Timozel."

Timozel felt a pang of shame pierce his heart. Did the man somehow know of his pact with Gorgrael? He gritted his teeth; how could he? "I live for her, Sentinel. I will let no harm come her way."

Jack nodded. It would have to do. "Then go in peace, boy. Gorkenfort will be a dangerous place. Protect her with all you have."

"You can be sure that I will," Timozel said tightly and dropped Jack's hand.

"Then," Jack said lightly to the women. "I will collect my pigs and be off. May the sun shine over all of us again one day."

Faraday nodded, unable to speak, but Yr raised her hand in salute. "May we all find peace together in the light one day, Sentinel."

Jack nodded, then he and his pigs were gone in the swirling snow.

Timozel watched the place he had disappeared for a moment, then he patted the mule standing patiently behind him. "We have no time to waste if we want to find shelter and a bed tonight," he said shortly. "Let's be off."

Timozel led them down to the ferry, the two women holding onto the straps of the mule's packs to avoid being separated in the snowstorm. Both women, protected by the falling snow and the deep shadow of their hooded cloaks, cried a little. Most of the Sentinels had been separated for at least two thousand years, and, as they only felt whole when they were together, the parting was especially painful for Yr. Faraday, on the other hand, felt the loss of a valued companion, a man she had come to lean on for support over the past few weeks. Since her experiences at Fernbrake Lake, Faraday had let go her vague mistrust of the man. The Prophecy manipulated them all, and Jack was as much a victim as she. Faraday had lost her mother and the man she loved, and for a while Jack had begun to fill both roles. She knew she would miss him terribly over the coming months. How could she cope with Borneheld if Jack were not there? Faraday raised her chin and gritted her teeth. "Mother, aid me," she whispered, and felt a small twinge of reassurance deep inside her. If they had a room tonight, Faraday vowed, she would use the sacred bowl.

The River Nordra was wide but slow where it bent its massive course southwards. Both traders and locals used the Tailem Bend ferry to travel from Ichtar into Skarabost, and some stayed to catch one of the river boats that plied their way to and from Carlon. The ferryman was just about to push the ferry out for the far bank and home when he saw the group of three struggling down the path cut deep in the Nordra's bank. He cursed a little; he had wanted to push off early and get home to bed before this storm thickened any further. For a moment he considered pushing off regardless, but he saw the glint of steel at the hip of the tall man leading the mule, and relaxed his grip on the pole. He called out to his three assistants to wait. Best not to anger one of Borneheld's captains.

The man led his mule down to the ferry and the ferryman's eyes widened a little. The man wore the uniform, albeit a little tattered, of an Axe-Wielder, and the ferryman was a religious man. He made the sign of the Plough before the Axe-Wielder.

"Good sir, may I offer you passage across the river this evening? 'Tis cold and blustery, and I'm sure that you're keen to reach your rooms this night." The ferryman's eyes widened a little further when he saw the two women follow the Axe-Wielder onto the ferry. They were both very beautiful, but the ferryman's mouth curved just a little bit more appreciatively at the blond wench as she walked past. Yr dipped her eyes coquettishly at the ferryman; it never hurt to turn a man's mind from money to lust and she did not know how Timozel was going to pay the man once they reached the other side.

But the ferryman had no intention of waiting until they reached the other side before he saw his gold.

"My lord," he groveled at Timozel's side, his stained teeth bared in a smile. "For yourself and the two lovely ladies 'tis only four marks for the journey across to Jervois Landing." His smile faded a little and his face assumed a sad expression. "I am sorry that the price should be so dear, my lord, but it costs so much to hire decent help to work this ferry in such bad weather. I know you will understand."

The ferryman was reassured by the smile that spread across Timozel's face, but his reassurance disappeared as Timozel's gloved hand seized his throat and half lifted him off his feet.

Timozel's pleasant smile never wavered. "My good

man, I can only assume that you do not recognize the Lady Faraday of Skarabost, betrothed to Duke Borneheld, and on her way to him at this moment for their wedding. Would you like me to pass onto Borneheld himself that you were churlish enough to demand payment from her as she hurried to meet her lord? And yours," he added to drive the point home.

The ferryman's eyes rolled in his head. Beautiful the girl might be, but he had never seen a less pretentious escort for what this Axe-Wielder claimed was Borneheld's betrothed. And the girl was dressed in country worsted! "My wife dresses better than that girl, my lord," he whispered, trying to put on a brave aspect in front of his assistants. "I hardly think she be the Duke's betrothed."

Faraday stepped forward, intending to show the man her ring, but before she managed to come close Timozel's face twisted and his fingers gripped the man's throat so tightly that the ferryman gave a strangled sound. His three assistants, all young lads, were kept well back by one fierce glare from Timozel.

"I'm sorry," Timozel whispered so threateningly the ferryman thought he was dead. "I thought I heard you say that you didn't believe me. You may even have insulted the lady by comparing her to your wife. I don't like that, ferryman!"

Faraday stopped and gazed at Timozel in amazement.

The ferryman's eyes bulged and he squeaked in fear. "I misunderstood, my lord! The passage is yours, free!"

Timozel dropped him and the man cowered on the deck of the ferry for a moment before scrambling away from Timozel as fast as he could on his hands and knees. "Pole, you witless idiots!" he yelped to his assistants. "Pole!"

The ferry began to move away from the river bank and Faraday turned to Timozel. "Timozel, was that much force necessary?"

Timozel turned to stare at her and Faraday stepped back at the look in his eyes. Timozel's expression softened, but his voice remained hard. "No one insults you before me and gets away with it. The man is lucky that he lives."

"If this is what you do to win us passage across the Nordra, then I dread to think what you will do to win us a bed for the night," Yr grumbled.

Yet, in the end, bed and a promise of transport was arranged more easily than any of them could have imagined. When the ferryman docked at the landing leading to the main street of Jervois Landing Timozel and the two women could not get off fast enough for his liking. He mouthed a curse as the Axe-Wielder strode by him, but he made sure his face was in shadow as he did it.

The main street was abuzz with activity even though dark had fallen. Faraday had arrived only just in time, since the last major contingent for Gorkenfort had arrived that morning and were due to pull out in two days. Faraday and Yr stuck close to Timozel's side, avoiding the lewd suggestions that were thrown their way by the rough soldiers. Timozel's back stiffened at the insults, but there was no way he could attack the entire street of soldiers passing by. He stopped one of the locals, a merchant by the cut and quality of his clothes. "Good man, is there an inn where we could rest close by?"

The merchant laughed. "Young man," Timozel's face stiffened, "there is no room to be had for gold or threat here tonight. Can't you see about you? The place is crawling with troops." He turned and grinned at Faraday and Yr. "Now, the young lasses might be able to find themselves somewhere warm for the night, if they're prepared to work a little for it, but I'm afraid you'll have to suffer the indignity and cold of a night in the streets."

Faraday grabbed Timozel's arm. "Tim! No! He does not realize who we are. I ask you not to lose your temper here!"

Timozel's mouth tightened so that his lips had almost

completely disappeared, but he jerked his head and waved the man away. "Faraday, I do not know what we can do," he began.

"Timozel?" A horseman hauled his mount to a sudden halt before them, "Timozel, is that you?"

Timozel stared for a moment at the man before he recognized him.

"Gautier!" Timozel said, relief relaxing his voice. He had met Borneheld's lieutenant in Carlon when the Axe-Wielders were preparing to ride east to Tare and the Silent Woman Keep. They had struck up an easy acquaintance, even though Gautier had won Timozel's best cloak from him at dice. At last fortune had favored them; there was no one save Borneheld himself who would hurry Faraday north faster than Gautier.

Gautier swung down from his horse, holding tightly to its reins as men surged past on their way to their overnight billets. Despite the cold he was wearing only his regulation brown leather uniform, his short cropped blond head bare to the wind. Light gray eyes in a sharp and narrow face made Gautier look constantly secretive, yet he was a man that few trusted with their own secrets. "Timozel! I'd heard you were dead! Word reached Carlon that you . . . oh, Artor!"

Gautier had finally caught sight of Faraday. "My lady!" he breathed, surprise softening his features somewhat. "How . . . what . . . who?"

Faraday forced a light laugh. She did not particularly like Gautier. She looked at Timozel, her eyes pleading with him silently to let her do the talking. "Timozel saved myself and my maid from the earthfall. We struggled free, and have been working our way north ever since. Hence our clothes," she grimaced, fingering her dress. "We had to purchase our dresses from a peasant woman. Ah, Gautier," and here goes my story on its first real test, she thought to herself, "after escaping death so narrowly I could not bear the thought of being separated from Borneheld any longer. I pleaded with Timozel to escort me north, instead of back to Carlon or Skarabost." She shrugged prettily, flirting with Gautier, playing to the admiration in his eyes. "Surely you can understand that I wanted to be with my intended husband? Perhaps you can help?"

It took only a moment for Gautier to recognize the possibilities. He imagined himself striding into the audience chamber of Gorkenfort, Faraday behind him, and taking all the credit for finding her and bringing her to Borneheld. His eyes flickered behind Faraday to her pretty maid, and further opportunities filled his mind. Why! The wench was panting for him! She'd be far hotter sport than the tired old crones who plied their trade in Jervois Landing.

Faraday watched the drift of Gautier's eyes and hoped that Yr wasn't playing the lustful wench too heartily. "We would all be very grateful should you be able to find us beds for the night. And I'm sure Borneheld would appreciate it too."

"Done!" Gautier grinned. "My Lady? With your leave?" He thrust the reins of his horse at Timozel who took them with studied bad grace.

Faraday accepted Gautier's proffered arm and he led her along the street, shouting for the crowds to make way, Timozel and Yr hurrying along behind as best they could with the mule and Gautier's horse. At least they were going to have rooms for the night and a decent bed, Yr thought to herself, although she wondered if she might still have to work a little for her share of the warmth. For a moment she had thought Gautier was going to wrestle her to the muddy street and take her there. Yr's lips parted in a smile. And perhaps she would not have minded. Well, she thought, as she hurried to keep pace with Faraday and Gautier, it was the least she could do to make sure that Faraday arrived in Borneheld's bed as quickly as possible.

Gautier led them to an inn called the Tired Seagull and, with only a minimum of shouting and fuss, arranged three rooms for them. The previous incumbents, at first disposed to complain about their eviction, were silenced by Gautier's threats and maids moved in quickly to change linen

and remove the luggage of the previous occupants. Faraday
forced a smile to her face again.

"Lieutenant Gautier. We have been traveling in these
clothes for close on four weeks. Do you think you could
manage to persuade the innkeeper to find us something
else to wear? And perhaps a seamstress for the morning? I
cannot appear before Borneheld like this."

"My Lady," Gautier bent over her hand. If she was going
to marry Borneheld, then she was almost as important to
impress as the Duke himself. "I will have clothes and water
brought to your rooms immediately. Perhaps you would do
me the pleasure of joining me below in the private dining
room once you have rested?"

Faraday dimpled prettily. "It would be my pleasure,
Gautier. I shall not hesitate to inform Borneheld that you
have been so helpful."

Much later that night Yr helped unlace Faraday from the
yellow silk gown that Gautier had somehow found for her.
He had not stinted in his efforts to find them clothes for
that evening and a bevy of seamstresses for the morning.
Faraday would leave in two days' time with virtually a
complete wardrobe. It was fortunate that Jervois Landing
was such a major trading post—once the merchants in residence heard that Duke Borneheld's betrothed was staying
at the Tired Seagull, bolts of silks, satins and velvets
started to arrive by the cartload, all with the assurance that
the trifling details of payment could wait until the Lady
Faraday had completed her nuptials.

Faraday breathed a sigh of relief as Yr removed the last
lace. Although the worsted peasant dress had been of rough
material, its loose cut had made wearing it extremely comfortable. Faraday had almost forgotten the restrictions of
high-fashion gowns.

"You do very well as a maid, Yr," she smiled as she
slipped the silk off her shoulders.

"It would not be my chosen profession, Faraday. Here,

don't throw the gown on the floor like that. Let me drape it over a chair."

Faraday unpinned her hair. The meal with Gautier had been reasonably pleasant. He was determined to please her, and even Timozel accepted his attentions as those due to Faraday as Borneheld's intended wife. She shivered in her thin linen shift. They were leaving within the next two days. Gautier had said that at the most they would take ten days to ride to Gorkenfort. The route was well-marked and well-provisioned. Within two weeks she could be Borneheld's wife.

"Shush, sweet one, sit on the bed and I will brush your hair out for you. Don't fret, I will not leave you."

For some time Faraday closed her eyes and surrendered herself to the soothing feel of Yr stroking the brush through her hair. "Yr?" she said, after a while.

"Hmm?"

"Yr, I want to try to reach the Sacred Grove tonight. Will you help me?"

Yr's hands stilled in Faraday's hair. "Are you sure, my sweet?"

Faraday twisted around to look at Yr. "Yr, I have almost lost the feel of the Mother. If I don't try tonight I'm afraid that I'll lose Her altogether."

Yr gently kissed Faraday's brow. "Never that, my sweet. The Mother will stay with you always. You must simply train yourself in the arts of reaching Her."

Faraday stood up and rummaged through her pack until she found the wooden bowl the Horned Ones had given her. "Yr, do you know how to use this?"

Yr nodded, putting the brush aside. "I have some idea. Come, we will need some water."

Yr put the bowl on a small table and told Faraday to fill it almost to the brim with water from a china pitcher.

"Now, the Mother always demands blood, a small sacrifice to show that you are prepared to give of yourself to be with Her. Here," Yr handed Faraday a small knife.

Faraday stared at Yr a moment, then nodded. The idea of

38

Sigholt

Axis stood on the flat roof of the Keep at the garrison of Sigholt and let the wind ruffle through his hair. He rested his hands on the ancient stone parapets of the Keep and gazed north, his eyes narrowed against the wind. On the horizon he could just see a faint smudge of purple—the Icescarp Alps. Cold as it was, the air was invigorating and Axis closed his eyes and filled his lungs. He had never been further north than Aldeni previously—Jayme had always kept him south of Ichtar—and the sight of the distant Icescarp Alps exhilarated him.

"The Princess loved to stand here, just as you do now," a soft voice said behind him. Axis opened his eyes, and turned to the old man behind him. They were alone on the roof of the Keep.

Reinald, retired chief cook of the garrison, was old and infirm. Rheumy eyes watered in the wind, and his all but bald pate shone in what weak late autumn sunlight managed to struggle through the clouds. He grinned amiably at the BattleAxe. Most of his teeth had gone.

"I was undercook then, BattleAxe, and one of my tasks was to supervise the Princess' meals. She would spend most of her time up here during the summer and the early autumn, and I and the kitchen hands would have to climb the steep stairs balancing hot bowls, sharp knives and fine china and crystal. Three times a day."

Axis smiled at the old man. "You must have cursed her."

"Ah," Reinald remembered, " 'twas hard to curse your mother, BattleAxe." Reinald was the only person Axis had met, apart from Faraday, who was comfortable with the fact that Rivkah was Axis' mother. "She would smile so prettily, and apologize for all the trouble she had caused, and then she would turn to the view and invite us to see what it was that had enthralled her."

"And that was?" Axis prompted.

Reinald stepped up to the parapets with Axis. "Why, the Icescarp Alps, BattleAxe. She used to tease us. Ralf, the youngest of the kitchen boys, had no head for heights and would often turn green with dizziness. Princess Rivkah would laugh, and say that one day she would fly away to the Alps and no one would ever see her again. I like to think that is what her soul did, BattleAxe, when she died during your birth. I have always comforted myself with the thought that finally she was free to visit the mountains she had always wanted to see. She was closer to the Alps then, you see, when you were born."

Axis could not say anything for a moment; sometimes graciousness and comfort could be offered from the most unexpected of places. "Thank you, Reinald," he managed finally. He turned his eyes back to the faint smudge on the horizon. "It is hard to see them from this distance."

"Oh, during the summer, on a clear day, they stand out as if there's only a league or two between here and there."

"She must have been very unhappy here," Axis said quietly, "if she wanted to fly away."

Reinald thought hard about what to say. "She was unhappy when Searlas was here, but when he was absent, then she would laugh."

"When my father was here?" Axis asked.

Reinald remained quiet for a very long time, staring out toward the Icescarp Alps. He remembered the terrible weeks when Duke Searlas had returned home from Gorkenfort to find his year-long absence had left Rivkah eight months pregnant. Without thinking he looked down at his own hands. His fingernails had never grown well again after Searlas had personally pulled them out one by one with a pair of rusted kitchen tongs, trying to find out what the undercook knew about the father.

Reinald, despite the pain, or perhaps because of it, had never told. In his own way he had loved Rivkah and if he could help her by remaining silent, then he would do so with the joy that he could in fact serve her.

Axis remained quiet, leaving the man to think. He would tell, or he would not. Either way Axis was glad that he had found this old man. Through his memories he could reach the mother he had never known.

"Searlas was so . . . so hard. Rivkah came here as a young bride, still a girl. Above all else she needed love and laughter, the two things Searlas could not give her." The man paused again for long minutes. "I learned to wait at the door to the roof, learned not to disturb your mother until she called. Sometimes I waited long hours, the food turning to a cold congealed mess about me. I would send the kitchen boys away." Reinald turned to face Axis. "I never saw your father, BattleAxe. But I heard him speak, and I heard him sing. He had a voice that one could listen to for hours." The old man smiled at the memory. "He gave her both love and laughter, BattleAxe. For close to eight months he came almost every day and stayed for hours. Who was he? I do not know. How did he reach the roof? No one ever passed me on the stairs."

Axis nodded absently, his mind drifting. This would be a lovely spot in summer with the green Urqhart hills in the foreground and the purple Icescarp Alps far away in the distance. Over the past few days Ogden had told him far more about the winged Icarii. Had the Icarii Enchanter flown each day from the Alps? Or did he have a haunt in the Urqhart Hills themselves? Axis relaxed as he thought of his mother and her Enchanter lover. A lilting melody ran through his head, and without thinking he started to hum it, enjoying the way it ran about his mouth. He closed his eyes for a moment, feeling the summer warmth upon his face, smelling the climbing roses that in summer crept up the Keep to its very roof. He did not see Reinald's face drop in stunned amazement.

"StarDrifter!" A young woman called, love deepening her already low voice, and Axis opened his eyes. The roof was bathed in sunshine and across from him a lovely young woman stood, laughing in the sun, holding out her arms to him. "StarDrifter! You said you would not come today." She was barefoot under a loose gown of lavender linen, and Axis could see that her waist was thickened with midterm pregnancy. Her long auburn hair drifted about her back, flicking slightly in the gentle breeze. She took a long step toward him, hands open in supplication. "StarDrifter," she called again, and then her face frowned a little. "Is that you, my love? What is that you wear?" Her voice was puzzled.

Axis took an involuntary step toward her, reaching out his own hand. Tears began to slide down his cheeks. "Mother?"

The vision wavered and Rivkah took a step backwards. "Who are you?" she whispered, her hand pressed protectively to her belly, and then the image wavered again before folding in on itself and disappearing.

"Mother!" Axis called, taking another step to where she had stood, but now only the wintry wind gusted across the roof, and the balmy air and smell of roses was gone. He turned to Reinald, his face pleading. "Did you see?"

Reinald's face was white. "Yes, BattleAxe. I saw. That was Rivkah. That was your mother," he whispered.

Axis whipped around, hoping that she had reappeared, but the roof was barren. He gave a cry of anguish and Reinald hobbled over to him. "Axis," he said intently, grasping the BattleAxe's arms, "you are truly your father's son! Look," he fumbled inside his gown for a moment and pulled out a long chain. There was a ring dangling at the end of it. He slipped it over his head and held it out for Axis. Axis blinked away his tears and took the chain and ring.

"Your father gave her this, young man. When Searlas returned Rivkah was terrified he would seize the ring and somehow find the father through it. So she left it in a bowl of uneaten trifle for me to find and look after. I suppose she thought she could always ask me to return it later. But she never did—Searlas had her transported to the Retreat in Gorkentown where she died. BattleAxe, I never knew what would happen to this ring when I died. What could I do with it? But I never thought that I would meet Rivkah's son, nor that I would ever see Rivkah again, laughing and smiling with love and joy atop this roof. You have brought wonder and joy back into *my* life, young man, and I would now pass on a little of that to you with my heartfelt thanks."

Axis' fingers closed over the ring. "Thank you, Reinald, thank you," he whispered, and he did not mean only for the ring.

After Reinald had gone Axis stood for a very long time atop the Keep. "StarDrifter," he whispered. "My father, StarDrifter."

A name. He had a name. And he had the memory of the love on his mother's face as she turned to gaze at his father. He opened his fist and gazed at his father's ring. It lay heavy and golden in his palm. It was a wide gold band, slightly reddish in tinge, and star patterns were picked out in tiny diamond chips around its circumference. The detail was incredible. The closer Axis looked at it the more patterns and stars he could see and no matter how hard he looked he could not find the same pattern twice. He un-

clasped the chain and slid the ring off before slipping it on
the middle finger of his right hand. It fitted beautifully, as if
it had been made for his hand alone.

Belial looked from the assembled and mounted Axe-
Wielders to the garrison of Sigholt as he waited for Axis to
come out of the Keep. They had stayed only long enough
to reprovision and rest and water the horses. Axis had
brought almost all of the Axe-Wielders with him from
Smyrton. Despite the vocal fears of the villagers Axis had
told them shortly that they had almost nothing to fear from
the Shadowsward, and had left them only thirty men to
protect them from whatever ghouls their own fears might
engender. Belial smiled as he remembered the looks on the
faces of those thirty men left behind. They had been livid
that they were left to guard a flock of superstitious peasants
when the rest of the Axe-Wielders were off to fight the
forces of Gorgrael at Gorkenfort.

It was fortunate, Belial mused, not only that the story of
the Prophecy had spread so quickly among the men but
that they had also so quickly accepted it. With the tacit
consent of Axis, Ogden and Veremund had spent a good
deal of time among the Axe-Wielders, speaking of what
they knew about the Icarii and Avar. They did not directly
reveal themselves to the Axemen as the Sentinels of the
Prophecy, but the understanding grew among the Axe-
Wielders that the two old men were more than they had
originally appeared. On the journey from Smyrton to
Sigholt the Axe-Wielders had asked a myriad of questions
about the Icarii and Avar. Gradually, at first in their own
minds and then openly about the campfires at night, the
men had begun to question the prejudices the Seneschal
had instilled in them. While the Seneschal had preached
hatred of the forbidden for the past thousand years, the
Acharites, Icarii and Avar had lived in harmony for thousands of years before the Wars of the Axe. Ogden and Vere-

mund, using their own gentle arts and the stronger enchanted powers of the Prophecy, appealed to the ancient
memories that all three races shared.

Whether it was the efforts of Ogden and Veremund, the
brief glimpses of long repressed race memories, or the
power of the Prophecy itself, by the time the Axe-Wielders
reached Sigholt they clearly understood that they rode to
face Gorgrael and his Ghostmen. The Icarii and Avar—and
the Axemen no longer even referred to them as the Forbidden—were in as much danger as the Acharites. Many were
already openly discussing the identity of the mysterious
StarMan who was supposed to lead them to victory against
the Destroyer. That was good, Belial thought. That meant
that, when the time was right, they would the more readily
accept Axis in his new guise. Axis had always been different and perhaps a brilliant commander because of that.

Belial turned away from the Keep and surveyed the Axe-
Wielders. For the three days they had stayed at Sigholt they
had camped in the wide depression that lay at the foot of
the garrison. Sigholt was situated at the mouth of the Hold-
Hard Pass in the Urqhart Hills; the Pass itself led to the
southern WildDog Plains and, eventually, to Smyrton as it
lay on the banks of the Nordra. The garrison had been built
many centuries previously, some said it was the oldest
fortress in Achar, and the Keep was by far the most ancient
part of the fortress. It sat on the rising slopes of the Hold-
Hard Pass above a deep depression which stretched in a
westerly direction. After three thousand men and more
horses had trampled all over it for three days and nights the
snow was packed hard, and to Belial's curious eye it
looked as though this had once been the bed of a wide lake
at the foot of Sigholt Keep and HoldHard Pass. Perhaps a
long, dried-up tributary of the Nordra had once flowed
through the pass into a lake in the basin of the Urqhart
Hills. Belial had seen Ogden and Veremund staring at the
depression one day, muttering darkly to themselves, and he
assumed they were as curious about the depression as he
was. But Belial had paid the two Sentinels little attention;

like Axis, he had grown somewhat used to their mutterings. Turning from the assembled Axe-Wielders before him, Belial's eyes focused further afield. Several leagues away lay Hsingard, the main city of Ichtar and the official residence of the Dukes of Ichtar. Axis planned to ride straight by it.

The ride to Gorkenfort from Sigholt was straightforward if hard. Snow and ice lay thick on the ground in Ichtar, and, if you listened to the locals, had remained all the previous summer. Gorgrael was indeed spreading his ice clouds further south. Yet Borneheld had been moving troops north for months, and once the Axe-Wielders hit the main trail leading north from Jervois Landing to Gorkenfort the going would be faster. Borneheld had established regular provisioning stations along the trail so the Axe-Wielders would not have to burden themselves with added supplies. Barring misfortunes, they should be there in about two weeks.

Belial rubbed his arms in the frosty air. Where was Axis? They were all ready and waiting, and for once the BattleAxe himself was late. Ogden and Veremund patiently sat their white donkeys to one side, Ogden's cherubic face and Veremund's ascetic one showing no sign of their true identity and powers. Belial snorted under his breath. How many other faces about him held mysteries that he could only guess at? He wondered for a moment about Azhure and where she was. There was a pretty face that held hidden depths of determination. Belial smiled ruefully and rubbed the back of his head. Even now he still suffered biting headaches when he got too tired.

A movement caught his eye and he spun around toward the Keep. Axis was striding down toward him, face relaxed, pulling on gloves to keep the cold out, his black cloak billowing out behind him.

"Is everyone in formation, Lieutenant?" he asked mildly, swinging into Belaguez's saddle and nodding his thanks at the stable boy holding the stallion's head.

Belial kept a straight face. "All cohorts are in formation, sir. In line. Packhorses loaded. Supplies accounted for.

Geared up, fed, watered, weaponed, and ready to go." He paused. "As they have been for the past half an hour."

Axis smiled down at him. "Then what are you doing still on your feet, Lieutenant? Mount up." He swung Belaguez around to face his Axe-Wielders. "Axe-Wielders, are you ready?" he cried in a clear and penetrating voice.

From the basin below him rose a single shout. "We follow your voice and we are ready, BattleAxe!"

"Then let us ride!" Axis cried, and a shout rose from his men as they swung their horses' heads toward whatever fate awaited them at Gorkenfort.

39

Rivkah Awakes

The group travelled north through the Avarinheim for over ten days, tracing the forest paths that ran beside the Nordra as it wound its way south from the Icescarp Alps. Grindle and his son had cut a lightweight but strong sled from dead branches of a Timewood tree floating down the Nordra river, and Raum was packed in every morning atop the folded leather tents. During the day Grindle and Helm, strong even at his youthful age, shared the work of pulling the sled through the Avarinheim.

The going was made easier by the smooth paths and calm weather. The Clans kept the paths they travelled clear of dead wood and leaf litter for those who followed. When Azhure asked why the unseasonable bitter cold and winds that swept Achar did not penetrate the Avarinheim, Gold-Feather smiled enigmatically and said that the trees of the Avarinheim kept the Avar people safe from all but the worst winter weather. "The trees have their own power," she said, "even though in these times it mostly lies quiescent."

As they travelled Pease and Fleat instructed Azhure in the uses of the plant life of the Avarinheim: the bark of the Alefen tree could be boiled for a stimulating and refreshing tea, while the bark of the Bearfoot tree, if shredded and dried, could be woven into baskets and mats and long-wearing soles for leather boots. Under the shelter of the evergreen trees grew a vast variety of bushes and herbs that assisted the Avar in their daily life. Azhure, so used to the Seagrass Plains that supported nothing but grain and vegetable crops, was constantly amazed and delighted by the new discoveries she made around each turn of the forest path. The Avar collected their daily food from the variety of berry bushes, malfari shrubs, small wild fruit and nut trees and even, whenever one draped low enough for the more agile of the children to reach, the great vines that roped between the treetops of the forest canopy. The pulp of their leaves provided a sweet additive to malfari bread and, although she knew the Avar children were skilled climbers, Azhure would watch with her heart in her mouth as Skali and Hogni scaled the great trees for upwards of thirty or forty paces to reach the prized vines.

Both Fleat and Pease were fascinated with Azhure's soft blue dress woven from sheep's wool. The Avar kept a small number of goats and sheep for their meat, milk, and skins, weaving their clothes from goat hair and sheep wool. But Azhure's dress had a different feel and a different weave than the Avar were used to, and Azhure quickly arranged to swap her apron and full-skirted dress for an Avar tunic and leggings, much more comfortable and suitable for the trek through the forest. As she slipped on dark red leggings and a thigh-length gray tunic with the Clan pattern of intertwined branches about its hem, Azhure felt as though she were casting off what remained of her life as a Smyrton villager. Fleat and Pease were more than pleased with the swap as the blue dress would provide them with the material for a tunic each and some items of clothes for the children. Only Barsarbe and GoldFeather among the females of the group wore long skirted robes of pastel shades.

GoldFeather spent most of the day walking beside Azhure, only talking when Fleat and Pease darted off to assist Grindle or Helm, or to collect some leaves or berries they'd spotted growing away from the path. She carefully explained the Prophecy of the Destroyer to Azhure, as well as some of the Avar practices and beliefs that had puzzled Azhure during her first days with the GhostTree Clan. Although Azhure was fascinated with the story of the Prophecy of the Destroyer, she was more enthralled with GoldFeather herself. Ever since she had known Gold-Feather Azhure had been curious about her past, but previously there had never been the time or the opportunity to question her closely about her origins and life.

GoldFeather told her nothing about her youth in Achar, but she did explain something of her life with the Icarii and Avar. "I am fascinated by both races," she said one evening as they set up camp in a small glade. "Originally I spent time with the Avar simply to familiarize myself with their way of life. But soon I realized I could help with the struggle to take their chosen children to be bonded to the Mother. For many years now I have helped take the children through the Seagrass Plains." She shrugged. "Some years I spend more months with the Avar than with the Icarii."

"Do you always travel with the GhostTree Clan while you are in the Avarinheim?"

"Over the past three or four years, yes, although I have lived with other Clans."

Azhure switched her line of questioning to the as yet mysterious Icarii. "Who do you live with among the Icarii?"

GoldFeather smiled at Azhure's persistent questions, but she did not resent them. "Why, with my family, of course."

"You have a family?" Azhure asked.

GoldFeather smiled. "A husband and a daughter. Listen," she said softly. "Do you hear that bird?"

Azhure paused from stretching leather hides over the supports of one of the tents and listened. In the distance she could hear the beautiful song of one of the forest birds. "What is it?" she asked.

"It is the Evensong lark," GoldFeather said, her eyes distant with memory. "I think it is one of the most beautiful songsters of the Avarinheim forest." She turned to Azhure and smiled a little. "I named my daughter after the bird— EvenSong."

Azhure smiled back at the woman. "What a lovely name. Do you have other children?"

GoldFeather's face clouded over. "I had two sons, but I lost them both," she said shortly, turning away from Azhure.

"I'm sorry," Azhure said softly, but GoldFeather had walked over to Fleat to help prepare the evening meal and did not hear. Azhure watched her for a moment. Obviously the loss of two sons still hurt her deeply.

That evening about the fire the conversation returned to the puzzling BattleAxe.

"Azhure," Raum said. "What do you know of the man?"

Raum was growing stronger day by day, his color now healthy, and was starting to insist that he could spend part of each day walking with the aid of crutches to relieve Grindle and Helm of the burden of pulling him on the sled. But Barsarbe still insisted that he protect his leg as much as possible.

"I know relatively little about him," she said slowly. "He only rode into Smyrton the afternoon before I managed to free you and I did not have very much to do with him."

"You know nothing about his past?" Raum asked.

Azhure shrugged, taking a sip of Alefen bark tea. "Only the old scandal that is repeated by some of the Brothers of the Seneschal."

"What is that?" Barsarbe asked impatiently, carefully turning over leaves of the waxflower shrub to dry before the fire. Waxflower leaves, when dried and powdered, made a good stimulant for aged and weak hearts. Barsarbe knew a woman of the FootStrong Clan who had need of such powder.

"That he is Axis Rivkahson, born of the shame of the Princess Rivkah."

"What is the shame of . . ." Raum began, but stopped immediately, appalled by GoldFeather's low wail of distress.

GoldFeather sat, her hands pressed to ashen cheeks, staring at Azhure, her gray eyes huge and shocked. She had gone so pale that her thick silver hair had more life in it than her face. Her lips moved soundlessly and she had to try again and again before she could force any words through.

"What?" she whispered. "What did you say?"

Azhure looked across to Raum and Barsarbe for a moment, but they looked as mystified as she felt. She turned back to GoldFeather. What was wrong with her? Pease moved over to GoldFeather and put her arms about her shoulders trying to comfort her. GoldFeather hardly noticed.

"The BattleAxe, Axis, is the son of Rivkah, sister to King Priam." Azhure said again. "GoldFeather, what is it?"

"But he died," GoldFeather whispered around her fingers. "He *died*!"

No one else about the fire could understand what had upset GoldFeather so much. Barsarbe leaned forward and spoke firmly. "GoldFeather—what is it?"

GoldFeather blinked her eyes and seemed to refocus on the group about her. She lowered her hands and clenched them in her lap. "*I* am Rivkah," she said bluntly. "And my son died at birth. *They told me he died!*"

"But it is said that *you* died," Azhure said slowly, beginning to understand. No wonder GoldFeather had always appeared so courtly and gracious, so sure of herself.

"They tried to murder me," GoldFeather said, her voice becoming harsh, "but they did not succeed. But they told me he was dead!" Her voice cracked with grief again.

Raum turned to Azhure. "Azhure, we do not understand. What is this story of Rivkah?"

Azhure told them what she knew of the story. Of Searlas' young bride who fell pregnant to an unknown lover. Of the birth in Gorkentown that left the mother dead and the son barely alive.

Raum spoke very quietly to GoldFeather . . . Rivkah. "GoldFeather, was StarDrifter your son's father?"

GoldFeather nodded. Pease tightened her hold about GoldFeather's shoulders and whispered comfortingly into her ear.

"So," Barsarbe said softly, "now we know how the BattleAxe carries Icarii blood. StarDrifter is of the oldest and strongest line of Icarii Enchanters, the SunSoars."

"He was dead when they carried him from the chamber," GoldFeather whispered. "He was so blue, so still. They told me he was dead! Azhure," she raised her eyes to the Nors woman. "Who raised my son? Who cared for him?"

Azhure thought for a moment, remembering the gossip she'd heard when the Plough-Keepers of neighboring villages visited Hagen. "Why, Brother Jayme, I think. He is Brother-Leader now."

GoldFeather took a sharp intake of breath and her eyes glittered. "Jayme and his comrade Moryson were the two who abandoned me in the Icescarp Alps to die," she said bitterly. "And now I find that they not only tried to murder me, but stole my son as well." Her face crumpled again. "How could I stand so close to him and not know," she whispered, her voice losing all its strength. "How could I have raised my hand and stopped before I touched him? *How could I not have known he was my son?*"

GoldFeather lowered her face into her hands and began to cry.

"Our need to reach the groves for Yuletide is now even greater," Raum said quietly to Grindle. "We must share this news."

GoldFeather heard him. "I must tell StarDrifter," she said, "I must tell my husband that our son lives." A great sob wracked her body. "How could I have stood so close and not known that he was my son?"

40

Gorkenfort

Gautier drove his troops north as fast as he could, keen not only to deliver Faraday to Borneheld personally, but also to reach Gorkenfort after months of delays. They stopped only the minimum time needed to prevent complete exhaustion of both horses and riders, to warm a thin meal of gruel and the stale bread they carried with them, and to reprovision and feed the horses from the supply depots along the road to northern Ichtar. First and foremost a fighting man, Gautier could almost smell the approaching battle as they rode closer to Gorkenfort.

His sharp face pinched and whitened by the cold, light gray eyes peering out from above his scarf, Gautier spent much of the day spurring his flagging horse up and down the column of troops, cursing and shouting at them to push their horses just that little bit faster. Any horses that were plainly too exhausted in the morning to go any further were slaughtered on the spot. His troops, witnessing Gautier's treatment of the horses, made sure that they never looked too exhausted to go on when their lieutenant rode by.

The weather, cold and snowy since southern Skarabost, had now degenerated into the worst weather Faraday had ever seen. The blacksmith traveling with Gautier was forced to screw thick spikes into the horses' shoes so that they could grip the icy road more easily and, when she rose in the mornings after another night spent shivering sleepless beneath her covering of blankets, Faraday could hear the outer layer of blankets crack and splinter with the thin film of ice which spread over her during the night. Few spoke during the day as they rode, their faces wrapped in thick woollen scarves to keep the frozen air from searing their lungs raw, their eyes almost squinted shut against the snow glare whenever the sun managed to struggle through the thick and low cloud layer. But no matter how many layers they wrapped about themselves the wind managed somehow to pierce right to the very marrow of their bones, and the horses' heads hung low as they trotted like automata along the road, long ropes of ice hanging down from their muzzles and tangled through the thick hair of their manes.

Numerous bands of citizens from Gorkentown passed them as they fled south. Frightened by the obvious preparations for war and the increasing attacks on patrols by the wraiths, those townsfolk who could were escaping as far south as fast as they were able. Their wagons piled high, the fleeing citizens often blocked the road, and Gautier had to force them into the snow at the side of the road to allow his troops through. The wagons trapped in snow drifts were simply left, their owners seizing what food and blankets they could and continuing the trek south on foot. Faraday wondered how many of them would survive.

Stranger still were the occasional bands of Ravensbund people. Faraday had heard vague stories of the wild and barbaric tribes that hunted among the ice packs of the extreme north, but the men and women that passed her on short and ugly yellow-haired horses were even more wild than Gautier's description. Every one of them had their faces tattooed with a tangle of blue and black lines, while

t as high or as thick as those of the fort itself.
ered with apprehension as they halted their
first guard post outside the walls. While she
iate nothing better than a warm bed out of the
and ice, that warm bed also meant Borneheld.
briefly about Axis, something she had rarely
elf to do over these past weeks. Was he all
e managed to reach the fort before her? If so
t be lost. "Pray that I am here in time," she
herself.

ooked at the shadowy figures of the watch pa-
g the walls rising high above her. Gorkentown
sprawling mass about the southern and west-
f Gorkenfort, and Faraday strained her eyes
dusk in an effort to catch a sight of the famed
where Axis was born and Rivkah died, she
here is where I must try to keep his life safe
ther.

!" Gautier suddenly shouted, making Faraday
rprise. Gautier leaned back and grabbed her
le, forcing the tired animal forward at a canter.
Lady Faraday, the sooner we reach the fort the

rds stood back from the town gate that was
ging open, and in a matter of moments Gautier
day's mount through and into the streets of
n itself. Timozel, his mouth grim, spurred his
them with Yr close behind.

deserted of citizens, Gorkentown was clearly
for a siege. Streets had been partially blocked
led masonry in case the fighting came down to
treet warfare and Gautier was forced to slow
s down in order to work their way through. Fara-
glimpse the front rooms of houses and
piled high with provisions, soldiers bedding
he night in homes close to the barricades. The

they plaited slivers of blue and green glass and tiny bells into their hair and the manes of their horses. One of Gautier's scouts reported even larger bands of Ravensbund people moving south through the plains of western Ichtar, and Faraday wondered at the forces that could make an entire people abandon their homeland.

Timozel rode just in front of Faraday, trying to protect her from the worst of the wind. His only thought was to get her safe to Borneheld, though he found himself wondering just how sane Faraday's determination to reach Borneheld really was. But Timozel knew he had made the right choice in dedicating himself to her. It must have been through Artor's personal intervention, Timozel thought, that he had been separated from Axis and the Axe-Wielders. Now that he was distant from his former commander, Timozel could see how his talents had been stunted and wasted among the Axe-Wielders. Axis had not only dishonored his mother and the memory of his father, but had also never given him the opportunity he needed to let his talents shine through. Timozel straightened as he thought about his new path in life. He was a Champion and would one day serve at the head of the most powerful army this land had ever seen. He would serve the WarLord as he would serve his lady wife. Yes, Timozel thought as he glanced at Faraday, riding silent and miserable in her wrappings and blankets, his cause was far more important, far more manly, than it had been in the service of the BattleAxe.

As he rode through the snow, wrapped in his own thoughts, Artor graced Timozel with a further glimpse of the glory that would be his.

A great and glorious battle and the enemy's positions were overrun. Timozel lost not one soldier.

Another day, and another battle. The enemy used foul magic this day, and Timozel's forces were grievously hurt . . . but Timozel still won the field, and the enemy and their crippled commander retreated before him.

Another day, and the battles were over. Timozel sat before the leaping fire with his Lord, Faraday at their side.

All was well. Timozel had found the light and he had found his destiny.

All was well.

Borneheld would help him to achieve greatness and glory. Timozel was sure, *sure*, of it. He would be the Lord that Timozel would fight for.

Timozel wondered whether he should tell Borneheld what he knew about the Sentinels and the Star Gate. If he told Borneheld about the strange creatures he had met and the places he had seen, Borneheld might suspect him. Worse, if Timozel told Borneheld that much, then he might also tell the WarLord about Gorgrael and the pact he had made with the Destroyer. And then Borneheld would never give Timozel command of his armies. No, safer, much safer, to keep his silence. Dark despair still enveloped Timozel whenever he thought of his pact with Gorgrael. But it would be all right so long as he was Faraday's Champion. He would prevail. Legend would remember him.

Day by day, Timozel was changing. The vision that had first accosted him in the tomb of the ninth of the Enchanter-Talons—a Talon so terrible that the Icarii could not bear to speak of him—darkened his heart and warped his soul. The mild resentment Timozel had once harbored toward Axis now festered into an open wound. His ability to judge between right and wrong and between truth and lies cracked beyond repair.

Finally, when it seemed the whole world had frozen beneath a sunless sky, they reached their destination. Gorkentown and Gorkenfort lay almost smothered in snow and ice, the spires of the town and the towers of the fort glittering under a thin layer of ice. Gorkenfort sat defiantly on a small rise, the town huddling about its steep-walled skirts. It was a massive fort with twenty-pace-thick black stone walls mined from the foot of the Icescarp Alps and foundations sunk into such deep bedrock that the fort's walls could not be undone by tunnelling beneath them. Ranged

along the parapets and ba
ready to wreak destruction
simple arrow slits, protecti
mies and the bitter winds
north. Only the southern wa
was so well fortified and de
direct an attack against it. B
ral weather to his advantag
night pour water down the
were encased in a thick slick
ally unscaleable—to flesh an

The awe-inspiring peaks
dramatic backdrop to the tow
to the steep mountain peaks
black from the gentler ice-c
slopes of the mountains. Th
highest peak in the mountain
any of its neighbors and, acco
was the home of the Dark L
Gorkenfort its peak was rarely
and mist that clung to it.

Gautier led his men down t
ten days since they had left J
had not allowed his men to stop
to spend another night out in
daydreaming about Borneheld
face when he presented him w
bride.

The town of Gorkentown la
Although Borneheld had over
tioned in the town itself, he did
cious fuel on fires or for torcl
bedded down with the sun. Exp
held that he could partially cou
creatures with fire, so it was impe
stores of oil and peat be saved
mounted their expected major off

Gorkentown was walled with

walls were n
Faraday shi
horses at th
would appre
cursed wind
She thought
allowed her
right? Had
all might y
whispered t

Faraday
trolling alo
huddled in
ern walls
through the
fort. Here
thought, ar
from his br

"We rid
jump in s
horse's bri
"Come, m
better."

The gu
slowly sw
pulled Fa
Gorkentov
horse afte

Virtually
preparing
with tum
street-by-
their hors
day cou
shopfron
down for

market square was a virtual tent city, again the number of troops and amount of piled provisions making rapid progress impossible. Faraday looked around anxiously for any sign of the distinctive light gray of the Axe-Wielder uniform, but could see none. For the first time she felt a small twinge of concern for her own safety. A heavily bearded soldier, bedded down in his blankets amongst the hay for added warmth, cursed her as he rolled out of the way of her horse's hooves.

"Here! You!" Gautier yelled at a soldier lounging against the support of a tent. The soldier peered through the gloom, then straightened with a snap. "Lieutenant Gautier!" he said, saluting as smartly as his cold-stiffened limbs would allow.

"I've got four hundred men following me into this Artor-forsaken town. They need to be fed, bedded down and their horses attended. Who's in charge of this sorry camp?"

"Ah, Goddars, sir."

"Then find the damned man and tell him that if I return in the morning and find that a single one of my soldiers or horses has gone cold and hungry for lack of his personal attention then he will be eating hay for the rest of his life," Gautier snapped, then tugged Faraday's horse savagely. "Come, my lady, the Duke awaits."

Gautier spurred their horses down a narrow street, not checking to see if Timozel and Yr followed safely. Faraday clung onto the pommel of her saddle, seeing the dark streets only through an increasingly thick gray mist of exhaustion. Men, dogs and horses skittered out of the lieutenant's way, and curses were bitten off hurriedly as men saw who it was who rode so recklessly through the streets of Gorkentown at night. Gautier got almost as much respect, and as much fear, as the WarLord himself.

The town backed up against the southern wall of Gorkenfort and within a few minutes they were picking their way along a massive stone wall rising to unseen heights in the darkness. Its top was too high for Faraday to pick out any movement of the watch. She turned slightly in the saddle, almost falling as she did so, trying to see if Timozel and Yr were still with them.

Timozel nudged his horse up beside Faraday's, catching her arm. "Curse it, Gautier, slow down!" Timozel called out to Borneheld's lieutenant in front of him. "There's no point rushing the Lady Faraday to Borneheld's side if she gets there in pieces!"

Gautier glanced contemptuously at Timozel, but pulled his horse in a little as he caught a glimpse of Faraday's white face. The scarf had fallen around her neck, and her skin was pale and pinched in the dim light, her eyes great dark holes of exhaustion. The reins of her horse's bridle had all but fallen from hands shaking so much with cold and tiredness that they could barely maintain their grip on the pommel of the saddle. "The gate's but a few more minutes," he grunted. "Hold on, my lady."

But Faraday's exhaustion, now that the journey had ended, hit her savagely. Shapes and voices passed her by in a blurred haze, and finally she weaved so badly that Timozel hauled her across to his own horse. Gautier looked back with a frown upon his face, but he was so involved with the complicated password requirements to get them through the massive iron-plated gates of the fort that he could do nothing. He let Faraday's now riderless horse go with a muttered curse and turned back to the standing watch at the gate.

"Timozel?" Yr edged her horse close to Timozel's; she was close to exhaustion herself. "Is she all right?"

Timozel glanced at Yr and nodded. "It is lucky that we arrived when we did. I doubt she could have ridden another day." He looked dispassionately at the Sentinel. "Surely your magic could have helped her before this?"

"I have done what I could, Timozel, but I am no healer." Yr paused, her blue eyes flickering over Timozel's face. "And be careful what you say here, Timozel, your loose tongue could have us *all* killed."

Timozel's face tightened, but his retort was stopped by the sound of the gates opening. He spurred his horse after

Gautier, leaving Yr standing until she could summon the strength to kick her horse after them.

The fort was crowded with men and provisions. As Gautier reined his horse to a stop in the center of the courtyard a tall and powerfully built man stepped out of one of the shadowed doorways of the Keep.

"What is going on here?" he shouted furiously. "I gave orders to close those gates at dusk and to let *no one* through once they were closed for the night!"

Gautier slid off his horse hurriedly, dropping to his knee in the muddy slush of the courtyard at Borneheld's feet. "My Lord," he said a trifle breathlessly, "it is I, Gautier. And look what I have brought you!" Gautier flung his hand out dramatically behind him and Borneheld looked toward the indistinct shadow of Timozel holding Faraday close on his horse.

Borneheld stepped past his lieutenant toward the horseman. "What could be so important that you could not spend the night in Gorkentown without disturbing the watch? Well, I'm not going to be . . ." He stopped in amazement as he reached the horse, recognising Timozel first, and then, unbelievably, the woman he held in his arms.

"My Lord," Faraday said with the last of her strength. "I simply could not wait for you to return to me, and so I have come here to you." Then she fainted.

41

The Duchess of Ichtar

Faraday woke close to noon the next day in an austere room, the only furniture unadorned serviceable chests and chairs and the bed in which she lay. The walls were of undressed stone, naked of any hangings or tapestries to relieve them of their stark lines. A single narrow window let in dim light through its opaque glass panes.

Gorkenfort. Gradually Faraday recalled her arrival the night before, the astounded faces of Borneheld, Earl Jorge and Duke Roland—all of whom had believed she and Timozel had died in the earthfall at the Ancient Barrows. She dimly remembered Borneheld carrying her inside to the fire where she had murmured the story she had told Gautier in Jervois Landing, Timozel filling in some of the gaps. She'd remembered, with a supreme effort, to squeeze Borneheld's hand as he knelt beside her chair. Then, as she had finished speaking, everything had dimmed again.

"Well, sweet child, do you feel better?"

Yr was sitting on the far side of the bed. Faraday rolled over and smiled at her. Yr had obviously managed to have the baggage containing their new clothes brought into the fort and was dressed in a light gray woollen dress, its plain cut suitable for a maid. She had pulled her fine blond hair into a staid roll and her hands were folded primly in her lap, but with her all-knowing eyes Yr looked anything but demure.

"Where are we?" Faraday asked, looking about. A small fire blazed in a grate along one wall, lending some warmth and cheerfulness to the chamber.

"Nowhere but Borneheld's own chamber, dear one. No doubt the WarLord has had to spend a cold night in less comfortable surroundings."

Faraday sat up. "Yr," she frowned, "I can remember so little of last night. What did Borneheld say to our story? Did he believe it?"

Yr laughed, a throaty pleasant sound. "Dear one, he was so astounded to find you alive that had you claimed to have floated down to Gorkenfort on a moonbeam he would have believed you. Now, you had better get washed and dressed so you can continue to play the part of the lovelorn girl for his benefit." Yr's face became serious. "Faraday, we have no time to lose. At the most we can be only a week or so ahead of Axis. I was talking to one of the watch last night and he told me that the fort received word a few days ago that the Axe-Wielders had left Sigholt and were riding for Gorkenfort. You must be married by the time he arrives. You *must* be able to temper Borneheld's jealousy of his half-brother. Remember, Tencendor's fate rests . . ."

"On my becoming Borneheld's wife, not Axis'," Faraday wearily finished for her. "You do not have to remind me every day."

Yr dropped her eyes and stood up, turning to fetch a pitcher of water that had been warming by the fire.

Borneheld met with Earl Jorge, Duke Roland, and Lord Magariz in the stone flagged Great Hall of the Keep. Although the Hall was not overly large for such structures it was barely warmed by the coal fire in the massive fireplace at the end of the Hall. The great dining table was covered with maps and reports and had been placed close to the fire; but even though they stood in close proximity to the fire all the men needed the extra layers of clothing they had on. Timozel stood to one side of the hearth, excited at being able to listen and occasionally advise the deliberations of such important commanders; *Axis* had never asked his advice or invited him to his consultations. Gautier stood by him, his face calm and patient. Borneheld had already rewarded him well for escorting Faraday to his side and Gautier was feeling very hopeful for his future prospects. The conference had been going almost an hour, and the War-Lord and his three commanders were arguing over whether or not to risk men's lives by sending out extra patrols, when Faraday entered the Hall from the doorway at the far end.

Her entrance stunned the warriors into silence. The sight of a lovely woman, dressed in an exquisite emerald and ivory silk gown that revealed more than it concealed, left them with their mouths open and their eyes gleaming in appreciation.

Faraday smiled as she made her way gracefully toward them, her skirts rustling musically as she moved. Thank the Mother they're standing by the fire rather than the other end of the Hall, she thought to herself, not letting the smile slip from her face and tilting her head slightly to display as much of her elegant neck as she could. Long sleeves and thick full skirts notwithstanding Faraday was close to freezing. Still, she wanted to entice Borneheld into marriage as quickly as possible, and she could do it better in this dress than wrapped in a thick woollen cloak.

Faraday stopped three paces short of Borneheld and sank into a deep curtsey. "My Lord Duke," she said, "I am sorry if my sudden entrance has disturbed you. Say the word and I will leave."

"No, no," Borneheld stammered, leaning forward to take Faraday's hand and help her to her feet. "You are not disturbing us at all. Please, do not go." By Artor, Borneheld breathed to himself as Faraday rose, she's even more lovely than I remember. And to think that she risked her life to journey to Gorkenfort to be by my side. She is as brave as she is beautiful, he thought. And she is mine.

Faraday stood quietly for a moment, regarding Borneheld as objectively as she could manage. He seemed larger and more powerful than she remembered. His auburn hair was cut even closer than before; now it was little more than a dark red shadow across his head. His gray eyes, his best feature, glowed with approval and Faraday could see herself reflected in their depths. He looked immeasurably pleased to see her, but was obviously struggling to find the right words. Remembering her girlish dreams of turning Borneheld into a gentle and articulate courtier, Faraday now wondered if he could ever be anything but the gruff and blunt fighting man he was. She broadened her smile at him and then turned to the other men present. Best to press the advantage of surprise home while she still held it.

"Earl Jorge, it my deepest pleasure to see you again." In past years the gray haired Earl Jorge had twice visited her father's home in Skarabost and had been kind and courteous to her, treating her with respect. She inclined her head; her position as betrothed wife to Duke Borneheld now meant that she outranked the man and did not have to curtsey to him.

Jorge stepped forward and lightly kissed her free hand. "My Lady Faraday, I will not pretend that I am not surprised and a little alarmed to see you here." His deeply seamed and weather-beaten face crinkled into a bare smile as he spoke and his hawklike eyes pondered her reflectively. Faraday hastily turned away to Duke Roland, lest those eyes see too much.

"My Lord," she smiled and sketched him the curtsey owed to his rank. Duke Roland bowed as elegantly as his bulk would allow and returned her smile cheerfully. "My Lady Faraday, you are looking lovelier than any of us remember. How fortunate that you survived that dreadful earthfall."

The other nobleman present stepped forward. He must be Lord Magariz, Faraday thought as she smiled and offered him her hand. His dark hair was liberally speckled with silver and a red and angry looking scar ran down his left cheek. His face was darkly handsome, almost mysterious, certainly provocative. Faraday tore her eyes away from his face and noticed he was heavily favoring one leg. She remembered hearing that he had been badly injured in an attack on Gorkenfort at the beginning of DeadLeaf-month. He had the spare look of a man who lived only for battle, but his face hinted at hidden depths of untapped ardour and his dark eyes sparkled at her with unexpected humor.

"My Lady," he smiled as he straightened after brushing his lips across the back of her hand. "We had hoped that Gorkenfort was impregnable to surprise attack, but here you have the best military commanders in Achar struggling to regain the advantage after your unexpected entrance. Be well and welcome to Gorkenfort, Lady Faraday."

Faraday smiled at his gracious remarks then reluctantly pulled her hand from his and turned back to Borneheld, giving Timozel and Gautier a brief nod as she did so. "My Lord, please do not tell me that I was wrong to come here."

"Well," Borneheld began, but Earl Jorge broke in.

"My Lord Duke, Gorkenfort is hardly the place for such a gently bred lady. We are a military establishment and we expect attack any day now. Borneheld, I beg you, now is the time to return your Lady to safety in Carlon."

"Oh no!" Faraday said hurriedly, genuine concern shadowing her eyes. She placed her free hand over Borneheld's fist where it held her other prisoner and spoke pleadingly. "Borneheld, my love. My mother is dead, and I only barely escaped death myself. In my grief and loneliness my first thought was to join you. Please, I beg of you, do not send me away now." She drew deep on the seed of power that the Mother had given her and stepped closer to Borneheld, smiling into his eyes and gently squeezing his hand between her own.

Borneheld took a sharp intake of breath, as did most other men in the room. Already beautiful, Faraday had assumed an aura of such allure that all the men present felt themselves responding to it in some measure. Borneheld had no intention of trying to resist; if the woman desired him so much, then why deny her?

Faraday saw Borneheld's eyes darken and pressed her advantage home. "My Lord," she breathed, "have I come all this way for nothing? Please, Borneheld, let us not delay our marriage any longer. Who knows what tomorrow will bring?"

By the Plough, Jorge thought, breathless himself, could I have refused so beautiful a woman who rode through snow and danger to be by my side?

All Borneheld could see was the lovely young woman in front of him, declaring before all these men that she had risked her life to simply be by his side. All his life he had suffered the indignity of watching women smile and compliment him on his fighting skills, while all the while their eyes had followed his half-brother. Well, now he had won a prize that even that fatherless bastard would doubtless hunger after. She had come to *him*, not Axis!

"No doubt you thought only of me after the BattleAxe failed you so dismally," he said. "I shall have him flogged for his incompetence when he arrives here."

Faraday quailed at the image Borneheld's suggestion brought to her mind, yet she knew that she could not plead for Axis now. "I should have stayed in Carlon with you, my love. My father was wrong to send me with the BattleAxe. Perhaps," she smiled coquettishly, "we should have my father flogged instead?"

Borneheld burst into hearty laughter. "What a mischievous lady you are, Faraday. A surprise, I must say. Well gentleman," he said turning to the three lords, "could you resist such a beauty as this? I admit that I cannot. Gautier!"

Gautier snapped to attention. "Sir?"

"There is a decrepit old Brother still lingering about the fort, eating his way through stores that would be better spent on a fighting man. Go find him."

"I will find him *instantly*, my Lord Duke," said Gautier, wondering where the man could be in the maze of the fort.

Borneheld turned his eyes toward his lieutenant momentarily. "See that you do, Gautier." He looked back at Faraday. "For I think we will be needing his services at a wedding this afternoon."

Faraday felt her stomach knot, but maintained her smile. "My Lord," she breathed, "I can hardly wait."

Magariz turned and caught Gautier's arm as the lieutenant strode past him. "Gautier," he said quietly, "you will find the Brother dozing in front of the kitchen fires."

Gautier's face relaxed in relief. "Thank you, my Lord."

Timozel, quiet up to now, stepped forward. "My Lord Duke," he began, and Borneheld turned toward him with mild impatience. What did the Axe-Wielder want now? He had done a service rescuing Faraday from the earthfall and escorting her northwards, but surely it was time for him to depart gracefully. Borneheld's eyes narrowed in thought as he looked more closely at Timozel. The charming youth had grown into a striking man and a nasty suspicion flowered in his mind. The journey north would have taken this pair weeks—just how had they amused themselves at night? Was he about to get something less than he had bargained on?

"My Lord Duke," Timozel went on, "I do not think you yet quite realize the deep bond between the Lady Faraday and myself." Borneheld tensed and Faraday felt his fist close tight about her hand. Oh, dear Mother, she prayed even as her face flinched from the pressure of Borneheld's fingers, do not spoil this now, Timozel. "My Lord Duke, after our fortunate escape from the earthfall I realized that one of the best ways that I could protect the Lady Faraday and bring her to your side unharmed was to pledge myself to her as her Champion."

Borneheld gaped in surprise and he almost laughed. Champion? No one did that now! Mingled with his amusement was some degree of relief; perhaps Faraday was not as spoilt as he had thought a moment ago. Behind him Jorge and Roland exchanged surprised looks. The last Champion they had known had been of their grandfathers' generation. Unlike Borneheld, however, neither of them were prepared to dismiss Timozel's pledge so lightly. What was this girl that she had managed to win herself a Champion?

"My Lord," Timozel dropped to his knees in front of Borneheld. "My pledge of service also extends to my Lady's husband. Know that I will serve you as loyally and with as deep a fervour as I serve your Lady wife. I pledge to always put your honor and your cause before my own and before any other vow that I may have made previously. My Lord Duke, will you accept my service?"

Suspicious a moment ago, now a glow of triumph began to suffuse Borneheld's face. Not only had Faraday fled Axis' protection to be at his side, but now Timozel had cast aside his vow of loyalty to Axis and the Axe-Wielders in favor of service to Borneheld. And to think that in a week or so Axis himself would be here to witness Borneheld's triumph—and to hand over control of the Axe-Wielders. Borneheld dropped Faraday's hand and smiled at Timozel's bowed head.

"Timozel," he said, not bothering to hide the triumph in his voice. "Take my hands." Timozel looked up and placed his hands between those of Borneheld. "Know that I, Duke Borneheld of Ichtar, do accept your vow of service and loyalty. Be welcome."

Faraday was shocked by Timozel's actions, but forced a smile to her face. "My Lord, you are so generous. 'Tis no wonder the troubadours sing your praises far and wide," she said, noticing that Earl Jorge was looking at her strangely. She smiled lightly at Jorge and hoped that he hadn't noticed her shock at Timozel's disloyalty to Axis.

"My Lord." Gautier's voice called from the doorway. At

his side stood an old man, his frame so fragile he looked almost ethereal, dressed in the habit of the Brotherhood of the Seneschal. "I have found Brother Francis."

"Brother," Borneheld said jovially as they joined them. "I hope you can remember the Nuptial Service. I have a marriage I wish to transact."

Brother Francis smiled at Borneheld and Faraday and nodded his head. "It has been many years, my Lord, but it is a Service that all brothers hope they will be called upon to perform one day. I am honored that I should be asked to join the lives of the Lady Faraday of Skarabost and Duke Borneheld of Ichtar." Gautier had obviously briefed him on the way up the stairs from the kitchen.

Borneheld turned to Jorge, Roland and Magariz. "My Lords, I would be honored if you would witness my marriage."

They inclined their heads graciously, although each was growing just a trifle impatient to return to the more desperate dealings of war.

"Faraday?" Borneheld turned back to her. "Are you ready?"

"Yes," Faraday said simply. She did not trust her voice for any more. Axis, forgive me, she prayed silently. Please understand what I am about to do. For an instant she let herself recall what it had been like folded in his arms, but then she thrust the thought from her. I must never think of that again, she told herself firmly. Never.

"My Lords and Lady," the Brother said, and then slipped smoothly into the words of the Nuptial Service. Faraday felt as if she were in someone else's dream, watching proceedings from a great distance. Ah, she thought to herself, neither Axis nor myself are our own people any longer. The Prophecy of the Destroyer demands a cruel price from those who must serve it.

Abruptly she realized that the Brother had fallen silent and that now Borneheld was holding her hand and speaking.

"I, Borneheld, Duke of Ichtar, do stand by my promise

of marriage to thee, Lady Faraday of Skarabost, and in front of these witnesses I do promise to honor you, to remain loyal to you, and to pledge to you my respect, my possessions, and my body for as long as we both shall live. To this I do freely consent and will. You have my pledge of marriage, Faraday, and to this may Artor bear holy witness."

He stopped and Faraday realized with a start that he was waiting for her vows. She had to clear her throat before she repeated the vows.

Brother Francis still had a few words of the Nuptial Service to utter, but Borneheld had enveloped Faraday in a powerful embrace. Neither heard him impart the blessing of Artor upon them and pronounce them husband and wife. Jorge looked at the pair, musing over the events of the past hour. He wondered if Faraday had been as sure as he had first believed. The girl had hesitated slightly before she spoke the holy vows and even now she appeared a little too rigid in Borneheld's embrace for a woman who had risked death to join her lover. Well, if she had doubts, then it was now too late. They were as legally and as tightly married as could be. Only death would sever that bond now. So he had witnessed. So he would attest.

"Listen to me," Yr said very quietly, "no matter what he does to you physically, he can never touch your soul—not if you refuse to let him. Do you understand what I am saying?"

Faraday nodded, her stomach tight. For weeks she had avoided thinking past the marriage ceremony itself; avoided thinking of the duties of a wife to a husband. Yr stood behind her unlacing her silk gown. Poor sweet girl. Borneheld was the last person who should induct her into the arts of love. Yet . . . it was necessary. She and Jack had fought long and hard to get Faraday to this point. Thank the Prophecy that they had reached Gorkenfort before Axis.

"Artor, girl, have you not finished with my Lady yet?" snapped Borneheld, standing by the fire of their bedchamber.

"In a moment, my Lord," Yr said softly as she touched the pale skin of Faraday's back, trying to give her some reassurance. But Faraday was too rigid to respond even to the Sentinel's touch.

As Borneheld continued to shift impatiently behind them, Yr swiftly unlaced Faraday's gown and helped her slip into a robe. She met Faraday's huge and apprehensive eyes for an instant, tried to impart some reassurance with her own eyes, then turned and walked for the door.

In the pale gray light of dawn Faraday eased her aching body as far away from that of her husband's as she could, praying that her careful movements would not awaken him again. Despite her best efforts tears finally forced themselves past her eyelashes. She knew that Borneheld had not meant to be unkind, but his own fierce desire for her had made him unwittingly impatient and thoughtless. She had tried her best to please him, but her lack of knowledge had confused Borneheld, and his lovemaking had turned out to be every bit as clumsy and unpleasant as his conversation.

She had wanted to think of Axis, had wanted to use the memory of his arms about her as a talisman against the reality of Borneheld. But Borneheld's presence was too powerful and his demands on her body too great for her to be able to retain any image of Axis in her mind at all.

But Borneheld had been pleased, and for that Faraday was grateful. Then she frowned. When it had finally been over, Borneheld had patted her belly hopefully. "Perhaps I have planted a son there tonight," he had panted, then had rolled over and immediately gone to sleep.

No, Faraday thought, her own hands on her belly now. No. I married him to serve the Prophecy but I will not bear him a child. I do not have to give that much. "Mother, hear me," she whispered, "let me remain barren. I will conceive no child of his." For a moment the heavy ruby ring pinched on her finger and she twisted it to relieve the pressure. It was every bit as heavy and uncomfortable as Borneheld was. "Grant this my wish."

"Faraday?" Borneheld's voice whispered sleepily. "Is that you? Are you awake?"

Faraday heard him turn over toward her and bit her lip to stop herself from tensing when she felt his hand fumbling at her breast.

"Come now, my dear. Your husband needs you."

42

Reacquaintances

In the end Faraday had well over a week before Axis arrived in which to accustom herself to marriage and to ensure that Borneheld continued to believe that she loved and wanted him. She learned to accept Borneheld's nightly demands upon her body, asking him to show her what she could do to please him. Very reluctantly, Faraday had to admit to herself that if it hadn't been for her love for Axis, if it hadn't been for those brief moments under the stars at the Ancient Barrows, she might have come to tolerate her marriage to Borneheld. In his own way, Borneheld wanted to please her. If his efforts at lovemaking were sometimes brusque and uncompromising, then those were qualities admirable in the soldier if not the lover—and Borneheld had never pretended to be anything else than what he was.

Borneheld had no use for Faraday during most of the day, locked as he was in discussions with his military commanders or occupied with leading patrols into the northern wastes. He did like her to come and watch him at weapon training in the mornings, though, and there Faraday made complimentary remarks as she watched him swing his heavily muscled body, bared to the waist, through sundry complicated maneuvers with sword and staff. He was a powerful man, as Faraday now knew in more intimate detail, but sometimes as she watched him her mind drifted to another man she had once watched at weapon practice early in the frosty mornings on the Plains of Tare.

On the fourth day of the first week of Snow-month she slowly paced the parapets of the walls of Gorkenfort, wearing a heavy cloak hugged tight over her black silk gown, the hood drawn far over her face as she gazed over the town of Gorkentown toward the road that led south. She never admitted what she was looking for walking along the parapets. Whenever anyone asked, she simply said that she was whiling away the lonely hours while Borneheld was otherwise occupied. Today Timozel walked by her side, although Borneheld increasingly gave him responsibilities about the fort. Pity, Faraday idly thought as she nodded at one of the watch, that Timozel's duties did not also extend to taking her place in Borneheld's bed. Her mouth curled in a private grin at the thought. Today Yr had also joined them for the fresh air, and Faraday glanced at the Sentinel, wondering if she'd caught her thought. It appeared she had. Yr was biting the inside of her cheek to keep her mirth in check, deliberately avoiding Faraday's eye.

The day was bitingly cold but relatively clear, for the past two days the snow clouds had held back, and it was Yr's sharp eyes that spotted them first. She stepped close to Faraday's side.

"Look," she said quietly, pointing toward a faint smudge on the southern road. "Can you see them?"

Faraday's heart leapt into her mouth and she strained to see. "Where?" she said breathlessly. "Where? I can't see them. Is it him?"

"Yes, sweet child, it is him. Are you ready?"

Her question might have had a number of meanings, but Faraday knew exactly what she meant. Could she restrain

Borneheld if it came to it? "If I am not then we will soon know, Yr," she said shortly.

"What is it?" Timozel asked impatiently, irritated by the way the two women whispered together. "What can you see?"

"The Axe-Wielders ride for Gorkenfort, Timozel," said Yr, turning her face toward him. For the past week or so she had taken to twisting her long blond hair into a loose knot on the crown of her head, leaving tendrils to float about her face like a shifting golden cloud. Since their arrival at Gorkenfort they had resumed their affair, and it pleased Timozel that Yr chose his company before that of Gautier's. "Are you ready to meet your BattleAxe, Timozel?"

"Not *my* BattleAxe any longer," Timozel replied. "My Lady has chosen to marry Duke Borneheld, the most powerful WarLord Achar has ever had. I serve Borneheld now."

Faraday's mouth twisted grimly. As she betrayed Axis, so too did Timozel. How could she blame him for that?

"Besides," Timozel added after a moment, thinking back on the moment in the tomb of the Icarii Enchanter-Talon, "Will not Borneheld be the one to save us from Gorgrael the Destroyer?"

Faraday's hands gripped the stone compulsively. She remembered that both Jack and Yr had been deliberately ambiguous when Timozel asked if Borneheld had been the one to save Achar. No one had known that the next instant he would be on his knees pledging his oath of Championship to Faraday. Oh what a pit we dig for ourselves, Faraday thought, with the shovel of our lies.

"Who knows who he is," said Faraday, reaching out for Timozel's hand. "Come, let us watch for the Axe-Wielders."

The Axe-Wielders took another hour to wend their way toward the gate of the town, and then through the town itself. Most of them stopped in the town square to organize billeting and food for themselves and their horses, but soon the Axemen who were left to ride for the fort were close enough for Faraday to make out individual faces. There was

Belial, looking thinner but more relaxed than she remembered. Behind him rode Arne, a man Faraday hardly knew.

"Yr," she said, pointing with her hand.

"Yes," Yr smiled. "They are still with him." Ogden and Veremund rode huddled into cloaks that billowed about their white donkeys. Yr was delighted to see her companions; she could barely wait to find out how they were doing with Axis, if they had seen Jack, if they had found the fifth Sentinel, if Gorgrael had struck again.

And then Axis rode into sight from behind a corner of the twisting streets. He was chatting with one of the Axe-Wielders who had lagged behind, and Faraday, hands clutched to her breast, thought her heart would seize at the sight of him. Did he mourn me? she wondered. Or did he shrug his shoulders at the pile of dirt that covered my grave and turn to joke with Belial?

Yr slipped her arm about the girl's waist again and whispered in her ear. "Doubtless you have both grown different ways since you last saw each other, Faraday, but if he said that he loved you, then do not doubt it."

Faraday watched Axis' black-clad form far below her as he rode toward the fort's gate.

Mother help me, but I love him, she thought.

I know, sweet child, I know, Yr replied, and Faraday did not wonder that she could hear Yr's thoughts within her own head.

Belial halted the small group of Axe-Wielders before Gorkenfort's gate, waiting for Axis to catch them up. Axis pulled Belaguez to a halt by Belial's bay stallion, his face tight with tension. Ahead of him lay the ultimate embarrassment, admitting to Borneheld's face that he had lost Faraday. And within minutes he would also have to surrender outright control of the Axe-Wielders to Borneheld as he had promised Jayme.

Axis had not been looking forward to this day.

"Remember, Axis, no matter what happens in Gorkenfort," Belial said quietly, his steady gaze fixed on Axis' face, "Our loyalty is to you and only to you. We will follow wherever you lead and fight in whatever cause you choose."

Axis looked over at Belial. Over the past few weeks the man had been a rock, always there with advice and reassurance, always there with a smile and a joke. On the road north Axis had spent hours discussing his doubts and uncertainties with Belial; had he not been there, Axis did not know how he'd have coped with the changes in his life.

Axis did not know how much longer his loyalty to Jayme could last. Already his trust in the Brother-Leader had been seriously undermined, first by Jayme's insistence that Borneheld assume control of the Axe-Wielders, but more recently by the things he had learned about his own origins and about the Icarii and the Avar. He had not been able to put the woman who had pleaded for Raum's life near the forest out of his mind. "You need do only what your heart tells you to do. Not what the Seneschal has taught you must be done. Your duty should always be to do what *you* feel is right." Axis took a deep breath. Did what she say make sense? Dare he trust his own heart? It certainly did not feel right to pass his Axe-Wielders over to Borneheld's command . . . but who was he to complain about the WarLord assuming control of the Axe-Wielders when so many of them had died needlessly in Gorgrael's storm?

"Axis! BattleAxe! It is good to have you here!"

Axis turned his head toward the sound. Duke Roland was striding over as fast as his fat would allow. Axis swung off Belaguez and grasped the Duke's hand and arm. Obese the man might be but Axis believed he was one of the best commanders in the army. Like Jorge, Roland had been one of the very few nobles at court who had not sneered or condescended to Axis because of his birth. Roland nodded at Belial and peered curiously at Ogden and Veremund but turned back to Axis. He gripped the BattleAxe's hand and forearm enthusiastically.

"Welcome, Axis. Artor be with you."

"And with you, Duke Roland, and with you," Axis smiled back at the man. "How go things?"

Roland shrugged. "Gorkenfort still stands, Axis. Raids have still taken their toll . . . no!" Roland let Axis' hand go and raised his own in front of him defensively at the questions he could see bubbling to Axis' lips. "No, I am not going to stand here in the wind and answer all your questions, my boy. Come inside. Borneheld and Jorge are meeting with Magariz, and they will want to hear what you have to say first. Did you discover anything at the Silent Woman Keep?"

Axis kept his face bland with a supreme effort, a thousand retorts springing instantly to mind. He waved at Ogden and Veremund. "I have brought these two elderly brothers with me, my friend. Perhaps they can help us, perhaps not."

Roland's round face dropped in amazement. "They rode all the way to Gorkenfort from the Silent Woman Woods on *those*? What were you thinking of? Did you have no spare horses?"

"A Brother and his donkey are hard to part," said Axis dryly. "Come, take me to your war council. Belial? Bring those two . . . gentlemen with you. We are off to meet Borneheld."

Roland put his hand confidentially on Axis' shoulder as they walked into the fort and talked rapidly and quietly to him about the defense systems already in place about Gorkenfort. Neither noticed the cloaked woman standing on the parapets watching them.

Borneheld looked up from the papers spread about the table in front of the fire and saw Roland and Axis walk in the door at the end of the Hall followed by the BattleAxe's lieutenant, Belial, and two ancient Brothers of the Seneschal. So. The BattleAxe had arrived. Now all would see who was the stronger, who was the more brilliant strategist, the better commander. Today he would assume control of the Axe-Wielders. Borneheld felt very sure of himself. Very powerful.

Jorge and Magariz, standing to one side of the table, exchanged anxious glances. Together with Roland, they had worried what the rivalry between Axis and Borneheld would mean to the defense of Gorkenfort. All three hoped Axis would not push Borneheld into an outright confrontation, and that Borneheld would not lose complete control and forget the defense of Gorkenfort in the pursuit of his hated half-brother. Axis and Borneheld supping together brought with it the risk of violence. What they might do in their current hostility during the dangerous stress of a military campaign was unthinkable.

"BattleAxe," Borneheld smirked as Axis reached the table. He had been looking forward to this moment for a long, long time. Finally he would see his brother humbled before him.

"WarLord," Axis said simply, his face expressionless. Neither man offered the other his hand.

"I received the report on your loss of the Ladies Merlion and Faraday north-east of the Silent Woman Woods, BattleAxe. I am somewhat surprised to see that you still think yourself fit to lead the Axe-Wielders."

Magariz, Jorge and Roland all stared at Borneheld, but they held their tongues at a quick glare from their War-Lord.

Axis hesitated, stung by the remark. "I have nothing to add to my report," he said tightly.

Borneheld rested his hands on the table and leaned forward slightly. "Your incompetence appals me!" he hissed. "Two innocent women trusted you!"

Axis' eyes narrowed. That Borneheld had every right to admonish him only made his anger more intense. Should he tell him that Faraday possibly lived? But he had no proof save the word of an Avar man, and Axis knew Borneheld well enough to know he would never accept the word of one of the Forbidden.

Roland spoke quickly, concerned that Borneheld was

wasting time in pointless hostilities. "My Lord Duke. Perhaps this matter could wait until later to be discussed . . . in more detail."

Borneheld spared him a quick, hard glance, but changed the subject. Time enough for Axis to discover that Faraday had not only survived, but had journeyed north to be with the man she loved. "Have you brought me my Axe-Wielders?" he asked.

Axis' face hardened. It was all he could do to stop himself reaching across the table and throwing Borneheld into the fire. The two men stared at each other, both unwilling to be the first to drop his eyes.

Roland, Jorge and Magariz held their collective breaths, but in the end Axis felt Belial step up behind him, lending his BattleAxe his silent support.

"I stand here for the Axe-Wielders," Axis said finally. "I put myself under your command and, through me, you command the Axe-Wielders."

Borneheld opened his mouth. It was not what he wanted. He wanted Axis completely out of the way and himself in daily control of the Axe-Wielders. Better, Borneheld would like to have broken the Axe-Wielders up completely and spread the individual men among his own units and cohorts, shattering the spirit and legend of the Axe-Wielders with one clean stroke. But Jorge stepped forward and spoke first. He knew exactly what Borneheld wanted to do and he also knew that Axis was unlikely to placidly stand by and watch his command destroyed before his eyes.

"We are all grateful for your support here, BattleAxe," he said smoothly, "and that you should so willingly put yourself under Borneheld's command. Through you the Axe-Wielders will be a useful adjunct to the WarLord's brilliance."

It was a masterstroke. Jorge had not only complimented Borneheld and pandered to his vanity, but had also put Borneheld in the difficult situation of appearing churlish if he now insisted on a complete surrender of the Axe-Wielders to his personal command. Borneheld gaped a little, unsure of how to take Jorge's intervention, and before he could decide how to react Roland followed Jorge's lead.

"We have all placed ourselves and our men under Borneheld's command," he said jovially to no one in particular. "Through all of us the WarLord controls an entire army but does not waste his time on the daily mundane activities of keeping thousands of men fed, watered and exercised. We are all grateful for his foresight in insisting we act as the conduits through which his commands pass to our own men. And to think of it," he turned and beamed at Borneheld, "the Duke Ichtar will be the first WarLord to command the Axe-Wielders."

Borneheld closed his mouth and thought about it. Yes, Jorge and Roland made sense. He didn't want to waste time worrying about which dullard groomed the horses. Better that lesser men, men like Axis, do that. Besides, as Roland had said, he *would* be the first man outside the Seneschal to command the Axe-Wielders.

"Yes," he nodded, "I accept the surrender of your command, BattleAxe. You may remain in daily control of the Axe-Wielders and I shall use you to relay my wishes to them."

Don't fight it, Axis, Belial thought desperately, keeping a pleasant expression on his face. Don't fight it. Be grateful to these two old men that you've retained as much control as you have.

To tell the truth, Axis was mildly amused by the way Jorge and Roland had flattered and manipulated Borneheld. "As you please, WarLord," he said neutrally, bowing slightly in Borneheld's general direction. "I accede to your wishes."

Borneheld smiled in complete satisfaction. For the first time since Jayme had appointed Axis BattleAxe, Borneheld felt as though he had firmly established his own superiority. "Well, BattleAxe. What have you learned at the Silent Woman Keep to help us drive back these wraiths and icemen that nibble at our flanks?" He sat down in a high-backed wooden chair and waved at the other men in the room to pull stools up to the table. Borneheld was feeling generous.

Ogden and Veremund, until now quiet and unobtrusive, stood forward. Axis glanced at them as he stretched his legs out underneath the table. "I have brought with me two Brothers who have studied long and hard the records of the Silent Woman Keep. Ogden, Veremund, perhaps you would like to inform the WarLord what you feel opposes Gorkenfort?"

All eyes swivelled toward Ogden and Veremund, who played the part of Brothers of the Seneschal to perfection.

"Artor save you and keep you always in His care," they said in unison, bowing to Borneheld.

"And you," Borneheld muttered impatiently, running a hand over the short stubble of his auburn hair. "On with it."

"My Lord Duke," Ogden began, "we believe that many of the answers you seek lie in an ancient Prophecy that dates from a time long before the Acharites forced the Forbidden behind the Fortress Ranges."

For the next half an hour the pair spoke, reciting the first two verses of the Prophecy of the Destroyer and explaining what they knew about Gorgrael and his Ghostmen. Listening to them, Axis found it hard to believe that the rest of Achar as yet had no idea of the revelations he had encountered in recent months. As far as Borneheld and his command in Gorkenfort were concerned, the strange wraiths they encountered could *only* be the Forbidden. They had no other explanation for them. Yet now Ogden and Veremund were providing Borneheld with an alternative. In the end, Borneheld reacted exactly as Axis suspected he might.

"Foolishness," Borneheld finally spat. "It is the Forbidden we face. The Seneschal teaches they are our enemies, not these creatures that some worm-ridden prophecy speaks of."

Magariz leaned forward, frowning at Borneheld's words. In the firelight the livid scar on his cheek glowed with an almost maniacal fury. "My Lord, I beg to differ. The ice creatures the Prophecy describes sound all too much like the creatures which attacked our patrols and the Retreat in

Gorkentown. And some of the Ravensbundmen who have been fleeing south have mentioned this name—Gorgrael. They say they have heard it whispered on the wind by the wraiths which attacked their homes and families."

Borneheld continued to look skeptical, but Jorge and Roland nodded thoughtfully. "Tell me, Brothers, if you can. If these are Gorgrael's creatures that push down from the north then how can we keep them back?" Jorge asked.

Ogden and Veremund looked at each other, both careful not to look at Axis. "If we listen to the Prophecy, Earl Jorge, then the three races of Tencendor must unite under the Star-Man to defeat the Destroyer. Nothing else will stop him."

Borneheld looked at them incredulously for a moment, then he leaned back in his chair and roared with laughter. "You bring me news that would entertain old women and young girls. You tell me nothing that will keep Gorkenfort and Ichtar secure from the creatures that swarm out there in the snow." He leaned forward again, his voice growing angry, his gray eyes glittering dangerously. "Your talk of this demon savior is nothing but the ramblings of old men in their dotage, while your talk of uniting Acharites with the Forbidden is heretical and I will have none of it! Artor-fearing men will drive back these invaders, not the ensor-celled souls of the Forbidden! You're lucky I don't have you summarily executed for subversive rumormongering!" He was shouting by the time he'd finished.

Both Ogden and Veremund stepped back, hands flapping anxiously among the skirts of their habits, their alarmed eyes flying to Axis for help. But Borneheld was not yet finished.

"I will have none of this talk of prophecy in Gorkenfort or the town, do you hear me?"

Axis waved the two old men back a few paces out of the way while Belial pondered the fact that even now over three thousand Axe-Wielders were undoubtedly sharing news of the Prophecy around the campfires of Borneheld's army. Borneheld would not be very pleased if news of the Prophecy and of the StarMan gained acceptance as quickly among his own men as it had among the Axe-Wielders. Jorge, Roland and Magariz all studied their hands and fingernails with deep fascination. They all believed that the Prophecy needed further discussion. But perhaps this was not the time to say so in front of Borneheld.

Borneheld finally dismissed Ogden and Veremund with a curt wave. They barely managed to keep their gait to a walk as they fled the Hall.

"Axis," Magariz said. "We have only one or two pieces of information ourselves. The wraiths, led by these ice creatures, have staged more numerous and more daring raids over the past few weeks as the weather has deteriorated, but they have not seriously threatened Gorkenfort or Gorkentown since the night they staged their extraordinary raids into the fort and Retreat themselves."

"Do you have any idea how they managed to break through your defenses on that occasion, Magariz?" Axis asked.

Magariz's handsome face suddenly looked gray and haggard. "I had been on patrol all day, BattleAxe, and I had gone to sleep here in front of the fire. I awoke late in the night, cold and stiff, the fire burned down to embers, to find the creatures about to strike. When I cried out the sentries rushed in and tried to defend me—but they were cut to shreds while I barely escaped with my life. The nightmare creatures left me unconscious and bleeding. How did they get in? I do not know, BattleAxe. Perhaps they used dark enchantments to pass the guards and breach the defenses." Magariz shuddered for a moment, remembering. "They had wings, Axis. They must have attacked from the sky." He smiled a little at the expression on Axis' face. "Yes. Wings. Since that night the sentries watch the sky as assiduously as they watch the ground."

"Our patrols have seen them from time to time, leading bands of the wraiths," Borneheld said quietly, his anger at the two Brothers forgotten as he recalled those times he had led the patrols outside the walls of Gorkenfort. "I have seen them myself when I have led patrols. They are . . . solidifying. Since the attacks began both the wraiths and their ice-creature leaders are becoming more flesh than ghostly apparition. We are losing many men and have yet to make a significant impression on the wraiths."

Jorge considered his WarLord for a moment. Borneheld might have his moments of ill-considered anger, and his jealousy of Axis might sometimes mar his judgment, but no one could call his bravery into question. He had done a superb task in organizing Gorkenfort's defenses. For that alone he commanded their respect, while his position as WarLord demanded their loyalty. Borneheld was a hard commander, demanding instant obedience and respect from his men. But he was, as yet, a largely untried combat commander and had gained his position as WarLord principally through his position as heir to the throne. Did he have the level head and the skills to see them through this crisis? Could he rally men the way the BattleAxe had already proved he could? Jorge's eyes flickered to Axis.

"Have the Ravensbundmen brought anymore news from the north over the past few weeks?" Belial asked, impressed that Borneheld had risked his life with that of his men.

Magariz slowly tapped the table with his fingers. "They have told us these Skraelings—their word for the wraiths—continue to flood south, keeping close to the Alps. They dislike the Andakilsa; the Ravensbundmen saw some of the wraiths become trapped and dissolve in the water."

To one side Borneheld frowned but did not speak. The wraiths did not like running water. For days his mind had worried at that, wondering if a moat could protect Gorkenfort. He sighed inwardly; it was a shame the river was too far distant to try and divert any of its waters.

"But unfortunately the Ravensbundmen can no longer provide us with information," Magariz continued.

"Why?" Axis asked.

"The flood of refugees from Ravensbund has suddenly dried up," Roland explained. He had found it difficult to balance his massive bulk on a small stool and was now standing by the fire, his body throwing gigantic shifting shadows onto the far wall as he eased his weight from leg to leg. "We think it is not because all the Ravensbundmen have fled their icy home, but because they have been cut off from their southerly escape route."

"That, or they've all been eaten," Jorge remarked. "Axis, we've discovered one slight defense against these creatures. In small groups they can sometimes be repelled with fire, although if they attack in force they can overwhelm burning brands. Now we equip all our patrols with burning torches—it provides some protection."

"That is all you've discovered?" Axis asked, realizing as soon as the words were out of his mouth that his question sounded insulting.

"Do you think you could learn more, BattleAxe? Do you think you can do better than those dozens of my soldiers who have died over the past months?" Borneheld snarled, enraged.

Axis began to apologize but Borneheld was not done. "Will you lead the morning patrol, BattleAxe? Then perhaps you can discover what it is that we have so dismally failed to perceive. After all, a man who could lose so many of his men to a sudden rain squall, not to mention the Lady Faraday and the youth Timozel to an earthfall, should have no trouble dealing with a few dozen wraiths in the snow!"

Axis leapt to his feet. Belial rose beside him and grabbed his arm, trying to restrain him, but Axis threw him off. "No one calls my courage into question, brother! You have your patrol leader!"

"This is hardly necessary, Axis," Roland started, but was interrupted by a voice from the back of the Hall.

"Borneheld," Faraday said clearly and sweetly, "how mischievous of you to infer that Timozel and I were dead." She slowly started to walk toward the group at the other end of the Hall, her entire will bent to keeping her eyes on Borneheld and not letting them drift toward Axis.

"Faraday!" Axis whispered, stunned by the sight of her. She *was* alive! What was she doing here? He turned slightly to see the look on Borneheld's face. Oh, dear Artor, no! She wouldn't, *couldn't*, have done this to him!

"Ah," Borneheld said, more than pleased by Axis' reaction. "Perhaps you remember my wife, BattleAxe. You lost her some weeks past." Faraday joined Borneheld at his side and the Duke placed a proprietorial arm about her waist. Faraday smiled at him, and then, finally, looked at Axis. Only with an extraordinary effort did she keep her expression impassive as she ran her eyes over his shocked face.

Axis' distress at seeing Borneheld's arm resting around Faraday found release in anger at her. "How *dare* you!" Axis suddenly shouted, making everyone in the Hall jump. "How dare you wander off without letting anyone know that you were alive! Do you have any idea how much grief you have caused? Do you?" His fist thumped on the table between them, papers and maps scattering across the wood and drifting down to the floor. Faraday paled and Borneheld's arm tightened about her waist.

"BattleAxe!" Borneheld began, but Axis completely ignored him. "I suppose that young idiot Timozel is here with you," he seethed, turning around from glaring at Faraday and looking down the Hall. Timozel was already halfway up the Hall, drawn to the defense of his Lady by Axis' anger.

"And do you have any idea how much pain you have given your mother, Timozel?" Axis hissed. "Have you thought to contact her since you so wondrously rose from the dead? No? Why am I not surprised? You may return to your unit, Timozel. I will finish with you tomorrow when I am returned from patrol. Until then you are confined to sentry duty within your unit."

Timozel calmly looked him in the eye. "No."

Belial thought for one moment that Axis was going to strike Timozel. The youth's arrogance was appalling. He stepped forward, ready to intervene if he had to.

"Axis," Faraday said urgently, "when Timozel saved me from the earthfall he pledged to become my Champion. His oath breaks all others that went before."

"And now he has pledged himself to my service," Borne-held said smoothly, revelling in his triumph.

All the tension went out of Axis' body and he suddenly laughed mirthlessly, his shoulders sagging. "Champion," he chortled, the sound so dreadful that Faraday flinched inwardly although she managed to keep the pleasant smile on her face. "Champion. Now I have heard everything. Well, at least this new Champion has managed to cut his hair and grow a beard since I saw him last. Just tell me, Faraday," he said, turning back to her and dropping the dreadful smile from his face. "Why did you not let us know that you were all right? Why . . . why come here?"

Faraday knew what he was asking. More than anything else she wanted to run to him and ease the pain in his eyes, reassure him that she still wanted him more than life itself. But that she could not do. "I came here because I wanted nothing more than to be Borneheld's wife as quickly as possible, BattleAxe. I had . . . I had no thought that you might be worried for me." And please Mother let him see the lie in my eyes, she pleaded silently. Please Mother make him realize that what I did, I did for him.

Axis stared at her for a long moment, his wretchedness and misery plain for all to see. He watched Faraday, watched her held within the circle of Borneheld's arms, watched the knowing smirk stretch across Borneheld's face and the apparently contented smile on Faraday's own, and finally he could take no more. He turned on his heel and, pushing past Timozel, walked toward the far doorway, every movement of his body stiff with anguish.

Borneheld's triumphant laughter followed him out the doorway.

43

The SkraeBold Speaks

Axis wheeled Belaguez around in a tight circle, his eyes scanning the snow fields about them. They had ridden out into the blessedly clear morning some two hours ago and now they were almost two leagues deep into the flat snow plains that stretched north from Gorkenfort. One league further to the northwest lay the River Andakilsa, now so dangerous it was impassable to shipping; Gorkenfort was cut off from the sea. To the northeast rose the Icescarp Alps, much, much closer now than at Sigholt, most of their black peaks lost in the clouds. Axis stared at them, narrowing his eyes to cut out as much of the glare from the flat snow fields as he could. The Alps rose abruptly from the flat plains, the massive mountains scarred with towering cliffs and deep crevices of black rock and ice.

"It is said that life is so barren within the Icescarp Alps that even the rivers are of ice. When I was first assigned to Gorkenfort an old shepherd told me that once he had driven his flocks so close to the base of the mountains that he could hear the rivers groaning and splintering their way through the passes," Magariz said quietly from behind Axis.

Axis turned around. Magariz had insisted on riding out with him, saying only when both Borneheld and Axis had tried to stop him that it was foolish to send out a Patrol Leader inexperienced in the ways of the snow fields and the wraiths without an experienced backup. His injuries did not hinder him on horseback, although Axis noticed that occasionally he raised a gloved hand to the scar on his cheek.

Behind Magariz rode Belial, Arne and the rest of the patrol, some fifteen men composed of Axe-Wielders and regular mounted soldiers. Axis had been coldly angry with Belial, arguing that his second-in-command had no right to be risking himself too. But Belial merely listened passively to Axis' arguments, then mounted his horse. Belial had seen Axis' reaction to Faraday the night before, had known that Axis had spent a sleepless night wrapped in his cloak on top of the battlements gazing silently toward the Icescarp Alps. He'd known Axis felt something more for Faraday than simple attraction, but he hadn't realized that emotions ran so deep. He was not going to stay behind and eat his heart out with worry wondering if his possibly suicidal BattleAxe would return from his patrol.

Arne had similarly ignored Axis' protests and his usually dour expression was now frozen even more firmly into place by the cold. For many weeks now, ever since they had ridden out of the Silent Woman Woods, Arne had been driven to protect Axis, to watch his back, to scan the faces of those about him for subtle signs of treachery. He was beginning to suspect many people about Axis, and sometimes his face broke out in a sweat of frantic anxiety if he saw Axis surrounded by too many unknown people.

Borneheld had been deeply satisfied when both Belial and Arne mounted their horses despite Axis' protests; the BattleAxe's authority seemed to be splintering about him. Borneheld did not realize that both Belial and Arne disregarded Axis' anger, and even his orders, simply because they would prefer to die for him than see him die before them. Borneheld would have been hard-pressed to expect similar devotion from Gautier.

All the patrol were dressed in shades of white and light gray; even Axis had discarded his usual black uniform for the gray and white of the Axe-Wielders. No one wanted to make themselves anymore conspicuous than possible. All were armored under their cloaks, even though armor was not always effective against the wraiths. Despite the cold, cloaks were kept well clear of sword hilts and axe hafts. Fingers were constantly flexed within gloves to keep them as warm and as limber as possible. All were tense and alert.

Five of the men carried burning brands. Magariz gave them terse instructions as they rode across the frozen snow, while Axis make sure they were as compact a group as possible. "Fire will sometimes make the wraiths think twice about attacking, but if there are large numbers of them it won't stop them," said Magariz. "If it comes to a fight, remember this. The wraiths have little flesh and blood, but they are vulnerable through their Artor-cursed silver eyes. Strike them cleanly through those orbs and you will kill them. As pale as they are, when you burst those orbs they bleed red blood as profusely as any man stuck through the gut."

He paused to let the men absorb this then continued, "And remember, they go for your face and throat, or sometimes your hands and wrists. Those are the parts of you that are most exposed. They smell flesh, and they hunger for it. They have the sharpest teeth, as long and as pointed as the man-eating fish that follow the ships in the Andeis Sea. Once they have fastened themselves into your flesh nothing will save you."

Magariz watched the unease, particularly among the Axe-Wielders, none of whom had yet experienced attack by these wraiths. "But they also feed on fear, gentlemen. If you can remain calm when under attack then you will have a chance. Do not let yourselves be overwhelmed by panic.

Panic, unreasoned fear, will kill you quicker than a spreading fire will consume a swaddled infant left by the hearth." He gave a harsh bark of laughter. "Stay calm? A tall order, comrades, when you are attacked by such nightmarish creatures.

"They seem to be becoming more substantial," Magariz continued, "as if, having fed on so much flesh and blood, they are recreating their own bodies from those they have slaughtered." Axis glanced sharply at the man: his words stirred some dim thought at the back of his mind, but it evaded his attempts to catch it. Magariz's own gloved hand now fingered the hilt of his sword. "Over the past weeks more and more of our patrols have been attacked."

Magariz was silent for a moment before he spoke again, reluctantly. "But the wraiths are not the worst you will face, my friends. Increasingly bands of the wraiths are led by the creatures that attacked Gorkenfort and the Retreat in Gorkentown."

They rode silently for another half an hour, each man wrapped in his own thoughts. Artor help those Ravensbundmen still left alive in these frozen wastes, Axis thought to himself. I would not want to venture more than a half day's gallop any further north from Gorkenfort. He pulled his cloak a little closer, careful to leave his sword hilt free. A soft mist was drifting down from the north, and the wind was now damp as well as cold.

"BattleAxe! Beware!" Magariz hissed suddenly, and Axis glanced at him sharply. The man was rigid on his horse and had drawn his sword. "Remember, they attack from mists such as this!"

Swords rattled out of scabbards and the five men holding the burning brands hoisted them a little higher. The horses skittered across the snow, their riders' increased nervousness communicating itself to them. Axis tightened his rein on Belaguez.

Something whispered along the wind and Axis felt the fine hair down the back of his neck stand on end.

"Skraelings!" Magariz hissed.

"Tighten your formation." Axis called calmly. "Back your horses into a circle."

But both men and horses were now fighting to keep their panic down and the horses were not easy to control now that each rider had either a sword or flaming brand in one hand.

"Magariz, advise me," Axis said conversationally, as Belaguez jostled against the lord's own stallion. "Do we attempt to flee, or is it better to stand and fight?"

"Fight," Magariz said tersely. "The Skraeling wretches want us to flee. If we flee we give in to panic and fear. And then we are dead."

Axis nodded briefly. "Then we fight." He suddenly felt very calm. He badly wanted to strike out at something in order to release his own pent up anger and frustration at Faraday's betrayal in the thrill of the sword thrust and the kill.

Whispers surrounded them, words distorted by the damp mist so that they lay just outside the boundaries of comprehension. Whispers, running along the edge of the wind and into their very souls.

"BattleAxe!" one of his Axe-Wielders cried, fear drifting through his voice despite his attempts to quell it. "They are everywhere!"

The mist thickened about them, enveloping the men and their horses in a gray fog of despair, and concealing the creatures that wanted to kill them.

Behind Axis Arne hissed in surprise. Shapes were drifting out of the mist in front of them. Tall and vaguely man-shaped, the wraiths were so insubstantial that the men of the patrol could see the shapes of other Skraelings milling behind those in the front ranks. Huge silver orbs floated inside their deep eye sockets. Their clawed hands and their skull-like heads, long pointed fangs hanging down from oversized jaws, were the most solid parts about them.

Axis hefted the sword in his hand. "Are you ready, my friends?" he called in a clear voice, his tone light. "Will you stand at my back?"

Axis' voice gave the others heart. The wraiths milled among themselves, unsettled by the aura of assurance surrounding the leader of the patrol. They preferred overt fear to this disturbing sense of boldness and daring. There was something unusual about this man. What was it?

"We stand with you, Axis Rivkahson," Belial called, his voice strong and confident. Magariz joined his voice to that of Belial's. "We place our trust in you, BattleAxe."

"Then let us not wait for attack, let *us* attack! To me!" Axis spurred Belaguez forward, feeling and hearing the others behind him, and then they were among the Skraeling wraiths.

The unsettled wraiths fell back. They preferred sneaking attacks to standing defense. Axis dropped Belaguez's reins, controlling the stallion with only knees and voice, and struck with his sword at the nearest wraith, feeling the pressure against his blade as it sliced through the creature's eye, revelling in the bright blood that spattered across his own body and down the neck of the gray stallion. "It bleeds!" he screamed and lunged down with his free hand to grab the stringy hair on the wraith's head, twisting his sword deeper and deeper. He felt so powerful, so in control, that he did not even think to sing the Icarii ward of protection.

The wraith wailed and grabbed helplessly at the blade as Axis rammed the sword home, writhing and twisting on the cold steel. The moment the blade drew free the wraith fell apart, disintegrating into a mass of gray slimy muck in the snow underneath Belaguez's plunging hooves.

Now that he was among them the wraiths knew what he was, knew *who* he was. Even though the man did not use his power, the Skraelings recognized it, and they were afraid. They had not expected *him* here!

"They die!" Axis called, joy strengthening his voice, and reached for the next wraith. About him his men stayed in close formation, Axis' blood lust communicating itself to them but not tempting them to break rank, flaming brands and swords rising one after the other before plunging deep into the silver orbs of wraith after wraith. Magariz also found himself screaming with excitement, each thrust of his blade one more stroke in revenge. Belial, calmer but equally deadly with his sword, kept his horse close to Axis, one eye on his BattleAxe in case he got too far ahead of the other men and horses and was isolated among the writhing, screeching pack of wraiths.

Borneheld's soldiers followed, amazed as the BattleAxe of the Axe-Wielders led them into such an all-consuming deadly attack that for the first time it was the wraiths who were experiencing the rout rather than them. Each and every one of them rallied behind the BattleAxe's back, drawing strength from his incredible courage and daring. All traces of fear fell away; all revelled in the feeling of power that came from a successful attack rather than a desperate retreat. "To Axis Rivkahson!" one of them cried, and his companions took up the cry, using it almost as a mantra of death as they struck deep into the wraiths time after time. The Axe-Wielders grinned at their companions, and soon all shouted Axis' name as they killed again and again.

And then, almost as suddenly as the wraiths had appeared they were gone and the mist began to clear. Belial reached forward and grabbed Belaguez's bridle, twisting so hard the horse almost fell; Belial had seen the bloodlust in Axis' eyes and did not want him spurring after the wraiths as they fled.

"Enough, Axis!" he snapped. "They have gone."

Axis turned to him, normality gradually returning to his eyes. "By Artor, Belial, that felt good. I needed that." Belial grinned and then laughed, releasing Belaguez's bridle. "Remind me not to come along with you the next time you feel like a little emotional release, my friend. I thought you were going to skewer me at one point!" His eyes drifted down to Axis' hands and he suddenly paled, his laughter dying as quickly as it had begun.

"Axis," he breathed. "Look what you hold!"

Axis glanced down. In his left hand he held the head of

one of the Skraeling wraiths, surprisingly solid but utterly dead. One of its silver eyes was punctured and drained of fluid, the other staring sightlessly into eternity. Its mouth hung flaccidly, teeth still gleaming wickedly in the reemerging sunlight. Its ashen skin was so thin that the bone of its skull threatened to break through its faint overlay.

Axis hefted it in his hand and held it high for all the men to see. "See!" he cried, his voice drifting triumphantly across the frozen wastes. "They can die too." He lowered his voice and looked at Magariz. "A gift for Borneheld, methinks," he said, and Magariz flinched a little at the harshness in Axis' eyes and voice.

Of all present, Arne was the only one not with his eyes fixed on Axis' face. He kept his eyes drifting across the frozen wastes about them, ever vigilant for fresh treachery and attack. "BattleAxe," he hissed. " 'Ware behind you!"

Axis swung Belaguez about, his face tightening. Walking fearlessly toward them was a creature conceived in someone's nightmare. Magariz inhaled convulsively. "Is that one of the creatures that attacked you?" Axis asked softly. Magariz nodded. "Yes, but more so. They have grown, changed, since they attacked Gorkenfort."

Axis' hand tightened on the hilt of his sword.

About fifteen paces away the creature stopped. It was both massive and graceful at the same time, taller and more heavily muscled than a man, but with a movement so sinuous that it reminded many of those watching of a stalking cat. Its head was a horror—part bird, part man, part beast. It had a hooked beak for a mouth and vicious tusks protruding from its cheekbones. Its eyes and forehead were man-shaped, but its skull was covered by a crazy mixture of fur and feathers, while its naked body was scaled like that of a lizard. Its hands and feet were tipped with massive black claws, and from its back extended two leathery wings that were similarly tipped with lethal black talons.

Axis sat Belaguez quietly, looking unconcerned by the dreadful creature that confronted them. Inside, however, he remembered the face of Gorgrael in the clouds at the Ancient Barrows. This creature shared many of its features.

Gorgrael's creature regarded them for a moment, its head tilted inquisitively like that of a bird although its silver eyes glinted with the deadly madness of a cornered boar. The wind ruffled the fur and feathers atop its elongated head. It focused on the head of the Skraeling that Axis held in his gloved hand.

"Sssss!" it hissed, then raised its beady eyes to Axis. "You are Rivkahson?"

Its voice was half-bird's chirp, half-hiss, and hard to understand. It had to speak slowly, as if it were an effort to get the words past its over-large tongue.

Axis nodded and edged Belaguez forward a step. "Who are you? What do you want of us?" he asked.

The creature laughed, a horrible gurgling hiss. "I? I am one of the favored five—we are the SkraeBold. We serve Gorgrael. What do we want? We want Tencendor, Rivkahson. We want to see your fields and forests stained dark with the blood of your peoples. We are sick of inhabiting only misty frozen wastes. We grow solid with our need, our hate."

"We will stand before you," Magariz said flatly behind Axis. "We will keep you to your frozen wastes."

The SkraeBold tilted its head, opened its beak, and howled its amusement to the sky. All the men shifted nervously as the sound crashed about them. The SkraeBold abruptly shut its beak with an audible snap and looked back at them.

"You will not be able to stop us," it hissed angrily. "Gorgrael gives us strength. Gorgrael recreates us from the flesh and blood that we kill for him. Once we were mist, now we can walk."

Again a maddening thought hovered at the back of Axis' mind.

The SkraeBold continued. "The day will come, soon, when your blood will feed my brothers, when your daughters and sisters will offer us the use of their bodies in exchange for their lives, when *you*, Rivkahson, will beg for mercy before Gorgrael!"

Axis smiled coldly and leaned forward over the pommel of his saddle. "I have a message for your Gorgrael, Skrae-Bold. Tell him that my father loved me. Ask him, did his father love him?"

The creature took a step forward in fury and both Magariz and Belial lifted their swords, but Axis did not move, keeping his smile on his face. "I and my four brothers love Gorgrael!" it screeched in fury. "He needs no father but us! We were the ones who midwived his birth!"

Then it simply faded. One moment it was there and the next it was not. With it went the final vestiges of the mist.

Axis wheeled Belaguez about and smiled at his patrol. "I think we have done enough this day, my friends. Shall we ride for Gorkenfort?"

Borneheld was at weapon practice in the fort's courtyard when the patrol returned, his bare chest glistening with sweat even in the frigid air, his skin steaming, the heavy sword hanging from both hands. To one side of the quadrangle Faraday watched, wrapped in her dark-green cloak.

Nineteen men had ridden out early in the morning, including Axis, and nineteen returned. They must have evaded all the wraiths, Borneheld thought as he swung around to receive them. Cowards. Women. He failed to notice that all nineteen rode with straight and proud backs and that whatever demons Axis had carried out with him earlier in the morning, he seemed to have lost them somewhere in the snow fields. Borneheld also failed to notice that the neck of Axis' gray stallion was spattered with blood, or that a goodly crowd of men had followed the patrol up to Gorkenfort's gates. He most certainly did not notice the object that Axis carried half-hidden in his cloak. Perhaps if he had noticed all these things he would have been a little more circumspect in what he said in front of the many witnesses who crowded the large courtyard of

Gorkenfort. Jorge and Roland looked on from the parapets, while, unseen to most eyes, the three Sentinels watched from behind a half-unloaded cart of supplies. They had feared deeply for the StarMan's life out there this day.

Borneheld leaned on his sword, proud of his physique, as Axis stopped his horse some ten paces away. "Did your horse run too fast for the wraiths to catch you, BattleAxe?" he sneered. "Did you discover for yourself that only *men* can deal with these creatures? If you yet have the bravery to admit your nerve has completely abandoned you I will summon enough sympathy to find you a job cleaning the pots in the kitchens. You should be safe enough there." He allowed himself a small laugh at his wit.

With his words Borneheld instantly lost the respect and loyalty of the nine of his own men who had ridden in the patrol. Later he would lose the trust and respect of most of those the nine spoke to. Axis simply smiled benignly and glanced across to Faraday, sketching a courtly bow to her from Belaguez's saddle. "Greetings, Duchess. I trust you slept easy last night?"

Faraday stiffened, stung by his words. Her guilt at her betrayal of the man had kept her sleepless long after Borneheld had rolled his heavy body away from hers.

Axis held her eyes for a moment, then glanced back toward Borneheld. He pushed the hood of his cloak down about his shoulders so that now the weak noon sun caught the gold of his hair and beard. His proud bearing and innate grace commanded the attention of all in the courtyard. If a stranger had walked into the courtyard at that moment he would instantly have assumed the golden-haired man on the gray stallion was a king and the more heavily muscled man who faced him his subordinate.

Just as Borneheld opened his mouth, Axis raised his left hand and held the ghastly object high for all to see. There was a collective gasp of repugnance. Axis' eyes had not left Borneheld's. "Gorgrael sends greetings, brother, and I present you with this wedding gift. Enjoy."

He hurled the head at Borneheld's feet and Borneheld

jumped out of the way, his face recoiling with horror as the Skraeling head slid by him on the slippery cobbles to stop just short of Faraday's feet. She took a huge breath and closed her eyes for a moment, but she held her ground and finally looked away from the head and back at Axis. Her face was tightly impassive but her eyes were dark with emotion. Her knuckles were white where they gripped her cloak.

"I thank you, Axis Rivkahson," she said, her voice calm and dignified, "that you thought I should have deserved such a gift."

Axis' face hardened and he held her stare for a moment longer before he turned Belaguez back toward the crowd gathered at the fortified gateway.

Borneheld's face darkened in fury as he stared at the repulsive head lying at his wife's feet and heard the cheers of the crowd as they saluted Axis.

44

Vows and Memories

Five days later Axis wrapped himself in a thick cloak against the cold, pulled the hood down far over his face and stepped out through the gates of Gorkenfort, walking quickly down through the streets of Gorkentown. Even though it was only midmorning the streets were almost bare of soldiers, the weather now so frigid that most only ventured outside for essentials. Death lurked in the wind.

Axis did not see the two hooded and cloaked shadows following him from Gorkenfort, one trailing the other by twenty or twenty-five paces.

He walked for fifteen minutes until he reached the all-but-deserted Retreat of the Brotherhood of the Seneschal close to the outer wall of the town. The two surviving Brothers had long since moved into the fort itself, but Axis had specifically asked the older Brother to meet him here this morning. He had questions to ask. Here was another link with his mother.

The heavy wooden door was standing open, half off its hinges, and Axis quickly stepped inside, grateful for the protection from the wind even though it was almost as cold inside as it was out. He looked about him. The Retreat still bore the scars of the attack by Gorgrael's creatures, the SkraeBolds and the Skraelings, several months previously. Once a comfortable residence for brothers who desired to spend their lives in quiet meditation in northern Ichtar, now torn hangings of drapes and tapestries flapped in the stiff breeze that wafted in through the open doors, while the furniture was broken and strewn about the floors. Axis shrugged deeper inside his cloak and wandered through the main apartments of the lower floor, occasionally coming across fragments of torn books and pottery, and a spare habit or two left to hang behind a door or on a nail in the wall, its owner long since dead.

Brother Francis was waiting for him in the kitchens. Stooped over an overturned cauldron when Axis entered, he slowly straightened his arthritic spine and faced the BattleAxe.

"Greetings, BattleAxe." He looked about the room for a moment, his transparent blue-veined skin stretched tightly over the frail bones of his face. "This was where so many of the brothers died the night the creatures attacked. It was the only place they thought to find weapons." He picked up a poker and held it for a moment, his face sad. "But pokers and pan ladles are no match for the powers of such beasts as we faced that night."

"Yet you escaped," Axis said softly, moving around to the old man.

Brother Francis' eyes dimmed a little, as though he felt guilty. He nodded. "Brother Martin, young and of quick presence of mind, pulled me into a linen closet where we huddled, listening to our family being torn to pieces outside. Pray you never have to listen to such as that."

For long moments there was silence, Axis standing deep in thought as Brother Francis pottered about the kitchen, picking up the various pots and pans lying about the floor and placing them neatly in ranks upon the bench spaces.

"Brother Francis, do you know who I am?" Axis finally

asked, lifting his head to look at the man. Brother Francis stopped his useless efforts at tidying and stared a moment at him.

Finally he nodded. "Yes. I know who you are. The soldiers in the streets speak of no one else, of your patrols, of your courage, of your leadership. Your name is Axis Rivkahson and you have come to ask me about your mother."

"She died here."

Francis looked surprised for a moment, but he quickly recovered. "She gave birth to you here, Axis. Yes. But she died elsewhere, not here." He smiled a little sadly at the shock on Axis' face. "I am an old man now, Axis Rivkahson, and I am not frightened of the things that I once was. For many years I have held my silence, each year burying another of my fellows who knew the secret. Now only I am left with the memory." He paused before continuing. "All of us were so scared of the king, old King Karel it was then, and of the fury of Duke Searlas, that none of us ever spoke again of the events that surrounded your birth. But now I have seen such horrors that the fury of earthly creatures no longer frightens me. And now stands before me the young babe who lost his mother. I will speak, if you wish it."

Axis considered. "No, Brother Francis. Perhaps the danger for you is not yet past. The Duke of Ichtar still walks the streets of Gorkentown. I will not knowingly put you in danger. All I ask is that you show me the room where I was born."

"That is all? Very well. Follow me."

Francis led Axis back through the ground floor apartments until they reached the entrance hall, then he started to climb the great curved stone stairway that led into the upper reaches of the Retreat. His breath wheezed a little in his throat as he climbed and Axis stepped forward, supporting his arm. "Thank you," the Brother gasped, pausing to catch his breath. "They carried your mother in through the main doors," he said, ignoring Axis' injunction not to risk saying anything. After so long holding his silence, Francis felt that he had to mention something about those few days at the end of Wolf-month of that winter thirty years ago; it was almost a confession for him. "I was young and strong then, and I was one of the ones who helped to carry Rivkah. Searlas had brought her to Gorkentown in an old wagon, and the journey was hard. She had gone into labor fifteen hours out from the town, and those last few leagues across the pot-holed road must have been agony for her."

They reached a landing and Francis turned into a long corridor which stretched the length of the building. "One of the brothers hurried for midwives, while another and myself carried her to a room we always left prepared for guests."

Brother Francis stopped at a room at the very end of the corridor. His hand, papery skin stretched tight over the swollen joints of his fingers, closed about the doorhandle, but Axis' own hand closed gently over his and stopped him from opening the door. "Thank you, Brother Francis. Thank you. I will be alone now, if you please."

Francis turned and looked at the face of the man who leaned over him. BattleAxe he might be, mighty warrior he perhaps was, but all Francis could see was the face of a man who was searching for his past. He nodded.

"Go with Artor, young man. Furrow wide, furrow deep."

Axis bent his head and smiled gently at the old man. Reinald had shown him the rooftop where he had been conceived, and now this old man had brought him to the place where he had been born. "Go with Artor, father."

Brother Francis nodded and walked back down the corridor and stairs. Halfway down the stairs he blinked in surprise at the person he met coming up them, but after a moment he simply nodded and continued on his way. He was an old man, and the only real surprise left in his life was that death had not already claimed him.

Axis left his hand on the door knob for long heartbeats before he could summon the courage to turn it to one side.

It clicked softly in his hand, and for a moment he could hear labored breathing. The door swung open slowly and Axis stepped inside. It was a relatively large chamber, probably the one the brothers kept for their most important guests. Nevertheless, it was bare and dismal now. Two high and small windows let in a minimum of light. Even had she been capable of it, there would have been no escape for Rivkah once the door was bolted behind her. To one side a bed, its lumpy mattress hanging half off broken springs, was pushed against the wall, a stool standing at its foot. A fireplace arched into the room from the opposite wall, the side furthest from the windows throwing deep shadows into the extreme corner of the room. A chest stood underneath the windows, a chipped and dusty china pitcher and wash basin sitting on its flat lid. Axis walked a few steps into the room, lost in his thoughts. It was a barren place to start a life.

Axis turned back to the door and saw Faraday standing there, wearing her green cloak thrown over a high-necked black dress. So stunned he could not speak for several moments, Axis stood there and stared at her.

More composed, Faraday folded her hands before her and drank him in with her eyes. Alone, finally.

"I almost tore that Barrow apart with my bare hands to reach you," Axis said eventually, so quietly that Faraday had to step forward to hear him. He paused and took a half step toward her. "And then I mourned you for weeks, only to find that you had survived and fled to Borneheld's bed. Can you tell me why?"

"Axis, I have to explain to you."

"Then explain!" Axis shouted, turning on his heel and marching over to the far wall underneath the high windows. "Explain," he said in a quieter but no less intense voice, "why you told me one night that you wanted me more than life itself and yet within days had left me mourning you dead while you fled to Borneheld."

"Axis," Faraday said in a broken voice, taking a step toward him until his furious gaze stopped her in the middle of the room. "I live only for you. I love you with every breath I take, with every beat of my heart. But I could not marry you. Not once I had been betrothed to Borneheld. He would have killed you, and I would rather have you alive than dead."

Axis' face did not soften. "I am not afraid of my brother!"

"Axis! I know!" Faraday said desperately, wondering if she should have risked coming here. "But it is so important that you live. I could not be the one responsible for making it Borneheld's life ambition to track you down and kill you!"

Axis' eyes narrowed. "What do you mean, 'it is so important that you live'?"

"Because I believe that you are the StarMan spoken of in the Prophecy of the Destroyer," she said finally. There. Let him make of that what he would.

Axis stared at her for a moment, then his face slowly relaxed and he laughed gently. "I have been told that by others. Belial would have me crowned this evening if he thought I would accept the diadem. This damned Prophecy spreads like wildfire, and I think I have been too firmly caught up in it to shake myself loose just yet."

"And do you believe it?"

Axis' smile died. "I must, if we are to survive. But, oh Faraday, it is so difficult to understand. It is so damned difficult to understand the changes in *me*!"

Faraday was horrified by the frustration evident in his voice. "Axis, I . . ." but he did not give her the chance to finish.

"You have heard the Prophecy, Faraday. *You* tell me what it means. Ah," he turned his face away and finished on a whisper. "It frightens me."

Faraday did not know what to say, and for a minute there was silence between them.

Axis eventually looked back at her. "I have discussed the Prophecy with Ogden and Veremund, but they profess ignorance. Belial . . . well, Belial is as bewildered as I. The first verse is so straightforward, but the second and third frighten me. I am the StarMan, Faraday. I try to accept that. But the second verse tells me that I must wait until all its riddles are fulfilled before I can wield my power against Gorgrael, otherwise it will kill me. Faraday," he laughed dryly, "the prophecies of the second verse are so enigmatic I would not recognize most of them if they solved themselves before my very eyes. And the third verse . . . the third verse tells me I have a traitor in my camp who will betray me. Who? Who?"

"I have not heard the third verse." A traitor, she thought. Mother, protect him!

"No. No one knows it except I." And what else does that cursed third verse tell me, he wondered. My Lover's pain could destroy me. Are you my Lover, Faraday? Will your pain so distract me that Gorgrael can strike the killer blow? For an instant a picture of Faraday lying broken and bleeding sprang to his mind.

He forced his mind away from the terrible image and regarded Faraday. He remembered how she had treated his parentage with respect and dignity when so many sneered at his birth. "But if the Prophecy confuses me, Faraday, then some of the mystery surrounding my father has been solved. Look," he said, pulling the glove from his right hand, the ring gleaming from his middle finger. "This was my father's. He gave it to Rivkah as a token of his love."

Faraday stepped over and took his hand to examine the ring more closely. Its workmanship was marvelous. Axis' eyes darkened as she ran her gentle fingers over his hand. "What kind of man was he to own such a ring as this?" she asked finally, looking up.

"My father is an Icarii Enchanter, my love. His name is StarDrifter. One day I will find him." He lifted his hand from hers and caressed her cheek. For a moment Faraday rested her cheek in the palm of his hand, feeling the Enchanter's ring cool against her skin. He had called her love, he *did* love her! Ah, Mother, to have the love of such a man to support her.

"The son of an Icarii Enchanter," she whispered. "No wonder you bound my soul with enchantments the moment I first saw you."

Axis stepped closer and cupped her chin in his hand, bending his head down to hers, but the instant before their lips met Faraday turned her head to one side. "I cannot, Axis, I cannot," she said tightly. "I have vowed to be true to Borneheld. I cannot break those vows."

And curse the Prophecy, she thought, that forced those vows upon me. She turned her eyes away, unable to bear his expression.

Axis' fingers tightened about her chin. "Is your damned sense of obligation and duty going to keep us apart for a lifetime, Faraday? Does what we feel for each other mean nothing to you?"

"I vowed to him, Axis. If I leave him now, then he will track you down and kill you. If I break my vows then my punishment will be your death! Whatever gods now walk this land will see to that. A vow is a vow, whichever god it is made before, Axis."

Axis suppressed a curse. Here she stood, almost touching him, yet determined to remain true to Borneheld. Axis had thought her loss at the Ancient Barrows was a torment, but this was even worse.

He released her chin and let his hands rest lightly around her waist, unsure if he could resist the temptation to pull her against him despite her determination. He had never wanted a woman like he now wanted Faraday. He should have never let her go at the Barrows. Now Borneheld had her.

Axis' hands tightened slightly. The nights were the worst. At night he lay sleepless, imagining, wondering, wanting.

"Does he treat you well?"

She shrugged. "He tries. He says he loves me and wants what is best for me. He can be tiresome at times and I wish he would laugh more." She paused. "He means well."

Axis' entire body tensed as she spoke. He wanted to hear

Faraday say that Borneheld beat her and abused her. He wanted an excuse to challenge Borneheld to fight to the death now, but she would not give it to him.

He breathed deep. She said that Borneheld loved her. How did *she* feel? Jealousy gripped Axis in tight claws. Did she *enjoy* the touch of Borneheld's hands?

Faraday understood what he was thinking. "He does not make me feel the way you made me feel under the stars. *You* are the StarMan, he is simply the man I married."

"Yet you will not break your vows." Axis was not comforted by her words.

"No," she said, her eyes steady. "No, I will not."

Anger began to replace Axis' jealousy. "Then listen to my vow, Faraday. What lies between Borneheld and myself will one day lead to the death of one of us. I vow that . . ."

"No!" Faraday cried. "No!" She tried to twist away, her hands on his arms, but Axis held her firm.

"Listen to me," Axis said savagely. "I will make this vow to you and may whatever gods the Icarii Enchanters pray to witness it for me. The day that Borneheld dies, that blessed day I run my sword through his body, Faraday, I will ask you to be my wife. Do you hear me?"

Faraday stared at him, horrified. All she could think of if Axis challenged Borneheld was the vision the trees had given her, the blood dripping through Axis' hair and over his body, Axis dead instead of Borneheld, the blood dripping between her breasts, the torn body at her feet, its spirit rising slowly behind it. "No!"

"You made your vows, now you can listen to mine!" Axis was furious, and it showed in his face and voice. "One day, Faraday, when Borneheld lies dead at our feet, I pledge that I will ask you to stand by my side as my wife. And what will you say, then, my sweet child? How will you answer?"

"You must not challenge him, Axis! Not here, not now!" Oh Mother, Faraday thought frantically, was I wrong to come here?

"One day I will have to, Faraday. No, hear me. You

know the hatred that we hold for each other will eventually end in bloodshed, but doesn't the Prophecy predict my victory?"

"What do you mean?"

Axis smiled grimly. "A wife will hold in joy at night the slayer of her husband, Faraday. Who else can that refer to but you and me? Our marriage is prophesied, Faraday. When Borneheld is dead, will you marry me? Will you hold me in joy?"

His impassioned arguments gave Faraday hope, but she knew that he still had to survive Gorkenfort. "Axis," she said very softly. "Promise me this. Promise me that you will stay your hand until after Gorkenfort is either won or lost. And promise me that if you *do* challenge Borneheld, you have just reason for it. I do not want you to murder him." Nor do I want his murder on my conscience, she thought, clinging to the belief that all the Sentinels wanted her to do was to keep Borneheld from Axis until after Gorkenfort. Only until then.

"I will not murder him, Faraday, for I am certain that one day Borneheld will give me just reason to challenge him. And you are right, Gorkenfort will need every commander it has to survive Gorgrael's inevitable attack." And if the fort falls and I die, he thought bleakly, then you will need him to save you.

Faraday breathed a sigh of relief and caressed his face. All might not be lost, after all, and she might yet have the man she loved. "When I am freed from my vows to Borneheld I will willingly stand by your side for the rest of my life," she whispered, "for then there will be no barrier between us. I swear it by the Mother and by the Enchanter's ring you wear on your hand." She tapped his ring gently with her fingertip. "Let the ring bear witness. My vow binds me to you. On the day that I am freed from my vows to Borneheld I will come to *you!*"

Axis released her quickly before he lost control. "You vow before 'the Mother,' Faraday? One day, when we have our lives to ourselves, we will have to explain each to the other what we have done, what we have seen, while we have been out of each other's sight. I have become the son of an Icarii Enchanter while you, you . . ." Axis smiled at her. "While you have been running about with an Avar Bane named Raum, have you not?"

Faraday gaped in surprise. "How did you know that?"

"I met him in Smyrton—but that's a story that will have to wait. No, never fear, Raum and the girl are well and are now in their homeland."

Faraday walked over to the bed, shifting the mattress back onto the springs and sitting down. "I owe you some brief explanation, Axis Icariison," she said mischievously. "If you know enough that Belial is already calling you the StarMan then you must know of the Sentinels?"

Axis nodded. "Of course. Ogden and Veremund."

Faraday laughed in anticipation of the shock she was about to give him. "And Jack the pig herder who you noticed about the Silent Woman Woods, *and* that white cat that followed you about everywhere! She is now masquerading as my maid, Yr."

But Axis did not laugh as she expected. "Two Sentinels spirited you away from me at the Barrows?"

Faraday nodded. "And helped me here." She dared not think what he would do if she told Axis that the Sentinels had virtually forced her to honor her vows when she was thinking of breaking them and following Axis. Still, Faraday knew she had done the right thing. Borneheld was currently so jealous of Axis and his reputation among both regular army and Axe-Wielders that only Faraday's whispered endearments and entreaties kept Borneheld from seizing the nearest axe or sword and hurling it between Axis' shoulder-blades the moment his back was turned. However much it cost her in personal happiness she knew that she was daily saving Axis from death. If only Axis could now be kept from Borneheld's throat.

Axis did not notice her introspection. "What does it mean, Faraday, when the Prophecy tells us that power will one day corrupt their hearts? Will they betray me?" Now that the talk had turned to the Sentinels Axis once again began to worry about the Prophecy and its hidden meanings.

"Oh, Axis, surely not! The Sentinels are the only ones who can guide us at the moment!"

And yet they are couched about with as many riddles as the Prophecy is, Axis thought. He walked over to the fireplace, studying the intricate pattern of the bricks. "We have both been caught by this Prophecy, Faraday. Pray only that it will one day let us plan our own lives," he said softly.

Faraday did not like the morbid turn of conversation. "What did you come here for, Axis? I had no idea you were going to walk this far when I followed you from the fort. And you met Brother Francis here?"

Axis held out his hand. "Let me show you what I have come here for."

Faraday stood and took his hand, hesitating slightly. "You are safe with me," Axis said good-humoredly, "I have another woman on my mind now."

Faraday looked at him, puzzled, as he led her to the dark corner where the fireplace and its mantel cast a deep shadow. "I was born in this room, Faraday. Perhaps it still contains memories of my birth. Come, stand close beside me." He slipped his arm about her waist and pulled her in close to his body so that they were both enclosed in the shadow. "Whatever happens, Faraday, do not make a sound. Now, let me make some Icarii magic for you."

For a moment he did nothing, and Faraday glanced up at his face. His eyes were focused on the bed pushed against the far wall, remembering the tune he had sung on the roof of Sigholt. Then he began to sing, very slowly, very softly, strange words and music that all ran together until the melody began to spin in Faraday's head. She closed her eyes and leaned in against his body, listening to the enchanted music he spun about her.

Her eyes flew open at the low but agonized groan of a woman. The room was now night-darkened and lit by two candles, one on the mantel above the fire, the other on the stool by the foot of the bed.

A woman writhed on the bed, her slender arms raised behind her to grasp the iron railings of the bedhead. Her long auburn hair, loosely plaited, was dark and dank with sweat. Her face was turned away from them toward the wall, but Faraday did not have to see it to know who it was. Rivkah. She wore a light linen nightgown, once white, now stained with sweat and blood. She was struggling to give birth, her nightgown pulled to her hips over the mound of her belly, her legs raised and bent so that her feet pushed against the mattress every time she was convulsed with a contraction. Two women, middle-aged and dressed in dark dresses and black-weave aprons, huddled at the foot of the bed, their faces lined with worry, their eyes anxious.

Axis' arm tightened about her waist and Faraday leaned closer and wrapped her own arms about him, lending him her support as he watched his mother struggle to give birth to him. He had stopped singing now, and was only humming the melody in broken snatches.

The door opened next to them and Faraday only just managed to stifle her gasp of surprise. How it was that none in the room saw them, she was not sure. A tall and powerfully built man, heavily bearded, strode through the door and over to the bed. He stood watching the woman writhe for a moment.

"My Lord Duke," both the midwives gasped, standing back from the bed.

"How goes it?" he asked. "How goes the lady bitch my wife giving birth to her fatherless son of the night?"

The midwives exchanged worried glances. What did he want to be told? Finally the older woman, the senior midwife, spoke as Searlas shot a hard glance their way. "The babe sits wrongly in the womb, Lord Duke. He is twisted about so that his hip blocks the birth canal. We cannot turn him. Your wife has labored now for close on two days. She cannot go on much longer."

It wasn't until the midwife addressed the Duke that Faraday remembered that Rivkah was the previous Duchess of Ichtar; and the man was her father-in-law, Searlas. Then, as it had her marriage night, the ruby ring pinched her finger. *This line deserves to die with Borneheld*, Faraday thought very clearly, then blinked, startled. Where had that thought come from? Why did Borneheld's line deserve to die with him? Why did her ring bite so?

Rivkah looked at her husband. Hate and loathing twisted her lovely face. "I curse the day I agreed to marry you, Searlas. I am glad I dishonoured your name!" A moan escaped her as another pain wracked her body.

"Bitch!" Searlas spat. "You die the death of a careless whore, Rivkah. Wonder, while you lie dying, if your lover was worth your life."

"Twice and twice over," Rivkah whispered fiercely. "I would die a hundred deaths for one more hour cradled in his arms!"

Searlas cursed Rivkah so foully that the midwives blanched. Then he leaned down and seized her left hand, tearing a ring from her heart finger. "Then give me back what is mine and Ichtar's," he said harshly. Faraday caught a glimpse of the ring he held; it was the same one she now wore. The Duke turned to the midwives, pocketing the ring. "I care not if they both die. Don't save them for my sake."

Then he was gone. The door slammed behind him so hard it reverberated on its hinges.

The older of the two women, the one who had spoken to Duke Searlas, sat down beside Rivkah on the bed. She took Rivkah's hand and spoke softly but urgently. "Lady, we can still save your life. Let us dismember the babe. He is surely dead already. If we can remove him from your womb then you will live." Her voice broke. "Please, let us do this for you!"

Rivkah hauled herself up from the bed and fastened her free hand into the startled woman's hair. "If you do a single thing to harm the baby I will come back from the grave to haunt you and yours for eternity. Do you understand me? You will do *nothing* to hurt the baby!"

The frightened woman nodded. "Then try to turn him

again," Rivkah grated, "try, damn you!" The midwife knelt down at the end of the bed and took a deep breath.

The next few minutes were a nightmare. Rivkah's screams echoed about the chamber until it seemed there was no escaping them. Faraday felt Axis' whole body convulse in her arms in sympathy with his mother's agony and Faraday held him as tightly as she could, trying to block the tormented woman's cries from her own ears against his chest.

Finally the midwife stood up from the end of the bed, her right arm bright with blood to the elbow. "Artor knows, it is done," she said hoarsely. Rivkah was still sobbing in pain and the midwife rinsed her arm and sat down by the woman again, stroking her forehead in a vain effort to soothe her. "He has been turned, Lady. If he is still alive I do not know. If you have the strength, then birth him. But do it quickly or you will both die."

Rivkah bit down on her lip and strained as hard as she could. The other midwife looked up. "He comes, Marta." A show of blood stained the sheets about Rivkah's hips. Marta hurried to help and, moments later, the baby slithered into her waiting hands. "The cord is about his neck," she said urgently. "Quick, hand me the knife!" She sliced the knife around the cord, releasing the baby's neck so he could breathe.

With the last of her strength Rivkah struggled onto her elbows. "Please . . . is he alive?"

The door opened slightly, and the two midwives looked up. What they could see Faraday did not know, but Marta nodded imperceptibly and, seizing a waiting sheet, wrapped it about the baby, blue and still in her hands. She hugged the bundle to her chest. "I am so sorry, my Lady, but he is dead. The cord strangled him."

Rivkah moaned and held out her hands. "Please, let me hold him! Please!"

But the midwife rose to her feet, clutching the baby close to her. "No, my Lady. Best you do not see him.

Come," she said to her assistant, and the pair of them hurried out of the room without a backward glance.

"*Nooo!*" Rivkah screamed. "Bring me my child! Bring me my baby!" She half fell out of the bed, trying to reach the women as they passed her, but she was too weak to do anymore. She lay there, panting and sobbing, twisted so that her head and shoulders hung below the level of the mattress. Faraday moved as if she would go to her, but Axis held her tight. "No," he whispered. "I must see what happens now."

For a moment or two Rivkah hung there, then she pulled herself back onto the bed. "Help," she whispered to no one in particular. "Help me! They have stolen my son!" The door slowly swung open and Rivkah turned to look. "You," she said woodenly, all hope draining from her face. "I might have known it would be you. Have you come to kill me then?"

Two Brothers entered the room, walked over to the bed and stared at Rivkah dispassionately. Neither said anything. They looked at each other, then the larger bent down, wrapped Rivkah in one of the stained blankets she lay on, and picked her up. As they turned from the bed Axis and Faraday had a clear look at their faces. Even Faraday recognized them. Jayme and Moryson.

"You have advised me well," Jayme said in a conversational tone to Moryson. "We will take her to the foot of the Icescarp Alps and dump her there. Let the crows eat her tainted flesh."

"Quite," replied Moryson as they left the room. "We need her no more."

Faraday released Axis and stood back to look at him. His face was hard and brittle. "If there was a body in the crypt here it wasn't my mother's," he said harshly. "The ravens have undoubtedly picked her bones well-clean by now." His face turned to Faraday's. "I trusted that man for almost thirty years, Faraday. He was the only parent I ever knew. And now I find that he and Moryson murdered my mother."

Faraday started to speak but her mouth was so dry that she had to clear her throat. "Axis, why didn't they murder you as well? Why keep you alive?"

"I don't know. But rest assured that one day I will ask them both—just before I slit their throats."

Faraday leaned close again and hugged him, but this time Axis' arms hung limp by his sides and his eyes stared into space. The lies that had bound him all his life were shattering about him.

Below them, hidden deep in the shadows, Timozel waited, dark with anger, for Axis and Faraday to emerge from the Retreat. An hour or so ago the old brother had trotted out the door and back up the street toward the fort, but Axis and Faraday remained within. What was she doing in there with the BattleAxe? Only the fact that his Lady Faraday had walked into this building of her own free will kept him from decisive action.

He would have to remind her that her future lay with Borneheld. She was weak, and she needed a strong hand to guide her.

The battles were over. Timozel sat before the leaping fire with his Lord, Faraday at their side. All was well. Timozel had found the light and he had found his destiny.

They drank from crystal glasses, sipping fine wine, Faraday in her wedding gown.

All was well.

Unseen by Timozel, a Dark Man stood behind him, a hand on Timozel's shoulder.

He was crying with silent laughter.

45

The Groves

At the beginning of the third week of Snow-month, four days before the most sacred festival of Yuletide, the GhostTree Clan arrived at the groves of the northern Avarinheim at the foot of the Icescarp Alps. Over the past week they had met up with the last of the other Avar Clans who were moving toward the groves and by the time they arrived their group was some eighty strong. Barsarbe cautioned Azhure not to speak with the other Avar until after the Clans had met to discuss her case. Mindful of Barsarbe's cold eyes Azhure avoided the other Avar Clans, sitting lonely by a small campfire at night while the Avar gossiped and passed news about, joined only by Gold-Feather, and occasionally Pease and Shra or Raum. She was glad to have left Smyrton behind her, but daily wished she had found some better way to free Raum and Shra.

Sometimes GoldFeather worried that Azhure was unnaturally quiet, but she had grown into such a reserved woman herself that she easily accepted reticence in others. And since Azhure had revealed the shocking news that the BattleAxe, Axis, was her son, GoldFeather had thought of little else. Rivkah. She thought she had buried Rivkah on the slopes of the Icescarp Alps. Over the past thirty years GoldFeather had rarely let herself think back on her last year of life as Rivkah, burying her old life with her dead son. She had established a new life as GoldFeather, finding a new meaning and a new happiness.

Now she let herself think back to the day when StarDrifter had landed on the roof of Sigholt. GoldFeather had known instantly what he was. An Icarii Enchanter. Although she had listened to the Seneschal's teachings about the Forbidden, GoldFeather—Rivkah as she had been then—had developed a fascination for the Forbidden in her early teens. A new troubadour had arrived in Carlon, a handsome man with coppery hair, and he spent many days performing before King Karel and his court. But he had also entertained the young Princess, singing songs for her ears alone. Songs about the lost Icarii and Avar and their magical lives. He was a very unusual man, sitting wrapped in a dark cloak even on the warmest days, but Rivkah had been fascinated by the songs he sang . . . and she had remembered them for years after the troubadour had left Carlon. So she had not been afraid when StarDrifter alighted before her; she had looked up from the baby she nursed, looked into his eyes, and was lost. They had conceived their magical child that day, and both had yearned for the moment when they could hold him in their arms.

But Jayme had deceived her! GoldFeather's lips curled in fury when she thought of how Jayme had stolen her son and tricked her into believing he was dead. Her gray eyes hardened when she thought of how the midwives had fled the room with her son still breathing in their arms. She had thought that she would have died, except that somehow, from somewhere, enough strength and love flowed into her to enable her to survive her trial on the mountain.

Within two hours of CrimsonCrest dropping to her side and asking politely, with the utmost arrogance, as was the Icarii way, if she truly intended to die beneath his favorite roost, StarDrifter had held her in his arms. Soothing her, loving her, healing her, crying with her at the death of their son, he had carried her personally back to Talon Spike, refusing all help from his fellows. Her healing had taken weeks, weeks during which StarDrifter had not left her side, refused to let her die, refused to let her give in to self-pity. "We have our lifetimes to create other sons," he would whisper, and in the end GoldFeather had believed him.

Yet neither had ever totally recovered from the loss of a son who had been conceived among the joy of newly discovered love. StarDrifter had been enthralled with the growing babe, spending hours with his hands planted on her belly, feeling his son wake to awareness within her womb. He would sing to him for as long as Rivkah could sit still without her legs cramping, and one day during her sixth month of pregnancy he had lifted his remarkable face from her belly in astonishment. "He sings back!" StarDrifter whispered, amazed. "He sings back to me! Truly, Rivkah, you have conceived a child that will wake Tencendor with his voice!" They had laughed then, but the laughter had died when Searlas had returned. Before StarDrifter could act Searlas had spirited her away to the Retreat in Gorkentown.

GoldFeather had eventually come out of her healing process in Talon Spike with her body completely healed of its injuries. The Icarii Healers had even managed to return the blood flow to her frozen extremities so that she lost none of her fingers or toes. The only sign of her physical ordeal was her magnificent auburn hair which had turned completely silver except for a golden streak where StarDrifter had rested his hand on her brow. But even safe within Talon Spike at StarDrifter's side GoldFeather could not find complete happiness. The Icarii were a prickly lot with their damnable pride and haughtiness and their obsession with enchantments and mysticism, and though they quickly overcame their initial suspicion of her and tried to be kind, GoldFeather could often sense their pity for her not far below the surface. And StarDrifter's insistence on taking a Groundwalker for his wife caused more than a few raised eyebrows.

Now StarDrifter and she shared another sorrow. One that they never, never spoke of, yet one that nevertheless caused them deeper unhappiness with each passing year. The Icarii were a race of remarkable longevity. They easily lived five or six times the span of a human or Avar life. StarDrifter was an Icarii Enchanter still early in his life and his natural lifespan would carry him hundreds of years past her death. The knowledge that she would age and die before he had reached the middle years of his life was a knowledge that both refused to ever mention. Already GoldFeather was aging before his loving eyes. She found that difficult to accept. Part of the reason she was spending longer and longer periods away from Talon Spike with the Avar was her discomfort in the disparity in their aging and in the as-yet-unconscious pity she could see in StarDrifter's eyes. It is difficult, she mused, for a human woman to love an Icarii. The love will never last. Already she had doubts about StarDrifter's continued commitment to her. She sighed. What would she do once she could no longer tolerate the pity in his eyes? GoldFeather shivered and turned her thoughts to her daughter.

Four years after she had joined StarDrifter in Talon Spike GoldFeather had given birth to EvenSong. Her birth brought them great joy and EvenSong was a beautiful daughter, her voice reflecting the soaring notes of the bird she had been named after. She was now approaching her twenty-fifth year, the year of coming of age for the Icarii. Soon she would join the Strike Force for the obligatory five years of military service. Stars help her if she was in the Strike Force during the time of the Prophecy of the Destroyer.

EvenSong had inherited little from her mother; her Icarii blood ran stronger than her human. Though all Icarii children were born as human babes, at about the age of four or five the children started to develop the buds of their wings which, by age seven, were developed enough to carry them. Because of her human blood EvenSong literally had to have her wingbuds coaxed out of her, and when she was a child StarDrifter had spent many a long hour singing to her, stroking her back, encouraging the wings to form.

Would her son have developed wings too, had StarDrifter been there to assist him? Had he inherited the Icarii longevity, as EvenSong had in its entirety? What other Icarii characteristics were coursing about in his blood? He had not forgotten to sing, if he had sung the Song of Re-creation for Shra. GoldFeather breathed deeply, thinking of that. No Icarii Enchanter, not even StarDrifter, the most powerful of them all, could sing the Song that well. Yet . . . Axis . . . had not had a moment's training, had not had the benefits of years of preparation and study that all other Icarii Enchanters had. What had she and StarDrifter bred?

Axis. GoldFeather's mouth slowly lost its hard line and curled softly. What an unusual name. It was not an Acharite name. Who had given it to him? Jayme? She and StarDrifter, like all joyous parents, had discussed names as they waited for the birth of their son, but had left it too late to fix on one or the other. Well, Axis it would have to be. It was, somehow, appropriate.

Now as GoldFeather helped Azhure and Grindle's two wives set up the tents in the trees beside the groves she fretted for StarDrifter's arrival. It had been almost three weeks since she learned that her son had not died, and in those three weeks she had not been able to get word to StarDrifter. All her thoughts were now of Axis and StarDrifter. Azhure had told GoldFeather all she knew about the BattleAxe, but it was not much, and it left GoldFeather hungering for more information.

Had GoldFeather not been so lost in her own thoughts and tumbling emotions she would have seen that Azhure was suffering much the same way that she herself had when she first joined the Icarii. All races, whether the haughty Icarii, the suspicious Avar, or the blinded Acharites instinctively regarded newcomers with some degree of intolerance or pity.

Azhure looked about her curiously as they set up camp about thirty paces into the tree line that surrounded the groves. She and Pease were staking down the first tent while Fleat and GoldFeather were starting on the second, lifting the heavy leather covers over the rigid framework of wooden poles. Around them the Avar Clans that had joined them during the last few days were also setting up their tents, and there was an air of suppressed excitement that was impossible to ignore. Both Pease and Fleat had been very quiet since arriving at the groves; even the children moved quietly about the GhostTree camp, helping their mothers clear a space for the campfire and lay out some cold food for a simple supper. Raum and Barsarbe had left to meet with the other Banes, while Grindle and Helm had vanished into the trees almost as soon as they arrived.

Pease noticed Azhure looking about and smiled at her. "You have felt the excitement, haven't you?"

Azhure nodded. "Everyone seems very quiet, though. I would have expected, oh, I don't know, people greeting each other, exchanging news, that sort of thing. The Clans don't normally meet together very much, do they?"

Pease shook her head, sucking her thumb to relieve the sting where she had caught it between one of the leather thongs used for tying the tent flaps down and a tent pole. "No. We only congregate in these numbers for the Yuletide and Beltide Meets. This evening we will all gather in the Earth Tree Grove and exchange greetings and news. Tidings will have to wait until then."

Azhure thought for a moment, her eyes downcast. "And will you discuss my case then?"

Pease moved over to Azhure, her dark eyes gentle. "Azhure, we do not mean to be rude or unwelcoming to you. But you must understand that we are a cautious peo-

ple. You are one of the Acharites, one of those who drove
us from our homes and murdered the forests that once
stood as far as the Widewall Bay. And," Pease did not particularly like to mention this again, but perhaps Azhure still
did not realize how seriously the Avar regarded those who
caused another's death, "you have committed violence.
The killing of *anyone*, let alone a father, we regard as ab-
horrent. Yes, I know that you killed him accidentally and in
defense of Shra—but there is also the fact that you struck
the Axe-Wielder. Two acts of violence, one through carelessness, one premeditated." She shrugged. "For the Avar
to allow one who has committed violence to walk the paths
of the Avarinheim is extremely rare. Your people have murdered with their axes most of the once great Avarinheim as
they once murdered the Icarii and Avar. Now you have
killed your father. Don't you see that we believe that your
people are inherently violent?"

"Pease, I have nowhere else to go. If you reject me, then
where can I go? I have no one who wants me." And that
was the crux of the matter, she thought. No one except her
mother had ever loved her, and her mother chose to leave
her with Hagen. After a lifetime of rejection and ill-treatment, Azhure yearned to be loved, needed, and valued.

"Azhure!" Pease was distraught at the distress in
Azhure's face. "We thank you from the depths of our souls
for the life of Raum and Shra. But if you want to be accepted among the Avar and make your home among us
then it must be by the acceptance and invitation of the entire Meet."

Azhure nodded.

The entire congregation of the Clans of the Avar met that
night in the grove of the Earth Tree. The Icarii would not
be joining them for another day or so, and tonight was reserved for the Avar people alone. There were several
groves used for the religious rites of both the Avar and
Icarii peoples in the northern Avarinheim, but of them all

the Earth Tree Grove was the most venerated and played the most important role in both Yuletide and Beltide rites. At dusk the Avar people, having eaten light meals in their own camps, began to move reverentially through the groves, their feet soundless on the carpet of soft grass and pine needles.

All the groves were circular, open to the night skies. The tall secretive trees of the Avarinheim surrounded them, keeping the mysteries of the groves safe from outside eyes. Azhure walked with the GhostTree Clan, her eyes downcast. Raum and Barsarbe rejoined them, and Barsarbe stared at Azhure so coldly that Azhure's feelings of shame and remorse deepened. GoldFeather finally caught something of the woman's heartache, and as they approached the Earth Tree Grove she stepped up beside Azhure and took her hand.

"I have been too preoccupied with my memories and the news of my son to think much of your troubles, Azhure," GoldFeather said very quietly. "Do not fear the Meet too much. Already it stands well in your favor that the Ghost-Tree Clan have allowed you to walk with them this far. Azhure, know that I will stand with you, and Raum will speak as strongly for you to this Meet as he did to the GhostTree Clan."

Azhure squeezed GoldFeather's hand slightly and managed a smile. "Thank you, GoldFeather. I appreciate your support."

Ah, the poor girl, GoldFeather thought. I should have known how she felt. But what could I tell her? That even I, loved by StarDrifter as I am, still find it hard to find a place that I can call home? "Sometimes I think we dream too much of safe haven in a world where few truly find it, Azhure. Azhure, if the Avar people decide against you this night then do not let it harden your heart, not after what you have already endured. And who knows, Azhure. The Icarii value excitement and daring far more than do the Avar." She paused. "And beauty."

Azhure laughed quietly, allowing GoldFeather to cheer

her. How could she complain when GoldFeather had endured so much loss? "Then I shall grow wings and fly, GoldFeather, and knock at their front door. I have no wish to return to Smyrton."

Barsarbe frowned at their conversation and cautioned them into silence. "We approach the Earth Tree Grove," she whispered. "Be silent now in respect for the Earth Tree."

Even though Azhure had grown used to the beauty of the Avarinheim, she gasped in wonder at the Earth Tree Grove. It was massive, easily holding all the Avar people gathered there. On one side it was bordered by the semicircular black cliff face of the first of the Icescarp mountains, on the other by the encircling Avarinheim. In its precise center stood a huge circle of upright stones, each stone ten paces in height and three in width. They were joined by similar stones laid horizontally above them, so that the circle consisted of a series of stone archways that led into the space inside. In the center of that space stood a gigantic tree, larger than Azhure had seen anywhere else in the Avarinheim. It soared above the encircling stone and reached its spreading branches to the very stars above. Flaming torches placed in niches in the stone circle gave enough light to show that the tree had large pointed oval leaves, dark olive in color and waxy in appearance. From the ends of the branches drooped fat trumpet-shaped flowers, some gold, some emerald, some sapphire and some ruby in hue. In daylight the Earth Tree would be as colorful as a rainbow.

GoldFeather gripped Azhure's hand tighter. "The Earth Tree is the Avar people's most sacred object," she whispered, defying Barsarbe's reprimand for silence. "For them it symbolises the harmony that exists between earth and nature."

Azhure nodded, unwilling to speak before the power of the grove. Even though her hatred of the Seneschal and her fear of Hagen had made her largely indifferent to religious matters, Azhure was deeply affected by the atmosphere in the grove and the haunting beauty of the Earth Tree within its circle of fire-rimmed stone.

The Avar had gathered about the stone circle, sitting themselves about twenty paces away from it. Banes, both men and women in long pastel robes with leaping deer about their hems, passed silently in and out of the stone archways, bringing with them bowls of fluid of which all the Avar partook. Barsarbe and Raum joined the other Banes inside the stone circle, Raum hobbling awkwardly. Azhure noticed a Bane, old and silver-haired and carrying a wide flat wooden bowl, approaching the area where the GhostTree Clan had sat. Azhure caught a brief glimpse of a thick black liquid within the bowl.

The Bane stooped by Grindle and offered him the bowl. "Drink sweet and deep, brother, and may the nectar of the Earth Tree guide your steps down the paths to the Sacred Grove when your time comes," the Bane murmured as Grindle took a mouthful. Then the Bane moved on to Fleat and Pease, calling them sister, and offering them the bowl. Even the children were greeted and received a sip of the nectar. GoldFeather smiled as the Bane bent down to her. "Greetings, Enchanter's wife," the Bane smiled. "Drink sweet and deep, and may the nectar of the Earth Tree help you to remember the Star Song when your time comes." GoldFeather took a deep draft and Azhure watched fascinated as peace and joy spread across GoldFeather's face. Her fingers let the bowl go only reluctantly. The Bane turned to Azhure and frowned slightly. "Greetings, sister." He paused. "I am afraid that until the Meet accepts you into the Avar I cannot offer you the nectar of the Earth Tree."

Azhure's face dropped in disappointment, but she understood the Bane's reluctance.

The Bane felt for her, but after a moment he stood and moved stiffly toward the next group of Avar.

GoldFeather stretched a hand toward Azhure, but just as she was about to speak a clear voice called from among the circle of stone. Azhure could only barely see the speaker, a woman in late middle-age with hair almost as silver and thick as GoldFeather's.

"Bane Mirbolt," GoldFeather murmured to Azhure. "The most senior of the Banes."

"Welcome to the Earth Tree Grove," Mirbolt called, walking about just inside the circle of stone. Although she quickly moved out of eyesight Azhure could still hear her perfectly. "Welcome to the Clans of the Avar, who have walked the trails of the Avarinheim since last we met. In four short days we will enact Yuletide with our brothers and sisters the Icarii, and dance and sing the sacred rites together. But tonight, brothers and sisters mine, we have other matters to discuss. Bane Raum has returned from the Mother with startling news. The Prophecy of the Destroyer walks the earth. Already the Sentinels are abroad." There were disturbed murmurings among the Avar. Rumors had been spreading for many months, now they had the dreadful confirmation. The murmurs died as the woman continued. "Tree Friend has been found and has been presented to the Mother and to the Sacred Horned Ones." Cries of amazement erupted about the grove. Tree Friend! The Avar turned each to the other and gripped hands in excitement. Tree Friend! "All these matters we must discuss in concert with our Icarii brethren because they concern them as much as us. This will be a Yuletide when matters are truly turned on their head, my people."

For some time Bane Mirbolt remained silent, walking around the inside of the circle of stones, the light from the burning torches illuminating her handsome face as she listened to the Avar people exclaim and discuss among themselves. The news that the Prophecy of the Destroyer walked was news the Bane had hoped she would never live to utter. What she had to say to them next was bitter gall. Her voice was very, very soft, but the command ringing through its tone brought complete silence to the grove.

"My people. Gorgrael lives and breathes and will shortly bear his might down on the lands that were once united as Tencendor. Remember the words of the Prophecy—the

Destroyer is of our blood, ours and the Icarii intermingled. One of our women, or one of the Icarii women, did not abort a baby that was in all probability conceived here in this grove, under the shade of the Earth Tree during the joy that is Beltide. We all bear the shame that is Gorgrael. Grieve with me that through our carelessness we should bring destruction down upon ourselves."

Many of the Avar hung their heads, some wept. That the Destroyer was of their blood was shameful news, and though the Prophecy had long predicted it they found it hard to bear. To think that one of their blood would direct such violence and hatred to rain down upon them was bitter news indeed.

"And yet out of sorrow perhaps there is good news as well," Mirbolt continued in a stronger voice. "The StarMan is of the Destroyer's blood, and perhaps we can hope that our shame can be redeemed if he is also of Avar blood." Although Mirbolt had been informed of the news regarding the BattleAxe, his parentage and his ability, the Banes did not feel that this news was yet anything but a private matter between StarDrifter and GoldFeather. If the BattleAxe was connected to the Prophecy then the Banes wanted to be very careful before they broached the news to their people. By the Horned Ones! It would be a grievous truth indeed to accept that one born of Icarii man and human woman was in fact the StarMan.

For a while Mirbolt talked of Faraday Tree Friend, giving her people some background on the woman. Many of the Avar spoke, standing and bowing respectfully toward the Earth Tree, wondering how it was that the Avar should be so shamed that one of them was not chosen by Earth Tree for this honor in their hour of need. To that the Banes had no answer. Raum spoke at length, telling of his testing of Faraday, of her instant and strong bonding with the Mother and of the present of the enchanted bowl the Horned Ones had made her. One day, he said, she will stand before the Earth Tree and lead the Avar to safety and to their promised home. One day, he pledged, she would present to them the StarMan. One day. Meanwhile Gorgrael brewed his terrible hate to the north.

All will be well, Raum finished, and all feet will find their way to the paths of the Sacred Grove. And to that, no one had anything to say for a long while.

Finally the silver-haired Bane stepped forward again. "We have one more issue that must be discussed and decided here tonight, my people. We have with us a guest, Azhure, daughter of the Plough-Keeper of the village of Smyrton just beyond the Avarinheim." As all eyes swivelled her way, Azhure's stomach turned over with nervousness. "Azhure, step to me, please."

GoldFeather gave Azhure a little shove and Azhure stood, picking her way a lot more calmly through the assembled Avar than she felt. Despite her fear, she kept her face composed as she walked up to Mirbolt who had stepped out of the stone circle to greet her. The Bane had a kindly face, but looking into her eyes was like falling into a lake where you did not know what lay below the surface waiting for you—hard rock a handspan below the surface to shatter your bones? Or soft, comforting water to cushion your fall? The Bane took Azhure's hand and led her around the outside of the stone circle so that all the Avar could see her.

"Azhure comes to us with both hope and pain in her heart," the Mirbolt spoke gently. "She helped Bane Raum and Shra escape the Plains Dwellers when it seemed that all hope was lost." Many of the Avar smiled at Azhure. "But Azhure committed violence to that purpose, violence that we could not normally condone." The Bane described how Azhure had caused the death of her father and attacked the Axe-Wielder Belial—and as she did so the faces of the Avar closed to Azhure.

Raum stepped forward and took Azhure's other hand, smiling at her encouragingly and speaking to his people, describing how he would almost certainly have died had it not been for Azhure's assistance, describing her attempts to care for himself and Shra when all her kindness had earned her was a beating from her father. He described the scars on Azhure's back, described the ill-treatment she had endured at the hands of her father, and the eyes of the Avar softened a little in sympathy and Azhure dared let herself hope. Raum also described Shra's puzzling acceptance of Hagen's blood as a gift to the Mother. The Banes had discussed this at length, but no one had known quite what to make of it. At the end Raum turned to Azhure. "Speak, Azhure," he said, his hand warm about hers. "Speak about what you want, about what you feel."

Azhure blinked. She had not expected to be asked to speak, and she felt shy in front of these people and in this sacred place. But she did not lack courage, and so she stood even straighter and addressed the Avar people.

"I thank you for being allowed here tonight and for being given the opportunity to speak to you. I would ask that I be allowed to join your people. I know that my people have treated yours harshly and that I have myself acted with violence. I can only vow before the Earth Tree tonight that I will never offer you or yours any violence. Please, let me stay with you. I have no people and nowhere to stay. I have lived for weeks with the GhostTree Clan and have learned to respect your way of life deeply. What I have witnessed here tonight has only increased my respect. I felt nothing but hollowness and pain when I lived in Smyrton. The Avarinheim has given the closest thing to peace that I have yet known. Please, let me stay with you," she repeated.

Bane Mirbolt nodded at her. "Thank you for your words, Azhure. Please, Raum, would you take her inside the circle of stone while we discuss with the Avar what their decision will be?"

Raum drew Azhure slowly underneath the nearest stone arch as the Bane started to walk among the Avar, leaning down to talk quietly with them as she passed through their ranks. Azhure turned to Raum, hope and pain softening her blue eyes. "What do you think, Raum? Will they accept me?"

Raum avoided answering and drew Azhure closer to the Earth Tree. "Come, Azhure. Let me present you to the Earth Tree."

"Are you allowed to do that?"

Raum grinned, his teeth white against his swarthy complexion. "I hardly think the Earth Tree will gather her roots and flee, Azhure. She has seen worse than you in her lifetime. Come."

They walked the twenty or so paces to the tree. Its girth was immense, fifteen men holding hands could not have encircled it. Slowly Azhure reached out a hand and touched its bark. It was smooth, like silk, and slightly cool to the touch. She smiled and rubbed her fingers up and down. It felt alive, almost as if it breathed. And to think that the Seneschal taught that trees, forests, were evil. None of them had ever touched the Earth Tree. She looked at Raum inquiringly.

"The Earth Tree has stood as long as the Avar have been here to tend it," he said. "We believe that the health of the Earth Tree is intimately connected with the health of the entire Avarinheim. When, so many years ago, your people," Azhure turned her eyes away from him, "embarked on the wholesale slaughter of the Avarinheim below the Fortress Ranges it is said that the Earth Tree sickened near unto death. It has taken many generations to recover and is now not so green and verdant as it once was. If the Tree should die, then we believe the Avar people would also be destroyed." Raum touched the Tree himself. "We could not live without it," he said quietly, but then smiled. "Ah, Azhure, ever since the destruction of so much of the Avarinheim the Earth Tree has sought refuge from her pain in sleep, absorbed in her dreams of great mysteries. Can you imagine her power and beauty should she wake? We all live for that day."

"Azhure." The voice behind her made Azhure jump. She turned around. Mirbolt stood there.

"My dear." The Bane's face was sad and Azhure's heart sank. "Our people have reached their decision. They sym-

pathize with your plight, and they are deeply grateful to
you for Raum and Shra's lives. But . . . your acts of violence still upset them. Yet they are prepared to be forgiving.
You may freely walk the paths of the Avarinheim, Azhure,
and you can continue with the GhostTree Clan for as long
as you will, but you will not be accepted as Avar. I am
sorry, my dear."

Azhure physically swayed on her feet and Raum's hand
grabbed her elbow to steady her. The villagers of Smyrton
had tolerated her presence, but they had never accepted
her. Now the Avar would do the same thing.

"I understand," she said eventually. "Thank you for allowing me to stay with you."

46

In the Hand of Artor

"Gorgrael!" the wraith whispered ecstatically and reached its hungry claws for the man on horseback.

Borneheld struck the Skraeling a death stroke through the eye, cursing the sweat that dripped in his own eyes as he did so. About him his men fought feverishly. They had been attacked by the Skraelings an hour into their patrol and for a time Borneheld thought the wraiths would overwhelm him and his men.

But his men fought bravely, and after half an hour Borneheld swung his horse about, looking for more wraiths, and noticed that the deadly mist was dissolving about them. He breathed easier and took the time to wipe his brow, running his eyes across his patrol. How many were left?

"They're going, my Lord Duke!" Gautier screamed by his side. "We've won through!"

Borneheld stared coldly at him, then indicated the reddened snow under their horses' hooves. "And how many men have I lost, Gautier?"

It had been only a small mass of Skraelings, but they had been vicious and deadly. Many of the men had died, their brands and swords ineffective against the ferocity of the wraiths. We've survived, not won through, Borneheld thought grimly as his horse sidestepped a headless corpse. How is it that Axis' patrols return unscratched while I lose man after man? Every patrol that Axis led only furthered his reputation, while every patrol Borneheld led fought and came home, but came home with casualties.

"Eight men are dead, two more injured," Timozel said, reining his horse to a halt beside Borneheld.

Besides Gautier's flushed face, Timozel appeared cool and composed. Borneheld eyed him speculatively. His respect for Timozel had grown four-fold since the man's appearance at the fort. This was the second time Timozel had accompanied Borneheld on patrol, and Borneheld was impressed with the man's fighting skills. Again he pondered the fact that the twenty-year-old Timozel had the assurance and manner of a man much older and more experienced. He was a good fighter, very good, and Borneheld thought he would give Timozel still more responsibility about the fort.

Yet more than Timozel's fighting skills, Borneheld valued the man's patent loyalty and admiration. He had brought Faraday to Borneheld. He preferred to ride on Borneheld's patrols. He conspicuously disliked Axis. Borneheld decided he liked Timozel very, very much.

"My Lord?" Gautier's voice cut across his thoughts. "Do we leave them here?"

"Of course, Gautier," he snapped. "Would you have me load down the living with the dead? We are only an hour into our patrol and have another four hours to go. Leave them here, but share their brands among the soldiers left."

He swung his horse away and shouted curt orders, pulling his men back into formation, and led them deeper into the northern wastes.

Although Borneheld remained alert for Skraelings, his thoughts drifted to Faraday. She was never far from his

thoughts, even in battle. Remembering the pain in Axis'
eyes when he saw Faraday encircled in his arms, Borneheld almost laughed. He knew Faraday truly loved him.
Whenever Faraday was in the same room as him and Axis,
her eyes never drifted toward the BattleAxe. No. She constantly leaned to *him*! Whispered endearments to *him*!
Borneheld felt very, very in control.

But he wished his patrols enjoyed the success that Axis'
did.

He wondered if he should have sent Faraday south as
Jorge had suggested. Would she be safe in Gorkenfort?
Borneheld reviewed the defenses of the fort and town. He
knew he faced a desperate battle if—when—the Skraelings
attacked in mass. The town walls were the weakest link in
the defenses. They were not so high nor so heavily defended as those about the fort, and they needed a capable
commander to defend them.

Axis.

Now Borneheld did smile. Axis *was* a capable commander, Borneheld was prepared to admit that, and he *was*
the best person to trust the town's defense to.

But if the town fell then Axis would almost certainly die.

There was a shout among his men and Borneheld swung
his horse about.

"Skraelings," a man cried, and the entire patrol tensed
again, their swords and brands held ready.

But it was a simple drift of snow kicked up by the
horses' hooves that had spooked the man, and Borneheld
reprimanded him.

Skraelings. Borneheld had finally and extremely reluctantly admitted to himself that the creatures he faced were
not the Forbidden. Increasingly the wraiths whispered the
name of Gorgrael among themselves, and their appearance
was too similar to the description of the Ghostmen of the
Prophecy. But was the rest of the Prophecy true?

Artor, no! I will not believe it! Borneheld prayed, invoking the sign of the Plough under his cloak. Although he
found the Brotherhood of the Seneschal irritating at times,

Borneheld was a devout man and believed utterly the word
of Artor as revealed in the Book of Field and Furrow. The
Forbidden were evil. They worked magic. They harbored
foul ambitions. Borneheld believed the Prophecy was of
their creation, designed to trap Artor-fearing Acharites. But
Borneheld was not deceived. The Forbidden had taken a
single sliver of truth—Gorgrael's invasion—and embel-
lished it with lies in order to accomplish their own invasion.

Whatever happens, he vowed silently, *whatever* happens, I will never consider an alliance with the filthy Forbidden. *He* was the WarLord. *He* was the heir to the throne.
And *he* would be the one to save Achar.

Not Axis. Borneheld was beginning to wonder if Axis
had begun to believe the Prophecy—why else should he
have the Brothers recite it in front of him?

"Before Artor," he whispered, "I vow that I will save
Achar from both the Gorgrael's Ghostmen *and* the Forbidden. *I* will be the one to save Achar."

"You *will*," Timozel said intently, pulling his horse close
to Borneheld's and leaning over to stare his Duke in the
eyes.

Borneheld frowned at Timozel's intrusion, but Timozel
took no notice of his Duke's irritation. "I have had a vision
from Artor," he said, his voice low but fanatical. "I have
seen great victories. I have led great armies for your cause.
And we will win through. Our enemies will cower before
us. We will sit beside a leaping fire and drink fine wine,
you and I, Faraday by our side."

By Artor! Borneheld thought, the man is touched! But at
the same time he felt the thrill of power run down his spine.
Was Timozel truly Artor-inspired? He had appeared at his
side just as he had vowed to Artor. Did Timozel speak with
Artor's authority? Borneheld struggled to make sense of it.

Timozel reached across a gloved hand and grabbed
Borneheld's arm.

"Artor has vouchsafed me this vision time and time
again," Timozel said fiercely, his eyes daring Borneheld

not to believe him. "*You* will be the one to save Achar from both Gorgrael and the Forbidden! Believe me!"

"Yes," whispered Borneheld. This is what he needed to hear. "Yes. I believe you. *I* will save Achar and I will not need an alliance with the dark Forbidden to do it."

Timozel released Borneheld's arm and sat back in his saddle. "You will win through," he said softly. "Not Axis. We do not need Axis."

Borneheld's eyes hardened with conviction. Timozel spoke the truth. "Yes. We do not need Axis. Yes, I will win through."

"Yes, we *will*," Timozel said, his eyes flaring with fanaticism again, "because we fight in the hand of Artor!"

They met no more Skraelings that day.

47

In the Hands of the Mother

With both Borneheld and Timozel gone Faraday took full advantage of her spare afternoon. Since she'd met with Axis in the Retreat Faraday felt much calmer, much more at peace with herself. She could feel the tension in the garrison, knew that the general feeling among commanders and soldiers alike was that a major attack from the Skraelings against Gorkenfort was imminent, but Faraday was at peace knowing Axis loved her, knowing he knew she loved him.

Now Faraday and Yr were safely cloistered in Faraday's bedchamber. Faraday had swept about the chamber and removed the few traces of Borneheld that there were, dumping an old comfortable pair of boots, an undershirt that needed mending, his second best tunic and his shaving gear into one of the chests.

"There," she said in satisfaction, turning to Yr. "He's gone." She smiled. "We're finally alone, Mother be praised." She knelt down at the chest where she kept her clothes and rummaged about for a moment, finally lifting the enchanted bowl from its hiding place. "Ah," she said softly, rubbing her fingers gently around its rim, "finally we have time, you and I."

Faraday had found no opportunity to use the bowl since Jervois Landing. Either Borneheld had been too close for comfort, a meeting with Axis too important, or she had felt too depressed to try to reach the Mother. But Faraday felt in the marrow of her bones that if she didn't use the bowl soon she might never do so again.

She waved Yr over to the bed. "Sit down, Yr. I won't need your help." Faraday wore a loose gown she could slip out of easily and had water standing ready in a pitcher close by. She unpinned her hair, then shrugged out of the gown, tossing it to Yr. She was thinner and paler than she had been before her marriage to Borneheld; her anxiety about Axis suppressed her appetite and Borneheld often kept her awake long into the night.

Faraday looked briefly at Yr; today the Sentinel's eyes and mind were unreadable. Lately Faraday had been learning, to Yr's discomfort, how to read the woman's mind the way that Yr read hers. She occasionally learned some surprising things from Yr's unguarded thoughts. Faraday suppressed a smile; Yr's tastes and talents could wait to be discussed and explored another day.

She placed the bowl on the floor at her feet and then slowly poured water from the pitcher into it. Then she squatted down, cut her thumb and suspended the drop of blood over the water.

"May this blood serve to renew my bond with the Mother," she intoned softly, her eyes almost unfocused in their concentration. "May it serve to remind me of my pledge of faith and service to the Mother, and may it serve to bring me closer to the Mother."

She tilted her hand and the drop of red blood rolled into the water. "Mother, with this my blood may you wake for me this day," she said, as the water in the bowl flared emerald and strength and power flowed through her. She picked the bowl up gently in her hands and slowly stood. Once straight she extended the bowl out before her. The emerald glow suffused the room.

"Mother," Faraday said clearly, her voice joyous, then she closed her eyes, let the power flare and race through her body, and stepped through the Gate.

Suddenly she vanished from the room, the bowl suspended in the air, the light pounding from it with the strength and rhythm of a gigantic heart. Yr's mouth fell open and she half stood. This was not supposed to happen! By the Prophecy, what was going on here? She slowly walked over to the bowl, careful not to touch it. If the emerald light still throbbed then the connection must not yet be broken.

Faraday walked through the light, feeling its power throb through her, feeling its love enfold her. For a while she laughed and skipped her way, she felt so alive, so free, but eventually she settled down to a more sedate walk. Perhaps the Mother did not appreciate such irreverent activities. But who could not help feeling joyous this close to the Mother?

The light began to change about her, resolving into shapes and shadows, and her feet stepped onto the grassy paths that led to the Sacred Grove. She was so happy she hummed a silly little melody which rippled through her head. The trees formed about her and above the stars whirled in their god-driven interstellar dance. Faraday felt very contented, very happy. She never wanted to leave this place. Exultation filled her.

She stepped into the Sacred Grove. Soft whispers of wind cradled her body as she walked across. Power drifted through her. Shapes shifted and slipped through the deep shadows behind the trees. There was no fear, no loathing in this place, only peace and happiness. At the far side of the Grove a Sacred Horned One appeared. He was the silver pelt that had greeted her and given her the bowl on the night Raum had brought her here. He greeted her again, his hands on her shoulders, his soft furred cheek against hers.

"Tree Friend. We have waited long for you to come back to us."

Faraday's face dropped and tears sprang to her eyes. "Forgive me, Sacred One," she whispered. "But it has been so difficult."

The Horned One gently nuzzled his damp nose into her hair. "I know, child. We have been with you and we know what you do to serve the Mother and to serve the Prophecy."

He turned her slightly to one side. "Faraday. On this visit the Mother would see you too. See? She waits. Go with love and peace, child." And suddenly he was gone.

Faraday looked to where he had indicated. Another path stretched out of the Grove. Strange, it had not been there previously. It stretched for many paces into the surrounding forest and at the end Faraday received an impression of light and warmth, of love and comfort, and the dim figure of a woman who stood at the very end of the path. "Mother," she whispered in awe.

As she walked down the path the light at its end got stronger, more compelling. Finally it became so blinding she had to close her eyes. Heat struck her face as though she were standing under the strong sun of a southern land.

"Daughter," a woman's voice said, and warm strong hands grasped hers. "Come into my garden." The impression of searing light and heat suddenly faded and Faraday opened her eyes.

Before her stood a pleasant-faced woman in late middle-age, her dark-brown hair graying and coiled loosely about her head. She had cheerful blue eyes and a friendly smile with slightly crooked ivory teeth. She wore a soft pale blue robe, belted about her waist with a rainbow striped band. Behind her stretched the most beautiful garden Faraday had ever seen. Smooth paths led between flower beds containing flowers of every shape and hue imaginable. Tall trees shaded the flower beds from the sun that shone overhead. Water tinkled from an unseen stream, and insects and birds buzzed and sang about the flowers and trees. Seats were placed invitingly under trees and across green lawns. It was a garden which invited company and friendship.

"Mother," Faraday smiled.

"Faraday," she replied. "The Horned Ones may call you Tree Friend, and other men may call you wife and lover, but I will call you Daughter."

"Ah," Faraday's eyes filled with tears. "Thank you, Mother."

"Come, child." The Mother linked Her arm with Faraday's and led her slowly down one of the paths. "I would talk with you a while." Yet despite Her words, for a long time they did nothing but walk, Faraday entranced by the beauty and the peacefulness of the garden. Every so often she would turn to smile at the Mother who squeezed her arm affectionately in reply.

"Look, Daughter, a pool. Shall we bathe?" Faraday looked at the charming pool hidden among rocks and ferns and laughed delightedly. She slipped into the water as the Mother folded Her gown carefully and left it on a rock. When the Mother joined her in the water She brought with Her fragrant soap. Slowly She washed Faraday, Her fingers soothing and gentle as they traced over Faraday's body. Faraday closed her eyes and leaned back into the Mother's arms in the water, letting both water and the Mother's hands support her as she floated.

"Mother," she whispered, unable to believe the sensations that the Mother's hands caused her, "that feels so good!"

The Mother smiled and lifted Her hands to massage the girl's scalp, soaping her hair and rubbing Her fingers softly yet firmly across the girl's temples. "You have known only the awkward touch of your husband, Daughter. I have the hands of love."

For a long time Faraday lay there in the water, letting the Mother minister to her, letting the Mother's love sweep through her. "Mother," she said finally, when she thought she could bear no more. "I must beg a favor of you."

"My Daughter?"

"I do not want to bear Borneheld a child. I do not think I could tolerate it."

The Mother bent and kissed Faraday's brow. "You will bear only children given and received in love, Daughter."

For a long time Faraday lay in the water under the Mother's touch, then, finally, regretfully, sat up in the water. "Ah, thank you Mother."

The Mother grinned cheerfully at her. "Have I made you feel better, Daughter?"

Faraday grinned back. "Much better, Mother."

"Then, let us continue our walk." When Faraday reemerged from the pool she found another robe folded neatly on the rock besides the Mother's blue gown. It was a beautiful gown of a soft material, colored in shifting shades of green, blue, purple and brown. It reminded her of the shapes and shades of the emerald light as it shifted and darkened and formed into the shapes of the trees down the path to the Sacred Grove. "It is beautiful," she said as she belted it about her waist. It left her shoulders bare and felt delightfully cool in this warm garden.

"Yes, it is," the Mother nodded. "You must wear it for special occasions. You will know when. Keep it safe until then. Now, come."

As they walked, again arm in arm, they talked of inconsequential things for a while: the garden, the birds, the quality of the water gurgling beside the path in a small streamlet. But gradually the Mother's face turned more serious, and She stopped Faraday beside a weeping silver birch tree.

"Daughter, I have another gift to give you and some advice before you return to your husband."

"Return? So soon?"

The Mother smiled lovingly at Faraday and caressed her cheek. "You have been gone some three hours. Your maid grows frantic. Soon you will have to return. But first I have another gift for you."

She held Faraday's head firmly in Her hands and Faraday felt the Mother's love flow through her. Then the warm glow of power that she had felt ever since she had entered the emerald light flared and seared through her body, as though fire consumed her flesh, and Faraday cried out and fell against the Mother. "Shush," the Mother soothed, letting Faraday's head go and cradling the weeping girl in Her arms. "It is better now, see?"

Faraday realized that the pain was indeed seeping away, and she nodded and stood up. "What did you do?"

"I gave you the power that My Daughter will need. It is power, unusual power, power to love and comfort, to nurture and enhance, to protect and endure. It is My special gift to you. You will learn how to use it. Follow your heart." She paused. "Hark!" The Mother's head tilted to one side for a moment. "Your husband's patrol returns. No . . . don't fret, shush and listen to me. I have more to say and not much time to say it. Faraday, dear Daughter, it will be some time before you come back to Me, but come back you will, never fear. Now, listen to My words." She caught Faraday's head between Her hands again and Her eyes burned, searing Her words into Faraday's memory. Her eternal happiness would depend on it.

"Remember, I will always be here for you. Daughter, *listen* to me! When your life drains away from you with your heart's blood, call My name and I will come. When pain tears at your mind until you are no longer sane, call My name and I will come. You are My Daughter."

She paused and Her voice became softer as She started to intone a short verse.

When all seems lost and dead and dark,
Of this I can assure you—
A Mother's arms will fold you tight,
And let you roam unfettered.

"Repeat it," She hissed fiercely, and Faraday mumbled the verse through again. "Never forget it, Daughter, *never, never* forget it! Remember to call my name . . . remember!" The Mother's eyes filled with tears and She leaned forward and kissed Faraday hard on the mouth. "Remember!"

Then everything faded.

Yr's arms folded about her fiercely, hugging her tight. "Thank the Prophecy, Faraday! I thought I had lost you forever."

Faraday opened her eyes and blinked. She was back in her chamber in Gorkenfort, the bowl held in outstretched hands before her, the emerald light fading as she watched. She still wore the gown the Mother had given her.

"Quick!" Yr hissed, "Borneheld has ridden into the courtyard and even now calls your name. Off with this gown—where did you get it?—and into this robe. Here, let me take the bowl, where's that pitcher? Good girl. The robe, the robe! Good. Ah, I can feel him striding down the corridor. Quick, there is no time, on the bed, I've rumpled it for you. Do your best to look sleepy . . . well, all right, a muddled look will do as well. Now, let me fold this gown about the bowl and, ah!"

The door opened and Borneheld strode into the room, his face lit with a strange light. Faraday sat on the bed, just risen from her nap, rubbing puzzlement and sleep out of her eyes. That maid, always too damn close, was folding some old clothes into the chest at the side of the bed.

"Out!" Borneheld shouted at Yr.

48

Yuletide Morning

It was early in the morning of the seventh day of the third week of Snow-month, and if the defenders of Gorkenfort and the town that lay beneath it had still followed the same yearly calendar of festivals as the Avar and Icarii, they would have known it was the morning of Yuletide, the night of the winter solstice. The winter solstice was the most critical night of the year for the Icarii and the Avar; if their rites did not help the sun survive the solstice and rise again the next morning then winter could well last forever.

For the past two days blizzards had pushed down through Gorken Pass, so bad that none could venture past the walls of either town or fort. Water froze in barrels. Men had to take to meat with axes. Tent flaps not tied down were frozen into whatever weird shapes the wind blew them. Not even Brother Francis could remember the fort and town being struck by such a severe storm. Yet the coal for fires had to be rationed. With almost fourteen thousand men crowded into the fort and town, fuel was in short supply. Life was appalling, and Borneheld feared fighting would be nigh impossible if the Skraelings attacked during the height of the blizzard. Tension kept men awake at night, expecting attack any moment.

The defense of Gorkentown was going to be a nightmare. It was critical for the town walls to hold against any attack, because the entire army could never fit inside the walls of the fort. If the town fell, then almost eight thousand men would perish; Gorkenfort might well hold, its walls and defenses were three times as strong as the town defenses, but at a dreadful cost to those trapped outside. As commanded by Borneheld, Axis had assumed responsibility for the town walls. Although he did not fear the responsibility, Axis feared the eventual attack. The Skraeling attacks on patrols would be nothing to what Gorgrael would unleash on town and fort.

If this was a normal siege the triangular battlements jutting out from the walls could be used to direct flights of arrows, even pour fiery oil, onto the besieging forces as they beat against the town walls. But no one knew what sort of attack they would have to prepare for against Gorgrael's forces. Atop one of the battlements, Axis, Magariz and Jorge huddled deep in their cloaks, their backs to the wind, trying to peer into the snowstorm. They had stood there ten minutes, their beards and eyebrows already frosted with ice below their tightly drawn hoods. Magariz tugged at Axis' cloak and tipped his head toward the trapdoor leading down into the battlement tower. Axis nodded, and the three men moved as quickly as they could on the icy footing through the trapdoor and down the ladder into the room beneath where the war council awaited them.

All breathed easier once they were out of the immediate wind, and aides helped the three men out of their ice-stiffened cloaks. A small fire blazed in a grate and they stood about it, not talking as they tried to warm their bodies before the inadequate flames, rubbing the ice away from their brows and beards with fingers so cold that the fire hurt where it warmed them. The room was bare of all furniture save the racks of lances and bows and quivers of arrows lining the walls. A single narrow window looked out over the territory beyond the town, but in this storm it was tightly barred shut.

"Well?" Borneheld demanded. "What do you think?"

Magariz glanced at Axis, then turned to face his War-Lord. All the men were dressed for battle, mail shirts over thick felt and leather tunics and trousers, light metal plate protecting arms, thighs and shins. In this weather men had learned not to touch their armor with bare fingers; all had lost patches of skin on their finger tips to the frozen metal. Borneheld and Roland were joined by several of the commanders' lieutenants, including Belial and Gautier.

"The blizzard is as fierce as it has been for the past two days, WarLord," Magariz said for the three of them. "It is a cursed storm, driven by the Destroyer himself. Its cold eats at men's joints and flesh, its evil eats at their souls and their courage." All present knew what he meant. A great part of the storm's deadly ferocity lay in its malevolence; it was as if the storm was alive and hungered for the death of all it encountered.

"We cannot attack through such weather," Borneheld muttered, stamping his freezing feet. "If we send men outside in this they will die in five minutes, frozen to their horses."

"I doubt Gorgrael can attack through this blizzard either," Axis said quietly, his back to the fire. "Have not the wraiths always attacked in relatively calm weather?"

Borneheld glared at him, but both Magariz and Jorge nodded. "We have had patrols outside in fierce weather, although never as bad as this, and they have not once been attacked." Magariz said. "You may be right, Axis, the attack may not happen until the storm abates."

"Then why the storm?" Roland asked. His bulky clothes and armor made him look even more massive than usual. "If Gorgrael has caused the storm, why do so if he cannot send his minions against us while it rages?"

"To sap our strength and courage," Jorge said softly. "Or simply to show us his power. To let us know what we face."

"Perhaps he simply enjoys its fury, revels in its hate," Axis muttered to himself by the fire.

Borneheld cursed. "It will not matter when he attacks if all he has to counter is a mound of frozen corpses. Gautier, when the stocks of coal run out tell the unit commanders they can tear down the doors and shutters of unoccupied houses and use them as fuel for fires. And let us hope that this storm doesn't keep up for too much longer."

If he had reluctantly admitted that it was Gorgrael they faced, then Borneheld had been furious to learn that word of the Prophecy had spread like wildfire among his own troops and now all were talking about it. He demanded that they direct their attentions to the forthcoming battle rather than trying to decipher the useless riddles of an Artor-cursed Prophecy. But his demands had little effect. Men still talked. Heated discussions were held about fires at night, or under blankets when coal was not available for fire. Who was this StarMan? Would he help Achar free itself of the threat from the north, or should they trust to Borneheld? Men muttered about the Forbidden, uneasy that the Prophecy declared in unambiguous terms that the Acharites would have to unite with them to defeat Gorgrael. Opinion was sharply divided about whether it would be wise to admit the Forbidden back into Achar. In many minds, old prejudices refused to die. In others, new possibilities suggested themselves. The AxeWielders were silent as the arguments were tossed back and forth. When asked by regular soldiers for their thoughts, the Axemen said simply that they trusted their BattleAxe. He had saved them from Gorgrael before and would again. They would follow where he asked.

All agreed on one thing. At the moment Borneheld's army was all that stood between Gorgrael and Ichtar.

Even if they would help, no one knew where the Forbidden were. This battle they would have to get through on their own. And if they could not venture past the fort or town walls, then all present knew that it would turn into a siege rather than a decisive battle. Gorgrael would have to break Gorkenfort if he wanted uninterrupted access to Achar. He would not be able to afford having a well-garrisoned fort behind his own army.

GoldFeather shivered and wrapped a soft goat hair shawl about her. "It does not usually get so cold in the Avarinheim, Azhure. Even so far north. At Yuletide, we could normally still go about without extra wraps. But this," she shivered and looked about the small grove near where the GhostTree Clan was camped, "is unusual."

Azhure nodded indifferently. GoldFeather had tried her best to cheer Azhure since the decision at the Sacred Tree Grove, but she remained impervious, the spark gone from her eyes.

Now, as she paused to adjust a bootstrap, GoldFeather let her mind drift back, as it often did these days, to her son and to the imminent arrival of her husband and daughter. About a third of the Icarii nation should arrive to celebrate Yuletide with the Avar—more always flew down for Beltide—and GoldFeather could barely wait to see StarDrifter and EvenSong again.

But the Icarii were late, and GoldFeather was not the only one fretting about it. All the Avar whispered among themselves. Here it was Yuletide Eve, only eight or nine hours away from the time when the rites would have to begin, and there was no sign of them. The rites would be a disaster without the Icarii, and particularly without their Enchanters. What was happening in Talon Spike to so delay her people?

GoldFeather and Azhure continued wandering through the groves, both preoccupied, their eyes occasionally checking the skies. It was always better if Yuletide could be conducted under a clear sky. Azhure dropped her eyes from another brief scan of the sky, and stopped, puzzled. A strange noise filled the air, getting louder every minute. It was almost identical to the sound the River Nordra made when it cascaded through the chasm of the Forbidden Valley. Azhure turned to GoldFeather, but was stopped from saying anything by GoldFeather's face. Normally a reserved woman, GoldFeather had an expression of intense excitement on her face. Her eyes shone and she laughed in both joy and relief, clapping her hands like a small child. "The Icarii!" she cried, grabbing Azhure's arm and forcing her to run toward the inner groves, "they've come!" Her hand twisted in Azhure's sleeve, dragging the surprised woman along the grass toward the entrance to the next grove. "StarDrifter!" she yelled. "Where are you?"

"Behind you," an amused and deeply musical voice said, and Azhure was almost knocked to the ground as Gold-Feather whipped around to stare behind her. Settling down on the ground was the most amazing creature Azhure could ever imagine existing, while above them the air was filled with the sight and sound of beating wings so profuse they almost blotted out the sky. GoldFeather gave a wordless cry, picked up her skirts and dashed madly across the distance between herself and the birdman, throwing herself so violently into his arms that he almost fell over, laughing. "GoldFeather," he said softly, and wrapped both arms and wings about her as he bent his head to kiss her mouth.

Azhure took a deep breath and stared. StarDrifter. There was no one else that GoldFeather would cling to so desperately. Azhure knew she was staring and knew that it was probably considered very impolite, but she could not tear her eyes away from the pair in front of her. Besides, they were so completely enveloped in each other she doubted they were aware of anyone else. Around her other Icarii drifted out of the skies and even more were pouring over the top of the cliff face of the Icescarp mountain and drifting down into the groves.

Azhure was utterly captivated by StarDrifter. He was tall and of a lean and muscular build, and while his torso was bare he was clad from the waist down in a pair of tight golden breeches and boots. His head was covered in shimmering golden hair which curled down from the back of his head, lightening into pale gold and then into silver as it gave way to feathers and then to the luminous white wings that sprouted from his back at the level of his shoulder blades. Although his wings were now wrapped about Gold-Feather, Azhure had caught a glimpse of them as he'd landed. Fully extended they were wider than three men laid out head to foot. Azhure blinked and looked about. The groves were now full of excited Avar and Icarii, wings beating and then folding as Icarii after Icarii landed, loose downy feathers drifting through air filled with the sound of shouted greetings.

GoldFeather tilted her head back and stared into the face of her beloved StarDrifter. Relaxed with love and joy she looked younger, as beautiful as the young girl the Enchanter had fallen in love with so many years ago. StarDrifter laughed and raised a gentle hand to her face, his wings holding her so tight that both were cocooned in their soft strength and warmth.

"I have missed you, woman of my roost. My heart and my bed have been cold these past few months." StarDrifter's face was extraordinarily beautiful, fine pale skin stretched tightly over high narrow cheekbones and a thin, jutting nose. Tilting and utterly compelling pale blue eyes gazed lovingly at GoldFeather from under flaxen brows and a high forehead that sloped gently back into his golden curls. The entire shape of his face and head was narrow and very slightly elongated, but the alien aspects of the bone structures of his skull and face gave him an air of mystery, perhaps even of arrogance, rather than of unnaturalness.

GoldFeather found his physical attraction irresistible. The first time she had seen StarDrifter he had but to hold out his hand and smile, speaking not a single word, and she had gone to his arms then as she did now.

GoldFeather glanced over StarDrifter's shoulder. "Even-Song?" she asked, her voice breathless with excitement and love.

"Following later, my love," StarDrifter smiled. "She preferred to fly with FreeFall."

GoldFeather rested her hands against StarDrifter's chest and stared into his eyes. "StarDrifter," she whispered, "I have something that I . . ."

"Not yet, my love, not yet," StarDrifter whispered and stopped her words with his mouth. Azhure finally turned away and left them alone, wandering away to the side of the grove and sitting beneath a tree. She felt unutterably lonely, the alien outcast among the two races of the Forbidden. The joy of the reunion between the Avar and the Icarii, and between StarDrifter and GoldFeather, drove home as nothing else could the truth that she had no one to worry over her and hold her tight when she returned home.

GoldFeather finally managed to tear her mouth away from StarDrifter's. "StarDrifter," she said, her voice tight with urgency, "I have to talk to you. Our son did not die! I was tricked by Jayme, may his soul drift for eternity! *Our son lives!*"

StarDrifter's grip loosened slightly around GoldFeather and he leaned back to study her face. So long had it been since the loss of their first child that for a moment StarDrifter could make no sense of her words. After a while he shook his head in bewilderment, almost denial. "No, no . . . what do you mean? Our son? He died . . . you saw him . . . our son died . . ." His voice trailed off into silence.

GoldFeather's chest heaved with great sobs. "Jayme stole him and raised him and our son is now BattleAxe of the *Seneschal!*"

StarDrifter let GoldFeather go completely and stepped back. "No, no, it cannot be. Our son? The *BattleAxe?*"

Raum, who had been watching carefully from some distance away, now hobbled forward. He hadn't been sure how StarDrifter would react to the news and he was not entirely surprised at the look of horrified denial across the Enchanter's face.

"Enchanter, it is true." He said quietly, and StarDrifter spun his head toward Raum. Raum raised his hand. "Peace,

Enchanter! Listen to me. I have met the BattleAxe. He names himself Axis Rivkahson, and . . ."

"Imposter!" StarDrifter hissed, black anger now spreading across his face. This *must* be a foul trick of the Seneschal, designed to trick and then trap the Icarii Enchanter!

Raum stood his ground. "No, Enchanter. Not that. He has your eyes, and the cast of your features. No! Wait! There is more. Beneath the black of the BattleAxe dwells the soul of an Icarii Enchanter, StarDrifter SunSoar." Raum stepped up to the Icarii and grabbed his arm. It was rigid with tension. Raum forced himself to stare unwavering into StarDrifter's furious eyes. "Before me your son sang the Song of Re-creation. He recreated the Avar child I had with me, StarDrifter, when she was all but dead. Do not tell me the Seneschal can create an imposter with such powers!"

StarDrifter's stared at Raum a moment longer, then he turned to GoldFeather and opened his mouth, but he couldn't say anything.

GoldFeather threw her arms about him and pressed her face against his chest. "It is true, my love, it is true. I stood no further from him than Raum now stands from you, *but I did not know it was our son!*" She started to sob again, and StarDrifter pulled his arm from Raum's grasp and wrapped it around GoldFeather. "What are we going to do?" he whispered to no one in particular. "How can we get our son back? How can I leave my son with the Seneschal?"

My son, he thought. I have a son. It was a thought which altered his entire existence. I have an Enchanter son.

Crest-Leader FarSight CutSpur strode through the crowded groves, his raven-backed wings folded carefully out of the way, his sense of military organization and discipline offended by the excited jumble of Avar and Icarii about him. His black brows frowned as he peered about for

StarDrifter SunSoar, his brother wanted him, and what RavenCrest SunSoar wanted he generally got if FarSight had anything to do with it. RavenCrest SunSoar was the Icarii Talon, and the direct commander of the Icarii Strike Force. Under him ranged twelve Crest-Leaders, of whom FarSight was the most senior. Each of their Crests was composed of twelve Wings, the basic unit of the Strike Force, themselves composed of twelve Icarii males and females. Those Icarii in the Strike Force had come to the Yuletide Meet in their guise as military personnel rather than as individual Icarii participating in the Yuletide rite. The Icarii had grievous news to impart to the Avar, but the Talon was insisting that his brother StarDrifter join the Combined Council of Elders, Crest-Leaders, Banes and Enchanters that was now convening within the magical circle of stones surrounding the Earth Tree. Thus Crest-Leader FarSight CutSpur strode purposefully through the crowds, ignoring cheerful greetings and those Avar who fell quiet when they noticed he was fully armed for war with his bow slung over his shoulder and his quiver of war arrows hanging ready down his back between his wings.

No one had brought weapons to the Avar camps and the groves in living memory.

FarSight found StarDrifter, GoldFeather clinging to his side, in the farthest clearing. The Avar Bane Raum was talking to them earnestly, and FarSight could see that something seriously troubled the Enchanter. Well, these were seriously troubling days, FarSight thought grimly.

"StarDrifter!" he called several times, before having to virtually shout directly into StarDrifter's face to get his attention. "StarDrifter, the Talon wants you. He has convened a Combined Council in the Sacred Circle, and you must be there."

StarDrifter was definitely distracted, and GoldFeather distressed, but FarSight was unmoved. If they had family troubles then they would have to set them aside. "Now," he said firmly and turned his gaze upon Raum. "You must come too, Bane. There are matters that need to be discussed before the rites begin this evening. *If* the rites begin this evening."

That got Raum's attention and his dark eyes deepened in concern. "FarSight, StarDrifter has received shocking news, but I think it may be news that the Council should hear as well. StarDrifter, come. We must go. You too, GoldFeather. You may be able to help the Council."

They were the last to join the Council and the Talon, RavenCrest SunSoar, was clearly impatient to start proceedings. He was a beautiful birdman with vivid violet eyes, his hair as dark as his younger brother StarDrifter's was light, and with the underside of his raven-backed wings dyed a brilliant speckled blue. Although Icarii rarely changed the color of their hair or their wingbacks, they tended to dye their underwings as the impulse took them. RavenCrest's breeches matched his underwings and about both his upper arms shone the twin silver armbands of his rank. RavenCrest had led the Icarii for over fifty years, since the death of his and StarDrifter's father RushCloud, yet the past few days had been by far the most harrowing he had ever experienced.

As soon as his brother and GoldFeather joined the group of about one hundred and twenty Avar and Icarii gathered about the base of the Earth Tree, RavenCrest began speaking. As he spoke he strutted up and down beneath the Earth Tree. Behind him and slightly to one side stood his only son, FreeFall SunSoar, who had his uncle's golden hair but his father's violet eyes.

"My friends and neighbors," RavenCrest began, "the Strike Force has brought me disturbing news. Our farflight scouts have reported great numbers of Skraelings, as well as other unknown creatures, massing in the southern parts of Ravensbund at the River Andakilsa. They are preparing to strike the Groundwalkers' fort in Gorken Pass. That is the reason we are so late; we did not want to leave our observation of northern Ichtar until the last moment possible. Currently it lies under a fearsome storm of some dark sorcery that we do not yet understand." RavenCrest held up his hand to silence the nervous chatter that broke out and went on. "There is more. Storm clouds build to the north of the groves, and the Skraelings are also massing along the northern borders of the Avarinheim. My cousins Avar, I fear that the Avarinheim will shortly suffer the same action as Gorkenfort."

"But that's impossible!" cried Bane Mirbolt. "The Skraelings have ever been loathe to enter the Avarinheim. They cannot stand the trees, nor the closeness of the groves to the northern borders of the Avarinheim."

"Gorgrael now lends the Skraeling wretches the benefit of his power, Mirbolt," Raum said quietly, standing so that his words could be easily heard. "Who knows what they will do now? RavenCrest SunSoar, before you go any further, there is something you must know. The Prophecy of the Destroyer walks the earth."

RavenCrest rocked on his feet, horror sweeping his beautiful strong face, and all the Icarii present looked deeply shocked. "Ah, no," StarDrifter whispered, and rested his head briefly in his hands. This as well as the news of his son.

Raum quickly described what he had learned from the Sentinels at Fernbrake Lake and his contact with the Tree Friend. Then, with a glance at StarDrifter, who stared at the ground, Raum told them about meeting with the BattleAxe of the Seneschal, and how, incredibly, he carried the soul of an awesomely powerful Icarii Enchanter—powerful enough to sing the Song of Re-creation as though he were humming a simple ballad. As that news sank in, and as those Icarii elders and Enchanters who were present turned to whisper to each other, Raum paused and looked pityingly at StarDrifter. "Perhaps now StarDrifter must tell you something," he said softly.

Slowly StarDrifter raised his face and looked about the assembled group before his eyes locked into those of his brother's. "RavenCrest, my brother, the BattleAxe is my son. GoldFeather's child, stolen from her at birth by the man who has become the Brother-Leader of the Seneschal. I have only just found out myself."

"What is going on here?" RavenCrest exclaimed, confusion turning his temper toward anger. "How can an Icarii Enchanter be raised among the Seneschal filth?"

Raum stepped forward, holding his hand up for quiet among the hubbub of noise. "There is one more thing I must say. The Prophecy walks and Gorgrael gathers his forces to strike south. The Sentinels walk abroad, as does Tree Friend. An Icarii Enchanter lives in the ghastly clothes of the BattleAxe of the Seneschal. My friends, why should four of the Sentinels and Tree Friend all be gathered, at one time or the other, about the person of the BattleAxe? Who carries Icarii blood and has the makings of the greatest Enchanter that has ever lived? We all know the Prophecy. Gorgrael is of mingled Avar and Icarii blood. The StarMan is related to him, a half-brother who shares the same father with Gorgrael."

"No," StarDrifter whispered to himself, his hands clenching by his sides in horror as the implications of what Raum was saying struck home with dreadful force. "No, no, no, no!"

"My friends," Raum continued, his eyes half on StarDrifter. "Must I spell it out for you? Who else can the StarMan be but the BattleAxe, the Icarii Enchanter lost in the lies of the Seneschal that bind him tight? And if that is so, as I believe it must be, then, StarDrifter, have you also fathered Gorgrael?"

StarDrifter lifted his head back and screamed, a primeval sound of pure anguish, and leapt to his feet. He stared wildly at Raum, his wings raised and outstretched as if he would leap into flight, then Crest-Leader FarSight grabbed him and wrestled him to the ground, their wings thrashing together as they struggled. Both Icarii and Avar stumbled out of the way. RavenCrest flapped his wings in a single powerful movement and landed beside his brother, seizing his golden hair in his hand and forcing StarDrifter to look him in the eye. "We need to know," RavenCrest ground out between locked jaws. "Is it possible?"

"Before I met GoldFeather anything is possible," StarDrifter whispered, his entire body slumping. "You know as well as I that during Beltide unions between Icarii and Avar often occur."

RavenCrest turned back to the Avar present, his hand still buried in his brother's hair. "Do any of you know of a child born to one of your women from a Beltide coupling?" he asked fiercely. Now the Avar looked shamed as they considered the unthinkable. Had one of their women not aborted a Beltide babe?

"StarDrifter," Raum said softly, his eyes sorrowing for his people. "Tell us. Which of the Avar could you have fathered Gorgrael on?"

StarDrifter's wings drooped. He had no more resistance to deny the obvious truth. "The Beltide night before I flew down to Sigholt," he whispered, "there was an Avar woman. Beautiful."

"StarDrifter!" RavenCrest hissed again, impatient, his hand giving StarDrifter's head a slight shake. *"Who?"*

"Ameld," StarDrifter whispered so quietly that the others could barely hear. "Her name was Ameld."

Mirbolt gave a horrified cry and RavenCrest turned his piercing eyes on her. "What do you know, Mirbolt?"

"My sister Ameld disappeared some five months after Beltide that many years ago," she said, her hands to her face. Her sister had given birth to Gorgrael? "My sister, my poor beautiful Ameld! How did she die?"

Raum watched the group for a few minutes before squatting down by StarDrifter, wincing as his ankle flared in pain as he shifted his weight, and put a hand on the Enchanter's shoulder in comfort and friendship.

"My friend, there is no blame to be apportioned here. The Prophecy has chosen its time to awaken, and you are merely one of its instruments. Think not of the horror of siring Gorgrael, but the joy and wonder of siring the Star-

Man, joy and wonder that GoldFeather can share with you. Remember, the StarMan must unite all three races of Tencendor, and your son carries within him the royal blood lines of both Icarii and Acharite people. He has been well-bred." He stood again and turned his eyes to the others. "We can only grow strong from the knowledge that this afternoon has given us. We know something of Gorgrael, we know he wields powers similar, if greater, to an Icarii Enchanter. We know who the StarMan is. And we know where he is."

StarDrifter looked up suddenly, his face losing a little of its gray horror. "Where?"

"Gorkenfort. He is in Gorkenfort with Tree Friend."

49

Yuletide

Axis and Belial, swathed in heavy cloaks, walked down one of the narrow alleyways that separated the town walls from the outer blocks of houses. The storm raged overhead, but the walls on either side of the men protected them from the worst of Gorgrael's wind. Sentries stood shadowed in the eerie twilight, and Axis stepped close to one man to speak with him.

"Higginson," he said, recognizing the soldier as one of the regular troops helping the Axe-Wielders reinforce the wall, "a cold afternoon. Have you been on duty long?"

Higginson nodded at the BattleAxe, impressed he had remembered his name. "Some hours, BattleAxe. But I have this doorway to shelter me, and Gorgrael's storm does not concern me."

"Good man," Axis said, seeing the glint of fear in his eyes, but clapping him on the shoulder. "Make sure you get some warm food in you once you stand down."

As they strode further down the alleyway Axis turned to Belial, shouting from underneath the hood of his cloak.

"This storm saps our strength, Belial, yet I fear its cessation almost as much as I fear its fury."

Belial could only just catch his words amid the howling from the rooftops. He nodded, then indicated a doorway some paces further down the alley. There was little point in them trying to inspect the defenses at this stage.

After Borneheld and his commanders struggled back to the fort via houses and sheltered alleyways, Axis and Belial spent hours inspecting walls and talking to men. Men were positioned in the battlements, ready to man the walls once—if—the storm abated, while other units sheltered in the houses adjacent to the walls. All had orders to keep as warm as they could, but no orders that Axis gave could stop the fear that grew with each passing hour.

Grateful to be out of the frigid air, Axis and Belial hurried through the door, slamming it behind them. The room, once a cobbler's workshop, was now set up as a kitchen, and a small fire burned in one corner, a pot hanging from a tripod above it. Pulling off his cloak and gloves Axis sat on a small stool before the fire and motioned Belial to do the same. The unit's cook took one look at them, ladled out bowls of gruel, then retreated to a storeroom in the back of the building.

"I'm afraid," Axis admitted quietly as he finished the gruel.

"There is no shame in that." Belial threw the few remaining lumps of coal onto the fire and sat back, rubbing his hands. "All are afraid."

"None can escape the venomous intent of this storm, Belial." Axis paused, listening to the fury of the wind. "Even Belle wouldn't insist her husband venture outside to save Cow Crumbocke. Not unless she truly desired a widowed old-age."

Belial tried to smile reassuringly at Axis, but it didn't work.

Axis sighed. "What will Gorgrael throw at us, Belial? What tricks does he have waiting for us beyond the walls?"

Earlier both men had tried to peer through one of the arrow slits, but could see nothing.

"I think we will not have to wait very much longer to find that out," a voice said behind them, and Axis and Belial swung about in surprise to see Ogden and Veremund hurrying through the door.

Belial frowned. "What are you two doing here? Return to the fort where you will be safer."

But Axis moved his stool to one side to make room for the Sentinels by the fire. "Have you come to tell me how to use my powers, old men? Have you come to tell me how to save these walls and my men?"

Belial did not like the tone in Axis' voice. "You will do as you have always done, Axis. You will fight to the best of your ability and lead your command to the best of your ability. It is all you can do."

"Damn it!" Axis said intensely, staring at the flames. "If I am the StarMan, I should be able to do more than what I have simply done before. Ogden, Veremund," he lifted his eyes to the Sentinels, "can you help me?"

Ogden spread his hands, apologetic. "We are only servants, Axis, and as the Prophecy unfolds we can only stand and watch. We have no powers to save this town and fort. We cannot teach you how to use your power."

"Then what are you doing here?" Axis said harshly. "Why did you come?" His deep sense of helplessness in the face of the horror that waited beyond the storm found release in anger.

"We have to witness, dear one," Veremund said gently. "And we must do our best to make sure that you live through this. The Prophecy must grow at its own pace. If it had wanted you at your full power for Gorkenfort then it would have moved sooner."

Axis stared at Veremund for a moment, then gestured toward the door in an abrupt, angry movement. "And tell me, Sentinel, will you and your Prophecy make sure that these fourteen thousand live through this as well?"

Veremund held Axis' stare, his face impassive. "Who lives and dies is not my decision. I only know that you must live."

Axis dropped his eyes. "Is my father close, Veremund? Ogden? Will he tell me what to sing to drive these wraiths back?"

"I cannot say, dear one," Veremund replied. "We cannot know that."

For long minutes Axis stared into the fire. Would the BattleAxe be enough to save this town? Or did he need the powers of the StarMan? StarDrifter, he thought, where are you? Where are you?

Belial leaned across and rested his hand on Axis' arm. "You will do your best, Axis. It is all you can do."

Axis took a deep breath and looked at the Sentinels. "Perhaps it were best if you returned to the fort, my friends. If you stay around here any longer you may be required to perform the Service of the Dead more times than you might wish."

"And we must . . ." Belial began, rising to his feet, then stopped. "What?" he said, bewildered.

As Axis stood up, his face toward the door, the Sentinels looked at each other. It was time.

"The storm has broken," Axis whispered, his face white. "Gorgrael is ready to strike!"

Without another word Axis and Belial grabbed their cloaks and gloves and rushed for the door.

The sacred and ancient rituals of Yuletide began as the first stars glittered through the gaps in the cloudy sky. The combined council had debated fiercely whether or not to conduct the rites given the recent ominous news, but had finally agreed that it was essential. If Gorgrael disrupted the rites of Yuletide the winter might never lift and his creatures of ice and cloud would drift unhindered ever lower into the lands of Tencendor.

The damnable thing was, Yuletide was the ideal time for

Gorgrael to strike since many of the Icarii and most of the Avar were gathered in one spot, together with their Enchanters and Banes. Recognizing the danger, the Icarii and Avar took what precautions they could. Crest-Leaders posted sentries about the forest and the cliffs to give advance warning of any attack, while all Avar children under the age of twelve years were taken as far down the paths into the southern Avarinheim as they could in the time available; the Icarii never brought their children to the groves. No people could survive if their helpless children were slaughtered.

As dark fell the rites began. Azhure, watching from the very fringe of the assembly gathered in the Earth Tree Grove with GoldFeather, her daughter EvenSong and Pease by her side, felt and saw the Avar and Icarii relax a little as the familiar and ancient words of the ritual began. The Icarii Enchanters, StarDrifter prominent among them, gathered with the Avar Banes in a circle about the stones surrounding the Earth Tree. Enchanters and Banes were both dressed in crimson, the Icarii with half-length robes that fell from their waists, even the women leaving their breasts bared, the Banes with full-length robes draped gracefully from their shoulders. Bearing the image of a blazing sun suspended across his chest, StarDrifter stepped forward from the circle and lifted an unlit brand from one of the stone pillars. For a moment he stood, head bowed in thought or prayer, then he passed one of his hands over the brand and it burst into flames. He held it forward to the assembly, walking slowly about the circle of stone so that all could see. He stopped in front of a young female Bane who held a harp in her lap, smiled a little, then as she struck the first chord on the instrument he opened his mouth and began to sing.

He sang in an ancient language that Azhure had never heard before, but after a moment's puzzlement she found she could understand what he was singing. StarDrifter sang of the glory of the sun, of the life it gave to those who lived in its light, of its yearly death and resurrection on the night of the winter solstice. He paused briefly, then sang of the dependence of the Earth Tree, as the earth itself and all life it contained, on the continued health and well-being of the sun. He sang of the mysteries of the sun and of the song it hummed to itself as it danced through the heavens, of the stars themselves, of the myriad of suns that all swayed and dipped to the notes of the Star Dance which itself remained one of the Seven Great Mysteries. The voices of his fellow Enchanters and Banes rose beneath his voice in supporting harmony, leaving StarDrifter's voice clear to soar strong through the hearts of all those listening and surge above their heads to drift with the stars themselves.

Azhure wept. His voice touched the very sinews of her soul and she could feel her blood vibrate to the music that he made.

Finally StarDrifter's voice faded and he turned to his fellow Enchanters and Banes. "What can we give the sun to encourage it to live again in the morning?" he asked.

The Enchanters and Banes replied as one. "We can give to the sun the strength to rise in the morning."

"We can," StarDrifter whispered, although his whisper reached all ears. "We can give the sun the strength to rise in the morning. We can give it blood." Azhure's eyes were caught by a sudden movement at the edge of the grove, the spot where the Avarinheim met the Icescarp Alps. Slowly, but with incredible dignity and grace, a huge Stag appeared. He was in the prime of his life, his pelt glowing dark reddish brown on his back, fading to creamy yellow on his underbelly. Massive twelve-point antlers swayed from his head. He paused slightly at the edge of the assembly, his huge dark eyes knowing, then he began to pick his way through the assembled Avar and Icarii toward the stone circle.

As the Stag neared the Enchanters and Banes they sang a song of love and support, of compassion and gratitude, their voices humble before the sacrifice of the Stag.

The Stag walked into the clearing below the stone circle, then through the Banes and Enchanters, stopping only when he reached StarDrifter. StarDrifter reached out a hand and touched the Stag briefly on the forehead in blessing. Then he turned to one side and Raum hobbled forward, a long knife in his hands. The Stag dropped to his knees and offered his throat, closing his magnificent eyes so that he would not have to witness the arc of the knife as it swung.

StarDrifter began to sing again, this time a song of wonder that the Stag should choose to offer its life in order to give the sun strength. As his voice died Raum placed one hand on the Stag's forehead and with the other placed the knife against its quivering throat. "Thank you for this sacrifice you are willing to make for us tonight. Tonight you will join with the Mother," Raum said quietly, then lifted his head and cried to the assembly. "Witness this sacrifice freely given by friend Stag to the sun, to enable the sun to waken at the end of this long night, to give it the strength it will need to strengthen toward spring. Friend Sun, accept this gift!"

And he dug the knife into the Stag's throat as hard as he could. A dark spurt of blood arched through the air and the Stag groaned, collapsing onto the ground. As the blood spurted free StarDrifter began to sing again, a high exultant note in his voice, and he threw the burning brand he had been holding spinning into the sky.

Instantly the great circle of stone about the Earth Tree burst into flame.

Axis paced along the wall, his face tight with apprehension. As the wind had died, so too had the snow stopped. Now the frightful mist that heralded the arrival of Skraelings was thickening about the walls. Dark had fallen, and the night increased the mist's impenetrability. Belial watched Axis as he paced back and forth along the wall, pausing now and again to peer uselessly into the night. Sentries in both town and fort had lit torches along the walls, but even the thin tracery of light could do nothing to allay the growing fear. All were tense and ready, some soldiers climbing the ladders to the parapets of the walls, others hefting weapons in their hands. Others stood scattered about in defensive positions throughout the town in case the walls should fail and the survivors be forced to retreat through the town's twisted streets toward the fort.

Axis slapped the wall with a gloved fist in frustration. What was out there? What? He recalled the night Gorgrael had rolled his cloud of fear over the Axe-Wielders and imagined he could hear the beat of great wings deep within the mist. He quickly scanned the sky. What if Gorgrael gave more of his creatures wings? The idea of Skraelings dropping from the sky made Axis' skin crawl.

What was Gorgrael doing? Why was he waiting?

Frustrated by his inability to see what was going on, and seized by a sudden impulse, Axis snatched one of the burning torches from its bracket and heaved it spinning high into the mist. Thousands of wraiths suddenly became visible as they fled the flaming brand spinning down toward the earth, their silver eyes throbbing in panic, their whispery voices wailing and weeping.

Then, as the light sputtered and died in the soft snow, Gorgrael's forces launched their attack.

Azhure's attention was caught by the spinning torch and the sudden conflagration of the stone circle and for critical instants she did not realize the Earth Tree Grove was under attack. Screams and shouts reached her ears, but it wasn't until Pease grabbed her arm and screamed with a strange guttural sound that Azhure abruptly realized something was dreadfully wrong. Two creatures, Skraeling wraiths, had hooked their clawed hands into Pease's upper body— their frightful jaws working at her neck and shoulders. Pease gripped Azhure's arm convulsively even as her body jerked. Her eyes pleaded for help; blood dribbled from her nose and mouth.

Azhure tore her arm from Pease's death grip, too terrified to scream herself. She slowly backed away, step by step, her eyes riveted by Pease's death agony, horrified by the nightmare creatures that tore convulsively at Pease's flesh. Pease's eyes rolled up into her eye sockets and her body began to collapse backwards, her hand still extended in appeal. One of the creatures lifted its head and hiccupped, its eyes on Azhure.

Finally, her terrified trance broken, Azhure turned and ran.

She ran into a landscape of chaos and terror, blood and frenzied feeding. As the stone circle had burst into fire the three SkraeBolds in charge of the assault on the Yuletide rites launched thousands of Skraelings into the Earth Tree Grove. The first the Avar and Icarii knew of the attack was the shocking sight of the sentries' bodies hurtling down from the cliff face above them, their dead bodies breaking the bones and wings of the living in a sudden, frightful crackling of pain. As Avar and Icarii screamed and milled in confusion the Skraelings massed out of the tree line and down the cliff-face into the assembly.

It took vital minutes for the Crest-Leaders to rally the Strike Force to their calls, vital minutes when the countless Skraelings literally ate their way through the crowd toward the stone circle, intent on reaching the Enchanters and Banes in the center of the grove, and then the Earth Tree itself.

FarSight CutSpur screamed in anger and frustration as his Strike Force lifted into the sky in pitiful dribs and drabs. He fitted an arrow into his bow, but then screamed again in frustration—how could he fire into the crowd and not kill his own? The scene below him was one of complete chaos, everywhere the Avar and Icarii were snarled with the Skraelings. Some of the Icarii were lifting out of the death below him, many with grievous wounds and torn wings, but the Avar were being massacred.

The SkraeBolds howled in delight. Every now and again they turned to strike down one of the Icarii who had managed to lift out of the tangled mess, their clawed hands and feet ripping wings to shreds in instants. They had a mission here this night, and it was not simply to disrupt the Yuletide rite. They flapped lazily toward the burning circle, keeping a prudent distance from the flames. They were angry now as their silver eyes searched the crowd below them. They had thought to disrupt the rite before it got this far, before the circle burned, but StarDrifter had hurled the flaming brand before they had a chance to act.

The Banes and Enchanters were as helpless as the Crest-Leaders and the tattered remnants of the Strike Force hovering impotently above. Even their wards of protection would do little against this savage attack. For long minutes StarDrifter stood with his fellows, encircled by dying Icarii and Avar, watching the gray mistlike wave of wraiths creep closer and closer to them. Then, before they had time to act, in whatever way they could imagine, the SkraeBolds struck.

The Skraelings rushed the walls in a massed attack, hooking their talons into the minute cracks in the masonry and gradually clawing their way toward the battlements, their silver eyes gleaming obscenely in the dim light that the torches threw down. Axis leaned over the battlements, his eyes and mouth grim, watching the creatures as they howled and whispered their way to the top of the walls. If anything they had become even more solid since he had last encountered them on patrol, flesh extended down to their shoulders and through most of their thin, sticklike arms and legs. Only their torsos were still misty, insubstantial. But their teeth, hanging sharp in their oversized loose jaws, looked real enough. Too real.

Axis strode along the battlements. "Stand fast!" he called. "They will be easy prey, my friends. They cannot clamber over in large numbers and we will stick their eyes before they manage to gain a hold on the battlements. Stand fast!"

Men responded and rallied as Axis strode among them.

"Are you ready?" Axis shouted above the increasing whisperings of the Skraelings.

"We hear your voice and we are ready, BattleAxe!" the men nearest him responded, and gradually the cry spread along the walls of Gorkentown. "BattleAxe! We hear your voice and we are ready!"

Then the killing began. The Skraelings clambered over the top of the battlements in wave after wave, almost overwhelming the thousands of men who lined the walls ready to meet them. But they were prepared, they had their BattleAxe among them, and they had been drilled repeatedly about what they must do. Hands grasped Skraeling hair before the creatures could grasp them, and swords, knives and lances were thrust time and time again into their plump silver eyes. Wraiths screamed and lost their grip as their eyes burst, their disintegrating bodies plummeting down to the snow below as their lives bled away.

But men screamed also. Scores fell, Skraelings clinging to their faces and necks, their teeth sunk deep into the sweet flesh of the manlings, almost delirious with joy as they tasted their flesh. Axis and Belial seemed everywhere at once. When one section of the wall looked set to fall to the Skraelings, then one or the other, and sometimes both, were there to plunge into the fray, rallying the spirit of their men, driving the attack back over the walls once more.

"Use the fire!" Axis screamed above the noise of the battle. "Use the fire!"

Men standing in wait lifted containers of oil to the battlements, tipping it over the edge, soaking the Skraelings as they climbed. Then they tossed torches, igniting whole sections of climbing Skraelings. Their flesh burst into gouts of fire and the creatures fell screaming to the snow, their bodies dissolving into gray sludge almost as soon as they hit the snow.

But fuel was in critically short supply and most of the defenders along the wall had to rely on their weapons to fight the wretches as they reached the top of the walls. More and more Skraelings emerged from the mists, but as

Axis strode the length of the walls it seemed that Gorkentown might hold. The Skraelings had yet to make a significant breach in his defenses. Axis permitted himself to hope
a little.

Then he saw two SkraeBolds walk out of the mist, a
mass of Skraelings parting like a sea about them. The
SkraeBolds stopped not twenty paces from the gates, their
posture relaxed, an amused expression on their dreadfully
mutated faces. One idly scratched its belly as the pair studied the gate.

Axis fought his way back along the battlements until he
stood looking down on them.

"Greetings, Axis Rivkahson," one of the SkraeBolds
called, its voice distorted as it hissed past its beak. "We
have come for you. Behold!" It waved its taloned hand to
something as yet hidden in the mist.

The SkraeBolds moved fast. Gorgrael knew well the relationship between Enchanter and Enchanter's son, and had
carefully instructed his SkraeBolds regarding StarDrifter's
fate.

The elder of the SkraeBolds, SkraeFear, directed his two
companions to continue the slaughter among the Banes
and Enchanters. He could deal with StarDrifter himself, he
hissed, his pride not letting him allow the three to attack together as instructed. SkraeFear wanted to be the one to
present StarDrifter to Gorgrael. He wanted Gorgrael to recognize SkraeFear as the leader of the SkraeBolds. It was
he, after all, who had rescued Gorgrael from the ruin of his
mother's belly.

StarDrifter's training as an Enchanter had never prepared him for this. He had never contemplated being alive
during the time of the Prophecy of the Destroyer and did
not have the powers to repel such an attack. Yet despite his
fear and his sense of impotence and failure he never once
thought that he could simply lift out of the battlefield. He

could not desert his dying brethren, even if it meant his own death.

StarDrifter heard a soft sound behind him and turned.

Five paces away stood something that should never have existed.

"StarDrifter," it hissed. "I have come for you." It flexed its clawed hands at its side.

StarDrifter lifted his head, his eyes calm.

SkraeFear took a step closer, tilting its dreadful head to one side as it contemplated the Enchanter. So, this was the Father. It was ugly, ugly, all white and gold.

"Do you love your son, Enchanter?" it asked, its silver eyes cold and calculating, its tongue lolling completely out of its beak.

StarDrifter hesitated only an instant. "Yes," he said, his voice strong. "Yes, I've loved Axis through all those years when I thought he was dead. Now that I find he is alive, I find my love confirmed and renewed."

SkraeFear hissed in anger, his clawed hands half raised. "No! No! I mean your elder son. Your heir. The one who will win such fame, such power, that he will be the one through whom you are remembered. Gorgrael. Do you love Gorgrael?"

StarDrifter's eyes became hard and cold. "I pity him. I do not love him. I do not honor him. I turn my back on him. He is not *my* heir."

The SkraeBold screamed and, ignoring all instructions to the contrary, attacked the Enchanter.

Axis heard Belial gasp in shock and turned and met his second-in-command's eye for a moment. Then he turned back to the horror working its way toward one of the western sections of the town walls. It had a head like a distorted horse's, with the silver eyes common to all of Gorgrael's creatures and an open mouth containing as many teeth as a Skraeling—except, on this huge head, they were almost as long as a man was tall. Ridged flesh like raised scales ran down its neck and back, and its body was ridged and sectioned like that of a worm. It was fat, its sides bulging and convulsing obscenely, as if it were in the throes of birth pangs. It had no limbs, and hunched and slithered its way toward the walls, running down those Skraelings that did not move out of its way fast enough. IceWorm.

"Axis, look!" Belial screamed at the BattleAxe's side, and Axis turned to where he pointed. Four more of the Ice-Worms slithered out of the mist.

"The gods help us if they're attacking along the length of the walls," Axis snapped. "Come!"

They ran to the spot the nearest IceWorm was aiming for. Axis snatched an archer's bow and a handful of arrows. "Here, my friend," he said, thrusting the bow toward Belial. "You're the archer, not I. Aim for its eyes."

Belial flexed his fingers and notched an arrow into the bow. "Luck guide me," he whispered, his face a mask of concentration, holding his aim until the IceWorm reared its body some ten paces above the battlements. Then he loosed his breath and the arrow at the same time. The arrow hit the IceWorm just below the level of its eyes and bounced harmlessly off the scaly armored skin of its cheekbone. Axis slapped another arrow into Belial's outstretched hand. Belial let fly again; this time the arrow flew true and struck deep into the IceWorm's eye, blood spattering down over the walls. The creature toppled over backward, screaming its anger and agony. Belial and Axis rushed over and looked down as the IceWorm crashed into the snow. It split apart in a dozen places as it hit the ground, and out of its sides writhed Skraeling wraiths.

Fear crawled down Axis' back and he turned and grabbed Belial's arm. "Quick, get the archers to work. We've got to stop these creatures before their heads top the walls and they disgorge their loads!"

Belial nodded tersely, and ran along the battlements, shouting for the archers to come forward.

Axis looked back at the disintegrating body of the Ice-

Worm, and then checked on the progress of the other four. His eyes slipped toward the two SkraeBolds and for one frightening moment he could not see them. Then his eyes caught a movement down at the gates.

Azhure collided with body after body, some Icarii, some Avar, some Skraeling. Sometimes blood-reddened hands reached out to her in appeal, sometimes blood-reddened claws reached out to her in a mad lust of hunger. Azhure stumbled ahead, her hands pressed against her face, her legs somehow carrying her through the throng, Pease's agonized, dying face before her always. A Skraeling reached for her and caught her by the shoulder, spinning her around. As Azhure felt the claw bite deeply into her shoulder rage suddenly flared and exploded through her numb terror. Her hand brushed the back of an Icarii warrior, slowly collapsing to the ground beside her. Her fingers tangled among the feathered arrows in the quiver on his back and, without thinking what she was doing, she grabbed one of the arrows and pulled it out of the quiver, plunging it toward the Skraeling's eye.

The arrow burst the silver orb as satisfactorily as a plague boil that begs to be lanced and bright blood spurted forth over Azhure's face and neck.

"The eyes!" she screamed, the triumph of her voice commanding more attention than the scream itself. "Strike them in the eyes! The eyes! They die!"

She tugged the arrow out of the disintegrating wraith's eye socket and turned to the wraith mauling an Avar man next to her. Grabbing the wraith's head until it bent back, she plunged the arrow into its eye. Then she turned again and again, screaming all the time, seizing wraith after wraith, plunging the arrow down again and again. Those who heard her took up the cry. Soon, in an ever-widening circle, the Avar and the Icarii began to fight back. Knives and arrows were loosed and used. Wraiths started to die. The Crest-Leaders could finally launch their Strike Force into action with orders to close on the Skraelings from above and behind, seizing their heads and plunging arrows directly into their eyes. Panic spread among the wraiths.

The SkraeBolds leaned into the two iron-barred wooden gates of Gorkentown, legs straddled, hands placed as far apart on the wood as they could. They sang a broken tune, horrible to listen to, dark and destructive music that split the air about them.

Axis moaned. Their song tore deep inside of him, and only by running the tune of the Icarii ward of protection through his mind could he stop the dreadful effects of their singing. For a distance of some twenty paces along the wall either side of the gates men dropped their weapons to tear at their ears, some screaming in pain, others writhing silently on the stone pavement of the battlements, blood trickling from their ears and eyes. More and more Skraelings clambered over the top of the wall, feasting well on the defenseless men.

Axis was powerless. The ward of protection kept the Skraelings from him but not his men, who collapsed into uselessness and death as the Skraelings hooked themselves into their flesh.

Axis turned back to the gates. The SkraeBolds had not moved, but frost ran from their hands across the wood. The wood splintered, the sound a dreadful crackling accompaniment to the SkraeBolds' music. Within minutes the gates would crack apart. Axis ran to the internal battlements, looking down at the unit of men stationed inside the gates. The SkraeBolds' music hadn't yet reached them in force, though many scratched at their ears as they stared in horror at the splintering wood.

Axis leaned down as far as he could, screaming at the men above the general hubbub of battle and the sound of the cracking wood. "Get back," he screamed. "Seek shelter." As one the men ran to look for defensive positions further into the town.

Axis turned back to the battle. Several of the IceWorms lay dead and split on the ground, but a hundred paces further west one of the IceWorms reared its head among a hail of arrows, wavered for a moment, then heaved obscenely, once, twice, a third time, and then spewed forth hundreds of Skraelings deep into the town. Axis felt sick to his stomach. He prayed that the units stationed among the twisting alleyways of the town would be able to contain the Skraelings, but even as he prayed he saw a second, a third, and, horrifyingly, a fourth IceWorm rear their heads above the walls and spew forth their cargo.

Below him the gates splintered completely, then fell, tearing from their hinges in a scream of tortured metal.

"Damn you, StarDrifter!" Axis screamed into the night, "why are you not here to show me what to do! Damn you!"

The defenses of Gorkentown were breached.

SkraeFear attacked StarDrifter in such a fury of razor-sharp beak and taloned hands, feet and wing tips that had the Enchanter not managed to pull his head back he would have been decapitated by the SkraeBold's beaked jaws. His ward of protection no use against the SkraeBold, he was pushed to the ground by the force of the creature's attack, and felt lethal talons pierce his flesh.

"Think that your pitiful wards are enough to withstand me, Enchanter?" SkraeFear hissed close to StarDrifter's ears. "Do you think that you are stronger than your son? Fool!"

StarDrifter's body was wracked with pain as the Skrae-Bold's talons sank deeper into his flesh, jerking and tearing as its claws clenched tighter. He fought to retain his grip on the power of the Star Dance but the pain was so dreadful that his mind slipped. His vision blurred even as the Skrae-Bold tore at his wings with his beak; there was nothing he could do against such an attack. A gray mist gathered at the edges of his vision.

Then the SkraeBold hissed and writhed in surprise and

pain and StarDrifter felt the grip of its talons loosen. With a final supreme effort he pulled himself free and rolled to one side. A woman was hunched over the SkraeBold, twisting an arrow into the base of the creature's neck.

The SkraeBold had its hands to the arrow, trying to pull it out, ignoring the woman for the moment. StarDrifter launched himself to help her, crying out in agony as he felt his wings flap uselessly behind him. He pushed himself forward nevertheless, grabbing the woman about the waist and hauling her away from the SkraeBold. Any moment it would attack the woman and she wouldn't stand a chance against its taloned malice.

StarDrifter, even as the SkraeBold had seemed within an instant of taking his life, had suddenly realized how he could help . . . if he lived long enough. Half dragging the woman, half leaning on her for support, StarDrifter stumbled toward the still burning circle of stone, sobbing in relief that the Skraelings had delayed their attack until the stone had lit. All that was keeping Gorgrael's creatures from the Earth Tree was the circle of enchanted flame.

"Do not breathe!" he croaked as he dragged the woman toward one of the burning archways, "do not breathe as we go through!" He clamped a hand over her nose and mouth as they tumbled through, feeling the flames sear his flesh and feathers, tucking his tattered wings as close to his body as possible—he did not want to go up as a living torch if his wings caught fire.

Still holding onto the woman he stumbled toward the Earth Tree. Raum ran toward him, catching him by the shoulders. Relatively unmarked himself, the Bane's face twisted with horror at the sight of the Enchanter's injuries.

"StarDrifter! Let me help you."

"No time!" StarDrifter muttered, close to collapse. He finally let go of the woman and leaned on Raum. "Quick. We have to get to the Earth Tree. There is a chance . . . a chance . . . if this Tree Friend of yours truly exists . . . that we can put a stop to this slaughter and save both our peoples and the Avarinheim."

Raum exchanged a stricken glance with Azhure. "Help me," StarDrifter cried, and between them Raum and Azhure dragged him to the Earth Tree.

"Raum, I will need you to help me reach this girl, what did you say her name was?"

"Faraday."

StarDrifter nodded, the gray haze closing in on him again.

Raum looked desperately at Azhure. "Azhure, support him—careful! His wings are terribly injured!"

Azhure knelt behind StarDrifter and helped him into a sitting position, carefully pulling his bloodied wings to either side of her. She could see that many of his wounds were open to the bone.

The pain woke StarDrifter from his mental fog and, after a moment, he leaned back against her, grateful for her support. "Thank you," he said quietly, looking at her. "What is your name?"

Raum started to speak, but StarDrifter seized his arm and forced him to silence. The Enchanter kept his eyes riveted on Azhure's face. His blood loss made him lightheaded, but there was something about the woman that called to him. Did he know her?

"My name is Azhure, StarDrifter."

"Azhure." StarDrifter nodded and turned back to Raum, wrapping the Bane's hand in his gently and placed his other hand on the Earth Tree's trunk. "Give me your support in this, Bane Raum, and help me to find Faraday. You know her, I do not. With her help, we will make Earth Tree sing as she has not done in millennium."

Through their interlinked hands Raum felt the Icarii Enchanter bend his mind and will to the Tree, loving it, calling to it, asking it for aid. Raum placed his own free hand against the Tree, called on the Tree, the Horned Ones and the Mother for aid, and summoned Faraday. The Earth Tree, rarely aware of what happened in the world of moving beasts, briefly turned her mind from contemplating those mysteries she found buried deep in the earth with her roots and those that ruffled past her leaves carrying the faint vibrations of the Star Dance and listened to both the Icarii Enchanter and the Avar Bane. Tree Friend? Tree Friend walked? For a while she contemplated this new mystery, then she drifted back into her slumber again.

Faraday, terrified, sat huddled in her chamber, holding tightly to Yr. Timozel stood guard at the door, his sword drawn, showing no obvious doubts about his ability to hold back a hundred of the Skraelings should they come swarming up the corridor. The attack on the fort and town felt like it had been going on for hours, yet Faraday was dimly aware that only an hour had passed since the Skraelings had launched themselves against the walls of Gorkenfort. The screeching and wailing of wraiths, the shouts and screams of men, tore at her ears, and she buried her head in Yr's shoulder. Yr's face was white and pinched, and her lips moved silently and unceasingly as she prayed to the Prophecy that they all might somehow survive this terrible attack. She rocked Faraday slowly back and forth, as much to comfort herself as to comfort the girl.

Suddenly she felt Faraday stiffen in her arms and cry out softly, almost as if in pain.

"Faraday?"

Faraday mumbled something very softly, and Yr felt the girl's hands clench at her back. "Faraday? What's wrong?"

Timozel turned from the door. "What is it?"

"Raum?" Faraday whispered.

Yr forced a smile to her face. "It is nothing, Timozel. Faraday merely fears, as do I."

Timozel frowned, then turned back to his post.

Yr bent back to Faraday and pulled her head back a little so she could see Faraday's eyes. The girl had a slack and vacant look on her face, as if her soul was elsewhere.

* * *

Faraday fought through a sea of pulsing emerald light, pulled by such a feeling of pure need that she could not resist. She had never feared the light previously, but now it was so strong, so angry, that she quailed. Faraday realized that the light was not angry with her, but with something else. She frowned. It was angry but it did not know how to strike.

A voice spoke to her. A low, musical voice, full of magical shadowed cadences. "Faraday?"

"Yes," she whispered, turning slowly through the pulsing light, trying to find the source of the voice.

Another voice spoke, and this one she knew. Raum.

"Faraday. We need your help."

"Raum!" she cried, her voice full of joy.

"Faraday. Listen to StarDrifter."

"Faraday." The voice spoke again, very close now. Beside her stood the most beautiful winged man, so pale skinned and feathered that he glowed almost silver in this emerald light. He was smiling and holding out his hand to her, his pale blue eyes compelling her to trust him. She could not resist. She took his hand.

"Tree Friend," he said. "Will you help your Icarii and Avar neighbors in their hour of need? Will you sing to the trees and ask them to live?"

"Gladly," she whispered. She would have laid down before the Skraeling host to have her throat torn out had he asked her.

His wings beat gently and she could feel him pulling her down a long spiraling tunnel of green and silver that swirled about them. They spiraled further and further until they were hovering over a huge glade; a massive tree stood at the center, surrounded by a flaming circle of stone. About the rest of the glade there was a battle going on, but Faraday could not see it very well, all but the tree and the circle of fiery stone was a blur.

"Faraday," said the Enchanter, StarDrifter. "This is Earth Tree. She is very powerful, very vital. To her is connected the life of the Forest Avarinheim. If she dies, or even if she remains indifferent, the Avarinheim will die. Faraday, will you sing to her? Will you wake her out of her indifferent slumber? Will you ask her to protect those who love her and who depend on her for their survival? Gorgrael strikes into the heart of the Avarinheim, Tree Friend. Will you try to save it?"

"Gladly," Faraday answered again. She could deny this Enchanter nothing.

They landed softly at the base of the tree. There she saw three dim figures, a woman crouched behind another of the Icarii, an Avar male holding the hand of the Icarii. Both the Icarii and the Avar had their hands on the tree and were concentrating on it with all their might. They paid her no attention, although the woman looked up, wonder on her face. Faraday smiled reassuringly at her, instinctively knowing she would like this woman.

"Come with me," StarDrifter said gently. "Come with me and touch the Tree."

Faraday laid her hand on the Tree, the Enchanter's hand warm on hers. "Sing," he commanded. "If you do not wake her with your song then all will die."

Faraday sang. She did not know where the song came from, but she could feel herself drawing on the power the Mother had given her in the garden. StarDrifter began to sing beside her, his voice weaving in and out of hers until they created wondrous patterns with their voices, patterns that hung about in the air between them, patterns that penetrated deep into Earth Tree.

Earth Tree had waited thousands of years with no one to sing this song to her. It was her own song, the song she had composed in her youth and then given to the Mother for safekeeping. She sighed, caught deep in the memories the song evoked, memories of when the Avarinheim was young, when all was hope, all was joy. Then she slowly, reluctantly, let go of the great mysteries she had been contemplating and started to rise to awareness. The closer she rose to the surface, the further distant from the great caverns of the center of the earth into which her roots hung,

the more she realized that something was wrong. The Avarinheim was under cruel attack, had been for centuries, and
was now under even worse. Loathsome creatures swarmed
in the very glade she called home.

Earth Tree screamed in fury.

Faraday almost lost contact with the Tree and her song
faltered, but StarDrifter's hand kept hers pressed close to
the Tree, and his voice missed not a beat, encouraging her
to keep singing as the Earth Tree's scream of rage reverberated about them. Faraday realized that it was imperative
that the Earth Tree not lose control to the point where she
would use her fury to destroy friends as well as foe. The
only way Faraday could do that was to speak to her with
Song, speak to her with enchanted music. Her voice
strengthened.

StarDrifter's song started to alter, first only a note here
and there, but then entire phrases. Faraday altered her own
song to support his, and, in the space of one incredible
heartbeat, Earth Tree joined them, her thunderous voice
lifting over the entire northern Avarinheim. As she caught
the song StarDrifter and Faraday fell silent, awed by the
majesty and power of the Earth Tree as she sang her Song.
The Song of her Making.

The entire Earth Tree Grove was blanketed by the awesome sound. All movement stopped, and then, as one, the
Skraeling mass broke apart. Skulls burst, eyes popped,
hands fell from arms, and torsos smashed to the ground as
legs broke asunder. The two SkraeBolds who were whole
dragged their stricken companion, still with the arrow protruding from his neck, back from the circle of fire, screaming defiance at the Tree, yet totally unable to challenge it.
Gorgrael had not given them the power for this. With a final scream of defiance they vanished.

Those that were left among the Avar and Icarii scrambled to their feet and turned to the tree, their weary faces
filled with awe and wonder.

"She sings, beautiful woman," StarDrifter whispered
and turned to Faraday. "Thank you, Faraday. Between us

we brought both the music of the Stars and the music of the Mother to wake the Earth Tree. She sings now, and she will ward the Avarinheim with the strength of her protection. Gorgrael will not have such an easy route south as he had hoped."

Faraday touched his face with gentle fingers. "You are StarDrifter, Axis' father. He looks for you, Enchanter. He needs you. Will you come to help him?"

"You know him?"

Faraday's beautiful smile spread across her face and she laughed innocently, still unaware of the power her smile could have on a man. "I love him, Enchanter. You have a beautiful son." But suddenly she felt the power fading, felt herself losing her grip on StarDrifter's hand. She spiraled gently upwards into the green and silver tunnel. "Help him, StarDrifter," she called desperately. "Help your son!"

"Help him, StarDrifter," Faraday mumbled, twisting in Yr's arms. "Help your son!" Then she gasped, her eyes flying open into Yr's, and fainted dead away.

50

The Streets of Gorkentown

Axis spent a desperate night rallying his forces about the five roughly semicircular lines of defenses radiating out from the fort's gates. He lost the larger portion of his men at the point when he ordered the evacuation of the walls and a retreat to the first line of defense. He'd desperately hung onto the battlements for as long as he could, watching more and more of his men die, until he realized that if they did not fall back soon then the growing numbers of Skraelings vomiting forth from the IceWorms could cut them off from their lines of retreat. As they fell back entire units died under the weight and teeth of wraiths who clambered onto their backs. More died falling from ladders in their desperation to escape. Axis and Belial, and all the remaining unit commanders, fought desperately to keep the men under some sort of discipline, fought to keep them obedient to orders.

As men faltered and died, more wraiths surged forward, newly confident. They had been afraid of the nasty golden man, but nothing would stop them this time. Not even the man with his power.

Axis remained on the walls until it would have been death to stay. Finally Belial dragged him toward one of the remaining ladders left standing.

"Axis! You can do no more here, and you will be less than useless to those left if you die in a futile stand on the battlements. Come!" Belial grabbed Axis' arm and hauled him toward the ladder. As they reached it Axis turned one last time to watch the slaughter of those still remaining along the top of the walls. Most were lost under a writhing gray and crimson mass of feeding wraiths.

Axis seized Belial's shoulder, leaning close, his pale eyes fierce. "*I* should have been able to stop this!" he yelled above the screams of dying men and the whisperings of Skraelings.

Belial almost toppled over as Axis' grip tightened painfully on his shoulder. He grabbed the top of the swaying ladder for support. "Damn you, Axis! Don't give in to self-pity now! Pull yourself together and rally your men—listen, they call your name!" Faint shouts of "BattleAxe" reverberated up from the alleyways as men did battle with the Skraelings who had reached the ground.

He shrugged free of Axis' hand and pushed him down the ladder before sliding down himself.

Axis jumped down onto the ground, slipping a little in the bloodied snow. "To me! To me!"

Thus began the desperate street battle of Gorkentown.

The narrow winding, twisting streets both aided and hindered Axis. On the one hand the Skraelings could not mount a mass charge without pounding against a strong line of determined defenders; on the other hand, lines of defense were often broken when Skraelings clambered over rooftops to fall upon the men as they watched the streets before them rather than the roofs above them. All fought bravely, with Axis rallying barricades when it seemed they might fall, standing shoulder to shoulder with his men as the Skraelings attacked. He tried firing the houses lying between themselves and the Skraelings, but too often burning walls fell upon his own men. They would have to save Gorkentown with their swords and little else.

On the other side of the barricades the two SkraeBolds rallied their writhing forces, directing the attack to the most vulnerable spots in Axis' defense lines, hissing and spitting at the Skraelings until the wraiths were driven to even greater measures to reach the men. The Skraelings were murderous foes. Barricades that would have held for days against an army of men fell in only minutes to the wraiths. The wraiths could climb, sinking their claws into the slightest hookhold in the barrier. Better than climbing was slithering through spaces that cats would get stuck in, their toothsome faces grinning in anticipation, their hearts emboldened by the sudden spurt of fear which crossed men's faces when they saw the wraiths emerge from impossible places.

The wraiths fed well. Barricades fell and were marked with the piled and torn bodies of the men who'd died defending them. There had been five lines of barricades in Gorkentown, but as the sun started to streak the eastern sky as crimson as the streets, Axis rallied those of his men that were left on the final line of barricades before the gates of Gorkenfort itself.

Weeks of relentlessly slicing the fort's walls with ice had made them much harder for the Skraelings to climb, and those that had reached the top of the fort's walls had been relatively easily disposed of. The IceWorms, who had wrought so much damage to the town's defenses, vomiting forth their Skraelings behind the walls, were too small to severely threaten the fort's walls, their heads rearing uselessly twenty paces below the battlements. Still, Borneheld's men had died as well, and the WarLord strode up and down the walls of Gorkenfort, cursing each and every one of his men, cursing Axis as the town's defenses were breached.

Atop the fort's walls Jorge and Magariz stood watching the desperate fighting in the streets below, their faces gray and haggard. They ached to seize weapons and rush out to aid Axis and his men. Yet they could not. Borneheld had ordered that the fort's gates remain closed no matter what happened in the streets below. Hard as it was, it was the correct decision. No matter the desperation of the men trapped outside, no commander should risk the safety of the entire fort.

Axis and all his remaining men were exhausted. They had been tense and alert for twenty-four hours, fighting desperately for almost twelve. All had wounds, and many were weak from blood loss caused by deep lacerations. Those not fighting leaned against walls, many slipping to the ground in exhaustion, knowing they were almost certainly dead if the Skraelings leaped on them while they were off their feet. Some pushed themselves wearily to their feet, others stayed down, beyond caring. Units had been decimated and men fought beside strangers, most in the gray of the Axe-Wielders, some in the brown of the regular Acharite forces.

At times during the street battles, Axis had desperately tried to reach within himself, reach within him to the power he *knew* was there. If he had once found the power and the knowledge to sing the Song of Re-creation, why didn't the deaths of his own men stir him to sing death and destruction upon the Skraelings? Through the haze of exhaustion and pain clouding his mind Axis realized that he needed his father, needed his knowledge. He felt like the five-year-old child he had once been, given a man's sword for the first time, knowing that it could kill, yet able to do no more than drag it uselessly behind him as he wobbled across the courtyard. He found himself screaming his father's name as he plunged his sword into a Skraeling's eye, as if that could somehow magically bring his father to his side.

But all he could do was use the sword he had finally grown into, and pray that he would live beyond this nightmare. As those of the men that were left, less than three thousand of the eight that had originally manned the walls, gathered outside the fort's walls, Axis was so exhausted he could no longer even maintain the Icarii ward of protection about him. Perhaps, after all, death would not be so bad— a kindness after all he had witnessed and the futility he had experienced this night. He leaned against a wall and slid wearily to the ground, his sword extended before him.

Belial slumped beside him, exhausted. Blood plastered his fine sandy hair to his forehead and exhaustion carved deep lines from nose to mouth.

Axis closed his eyes, but they flew open as a man screamed close by.

"They arrive," Belial said shortly, helping Axis to his feet again. "Have they not fed enough yet?"

Axis wavered a moment and Belial had to steady him. "They seek me, I think, Belial. Their appetites cannot be sated until they taste my blood. If they do that, then Achar lies open to them forever and you may as well fall upon your sword." Stricken by a horrifying thought, his eyes widened. "Belial! What will happen to Faraday should I fall?"

"Borneheld will keep her safe," Belial said shortly. "Come, the men need you now."

Axis followed him. "The gods must know she would be better feeding the hunger of a Skraeling than living out a long life with Borneheld," he muttered.

The Skraelings were massing behind the last line of barricades, and a number were already swarming over the top of the hastily built wall of carts and boxes. As Axis came closer to the barricade, Belial already well ahead, a bulky shape dropped out of the sky in front of him. Axis stopped dead, his eyes narrowing in surprise.

"Your men die, Axis Rivkahson," the SkraeBold hissed, "and you tremble close to death yourself." It stepped closer, wings extended behind it, taloned hands held ready to strike. Axis forced himself into a combative frame of mind, knowing that men depended on him. He would not die now, not yet. There must be more than this. He slowly raised his sword before him.

The SkraeBold gurgled happily as he saw the sword sway in Axis' battle-wearied hands. The kill would be easy. It crowed its triumph to the sky for a moment, then, lowering its head, leaped forward.

But Axis had a little more determination left than the SkraeBold had anticipated. He swept his sword before him in an arc, catching the SkraeBold across a shoulder, opening the creature's flesh until blood flowed. The SkraeBold screamed and twisted to one side, then changed the direction of its attack, driving in low below the arc of Axis' next sword swing, its taloned hands seizing Axis about the chest and waist and driving him to the ground. The creature worked its claws closer and closer to his flesh, tearing at Axis' tunic and mailshirt with its beak and tusks.

The strength of the SkraeBold was phenomenal, and although Axis was stronger than most men he could not free himself from the grip of the beast. Its breath, so close to his own face, smelled of rotten carrion, and Axis gagged, unable to fight back until he could catch his own breath. He tried to turn the sword in his hand, to turn it so that he could plunge the blade down into the SkraeBold's back, but as he readjusted his grip the SkraeBold's talons tore his mailshirt apart and sliced deep into his chest and flank. Axis went rigid with shock, his back arching off the ground beneath him, the pain too great for him to summon the breath to scream. His sword clattered from suddenly nerveless hands, and Axis knew he was dead. Perhaps it was as well that he would die where he had lost so many of his command. Better he die with them than survive without them.

The SkraeBold writhed and twisted as it lay upon Axis' body, digging its talons deeper, feeling them rip through the man's flesh, crowing its joy. Gorgrael would reward him well for this. It was still laughing and hiccupping with amusement when Belial swung his sword high in both fists and buried it deep between the SkraeBold's wings. The impact was so great that it almost knocked Belial off his feet, but he held on grimly as the creature writhed screaming below him. Pray I am not too late, Belial thought over and over in his mind, horrified to see glimpses of Axis' pale and still face, terrified by the sight of blood running away down the gutter.

"Die, you inhuman bastard!" he screamed, and twisted the sword down through the creature's flesh until he heard the flesh tearing away from bone. He let go the sword, still buried deep in the SkraeBold's body and, grabbing one of the leathery flapping wings, rolled the creature off Axis' body. As the SkraeBold flopped over onto its back the sword drove deeper until the tip of the blade suddenly emerged with a dreadful sucking pop from its breast. The SkraeBold gave one last hiccupping sigh, its blood pouring out from its beak. Instantly it started to dissolve.

Belial raised his head to look at the white faces staring down from atop Gorkenfort's walls. "Damn you!" he screamed. "Open the gates! Axis lies a-dying while you watch!"

He leaned down and lifted Axis' limp body across his shoulder, staggering as he took the full weight onto his own exhausted frame. Turning slightly toward the final desperate battle at the barricades he screamed to Arne, the most senior of the Axe-Wielders left alive. "Fall back, Arne! Fall back toward the gates!" Not waiting to see if Arne had heard him, Belial staggered toward Gorkenfort's gates, his feet slipping now and again on cobbles made treacherous with melting snow and blood.

Atop the walls Jorge turned to Magariz. "I hereby do take the decision to open the gates. You are not involved. I outrank you. I will take total responsibility."

"You are too late. I gave the order to open the gate minutes ago."

The two men stared at each other. Then they turned and slid down the ladders leading to the courtyard.

Borneheld was across the other side of the fort, close to

the walls of the Keep, when he saw the gates begin to open. He screamed in fury and ran around the battlements toward the gates, but he was tired and the footing treacherous and only a third of the way around he slipped and fell heavily, turning an ankle so viciously that he could not rise for several minutes. He lay there, his face red and furious, gasping unintelligible orders.

Belial struggled through the gates with Axis an instant ahead of a flood of soldiers, many of them dragging wounded colleagues. Confounded by the death of one of the SkraeBolds, the Skraelings failed to attack the retreating men. And the remaining SkraeBold was so surprised at the killing of its brother that for long minutes it failed to rally the Skraelings.

The combination of Magariz's humanity, Borneheld's unsure footing, and the Skraelings' confusion meant that only a few men were unlucky enough to be caught by wraiths as they turned to flee for the gates. All the others got through, and the iron-plated gates clanged shut in the faces of the first Skraelings to rouse themselves and race after the fleeing men.

The siege of Gorkenfort had begun.

Faraday walked through an enchanted forest, full of power and beauty, peace and serenity and strange diamond-eyed birds.

But the beauty, peace and serenity did not last and the diamond-eyed birds fled.

The sounds of a battle began to intrude upon her dream, and then, horrifyingly, the vision the trees had sung her flickered before her eyes again.

Axis, his sword clattering uselessly from his hands. Red, red everywhere. Heat. A Dark Man, crying with laughter. A woman, crying for release. A bloodied sun hanging over a golden field. Blood. Blood—why was there so much blood? Where was Axis? Faraday twisted away, gagging in horror. He was covered in blood—it dripped from his body, it hung

*in congealing strings through his hair and beard. He
reached out a hand, then a great gout of blood erupted that
covered her as well. She could feel it trickling down between her breasts, and when she looked for Axis all she
could see was a body lying before her, hacked apart, and a
golden and white form, as if a spirit, slowly rising behind it.*

A heart, beating uselessly . . .

The bloodied sun . . .

A heart . . .

Blood . . .

*The creature's claws and beak tearing deep into the
heart.*

"*Axis!*" she screamed and wrenched herself from Yr's
arms. "Axis!"

Yr tried to grab her but Faraday had already snatched a
cloak and was pushing past Timozel. He too tried to restrain her, but Faraday turned on him viciously. "Take your
hand off me," she snarled, and, shocked by the power in
her voice, Timozel let her go.

Faraday wrapped the cloak about her shoulders and ran
down the corridor, her hair flying, Timozel and Yr only a
step behind her. They shared an apprehensive glance. What
was happening?

Faraday ran into the courtyard just as Belial staggered
through with Axis in his arms. Even from her distance
Faraday could see the blood that covered Axis.

"Mother!" she whispered, appalled, certain he must be
dead, then picked up her skirts and ran toward Belial.

Yr raced behind Faraday, her face white with anguish at
what she could see.

Faraday slid to a halt beside Belial as he lowered Axis to
the ground underneath the eaves of the stables. Drained of
the last of his strength, Belial sank down beside Axis, his
face pale underneath his bloodied forehead.

Faraday pushed away the few men who reached down to
Axis and fell to her knees beside him. He breathed spas-

modically, his skin ashen from loss of blood that seeped from half a dozen deep wounds. If the SkraeBold had missed Axis' heart it nevertheless sounded as if it had torn his lungs apart.

"Faraday," Belial began brokenly.

Faraday raised her eyes from Axis' bloody body. "I am not going to give up while he has life left in his body, Belial! Give me your knife!"

Belial stared at her, not comprehending, and Faraday snapped her fingers impatiently. "Your knife! I have to cut these clothes from him!"

Yr dropped to her knees beside Faraday, her face stricken, cradling Axis' head in her hands. This was the closest contact she'd had with the man since she'd been in cat form; it felt as if his life force was all but gone. If it blinked out completely then all was lost; the world would tear itself to pieces under Gorgrael as the Prophecy shattered apart.

Faraday desperately cut and tore Axis' clothes from his body, paling as she saw the full extent of his injuries. The SkraeBold had dug its talons deep into his chest and left flank—seven or eight appalling lacerations gaped open revealing bone and spongy lung tissue. A dozen smaller cuts dotted his chest and belly.

"Leave his head," Faraday said quietly to Yr, "Help me staunch some of the wounds." Already her own hands were slippery with blood.

Axis was dying. "Damn it!" Faraday muttered, then took a deep breath. "Mother, help me save him," she whispered, and reached down into the very soul of her being to draw on the power the Mother had given her.

It seared up through her body and Faraday fought not to lose control, fought to direct the power to her purpose. Belial, who had struggled to a sitting position, was the only one with a clear look at Faraday's face and he noticed the change that came over her. He rocked back, shaken by the flash of emerald glow in the woman's dark green eyes as she called on the Mother's gift, but more so by the expression of sheer power that swept down over her face like a curtain.

Faraday dug her fingers deep into Axis' wounds until her hands were completely submerged in his body, the Ichtar ruby on her left hand burning as it was immersed in the BattleAxe's blood. The bystanders took sharp breaths in alarm; what was she doing?

As they probed, Faraday's fingers persuaded living tissue to bind itself together, enticed and in some cases seduced blood vessels into retying and replenishing themselves. She muttered to herself as she worked, wordless sounds, encouraging murmurs. Yr could feel what was happening and she leaned back, looking first at Faraday's face, then turning to share her amazement with Belial. She looked back down again. Already Faraday had dealt with the major wounds on Axis' body and her fingers were now closing the lesser lacerations. Finally Faraday trembled, her face losing concentration, her eyes losing their power and returning to normal.

She looked up at Belial, her chestnut hair tumbling down over her shoulders, her face pale and bewildered. "What have I done?" she whispered. Belial leaned across Axis' body and gripped her bloody hand. "You have saved his life," he said quietly, "and for that I thank you."

Axis took a deep breath and shuddered, and although his eyes remained closed his face was regaining some color, relaxing away from death.

"What's going on here? What piss-brained soldier ordered the gates open?" Borneheld had finally struggled down from the battlements, limping heavily. Didn't they realize that the Skraelings could have staged a mass charge and broken through?

There was a knot of men gathered about by the stables and Borneheld thumped over, shouldering his way through. Axis lay unconscious on the ground, bloodied and torn clothes about him. Faraday knelt to one side of him, her hands tearing strips from her cloak to wrap about his wounds, while the maid, Yr, sat cradling the BattleAxe's head in her lap.

"If those are the only wounds he has to show for the loss of Gorkentown then I would hazard to guess that he spent more time running than fighting," the WarLord observed derisively. "Faraday, come. The servant can see to those bandages. You should not be demeaning yourself out here in the cold and mud."

Faraday rose, her face drawn with the effort she had spent. "It is part of my duties as chatelaine of Gorkenfort to see to the wounded, Borneheld. And there are many more here for me to attend." She turned toward another group of injured men lying a few paces away.

Borneheld's fury returned in full force. "Who ordered the gates open?" he yelled.

Magariz opened his mouth, straightening his shoulders, as Faraday turned back to Borneheld. "I did, my husband," she said quietly. "I was sickened at watching men die needlessly when we could shelter them in here." Her eyes flickered to Magariz, daring him to contradict her. Magariz's mouth hung open, appalled at the risk she took. Even though Faraday was Borneheld's wife, in his present mood there was no telling what he would do to her.

Borneheld stared at his wife, furious with her. How *dare* she interfere with his orders! "You stupid . . . !" he started to shout, then stopped himself with a massive effort. He breathed heavily, the veins standing out on his forehead, struggling to bring his rage under control. If it had been anyone else Borneheld would have struck out. But Faraday was his wife and only a woman. She didn't understand military matters or the danger that could have seethed through the gate when she ordered it open. She was upset by the battle about her. She . . . she had saved Axis' life through her interference. "Do not meddle in matters beyond your concern!" Borneheld rasped finally. "Mop up the blood if you wish, but then go inside and sit by the fire where you belong. I don't want your sentimentality endangering this fort again."

He stared at her a full minute longer, then turned and stomped off toward the Keep. Faraday's face and body relaxed in undisguised relief. Her eyes met Magariz's briefly.

"You have won the respect and more from all here who witnessed what you did for the BattleAxe and what you just did for me," he said quietly, his striking face intense with undefinable emotion. "I am humbled by your courage and awed by the power that you carry inside you. I am your servant." He bowed jerkily, then turned to follow Borneheld into the Keep.

Faraday watched him for a moment, then turned to Belial. She leaned down to his forehead and touched him with her hands. "Let me help you," she said.

51

The Lake of Life

Jack stood still in the early morning air, the breeze ruffling his straight blond hair, his green eyes gazing intently to the north. He listened to the Song of the Earth Tree. Ordinary ears could not hear it, but to Jack's Sentinel ears the music reverberated through the crisp morning air, filling his soul with consolation. Earth Tree was awake, and the Avarinheim would be denied a little longer to Gorgrael. His entire force would have to flow into Achar through the Gorken Pass.

Jack had left his pigs in a sheltered valley in the southern Urqhart hills while he had spent the past week trudging further north, seeking out the fifth Sentinel.

The Prophecy had recruited and then recreated only the five of them. Jack, the wanderer and the one who largely bore the weight of responsibility for their mission; Ogden and Veremund; Yr. And Zeherah. No one had heard from Zeherah, felt Zeherah, for over two thousand years. It worried Jack. Since their creation they had largely stayed apart, happier not to congregate as five lest that in itself trigger the Prophecy. But their minds had touched even if hundreds of leagues had separated their bodies. All but Zeherah. She had vanished. If Jack could not find her in time for her to fulfil her assigned role in the Prophecy then all would be lost. She *should* have awakened and walked with the rest when Axis entered their lives.

Jack knew that Gorgrael had struck strongly the night before. Yuletide. Jack should have been able to feel the revitalised joy of the sun this morning as it rose. It had risen, but only half-heartedly, and winter retained its strong grip on the country north of the River Nordra. Jack feared in his heart that the Yuletide rites had not been completed. He could only hope that enough had been done for the sun to somehow struggle toward spring.

Tears sprang to his eyes as he contemplated the slaughter he had felt in the Earth Tree Grove. Each scream had torn at his soul. And yet . . . yet it had been worse at Gorkentown. Were Axis and Faraday still alive? He knew Yr, Ogden and Veremund were, for he could still feel them, and he could only hope that Axis had not perished along with so many of the others whose souls had passed him by throughout the night.

Jack had watched the dead as he sat through the river of the night. He had seen the Icarii, torn and some wingless; the Avar, shocked and bewildered; the mass of soldiers from Gorkentown, all wandering disconsolately through the night and along the River of Death toward the great Gate of the AfterLife. He had finally roused himself as the last of the soldiers killed in Gorkentown passed him by. At least Axis had not passed. There was still hope.

Jack stood on the southern face of HoldHard Pass in the Urqhart hills. The garrison of Sigholt sat on the northern face about a league away. While it stood there unviolated this morning, if Gorgrael moved through Ichtar then it might well be overrun if its ancient magic could not save it. But Jack's eyes did not linger on Sigholt, even though it was one of the remaining three ancient Keeps of Tencendor left standing. Instead Jack's eyes turned toward the wide basin at its foot, his eyes tracing the outlines of an ancient shoreline. There should have been a lake here. One of the four magical Lakes of Tencendor. Yet there was none. It was gone. And with it had gone Zeherah.

All the Sentinels had been tied in some way or another to the lakes. Yr with Grail Lake. Ogden and Veremund, inseparable, with Cauldron Lake. Himself with Fernbrake Lake, the Mother. And Zeherah with the Lake of Life, the most magical, some said, of all the Lakes. Sigholt had guarded its shores for millennia. Now it guarded nothing but a bowl of snow, and undoubtedly during summer held nothing but dust.

The Lake of Life had been drained—perhaps by one of the ghastly Dukes of Ichtar sometime during the past two thousand years. The Lake of Life was dead.

And the love of his life was dead with it, blown away with the dust that formed when the lake was drained. Zeherah. Jack bowed his head and wept. For the moment he did not mourn the Prophecy, but his own loss. Zeherah had, in another existence, once been his wife.

All the Sentinels had once been members of the lost fourth race of Tencendor. The Charonites. The Ferrymen who plied their boats along the waterways of the Under-World.

52

The Earth Tree Grove

He will live, GoldFeather, but he will not fly for some time. See, these two wounds have cut deep into the flight muscles of his chest. They will need time to heal." Barsarbe sighed, her face gaunt and ashen after the terrible night they had all endured. Those Banes left had spent the hours of the night tending to the wounded. "Once he gets back to the hot springs of Talon Spike he will heal faster and cleaner."

"I thank you, Bane Barsarbe. You have done more than your best here this night," said GoldFeather. Barsarbe had worked for over four hours on StarDrifter's wounds, stitching the muscles back into place, sprinkling herbs into the deepest wounds to help fight infection and aid healing.

A small group huddled about StarDrifter as he lay under the Earth Tree. RavenCrest, his son FreeFall, EvenSong and Azhure. GoldFeather sat by her husband's side, her face tight with worry. A few paces away stood a vigilant group of five of the Strike Force detailed by FarSight Cut-Spur to guard the Talon and his heir. RavenCrest and

FreeFall had been forced by CutSpur to lift out of the grove the night before as the Skraelings attacked, and the Strike Force had kept them well out of the way until the danger was over.

EvenSong had saved GoldFeather. As the Skraelings attacked Pease, EvenSong had grabbed her mother and, through a supreme effort, lifted her to the tree tops. Although the Icarii were very strong, few could carry the weight of another into the air.

Now EvenSong sat to one side, watching Bane Barsarbe work on her father. She was a striking woman, with her uncle RavenCrest's violet eyes and her father's golden hair; like all Icarii women, she wore her curls cropped close to her skull. Her wingbacks were the same gold as her hair, and she dyed her underwings to match her eyes so that in the air she was all gold and violet. Now her wings were tucked in behind her, the muscles of her back and chest strained and aching. She and GoldFeather had huddled terrified in the tree tops of Earth Tree Grove, watching the massacre below them, too scared to cry out even when StarDrifter was attacked, knowing they could not help him.

EvenSong was shocked by the attack on the grove and her father and numbed by the news of her elder brother. She knew that her parents had lost a child early in their relationship, and that it caused them great and lasting sorrow. Now it seemed her brother lived. EvenSong, so used to being an only child, found it strange to consider that she had an elder brother somewhere, and one who had inherited StarDrifter's powers. EvenSong knew StarDrifter had hoped she would inherit the mantle of Enchanter from him, but he had hid his disappointment well when it became apparent that the baby daughter Rivkah carried would wield no more magic than ordinary women. He loved his daughter nevertheless. But now her brother lived and would become an Enchanter, if StarDrifter could ever find him. EvenSong, always a little temperamental, was jealous.

EvenSong regarded Azhure with immense admiration and respect. As she and GoldFeather had huddled terrified in the trees Azhure had helped turn the tide of the battle, not to mention saving StarDrifter's life. No one else had managed to act with such decisive determination. Even-Song knew that many of the Strike Force had been shamed by Azhure's actions. While they had hovered, screaming their frustration, she had somehow managed to rally those on the ground. There would be soul searching among the Crest-Leaders over the next days.

RavenCrest was furious, both with his own inability to act and with the Crest-Leaders' impotence in the face of the Skraeling attack. What was the point, he had screamed earlier this morning as he had strutted about the grove before the assembled Strike Force, of having a Strike Force when his people died anyway? Was not the attack last night something they had trained for? But RavenCrest stopped short of totally humiliating his Strike Force and twelve Crest-Leaders. The Icarii, as the Avar, had lived in relative peaceful isolation for so long that they had forgotten the skills necessary to repel and counterattack. RavenCrest knew he had to assume as much responsibility for the number of Icarii and Avar dead as anyone else.

RavenCrest, although he loved and respected his brother deeply, felt ashamed that it had been StarDrifter who had salvaged the House of SunSoar's pride. In concert with the Avar, Bane Raum, he had managed to awaken the Earth Tree, and now she continued to sing over the grove and the entire northern Avarinheim. Her Song had repelled and destroyed the Skraeling attack. Still the price had been awful.

Many hundreds of Icarii and Avar had been killed, the Avar bearing the brunt of the attack because of their passivity and their inability to lift out of the grove. This evening the Icarii and Avar would build great funeral pyres in the lesser groves, commending their dead to the River of Death, the Avar praying that they reach the paths of the Sacred Grove while the Icarii prayed that their own would remember the Star Song so that their souls would eventually be reborn among the Stars themselves.

Azhure saw EvenSong watching her. She was fascinated

by the Icarii woman and hoped she would have the chance to know her better. But for the moment there was too much sadness to contemplate new friendships. Fleat's daughter Hogni had been killed by the Skraelings as well as Pease. At least Fleat had been well out of it, escorting the young children further south into the forest. Hopefully they had evaded attack. Despite the grateful and dignified thanks of the Icarii and Avar, Azhure felt more cast adrift than ever. Azhure lowered her eyes and studied her hands.

She wasn't sure what she should do now. Pease had been her strongest tie with the Clan, and now she was gone. The memory of her desperate, pain-filled eyes, her hand stretched out to Azhure for help, would be with her for always. Azhure sat beneath the singing Earth Tree and stared at her hands, trying to clean the dried blood out from underneath her fingernails, thinking about her future.

"StarDrifter. Can you talk?" RavenCrest squatted down beside his brother.

StarDrifter held out his hand and his brother helped him sit up. Although Barsarbe had neatly stitched his wounds, his torso still looked appalling, and Azhure winced in sympathy as a moan escaped his lips. His face was drawn tight with suffering, his injuries now felt worse than when they had gaped open. Barsarbe had been forced to pull great handfuls of feathers from his wings in order to stitch the lacerations there, and StarDrifter's Icarii vanity hurt almost as much as his wounds.

"Yes," he said, hoping that his voice did not croak too much. "We need to talk, RavenCrest."

RavenCrest was silent for a moment, looking thoughtfully at the ground, then he raised his proud head and stared StarDrifter in the eye. "How much damage did the Skraelings do, Enchanter?"

StarDrifter knew he was not asking about the physical damage. He took a deep breath, then flinched as his wounds screamed in agony at their misuse. "The damage was bad, yet it might have been worse, RavenCrest. We did not finish the Yuletide rites, but the SkraeBolds did not launch the attack until after the circle of fire was lit. The sun will be reborn, and has," he said, his eyes briefly checking the sky. "But it will be weak as it grows toward the spring thaw. Perhaps too weak. The earth will have to struggle hard if it is to break through the covering of snow and ice. Brother, it could have been worse. If the circle of fire had not been lit we could be facing perpetual winter."

RavenCrest nodded. "Gorgrael has gained ground."

"But not as much as he had hoped for," his son FreeFall said, standing behind his father. The young Icarii prince was starting to grow into his birthright, and over the past few years was admitted to all of his father's councils and allowed to take on some of the daily tasks of the position he would one day inherit. FreeFall was considered by many to have the makings of a great Talon in him; unlike his father, he did not sometimes let his innate arrogance get in the way of making the right decision.

StarDrifter nodded at his brother and nephew. "You are both right. Gorgrael had surely hoped for far more than what his SkraeBolds achieved. If they had done what he ordered then even now winter would be freezing over the Avarinheim, and I would be in the Destroyer's clutches."

GoldFeather, who had remained silent through this exchange, looked horrified. "What do you mean, 'in the Destroyer's clutches'?"

"I provoked the SkraeBold into attacking. I think that Gorgrael wanted me alive and brought to him," StarDrifter replied.

"Why?" RavenCrest glanced briefly at FarSight CutSpur who had just wandered up to the group. "Why would Gorgrael want you alive?"

GoldFeather felt a shudder pass through StarDrifter as she supported his shoulders. "Because all Enchanters need their parent to teach them," he said, his voice tight, "and Gorgrael, like it or not, is as much an Icarii Enchanter as is the StarMan."

"I don't understand," said FreeFall. "If Gorgrael needs you to teach him, then how has he achieved so much power already?"

"As Barsarbe stitched my wounds I thought about that, long and hard." StarDrifter grimaced. "It was one way to keep my mind from the pain. FreeFall, all Enchanters derive their power from the music of the Star Dance, the music that the Stars make as they dance through the heavens." RavenCrest and FreeFall nodded. "But I think Gorgrael, to this point, has derived his power from somewhere else," StarDrifter continued, turning to look slowly about the rest of the group. His eyes lingered momentarily on Azhure, sitting to one side, looking wan and dispirited. "I think that Gorgrael derives his power from the discord that also floats about between the stars. The disharmonies that are made when the Stars miss their step, when they crash one into the other, when they forget the Dance to the extent that they swell into great red giants and explode. There are two types of music among the Stars, my friends. The Star Dance is the loudest and it is the one that all Enchanters are taught to listen to and to derive their power from. But underlying the Star Dance is a subtle thread of discord, of disharmony, the dance that leads Stars to their death—a Dance of Death. Many Enchanters have feared that one day an Enchanter would learn to use that music as well. I think that one now has."

"But who taught Gorgrael to use that . . ." FreeFall began again, his pale brow knitted in confusion.

StarDrifter cut FreeFall off before he had the chance to finish the question that he feared most of all. "Perhaps Gorgrael now wants me to teach him how to use the Star Dance—the Dance of Life and of Harmony. If Gorgrael can control *both* harmony and discord then nothing will stop him. Not even his brother. And once he has conquered this world then he could move out into the universe. The Destroyer would step through the Star Gate."

StarDrifter's words were so shocking, so appalling, that

all were silent. StarDrifter watched the reactions about him—the worst he had not voiced. Gorgrael could not have simply learned to use the music of discord by himself. Someone had taught him. But who? *Who*? StarDrifter wanted to think about that longer and more deeply. And he also wanted to examine his other son, Axis. What talents did *he* display?

RavenCrest stirred and glanced at FarSight before looking back at StarDrifter. "Brother, you are about to receive a Strike Force guard strong as my own or that of FreeFall's. Your safety is now even more paramount than that of your son's."

"And what of Axis?" FreeFall asked. EvenSong sat forward a little.

"We must help him," StarDrifter said quietly. "The route south through the Avarinheim is denied Gorgrael for as long as the Earth Tree sings. She has laid such a powerful ward over the entire northern Avarinheim that even Gorgrael cannot break through. If he wants to push south then he will have to do so through Gorken Pass. And to do that he will have to destroy Gorkenfort."

"How can you suggest that we help the Groundwalkers?" FarSight was aghast. It was the Acharites, under the leadership of the Seneschal, who had pushed both the Icarii and the Avar behind the Fortress Ranges.

"We have no choice, FarSight," StarDrifter said quietly. "Remember the Prophecy. We must all reunite to defeat Gorgrael. And must I point out that Axis is also one of your Groundwalkers?"

"At least he has enough Icarii blood to sing as an Icarii Enchanter," FarSight retorted, not appeased by StarDrifter's arguments.

RavenCrest watched the exchange. He had his own reservations about helping the Acharites at Gorkenfort.

"StarDrifter," he said gently. "I know you want us to go to the aid of your son. But aiding the Acharites is not a decision to be taken lightly. It is not a decision to be taken in haste." He looked around the group, but particularly to FreeFall and FarSight. "We must convene an Assembly in the central chamber of Talon Spike to discuss this matter."

Although in most daily business the Talon's word was law, major decisions needed the approval of the Assembly of the Icarii, a body composed of all Icarii over the age of twenty-five. It was an unwieldy and raucous body, but RavenCrest was justifiably concerned that if he ordered the Strike Force to assist Gorkenfort without consulting the Assembly then the Icarii would rebel.

"By the Stars, RavenCrest! If the Skraelings have attacked Gorkenfort as they did here, then how can they hold them? The Earth Tree does not sing for them!" StarDrifter cried, grabbing his brother's arm. "Why can't the Strike Force fly to their aid *now*?"

"It is *not* a decision to take lightly!" RavenCrest hissed again at his brother.

"Then let us simply rescue my son! RavenCrest, listen to me!"

"Father, perhaps StarDrifter speaks some sense," FreeFall began. If Axis was the one to face the Destroyer than he would be in desperate need of StarDrifter's training, natural talent or not.

RavenCrest whipped around to his son, his violet eyes blazing. "I am not going to make a decision that overlooks a thousand years of hatred between our races, FreeFall! Axis or not, I am loath to go to the aid of those who would as willingly murder us as listen to us!"

FreeFall stood up and stepped back, glancing at Even-Song. "As you wish, father. As you wish." He strode away into the clearing, EvenSong hastening after him.

As the group broke up, Barsarbe approached Azhure. "I have not yet thanked you personally, Azhure," she said, her face expressionless, "for your actions last night."

Azhure stood up, straightening her tunic. "I know you don't approve . . ." she began, but Barsarbe interrupted.

"We do not like violence, yet your actions saved us. Azhure, I cannot pre-empt a decision of the Meet, but I am sure that at Beltide the Clans will reconsider favorably your request to join us."

Staring at her, Azhure wondered if the Icarii had pressured Barsarbe into making this offer. Azhure swallowed. She did not know what to say.

"Azhure." StarDrifter's voice interrupted her thoughts. He was leaning on GoldFeather's arm, smiling warmly at her. "Azhure, come home with GoldFeather and myself. I owe you my life, but I make this offer out of friendship."

GoldFeather added her plea to her husband's. "Oh, Azhure, please! I would love you to come. Talon Spike is a wondrous place."

Azhure couldn't resist StarDrifter's smile or the genuineness of both his and GoldFeather's invitation.

"Thank you," she said. "I would like to see Talon Spike."

53

Departures

Less than forty-eight hours after the tragedy of Yuletide Eve the Icarii assembled for the long flight home. Debate between the Avar and Icarii had continued about what to do, but RavenCrest remained adamant that he wouldn't commit to aiding Gorkenfort until the full Assembly of the Icarii met to discuss it in the Chamber of Talon Spike. RavenCrest had no qualms about pulling the Icarii Strike Force out of the Avarinheim. Earth Tree still sang strong and true and her Song would continue to protect the Avarinheim from the incursions of Gorgrael. No SkraeBold or Skraeling could come within range of the Song and live.

The flight across the Icescarp Alps to Talon Spike would be arduous. The seething winds between the sharp peaks of the Alps created dangerous gusts and shears that could drag an unwary Icarii to their death on the black cliffs below. They would have to fly high and fast through the thin air of the upper atmosphere, and because of the lack of suitable landing places they would have to make the entire distance in one continuous flight lasting almost twenty-four hours. Two farflight scouts had already left to alert the Icarii in Talon Spike of the tragedy of Earth Tree Grove.

RavenCrest watched the Icarii mass, anxious to return home, but wondering whether they should perhaps have waited another day or two. He had tried to weigh the value of the flightworthy Icarii resting muscles already sore and strained against the advantage of the winds which currently favored them on the way home. No, he decided, it was best they leave now. With most of the Strike Force in the groves, Talon Spike itself was badly underprotected, and RavenCrest needed to be back in the Spike to hear the reports of the scouts over Gorken Pass. Besides, none wanted to linger amid the scent of death. The Icarii and the Avar had cremated their dead the previous evening. It was a dreadful ceremony, watching so many comrades, friends and family members given up to the flames. Now the pyres were mere gray stains of shifting ash.

About the Earth Tree Grove lay some eighteen Icarii, StarDrifter among them, too badly injured to make the long journey home through the air. None of them would be fit to fly for days, perhaps weeks, and RavenCrest had to talk to StarDrifter about how they would get home. He watched StarDrifter, leaning against one of the stone uprights of the sacred circle, GoldFeather by his side. StarDrifter had insisted on leading the funeral rites the previous day, yet even after a day's rest RavenCrest could see how much the effort had cost his brother. EvenSong was leaning forward to kiss her mother and father goodbye, FreeFall at her shoulder. The two had already said their farewells to RavenCrest. He watched them, considering. They had been close for many years now and RavenCrest wondered idly if they would formalize their union after both had served their time in the Strike Force. It was not unusual for Icarii cousins to marry, and it would be good for both of them. He stretched his wings slowly, as the two turned and lifted off, waving as they flew overhead. Yes, it would be a good marriage. Perhaps EvenSong might be able to control his son's sometimes good-hearted impetuousness.

He walked over to StarDrifter and gently touched his shoulder, trying to avoid his injured wings. "Brother, how long will it be before you can fly home?"

StarDrifter glanced at GoldFeather before replying. "Too long. Many will not be able to make the journey for weeks, but I am reluctant to stay that long. All of us will be needed back at Talon Spike and, as you know, I want the chance to address the Assembly."

RavenCrest frowned, wondering at the look that passed between StarDrifter and GoldFeather. He knew that when GoldFeather left Talon Spike to wander with the Avar she followed the pathways of the Nordra from its birth place at the foot of Talon Spike through the Alps into the Avarinheim. The steep icy paths were passable only if extreme care was taken, and would kill many of the Icarii lying wounded here, and StarDrifter was certainly in no condition to travel them. Besides, travel along those paths took many, many days, and it would simply be safer and more sensible to wait until they could fly.

But sometimes StarDrifter was not entirely sensible. One only had to look at GoldFeather to know that.

StarDrifter knew his brother very well, and knew exactly what he was thinking. "I am not thinking of walking the icy paths, RavenCrest. There is a far simpler, quicker and more amenable route home to Talon Spike."

RavenCrest's frown deepened.

"We will seek the assistance of the Charonites," StarDrifter said quietly, his eyes steady on those of his brother.

RavenCrest took a step back, speechless. No one had heard from the Charonites for many thousands of years. He only knew of them because both his mother and his brother were Enchanters and had spoken of them to him. Few, if any, other Icarii would have known of what StarDrifter spoke.

"It is time that they knew that the Prophecy has awakened, brother. They have their own interests in what happens. And they can aid us and transport us to Talon Spike."

"Are you sure they still exist, StarDrifter? Stars knows, we can ill afford to lose you wandering about some cavern in the Alps. And what if they refuse?"

StarDrifter was prepared for his brother's objections. He had already talked it through with Raum earlier in the day. "Leave us a Wing of your Strike Force, RavenCrest. If we should fail, then they can see us safely back to the groves and fly on to Talon Spike to let you know our revised plans. But I think, with Raum's help, I can find them."

Raum had stepped out from behind the stone support to lend his own weight to StarDrifter's arguments. "Among the Avar Banes there is a belief that the Charonites still come out to drift along the Nordra on hot summer nights, Talon. Occasionally, once every hundred years or so, we think that they come out to gaze at the reflections of the stars in the night water. Perhaps they have not completely lost their taste for the OverWorld. There *must* be an entrance close by."

RavenCrest did not think this a very powerful argument in favor of trekking off to look for these semimythical Charonites, but he could see that his brother was determined on his course of action. "You will go with StarDrifter?" he asked Raum. Raum nodded, and RavenCrest looked puzzled. "But you are needed here, Raum. With Mirbolt dead, you are now the senior Bane. Shouldn't you stay with your people?"

"My people will reform into their Clans and drift back into the Avarinheim. Barsarbe can fill my place while I am gone. Besides, I may need to speak to your Assembly. I am one of the few here who have met Axis and spoken with him. You may need my advice."

RavenCrest was clearly unhappy with the situation, but finally he nodded, reluctantly. "I will send a Wing of the Strike Force with you, brother. I *cannot* afford to lose you. There is not another Enchanter among us strong enough to take your place."

"You will not hold the Assembly until I arrive?" StarDrifter asked anxiously.

RavenCrest paused, his face grim. "I will wait a week. A week only. And if you are not there to address them, then I do not know how they will vote." He paused as FarSight strode across the clearing toward him. "I must go now. When will you leave?"

"Tomorrow morning." ▸

They assembled in the hour before dawn. StarDrifter and GoldFeather, Raum, the other wounded Icarii, supported by members of the Strike Force Wing assigned to them— and Azhure. Azhure had slept better last night than she had in months, and was now clearly excited at the prospect of traveling to Talon Spike. StarDrifter eyed her with some amusement, pleased he'd thought to ask her to accompany them home. Along with Raum and GoldFeather she was one of the few who had seen and spoken to Axis. She was a link to his son.

Barsarbe rose to farewell them, relieved to see Azhure leave despite her words of the previous day. She repressed a shudder. It wasn't only Azhure's ready use of violence that made Barsarbe dislike the woman. There was something else about her. Something that made Barsarbe vaguely jealous and resentful of her.

But for now it was simply enough that Azhure was leaving the Avar. The Avar did not need her, and who knows, thought Barsarbe, perhaps the Icarii could find a use for her. After Barsarbe said goodbye to the group she gave Azhure bags of herbs as well as instructions on how to use them for the Icarii wounds she would attend on their journey through the UnderWorld. Barsarbe prayed she would never have to see the human woman again.

StarDrifter gathered the group together, and set off. Though he'd spoken confidently to RavenCrest yesterday, he was still doubtful about the success of his plan. What if they *couldn't* find the entrance to the UnderWorld? And even if they did, what if the Charonites refused to help them? Even before they had lost complete contact with the

Charonites, relations between the two races had been cool. By the Stars, I hope I have not committed us to a foolish course of action, StarDrifter thought as he led the group slowly northwards along the Nordra.

All wore warm clothing, but only Raum and Azhure carried packs. The members of the Wing spaced themselves along the line, their bows at the ready, their eyes continually scanning the sky. As they moved onto the paths that ran directly by the water's edge Raum and StarDrifter exchanged worried glances. The Nordra was at its lowest point for many years. The previous spring thaw had been a weak affair in the northern lands, and little new ice water trickled into the Nordra from the Talon Spike glacier. Now that winter tightened about the snow fields north of the Avarinheim and throughout the Icescarp Alps, water froze into ice rather than flowing into the streams that fed the Nordra. The Avar depended on the Nordra for much of their food, and fish stocks would run low if the water level dropped any further.

StarDrifter's thoughts quickly slipped from the water level to his pain. He ached from a dozen of his wounds, the deeper ones sending spears of fire through his chest as he breathed in the colder air by the river. GoldFeather spent the greater part of her time walking by his side, lending him her support, wincing whenever he cried out when she tightened her grip about his waist to prevent him slipping over.

They hiked until midday, a sad, sorry line that had to make frequent stops so the injured could rest. Both Azhure and Raum spent much of their time wandering up and down the line, giving encouragement, occasionally helping support one of the wounded. When StarDrifter finally called a halt at midday Azhure breathed in relief. At least now they would have time to brew some analgesic tea for the injured.

After Azhure and Raum had passed about the tea, Azhure took a cup of herbed tea and sat down to one side of the group. SpikeFeather TrueSong, the WingLeader, came and sat next to her after checking both forest and sky for danger.

Azhure smiled shyly at him. He was a handsome bird-man, not as beautiful as some, but he had striking, brilliant dark-red plumage and kind, dark eyes.

"I saw what you did in the Grove," he remarked. "You harbor great courage and resourcefulness within you."

"I could have moved sooner."

"As could we all," SpikeFeather said dryly. "But you moved first. Azhure, have you ever had any military training?"

Her fingers tightened about her cup. "No."

"Then perhaps you would consider training with my Wing when we return to Talon Spike."

Azhure felt sick to her stomach. "Oh no, I couldn't possibly—"

"Azhure," SpikeFeather's eyes were grave. "I know the Avar regard you with some concern. They are sometimes a strange people. But you have my admiration and the admiration of many of the Icarii. Think about it. The Avar may dislike your talents, but the Icarii will value them." His eyes crinkled in amusement. "I have some skill with the bow, Azhure, and I would enjoy teaching you the proper use of an arrow."

As Azhure hesitated the birdman stood up. "Think about it," he repeated, then moved off.

As he walked off Azhure noticed GoldFeather, who winked, and Azhure colored and looked away, wondering about SpikeFeather's words.

For some time the group sat silently, listening to the birds and the sounds of the Nordra. StarDrifter finished his, checking the position of the sun. Not too much further ahead the paths became dangerous, and he did not want to risk the wounded anymore than he had to.

Handing his empty cup back to GoldFeather, StarDrifter summoned SpikeFeather to his side.

"Wing-Leader," StarDrifter said, shifting uncomfortably and hoping the tea would have some effect soon. "From this point the undergrowth begins to crowd the banks of the Nordra. If we continue to scout on foot we could easily miss the entrance to the UnderWorld. It would be best if you take some of your Wing scout ahead by air."

SpikeFeather nodded. "Enchanter, what is it we look for?"

StarDrifter grimaced as pain bit deeply into his chest and had to wait for a few heartbeats before he had the breath to answer. GoldFeather exchanged a worried glance with SpikeFeather.

"A feeder stream, Wing-Leader," StarDrifter finally replied. "One that enters the Nordra from a cavern, most like. The entrance to the UnderWorld should not be too far away. A league from here the Nordra is hemmed in by the steep cliff faces of the Alps. GoldFeather, you have not seen anything like a stream issuing forth from the path by the Nordra as it flows through the Alps, have you?"

GoldFeather shook her head. "No. There is nothing like that in the Alps themselves. This section of the river I do not know well, I usually strike off to the east as soon as I get out of the Alps."

"Then fly, Wing-Leader. The entrance cannot be too far. Fly."

As the Icarii lifted off StarDrifter leaned back against GoldFeather and closed his eyes, relishing the chance to rest.

He did not get to rest long. SpikeFeather dropped down beside them not ten minutes after he had left.

"We've found a narrow channel of still water that runs between the river and a wide cavern mouth, fortunately on this side of the riverbank. You were right, Enchanter. None of us would have spotted it from the ground. There is a heavy growth of oldenberry bushes that lies across the channel's path as it curves into the Nordra. The cavern entrance is hidden by the undergrowth."

"Will it take us long to walk there, SpikeFeather?"

The Wing-leader shook his head. "Not more than half an hour, StarDrifter."

"Good," StarDrifter grunted as GoldFeather helped him to his feet.

Exactly half an hour later they stood in the cavern by the still water that led to the Nordra. Although the cavern was relatively close, the Icarii warriors had been forced to cut a path for the others through the dense growth of oldenberry bushes that hid the cavern mouth from the river bank. SpikeFeather had been right, no one wandering along the banks of the Nordra could possibly guess that this cavern existed.

The channel of water leading to the Nordra was no ordinary stream. Its regular banks were carefully lined with stone, and it was a uniform five paces wide its entire length. Once in the cavern the channel widened into a large rectangular pool, lined with massive slabs of gray stone that seemed to have been quarried from the nearby cliff face. The cavern, its entrance only some fifteen paces across, widened and deepened into a spacious chamber, its arching roof at least twenty paces high, and stretching back until the rear of the cavern was lost in darkness.

"Yes," StarDrifter said as he looked about him. "Yes. I think this is one of the entrances to the UnderWorld. Look!" he suddenly said, excited. Two small flat-bottomed boats were drawn up on a low shelf to one side of the cavern.

GoldFeather walked back a little further into the cavern, then turned to StarDrifter, her handsome face puzzled. "StarDrifter? The pool ends here. The water does not continue any further. How can this be the entrance to the UnderWorld?"

StarDrifter smiled and hobbled over to her as gracefully as his injuries would allow. "My love. The UnderWorld exists far below us. Not even the Charonites, magical sprites that they are, can make water flow upwards. They build stairs to the OverWorld which they climb whenever they feel the urge to feel once more the night air on their faces. Let us look."

SpikeFeather found several brands on the low shelf that held the boats. He lit them from his tinderbox and handed them to his command as they walked into the darkness of the cavern. The even stone floor continued smooth and surprisingly dustless for some fifty paces, then ended abruptly in a flat stone wall. Azhure, walking with Raum, turned and looked at him anxiously, but he only smiled and took her arm. "It is not for nothing that StarDrifter is accounted one of the strongest Enchanters the Icarii have bred for generations. Watch."

StarDrifter motioned the group to stay well behind him and then moved stiffly over to the stone wall, holding a flaming brand in one hand for light. For some time he moved slowly down its length, running his hand over the wall, his face frowning in concentration; he even extended the wing closest to the wall, running the tips of its feathers gently over the surface of the rock, the sound almost like the rustle of a silken gown.

Slightly to one side of the center of the wall he stopped, tapped the wall gently with his fingers, then turned his head to smile at the group watching him. In the leaping shadows thrown by the brand his face had a slightly rakish look about it, almost mischievous, like a small boy about to play a particularly satisfying prank.

"Here, I think. The Charonites hide their handiwork well, but not so well as to fool this Icarii Enchanter."

He turned back to the wall, humming softly, his fingers tapping in time against the stone. "Yes, yes, yes," he whispered suddenly, excitedly, "that's it, that's it!" StarDrifter's voice became louder, stronger, and now he added the occasional word into the music he was humming. It was a strange tune, compelling, the tune whirling around and around the cavern.

Abruptly StarDrifter stopped singing, closed his fist and struck the stone wall as hard as he could.

"Ecrez dontai Charon!" he cried, and the entire wall shattered beneath his fist. He leapt out of the way, his wings fluttering uselessly, but he was caught in a shower of stone fragments.

GoldFeather and SpikeFeather rushed to his aid. He was covered from head to toe in fine gray dust, the only color the pale but intense blue of his eyes and the small trails of blood that seeped from his wounds where he had torn them in the fall to the floor. But StarDrifter shook himself free from GoldFeather and SpikeFeather's hands, still grinning as excitedly as a small boy. "Look!" he cried, turning back to what the crumbling wall revealed.

Instead of a bare gray stone wall there now stood a screen carved out of translucent white marble into a delicate tracery of lace. It looked as thin as a child's finger, and was supported by delicate pillars rising to the roof. The incredibly fine and detailed carving of the tracery revealed a pattern of women and children dancing in long transparent robes. Such craftsmanship had gone into the carving of the screen that Azhure could almost see the marble figures move. In the center of the delicate wall was a wide pointed arch of golden marble about a closed bronze door.

StarDrifter shook his wings free of as much dust as he could and brushed the rest from his body. He seemed almost revitalized instead of tired by his exertions. He took GoldFeather's hand and smiled at her. "I remember that once I promised to show you wonders, my love. Take my hand and become the first of your race to walk through the door to the UnderWorld. Come."

StarDrifter turned to the bronze door and gently pushed with his hand. It yielded instantly, and he and GoldFeather walked through. SpikeFeather hurried his warriors after them while Azhure and Raum turned to help the other wounded Icarii into the entrance to the UnderWorld.

54

The Charonites

Beyond the bronze doorway the group found themselves in a massive circular well with a beautiful patterned translucent pink marble staircase winding around the wall of the well to depths unseen; a waist-high railing guarded against any unwary step. Azhure paused to gaze about her as StarDrifter led GoldFeather down the first of the steps—the craftsmanship of the well was extraordinary. StarDrifter saw her staring at the wall carvings. "Come Azhure. We have a long way to go."

Slowly they descended, the members of the Wing assisting Azhure and Raum with the injured. But the stairs were wide, the gradient gentle and the footing firm so that even the more severely injured among the Icarii could negotiate the steps relatively easily. After an hour or so StarDrifter started to talk softly, his words carrying easily to those who brought up the rear, sharing what he had been told of the Charonites.

"The Charonites and the Icarii are a related people, both born of the Enchantress."

"The Enchantress?" Azhure asked.

"The original Enchanter, Azhure, who discovered the power of the Star Dance," said StarDrifter. "Charonites and Icarii revere her as the founder of their races. As others should."

What did that cryptic remark mean? Azhure thought, but she bit down her question. She would ask GoldFeather later.

"The Charonites were always a reclusive people," StarDrifter continued, "inward rather than outward looking. Preferring the depths rather than the heights. Casting their eyes downward rather than upward. They claimed they gave up their wings because they no longer craved the feel of the thermals beneath them." StarDrifter paused, unable to believe that any would want to give up the thrill of the soar. "I know that some say the Icarii are too mystical, and a little arrogant." He looked quickly at GoldFeather, and although she kept her face impassive her eyes twinkled, "but we are nothing compared to the Charonites. Well over thirteen thousand years ago they descended to the depths, saying they preferred to explore the inner space rather than the outer, and over the millennia they explored and settled the waterways of the UnderWorld. It is said that the waterways not only stretch beneath all of what Tencendor used to cover but under the oceans as well." He shrugged. "Perhaps the waterways touch other worlds as well."

For some time there was silence as everyone pondered the Charonites and their waterways, wondering about the secrets the Charonites must know.

"Few know of the existence of these people," StarDrifter continued eventually. "Gorgrael himself may not know of them." He paused again, thinking deeply. "Legend tells us that in the center of this UnderWorld is a cavern with a crystal roof over a mirrored lake, the source for the magical lakes of Tencendor. From this lake radiate the waterways of the UnderWorld upon which the Charonites ply their ferries, seeking the answers to mysteries. I am hoping that there will be a waterway that stretches from here to the roots of Talon Spike, and I am hoping that the Charonites will agree to ferry us there, although what price they might ask in payment I don't know."

"Price?" PreenDeep, one of the injured Icarii, asked.

"It is said that the Charonites always demand payment, but that could simply be because Icarii speak of them with no small disdain for choosing the UnderWorld rather than the limitless freedoms of the skies."

For a long time after that there was no sound but for the soft shuffle of boots down the pink stairs. Eventually StarDrifter, glancing behind him, called a quick rest. As they settled down, SpikeFeather leaned forward. This talk of their lost cousins fascinated him.

"Why have the races lost contact, StarDrifter? I would have thought that each had many things they could teach the other. And besides, as you said, we are related."

"There was some coolness," said StarDrifter reluctantly.

"Coolness?"

StarDrifter wished SpikeFeather had never asked this question, but now all the Icarii looked at him curiously, and if he refused to answer then the question would simply fester in their minds.

"The Charonites claimed that one of our Enchanter-Talons treated them cruelly."

"Which one?" SpikeFeather asked innocently, and Star-Drifter mentally cursed him.

"The ninth," he said shortly and stared at SpikeFeather with cold eyes.

Azhure, who had been rebandaging one of the Icarii warriors' wounds, looked up at the sudden silence. Every one of the Icarii sat stiffly, their faces frozen. What had happened? Even GoldFeather's eyes were cast down.

"Oh," SpikeFeather said, then stood up. "Have we rested enough?"

They climbed down in silence now, StarDrifter refusing to say anymore about the Charonites. As they trod lower and lower a soft wind blew in their faces, and Azhure paused to lean over the balustrade to peer into the depths of the well. Warm wind rushed upwards, tugging at the pins holding her hair in place.

"StarDrifter!" she cried in amazement, delighting in the feel of the warm air upon her face. "What is that?"

"That is the breath of the world, Azhure. Every second day the world inhales, every other day it exhales. Today, apparently, it exhales." A pity he thought, a tail wind would have been nice. "All of these wells—there are many of them about the land that was Tencendor—are breathing vents for the world. I do not know if the Charonites built them, or merely built these staircases into fissures that already existed."

Soon everyone could feel the warm wind. It had a wonderful fragrance, like warm spices freshly picked and left to dry in the sun, and it grew stronger as they neared the foot of the stairs.

"How far have we come?" GoldFeather asked as they finally stepped out onto a flat gray stone floor.

"Who knows? But we have reached one of the outer waterways."

Azhure looked about her. They were in a wide cavern, walled and domed in smooth stone as gray as the floor. She heard the gurgle of water and walked some few paces toward the center of the cavern. "Ah!" she breathed in wonder. A river flowed gently through a wide channel, entering the cavern through an arch on one side, and exiting through another arch on the far side. It was perhaps ten paces wide, and the edges were marked with translucent white stone so that visitors should not step unwarily into the water.

The water glowed a deep emerald in color, and in its depths Azhure could see bright sparkles she was unable to define. She peered more closely, trying to work out what they were, before feeling a gentle hand on her shoulder. StarDrifter had stepped up to stand close to her, his eyes fixed on the water, his own expression one of awe. "The Charonites have not left the Stars behind them, after all," he said softly. "Look, they glow in the depths of the water."

StarDrifter was right. Stars glowed deep within the emerald water and impulsively she reached down to the water.

"No!" StarDrifter caught her hand in his own. "Do not touch the water. I do not know what it will do to you."

"And now?" SpikeFeather asked quietly as he joined them. "Now what?"

"Why, we summon the Ferryman, SpikeFeather!" StarDrifter pointed to one side. A large golden bell hung at shoulder height from a golden tripod. StarDrifter walked over, hesitated a moment, then struck it with his fingertips.

A clear chime rang out, once, twice and then a third time. Then the bell fell silent.

"And now we wait for the Ferryman to arrive," StarDrifter said to the others.

As they waited, most succumbed to weariness and sat on the floor, some of the injured stretched out asleep. Azhure and Raum did what they could for them, then Raum forced a nervously excited StarDrifter to sit down while he and Azhure tended his wounds. Raum and Azhure carefully cleaned his lacerations with some water they had carried down with them, wiped the clean wounds with an astringent lotion that even made StarDrifter forget who he was and what he waited for, restitched two of the wounds that needed it, making the Enchanter curse, and finally dusted all of StarDrifter's injuries with the herbs and healing powders Barsarbe had given Azhure.

"There," Azhure smiled at StarDrifter's wan face. "Presentable."

"Thank you very much," StarDrifter managed to say, the sting of the restitching and the astringent fading.

"StarDrifter!" SpikeFeather's tense voice called. "Something comes!"

Raum helped StarDrifter to his feet and they moved to the water's edge. Deep inside one of the tunnels carrying the waterway into the cavern they could see a light bobbing.

"The Ferryman," StarDrifter whispered. "Finally, after thousands of years, we are to meet our lost brethren again."

Azhure felt a little apprehensive, and as she gazed at StarDrifter's exhilarated face she hoped the Charonites would feel as excited about the reunion as the Icarii Enchanter obviously did. She looked back to the tunnel entrance.

A large flat-bottomed boat slowly emerged into the cavern, approaching the huddled group without any obvious means of propulsion, a deeply hooded figure seated at the stern with his hands folded in his lap. As the boat reached them it stopped.

"Who summons the Ferryman?" a gruff voice asked from beneath the hood of the ruby-red cloak. "Who rings the bell?"

StarDrifter stepped forward and bowed to the figure, trying unsuccessfully to see beneath the hood as he did so. "I, StarDrifter SunSoar, Icarii Enchanter, summon you, Ferryman. May the Sentinels one day return safe to their home."

The figure sat totally unmoved by the Enchanter's words. StarDrifter grew uneasy as the Charonite remained silent. He fought to keep from fidgeting, and instead stood tall, his spread wings drooping to the floor behind him in the traditional Icarii gesture of goodwill. Perhaps the Charonites had forgotten such polite gestures, StarDrifter mused, wondering if he should say anything more.

Finally the Ferryman spoke. "The Sentinels have forsaken their home forever, Enchanter. Have you not understood the Prophecy?"

By the Stars! StarDrifter thought bleakly, I was simply trying to be polite! "The Sentinels walk abroad now that the Prophecy has awoken," he said, wondering if the Charonites yet knew that the Prophecy itself walked. "Who knows how the Prophecy will turn. Perhaps the Sentinels will return to their home, in one form or another."

"You have a smooth tongue, Enchanter. Perhaps too smooth if it got you Gorgrael."

StarDrifter's face hardened. The Charonites knew too much. "Then you also know what else it got me."

The Ferryman stood up, slowly unfolding what turned out to be an extremely tall frame, and bowed to Gold-Feather as she stood slightly behind StarDrifter. "Greetings, Rivkah. I hope the Enchanter's arrogance will have been tempered by your humanity in your son."

GoldFeather smiled and inclined her head. "Greetings, Ferryman. I am ashamed that until this day I did not know what mysteries lay beneath my feet. I will strive to learn more so that my ignorance may not embarrass me again."

The Ferryman was pleased by her smile and her gracefulness. The Charonites had always been niggled by Icarii arrogance. He lifted pale age-spotted hands and drew the material of the cloak back from his head and down over his shoulders. The Ferryman's bald skull and cadaverous face bespoke great age, yet the resemblance to the Icarii shone through in the tilt of the eyes, the high cheekbones and the narrow nose. His eyes, however, belied his otherwise ancient appearance. They shone as lustrous and bright as those of a child, innocuous pools of violet in his desiccated face.

"You speak well, Rivkah," the Ferryman said, "for a member of those people who have forgotten the joy of the mysteries." Then, surprising all who watched, he turned and bowed deeply to Azhure, his hands covering his heart. "You are welcomed, Sacred Daughter and Mother of Nations," he said in tones of deep reverence. "Find peace." For long moments he stayed bowed in obeisance to Azhure. StarDrifter turned and gazed at her in amazement.

Startled, Azhure stared at the Ferryman. She recovered quickly however, noting how the Ferryman had responded to GoldFeather's gracious words. "I stand with Rivkah in shame that I have not previously recognized your mysteries," she said with a dignity her companions had not seen in her before. "Find peace, Ferryman." Sacred Daughter? Mother of Nations? she thought. What did he mean?

I speak of a time both before and beyond the Prophecy, the Ferryman's voice whispered in her mind as he raised himself from his bow, and Azhure only just managed to stop herself from rocking on her feet with surprise.

The Ferryman turned to StarDrifter. "Because of these two women who accompany you," he said softly, "the Ferryman asks no price. Where do you wish to go?"

"Talon Spike," said StarDrifter and then couldn't resist asking, "what is your usual price?"

The Ferryman stood back and gestured for GoldFeather and Azhure to step into the boat first. His eyes flickered to StarDrifter. "The normal price is a life, Enchanter. The greatest mystery of all." He paused and a merciless smile lit his face. "Who would you have picked to pay it?"

StarDrifter's face paled. Who *would* he have picked?

They loaded quickly, the flat-bottomed boat easily holding them all in comfort. They sank down on thin cushions, the Ferryman seating GoldFeather and Azhure on either side of him in the stern of the boat. Neither woman could see any means of steering or propulsion, but as the Ferryman folded his hands serenely in his lap, the hood remaining draped over his shoulders, the boat moved smoothly forward.

For a long time there was silence. The Ferryman's words regarding the price of passage had shocked them all, as did his obvious reverence for the two women, especially Azhure. Icarii pride was pricked. With them travelled one of their greatest Enchanters, someone toward whom the Ferryman should have been more respectful, and yet he seemed to prefer the two Groundwalker women. SpikeFeather's curiosity about Azhure increased.

They travelled through tunnels whose roofs only cleared the Ferryman's head by a handspan. Both walls and roofs were of the pale stone lining the walls of the wells, and light was given off by the emerald glow of the water. After a while Azhure shifted a little in her seat and said quietly, "May I speak with you, Ferryman?"

"Assuredly," he smiled, inclining his head a little. "But if you ask me questions do not take offense if I decline to answer some of them. There are some mysteries we will not speak of."

"I understand." She was silent for a few moments. "Will you speak to me of these waterways?"

The Ferryman considered, then nodded his head. "Of some aspects, yes. The waterways are corridors between real places, physical places, but they are also corridors linking the mysteries of time and lives past and future. Worlds that have gone and worlds that will be. Worlds that have never been and worlds that might only be. In themselves they are both a mystery and an answer. The waterways are always a means to an end."

Azhure frowned. At her feet, however, StarDrifter narrowed his eyes in thought.

"Are you the only ones who can travel them?" Azhure asked.

The Ferryman bit his lip. "No," he said flatly, refusing to say anymore on the matter.

"How does the boat move?"

"Of its own free will," the Ferryman answered promptly. "And because I have given it purpose."

"There seem to be stars in the water, Ferryman." She deliberately did not phrase it as a question.

"The waterways mirror the paths of the Stars, Lady, and the Stars are mirrored in the waterways."

StarDrifter smiled to himself. A mystery was beginning to clarify itself in his mind. He shifted in the boat, easing his aching wings. "And why the price of a life, Ferryman? Why such a high price to follow the path of the Stars?"

"You presume, Enchanter," the Ferryman said testily. "I shall not answer that." StarDrifter nodded, but he did not say anymore.

GoldFeather glanced at her husband, then also addressed the Ferryman. "You know much of the Prophecy, Ferryman, and of what has passed. Yet you live among these subterranean waterways. Your ability to know is astounding and again I am humbled. Will you tell us something of the Charonites and of the life you lead along the waterways?"

"We travel the waterways, Lady," he said briefly. "We seek to understand the Mysteries of the Universe."

StarDrifter nodded to himself. The Seven Great Mysteries.

The Ferryman's mouth twisted at the Enchanter's incomprehension. The Icarii always thought they knew everything and their Enchanters were the worst of all. "The Mysteries are neither great nor small, Enchanter, nor easily counted. They are myriad. Lady," he inclined his head slightly back toward GoldFeather, "I find it hard to talk to you of our lives, such as they are, along the waterways. Not because I do not wish to, but because I cannot find the words to explain to you. We are . . . different . . . to when we first began to explore the waterways so many millennia ago. Then we were close kin to the Icarii . . . now, I am not so sure. The waterways are strange, and they have led us places that we did not always want to go."

Raum, sitting halfway back in the boat, spoke. "Ferryman, may you find peace." The Ferryman bowed slightly at the Bane as Raum continued. "Have you mapped the waterways? Is there an easy way to find your way about them?"

The Ferryman considered. "Bane, you are welcome to my boat. It has been rare that we have one of your people visit. Map? Why do you ask? Is not the way of the waterways plain for all to see?" He sounded genuinely puzzled at Raum's question and again StarDrifter nodded slightly to himself, but wary now to keep his thoughts well-guarded.

Now the Ferryman spoke first. "You have seen the Sentinels, Bane?"

"Yes, two. Jack and Yr. At the Mother."

"Ah," the Ferryman's face broke into a wide smile. "Yr is my daughter. She was well?"

"Yes, Ferryman." Raum was genuinely astounded, as were most others who listened. "She looked well."

"Good." He paused, and an expression something like embarrassment crossed his face. "Lady," he addressed GoldFeather, "I have perhaps been remiss in not asking a price for the Ferryman." Her eyes widened, but the Ferryman continued. "Since it is now too late to negotiate a price, will you grant me a boon?"

GoldFeather's face remained wary. "What is it?"

"Lady, I would ask that you acknowledge your identity as Rivkah, not GoldFeather. Rivkah is needed to walk the land of Tencendor and to aid your son, GoldFeather is not. This is a heavy price I ask from you, but I fear it is a necessary one."

GoldFeather considered. When she had fled to the Icarii she had shed the name of Rivkah and adopted the name GoldFeather in an attempt to totally forget her former life and start anew with the Icarii. Rivkah? She had not thought of herself as Rivkah for thirty years. Rivkah was a young girl betrayed and murdered by the power games played in upper Acharite society. She looked at StarDrifter. He was considering her carefully, his face unreadable. She raised her eyebrows at him and he gave a slight shrug, as if to say it mattered not to him, it was her choice to name herself GoldFeather and it would be her choice to return to Rivkah. He had loved her as both.

Rivkah turned to the Ferryman. "I will grant you what you ask." But Rivkah had not lived almost forty-eight years amid the intrigues of both upper-level Acharite and Icarii societies without learning to exact blood for blood. If the Ferryman believed this would cost Rivkah a high price then Rivkah also determined to exact a price from the Ferryman. "As I have freely given you this boon I ask one of you. Grant that if my son Axis should need your assistance, in whatever manner, you will help him. Do this for Rivkah."

The Ferryman's nostrils flared and he barked sharply in harsh laughter. "You have learned well, Rivkah. Blood for blood. And for blood, your boon is granted. Now, I will not talk anymore. There is much to contemplate before we arrive at Talon Spike."

The Ferryman fell silent and refused to answer another question.

55

The Assembly of the Icarii

StarDrifter eased his aching muscles into the steaming water, holding his breath until his body had adjusted to the temperature, then relaxed and let himself float away from the side of the pool, his wings stretching down deep into the water and flexing slowly to keep him comfortably afloat. Over the past week most of his wounds had closed over, healing well, and only the deepest of the tears in his chest still kept him awake at night. Until this point in his life StarDrifter had always revelled in his youth and vibrant health, but the SkraeBold attack had brought him uncomfortably close to the death he had previously felt was so far away.

Death rarely entered the Icarii mind. They lived so long, and generally retained their health and mobility until the very end. Then, over a period of only a few weeks, they simply faded, as if some bright sun inside them had finally run out of combustible fuel. The dead were mourned briefly, intensely, and then the Icarii got back to living life to the fullest. Until the attack on Earth Tree Grove few

Icarii had met violent deaths over the past thousand years, and none were left alive from the Wars of the Axes to remind the younger generations what it felt like to watch friends and family struck down in the prime of their life by cold steel.

But since the return to Talon Spike all Icarii had done a lot of soul searching. There had been many dead to mourn. Children, roostmates, and parents had died. Others had been terribly injured and would carry scars for the rest of their lives. They had watched each other being torn to pieces. And what had they done about it? Virtually nothing but give in to blind panic. The vaunted Icarii Strike Force had been made to look incompetent. The Icarii searched for explanations. Crest-Leaders shouted at Wing-Leaders, Wing-Leaders shouted at individuals within their Wing and Talon RavenCrest shouted at everybody. Councils were convened to discuss what could be done, argued futilely for hours, and were then disbanded with nothing decided. The Enchanters, StarDrifter among them, met, wept over the dead farewelled in the groves of the Avarinheim, and wondered what they could have done differently. StarDrifter, in an agony of guilt, had all but abased himself before his fellow Enchanters for not realizing sooner that Earth Tree, if awoken, could help them. The other Enchanters had refused to let StarDrifter assume all the blame; in the end it had been his action, even when so terribly injured, that had helped save them. His and Azhure's.

StarDrifter, now completely relaxed, opened his eyes and looked about the Chamber of Steaming Water. Great hot mineralized waters bubbled up through the deep fissures of Talon Spike and fed this pool in its huge Chamber in the depths of the mountain. The Icarii loved the waters, and usually came here several times a week to soak their cares, such as they were, away. StarDrifter looked for Azhure and EvenSong. They had come down to the Chamber with him—Azhure had first seen the hot water the day that they had arrived in Talon Spike and had come back every day since.

The Ferryman had not talked again after GoldFeather—
Rivkah—had won his promise to assist Axis. StarDrifter
smiled as his eyes searched for his daughter and Azhure
among the Icarii disrobing at the steps leading down into
the water. Rivkah had thought quickly, and StarDrifter
doubted if any had won such a major concession from the
Charonites for a thousand years. Eventually the silent Ferryman deposited them in a Chamber seemingly identical to
the one that they had summoned him from, pointed to an
identical stairwell leading upwards, and floated off again.

A spasm of remembered pain crossed StarDrifter's face
as he recalled the climb up those Star-damned stairs to the
top. It had taken them almost half a day and by the end
their legs felt as though they would fall off. The stairwell
had opened out into a long disused tunnel that had, after
further long hours of walking, led into one of the storage
Chambers in the very deepest part of the Talon Spike complex. It had been another climb of several hours before they
had met anyone to alert them to their presence. They'd arrived in Talon Spike only hours after the last waves of
Icarii from Earth Tree Grove landed, and RavenCrest had
been astounded by the rapidity of his brother's journey and
impatient to hear an explanation. But StarDrifter did not
have to feign bone-deep weariness to wave him off and
promise to discuss it another day. If he did. StarDrifter felt
that it might be better to keep the details of the Under-
World secret a little longer. Perhaps he might discuss them
with FreeFall. The boy had a sharp mind and might see a
shadow and a movement where for StarDrifter there was
only brightness.

StarDrifter finally caught sight of EvenSong and Azhure
as they left their robes and towels on a granite bench and
stepped into the water. The two women, close in age, had
become friends since their arrival in Talon Spike and,
along with Raum, Azhure had moved into the apartments
shared by Rivkah, StarDrifter and EvenSong. StarDrifter's
mouth curved appreciatively as Azhure lifted her arms to
pin her hair on the crown of her head. She was a particu-

larly striking woman, even more so than Rivkah at her age, and StarDrifter had always had an eye for beautiful and sensual women—and he had been even more interested in Azhure since the Ferryman's deep show of respect for her. It was a pity about the ridged scars down her back. Perhaps the Healers among the Enchanters could do something for her. Azhure sank down as quickly as she could into the hot water and StarDrifter's smile widened a little. She had not yet become used to the Icarii habit of shared bathing of males and females and was more comfortable fully submerged than exposed to watching eyes. He found the Acharite modesty appealing—and more than a little challenging. Why had the Ferryman been so reverential of Azhure? Was it simply her beauty? No, not that. The Ferryman did not look as though he was capable of bedding a limp sack of grain, let alone Azhure.

StarDrifter turned his head away and closed his eyes again. How could he think of love when it hurt simply to stretch his wings? As he succumbed to the relaxing waters his mind turned to Rivkah. He had wanted her the moment he saw her. He had been very young then, only a few years out of his service in the Strike Force and in the midst of the hectic advanced stages of his training as an Enchanter under the tutelage of his mother, MorningStar. He had learned so quickly and shown so much early ability that he had been chosen to lead the Beltide rites for the previous two or three years. StarDrifter remembered the Beltide he had coupled with the Avar woman, Ameld, and shifted a little uncomfortably in the water. After Beltide he had flown south rather than north, saying he wanted some time to himself. And then, one bright morning, riding a low air thermal over Sigholt, he had seen the young woman feeding her baby on the roof of the Keep.

StarDrifter smiled, remembering. He had always been impetuous and, not thinking of the danger, he had spiraled straight down to the roof of the Keep and seduced the woman within fifteen minutes, her abandoned baby squalling angrily to the sounds of their lovemaking. Day after day he had gone back, careless of the danger, so fascinated with the woman that he could not return to Talon Spike. He still remembered the day she had smiled and told him she was pregnant. Even then, as such a young Enchanter, StarDrifter had known that the son Rivkah carried was extraordinary. When she had finally escaped her husband and told him that his son was dead StarDrifter had been stricken with grief.

StarDrifter had lavished love and attention on Rivkah, feeling deep guilt that she had suffered so much pain and loss while he had escaped Searlas' wrath. He had never regretted taking her for his wife, his roostmate, even though so many of his people strongly objected to the match.

He'd loved her, hadn't he? She was young and lovely and possessed a mind as lively and as inquisitive as his. But Rivkah had never settled well into Talon Spike. She tried, he tried, and the Icarii people as a whole generally tried, but it had been hard. After the birth of EvenSong when Rivkah had begun her habit of wandering for months at a time with the Avar, StarDrifter had been left to his own devices in Talon Spike with only his small daughter to remind him of his wife. For years he remained faithful to Rivkah, but over the past seven or eight years . . . well, ever a sensual creature, he had found some temptations too hard to deny himself, some seductions too hard to resist. Rivkah chose to leave him, did she not? And . . . StarDrifter twisted uncomfortably in the water as he confronted again the unpalatable truth that Rivkah was aging before his eyes. He was still a young man, he had a young man's desires, and while he still loved Rivkah, yes he did, and still found her desirable, certainly that, he sometimes caught himself looking at her and wondering what the future had in store for them. StarDrifter opened his eyes and drifted about the water, looking for Azhure again.

Like so many of the Icarii, he was a vain and selfish creature.

* * *

RavenCrest summoned the Assembly of the Icarii that afternoon and soon after the midday meal the Icarii filed into the central meeting Chamber of the Talon Spike complex. Talon Spike, the massive mountain that soared above all its brothers and sisters in the Icescarp Alps, had been the home of the Icarii people for the last thousand years, yet even before the Axe-Wielders had driven them out of the sunnier southern lands of Tencendor the Icarii had loved the place and had often summered there. Long dead volcanic activity had hollowed out winding and twisting mazes of passages and caverns in many of the mountains of the Alps, especially Talon Spike, and over the generations the Icarii had worked at these internal chambers to fashion out a home for themselves. Outside the air might be frigid, the climate inhospitable at best, but inside the great hot springs which fed the Chamber of Steaming Water kept the air that circulated within the mountain warm and comfortable. Perhaps the Icarii Enchanters were poor when it came to the art of war, but countless generations ago they had mastered the Songs needed to keep the interior of Talon Spike lit and the people fed and clothed. The Icarii, banned from their traditional homes further south, indulged their love of mysticism and magic, their love of the seduction, and their undoubted talent for interior decorating.

The huge Assembly Chamber of Talon Spike was one of the best examples of Icarii building and decoration. It was circular and tiered with scores of rows of benches on which the adult Icarii sat and fluttered and generally made raucous noise whenever they met in general Assembly. The Chamber, most of the elder Icarii agreed, was at its best both aesthetically and politically when it was completely empty. The walls and benches were faced with golden-veined white marble, the circular floor in the center of the Chamber of a peculiarly translucent and very beautiful golden marble veined with violet. Pale gold and blue cushions were scattered about the benches; never quite enough for the number of Icarii that squeezed into the Chamber, feathers often flying as they fought over the cushions. The lower three circles of benches were reserved for the Elders, the Enchanters and the family of the Talon. These benches were completely lined with crimson cushions for the Elders, turquoise cushions for the Enchanters, and the royal violet for those of the House of SunSoar. The very top six rows of benches were reserved for the Strike Force, and they were uncushioned as befitted the hard muscles of warriors.

The most spectacular part of the Assembly Chamber was not the rows of tiered marble benches rising three quarters of the way up the walls, but the circle of gigantic pillars soaring above the tiers which supported the domed roof of the Chamber. Their design was based on the shapes of the carved Icarii birdmen encircling the Star Gate, except these in the Assembly Chamber were five times as tall, far more spectacularly constructed and consisted of alternating male and female figures. In the Chamber of the Star Gate most of the birdmen statues had their arms folded and heads bowed, eyes closed. Here all the statues had their arms and wings extended joyously, their eyes open in wonder and mouths open in silent song. They had been gilded and enamelled in jewel-bright colors, real gems mined from the depths of Talon Spike in their eyes and in the golden torcs about their necks. Each individual hair on their heads and feather in their wings had been picked out in gold and silver and the muscles in their pale naked bodies were carefully defined in the ivory tones of pale flesh. They supported a domed roof completely plated in highly burnished bronze mirrors that, due to the enchantments bonded into their making, gave off a gentle golden light which illuminated the entire Chamber.

The Icarii entering the Chamber did so between the archways formed by the outspread wings and arms of the great pillars. According to inclination, they then either spiraled down gently though the air or walked down the tiers until they found the appropriate seat with, hopefully, a cushion still in place. On this afternoon in the first week of

Wolf-month, only a few days after the New Year, the Icarii took their seats within the Chamber with slightly less than their usual vocal enthusiasm. They knew they would have to make a decision involving war. That knowledge was emphasized by the entrance of the entire Strike Force, fully armed, all the Crest-Leaders and many of the Strike Force with both underwings and wingbacks dyed in the ebony of war.

Azhure watched silently from just underneath one of the arches of the encircling pillars at the very top of the Chamber. Raum stood beside her. Both were dressed in softly draped floor-length robes, soft gray for Azhure, dark green for Raum.

The Elders, Enchanters and members of the House of SunSoar entered last, filing silently into their seats from a small door secreted away in the bottom rows of tiers. RavenCrest and his son FreeFall were both draped in violet and ivory; RavenCrest had a jewelled torc about his neck like those worn by the lifeless statues. BrightFeather, RavenCrest's wife, followed dressed in a paler shade of violet. Close behind came MorningStar, RavenCrest and StarDrifter's Enchanter mother. Last of all came StarDrifter, draped in a crimson and gold toga embroidered across his chest with the motif of a blazing sun. All had bare feet.

It was a mark of his status as both a SunSoar and the most powerful Enchanter present that StarDrifter opened proceedings. The Assembly hushed as he halted in the center of the golden floor. StarDrifter circled the Chamber with his pale eyes, then he abruptly bowed to the assembled Icarii, his eyes downcast, both arms and wings swept low in a gesture both of respect and of abasement, swinging in a slow full circle so that all were included in his bow. The feathers of his almost healed wings swept the floor behind him and all could see the vivid scars among the feathers.

Azhure took a quick yet deep intake of breath; Star-

Drifter's salute to the Assembly was one of the most graceful and courtly gestures she had ever seen performed.

As he straightened out of his bow the Enchanter started to sing, very softly at first, although each word could be heard at the very topmost tier of seats, then gradually his voice strengthened and grew in passion until it soared to the very bronze mirrors of the domed roof.

Again StarDrifter sang in the alien ancient language. Again Azhure found she had no difficulty understanding his words—indeed the exotic intonation of the words and phrases made her blood sing.

He sang of the Icarii origins, of the time when the Icarii had finally learned the art of flight and of the day when they had first discovered the sun and the stars. He sang of their proud heritage, of their leadership of Tencendor, of the dances and the songs they had performed high in the summer sky above the magic lakes and forests of their homeland. He sang of a time when the Icarii could soar and drift the thermals from the Icescarp Alps to the Sea of Tyrre, a time when their children learning the Way of the Wing did not have to be guarded against deadly arrows loosed from below. He sang of their downfall, of their inability to realize that the Groundwalkers feared and resented their beautiful cousins, and of their inability to realize that this fear and resentment would eventually prove fertile ground for the whisperings of the Seneschal.

Tears rolled down many faces as the Icarii remembered what they had lost. Azhure found she wept with them.

StarDrifter sang of the Wars of the Axe, those dreadful decades when their ancestors had lost all they had gained, when the Groundwalkers had taken the axe to both feather and forest, when the Icarii had fled in the night with the Avar to huddle, senseless with grief, behind the Fortress Ranges. StarDrifter paid more attention to this part of the Song than he had the previous verses, describing in detail both what the Icarii had lost and how they had been unable to counter both the wicked lies of the Seneschal and the axes of the Groundwalkers who rallied to the Brotherhood. His voice was indescribably beautiful, yet so sad and haunting, so full of death and fear, that Azhure's tears turned from sadness and loss to shame and humiliation. *Her* people had driven these creatures of such incredible beauty and gifts from Tencendor?

StarDrifter sang of the new home the Icarii had built for themselves in the desolate yet welcome isolation of Talon Spike, of the ingenuity with which they had transformed their mountain home into both beauty and comfort. He sang of their years spent in peace here, of the mysteries they had unravelled, and the unparalleled vision of the Stars they had from the peak of Talon Spike. Then, lest the Icarii be lulled into thinking that they did not mind that they had lost so much of Tencendor, StarDrifter sang of the wonders and the sacred sites they had lost to the Groundwalkers—the larger part of the Avarinheim and the enchanted glades that it had contained, now ravaged under the deep bite of the Plough; the Sacred Lakes, dying through lack of love; the Enchanted Keeps, most of which had been destroyed or defiled with the touch of the Seneschal; the enigmatic Spiredore. The Island of Mist and Memory, where the Gods lay trapped by filthy and diseased pirates. The Nine High Priestesses of the Order of the Stars, doubtless raped and forced to bear the children of their captors. The Sepulchre of the Moon, bricked up and dark. The Ancient Barrows, now crumbling. Star Gate. Lost.

As one the Icarii moaned and wrung their hands, and Raum turned in surprise as a small moan escaped Azhure. Why did *she* weep? Had she understood StarDrifter? It had taken Raum many years of close study to be able to grasp the general meaning of the Icarii sacred tongue—yet here was Azhure weeping as if she had understood every nuance of StarDrifter's song. Puzzled, Raum turned back to watch StarDrifter.

"Now," StarDrifter whispered, abruptly switching to a

speaking voice. "There is a chance that you can regain all of this." He paused, closed his eyes, folded his hands upon his breast and began to sing again.

This time he sang the Prophecy of the Destroyer. The first two verses only, for all knew that the third verse was the province of the StarMan alone, but StarDrifter hummed that verse, his voice so rich and with so many complicated strands interwoven into the underlying music that it sounded as if a whole choir were singing a song whose words were only slightly out of focus. Raum grasped Azhure's hand, overcome by the splendour and power of StarDrifter's talent. Neither the Bane nor Azhure had ever come close to seeing the true extent of StarDrifter's gift, and even now they did not realize that they heard only a minute fraction of what he was capable.

After StarDrifter's voice had faded the Chamber remained totally silent for a full five minutes. StarDrifter had reminded them, more vividly than ever before, that they were a race who were mere shadows of their former selves. Talon Spike, no matter how beautiful and comfortable, could never replace what they had lost. StarDrifter had shown them how they could perhaps regain it. The Prophecy of the Destroyer was also, perhaps, a Prophecy of Hope.

StarDrifter stood with his head bowed, arms folded across his chest, listening to the silence. Rivkah stared at him with tears rolling down her cheeks. She had never loved him more than she did at this moment. Finally StarDrifter took a deep breath and raised his head. His movement broke the spell in the Assembly and a sound of whispering arose. StarDrifter let his hands fall from his breast and walked quietly over to the bench to sit between Rivkah and EvenSong, smiling at each of them. He folded his hands in his lap, although Rivkah desperately wanted him to reach out and hold her hand.

RavenCrest stood up and took the floor, the spare material of his toga draped over his left arm, his torc shining brilliantly in the light. "My fellow Icarii," he began, his voice clear and strong. "You all know of the events of the previous ten days, so I will not bore you with a repetition. You know that the Prophecy has awakened and walks the earth, so I will try your patience with repeating the details that have circulated among you for the past week. You know that Tree Friend walks and that Earth Tree Sings. You know that we face Gorgrael and that he is the son of StarDrifter SunSoar and the Avar woman Ameld of the FarWalk Clan." StarDrifter hung his head, but RavenCrest did not look at him. "You know also that the StarMan is the BattleAxe of the Seneschal, and that he is Axis, son of StarDrifter SunSoar and Rivkah, Princess of Achar. What we must decide today is whether we go to his aid in Gorkenfort and whether we can accept the BattleAxe of the Seneschal among us as the true StarMan."

A number of clear hisses drifted down from the Assembly. After StarDrifter had so clearly and wondrously reminded them exactly what they had lost to the cold steel of the axe, how could they accept the BattleAxe of the Axe-Wielders among them?

RavenCrest took no notice of the hisses. "But first we must hear the news of Gorkenfort. Crest-Leader FarSight CutSpur, your farflight scouts have now returned from reconnaissance around Gorkenfort. What news?"

FarSight stood up from his bench at the very top of the Chamber. He was a forbidding sight, his already swarthy appearance enhanced by his ebony-dyed wings.

"Talon, I bring grave news. Gorkenfort is under siege from an army of Skraelings twenty-fold larger than the force which struck us in Earth Tree Grove. The town is lost and a shambles, all the Groundwalkers who survive are in the fort." He paused. "The battle for the town must have been fierce and desperate. We lost many hundreds in the Earth Tree Grove, they lost many thousands. The dead are still piled high, the Skraelings so glutted they cannot feast anymore. Four SkraeBolds now lead the siege, tens of thousands of Skraelings mass in a gray mist about the town. Comrades, I am at a loss to describe the horror that must face those Groundwalkers whenever they peer over the battlements of their fort."

"Will it hold?" someone called from halfway up the tiers.

FarSight took a deep breath and considered. "No. I do not think so. In the end the cold and the lack of food—I suspect the fort is crowded with too many men—or perhaps simply the fear will mean the fort will fall. Gorgrael's army is too large. They cannot stop it from marching south. Gorgrael has the cream of Achar's army, or what is left of it, bottled up in Gorkenfort."

"And he has my son bottled up there, too," said StarDrifter quietly.

"Yes," FarSight said, "he has your son in there. The scouts have seen him, StarDrifter SunSoar. Walking the walls in the black of the BattleAxe. He has been injured in the fighting, StarDrifter, the farflight scouts say that even from the height they have been circling they can see that he has the ashen face of one who is only just managing to recover from massive blood loss."

StarDrifter moaned, and this time he did take Rivkah's hand; both looked stricken.

"The question," FreeFall strode into the circle of the floor to stand by his father, "is whether or not we go to Gorkenfort's aid. *I* say we *must*—can we let the StarMan, the one who can lead us to victory against Gorgrael, die on the walls of Gorkenfort for want of our help?"

"Peace," RavenCrest muttered, annoyed that his son should have entered the debate so precipitously. But FreeFall shook off his father's cautionary hand. He was hot for action, and his violet eyes flared at the Assembly, challenging them to disagree with him.

"I say we have *no* choice!"

His words sent the Assembly into an uproar. Relatively quiet until this point, now the Icarii turned to their neighbors beside, above and below them on the benches and argued back and forth. Feathers started to drift down along with the words and shouts.

"We *always* have a choice, that is what this Assembly is all about!"

"This is not a matter to be decided so lightly or quickly, we must think on this for days!"

"Would we do any good against the might of the Skraelings? Would we not be better simply to bolster the defenses of Talon Spike?"

"Perhaps all Gorgrael wants is Achar, perhaps we should let him have it."

"Help the Groundwalkers? You must be demented, boy! Where is the Icarii pride?"

"Burned with the bones and the flesh of our dead in Earth Tree Grove!" FreeFall screamed into the roar of voices, his hands clenched into fists at his sides, his wings raised behind him as if he would lift any moment.

RavenCrest grabbed FreeFall's arm with one hand and raised the other to silence the Assembly. It didn't work, the Icarii were in uproar. RavenCrest's lips twitched in anger a moment, then he screamed, "Silence!"

His voice penetrated to the very bronze mirrors, echoing back down through the Chamber. Everyone stopped talking at once.

"Do you think I come lightly before you to raise this issue?" he snarled. "Do you think that I have not twisted at night with the horrors that face us if we do not agree to help the Groundwalkers, and twisted with the horrors that we face if we do? Do you think that I have not considered the legacy of hatred that exists between the Groundwalkers and the Icarii? Well, think again. I want reasoned discussion on this issue, then I want a quick and painless decision. StarDrifter, you are more personally involved than any other Icarii present and you are far more knowledgeable. Speak to us."

RavenCrest stepped backwards, dragging FreeFall with him.

StarDrifter let Rivkah's hand go and stepped forward. "I speak both as a father and an Enchanter," he said, raising his face to the Assembly. "Gorgrael has moved, and so must we. Inaction will result in our ruin, and the ruin of all we hold dear. There is only one who can save us—Axis, BattleAxe of the Seneschal. The Prophecy speaks thus, and I know thus. He has grown to manhood without my support and has learned to view the world without my explanations." StarDrifter shrugged, a small smile twitching across his lips. "Perhaps that is as well. But I know my son from what I learned of him in the womb. Icarii fathers! You all sing to your children as they grow in the womb. But how many sing back?"

His last few words had stunned the Assembly, and StarDrifter waited for the whispers to die down. "My son sang his own Song of Creation. He created himself. Perhaps it was my seed that planted him, and perhaps it was Rivkah's womb that nurtured him, but my son took of us both what he wanted and made himself."

No one could speak for long minutes. This was unbelievable.

"Think on the power hidden in this man that waits for release," StarDrifter finally said. "I beg of you, do not let him die in Gorkenfort. He is all that can save us."

Murmurings arose from the Icarii—many were still not convinced. Perhaps he did have the makings of an Enchanter only dreamed about in legend. But could they trust this half-Icarii, half-Groundwalker? A *BattleAxe*?

Above them all, Raum stood forth, pulling Azhure with him. "Hear me!" he called and heads turned and craned to see who spoke.

"I have two things to say," Raum said, slightly unnerved by the many thousands of faces turned his way. "First, we should not forget that Gorkenfort contains others besides Axis BattleAxe. Within those walls also stand at least three of the Sentinels. I need not remind those familiar with the Prophecy that the loss of any one of those Sentinels, let alone three of them, would be disastrous itself. Also within those walls stands Tree Friend, Faraday, probably Duchess of Ichtar by now."

Far below Rivkah's hand crept to her throat. Again the faint memory of Raum turning to Axis outside the Avarinheim and calling something about Faraday back to her son niggled at her mind. What was it he had said?

"Can we afford to lose her as well? StarDrifter needed her to wake the Earth Tree, and without her the Avarinheim will never march forth to face Gorgrael. My friends, Gorkenfort virtually *is* the Prophecy at the moment with so many named by the Prophecy trapped within it. On these grounds alone you should assist Gorkenfort in whatever manner you are able. But there is another argument for aiding the Groundwalkers. My friends, please do not take what I am about to say amiss. I judge my own people as well as yours in this." Raum paused. "Both the Avar and the Icarii need a war leader. We need the StarMan to lead us against Gorgrael. I have seen Axis, albeit briefly. I have seen his command and the manner in which his men respond to him—he controls probably the best fighting force in Tencendor at this moment. I have seen his compassion—I am alive because of it. His name has become legendary within Achar in only the five years that he has led the Axe-Wielders. Azhure," he turned to the woman at his side. "Tell the Icarii what you know of Axis BattleAxe."

Azhure took a deep breath and looked down, her voice steady. "Our youths flock to the Axe-Wielders to train under his command. Toddlers seize twigs from firewood and wield them like swords, invoking Axis' name. Grown men speak his name both with approval and envy over their pots of ale. Women," she smiled slightly, "dream of spending the night in his arms." StarDrifter smiled also. His son had apparently inherited more than enchantments from him. Had this woman dreamed of Axis in this way? His smile faded and he frowned slightly.

"His is the name that Achar might well rally to," Azhure continued. "He has good men under his command, and I can think of no other war leader in Achar who could call on both the hearts and hands of so many of my countryfolk."

Raum spoke again before any of the Icarii could answer. "For all these reasons I add my supplication to StarDrifter's. Aid Gorkenfort and you will in the end aid yourselves. Let Gorgrael destroy all those within Gorkenfort and the Prophecy dies before us. Let Axis become our war leader. We have no other to lead us."

Almost before Raum had finished speaking the Strike Force, almost to a man and a woman, stood up and shouted objections. *They* would stand against Gorgrael! *Their* Crest-Leaders, FarSight CutSpur senior among them, would provide the leadership to win this holy battle. Talon RavenCrest would lead the combined might of the Icarii and the Avar to victory against the Skraelings!

Far below FreeFall stood forward again. "Yes, it will be a SunSoar who will lead us to victory!" he shouted. "But it will not be RavenCrest, nor StarDrifter, nor even myself! It *must* be Axis! Hold, my friends! Have you forgotten Earth Tree Grove so fast? Will you let Icarii pride drive us to our graves? *We need the battle experience and the leadership of Axis!*" He paused, his eyes burning bright. "And what better training could he have had than as BattleAxe?" he said softly into the silence. "Tell me, my people. What better training could the StarMan have had? Have not the BattleAxes kept us from Tencendor these long centuries?"

He paused once more, letting each and every word bite deep. "Then let a BattleAxe lead us back again."

FreeFall stepped back, drained, but his words had cut deep. StarDrifter nodded at him.

PerchSure HoldFast, one of the Elders, stepped forward. "But has not the BattleAxe lost the battle for Gorkenfort? If he has miscalculated this badly then how do we know he won't do it again?"

StarDrifter cut in quickly. "PerchSure, Axis would not yet know how to control his power or how to really use it until I show him. At the moment he is literally half a man, perhaps driven mad by the glimpses of power that he has."

"Your decision!" RavenCrest shouted, stepping back into the center of the golden circle. Most had forgotten he was there. "Do we aid Gorkenfort?"

"How?" a lone voice cried. "How do we aid Gorkenfort when we could not stop the slaughter in Earth Tree Grove?"

FreeFall stepped into the void. "We will send an envoy to Gorkenfort and initiate negotiations with the Ground-walkers . . . with Axis BattleAxe. Will we place ourselves under his leadership for the battles ahead?"

Again murmurings among the Strike Force began, but FarSight CutSpur raised his hand for silence among his command. "I have lain awake nights thinking on how badly we failed at Earth Tree Grove," he said quietly, the shame in his voice for all to hear. "It took a Groundwalker woman, Azhure, to show us how to use our weapons. Do I want to see the Strike Force led by a BattleAxe?" He laughed mirthlessly. "No. But we have no choice. If he is as good as some say he is . . . if . . . then I will stand aside for the man. But I want one of the Crest-Leaders to be among those who go forth to Gorkenfort."

"Do we agree to send a small number to meet with the Groundwalkers at Gorkenfort and to meet this Axis Bat-tleAxe? Do we agree to offer our aid?" RavenCrest threw open his arms to the Assembly, appealing for a quick decision.

One by one the Icarii stood, many still obviously unhappy with their lack of choice in the action ahead, others more sure that Axis could perhaps lead them out of the Prophecy of the Destroyer and back into Tencendor.

"Aye!" voices began to call singly, and then, as more and more joined in, "Aye!" thundered to the domed roof.

StarDrifter turned his head aside and wept, and FreeFall enveloped his uncle in an embrace.

56

Freefall SunSoar

Axis, Belial and Magariz stood in the cold dawn light on the roof of the Keep in Gorkenfort, wrapped in thick cloaks, gazing down at the Skraelings massing below them. It had been almost two weeks since the fall of Gorkentown and, for those inside the fort, the situation had steadily worsened. Axis shifted from foot to foot, still weak. But he was alive, and for that, according to Belial and sundry other witnesses, he had Faraday to thank. Under the cloak Axis' hands touched the side of his chest where the new scars still itched. No one could satisfactorily explain what Faraday had done, how she had healed him, and Axis had no chance to ask himself. For a week after the fall of Gorkentown she had been careful to avoid Borneheld's ire, staying within her room, whispering words of apology and endearment to her husband whenever he came to her. But Borneheld remained cold. She had disobeyed him in countermanding his orders, but Faraday knew that in Borneheld's eyes her worse crime was saving

Axis' life. She must not let Borneheld suspect her true feelings for Axis; he could still kill Axis in a fit of jealous rage.

As they stood there in the cold dawn, the northerly wind wrapping their cloaks even closer, Magariz felt that much of the coldness surrounding him emanated from Axis himself. Axis had been angrily incredulous that Magariz had allowed Faraday to accept the responsibility for the opening of the gates, and had hardly spoken to him this past week. Magariz could not blame him. He shifted his injured leg slightly and pulled his cloak a little closer, surreptitiously looking at Axis from the corner of his eye. Only a few weeks fighting alongside this man had twisted Magariz's loyalties out of shape. For years he had been Borneheld's right-hand man, his senior commander, trusted with Gorkenfort. But now Magariz, as others, wondered if Axis was not the better man to hold the supreme position of WarLord. He sighed.

Belial heard Magariz sigh and glanced at him. Artor! he thought silently, Axis and Faraday's pain touches and envelops us all. Was love worth this much pain? Would it not be better if Axis and Faraday simply forgot each other, turned their backs and accepted that their feet trod different paths? Let me never love a woman so desperately that I know only pain because of it, he prayed. Belial lived for his military calling and had never been tempted by the thought of marriage or children. Women passed in and out of his life like shadows, there for a night or a week, leaving no trace of themselves once they had left. Thinking about Axis and Faraday now made Belial sigh as well, wondering why some men let themselves love and suffer to this degree.

Axis heard both men sigh and turned away, irritated. Everyone was sunk in gloomy thoughts, sunk in contemplations of their own doom. Well, looking down on the Skraelings massed through what was left of Gorkentown and about the walls of the fort itself, Axis supposed that he could not blame men for such contemplations. The Skraelings had almost completely destroyed the town, piling rubble into tall piles and burrowing beneath. Axis shuddered to think what they might be doing underneath there.

The fort's gates, iron-plated, held fast against the Skrae-Bolds' attempts to crack them with their icy claws, the bolts remaining securely fastened. But the number of Skraelings grew day by day so that they were now a sea of undulating gray forms beyond the fort's walls, silver eyes and toothy jaws constantly raised to the walls in anticipation of the feed that awaited them.

Although starvation was a real possibility, and while most believed that the fall of Gorkenfort was inevitable, equally no one believed that Gorgrael would waste the time needed to starve them out. He would want to move south as soon as he could, grab as much territory as quickly as possible while Achar still reeled from the disaster of Gorkenfort. He would not want to move south while he had such a large number of enemies encased in the fort behind him, ready to burst forth for the attack once his lines were stretched. But what would he do? When would he attack? The waiting was wearing down men's nerves, nerves already shredded by the loss of Gorkentown.

Since he had crawled out of his bed and resumed his responsibilities as BattleAxe Axis had been almost impossible to be around. He infuriated Belial who had one night shouted at Axis when they were alone in their quarters, trying to make him understand that anyone else would have lost Gorkentown sooner and would have lost the lives of all who had defended the town. But Axis merely remarked bitterly that was all very well for Belial to say, wasn't Belial the one who had managed to not only save Axis' life, but the lives of those remaining in the street? Belial had truly lost his temper and had only just restrained himself from striking Axis, eventually turning and stalking out of the room.

The three men stood alone on the roof of the Keep. It was the highest point in the fort's defenses and all the other sentries were well below them on the battlements and walls. They were alone, wrapped in their own thoughts.

Alone, until all three men realized that they could hear the soft beat of wings. Magariz, memories of the SkraeBold's previous attack on him rushing to his mind, was first to draw his sword and crouch into a defensive posture, his eyes scanning the low cloud above, his left hand pushing his cloak out of the way of his sword arm.

Three forms dropped out of the cloud and onto the roof a safe distance away from the three men, all now with their swords drawn. Axis narrowed his eyes at the three winged men, dressed in warm woollen garments, standing across the far side of the roof. Two had jet-black wings, the third had snow-white wings, golden hair and the deepest violet eyes Axis had ever seen in any creature. None of them were armed and all held their hands well out from their sides to show that they carried no weapons, drooping their wings until they rustled along the splintery wood of the roof.

One of the black-winged creatures stepped forward and bowed slightly at the three men. "Greetings, BattleAxe Axis, StarMan," he said in a deep musical voice.

All three men started at the sure naming of Axis, but Magariz was especially stunned by the use of the title "Star-Man." His eyes momentarily flickered to Axis. StarMan?

"I am Crest-Leader HoverEye, BlackWing, commander in the Icarii Strike Force." Axis almost dropped his sword in astonishment. They are Icarii! he thought, his heart starting to bound in his chest. Icarii! "My companions," Hover-Eye continued, after a moment's pause, "are FreeFall SunSoar, heir to the Talon throne, and Wing-Leader Spike-Feather TrueSong." It had taken FreeFall hours of heated argument with his father to obtain permission to fly in with HoverEye and SpikeFeather and the Talon had been heartsick as he waved his only son goodbye from Talon Spike.

HoverEye stopped and looked expectantly at Axis who suddenly realized that HoverEye was waiting for him to introduce his two companions. "Ah, Lord Magariz, commander of Gorkenfort under Borneheld Duke of Ichtar," Magariz bowed slightly, his cautious but intensely curious dark eyes not leaving the group of the three Icarii, "and my lieutenant, Belial."

Belial sketched a bow, his eyes friendly. So these were Axis' father's people? "It is strange," he said, "that my first impression of the Forbidden should be that they are hardly forbidding at all."

Magariz gawked at the three creatures. Forbidden? They were nothing like the foul creatures of the Seneschal's teachings.

FreeFall walked forward, stopping only a few paces from Axis. Axis lowered his sword and turned to his companions. "We have nothing to fear from these Icarii. Put your swords away." He sheathed his sword and an instant later Belial did the same. Somewhat reluctantly, even though he believed the three Icarii were little threat, Magariz lowered his own sword and sheathed it. The scar throbbed on his cheek, reminding him of what injuries winged attackers could inflict.

Axis turned back to look at FreeFall. He couldn't believe how beautiful the Icarii was. No wonder his mother had loved one of them.

Magariz grasped Belial's arm, his eyes wide in shock as he looked between Axis and the Icarii. "Artor save us!" he whispered, "I think I can now see who, *what*, fathered Axis!"

"Indeed, my Lord Magariz. Axis is as much Icarii as Acharite."

Magariz dragged his eyes away from Axis and the Icarii and looked at Belial in amazement as he realized that Axis and Belial were already well aware of Axis' Icarii connection and of the idea that Axis might be the StarMan.

For their part FreeFall, HoverEye and SpikeFeather were equally enthralled with Axis. Could he be the One to save them? HoverEye thought he saw the lines of strain and self-doubt around the man's eyes and wondered if this could truly be the StarMan. Surely the One would be more confident?

FreeFall smiled at his cousin and held out his hand. Slowly Axis stepped forward and extended his own. FreeFall grasped it. "Greetings, cousin. StarDrifter and Rivkah send greetings and their love and would, had they been able, have come here to greet you themselves. But Rivkah, alas, has not the gift of flight and your father is only just recovering from cruel injuries inflicted by a SkraeBold at Yuletide."

Axis wavered on his feet and FreeFall's grip tightened about his arm. "Axis?"

Magariz looked, if possible, even more stunned.

"Rivkah is alive?" Axis whispered. His whole life had been built about the presumption of her death at his birth, yet now this Icarii—his cousin?—stood before him and smiled and said that Rivkah was alive. How had she survived Jayme and Moryson?

FreeFall blinked in some bewilderment, then laughed as he realized what had shocked Axis so much. "Of course, cousin. Ah, but I can see that there has been some confusion. Truth to tell, StarDrifter and Rivkah believed until very recently that you were dead, too. Ever since they found out the truth of your existence they have fretted to see you."

After all the cruel lies, after a lifetime of believing there was no one in the world for him, that he had no family, suddenly Axis discovered that his parents were alive and loved him. His parents . . . what a strange concept. He had never had *parents* before now. And this man had called him cousin? "Cousin?" he frowned.

FreeFall smiled more gently at the man. How strange he must be feeling. "StarDrifter is my uncle, brother to my father RavenCrest, the Talon." His smile broadened. "And you have a sister, EvenSong. So you see, Axis, you have an entire family that you knew nothing about until now. Welcome to the House of SunSoar." FreeFall hesitated an instant, then he leaned forward and embraced Axis.

Axis stood, completely overwhelmed, then he suddenly hugged FreeFall tightly. "FreeFall," he laughed, some of the tightly coiled emotions within him unwinding, "what a ridiculous name!"

"And what of Axis? There has never been an Axis Sun-Soar before. But it sounds good. It sounds good, cousin. And I am glad that we have found you."

All watching felt the emotion between FreeFall and Axis and none were unaffected by it. Belial stepped forward and briefly embraced Axis. "Axis SunSoar," he said grinning, "I like it. And a sister? I think I'd like to meet her! I hope she has not got your temper."

FreeFall grinned at this likeable man, but thought it best to banish any romantic thought about EvenSong from his mind. "She has the worst of the SunSoar temper, Belial. You would do better to avoid her. Besides, daily she torments me with the threat of becoming my wife."

Belial bowed slightly to the Icarii. "Then you have my apologies and my condolences, FreeFall SunSoar. I have lived with Axis' temper for many years now and can only imagine what it must be like in a woman."

Axis' smile faded a little. StarDrifter. "FreeFall. My father. I must get to my father."

"Yes. I understand, Axis. That is partly the reason why we are here. HoverEye? SpikeFeather?" FreeFall gestured the other two Icarii forward. All three had folded their wings against their backs now that the greetings were over.

"Axis SunSoar," HoverEye began formally. "We know of the Prophecy and, with so many of the Sentinels with you, then I can only assume that you do also." Axis nodded. "You are the StarMan," HoverEye said bluntly, "and you are the one who will bring Gorgrael to his knees. Here you are impotent," HoverEye gestured about Gorkenfort and Axis winced. HoverEye noticed the expression in Axis' eyes. "No, Axis SunSoar, do not blame yourself for this. No one could have prevented this rout. And perhaps you should know that both the Avar and the Icarii have stood as helpless against the Skraelings as you do now." He grimaced at the memory. "It took a Groundwalker woman, Azhure, to show us how to kill the wraiths."

"Azhure?" Both Axis and Belial said together in surprise, half that Azhure now apparently lived with the Icarii and half at the appellation 'Groundwalker.' "She's still good at the death stroke then," Belial muttered.

HoverEye ignored their reaction. "Axis SunSoar, it *must* be a combined force that meets Gorgrael's army, not a force composed only of Groundwalkers or of Icarii or Avar warriors." He shrugged, discomforted. "Our proud Strike Force could do little against the Skraelings. However much it galls many of the Icarii, we think we must fight with you at our helm. You have the experience, the blood and the power. BattleAxe, we ask for your aid in fighting Gorgrael. In return, we will give Gorkenfort aid."

"Axis," FreeFall said quietly, his violet eyes intense, his hand on Axis' shoulder. "You *must* be with your father if you are to reach your full power!"

"I know, I know," Axis said, then he looked up at FreeFall. "What am I, FreeFall?"

FreeFall stared at his cousin, then, acting on pure instinct, he reached out and took Axis' right hand, pulling the glove from it. He held the hand out for all to see, the strengthening light catching the gold and diamonds of the Enchanter's ring. "I think you already know what you are, Axis. Already you wear the Enchanter's ring. But only your father can bring you to your full potential, can make you strong enough to defeat Gorgrael. You are who you are, Axis. Accept it or we all die."

Axis stared into FreeFall's eyes. Then he nodded tersely. "I am Axis SunSoar, son of StarDrifter SunSoar," he said quietly, "and if I am to be an Icarii Enchanter who can lead the people of Tencendor to victory against Gorgrael then I need my father's teaching."

"Yes," FreeFall smiled, "yes! Welcome home, Axis, welcome home!"

Axis had the sudden, astounding feeling that he was indeed home. He had found his family. He had found what he needed to replace the lies with which the Seneschal had bound him.

"What's going on here? Have I finally caught you at your treacheries, BattleAxe?" an enraged voice called across the Keep.

Axis snatched his hand out of FreeFall's grip and spun around at the sound of Borneheld. He drew his sword, although Belial had the good sense to keep his sheathed. Magariz, still baffled by what he had witnessed, stood back a pace or two, his hand on the hilt of his sword but refraining from unsheathing it. Borneheld strode across the rooftop toward them. Jorge, Roland, Gautier and a number of fully armed soldiers followed him, Faraday and Timozel close behind. Borneheld had been at early morning weapon practice when he had espied the strange group on top of the Keep. Now he slowly weaved his sword before him as he halted a few paces away from Axis and the winged men, Gautier at his shoulder, his own sword at the ready. Timozel held Faraday back, his arm tight about her waist. His own eyes were cold.

The Icarii were instantly wary, their wings reflexively unfolding for flight. They had watched Gorkenfort for three days, waiting for a time when Axis was relatively isolated. They had no wish to antagonize Borneheld, knowing from their own observations and the reports of the Icarii farflight scouts that he was quick to anger. Some of the soldiers behind Borneheld had arrows, notched and ready for flight. This was too dangerous . . . too dangerous.

It was Lord Magariz, in the end, who spoke. "My Lord Duke, these are members of the Icarii who have offered us their aid in defeating the Skraelings." He did not think it prudent to mention that one of them was also closely related to Axis, or that it was one of the creatures from this strange race who had seduced Borneheld's mother.

Borneheld leaned back and laughed contemptuously. "So these are the Forbidden, then? Have we been afraid of such as these for so many years? Have we quivered under our beds at the thought that they would come to terrify us?

Why," he sneered at the three birdmen, "they are too pretty to be fearsome. I shall build me a cage and keep them to sing for me when I am an old man and weary of battle and women. Pretty, pretty." HoverEye stepped back, shocked and insulted to the core of his being. Surely no one who laid any claim to being civilized acted like this?

"We need all the help we can get, Borneheld," Axis said, only barely keeping his temper under control. His hand tightened about the hilt of his sword, a movement not missed by FreeFall. "Gorkenfort will fall if we cannot get assistance from outside. We *need* the Icarii!"

Borneheld stared at Axis, his face working as emotions battled inside of him. *"I will save Gorkenfort!"* he screamed abruptly, his face furious, his gray eyes glittering with hate. *"I do not need any help and I will not ally myself with the filth that stand here on this roof!"*

Behind him Timozel nodded. Yes. That was the message of his vision. Borneheld would save Achar.

Duke Roland glanced at Jorge and stepped forward. "My Lord Duke," he said placatingly, "it will not hurt to listen to what these Icarii have to say. Perhaps they have news that we should hear, reports of weaknesses in Gorgrael's lines."

FreeFall, swallowing his own sense of insult at Borneheld's words and actions (how could the gentle Rivkah have birthed such a son?), stepped past HoverEye and stood between Axis and Borneheld. "My Lord Duke Borneheld," FreeFall said politely. "I bring greetings from the Talon and offer the assistance of the Icarii Strike Force in driving the Skraelings from northern Ichtar. We stand ready to strike wherever you think we might aid you."

"I do not need the help of the Forbidden!" Borneheld rasped. "You are cursed beasts who should not have been allowed to live to breed beyond the Fortress Ranges. We misjudged during the Wars of the Axe, I think, in not burning you along with your demon-darkened forests. Once I am finished with the Skraelings I will ride into your mountain homes and burn your nests until only shifting ash and your memory remains."

FreeFall was shocked into silence, his great violet eyes locked unbelieving on the man in front of him. How could his people ally themselves with the Groundwalkers when they were filled with such unreasoning hate?

Roland tried one more time to make him see reason. "Borneheld, you know that we face Gorgrael. The Prophecy says that we must ally ourselves with the, ah, Forbidden. Who knows if it is right? But surely we should talk with these, ah, men. Hear what they have to say."

FreeFall felt Axis stir behind him and remembered that Axis had his sword drawn. He turned around, ready to stop Axis from attacking. "Axis," he said softly, intently, "you must not . . ."

And then Borneheld moved as fast as a striking viper. *"I give you this for your damned Prophecy!"* he screamed, and plunged his sword deep into FreeFall's back, the stroke so powerful it broke through bone and muscle before slicing open the heir to the Talon throne's heart. Faraday screamed as she saw the blur of steel plummet into FreeFall's back and would have rushed forward had not Timozel roughly hauled her back, tightening his hold about her. In that moment, that instant, as she saw the sword slice deeper and deeper into the defenseless Icarii man's back, Faraday's dislike and fear of Borneheld hardened completely into contempt and hate.

Borneheld grunted and yanked his sword out of FreeFall's back, putting his boot into the small of the birdman's back to give himself the necessary leverage to pull it free. The sword made a sound like rotten cloth giving way as it slid free of FreeFall's flesh.

All Axis saw was the blur of movement behind FreeFall, the shocked look on FreeFall's face, and then, unbelievably, the glint of a sword tip, reddened with blood, pushing through FreeFall's chest and then disappearing.

FreeFall collapsed into Axis' arms, Axis catching him,

unable to comprehend what had happened. His eyes met Borneheld's. "You're next, brother," Borneheld said softly but very, very menacingly. He took a step forward.

Axis looked down at FreeFall. The birdman was dying, his arms and wings hung limply at his side, his great violet eyes were glazing gray. Blood was beginning to pump from his mouth as he struggled to say something. Axis bent his head. "Find StarDrifter, Axis," FreeFall whispered. Then, as the last of his life pumped out of him, FreeFall said something very, very strange. "The Ferryman owes you, Axis." He had to force the words now and Axis could barely hear him. "Learn the secrets and the mysteries of the waterways and *bring me home*! I will wait at the Gate. *Bring me home to EvenSong! Promise!*"

Axis nodded. "I promise," he whispered to his cousin, then staggered with the sudden weight in his arms as FreeFall died. Even if he could have found the time in the midst of this nightmare to sing the Song of Re-creation, Axis knew it would be no use. FreeFall had gone.

With his death, FreeFall gave Axis the single most powerful motive he would need to push Achar into civil war. Axis had never before entertained the idea that with his heritage he could seize complete control in Achar; now, in his grief for FreeFall and his horror at Borneheld's action, he did. If Priam and Borneheld refused to unite the Acharites with the Icarii and Avar in order to fight Gorgrael, then Axis knew he was now ready to go to war against them. Civil war in Achar was inevitable.

Axis slid FreeFall gently to the roof, touching the birdman's forehead briefly in benediction, wishing he had known FreeFall for years instead of only moments, then he stood and looked back at Borneheld. Each knew at that moment that only death would bridge the gap between them. Neither was aware of the commotion about them.

The instant after Borneheld struck FreeFall, Belial had grabbed HoverEye's arm and hauled him backwards several steps out of the way of the violence. "Listen to me!" Belial whispered fiercely into the shocked birdman's ear.

"Listen to me! I will get Axis to the foot of the Icescarp Alps for you. Are you listening?"

HoverEye, still riveted by the dreadful sight in front of him as Borneheld wrenched the sword from FreeFall's back, nodded slightly. "Can you and yours meet him there? Birdman? *Can you*? Or will you let FreeFall die in vain?"

HoverEye finally looked at Belial. He nodded again, some understanding replacing the horror on his face. "Then fly, damn you, fly before Borneheld slaughters you as well!" Belial gave HoverEye a push. "Fly!" HoverEye stared again at FreeFall. Belial literally shook him in frustration. "You can do nothing! He is dead. Now fly! Watch the foot of the mountains for your Axis. Fly!" Belial seized an equally shocked and unmoving SpikeFeather. "Fly!" he whispered hoarsely. "I can do no more for you."

Both birdmen stretched their wings out and started to lift off; several of the soldiers behind Borneheld saw the movement and raised their bows. "Halt!" Magariz cried, finally shaking himself out of his own shock. "Unnotch those arrows! Let them go!" Reluctantly, the soldiers lowered their bows and watched the two birdmen rise off the roof and wing away toward the Icescarp Alps.

Axis and Borneheld still stared at each other. After a moment Borneheld started to laugh and, leaning down to where FreeFall's body lay on the roof, wiped his sword clean along the soft white feathers of his wings before sheathing it.

"You will wait till later, I think, brother," Borneheld said lightly. "I am in a good mood now that I have disposed of one of the filthy Forbidden."

Axis felt as if he should kill Borneheld here and now; raise his sword and wipe this piece of filth from the face of the earth and the minds of men forever. But, oh FreeFall, his heart cried, if I am to flee to the Icarii and StarDrifter then Borneheld must live to save Faraday! My hands are still tied. But one day . . . one day . . . "One day you will die for what you have just done, Borneheld. I swear that I will kill you in just combat for my cousin FreeFall Sun-

Soar's death. On that day you will join the carrion on the refuse heaps of Achar. Only the crows will tug at the flesh of the Duke of Ichtar, Borneheld, not the sweet words and lying ballads of troubadours. Priam has two heirs, Borneheld, you and I, but you will not live to enjoy your heritage. Eventually I alone will lead Achar against Gorgrael." Axis' voice was completely calm, and completely believable and chilling because of that. His eyes were steady, his body relaxed, his sword hanging loose at his side, and yet Borneheld suddenly felt very, very afraid.

"Seize him!" Borneheld cried, as Axis' final words burned into his memory. Cousin? He had called the dead Forbidden *cousin*? "Seize him! He is Forbidden himself!"

One of those filth had raped his mother?

Gautier and three other soldiers rushed forward and seized an unresisting Axis. Gautier tore the sword from Axis' hand and the axe from his belt and threw them across the roof. For weeks he had resented the adulation that Axis commanded from the men stationed in Gorkentown and Gorkenfort. Now he could participate in his downfall; it made him glad, it made him feel strong.

Borneheld stood back and tore his eyes away from Axis' continuing stare. "Throw him into the dungeons," he snarled at Gautier. "He will die tomorrow morning hanging from a gibbet like any common criminal!" He turned to the small knot of people behind him. "And throw the body of the Forbidden over the parapets. Let the Skraelings feast on it. I do not want it fouling up the roof of the Keep any longer."

He stared about him for a moment longer, then he stomped off the roof, Timozel hauling a shocked Faraday after him. Gautier and his men hustled Axis roughly toward the trapdoor.

Jorge and Roland stared at Magariz and Belial, lost. What could they do? Was Axis truly one of the Forbidden? And if so, how should they regard him? Slowly they, too, turned and followed Borneheld, shocked and sickened by the murder they had just witnessed but not yet ready to turn

against Borneheld because of it. They were men loyal to
the monarchy of Achar, and it was Borneheld who represented the monarchy here in Gorkenfort. Priam was not going to save Achar, but Borneheld just might be able to do
so. Axis could hardly be the one to save them if he was to
die in the morning. Brave as they were, Jorge and Roland
were too old and too set in their beliefs to turn their back
on the established and comfortable order in order to help
the birth of a new world.

Soon only Magariz and Belial stood on the roof, the
bloody body of FreeFall before them. Two of Gautier's
men had tried to drag the body toward the parapets to hurl
it down to the Skraelings, but Magariz snarled at them and
the men fled.

Magariz stared at FreeFall's body for a moment longer
then turned to Belial. "Are you with Axis?" he asked.

Belial knew what he meant. He nodded. "I and all the
Axe-Wielders who are left. We will follow Axis to the pits
of the AfterLife if he asks . . . and if it becomes necessary.
We believe, as do the Icarii, that he is the One named in the
Prophecy."

Magariz's eyes were thoughtful. "Then I am with you,
Belial. I am with you." He paused, uncertainty crossing his
handsome face. He had never pledged himself to treachery
before, yet, strangely, it did not feel as foul as he thought it
might. Indeed, it would have been a betrayal if he had denied Axis, especially after hearing the startling news about
Rivkah the Icarii had brought with them. "What do we do
now?"

Belial bent down to FreeFall and smoothed the golden
hair back from his dead eyes. "Now, Magariz? Now we
give FreeFall SunSoar the Office of the Dead that befits his
rank and honor, not the dishonor that Borneheld would
have him thrown to. Fetch Brothers Ogden and Veremund,
they will know what to do. If FreeFall cannot be with his
people for his farewell into the AfterLife, then we will be
his people for him."

57

Escape from Gorkenfort

FreeFall's death gave Axis the desire and the anger to live. As he sat alone and cold in the dark and dank dungeons of Gorkenfort he did not give in to self-pity as he had done after the fall of Gorkentown. He owed it to FreeFall to succeed. The dungeon and Borneheld's threat of death did not concern him. He would live for FreeFall, for the first of his family who had welcomed him home. He had Belial, and Belial had Faraday, and in the end it would be Faraday who would make sure that the way would be clear.

Belial argued with Borneheld, leaning forward from his chair, his face flushed with the force of his argument, knowing he was right, knowing that Borneheld could not resist agreeing with him. Knowing that Borneheld would see Axis' death in the plan.

"My Lord," he said forcefully. "I care not if I offend with these words. Gorkenfort will not hold. Not even the best commander, not even you, my Lord Duke, could hold it. There are too many men and not enough food. More Skraelings arrive each day while the IceWorms grow larger, in a few days they will be large enough to start disgorging their loads over the top of Gorkenfort's walls. Soon Gorgrael will strike, and Artor alone knows what he will strike with. It is best now to start thinking of retreating back into Ichtar, and perhaps trying to hold the Skraelings in the gap between the Rivers Azle and Nordra."

Borneheld's flinty eyes stared coldly at Belial, but he did not stop him. He had come to the same unpalatable conclusion. He would lose Ichtar, but better lose Ichtar and save the bulk of the army that was left to fight another day. The Skraelings did not like running water and there was a possibility that Achar could hold them back between the Azle and the Nordra. If Borneheld could get himself and his command there alive. "Continue," he said as Belial paused.

"My Lord Duke, in order that the bulk of the garrison can move south with some hope of arriving alive, there needs to be a force willing to draw the Skraelings away from Gorkenfort. The Axe-Wielders can do that—if Axis leads them, for they will follow no one else. We are still over fifteen hundred strong and most of our mounts are stabled here. If we can break through the ring of Skraelings we can draw them northeast, and you can . . ." Belial almost said "make a run for it", but realized they might be the wrong words to use before Borneheld, ". . . lead the remainder of the garrison south and regroup at Jervois Landing."

They were sitting at the table before the fire in the Hall of the Keep, Jorge, Roland and Gautier with them. Faraday stood behind Borneheld's chair, her hands resting lightly on the wooden head rest, her eyes steady on Belial.

Jorge tapped the table with his fingers. "Any decoy force, no matter how experienced, would face certain death under the circumstances you describe, Belial."

Belial nodded.

Borneheld glanced at Jorge, then looked back at Belial. "Is self-sacrifice part of your creed, Belial?"

Belial kept his eyes steady. He had to convince Borneheld. "To stay here is certain death, my Lord Duke. I, as my command, would prefer to die fighting in order that others might live. Who knows?" his voice became lighter, as if not even he believed what he said. "Some of us may yet live to dangle grandchildren on our knees, my Lord. If any of us do survive, then we will attempt to join you at Jervois Landing."

A cynical grin spread over Borneheld's face. There was only one question he needed to know. "There will not be much point in your sacrifice if you die within five paces of leaving the gates, Belial. Your plan demands that at the least you break through the massed Skraelings and lead them north so that we can move south. Can you break through? Will your force stay alive long enough for that?"

"Yes, I believe we can. The element of surprise will work for us. The Skraelings will not expect us to attack. But to make absolutely sure I want to issue most of the men with fire brands. I think that we can create enough fear among them with the fire to break through." His eyes briefly met Faraday's above Borneheld's head. Belial was placing his trust, as well as the lives of himself, his men and of Axis in her hands. The fire was her plan, and she thought she could make the fire just that little bit more frightening to the Skraelings. Enough, perhaps, to not only let them break through, but to save most of their lives.

Belial had told Borneheld that he and Axis would take only those Axe-Wielders left, some fifteen hundred. But both Belial and Faraday hoped that close to three thousand men would follow Axis out those gates. There was enough disloyalty to Borneheld amongst his men for almost another fifteen hundred, led by their garrison commander, Magariz, to rally to Axis' cause.

Borneheld looked to Timozel. Over the past days he had found himself relying more and more on Timozel's judgment rather than that of his more senior commanders. He did not like the glances Jorge and Roland threw each other's way, and he thought Magariz was not the man he had been before the SkraeBolds had injured him so badly. Even Gautier, although not suspect, flattered simply for advancement. But Timozel was true. Borneheld was certain of it. Timozel had told him that he thought treachery had been the undoing of Borneheld's plans to save Gorkenfort, and Borneheld believed him. Axis' meeting with the Forbidden atop the Keep only confirmed his suspicions. He had planned and commanded well, but deceit had undermined his efforts. Yes. If disaster now threatened Achar, then it was not Borneheld's fault.

Timozel smiled and nodded and Borneheld made up his mind. If the Axe-Wielders wanted to die so quickly, then that was their business. And it might, just might, give them a chance to escape. And it would dispose of Axis. Despite his words on the roof of the Keep two days ago Borneheld had not yet executed Axis. He could not test loyalty further with a public execution . . . or even a private one.

"So be it," he agreed. "When do you want to go?"

Belial sat back in relief. "Tomorrow."

Borneheld's eyes were cold. "I want to see Axis at the head of the Axe-Wielders as they pass through that gate, Belial."

"Good. We will go in the morning. At dawn. Will you give me permission to requisition the remaining fuel in the fort? For the brands? I want as many of my men to have them as possible."

"Tear apart this table if you want, Belial. I will leave nothing for the Skraelings to feast on. Come gentlemen, we all have much to do if we are to be ready to evacuate Gorkenfort."

Faraday, Yr, Belial, Magariz and a number of Axe-Wielders stood in one of the cramped stables. Horses had been moved outside so the stalls could be piled high with pieces of wood. At one end of the row of stalls three or four men patiently dipped each new brand in a specially prepared oil so it would burn bright and long. A bundle of green material in her hands, Faraday smiled at the doubt on Belial's and Magariz's faces, loving both of them for the love and loyalty they were showing Axis.

"Trust me," she said. "I can give you enough protection to break through the Skraelings, but I can also give you the means to destroy a good number of them once you have drawn them clear of Gorkenfort." Faraday turned to Yr. "Is Timozel still busy?"

Yr nodded. "Yes. Borneheld has him in the Great Hall, discussing the plans for the retreat."

"Good." Faraday shook out the material she was holding. Once it was unfolded the men could see that it had a peculiar pattern with shifting colors of green, blue, purple and brown. It shimmered before their eyes. For a moment Faraday stood, stroking the soft fabric.

"Mother protect them," she whispered, closing her eyes, and reached down into the very soul of her being for the Mother's power. It did not fail her, scorching up through her body more powerfully than she had felt it yet. Faraday moaned a little and Yr grasped her shoulders, steadying her. For a moment Faraday hung there before the men, then the gown suddenly flared a searing emerald and every man took a step back. Artor, protect me! Magariz thought silently, what is this woman? First to heal Axis as she did, and now this?

Faraday took a deep breath and hugged the gown tightly to her, remembering the anger of the emerald light as she had moved through it to reach Raum and StarDrifter the night of the first Skraeling attack. She remembered how it had wanted to strike out and not known how. "Mother forgive me if I misuse your power," she whispered, "but protection will need to be tempered with some action this time." She fought for control of the emerald light as it throbbed in her arms, talking to it, telling what she needed of it, giving it an outlet for its anger, asking it if it would answer her bidding.

The light abruptly flared three times as brilliantly as it had previously—the entire row of stalls was enveloped in the throbbing light. Then, as suddenly as it had flared, the light died, and Faraday was left standing with simply a voluminous robe of peculiar shifting colors gathered into her arms.

She looked at Yr, and Yr tightened her hold protectively; the girl looked wan and exhausted. But Faraday managed a small smile. "It is done, Yr. It is done." She turned to Belial and Magariz. "You will be protected as you move through the Skraelings, and you will kill more efficiently than you have ever done before. Now, we have work to do before morning."

Faraday put the gown on the floor and ripped about a third of the material away. "Tear this apart," she said, gazing up at the men. "Tear it apart until you only have threads left, then give each man who will ride with you a thread to tie about his arm. Tell them," her voice took on a steely tone, "tell them, as they tie it, to thank the Mother for Her protection and love, or else it will not work for them. *Tell them!*"

Magariz bent down and took the torn strip of cloth from Faraday's hands. "I will tell them, my Lady, and I will offer thanks to the Mother here and now that you are here to guide and help us."

Faraday sighed, both in relief and exhaustion. "Artor will not protect them out there, Magariz, only the Mother. Make sure they are told." Yr helped her to her feet and Faraday made a quick decision and laid a hand on Magariz's arm. "Wait, Magariz. I will come with you."

Magariz glanced anxiously at Faraday. He did not want her to get into even more trouble than she already had on his behalf "My Lady, Borneheld . . ."

"Borneheld is too busy tonight to miss me, my Lord Magariz. Come, let us see to your men."

They came for him in the hour before dawn. All night he'd heard the muffled sounds of men and horses preparing for action, and had paced about his cell in irritation. What was going on? Borneheld had allowed him no company since he had been thrown into this dark hole and had only reluctantly allowed a man to bring him food and a blanket to keep the worst of the chill at bay. Axis threw the blanket about his shoulders and paced back and forth, back and forth. Damn! Years had passed since he was simply a man at arms, waiting for the decisions and plans to be told to him by his superiors. How had I ever stood it then? Axis asked himself. How could I bear to have been one of the led?

Finally, as he was almost screaming with impatience and frustration, Axis heard one of the upper doors being thrown open and the sound of the footfalls of men coming down the stairs. A glow of light came toward him, gradually becoming brighter.

Axis blinked and shaded his eyes with his hand.

"Brother."

Borneheld. Axis lowered his hand and blinked, trying to adjust his eyes to the light. Borneheld stood the other side of the cage's bars, Gautier, Belial and Magariz slightly behind him. Dangling from Borneheld's hand was a ring of keys. He had a contemptuous smile on his face.

"Belial has decided your fate, like it or not," Borneheld sneered. "Your lieutenant seems to desire death and has offered your life and the lives of your men as well. Will you accept Belial's fate?"

Axis glanced behind Borneheld to Belial. Belial's eye lowered in a small wink and even Magariz nodded slightly at his side. It was not a hard decision for Axis to make.

"I would trust Belial with my life," he said quietly, shaking the blanket from his shoulders, his bearing proud and graceful even in the disgusting cell.

Borneheld rolled his head back and laughed loudly, although to Axis' ears the laughter sounded forced. "You would? Then do!" He thrust the keys into Belial's hands. "You ride in fifteen minutes, foolish man. Make sure that my brother is ready to ride with you—to lead you, if you have the courage. Magariz, Gautier, to me!"

He strode off down the dungeon corridor, Gautier and, after a slight hesitation, Magariz, hurrying after him. Belial unlocked the cell and embraced Axis. "With the Mother's help, we ride this morning through and beyond the Skraelings into Prophecy."

Axis felt a chill at Belial's words. "The Mother?" he asked. "Has Faraday converted you?"

Belial looked sheepish. "It appears the Mother, whosoever She might be, will save us this morning, Axis, while Artor lies sleeping. Here," Belial lifted a long piece of thread from his pocket and tied it about Axis' upper right arm. Axis saw that Belial wore one too. "Faraday says that this thread will protect you. We all wear them. But you must thank the Mother for Her protection and love, and place your trust in Her."

Axis fingered the thread for a moment. "From what you have told me, Belial, She has already given me life through Faraday's hands," he said quietly, "and I find it no hard task to thank Her and to place my trust in Her for this day. Belial," he raised his head and gazed into Belial's hazel eyes. "What is it we do today?"

"The Axe-Wielders ride through the gates in a few minutes' time, Axis SunSoar, to act as a decoy for Borneheld to evacuate Gorkenfort. We lead the Skraelings north and Borneheld and the rest of the garrison flee south to rally Achar at Jervois Landing."

"Pray that the Mother keeps watch over Faraday, Belial. We head for the Icescarp Alps?"

Belial nodded. "Yes. It is time that you went to your father, Axis. We need you with all your secrets unlocked to lead us against the Destroyer."

Axis buckled the weapon belt that Belial handed him about his hips, sliding his sword and axe into place. "I am not sure that I want all my secrets unlocked, Belial. They may be more frightening than what the Destroyer has to throw at me." He paused. "And how many men ride with us, Belial? How many men still want to follow me?"

"More than you think, Axis. You will see when we ride. Now, come say goodbye to your brother. For the time being."

As Axis and Belial emerged from the dungeons Arne fell into step behind Axis, handing his commander his cloak and gloves. There was hardly any space to move, and Axis and Belial had to push their way through units of men standing in formation. Everyone was under strict orders to be as quiet as they could so that the Skraelings would have little warning about what was to happen, but Axis heard his name being murmured in greeting as he passed the ranks of men, and many reached out their hands and touched his shoulder as he passed by.

By the gates what was left of the Axe-Wielders sat their mounts, firebrands burning brightly in their hands, Belaguez standing at their head, saddled and ready to run, impatient for his master and for the battle ahead.

To one side of the Axe-Wielders stood Borneheld, and beside him Faraday, Timozel at her shoulder, their own horses saddled and waiting behind them. Yr waited further back; she would remain with Faraday. Axis smiled, but as he crossed the courtyard toward them he spotted Ogden and Veremund sitting on their placid white donkeys.

"Well, Sentinels, who do you ride with today? Do you fight your way north with me or do you run south with Borneheld?"

Ogden sniffed. "We will tread our own paths for a while, Axis SunSoar. But you will not lose us for long, I think."

Axis regarded them for a moment. For so many months they had annoyed him. Now he found himself trusting them, despite the disturbing riddle of the Prophecy. "Then take care of yourselves, Sentinels. And of your ridiculous donkeys." He pulled the soft droopy ear of the nearest donkey affectionately. "I'm sure that you will return to annoy me as soon as you can."

Veremund leaned over and touched Axis' shoulder briefly. "Find peace, Axis SunSoar."

"Find peace, gentlemen," Axis replied softly, then he turned and strode over to Borneheld. For a moment they stared flatly at each other.

"I hope you die out there today, brother," Borneheld finally said, his voice thick with forced bravado. "It is the only reason I let you go." He suddenly wished that he had followed his original plan of having Axis hung like a criminal here in this courtyard.

"The only reason you let me go was because you knew you couldn't execute me without the entire garrison rebelling. I will not die out there, Borneheld. One day I will return. Wait for that day and know that it will arrive." Both Axis' eyes and voice were chilling and Borneheld only just managed to stop himself from stepping back. He forced a sneer to his face, but knew it was not very convincing. Axis' mouth curled in contempt and he turned away. The next time he saw Borneheld he hoped it would be at the point of his sword.

Axis stepped over to Timozel and stared at the man's gaunt face for a long moment. "You are a changed man, Timozel, and I do not think that I like what you have become. I hope that your loyalty to Faraday will not fade as quickly as your loyalty to me." He suddenly reached out and grabbed Timozel's tunic front, pulling the man close until their faces were only a handspan apart. "Look after her, Timozel! Get her safely away from this death trap! If you value the vow you swore her as Champion then *get her safely out!*"

Timozel's face hardened and he wrenched himself away from Axis' hand. "I live for Faraday," he said, his voice thick with anger, "and I do not need you to tell me how to protect her!"

Axis moved away from the man and his face softened as he looked at Faraday.

"Live, Faraday," he said quietly. "You know I could not bear it if you died."

Her eyes filled with tears and she reached out and touched the thread about his arm for an instant. "Mother be with you," she whispered, "and with me. I will strive to live, Axis, and hope that you will live for me." She no longer cared if Borneheld realized her true feelings for Axis. It no longer mattered. She had done her duty and kept Borneheld from killing Axis.

Borneheld looked between the two of them and frowned.

"Borneheld," Axis said lightly, "I have just realized that I have not claimed my brotherly kiss from your new bride. I apologize for being so tardy. I cannot think what could have come over me to forget my courtly manners so." Without giving Borneheld a chance to reply he leaned forward, seized Faraday by the shoulders, and kissed her hard on the mouth, once, and then once again.

He released her and stood back. "My Lady Faraday, Duchess of Ichtar, accept what will probably be my last salute as BattleAxe of the Axe-Wielders." He clenched his fist over the golden axes on his black tunic coat and bowed jerkily from the waist. "And remember your vows. Every last one of them." He turned away without waiting for a reply, brushed past Borneheld, who was still looking stupefied at Faraday, and mounted Belaguez.

"Axe-Wielders, are you ready?" he cried in a clear voice.

"Wait!" A dark figure rode forth on a black stallion, a burning brand in his hand. Lord Magariz. "I ride with the StarMan," he cried to all those assembled in the courtyard, ignoring Borneheld's furious shout of denial. "Who will ride with me?"

"We will!" the cry rang out behind him, and a long column of men who had been waiting behind the stable blocks now rode out to join Magariz. There were well over fifteen hundred of them, all wielding flaming brands, and each with a thread tied about his arm.

"You will die for this betrayal, Magariz!" Borneheld screamed in fury. "Ride with my unnatural brother now, but never think to receive any mercy from me when you crawl back begging for my favor! I will hunt you down and kill you for what you do here this day!"

Magariz reined his stallion to a halt in front of his former lord. " 'Ware, Borneheld," he said softly, "of the death penalty already hanging over your own head for the murder of FreeFall SunSoar. With that stroke you cut the ties that bound me to you. My own honesty compels me to ride with the man who commands my respect, not the man who has lost it." He wheeled his stallion over to Axis. "Will you accept my oath of loyalty and service, Axis SunSoar?"

Axis reached out and gripped his hand. "Gladly, Magariz, gladly. You and yours are welcome at my side." The man's support touched him deeply; Magariz and his men were risking ostracism, possible death, by joining him. He glanced at Belial, mounted and waiting behind him, and thanked whatever gods were listening that he had men like Belial and Magariz at his back.

He opened his mouth again to call to the Axe-Wielders, but he realized that he could not use that name. "My friends," he called simply, "do you stand ready?"

"We follow your voice and we are ready, SunSoar!" they cried as one, and emotion briefly threatened to overwhelm Axis.

He stared at Borneheld for a moment, still standing furious and disbelieving at Magariz's treachery. "I go now to claim my heritage, brother," he said softly, "and when I return, 'ware!"

Axis wheeled Belaguez around and the gates began to swing open, admitting the excited whispering of the Skraelings. "Then let us ride!" he cried, seizing a flaming brand from a guard standing close by. "Let us ride!" He brandished the fiery torch and spurred the dappled gray stallion forward through the gates.

SunSoar's command rode and fought as if possessed, as indeed they were, fighting for and with the Mother. Belial and Magariz had instructed them carefully and now that they had the StarMan at their head, how could they lose? The three thousand rode together in tight formation, their flaming torches held in front and to the side, burning their way through the mass of Skraelings in front of them. The gray mass writhed and screamed, falling back from the flames, weeping and wailing and whispering in horror at the nasty, horrid brights that the manlings thrust their way. The SkraeBolds screamed at their wraiths, for they had taught them not to fear fire, but these were no ordinary flames—they glowed emerald at their tips. Every so often a wraith was not quick enough to duck out of range, and as the flame touched the unlucky Skraeling it would flare into a bright pillar of emerald fire, then fizzle out of existence in the snow.

The soldiers screamed Axis' new name, SunSoar. Belial and Magariz had told them of the meeting atop the Keep roof, of Axis' heritage, and of his claim to be the StarMan. The One who would lead them to victory against Gorgrael. Few of the Axe-Wielders had any reason to doubt what they said, they had known and fought under Axis for years and they already knew that he was the man to die for, none other. The men who followed Magariz in his disloyalty to Borneheld were among the many regular soldiers who had no trouble believing it either. Many of them had ridden on patrol with Axis and had seen first hand how he could lead to victory against the Skraelings; their admiration of his leadership had spread.

As they rode through the town, the Skraelings leaping out of their way, Axis stood high in his stirrups and brandished his fire torch high. "SkraeBolds! Can you hear me?" he screamed. "Will you let me go so easy? Do you give up the chase so easy? Shall I tell Gorgrael how untrustworthy, how cowardly, his lieutenants are? Don't you want the chance to bring Gorgrael my head?"

The SkraeBolds heard and Axis' words inflamed them. They redoubled their efforts, driving the Skraelings before them to follow Axis and his company. The watchers in Gorkenfort could see the Skraeling mass turning to chase the riders.

Jorge, watching atop the walls, clutched the stone battlements in excitement. "By Artor!" he bellowed, not caring who heard his elation. "They're following him out of the town. See! Even now he swings north." At this distance Axis' command was simply an indistinct mass of light, but that was enough. That was enough. "We are saved!" He turned to Roland, gasping in breathless excitement beside him. "Axis has saved us!"

They rode until they could feel the horses tire beneath them, then they turned to fight the Skraeling host which had seethed out of the town after them.

"Shall we give Borneheld and Achar some breathing room, my friends?" Axis cried to Belial and Magariz, a grin of sheer excitement lighting his eyes. "Shall we make our stand here?"

Horses and riders milled about them and Belial shouted orders, getting the excited men in formation behind Axis. All wanted to stand and fight. They had been running before the Skraelings too long. Before them rode Axis Sun-Soar, StarMan. They knew he would lead them to victory, who could doubt it?

The Skraelings, emboldened both by the SkraeBolds' urgings and the sight of the riders running before them for two hours, did not wait. They could see that many of the burning brands had gone out. They could see the manlings' horses stumble as they tired. They knew that they outnumbered the men some fifty to one and they knew that there was some good eating awaiting them. They did not stop to think of the danger.

Axis waited until they were close, very close, waited until he could see the silvery orbs glistening in anticipation and the jaws working and slavering in the front ranks of the

Skraelings. He waited until their frantic whispers filled his ears, then he stood high in his stirrups, graceful and easy even though Belaguez skittered excitedly underneath him.

"In the name of the Mother," he called, his voice clear and powerful, "and of the Stars that watch above, lend aid to me and mine now."

Then he spun the brand high into the sky. Just as it reached the pinnacle of its arc, just before it started to spin down toward the Skraeling host, the brand exploded into an emerald ball of fire. As it fell it expanded and threw off smaller balls of spitting, hissing green fire.

The SkraeBolds, winging their way above and behind the leading ranks of the Skraelings, screamed in fear and frustration. They paused just long enough to hurl an order for dispersal at the Skraelings and then, as the emerald fire hurtled down toward them, they faded from sight.

The instant the fire hit the Skraeling mass it expanded and strengthened, feeding upon more and more of the wraiths. Thousands of Skraelings burned that clear frosty morning in the northern reaches of Gorken Pass, died screaming and whispering amid the Mother's anger and retribution. Others died as the men pushed their horses in among the confused mass, reaching down to grab their stringy hair and put out the light in their eyes with a vicious thrust of a sword. The emerald fire did not touch those who wore the threads about their arms.

It was a rout, and only when there were no more Skraelings left to kill did the men rein their horses in and watch the remaining wraiths flee back toward Gorkenfort.

"Pray we have bought them enough time," Belial whispered, his face drawn with exhaustion.

"Pray that Borneheld got them out of Gorkenfort before the Skraelings returned," Axis replied just as quietly. "Pray that he can rally Achar to hold them at Jervois Landing . . . until I return."

58

BattleAxe

In the cold evening air they sat their horses at the base of the Icescarp Alps.

"We will not follow you in there," Belial said quietly, his eyes on the massive black cliffs that reared out of the snow-covered plains before them. "That is for you alone."

Axis turned to him. The excitement of the morning had faded, and now his face was as exhausted as everyone else's. "And you?"

Belial was silent for a moment, his eyes drifting over the black cliffs. Then he dropped his gaze to Axis. "I will take your army and ride south through eastern Ichtar, the Wild-Dog Plains, until I find us a safe haven. I doubt the Skraelings will bother us overmuch. They will want to push south after Borneheld rather than east. We will wait in the southern WildDog Plains for you, Axis SunSoar, perhaps even Sigholt if it remains free of Skraelings. Do not take too long to rejoin us."

Axis' eyes shone with tears. He gripped Belial's hand

and arm. "I thank you for your friendship and support," he said quietly, "and I will rejoin you as quickly as I am able." He let Belial's hand go and slid off Belaguez, handing the stallion's reins to his lieutenant and patting the horse's neck in affection. "Look after my horse for me, Belial. I will need a good mount when I return."

He turned to Magariz and gripped the man's hand. "I thank you for your support as well, Magariz. I pray that you will not suffer for it."

"Then come back to us quickly," the scar-faced man smiled. "I do not know who will reach us first, Gorgrael or Borneheld, and I do not know which will be the most dangerous!"

Axis laughed and saluted his men, smiling and waving at their cheers. Then he turned and walked toward the base of the cliffs, not knowing what to expect.

His army sat their horses silently, staying to bear witness to whatever would happen next.

Axis' booted feet scrunched through the snow, and he threw his cloak back over his shoulders. He had been walking for some ten minutes, the black rock of the cliffs now only fifty or so paces away, when the five Icarii birdmen who had been watching his approach landed softly in the snow in front of him.

Axis stopped. Two he recognized, HoverEye and Spike-Feather, but the other three he did not. Two of them had the black wings that HoverEye and SpikeFeather sported, but like FreeFall the fifth had pure white wings, golden hair . . . and pale blue eyes. He wore no clothes over his upper body and Axis could see that his torso bore the scars of a recent battle.

Looking into his face Axis could see reflections of his own.

He opened his mouth to speak, to say something, but he could not find the words to say. He could not take his eyes from his father.

StarDrifter slowly stepped forward, his eyes locked into those of his son. That this man was his son StarDrifter had absolutely no doubt, the man's blood sang to him, called to him, screamed for him, and StarDrifter could feel his own blood calling back.

StarDrifter's mouth thinned at the black uniform that the man wore and his eyes glittered angrily. He stopped a pace from his son and they both stood and stared at each other. Axis' eyes were filled with tears, but StarDrifter's were utterly dry.

Slowly, hesitantly, StarDrifter reached out a hand and laid it flat on Axis' breast, feeling his son's heart beating frantically under his fingers. Then StarDrifter's fingers convulsively clutched into the black material of Axis' tunic and with one vicious twist he ripped the insignia of the crossed golden axes from his son's breast and hurled the piece of material away to flutter unwanted across the ice-bound wastes at the foot of the Icescarp Alps.

StarDrifter's anger faded as the hated emblem blew away. He hesitated, then stepped forward and embraced Axis, speaking the ritual words of greeting normally uttered only to a newborn baby.

"Welcome, Axis, into the House of SunSoar and into my heart. My name is StarDrifter SunSoar and I am your father. Sing well and fly high, and may nothing and no one tear your feet from the path of the Star Dance again."

Axis wrapped his arms about his father and held him tight, the tears finally sliding free from his eyes.

Glossary

ACHAR: the realm stretching over most of the continent, bounded by the Andeis, Tyrre and Widowmaker Seas, the Shadowsward Forest and the Icescarp Alps. (Achar is pronounced with a hard *ch*, as in "loch".)

ACHARITES: the people of Achar.

AFTERLIFE: both Acharites and the Forbidden believe in the existence of an AfterLife, although exactly what they believe depends on their particular culture.

ALDENI: a small province in western Achar, devoted to small crop cultivation. It is administered by Duke Roland.

ANDAKILSA, River: the extreme northern river of Ichtar, dividing Ichtar from Ravensbund. It remains free of ice all year around and flows into the Andeis Sea.

ANDEIS SEA: the often unpredictable sea that washes the western coast of Achar.

ARCEN: the major town of Arcness.

ARCNESS: large eastern province in Achar, specializing in pigs. It is administered by Earl Burdel.

ARNE: a cohort commander in the Axe-Wielders.

ARTOR THE PLOUGHMAN: the one true god, as taught by the Brotherhood of the Seneschal. According to the Book of Field and Furrow, the religious text of the Seneschal, Artor gave mankind the gift of the Plough, the instrument which enabled mankind to abandon his hunting and gathering lifestyle and to settle in the one spot to cultivate the earth and thus to build the foundations of civilization.

AVAR, The: one of the races of the Forbidden who live in the forest of the Shadowsward, or the Avarinheim as they call it. The Avar are sometimes referred to as the People of the Horn.

AVARINHEIM, The: the home of the Avar people, known to the Acharite people as the Shadowsward. See "Shadowsward."

AVONSDALE: province in western Achar. It produces legumes, fruit and flowers. It is administered by Earl Jorge.

AXE-WIELDERS, The: the elite crusading and military wing of the Seneschal. Its members have not taken holy orders but have nevertheless dedicated their battle skills to the Seneschal to use as it wishes. The Axe-Wielders were the main reason the Acharites managed to defeat the Forbidden in the Wars of the Axe and, over the subsequent thousand years, have enjoyed a well-deserved reputation for military excellence.

AXIS: illegitimate son of the Princess Rivkah and an unknown father. Currently he holds the position of BattleAxe of the Axe-Wielders. See "BattleAxe" and "Axe-Wielders."

AZHURE: daughter of Brother Hagen of Smyrton. Her mother came from Nor.

AZLE, River: a major river that divides the provinces of Ichtar and Aldeni. It flows into the Andeis Sea.

BANES: the religious leaders of the Avar people. They wield magic, although it is usually of the minor variety.

BARROWS, The Ancient: the burial places of the ancient Enchanter-Talons of the Icarii people. Located in southern Arcness.

BARSARBE: a Bane of the Avar people.

BATTLEAXE, The: the leader of the Axe-Wielders, appointed by the Brother-Leader for his loyalty to the Seneschal, his devotion to Artor the Ploughman and the Way of the Plough, and his skills as a military commander. See "Axis" and "Axe-Wielders."

BEDWYR FORT: a fort that sits on the lower reaches of the River Nordra and guards the entrance to Grail Lake from Nordmuth.

BELAGUEZ: Axis' war horse.

BELIAL: lieutenant and second-in-command of the Axe-Wielders.

BELTIDE: see "Festivals."

BOGLE MARSH: a large and inhospitable marsh in eastern Arcness. Strange creatures are said to live in the Marsh.

BOOK OF FIELD AND FURROW: the religious text of the Seneschal, which teaches that Artor himself wrote it and presented it to mankind.

BORNEHELD: Duke of Ichtar, the most powerful noble in Achar. Son of the Princess Rivkah and her husband, Duke Searlas.

BRACKEN RANGES, The: a low and narrow mountain range that divides Arcness and Skarabost.

BRACKEN, The River: the river that rises in the Bracken Ranges and which, dividing the provinces of Skarabost and Arcness, flows into the Widowmaker Sea.

BRIGHTFEATHER: wife to RavenCrest SunSoar, Talon of the Icarii.

BROTHER-LEADER, The: the supreme leader of the Brotherhood of the Seneschal. Usually elected by the senior brothers, the Office of Brother-Leader is for life. He is a powerful man, controlling not only the Brotherhood and all its riches, but the Axe-Wielders as well. The current Brother-Leader is Jayme.

BURDEL, EARL: lord of Arcness and friend to Borneheld, Duke of Ichtar.

CARLON: capital city of Achar and residence of the kings of Achar. Situated on Grail Lake.

CAULDRON LAKE, The: the lake at the center of the Silent Woman Woods.

CHAMBER OF THE MOONS: chief audience and sometime banquet chamber of the royal palace in Carlon.

CHAMPION, A: occasionally an Acharite warrior will pledge himself as a noble lady's Champion. The relationship is purely platonic and is one of protection and support. The pledge of a Champion can be broken only by his death or by the express wish of his lady.

CHARONITES: a lost race of Tencendor.

CLANS, The: the Avar tend to segregate into Clan groups, roughly equitable with family groups.

COHORT: see "Military Terms."

COROLEAS: the great empire to the south of Achar. Relations between the two countries are usually cordial.

CREST: Icarii military unit composed of twelve Wings.

CRIMSONCREST: an Icarii male.

CREST-LEADER: commander of an Icarii Crest.

DESTROYER, The: another term for Gorgrael.

DEVERA: daughter to Duke Roland of Aldeni.

DISTANCES:

League: roughly seven kilometers, or four and a half miles.

Pace: roughly one meter or one yard.

Handspan: roughly twenty centimeters or eight inches.

EARTH TREE: a tree sacred to both the Icarii and the Avar.

EGERLEY: a young man from Smyrton.

EMBETH, LADY OF TARE: widow of Ganelon, good friend and sometime lover of Axis.

ENCHANTERS: the magicians of the Icarii people. Many of them are very powerful. All Enchanters have the word "Star" somewhere in their names. The power of the Enchanters is blood-related, thus an Enchanter is not created, but born.

ENCHANTER-TALONS: Talons of the Icarii people who were also Enchanters.

EVENSONG: an Icarii woman.

FARADAY: daughter of Earl Isend of Skarabost and his wife, Lady Merlion.

FARSIGHT CUTSPUR: a Crest-Leader in the Icarii Strike Force.

FERNBRAKE LAKE, The: the large lake in the center of the Bracken Ranges.

FESTIVALS of the Avar and the Icarii:

Yuletide: the winter solstice, in the last week of Snow-month.

Beltide: the spring Festival, the first day of Flower-month.

Fire-Night: the summer solstice, in the last week of Rose-month.

FINGUS: a previous BattleAxe. Now dead.

FIRE-NIGHT, The: see "Festivals."

FLEAT: an Avar woman.

FLURIA, The River: a minor river that flows through Aldeni into the River Nordra.

FORBIDDEN, The: the two races, the Icarii and the Avar, that the Seneschal teaches are evil creatures who use magic and sorcery to enslave humans. During the Wars of the Axe, a thousand years before the events of the Prophecy of the Destroyer, the Acharites pushed the Forbidden back beyond the Fortress Ranges into the Shadowsward and the Icescarp Alps. It is part of Acharite legend that one day the Forbidden will try to reclaim their old lands.

FORBIDDEN TERRITORIES, The: the lands of the Forbidden, the Shadowsward and the Icescarp Alps.

FORBIDDEN VALLEY, The: the only known entrance into the Shadowsward from Achar. It is where the River Nordra escapes the Shadowsward and flows into Achar.

FOREST, concept of: the Seneschal teaches that all forests are bad because they harbor dark demons who plot the overthrow of mankind, thus most Acharites have a terrible fear of forests and their dark interiors. Almost all of the ancient forest that once covered Achar has been destroyed. The only trees grown in Achar are fruit trees and plantation trees for timber.

FORTRESS RANGES: the mountains that run down Achar's eastern boundary from the Icescarp Alps to the Widowmaker Sea. The Forbidden are penned behind these ranges.

FRANCIS: an elderly Brother from the Retreat in Gorkentown.

FREEFALL: an Icarii male.

FULKE, Baron: lord of Romsdale.

"FURROW WIDE, FURROW DEEP": an all-embracing Acharite phrase which can be used as a benediction, as a protection against evil, or as a term of greeting.

GANELON, LORD: Lord of Tare, once husband to Embeth, Lady of Tare. Now dead.

GARDEN, The: the Garden of the Mother.

GARLAND, GOODMAN: Goodman of Smyrton.

GAUTIER: lieutenant to Borneheld, Duke of Ichtar.

GHOSTMEN: another term for Skraelings.

GHOSTTREE CLAN: one of the Avar Clans, headed by Grindle.

GILBERT: Brother of the Seneschal and assistant and adviser to the Brother-Leader.

GOLDFEATHER: an Icarii woman.

GORGRAEL: the Destroyer, an evil lord of the north who, according to the Prophecy of the Destroyer, will threaten Achar.

GORKENFORT: the major fort situated in Gorken Pass in northern Ichtar.

GORKEN PASS: the narrow pass that provides the only way from Ravensbund into Ichtar. It is bounded by the Icescarp Alps and the River Andakilsa.

GORKENTOWN: the town that huddles about the walls of Gorkenfort.

GRAIL LAKE, The: a massive lake at the lower reaches of the River Nordra. On its shores are Carlon and the Tower of the Seneschal.

GREVILLE, BARON: lord of Tarantaise.

GRINDLE: an Avar man, head of the GhostTree Clan.

HAGEN: Plough Keeper of Smyrton.

HANDSPAN: see "Distances."

HELM: a young Avar male.

HOGNI: a young Avar female.

HORDLEY, GOODMAN: Goodman of Smyrton.

HORNED ONES: the almost divine and most sacred members of the Avar race. They live in the Sacred Grove.

HOVEREYE BLACKWING: an Icarii Crest-Leader.

HSINGARD: the large town situated in central Ichtar, seat of the Dukes of Ichtar.

ICARII, The: one of the races of the Forbidden, living in the Icescarp Alps. They are sometimes referred to as the People of the Wing.

ICESCARP ALPS, The: the great mountain range that stretches across most of northern Achar. It is home to the Icarii, one of the Forbidden races.

ICESCARP BARREN: a desolate tract of land situated in northern Ichtar between the Icescarp Alps and the Urqhart Hills.

ICHTAR, DUKE of: the lord of Ichtar, currently Borneheld.

ICHTAR, The Province of: the largest and richest of the provinces of Achar. Ichtar derives its wealth from its extensive grazing herds and from its mineral and precious-gem mines.

ICHTAR, The River: a minor river that flows through Ichtar into the River Azle.

ISEND, EARL: lord of Skarabost, a darkly handsome but somewhat dandified lord.

ISLAND OF MIST AND MEMORY: one of the sacred sites of the Icarii people, long lost to them after the Wars of the Axe.

JACK THE PIG BOY or JACK SIMPLE: pig herder of Arcness.

JAYME: Brother-Leader of the Seneschal.

JERVOIS LANDING: the small town on Tailem Bend of the River Nordra. The gateway into Ichtar.

JORGE, Earl: Earl of Avonsdale, and one of the most experienced military campaigners in Achar.

JUDITH: Queen of Achar, wife to Priam.

KAREL: old king of Achar, father to Priam and Rivkah. Now dead.

KASTALEON: one of the great Keeps of Achar, situated on the River Nordra in central Achar. Of recent construction.

KEEPS, The: the three main Keeps of Achar. See separate entries under Kastaleon, Sigholt, and Silent Woman Keep.

LEAGUE: see "Distances."

LORD OF SORROW KRAK: the highest mountain in the Icescarp Alps. According to Acharite legend, it is the home of the King of the Forbidden, the Lord of Sorrow himself. (Also see "Talon Spike.")

MAGARIZ, LORD: commander of Gorkenfort.

MAGIC: the Seneschal teaches that all magic, enchantments or sorcery are evil and the province only of the Forbidden races who will use magic to enslave the Acharites if they can. Consequently all Artor-fearing Acharites fear and hate the use of magic.

MAGIC LAKES, The: the ancient land of Tencendor had a number of magical lakes whose powers are now mostly forgotten. Also known as the Sacred Lakes.

MALFARI: the tuber that the Avar depend on to produce their bread.

MASCEN, BARON: Lord of Rhaetia.

MERLION, LADY: wife to Earl Isend of Skarabost and mother to Faraday.

MILITARY TERMS—Acharite (for both regular army and the Axe-Wielders):
Squad: a group of thirty-six men, generally archers.
Unit: a group of one hundred men, either infantry, pikemen, or cavalry.
Cohort: five units, so five hundred men.

MIRBOLT: a Bane of the Avar people.

MONTHS: (northern hemisphere seasons apply)
Wolf-month: January
Raven-month: February
Hungry-month: March
Thaw-month: April
Flower-month: May
Rose-month: June
Harvest-month: July
Weed-month: August
DeadLeaf-month: September
Bone-month: October

Frost-month: November

Snow-month: December

MORYSON: Brother of the Seneschal and friend and chief assistant and adviser to the Brother-Leader.

MOTHER, THE: either the Avar name for Fernbrake Lake, or an all-embracing term for nature which is sometimes personified as an immortal woman.

NEVELON: lieutenant to Duke Roland of Aldeni.

NOR: the southernmost of the provinces of Achar. Nors people are darker and more exotic than the rest of the Acharites. Nor is controlled by Baron Ysgryff.

NORDMUTH: the port at the mouth of the River Nordra.

NORDRA, The River: the great river that is the main life line of Achar. Rising in the Icescarp Alps, the River Nordra flows through the Shadowsward before flowing through northern and central Achar. It is used for irrigation, transport and fishing.

OGDEN: Brother of the Seneschal attached to the Silent Woman Keep.

PACE: see "Distances."

PEASE: an Avar woman.

PIRATES' NEST: a large island off the coast of Nor and close to Ysbadd and the haunt of pirates. Some say the pirates are protected by Baron Ysgryff himself.

PLOUGH, The: each Acharite village has a Plough, which not only serves to plow the fields, but is also the center of their worship of the Way of the Plough. The Plough was the implement given by Artor the Ploughman to enable mankind to civilize themselves. Use of the Plough distinguishes the Acharites from the Forbidden; neither the Icarii nor the Avar practice cultivation.

PLOUGH-KEEPERS: the Seneschal assigns a brother to each village in Achar, and these men are often known as Plough-Keepers. They are literally the guardians of the Plough in each village, but they are also the directors of the Way of the Plough and guardians of the villagers' souls.

PRIAM: King of Achar and uncle to Borneheld, brother to Rivkah.

PRIVY CHAMBER: the large chamber in the royal palace in Carlon where the king's Privy Council meets.

PRIVY COUNCIL: the council of advisers to the King of Achar, normally the lords of the major provinces.

PROPHECY OF THE DESTROYER: an ancient Prophecy that tells of the rise of Gorgrael in the north and the Star-Man who can stop him. No one knows who wrote it.

RAINBOW SCEPTER: a weapon mentioned in the Prophecy of the Destroyer.

RAUM: a Bane of the Avar people.

RAVENCREST SUNSOAR: current Talon of the Icarii.

RAVENSBUND: the extreme northern province of Achar, although it is rarely administered by the Acharite monarchy.

RAVENSBUNDMEN: the inhabitants of Ravensbund, generally loathed by the Acharites as barbarous and cruel.

REINALD: retired chief cook of Sigholt, undercook when Rivkah lived there.

RENKIN, GOODPEOPLE: farming couple of northern Arcness.

RETREATS: many brothers of the Seneschal prefer the contemplative life to the active life, and the Seneschal has various retreats about Achar where these brothers live in peace in order to contemplate the mysteries of Artor the Ploughman.

RHAETIA: small area of Achar situated in the western Bracken Ranges. It is controlled by Baron Mascen.

RIVKAH: Princess of Achar, sister to King Priam and mother to Borneheld, Duke of Ichtar, and Axis, BattleAxe. It is said that she died in Axis' birth.

ROLAND, Duke: also known as "The Walker" because he is too fat to ride. Duke of Aldeni and one of the major military commanders of Achar. He is commander of the Keep of Kastaleon.

ROMSDALE: a province to the southwest of Carlon that

mainly produces wine. It is administered by Baron Fulke.

SACRED GROVE, The: the most sacred spot of the Avar people, the Sacred Grove is rarely visited by ordinary mortals. Normally the Banes are the only members of the Avar race who can find the paths to reach the Grove.

SEAGRASS PLAINS: the vast grain plains that form most of Skarabost.

SEARLAS: previous Duke of Ichtar and father of Borneheld. Once married to the Princess Rivkah. Now dead.

SENESCHAL, The: the religious organization of Achar. The Religious Brotherhood of the Seneschal, known individually as brothers, direct the religious lives of all the Acharites. The Seneschal is extremely powerful and plays a major role, not only in everyday life, but also in the political life of the nation. It teaches obedience to the one god, Artor the Ploughman, and the Way of the Plough.

SENESCHAL, TOWER of: the headquarters of the Brotherhood of the Seneschal. The Tower of the Seneschal is a massive pure white seven-sided tower that sits on the opposite side of the Grail Lake to Carlon. It is very old.

SENTINELS: magical creatures of the Prophecy of the Destroyer.

SHADOWSWARD, The: the great forest that stretches north behind the Fortress Ranges. It is home to the Forbidden. See "Avarinheim."

SHRA: a young Avar child.

SIGHOLT: one of the great Keeps of Achar, situated in HoldHard Pass in the Urqhart Hills in Ichtar. One of the main residences of the Dukes of Ichtar.

SILENT WOMAN KEEP: the Seneschal houses a few of its brothers in the Silent Woman Keep to study the records left from the Wars of the Axe. The Silent Woman Keep lies in the center of the Silent Woman Woods.

SILENT WOMAN WOODS: the dark and impenetrable woods in southern Arcness that house the Silent Woman Keep.

SONG OF CREATION: a Song which can, according to Icarii and Avar legend, actually create life itself.

SONG OF RE-CREATION: one of the most powerful Icarii spells which can literally recreate life in the dying. It cannot, however, make the dead rise again. Only the most powerful Enchanters can sing this Song.

SKALI: a young Avar female.

SKARABOST: large eastern province of Achar which grows much of the kingdom's grain supplies. It is administered by Earl Isend.

SKRAEBOLDS: leaders of the Skraelings.

SKRAEFEAR: senior of the SkraeBolds.

SKRAELINGS: (also wraiths) insubstantial creatures of the northern wastes who feed off fear and blood.

SMYRTON: a large village in northern Skarabost, virtually at the entrance to the Forbidden Valley.

STARMAN, The : the man who, according to the Prophecy of the Destroyer, is the only one who can defeat Gorgrael.

SORCERY: see "Magic."

SPIKEFEATHER TRUESONG: an Icarii Wing-Leader.

STAR DANCE, The: the source from which the Icarii Enchanters derive their power.

STARDRIFTER: an Icarii Enchanter.

STAR GATE: one of the sacred sites of the Icarii people, long lost to them after the Wars of the Axe.

STRAUM ISLAND: a large island off the coast of Ichtar and inhabited by sealers.

STRIKE FORCE: the military wing of the Icarii.

SUNSOAR, HOUSE of: the ruling House of the Icarii for many thousands of years.

TAILEM BEND: the great bend in the River Nordra where it turns from its westerly direction and flows south toward Nordmuth and the Sea of Tyrre.

TALON, The: the hereditary ruler of the Icarii people (and once over all of the peoples of Tencendor). From the House of SunSoar for over six thousand years.

TALON SPIKE: highest mountain in the Icescarp Alps, the home of the Icarii people. (See "Lord of Sorrow Krak.")

TARANTAISE: a rather poor southern province of Achar. Relies on trade for its income. It is administered by Baron Greville.

TARE: small trading town in northern Tarantaise. Home to Embeth, Lady of Tare.

TARE, PLAINS of: the plains that lie between Tare and Grail Lake.

TENCENDOR: the ancient name for the continent of Achar before the Wars of the Axe. A name now forgotten by all except the Forbidden.

THREE BROTHERS LAKES, The: three minor lakes in southern Aldeni.

TIME OF THE PROPHECY OF THE DESTROYER, The: the time that begins with the birth of the Destroyer and the StarMan and that will end when one destroys the other.

TIMOZEL: son of Embeth and Ganelon of Tare, and a member of the Axe-Wielders.

TREE FRIEND: in Avar legend Tree Friend will be the person who will lead them back to their traditional homes south of the Fortress Ranges. Tree Friend is also the person who will bring the Avarinheim behind the StarMan.

TREE SONG: whatever Song the trees choose to sing you. Many times they will Sing the future, other times they will Sing love and protection. The trees can also Sing death.

TYRRE, SEA of: the ocean off the south west coast of Achar.

UNIT: see "Military Terms."

URQHART HILLS: a minor crescent-shaped range of mountains in central Ichtar.

VEREMUND: Brother of the Seneschal attached to the Silent Woman Keep.

WARLORD: title given to Borneheld, Duke of Ichtar, by King Priam in acknowledgment of Borneheld's *de facto* command of the armies of Achar.

WARS OF THE AXE: the wars during which the Acharites, under the direction of the Seneschal and the Axe-Wielders, drove the Icarii and the Avar from the land of Tencendor and penned them behind the Fortress Ranges. Lasting several decades, the wars were extraordinarily violent and bloody. They took place some thousand years before the time of the Prophecy of the Destroyer.

WAY OF THE HORN: a general term sometimes used to describe the lifestyle of the Avar people.

WAY OF THE PLOUGH, The: the religious obedience and way of life as taught by the Seneschal according to the tenets of the Book of Field and Furrow. The Way of the Plough is centered about the Plough and cultivation of the land. Its major tenets teach that as the land is cleared and plowed in straight furrows, so the mind and the heart are similarly cleared of misbeliefs and evil thoughts and can consequently cultivate true thoughts. Natural and untamed landscape is evil; thus forests and mountains are considered evil because they represent nature out of control and because they cannot be cultivated. According to the Way of the Plough, then, mountains and forests must either be destroyed or subdued, and if that is not possible, then they must be shunned as the habitats of evil creatures. Only tamed landscape, cultivated landscape, is good, because it has been subjected to mankind. The Way of the Plough is all about order, and about the earth and nature subjected to the order of mankind.

WAY OF THE WING: a general term sometimes used to describe the lifestyle of the Icarii.

WESTERN MOUNTAINS: the central Acharite mountain range that stretches west from the River Nordra to the Andeis Sea.

WIDEWALL BAY: a large bay that lies between Achar and Coroleas. Its calm waters provide excellent fishing.

WIDOWMAKER SEA: vast ocean to the east of Achar. From the unknown islands and lands across the Widowmaker Sea come the sea raiders that harass Coroleas and occasionally Achar.

WILDDOG PLAIN, The: a plain that stretches from northern Ichtar to the River Nordra and is bounded by the Fortress Ranges and the Urqhart Hills. Named after the packs of roving dogs that inhabit the area.

WING: the smallest unit in the Icarii Strike Force consisting of twelve Icarii (male and female).

WING-LEADER: the commander of an Icarii Wing.

WOLFSTAR: the ninth and most powerful of the Enchanter-Talons buried in the Ancient Barrows. He was assassinated early in his reign.

WORSHIP HALL: the large hall built in each village where the villagers go each seventh day to listen to the Service of the Plough. It is also used for weddings, funerals and the consecration of newborn infants to the Way of the Plough. It is usually the most well-built building in each village.

WRAITHS: see "Skraelings".

YR: sometime palace cat in Carlon.

YSBADD: capital city of Nor.

YSGRYFF, Baron: lord of Nor, and a somewhat wild and unpredictable man like all those of his province.

YULETIDE: see "Festivals".

A preview of Book Two
in Sara Douglass'
Wayfarer Redemption series,

Enchanter

Prologue:
The Ruins of Gorkenfort

Gorgrael stood in the deserted bedchamber of Gorkenfort Keep, his breath frosting about his tusks in the
frigid atmosphere. His bright silver eyes narrowed as he
absorbed the lingering memories and emotions of the
room. Bending, he scraped a hand across the bed, catching
and tearing the bed linen with his hooked claws. Hate and
desire, pain and satisfaction lingered here. He snatched a
handful of the material to his nostrils, crushing it between
his powerful claws. *She* had been here, had slept here, had
laughed and cried here. Gorgrael abruptly arched his body
back, his muscles rigid, and shrieked his anger, frustration
and desire. He hated and wanted this woman almost as
much as he hated and wanted Axis.

Outside the Keep's walls the Skraelings stilled and fell
silent as they heard their master's voice echo about the
frozen wastes. As suddenly as he had given vent to his
anger and desire Gorgrael stopped, straightening and relaxing his body. He dropped the fragment of sheet to the
floor, and glanced around the ruined chamber. This had

been *her* chamber, hers and that pitiful fool's, Borneheld. He was of no account; Gorgrael would brush him aside at the first possible opportunity. But the woman . . . she was the key.

Gorgrael knew the Prophecy almost as well as its maker. He knew that now Axis had escaped to his—*their*—father he would prove a far more formidable opponent. Enough to counter Gorgrael's command of the Dark Music? Gorgrael was not sure. Axis was certainly now too strong to be vulnerable to his SkraeBolds. But as the third verse of the Prophecy gave Axis the key to destroy Gorgrael, so it gave Gorgrael the key to destroy Axis. The Prophet had been kind.

The key was the Lover mentioned in the Prophecy. If Gorgrael could destroy her, he would destroy Axis. Axis was vulnerable to nothing but love, and eventually love could prove his destruction.

Gorgrael shrieked again, but this time in glee. It would take time, but eventually he would have her. The traitor was in place. All he needed was the opportunity.

Faraday. Gorgrael had gleaned much from this room. *She* was the one to whom Timozel had bound himself, *she* had given Axis the power of the emerald fire that had decimated Gorgrael's Skraeling force. For that alone she deserved to die. For the fact that Axis loved her Faraday would die slowly. For her alliance with the Mother and with the Trees she would die alone and friendless. Gorgrael dug his claws deep into the mattress and shredded it with a single twist of his powerful arm. This is what he would do to Faraday's body. After she had begged for her life, pleaded for mercy, screamed as she submitted herself to his will. He would *shred* her!

Gorgrael's eyes drifted toward the shattered window. Most of the hamlets and towns of Ichtar lay in ruins. Hsingard, the one-time seat of the Duke of Ichtar, was useless rubble. Tens of thousands of Ichtar's inhabitants had died. The Skraelings had fed well. But not all had gone according to plan, and satisfaction was still a way off. Axis had escaped, and in doing so had badly damaged Gorgrael's force.

If Gorgrael had enough Skraelings to occupy Ichtar then he did not have a strong enough force left to harry either Axis or Borneheld. The Duke of Ichtar had managed to flee south with almost five thousand men (and *her*) and even now approached Jervois Landing. There he would no doubt make his stand by the running waters.

Neither Gorgrael nor his creatures liked running water. It made music from beauty and peace, not darkness. It *tinkled*. Gorgrael screamed in frustration and completed his destruction of the bed. He was severely disappointed in his SkraeBolds. Borneheld's escape had been assisted by their inability to focus the Skraelings' attention on attacking the Duke's column as it fled south. While it was true that many Skraelings trembled at the SkraeBolds' screams and threats of retribution, many others did not. Long had the Skraelings hungered to drive into the pleasant southern lands, long had they resented their icy northern wastes. Now, as the defeat of Gorkenfort opened Ichtar to them, they spread across the province in largely unrestrained and undisciplined glee, a misty, whispery mob that destroyed without thought. The SkraeBolds had found it impossible to rally enough Skraelings to make any serious attempt on Borneheld's fleeing force, and had to confine themselves to harrying the flanks and rearguard of his column.

Not only were the Skraelings proving harder to control and the SkraeBolds less effectual than he had hoped, Gorgrael also had to admit that his forces had been so weakened by the fury Axis had unleashed on them above Gorkenfort that it would take him months to rebuild an army strong enough and disciplined enough to push further south than Hsingard.

And as the SkraeBolds trembled and wept at the thought of reporting their failures to Gorgrael, so Gorgrael himself began to construct the arguments he would need to convince his mentor that it *had* been the right time to strike Gorkenfort, it *had* been the right time to begin his drive into Achar. The Dark Man had cautioned him to wait a year or two more, to wait until his army had been built into a more formidable force and his magic was deeper and darker. But Gorgrael had been tired of waiting. While the Dark Man had taught him all he knew, had taught him the use of the Dark Music and crafted him into the power he was today, Gorgrael feared him as much as he loved him.

His claws twitching nervously, Gorgrael began rehearsing his explanations.

1

Jervois Landing — Arrivals

Ho'Demi sat his shaggy horse and contemplated the impenetrable fog before him. His scouts had reported that the Duke of Ichtar and what remained of his command from Gorkenfort drew close. For all Ho'Demi knew they were but ten paces away.

Ho'Demi shivered. He did not like these southern lands with their damp mists. He yearned for the northern wastes of the Ravensbund with its endless leagues of grinding ice. He yearned to be once more hunting the great icebears with the men and women of his tribe—not these Ghostmen whose very whispers defiled the wind.

However, the northern wastes were denied Ho'Demi and his people. For as far back as tribal memory stretched the Skraeling wraiths had existed. Until the past year they had been neither numerous nor brave, and as long as his people hunted in packs, the Skraelings had not attacked. But now, massed by the unseen yet powerful hand of Gorgrael the Destroyer, the Skraelings had driven them from the Ravensbund, down through Gorken Pass, past Gorkenfort

and town—where the Duke of Ichtar had stopped the invasion of Gorgrael's Ghostmen—and into these southern
lands. Ho'Demi had finally stopped his people's flight here
at Jervois Landing. It was here that Borneheld, having
somehow escaped the Skraelings, intended to make his
stand.

Ho'Demi and his people had always intended to help the
Southerners against Gorgrael and his Skraelings; it was
part of their heritage. But when he had offered his warriors
at Gorkenfort, Borneheld had laughed and said he had no
need for Ravensbund assistance. He, Duke of Ichtar, commanded a *real* army. Well, now the Duke and his *real* army
might not be so slow to accept the help of the Ravensbund
warriors.

Ho'Demi had led as many of his people out of the
Ravensbund as he could. But the Ravensbund tribes lay
scattered across the vast territory of the northern wastes
and Ho'Demi had not been able to get word to the majority
of the tribes to flee into the southern lands. Only twenty
thousand had pitched their sealskin tents about Jervois
Landing, a mere twentieth of the Ravensbund population.
Ho'Demi shuddered to think of what had happened to
those left behind. He hoped they had found a place to hide
among the crevices of the ice packs, there to await the day
when Gorgrael was defeated by the StarMan. He hoped
they had the courage for a long wait.

The Ravensbundmen were a proud and ancient people
who had adapted their culture and society to a life spent almost entirely within the ice-bound regions of northern
Achar. Few had any contact with the world beyond the
River Andakilsa. The King of Achar (whosoever he currently was) might fondly believe that he ruled Ravensbund
as he ruled the rest of Achar, but as far as the Ravensbundmen knew or cared, the Achar King had as much control
over them as he did over the Forbidden. Ho'Demi was their
Chief, and his was the law they obeyed.

But now, for the sake of the Prophecy and because it was

the only thing left for him to do, Ho'Demi would put himself under the command of Borneheld. Ravensbundmen had been aware of the Prophecy of the Destroyer for thousands of years, and Ho'Demi knew that, divided, no-one could defeat Gorgrael. Someone had to begin the alliance that would create Tencendor and crush the Destroyer. As the Skraeling threat grew infinitely worse, he had quickly realized this was a sign that the Prophecy had awoken and now walked. Of all the peoples of this land, perhaps the Ravensbundmen were more loyal to the name of the Star-Man than most. When he called, then they would rally.

In groups of never less than a thousand, the Ravensbund people had passed by Gorkenfort, many weeks before Axis had arrived. As yet they did not know where the StarMan was; they did not know who he was. Until they found him, until they could declare their loyalty and their spears for him, Ho'Demi had decided they would fight with Borneheld. *If* he would have them.

Borneheld knew what the bells were the instant their gentle sound reached him through the fog, and he hunched even further beneath his voluminous cloak.

It had been two weeks since they had fled Gorkenfort. As soon as Axis had drawn the Skraelings northwards away from the fort, Borneheld had ordered the gates opened and led his column out through the ruins of Gorkentown. The march south toward Jervois Landing was a desperate trek through icy conditions which hourly weakened his men's resistance to death. Many had died from the freezing cold or from the physical effort of the march. In the past week even more had died as the Skraelings made nibbling attacks on the rear and flanks of Borneheld's retreating column. Others deserted. Even those two old brothers who Axis had dragged north with him from the Silent Woman Keep and who had babbled incessantly about musty prophecies had disappeared one night. As far as Borneheld was concerned, the Skraelings could feed all they wanted on those two as on any others not prepared to stay with him.

Unaccountably, the Skraelings had left them alone for a critical five days after their escape from Gorkenfort. They had ridden as hard and as fast as they could—until the horses started to die beneath them—expecting an attack from Gorgrael's army at any moment. No-one in Borneheld's company knew that it was because Axis and his command had hurt the Skraelings so grievously in the icy wastes above Gorkenfort that the SkraeBolds had needed to regroup the decimated Skraeling forces.

All Borneheld and his company knew was that they'd had five days' start on the Skraelings, and that five days was the difference between life and death. When the Skraelings did finally reappear, they did not do so in force, and Borneheld's column had managed to keep moving further south toward the comparative safety of Jervois Landing. The Skraelings would not push so far south. Surely.

Yet every step they took southwards toward safety increased Borneheld's bitterness. It hadn't been his fault that Gorkenfort had fallen. Traitors had undermined his command and betrayed both Ichtar and Achar. Magariz's actions had confirmed that. His most senior, most trusted commander had chosen to ride with his bastard half-brother rather than fight for Borneheld and the cause of Achar. For thirty years Borneheld's jealousy of Axis had dominated his life; now bitter resentment twisted his gut. Artor curse him, he thought, I hope he died out there in the frozen wastes. Screaming for me to ride to his rescue, screaming my name as the wraiths chewed the flesh from his bones.

But even that thought could not bring a smile to Borneheld's cold-chapped face. Now, after the treachery of Gorkenfort, Borneheld trusted few. If Magariz could turn against him, then who else might prove treacherous? Even Jorge and Roland, riding silent and introspective further back in the column, did not enjoy the same depth of trust as they once had. No, Borneheld truly trusted only Gautier and Timozel. Who would have thought that such a young whelp—and an Axe-Wielder to boot—could grow into such a loyal and devoted servant to the Duke of Ichtar? Timozel had clearly demonstrated his worth on this march south, proving that he could harry men into obedience as well as Gautier, and fight with as much courage as Borneheld himself. Now he rode his horse slightly to the left and behind Borneheld, sitting tall and proud in the saddle, the occasional flare of his visionary eyes keeping Borneheld's own hopes alive.

Artor had graced Timozel with visions, and that meant Artor would eventually grace Borneheld's cause with victory as well.

Borneheld's eyes slipped to the horse that followed a few paces behind Timozel's. His wife, Faraday, clung to the saddle and to Yr, as she had since her horse succumbed to the cold three days ago. Could he trust Faraday? Borneheld frowned under the hood of his cloak. He had thought that she loved him, for had she not whispered words of love and devotion to him night after night, and fled to his arms when Axis had proved incapable of protecting her? But what was it she had murmured to Axis as they said goodbye in the courtyard of Gorkenfort?

Curse her, he swore silently. Her future would be with *him*, not with Axis. She would provide *Ichtar* with an heir, not whatever shadowland Axis currently ruled. He would rather see her dead than betray him as Magariz had.

The loss of Gorkenfort and, subsequently, Ichtar had hurt Borneheld to the core of his soul. As a young boy growing up in a loveless household, deserted by his mother, ignored by his father, Borneheld had always had Ichtar. And when his father died and Borneheld became Duke of Ichtar at only fourteen, he finally felt that his life had meaning. Ignored by so many when he was simply the son of Searlas, Borneheld revelled in the power he wielded as the new Duke. Power brought him the attention he craved, the respect he demanded, the command that was his due, and, eventually, the woman that he desired above all others.

Now most of Ichtar was lost to him, and Borneheld felt the loss as keenly as a physical wound. What power would he command as the man who had lost Ichtar? What respect? Even if he could win back Ichtar—and he *would*—he would still feel vulnerable. He would only feel safe if he commanded ultimate power over all of Achar, if he sat the throne itself. As King, Borneheld would have all the power, the respect and the love he craved. As King, he would surely be able to flush out the traitors about him once and for all. Desperate as he was to get it back, Ichtar was no longer enough for Borneheld.

And didn't Timozel's visions indicate that Borneheld *would* become King? Yes, it was Artor's wish that he take the throne.

Now, as he approached Jervois Landing, Borneheld reviewed the forces he still commanded. Despite the losses at Gorkentown—all of which had been the fault of either the demon-spawned Axis or that traitor Magariz—he still controlled a powerful force. The original column of five thousand he had led from Gorkenfort had been swelled by the refugees from Ichtar. As sorry as these refugees were now, they could work and some could be trained to fight. There were also troops still stationed in Achar that Borneheld could command. There was still a cohort of five hundred Axe-Wielders guarding the Brother-Leader at the Tower of the Seneschal. All these could be his. And, if those soft chimes meant what he hoped they did, he would also have the Ravensbundmen. Uncouth savages to be sure, but they had both spears and horses. If they could stick an enemy in the gut then they would be useful. Finally, there were the resources of the Corolean Empire to the south of Achar. If that simpering fool of a King, Priam, hadn't yet thought about arranging a military alliance with the Coroleans then Borneheld would make sure that he soon would.

Suddenly a stationary horseman loomed out of the mist and Borneheld barked an order to halt. He sat for a moment and looked at the inscrutable Ravensbundman's face. It was even more intricately tattooed in blue and black than most of his race. Dizzying whorls and spirals covered not only his cheeks, but his forehead and chin as well—although, strangely, there was a circular area right in the center of his forehead that remained naked and untattooed. As with all his race, the savage had tiny chips of blue glass and miniature bells threaded through his myriad greasy black braids. Even his mount—ugly, stunted, yellow-furred nag that it was—had glass and bells woven into its mane and tail. Uncivilised savages. Still, if they could kill they might yet serve a purpose.

Ho'Demi let the Duke stare at him a moment, then spoke, demonstrating a fluent command of the Acharite language. "Duke Borneheld. Gorgrael has taken my land and murdered my people. He drives his Ghostmen south. The Ravensbundmen live only to defeat Gorgrael. If you fight against Gorgrael then we will stand by your side."

Borneheld narrowed his eyes at the barbarian. "I *do* fight Gorgrael. But if you want to fight with me then you will place yourself and your people under *my* command."

Ho'Demi wondered at the implicit threat in Borneheld's tone, but it did not perturb him. He nodded. "Agreed."

"Good." Borneheld peered into the mists behind the Ravensbundman, trying to see how many men he had with him. "How many will you bring to my command?"

"Of the twenty thousand in my camp, eleven thousand can fight."

"You have done well to choose my cause," Borneheld said quietly. "Together we will make our stand here at Jervois Landing against whichever of our enemies attack first. This time, *I* will prevail."

2

Talon Spike

Four weeks after StarDrifter tore the crossed axes from his breast, Axis—BattleAxe no longer—sat in his favorite spot on Talon Spike letting the wind ruffle through his blond hair and beard. Every few days Axis found he had to spend time alone, to lose himself in contemplation of these beautiful northern alps rather than in the intricacies of the magical Star Dance, Icarii society and his new life.

From his eyrie perch on the rock ledge Axis gazed at the blue-white glacier a thousand paces below, crashing a path through the lesser Icescarp Alps beyond Talon Spike to calve its massive icebergs into the Iskruel Ocean. One month ago the bergs in the Iskruel Ocean would simply have been flecks at the edge of his vision. Now he could see that the huge icebear on the smallest of the bergs had lost an ear in some past ursine dispute.

He sighed. Even the wonders of his new-found powers could not make him forget that Faraday was still trapped with one half-brother while the other, Gorgrael, was un-

doubtedly remarshalling his forces to invade Achar. And if
Faraday or either one of his despised half-brothers did not
occupy his thoughts, then Axis found himself worrying
over the problems of his new life.

Father, mother, sister, uncle, grandmother. All exciting,
all troubling in their own right. But it was StarDrifter who
dominated Axis' days. His father, the man who had only
existed in court gossip and innuendo for almost thirty years
and whose conspicuous absence had given Gorgrael the
grist to torment Axis in his nightmares for so long, was as
compulsively drawn to Axis as Axis was to him.

Their relationship was not easy. StarDrifter was a forceful man with powerful expectations. He drove his son
from first waking until Axis, exhausted, lay down his head
late at night. And Axis, having been alone for so long, having been his own man for so long, both resented his father's intrusions and yearned for his father's attention. It
was not easy reconciling resentment and need every
minute of the day.

Axis' mouth twisted as he thought of their morning's
training session. After hours confined in the one chamber,
they had fought, bitterly, savagely. MorningStar, Star-
Drifter's mother and Axis' grandmother, who was often
present, had finally dismissed Axis as she tried to reason
with her son. Yet all Axis wanted to do was stay in that
chamber and ask StarDrifter another question about his
heritage and powers.

"You fought again."

Startled, Axis turned his head toward the voice. It was
Azhure, dressed in a pale-grey woollen tunic and leggings,
walking confidently along the narrow rock ledge. She
halted a few paces away. "May I join you? Am I intruding?"

Axis smiled. "No, you're not intruding. Please, join me."

She sat down gracefully, curling her legs underneath her.
"It is a superb view."

"Can you see the icebear?" He pointed to the distant ice-
berg.

Azhure laughed. "I have not your Enchanter's vision, Axis SunSoar."

Axis relaxed. Since he had come to Talon Spike, Azhure had become a good friend. She was the one person he felt he could talk to, who understood the problems he encountered as he embraced his heritage.

"You have developed a good head for heights since living among the Icarii, Azhure. Few Groundwalkers could even stand on this ledge, let alone wander along it as if strolling the flat plains of Skarabost."

"Why fear when I have an Enchanter to hand to save me should I tumble?"

Axis laughed and changed the subject. "How did you know StarDrifter and I had fought?"

"He came back to the apartments and snapped at Rivkah. She snapped back. I left them bickering and thought to find the source of such marital disharmony so that he could explain himself."

"Do you think I should have re-entered their lives, Azhure?" Axis asked.

"If there are problems between them, you are not the cause, Axis," Azhure replied. "I am sorry if I implied, even laughingly, that you were."

Axis leaned his arms on his raised knees and considered his parents. Tension marked the relationship between himself and his father, while with his mother there was nothing but warmth. When the five Icarii had escorted him into Talon Spike she had been the first to step forward. She had said nothing, just folded him in her strong arms. For long minutes they had stood, each weeping silently, holding each other as close as they could. Axis recalled how he had summoned the memory of her struggle to give him birth and fight for his life. For so long he'd believed that she had cursed him as she died in his birth. Those long minutes holding each other had been a time of healing for them both.

But things between Rivkah and StarDrifter were not idyllic. That they loved each other, Axis had no doubt. But their passionate affair atop Sigholt had not transferred easily to Talon Spike. Perhaps Axis had arrived in their lives only in time to watch the sad disintegration of their marriage.

"It must be hard to look into the face of your husband and see a man who looks no older than your son."

Axis' expression hardened a little. His Icarii blood ran much stronger than his human and, like his sister, he would live the full span of an Icarii lifetime—perhaps some five hundred years, should he be left in peace to do so. What would it be like to watch his friends age and die while he still enjoyed youthful vitality? What would it be like to see the sods thrown on their grandchildren's coffins before he had reached his middle years?

"Do I like it that in four hundred years I might still be sitting here watching the icebears hunt seals on the icebergs, trying desperately to recall the name and face of a lovely woman who had once sat here with me? Whose bones have turned to dust in some forgotten tomb? No, Azhure. I do not like it. I find it . . . hard."

Azhure reached out and took his hand. Axis stiffened briefly, then he forced a smile. "But these powers I daily learn as an Icarii Enchanter give me a few compensations. Such as making the woman who sits here with me a small gift for the friendship she offers me."

For an instant Azhure thought she caught the hint of a faraway melody in the wind. Then she was laughing in delight as the soft, velvety blooms of the violet Moonwildflower rained down about her. She let Axis' hand go and tried to catch as many as she could.

"How did you know?" she gasped. She had not seen a Moonwildflower for over twenty years—when she was a tiny girl her mother had occasionally taken her on walks during full moon to find the flower.

Axis plucked a flower out of the air and threaded it into her wavy black hair. He was mildly disturbed, for he had meant to shower her with soft spring roses. "A lucky guess, Azhure. You sometimes remind me of the Moonwildflower. Hidden in darkness, desperate not to be found or touched."

Suddenly awkward, Azhure gently cradled a flower in her hands. The cascade drifted to a halt and she spoke, changing the subject. "EvenSong wants me to join her at training this afternoon. She says I show aptitude."

EvenSong had been impressed by Azhure's extraordinary fighting ability so clearly demonstrated during the battle in the Earth Tree Grove at Yuletide. While the Icarii Strike Force had faltered helplessly, unsure of how to combat the Skraeling wraiths, Azhure had discovered the Skraelings' vulnerability—their eyes—and almost singlehandedly rallied the Icarii and Avar to fight back. During the battle she had also saved StarDrifter from certain death.

EvenSong admired Azhure for her cool head and bravery, and for some weeks she and her Wing-Leader, Spike-Feather TrueSong, had been pressing Azhure to join weapons training with the Strike Force.

Axis could see Azhure's doubts and knew the reasons for them. Had he not reviled her for the death of her father and the assault on Belial as she escaped into the Avarinheim with Raum and Shra? Had not the Avar rejected her, suspicious of her violence, even though she had saved so many of their lives?

"Azhure," he said gently. "You did what you had to. Now do what you want with your life. *Would* you like to go with EvenSong this afternoon?"

Azhure hesitated, then nodded. "I have seen the Strike Force practise at archery. They look so smooth, so graceful. I would like to try that. SpikeFeather has offered to demonstrate for me and," her mouth quirked, "teach me the proper use of the arrow." Again she hesitated, then forged on. "I am sick of feeling helpless, directionless. I feel as though I have spent my life in a deep, dark well. Now, after so long buried in Smyrton, I am starting to make my way toward the surface—but the surface is still so very far away. Each day away from Smyrton, each new experience, brings me a little closer, wakes me up a little more from the torpor of my previous life. You are right. I must seek my own path."

She laughed now, her good humor returning. "I am glad I'm not an Icarii Enchanter like you, destined for heroic deeds. That would be a heavy burden."

Axis turned away, his face expressionless. "I am no hero."

Azhure lowered her eyes to the flower she still held. If Axis had his moments of denial, then she did not blame him. Not a day passed that Axis did not grieve for those who had already died for him. He despised the thought that yet more would die. And it haunted him that his sister blamed him for FreeFall's death.

"You must bear with EvenSong. She has not yet reconciled herself to FreeFall's death. Her grief needs an outlet."

Axis knew his sister resented him for many other reasons besides his inability to prevent FreeFall's death. She had not begun to come to terms with having an older brother, and one who had inherited their father's powers in full. Where once StarDrifter had lavished attention on EvenSong, now she found herself virtually ignored by her father as he spent almost every waking moment with his son. EvenSong found her father's obsession with Axis difficult to accept.

It was fortunate, Axis mused, that Azhure was here to offer EvenSong companionship. He too appreciated the friendship and understanding she gave him as he fought to adjust to his new life and his new powers. Rivkah spent a good deal of time talking to her as well. If not for Azhure, StarDrifter's entire household might well have self-destructed by now.

"The SunSoars are difficult people to live with," he said, resting his chin in his hand.

"The Icarii people as a whole are," replied Azhure, her eyes distant. "They are very good at passions and very bad at friendships."

Axis studied her closely. This woman from Smyrton displayed more insight than many who had spent years in scholarly or diplomatic training. Where had she got it from? Not from her father, surely; Hagen had demonstrated as much insight as a sack of barley. Her mother? From what Axis knew of Nors women, they thought mainly of the pleasures of the flesh and very little else. And surely the woeful society of her village had contributed little to the inner depths she increasingly revealed.

Azhure shifted under his gaze—those pale-blue eyes seemed to reach to the core of her soul. Unthinking, she said the first thing that sprang to mind.

"Do you worry about her, Axis? Do you wonder if she is all right?" she asked, and then wished desperately she could snatch her words back.

Axis tensed at her side and Azhure could sense his withdrawal. He rarely spoke of Faraday and yet Azhure knew she was always in his thoughts.

Azhure stumbled on, trying to relieve the sudden tension. "I saw her, you know, at Yuletide. She is a woman who combines great beauty with great compassion and selflessness. It is no wonder you love her as you do."

"You saw her?" Axis frowned. "How?"

"Did StarDrifter not tell you how he and Faraday woke the Earth Tree at Yuletide as the Skraelings attacked the Earth Tree Grove?"

Axis nodded, still frowning, and Azhure hurried on. "I don't know what enchantment StarDrifter used, but Faraday appeared as if in a vision above the Earth Tree. No-one else saw her. StarDrifter and Raum were concentrating so hard on the Tree that they did not look up. I don't know if she saw me, but she looked down and smiled." Azhure gave a little shrug. "At least, I like to think she smiled at me."

Axis relaxed a little. "She would like you, and you her. It is a pity you are both caught in the web of this Prophecy."

"If *I* were married to Borneheld he would not have survived his wedding night," Azhure said tightly. Over the past few weeks she had learned much of Faraday's circumstances. "Why did she not escape with you to Talon Spike?"

"Because she honors the vows that she took when she became Borneheld's wife, Azhure. Even her love for me will not make her desert her honor." He sounded bitter. "Do I wonder about her? Do I worry if she is all right? With every breath that I draw, Azhure. I live for her."

"Axis."

They both swivelled toward the voice. StarDrifter stood on the ledge by the archway that led back into the mountain, his white wings a little outstretched to aid his balance.

Axis stood in one fluid motion, feeling his father's intrusion keenly.

StarDrifter held his gaze briefly, then dropped his eyes to Azhure and smiled warmly at her, his face breathtaking in its beauty. "You should not bring Azhure out here, Axis. She does not have our balance." He stepped forward and helped Azhure to her feet, clasping her hand as he led her back into the safety of the mountain.

As they stepped through the archway and down into the wide corridor, Azhure pulled her hand awkwardly from StarDrifter's grasp. "I followed Axis out there, StarDrifter. It was not his fault. And neither the height of the cliff nor the narrowness of the ledge bother me. Truly."

StarDrifter looked back at her. He wished she would abandon the Avar tunic and leggings and wear the loose flowing robes favored by the Icarii women; she would look superb in their jewelled colors and she had the grace to do their elegance justice.

Axis stepped down into the corridor behind them and StarDrifter glanced at his son. The tensions of their morning argument remained, and this afternoon's training session would not be easy. No doubt they would end this afternoon with angry words as well. Axis was so desperate to learn, but hated being the student.

Yet he learned so well, and so quickly. That was part of the problem, for Axis wanted to learn faster than

StarDrifter was willing to teach. While StarDrifter took pride in the knowledge that the Prophecy had chosen him among all Icarii to breed this son, he also found it hard not to resent Axis' power. As EvenSong resented losing her only and most favored child status, so StarDrifter was battling to come to terms with the fact that very soon Axis' power would surpass his own—and StarDrifter had long revelled in being the most powerful Icarii Enchanter alive.

StarDrifter looked back to Azhure with studied casualness. "Will you join us this afternoon, Azhure?" he asked. With her present, both Enchanters kept a tighter rein on their tempers. Neither MorningStar—who often helped with Axis' training—nor Axis had so far raised any objections to Azhure's occasional presence in the training chamber.

"I thank you for the invitation, StarDrifter, but I will refuse. I promised EvenSong I would spend the afternoon with her. If you will excuse me."

She nodded at both men, then walked down the corridor, disappearing around the first corner.

"Imagine the Enchanters she would bear," StarDrifter said, so quietly that Axis could not believe he was hearing correctly. "I am nothing if not a good judge of blood."

Then he turned his powerful gaze on his son. "Over the past thousand years the Icarii blood has thinned. Before the Wars of the Axe that severed our races many Icarii birdmen chose to get their sons on human women. It was said that human blood added vitality to the Icarii. You are proof enough of that."

Axis felt his anger simmering. Was StarDrifter planning another seduction?

"I love Rivkah," StarDrifter said slowly. "I demonstrated my love through marriage—even though I believed she had lost our son. In ages past Icarii birdmen simply took the babies of human—Icarii unions and never spared a thought for the women they had bedded who had struggled to birth their children."

Appalled at such evidence of Icarii insensitivity, Axis

TOR

Award-winning authors
Compelling stories

Please join us at the website
below for more information
about this author and other great
Tor selections, and to sign up for
our monthly newsletter!

suddenly understood the depth of hate and loathing that had led the Acharites to finally drive the Icarii from Tencendor.

The Icarii had a lot to learn about compassion.